I KILL GIANTS ™

Special Thanks:

To Gina, Claire, and Jack for their love
To Megan for her insight
To Barbara and Sophia for their friendship
To Ken for his mighty, mighty pen

-JK

To the Fagniez family, for the Paris experience.
To all those who were part of it.
To all those who weren't there but supported me all along.
To Joe for his help killing this giant.

-KN

IMAGE COMICS, INC.
Robert Kirkman—Chief Operating Officer
Erik Larsen—Chief Financial Officer
Todd McFarlane—President
Marc Silvestri—Chief Executive Officer
Jim Valentino—Vice-President

Eric Stephenson—Publisher
Corey Murphy—Director of Sales
Jeff Boison—Director of Publishing Planning & Book Trade Sales
Chris Ross—Director of Digital Sales
Jeff Stang—Director of Specialty Sales
Kat Salazar—Director of PR & Marketing
Branwyn Bigglestone—Controller
Sue Korpela—Accounts Manager
Drew Gill—Art Director
Brett Warnock—Production Manager
Leigh Thomas—Print Manager
Tricia Ramos—Traffic Manager
Briah Skelly—Publicist
Aly Hoffman—Events & Conventions Coordinator
Sasha Head—Sales & Marketing Production Designer
David Brothers—Branding Manager
Melissa Gifford—Content Manager
Drew Fitzgerald—Publicity Assistant
Vincent Kukua—Production Artist
Erika Schnatz—Production Artist
Ryan Brewer—Production Artist
Shanna Matuszak—Production Artist
Carey Hall—Production Artist
Esther Kim—Direct Market Sales Representative
Emilio Bautista—Digital Sales Representative
Leanna Caunter—Accounting Assistant
Chloe Ramos-Peterson—Library Market Sales Representative
Maria Eizik—Administrative Assistant
IMAGECOMICS.COM

IKILL**GIANTS**™

Written by **JOE KELLY**
Art & design by **JM KEN NIIMURA**

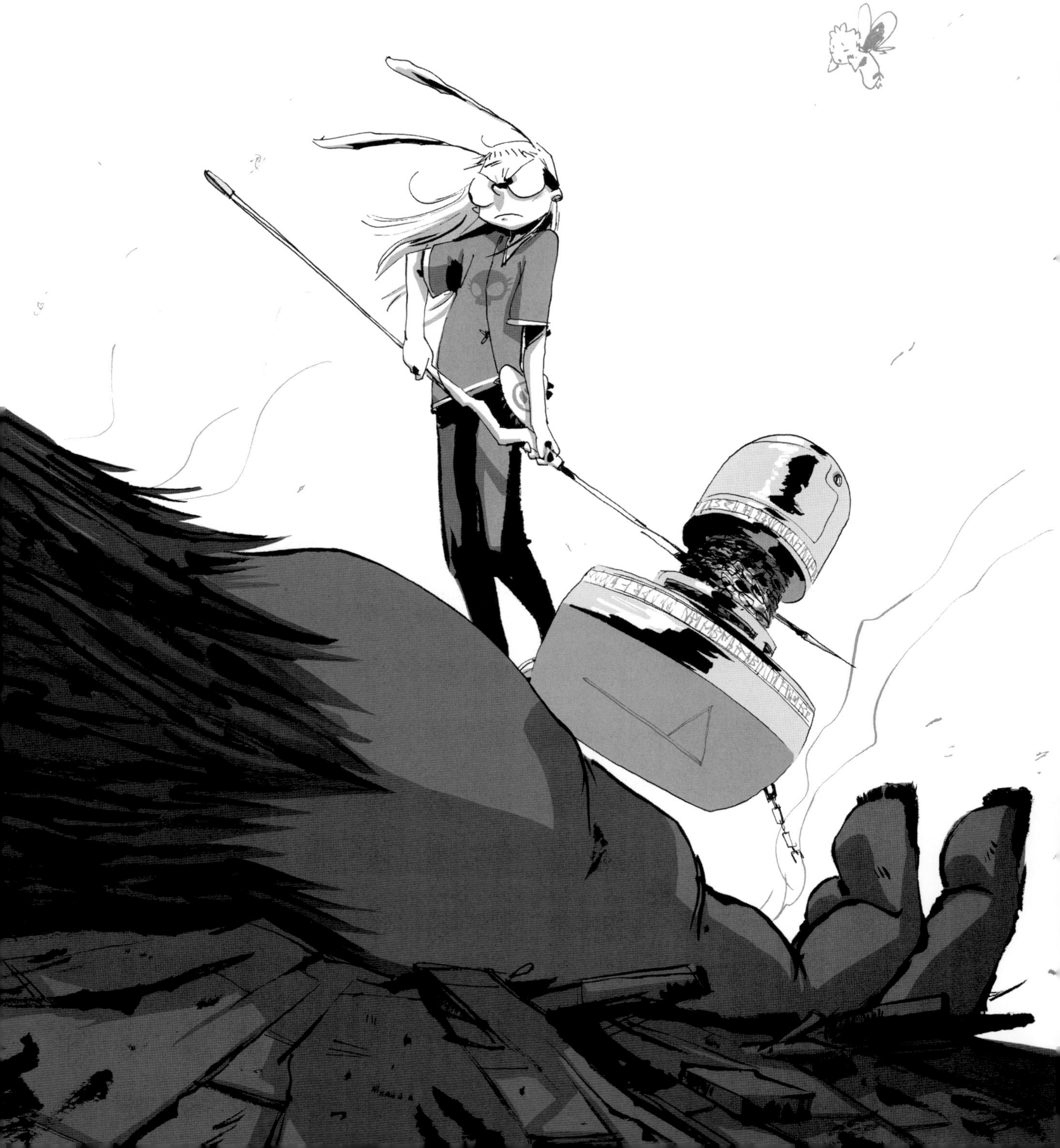

FOREWORDFORIKG

I walked into my local comic book store a few years back, a place called Comix Experience in San Francisco. I was browsing through the titles, grabbing the comics that looked interesting. There weren't many. The problem I have with a lot of the titles these days, is that you truly can't judge a book by its cover. Back in the Silver Age (am I that old?!), you could pop into a pharmacy (yes, I am that old!) pick up a handful of comics and discover an array of stunning, visceral covers drawn by the likes of Jack Kirby, Jim Steranko, Neal Adams, John Romita… And when you opened the pages you could almost guarantee that there would be 20 pages of countless panels, each one filled with a hand drawn, mind exploding piece of art drawn by the same hand that inspired you to pick up the book in the first place. These days when I reach for a comic, about 40 percent of the time I discover that the interior artist is completely different than the cover artist. Huge buzzkill. And the interior artwork ultimately feels generic and soulless, as if the characters were drawn by a machine.

But that all changed when I picked up "I Kill Giants".

I cracked it open, and not only did the art deliver on the promise of the book's cover, the writing was wonderful. Whip smart, funny and complex. When I finished the book, I felt the same way I did after watching E.T. in the theater for the first time. It was a profoundly moving experience, so real and honest, but with a dark magical heart.

Joe Kelly has written a deeply insightful story about a child using fantasy to navigate through a harsh reality. Barbara's character is a rarity among most graphic novels and comics. She is a damaged, not particularly likeable person, who is also a tangible, three-dimensional human being. At the end of her journey, by the time I got to the final pages, tears were streaming down my face. Not the result of cheap sentimental manipulation. No, this story earned my tears. It was raw and brutally honest.

JM Ken Niimura's illustrations are unlike anything I had ever seen in a graphic novel. To say that they are outside of the box doesn't even cover it. They're outside of the f--ing planet. They're visually arresting, tough and at times, whimsical. Ken's visuals perfectly compliment Joe's writing. His drawings transport us to a world we've never seen before, a unique fantastical vision.

After you've read this glorious book, you will almost certainly want to find a special place for it on your bookshelf. But I suggest you do something a bit more generous… pass it along to a family member or friend. It needs to be shared. It needs to be discussed. It needs to be experienced by everybody.

Do I sound obsessed? Yeah. Of course I am. I love this book. How often do you get to experience the work of great talents like Joe Kelly and JM Ken Niimura? These men truly walk in the footsteps of Will Eisner and Stan Lee and Roy Thomas and Steve Ditko and the many, many giants who came before them.

Thank you Joe and Ken, for giving me the opportunity to walk in the footsteps of Barbara. I felt her fears, her anger and frustration, her final victory. And it was one hell of a journey.

CHRIS COLUMBUS
Filmmaker
San Francisco, 2014

To those fighting their own giants,
You're stronger than you think.

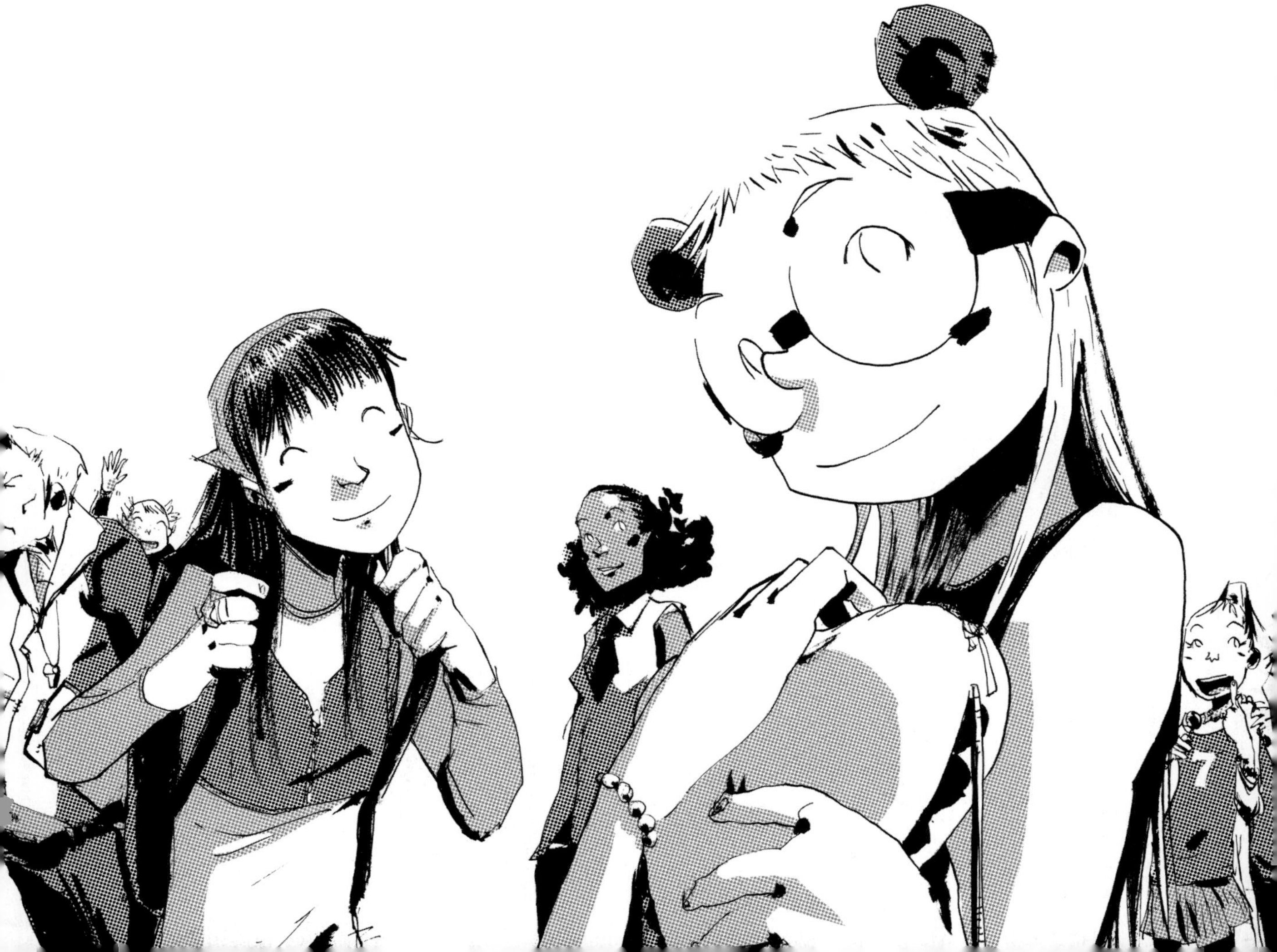

CHAPTER1: THE HAMMER

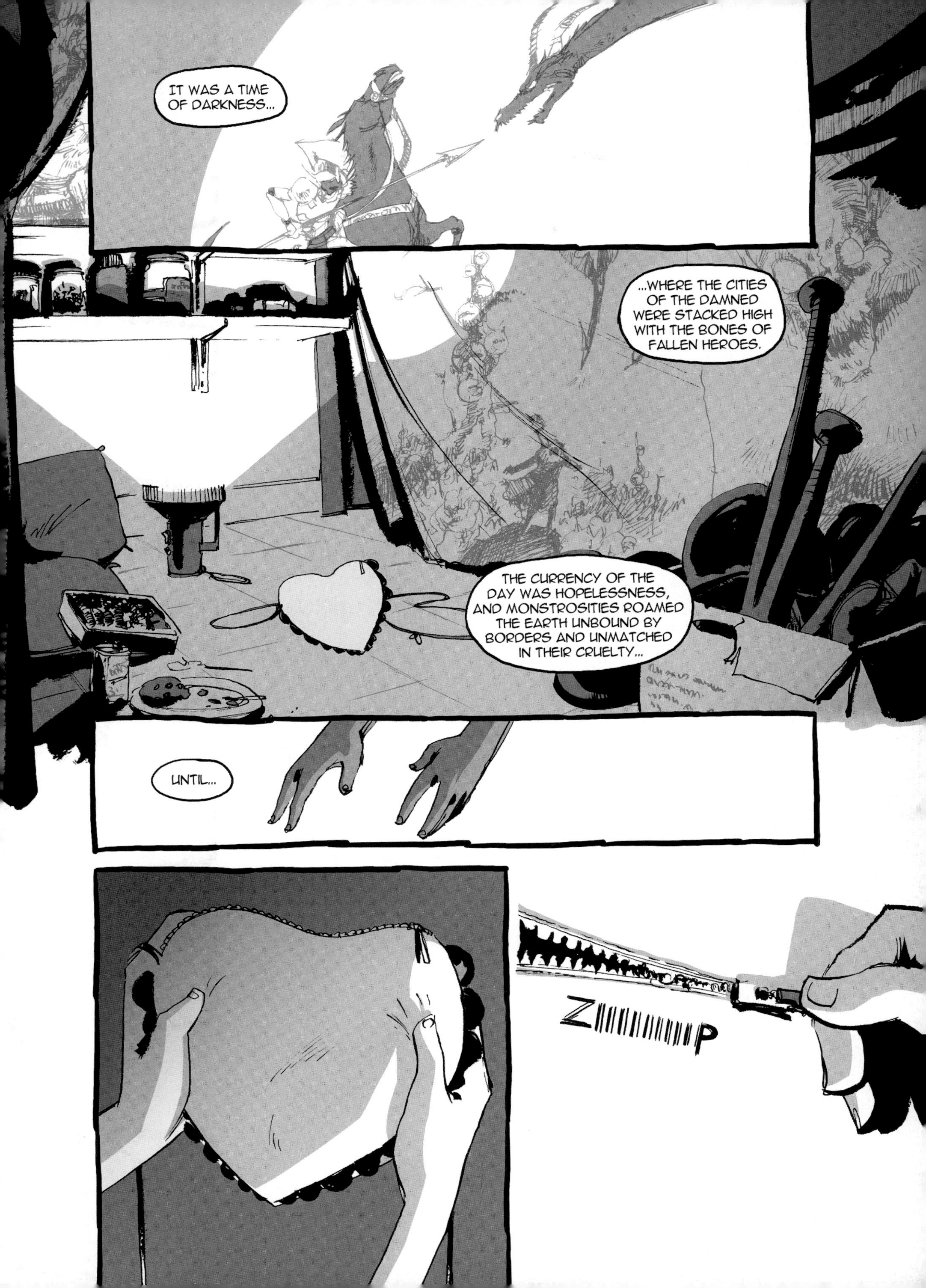
IT WAS A TIME OF DARKNESS...
...WHERE THE CITIES OF THE DAMNED WERE STACKED HIGH WITH THE BONES OF FALLEN HEROES.
THE CURRENCY OF THE DAY WAS HOPELESSNESS, AND MONSTROSITIES ROAMED THE EARTH UNBOUND BY BORDERS AND UNMATCHED IN THEIR CRUELTY...
UNTIL...
ZIIIIIIIIIIP

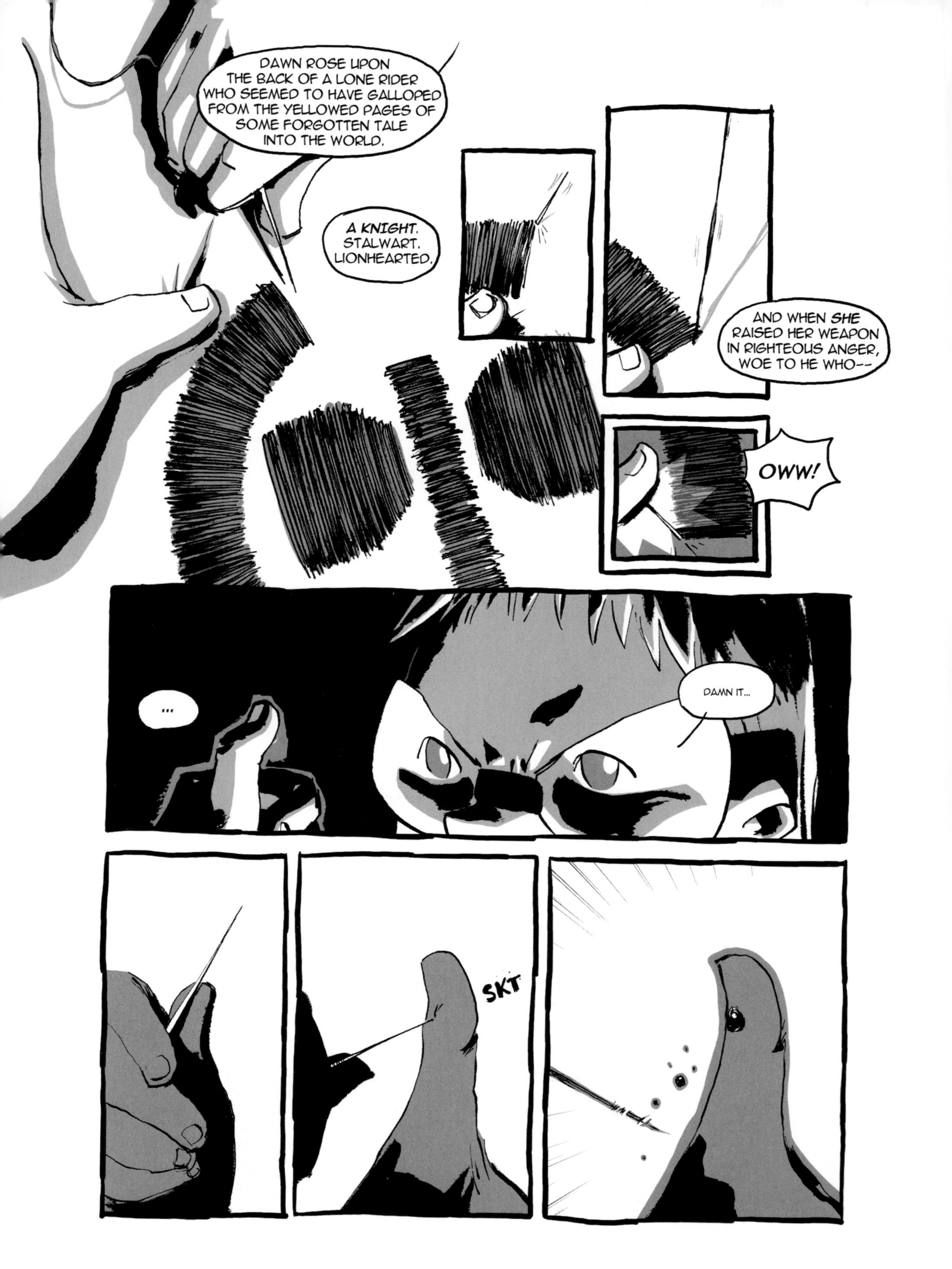
DAWN ROSE UPON THE BACK OF A LONE RIDER WHO SEEMED TO HAVE GALLOPED FROM THE YELLOWED PAGES OF SOME FORGOTTEN TALE INTO THE WORLD.
A KNIGHT. STALWART. LIONHEARTED.
AND WHEN SHE RAISED HER WEAPON IN RIGHTEOUS ANGER, WOE TO HE WHO--
OWW!
...
DAMN IT...
SKT

THURISAZ. THE THORN.
THE HAMMER.
TAKE THE FORCE OF MY ENEMY AND SEND IT BACK TO HIM A THOUSAND THOUSAND TIMES.
PLEASE.

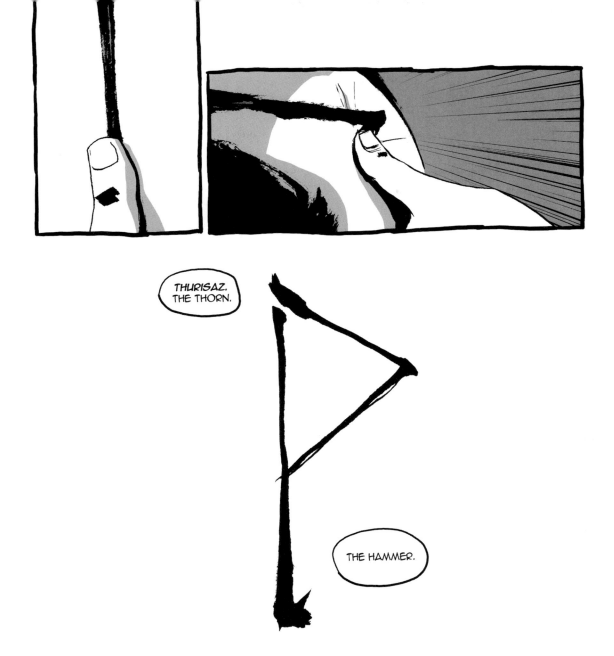

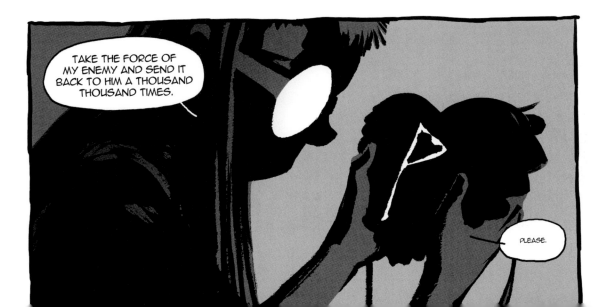

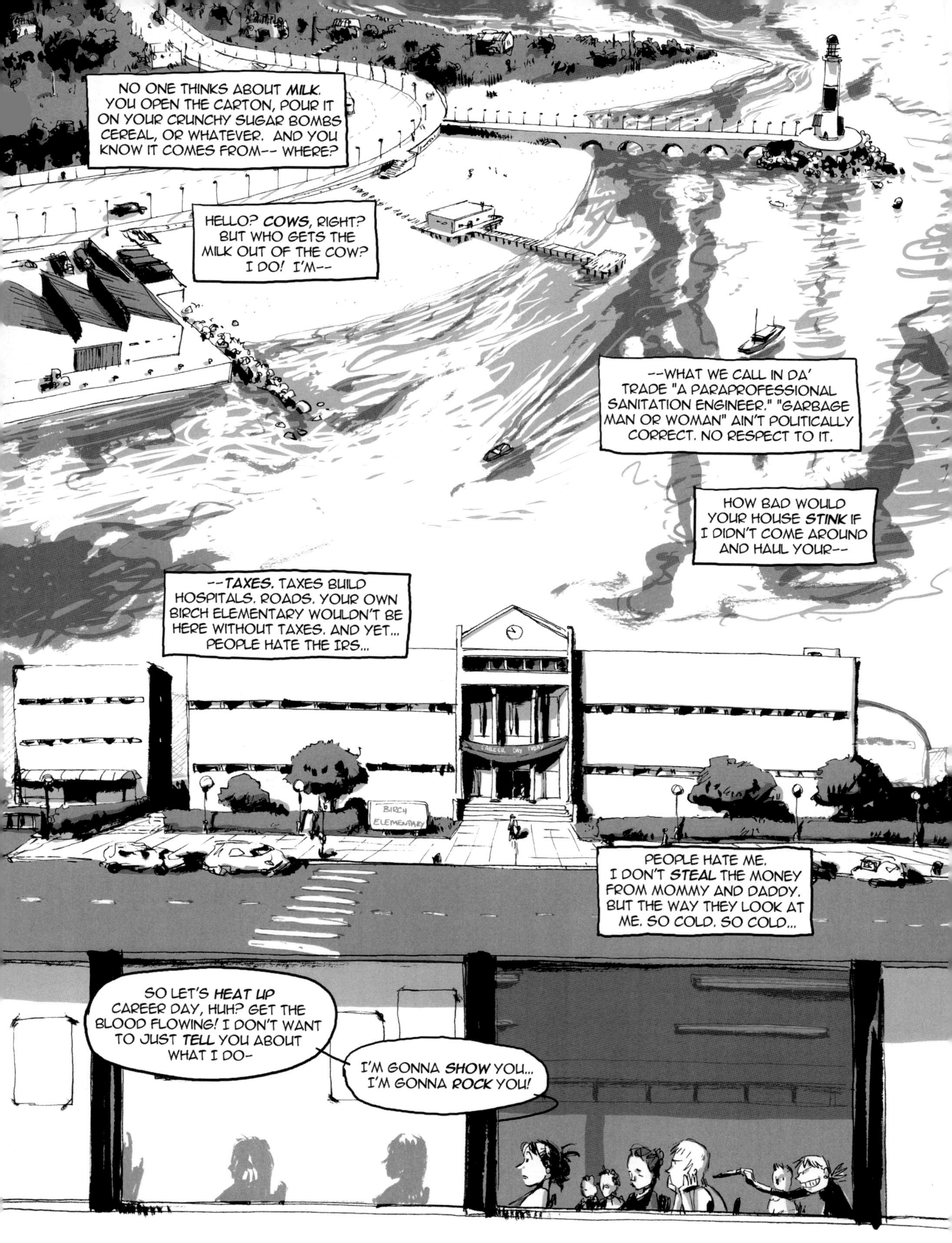
NO ONE THINKS ABOUT MILK. YOU OPEN THE CARTON, POUR IT ON YOUR CRUNCHY SUGAR BOMBS CEREAL, OR WHATEVER. AND YOU KNOW IT COMES FROM-- WHERE?
HELLO? COWS, RIGHT? BUT WHO GETS THE MILK OUT OF THE COW? I DO! I'M--
--WHAT WE CALL IN DA' TRADE "A PARAPROFESSIONAL SANITATION ENGINEER." "GARBAGE MAN OR WOMAN" AIN'T POLITICALLY CORRECT. NO RESPECT TO IT.
HOW BAD WOULD YOUR HOUSE STINK IF I DIDN'T COME AROUND AND HAUL YOUR--
--TAXES. TAXES BUILD HOSPITALS. ROADS. YOUR OWN BIRCH ELEMENTARY WOULDN'T BE HERE WITHOUT TAXES. AND YET... PEOPLE HATE THE IRS...
CAREER DAY TODAY
BIRCH ELEMENTARY
PEOPLE HATE ME. I DON'T STEAL THE MONEY FROM MOMMY AND DADDY. BUT THE WAY THEY LOOK AT ME. SO COLD. SO COLD...
SO LET'S HEAT UP CAREER DAY, HUH? GET THE BLOOD FLOWING! I DON'T WANT TO JUST TELL YOU ABOUT WHAT I DO-
I'M GONNA SHOW YOU... I'M GONNA ROCK YOU!

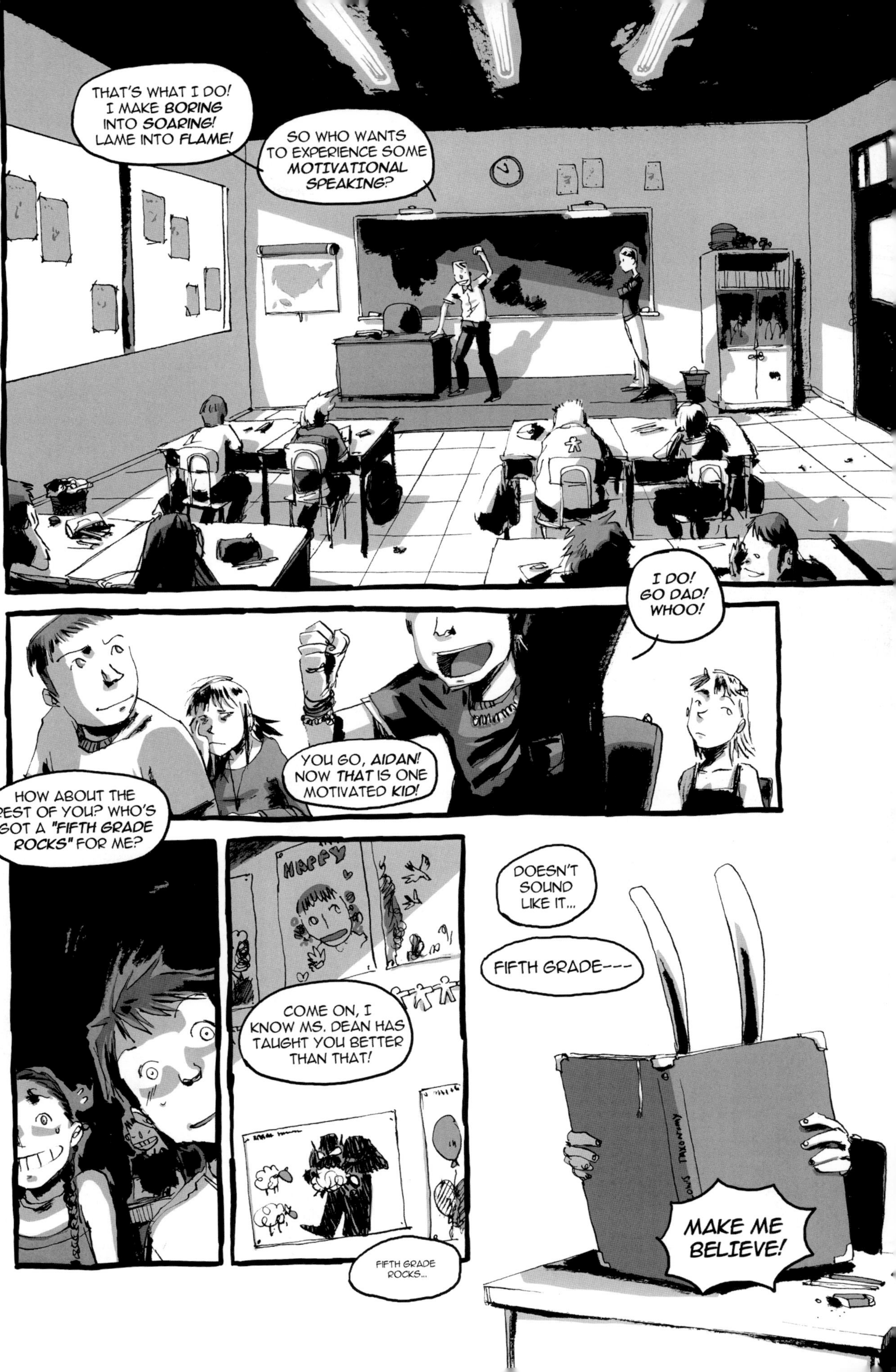
THAT'S WHAT I DO! I MAKE BORING INTO SOARING! LAME INTO FLAME!
SO WHO WANTS TO EXPERIENCE SOME MOTIVATIONAL SPEAKING?
I DO! GO DAD! WHOO!
YOU GO, AIDAN! NOW THAT IS ONE MOTIVATED KID!
HOW ABOUT THE REST OF YOU? WHO'S GOT A "FIFTH GRADE ROCKS" FOR ME?
HAPPY
COME ON, I KNOW MS. DEAN HAS TAUGHT YOU BETTER THAN THAT!
FIFTH GRADE ROCKS...
DOESN'T SOUND LIKE IT...
FIFTH GRADE---
MAKE ME BELIEVE!

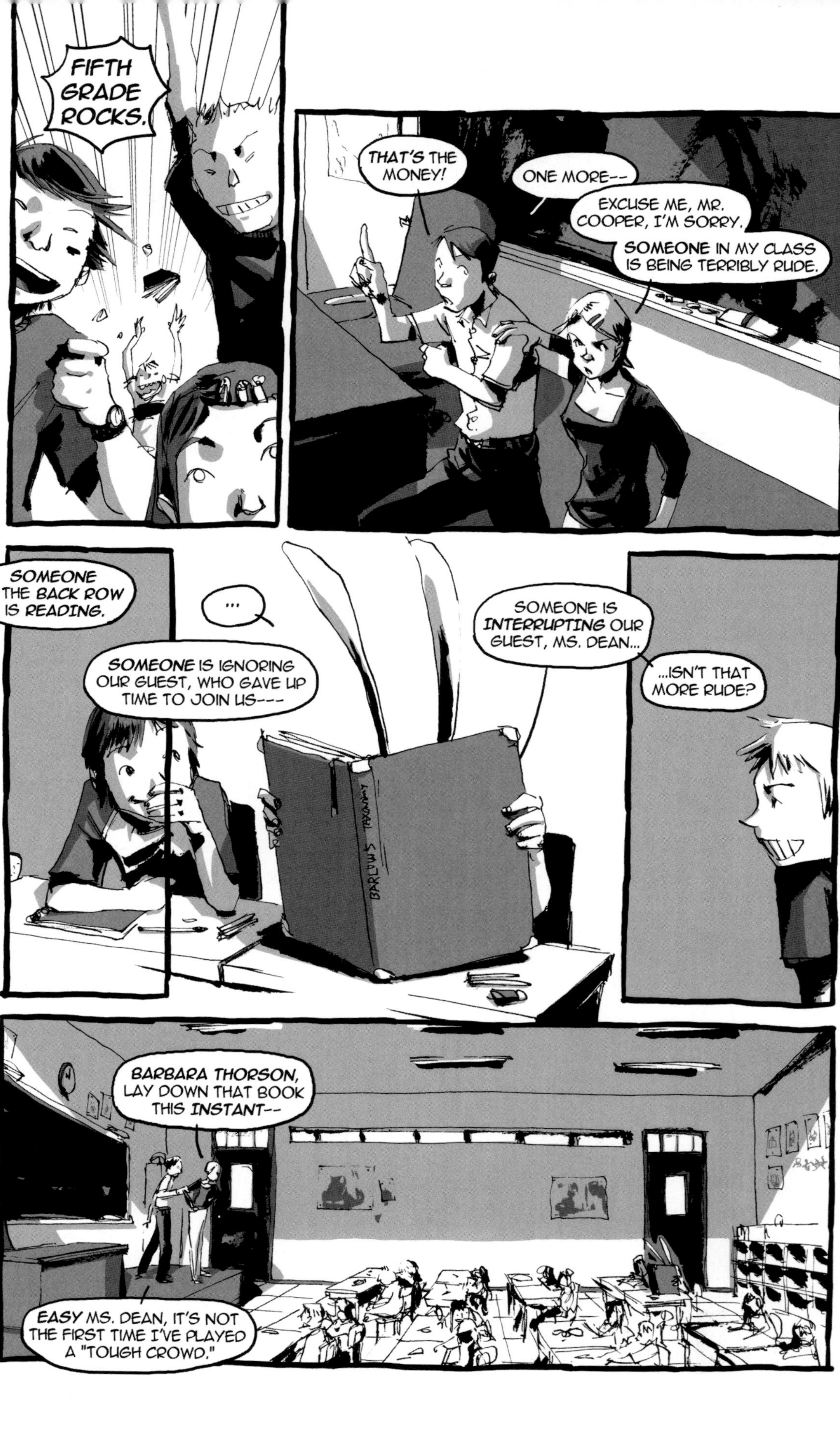
FIFTH GRADE ROCKS.
THAT'S THE MONEY!
ONE MORE--
EXCUSE ME, MR. COOPER, I'M SORRY.
SOMEONE IN MY CLASS IS BEING TERRIBLY RUDE.
SOMEONE IN THE BACK ROW IS READING.
...
SOMEONE IS IGNORING OUR GUEST, WHO GAVE UP TIME TO JOIN US---
SOMEONE IS INTERRUPTING OUR GUEST, MS. DEAN...
...ISN'T THAT MORE RUDE?
BARBARA THORSON, LAY DOWN THAT BOOK THIS INSTANT--
EASY MS. DEAN, IT'S NOT THE FIRST TIME I'VE PLAYED A "TOUGH CROWD."

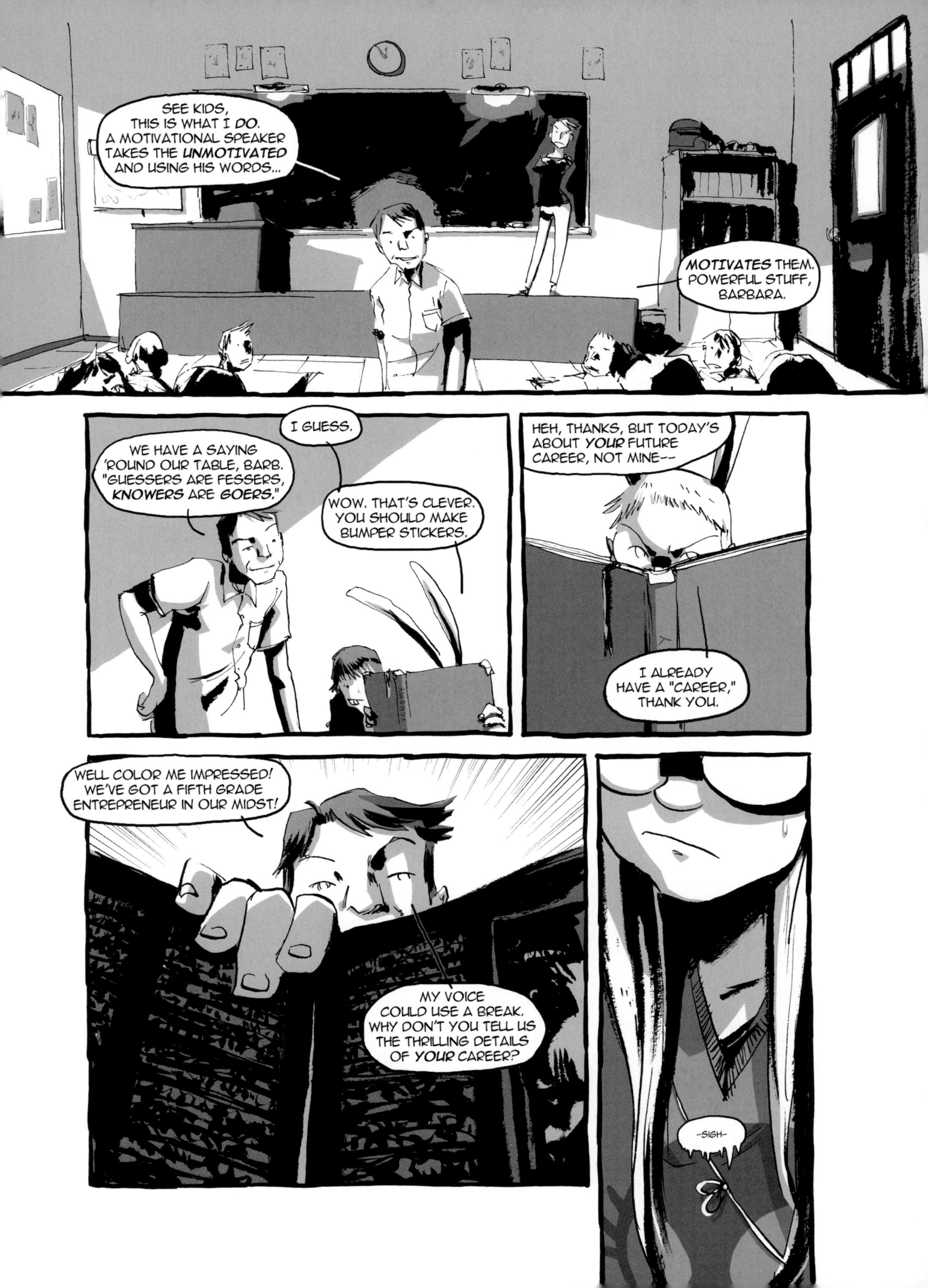
SEE KIDS, THIS IS WHAT I DO. A MOTIVATIONAL SPEAKER TAKES THE UNMOTIVATED AND USING HIS WORDS...
MOTIVATES THEM. POWERFUL STUFF, BARBARA.
I GUESS.
WE HAVE A SAYING 'ROUND OUR TABLE, BARB. "GUESSERS ARE FESSERS, KNOWERS ARE GOERS."
WOW. THAT'S CLEVER. YOU SHOULD MAKE BUMPER STICKERS.
HEH, THANKS, BUT TODAY'S ABOUT YOUR FUTURE CAREER, NOT MINE--
I ALREADY HAVE A "CAREER," THANK YOU.
WELL COLOR ME IMPRESSED! WE'VE GOT A FIFTH GRADE ENTREPRENEUR IN OUR MIDST!
MY VOICE COULD USE A BREAK. WHY DON'T YOU TELL US THE THRILLING DETAILS OF YOUR CAREER?
-SIGH-

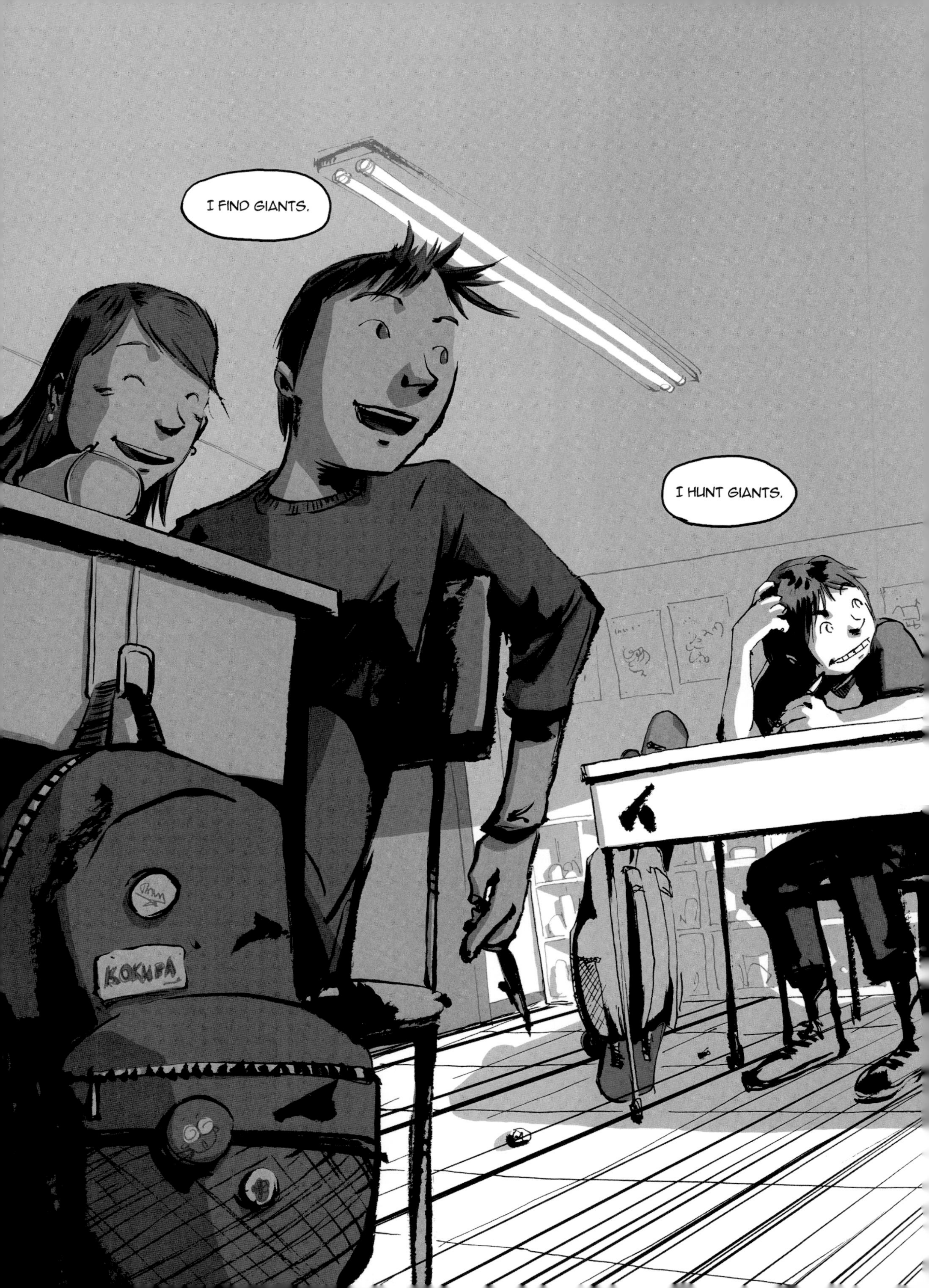
I FIND GIANTS.
I HUNT GIANTS.

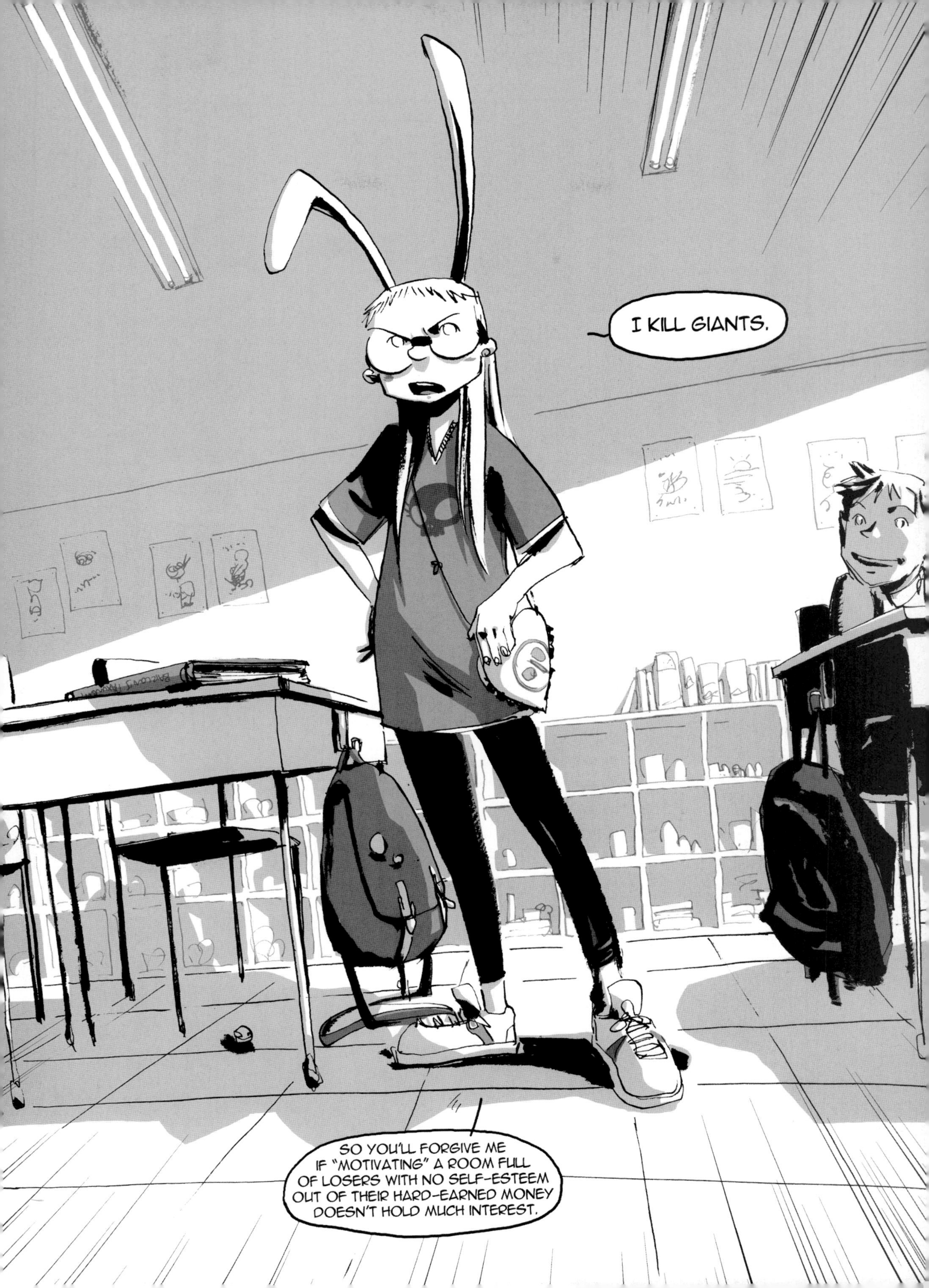
I KILL GIANTS.
SO YOU'LL FORGIVE ME IF "MOTIVATING" A ROOM FULL OF LOSERS WITH NO SELF-ESTEEM OUT OF THEIR HARD-EARNED MONEY DOESN'T HOLD MUCH INTEREST.

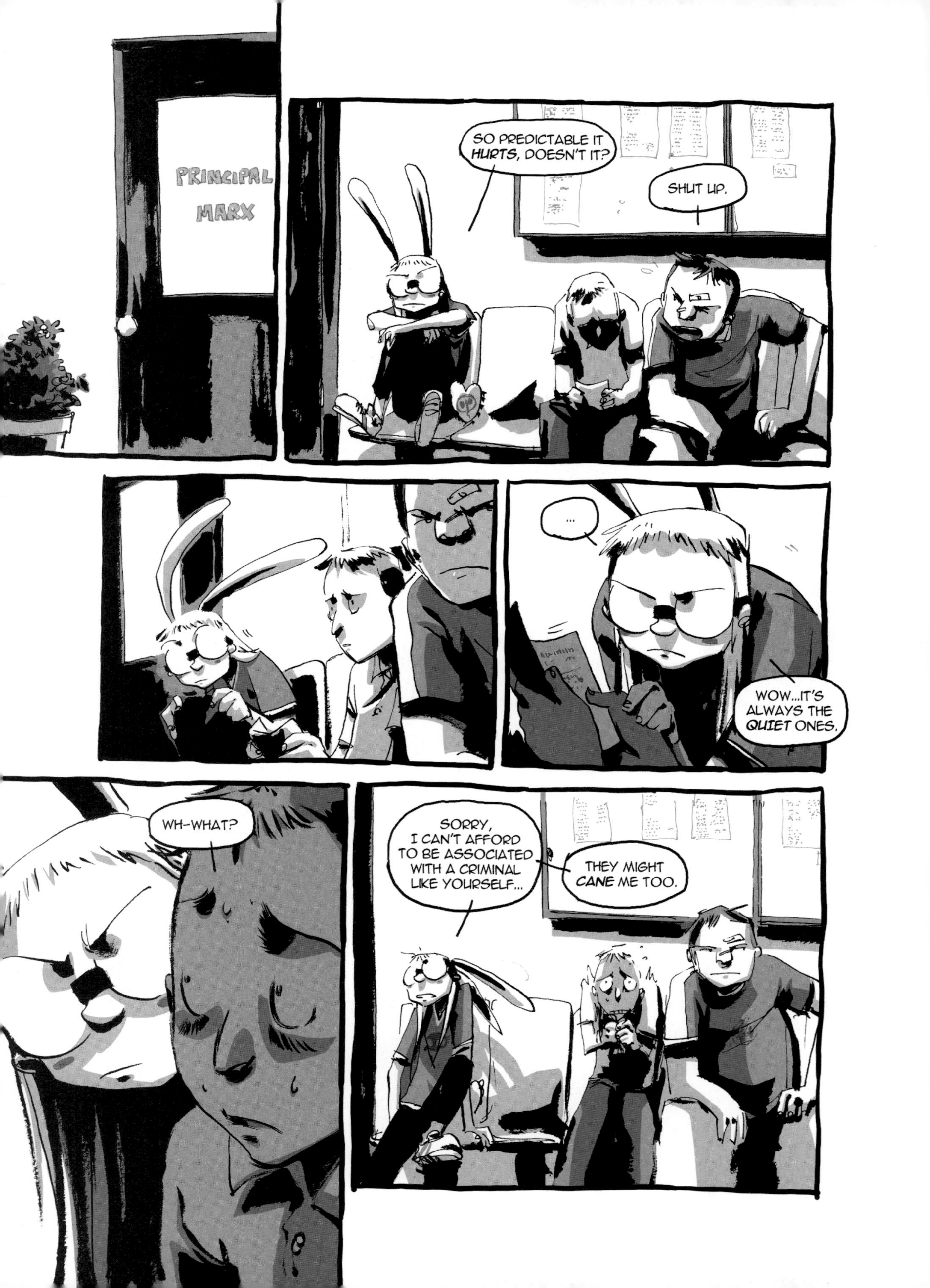
PRINCIPAL MARX
SO PREDICTABLE IT HURTS, DOESN'T IT?
SHUT UP.
...
WOW...IT'S ALWAYS THE QUIET ONES.
WH-WHAT?
SORRY, I CAN'T AFFORD TO BE ASSOCIATED WITH A CRIMINAL LIKE YOURSELF...
THEY MIGHT CANE ME TOO.

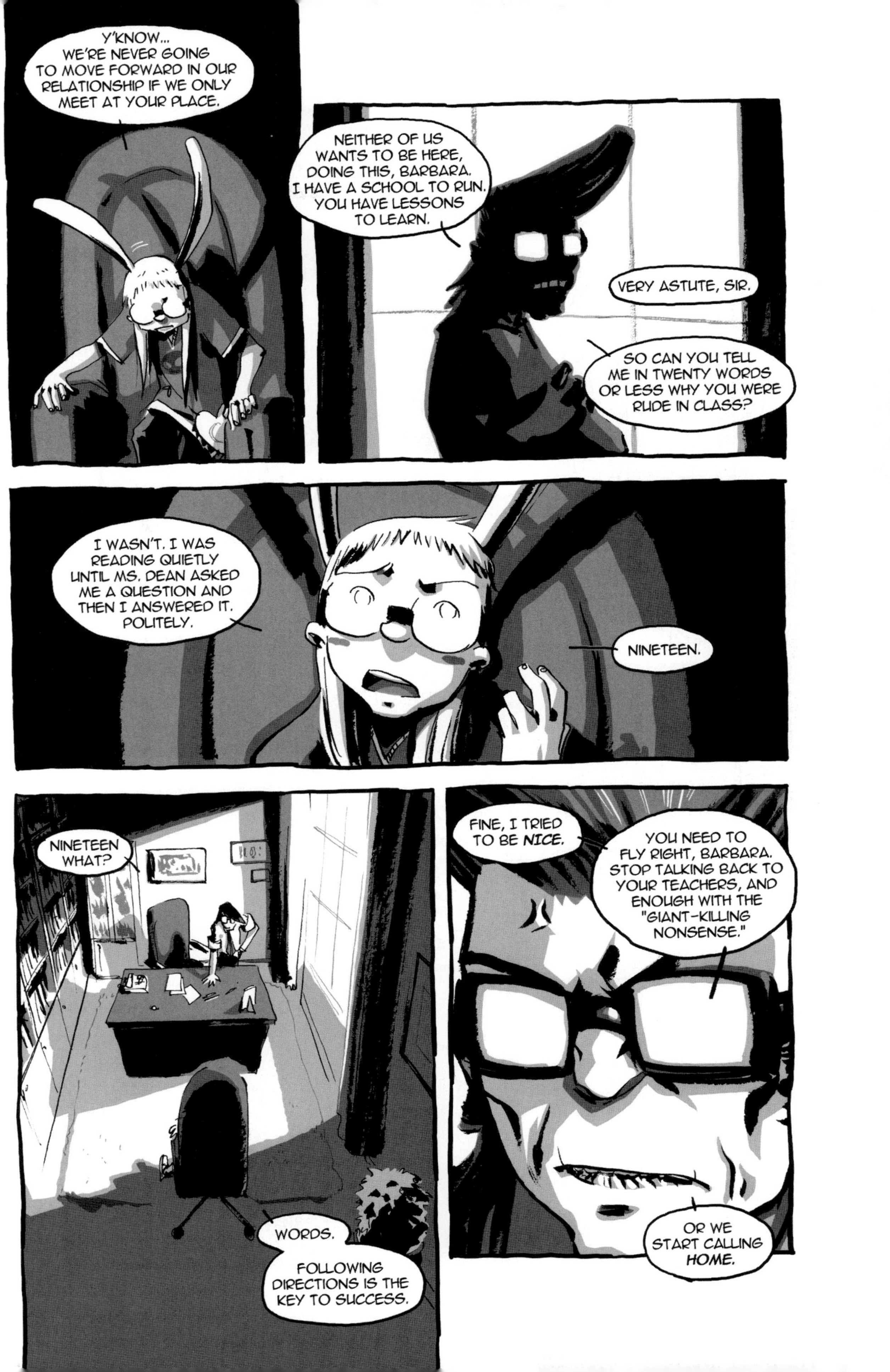
Y'KNOW... WE'RE NEVER GOING TO MOVE FORWARD IN OUR RELATIONSHIP IF WE ONLY MEET AT YOUR PLACE.
NEITHER OF US WANTS TO BE HERE, DOING THIS, BARBARA. I HAVE A SCHOOL TO RUN. YOU HAVE LESSONS TO LEARN.
VERY ASTUTE, SIR.
SO CAN YOU TELL ME IN TWENTY WORDS OR LESS WHY YOU WERE RUDE IN CLASS?
I WASN'T. I WAS READING QUIETLY UNTIL MS. DEAN ASKED ME A QUESTION AND THEN I ANSWERED IT. POLITELY.
NINETEEN.
NINETEEN WHAT?
WORDS.
FOLLOWING DIRECTIONS IS THE KEY TO SUCCESS.
FINE, I TRIED TO BE NICE.
YOU NEED TO FLY RIGHT, BARBARA. STOP TALKING BACK TO YOUR TEACHERS, AND ENOUGH WITH THE "GIANT-KILLING NONSENSE."
OR WE START CALLING HOME.

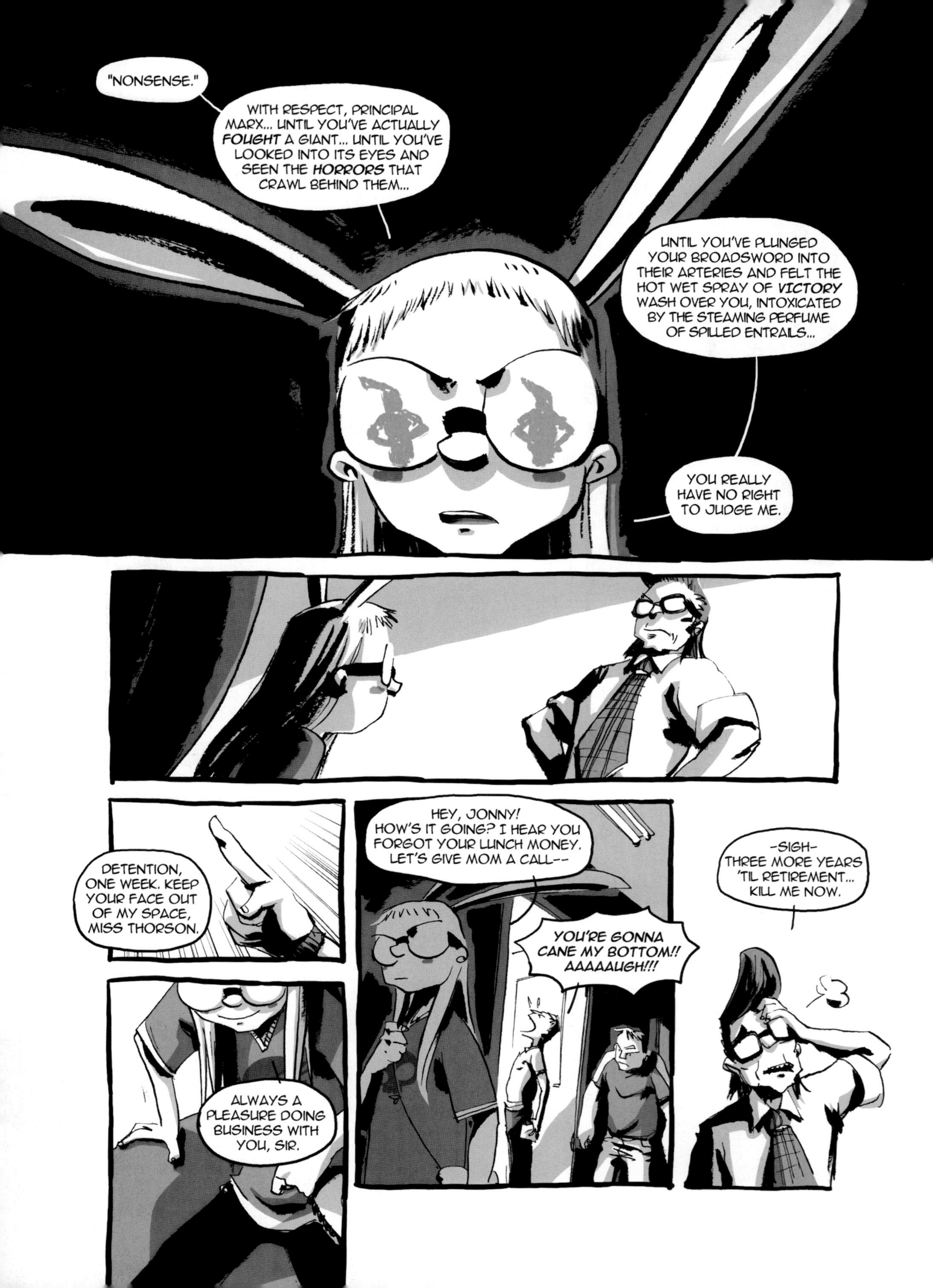
"NONSENSE."
WITH RESPECT, PRINCIPAL MARX... UNTIL YOU'VE ACTUALLY FOUGHT A GIANT... UNTIL YOU'VE LOOKED INTO ITS EYES AND SEEN THE HORRORS THAT CRAWL BEHIND THEM...
UNTIL YOU'VE PLUNGED YOUR BROADSWORD INTO THEIR ARTERIES AND FELT THE HOT WET SPRAY OF VICTORY WASH OVER YOU, INTOXICATED BY THE STEAMING PERFUME OF SPILLED ENTRAILS...
YOU REALLY HAVE NO RIGHT TO JUDGE ME.
DETENTION, ONE WEEK. KEEP YOUR FACE OUT OF MY SPACE, MISS THORSON.
ALWAYS A PLEASURE DOING BUSINESS WITH YOU, SIR.
HEY, JONNY! HOW'S IT GOING? I HEAR YOU FORGOT YOUR LUNCH MONEY. LET'S GIVE MOM A CALL--
YOU'RE GONNA CANE MY BOTTOM!! AAAAAUGH!!!
-SIGH- THREE MORE YEARS 'TIL RETIREMENT... KILL ME NOW.

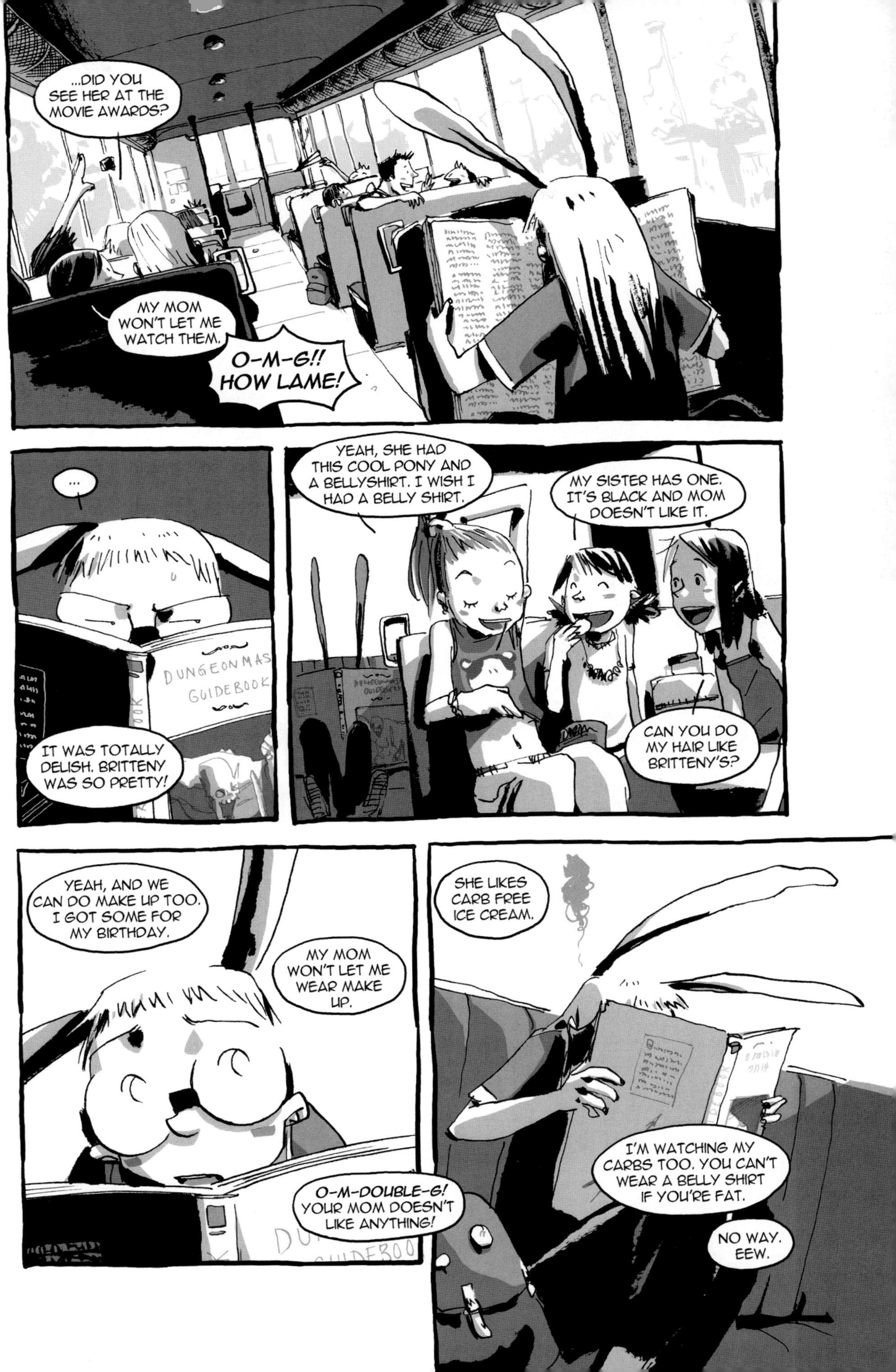
...DID YOU SEE HER AT THE MOVIE AWARDS?
MY MOM WON'T LET ME WATCH THEM.
O-M-G!! HOW LAME!
...
IT WAS TOTALLY DELISH. BRITTENY WAS SO PRETTY!
DUNGEONMAS GUIDEBOOK
YEAH, SHE HAD THIS COOL PONY AND A BELLYSHIRT. I WISH I HAD A BELLY SHIRT.
MY SISTER HAS ONE. IT'S BLACK AND MOM DOESN'T LIKE IT.
CAN YOU DO MY HAIR LIKE BRITTENY'S?
YEAH, AND WE CAN DO MAKE UP TOO. I GOT SOME FOR MY BIRTHDAY.
MY MOM WON'T LET ME WEAR MAKE UP.
O-M-DOUBLE-G! YOUR MOM DOESN'T LIKE ANYTHING!
SHE LIKES CARB FREE ICE CREAM.
I'M WATCHING MY CARBS TOO. YOU CAN'T WEAR A BELLY SHIRT IF YOU'RE FAT.
NO WAY. EEW.

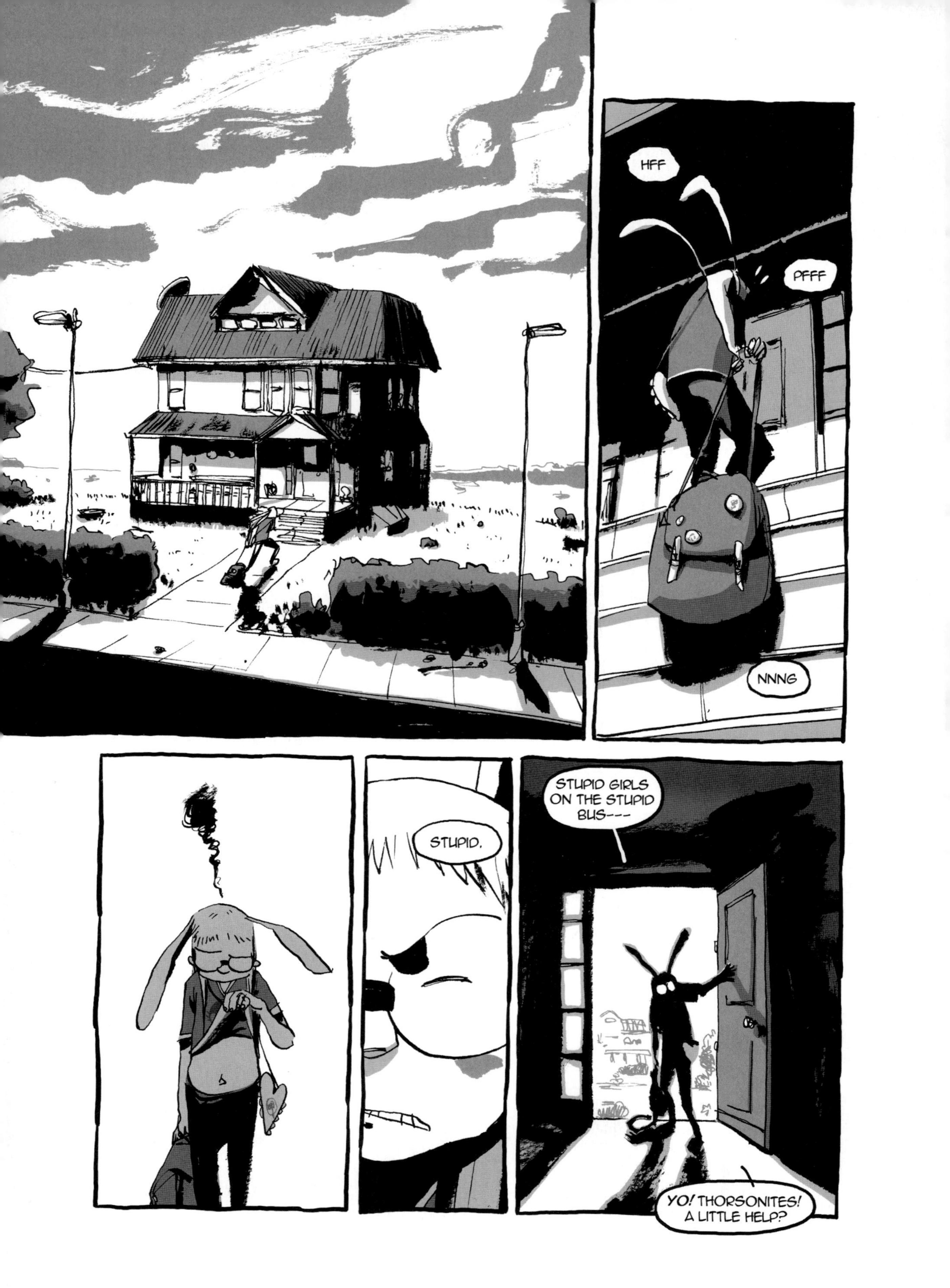
HFF
PFFF
NNNG
STUPID.
STUPID GIRLS ON THE STUPID BUS---
YO! THORSONITES! A LITTLE HELP?

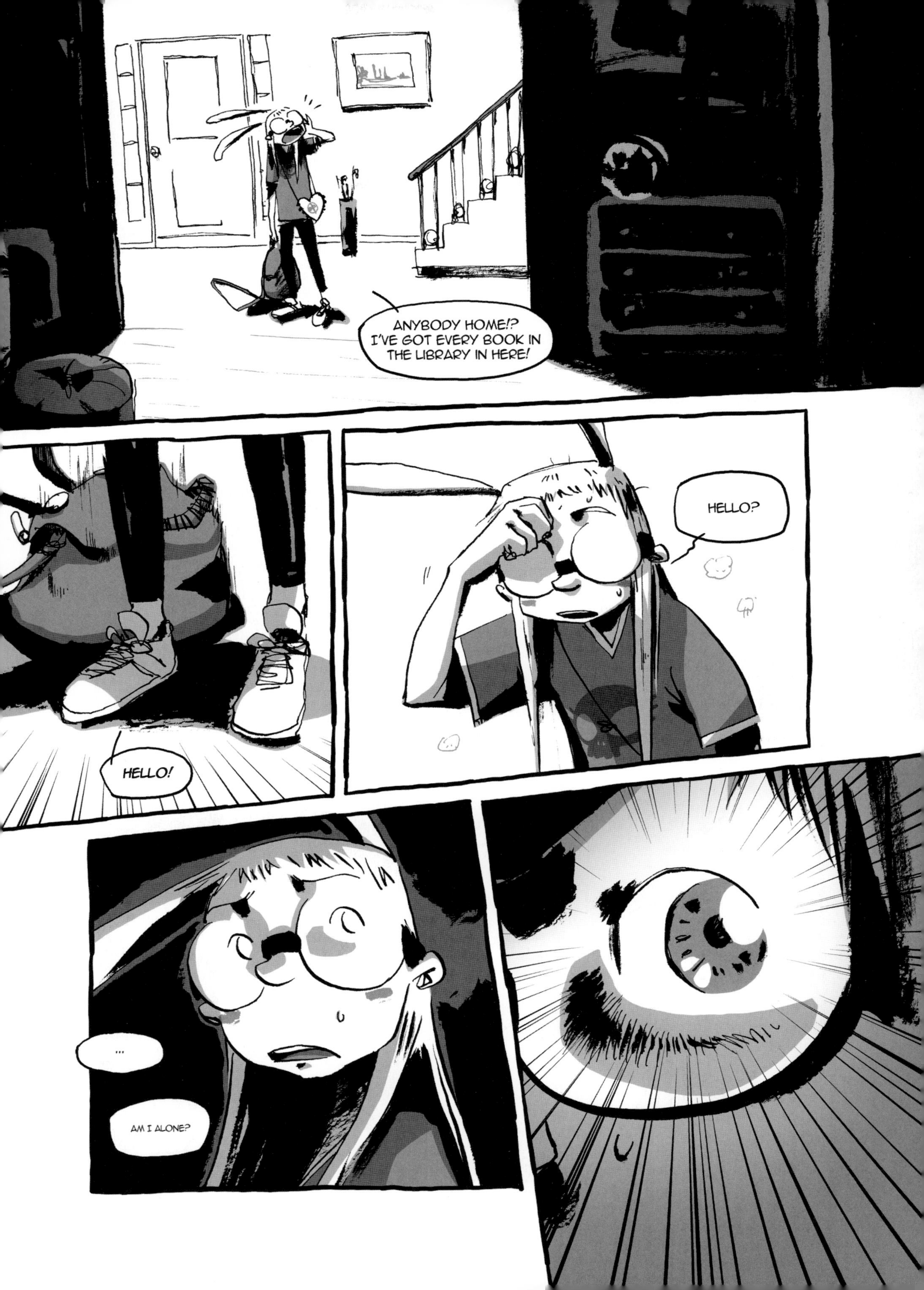
ANYBODY HOME!? I'VE GOT EVERY BOOK IN THE LIBRARY IN HERE!
HELLO!
HELLO?
...
AM I ALONE?

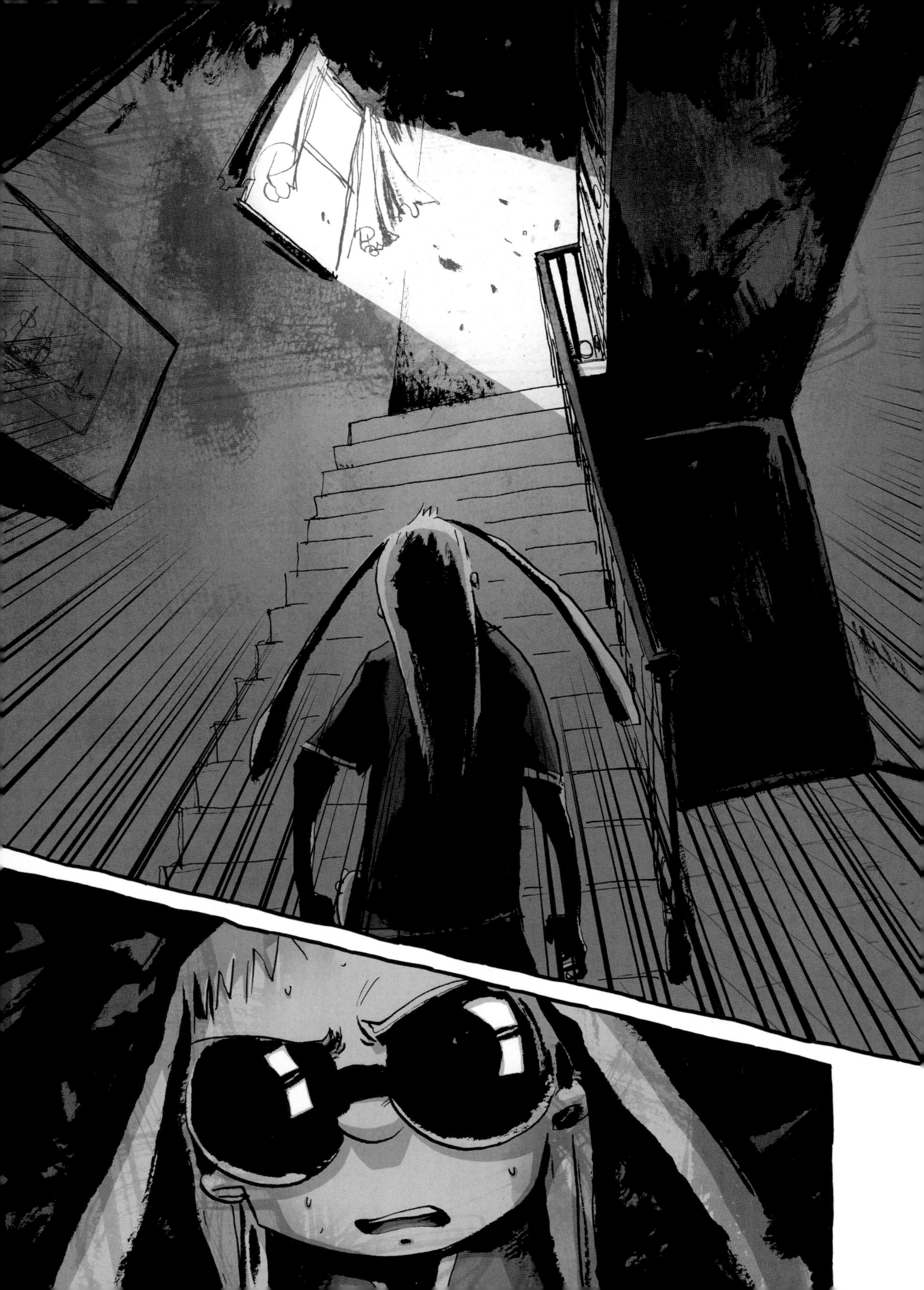

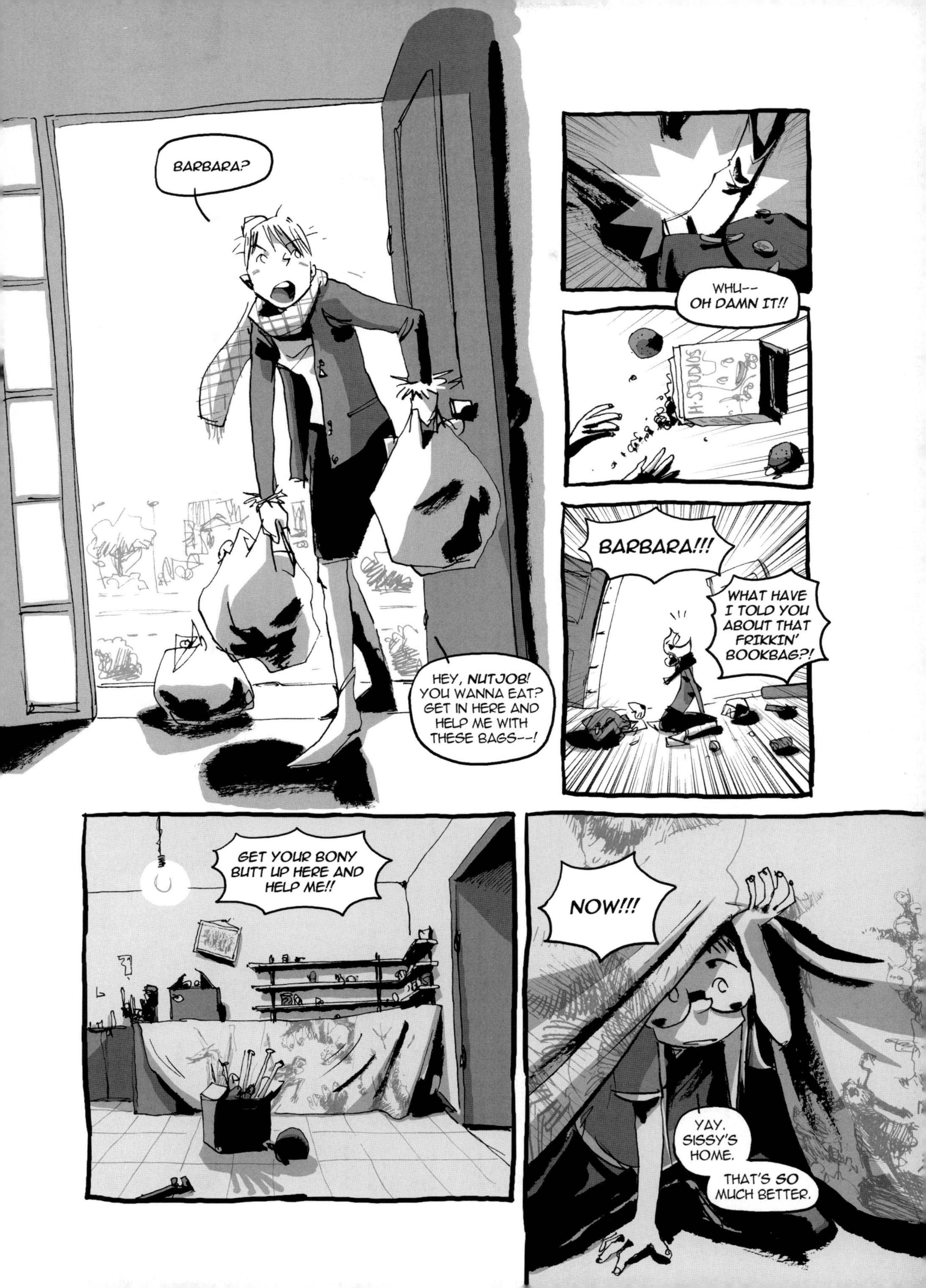
BARBARA?
HEY, NUTJOB! YOU WANNA EAT? GET IN HERE AND HELP ME WITH THESE BAGS--!
WHU-- OH DAMN IT!!
H·STUDIOS
BARBARA!!!
WHAT HAVE I TOLD YOU ABOUT THAT FRIKKIN' BOOKBAG?!
GET YOUR BONY BUTT UP HERE AND HELP ME!!
NOW!!!
YAY. SISSY'S HOME.
THAT'S SO MUCH BETTER.

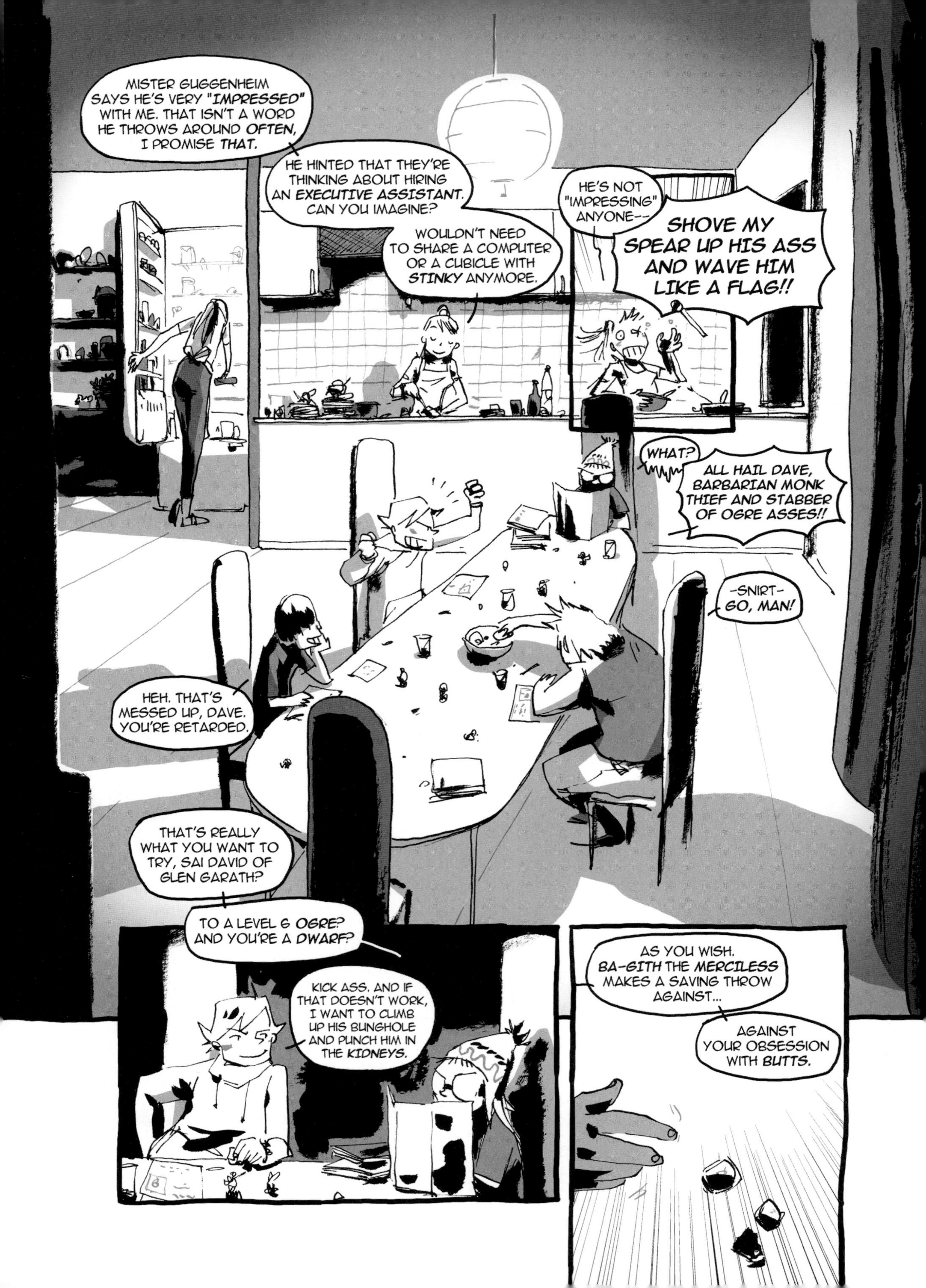
MISTER GUGGENHEIM SAYS HE'S VERY "IMPRESSED" WITH ME. THAT ISN'T A WORD HE THROWS AROUND OFTEN, I PROMISE THAT.
HE HINTED THAT THEY'RE THINKING ABOUT HIRING AN EXECUTIVE ASSISTANT. CAN YOU IMAGINE?
WOULDN'T NEED TO SHARE A COMPUTER OR A CUBICLE WITH STINKY ANYMORE.
HE'S NOT "IMPRESSING" ANYONE--
SHOVE MY SPEAR UP HIS ASS AND WAVE HIM LIKE A FLAG!!
WHAT?
ALL HAIL DAVE, BARBARIAN MONK THIEF AND STABBER OF OGRE ASSES!!
-SNIRT- GO, MAN!
HEH. THAT'S MESSED UP, DAVE. YOU'RE RETARDED.
THAT'S REALLY WHAT YOU WANT TO TRY, SAI DAVID OF GLEN GARATH?
TO A LEVEL 6 OGRE? AND YOU'RE A DWARF?
KICK ASS. AND IF THAT DOESN'T WORK, I WANT TO CLIMB UP HIS BUNGHOLE AND PUNCH HIM IN THE KIDNEYS.
AS YOU WISH. BA-GITH THE MERCILESS MAKES A SAVING THROW AGAINST...
AGAINST YOUR OBSESSION WITH BUTTS.

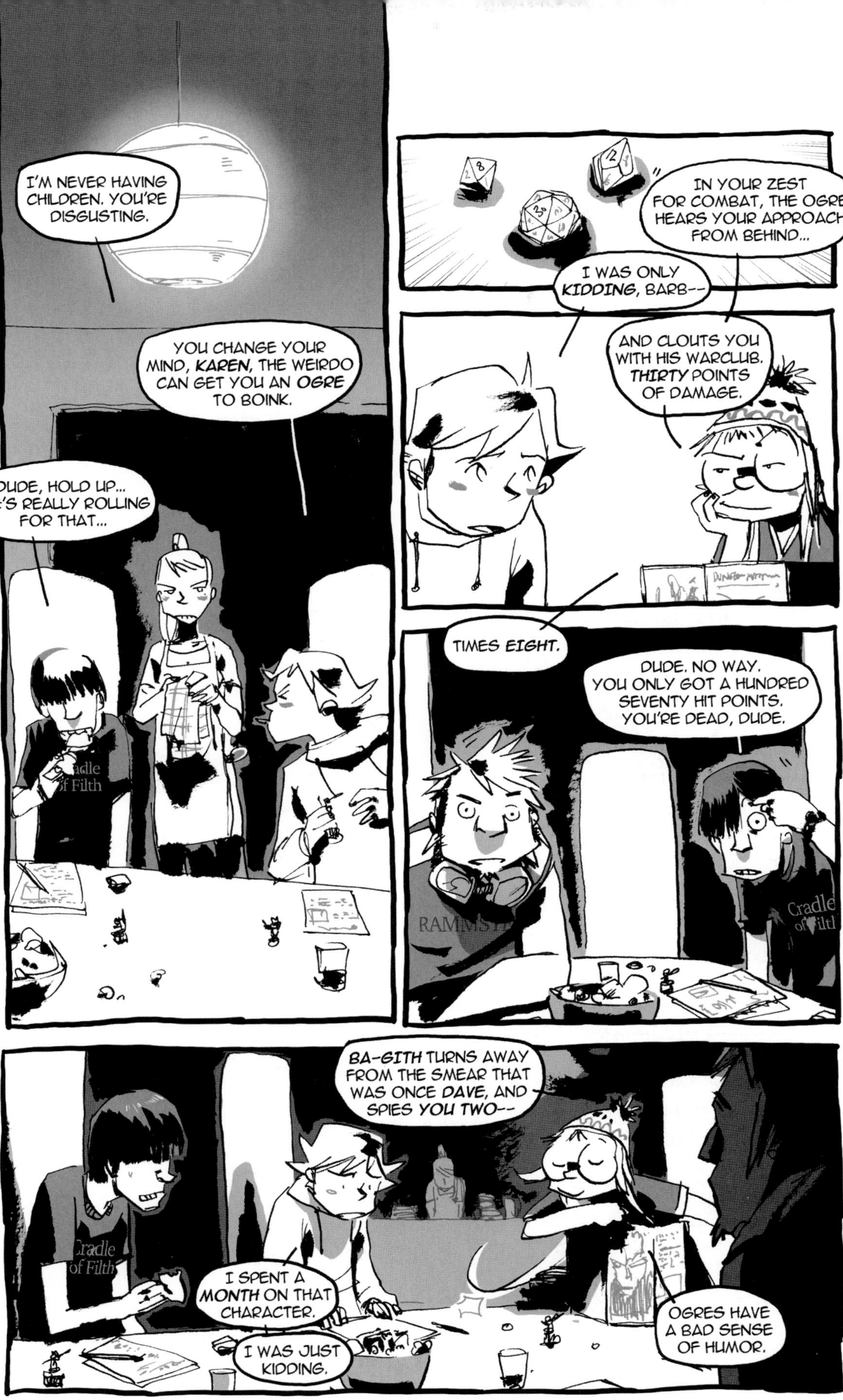
I'M NEVER HAVING CHILDREN. YOU'RE DISGUSTING.
YOU CHANGE YOUR MIND, KAREN, THE WEIRDO CAN GET YOU AN OGRE TO BOINK.
DUDE, HOLD UP... SHE'S REALLY ROLLING FOR THAT...
Cradle of Filth
IN YOUR ZEST FOR COMBAT, THE OGRE HEARS YOUR APPROACH FROM BEHIND...
I WAS ONLY KIDDING, BARB--
AND CLOUTS YOU WITH HIS WARCLUB. THIRTY POINTS OF DAMAGE.
TIMES EIGHT.
DUDE. NO WAY. YOU ONLY GOT A HUNDRED SEVENTY HIT POINTS. YOU'RE DEAD, DUDE.
Cradle of Filth
BA-GITH TURNS AWAY FROM THE SMEAR THAT WAS ONCE DAVE, AND SPIES YOU TWO--
Cradle of Filth
I SPENT A MONTH ON THAT CHARACTER.
I WAS JUST KIDDING.
OGRES HAVE A BAD SENSE OF HUMOR.

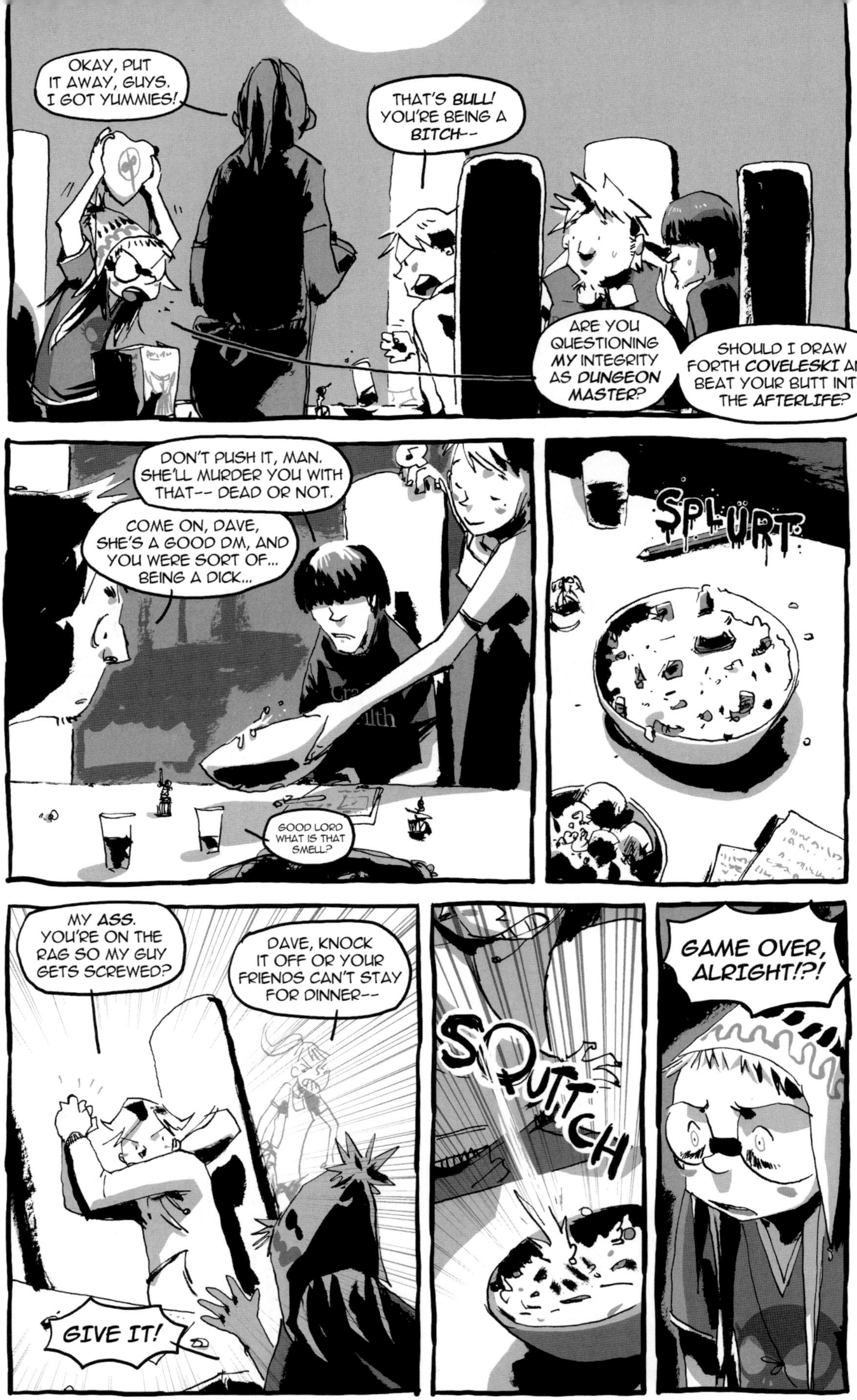
OKAY, PUT IT AWAY, GUYS. I GOT YUMMIES!
THAT'S BULL! YOU'RE BEING A BITCH--
ARE YOU QUESTIONING MY INTEGRITY AS DUNGEON MASTER?
SHOULD I DRAW FORTH COVELESKI AND BEAT YOUR BUTT INTO THE AFTERLIFE?
DON'T PUSH IT, MAN. SHE'LL MURDER YOU WITH THAT-- DEAD OR NOT.
COME ON, DAVE, SHE'S A GOOD DM, AND YOU WERE SORT OF... BEING A DICK...
GOOD LORD WHAT IS THAT SMELL?
SPLURT
MY ASS. YOU'RE ON THE RAG SO MY GUY GETS SCREWED?
DAVE, KNOCK IT OFF OR YOUR FRIENDS CAN'T STAY FOR DINNER--
GIVE IT!
SPUTTCH
GAME OVER, ALRIGHT!?!

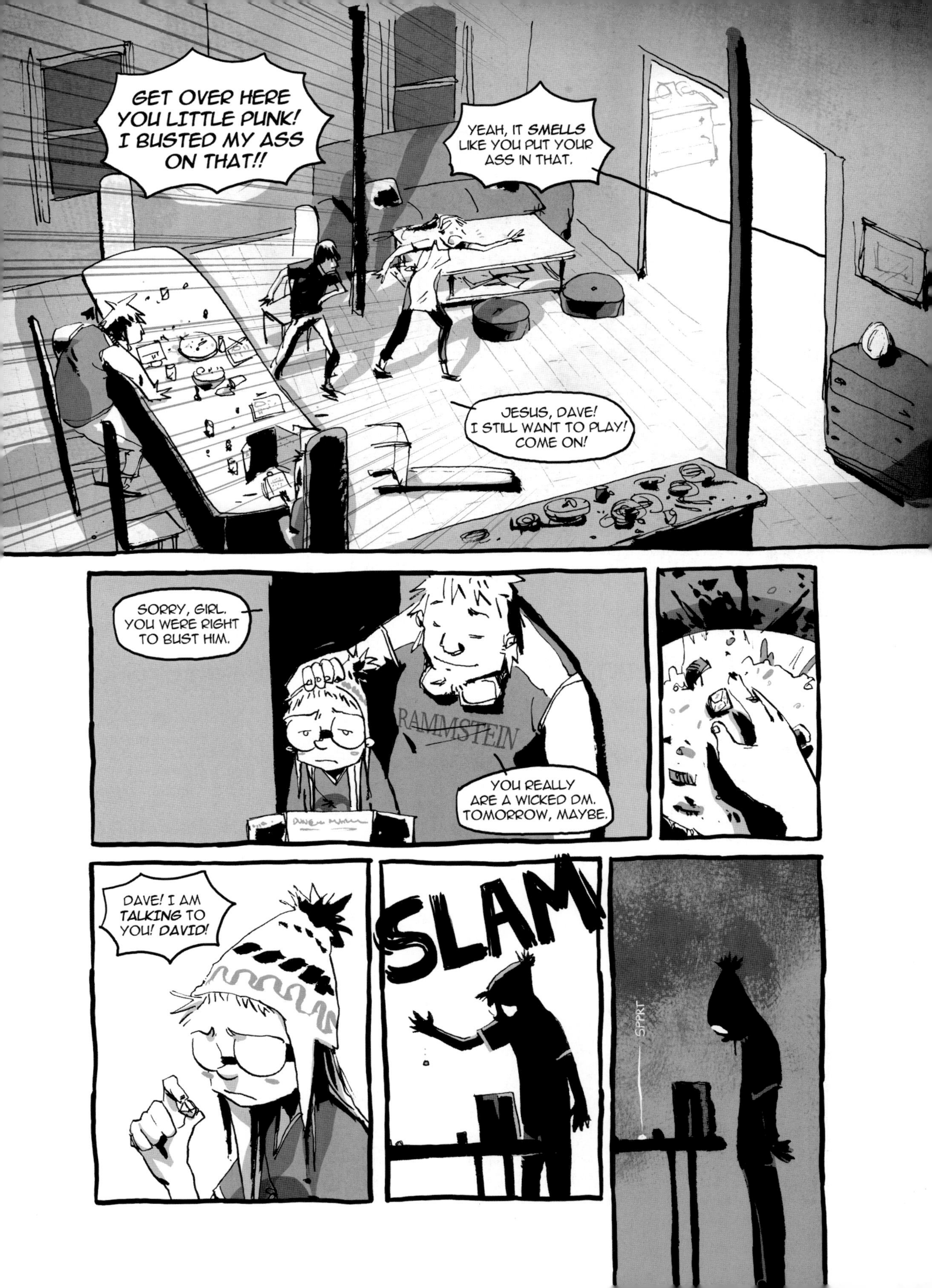
GET OVER HERE YOU LITTLE PUNK! I BUSTED MY ASS ON THAT!!
YEAH, IT SMELLS LIKE YOU PUT YOUR ASS IN THAT.
JESUS, DAVE! I STILL WANT TO PLAY! COME ON!
SORRY, GIRL. YOU WERE RIGHT TO BUST HIM.
RAMMSTEIN
YOU REALLY ARE A WICKED DM. TOMORROW, MAYBE.
DAVE! I AM TALKING TO YOU! DAVID!
SLAM
SPPRT

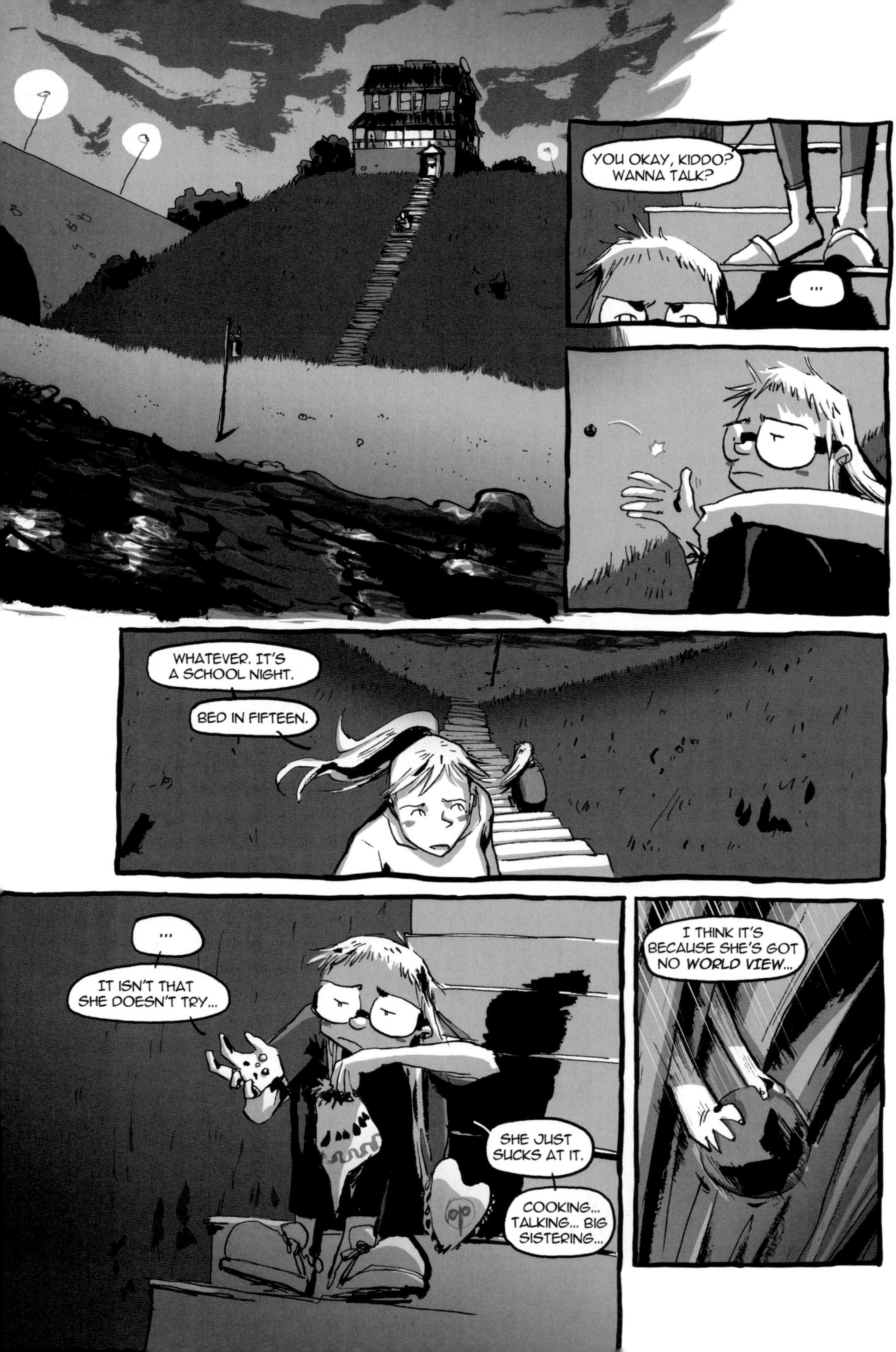
YOU OKAY, KIDDO? WANNA TALK?
...
WHATEVER. IT'S A SCHOOL NIGHT.
BED IN FIFTEEN.
...
IT ISN'T THAT SHE DOESN'T TRY...
SHE JUST SUCKS AT IT.
COOKING... TALKING... BIG SISTERING...
I THINK IT'S BECAUSE SHE'S GOT NO WORLD VIEW...

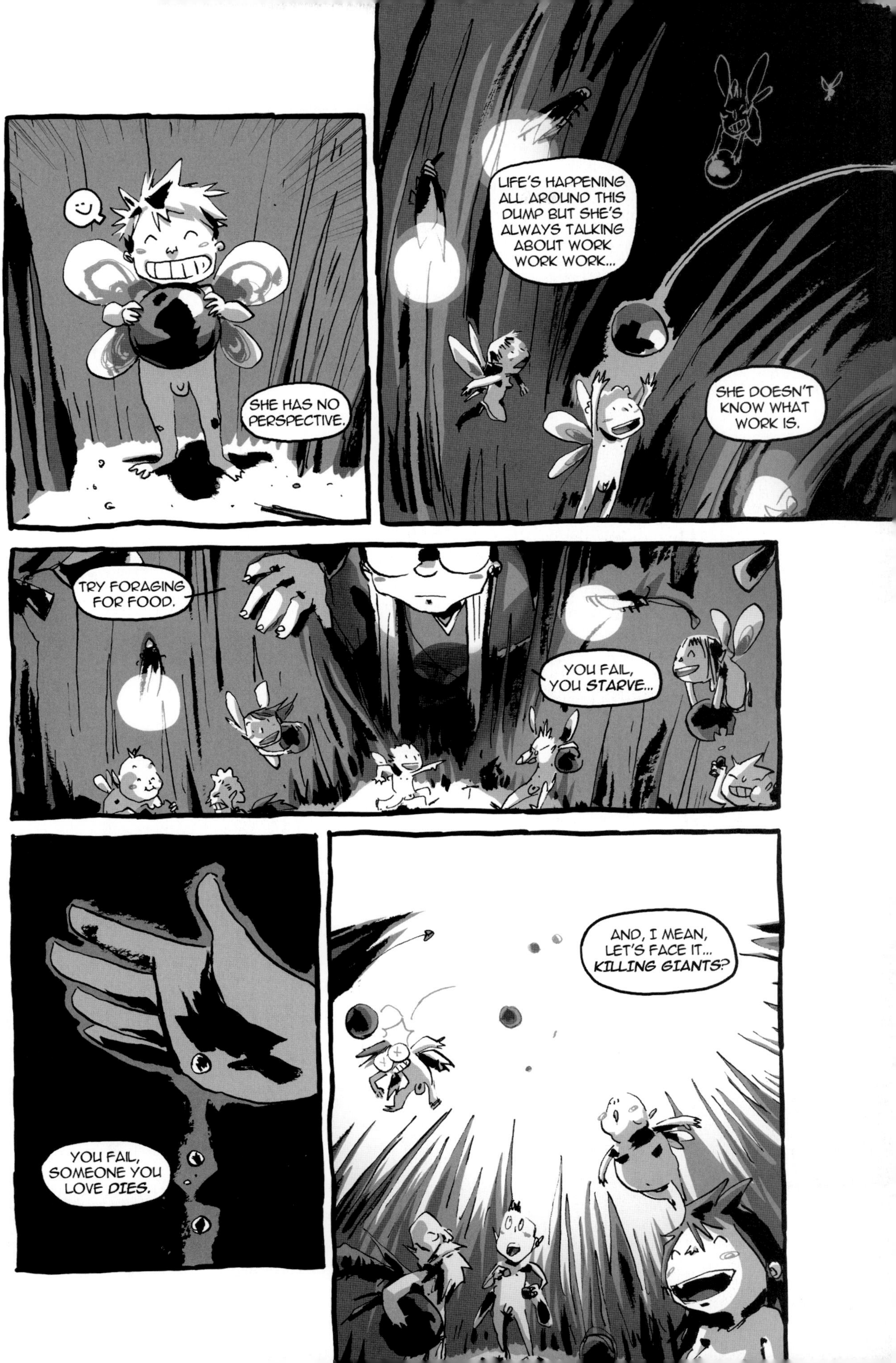
SHE HAS NO PERSPECTIVE.
LIFE'S HAPPENING ALL AROUND THIS DUMP BUT SHE'S ALWAYS TALKING ABOUT WORK WORK WORK...
SHE DOESN'T KNOW WHAT WORK IS.
TRY FORAGING FOR FOOD.
YOU FAIL, YOU STARVE...
YOU FAIL, SOMEONE YOU LOVE DIES.
AND, I MEAN, LET'S FACE IT... KILLING GIANTS?

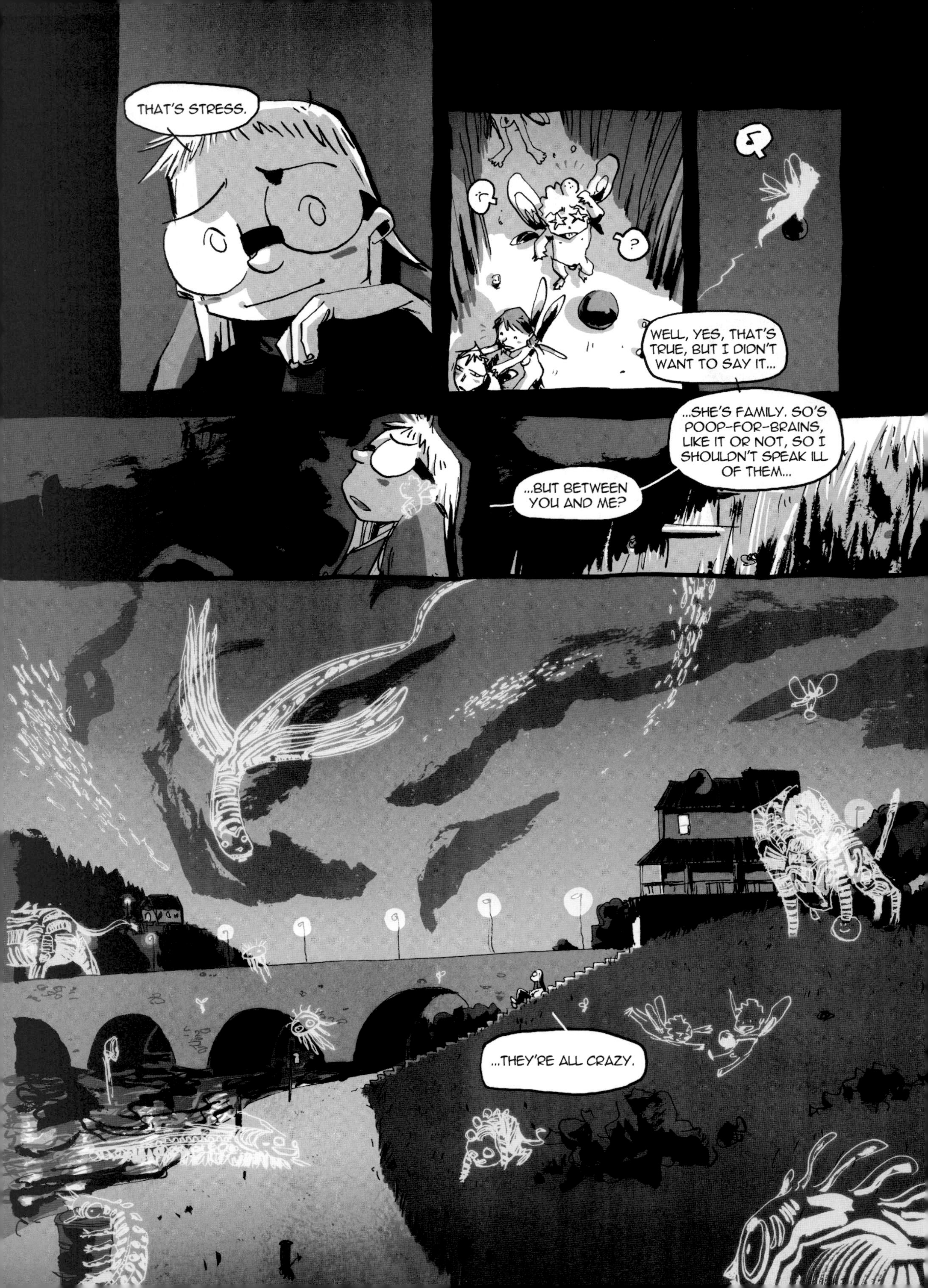
THAT'S STRESS.
WELL, YES, THAT'S TRUE, BUT I DIDN'T WANT TO SAY IT...
...SHE'S FAMILY. SO'S POOP-FOR-BRAINS, LIKE IT OR NOT, SO I SHOULDN'T SPEAK ILL OF THEM...
...BUT BETWEEN YOU AND ME?
...THEY'RE ALL CRAZY.

CHAPTER2: THE SPARK

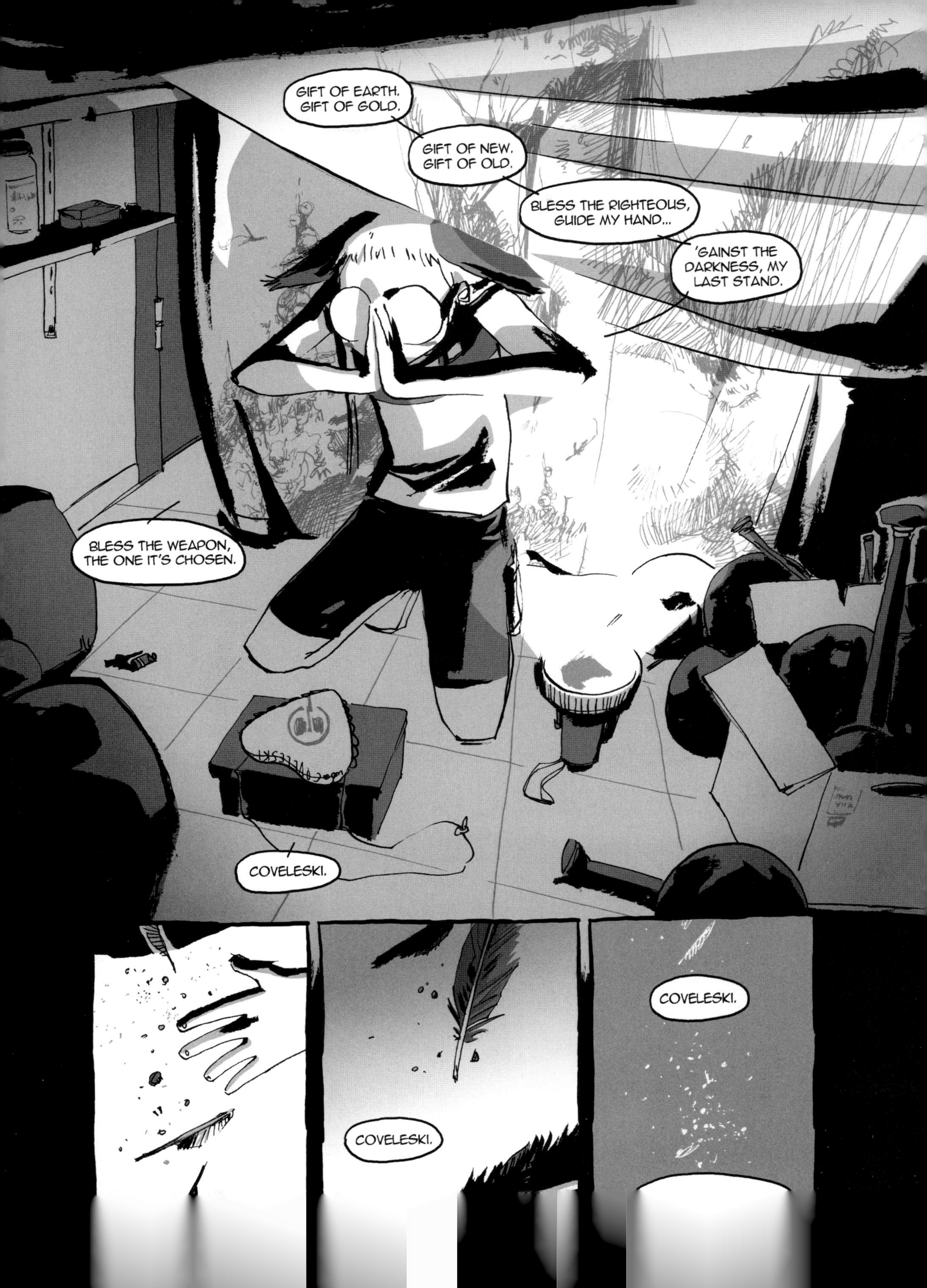
GIFT OF EARTH. GIFT OF GOLD.
GIFT OF NEW. GIFT OF OLD.
BLESS THE RIGHTEOUS, GUIDE MY HAND...
'GAINST THE DARKNESS, MY LAST STAND.
BLESS THE WEAPON, THE ONE IT'S CHOSEN.
COVELESKI.
COVELESKI.
COVELESKI.

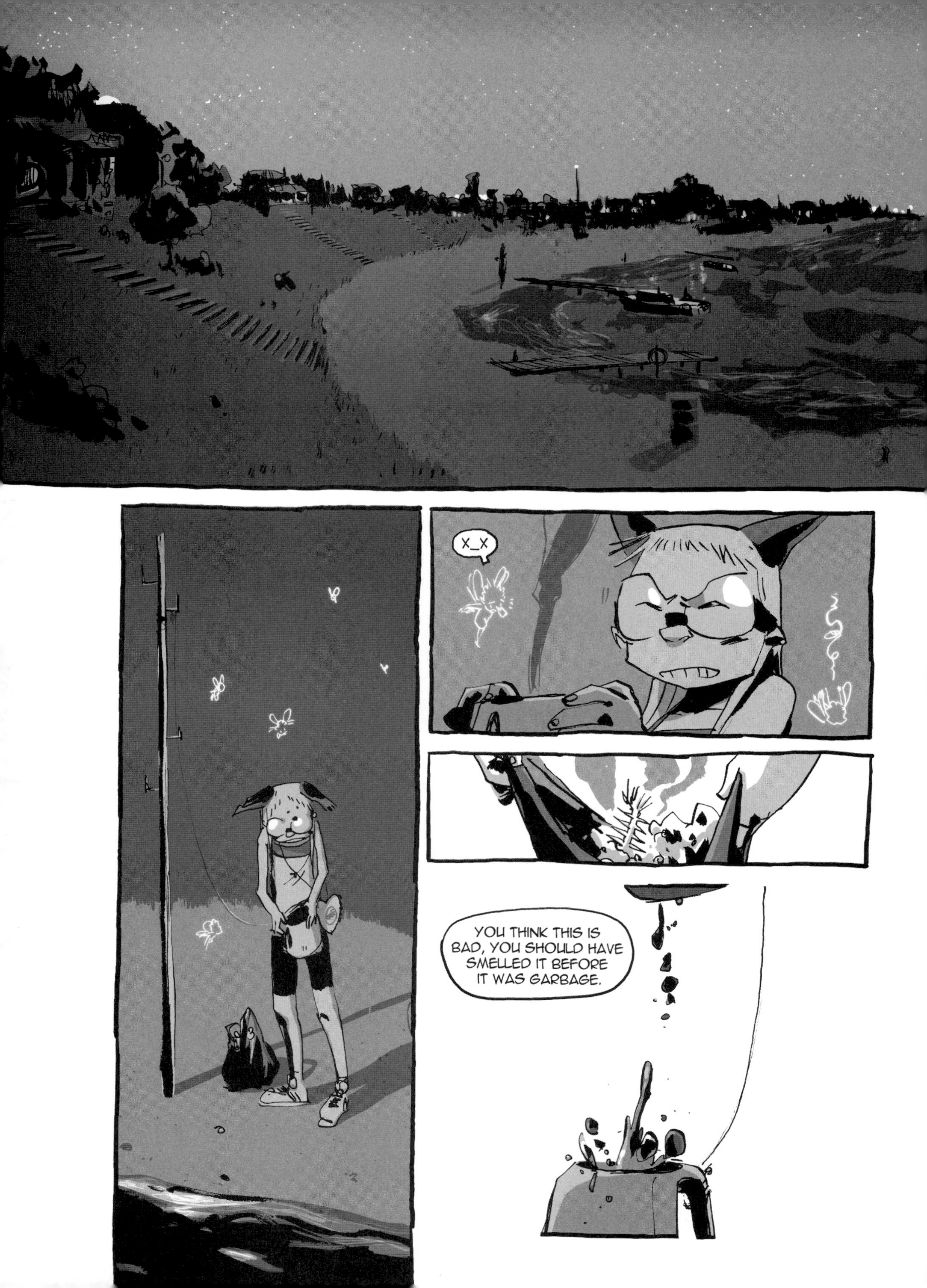
X_X
YOU THINK THIS IS BAD, YOU SHOULD HAVE SMELLED IT BEFORE IT WAS GARBAGE.

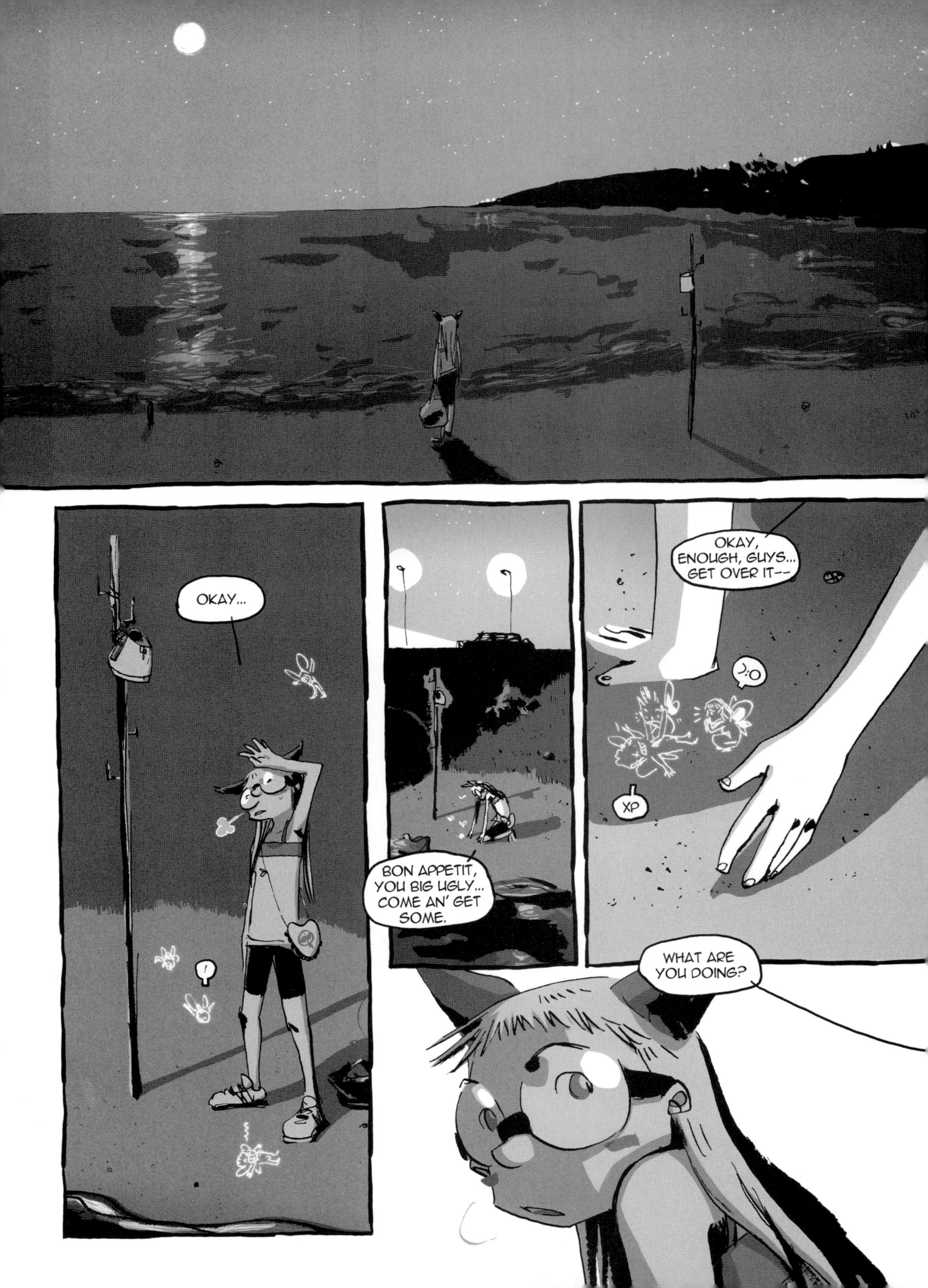
OKAY...
!
BON APPETIT, YOU BIG UGLY... COME AN' GET SOME.
OKAY, ENOUGH, GUYS... GET OVER IT--
):O
XP
WHAT ARE YOU DOING?

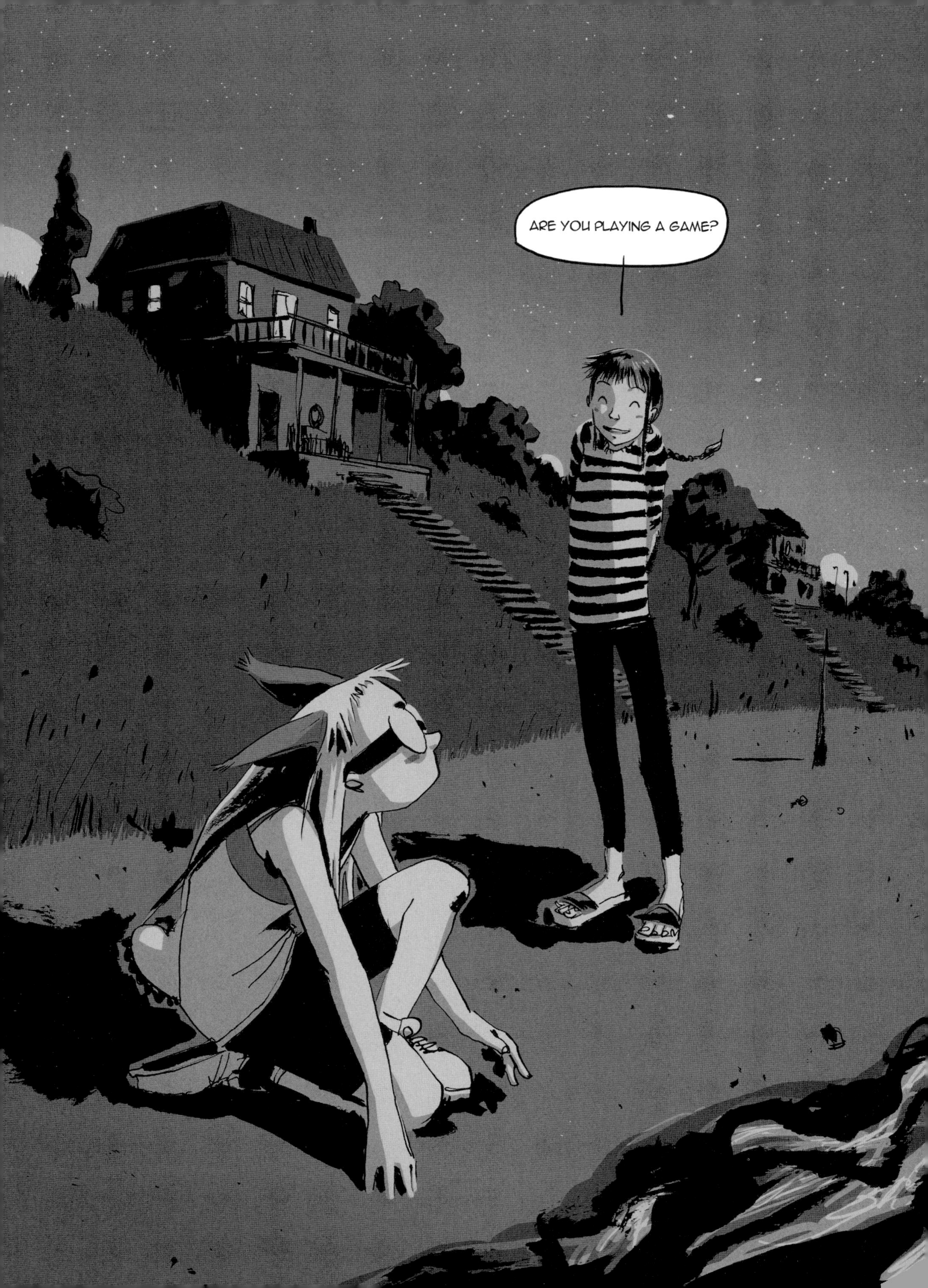
ARE YOU PLAYING A GAME?

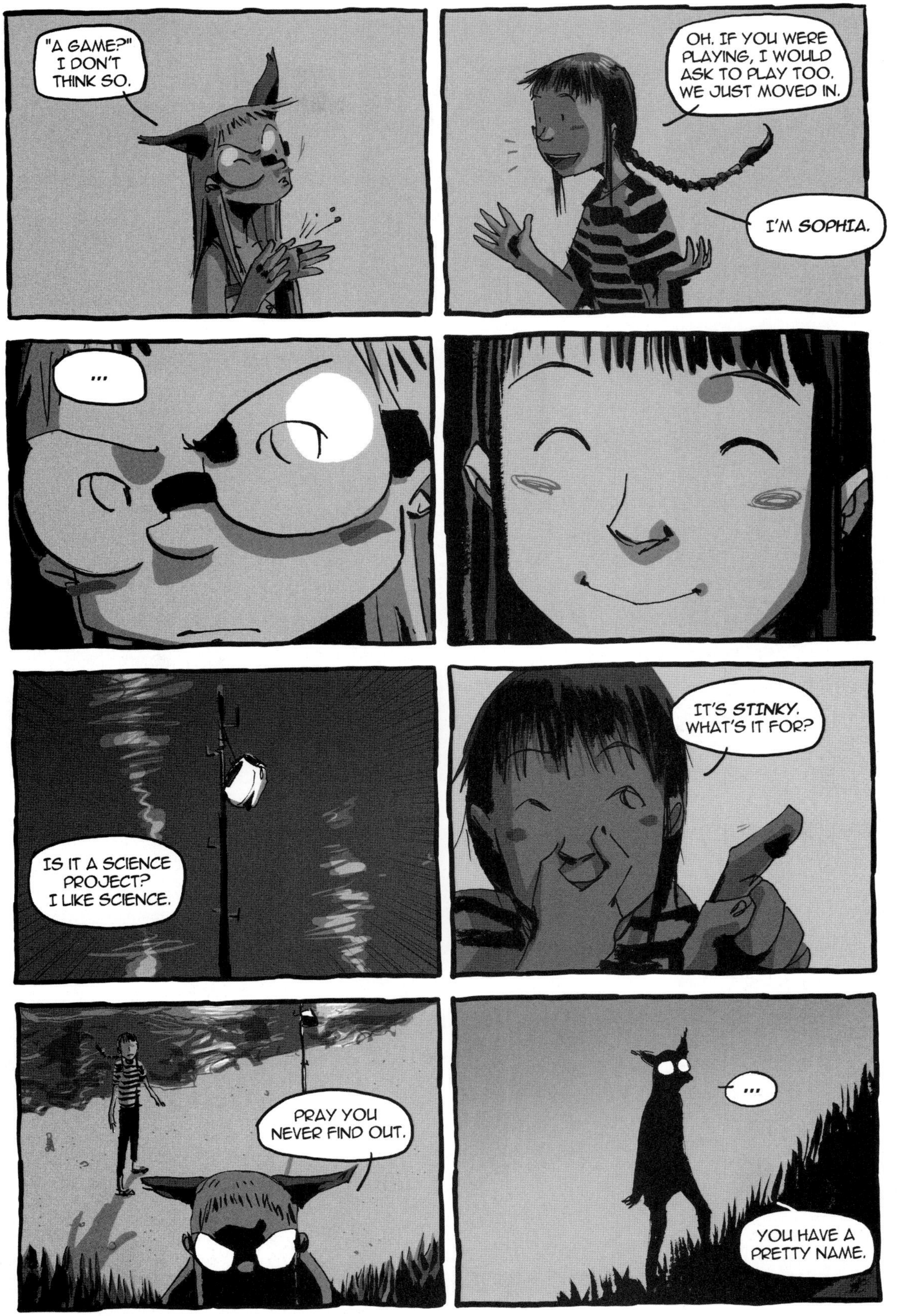
"A GAME?" I DON'T THINK SO.
OH. IF YOU WERE PLAYING, I WOULD ASK TO PLAY TOO. WE JUST MOVED IN.
I'M SOPHIA.
...
IS IT A SCIENCE PROJECT? I LIKE SCIENCE.
IT'S STINKY. WHAT'S IT FOR?
PRAY YOU NEVER FIND OUT.
...
YOU HAVE A PRETTY NAME.

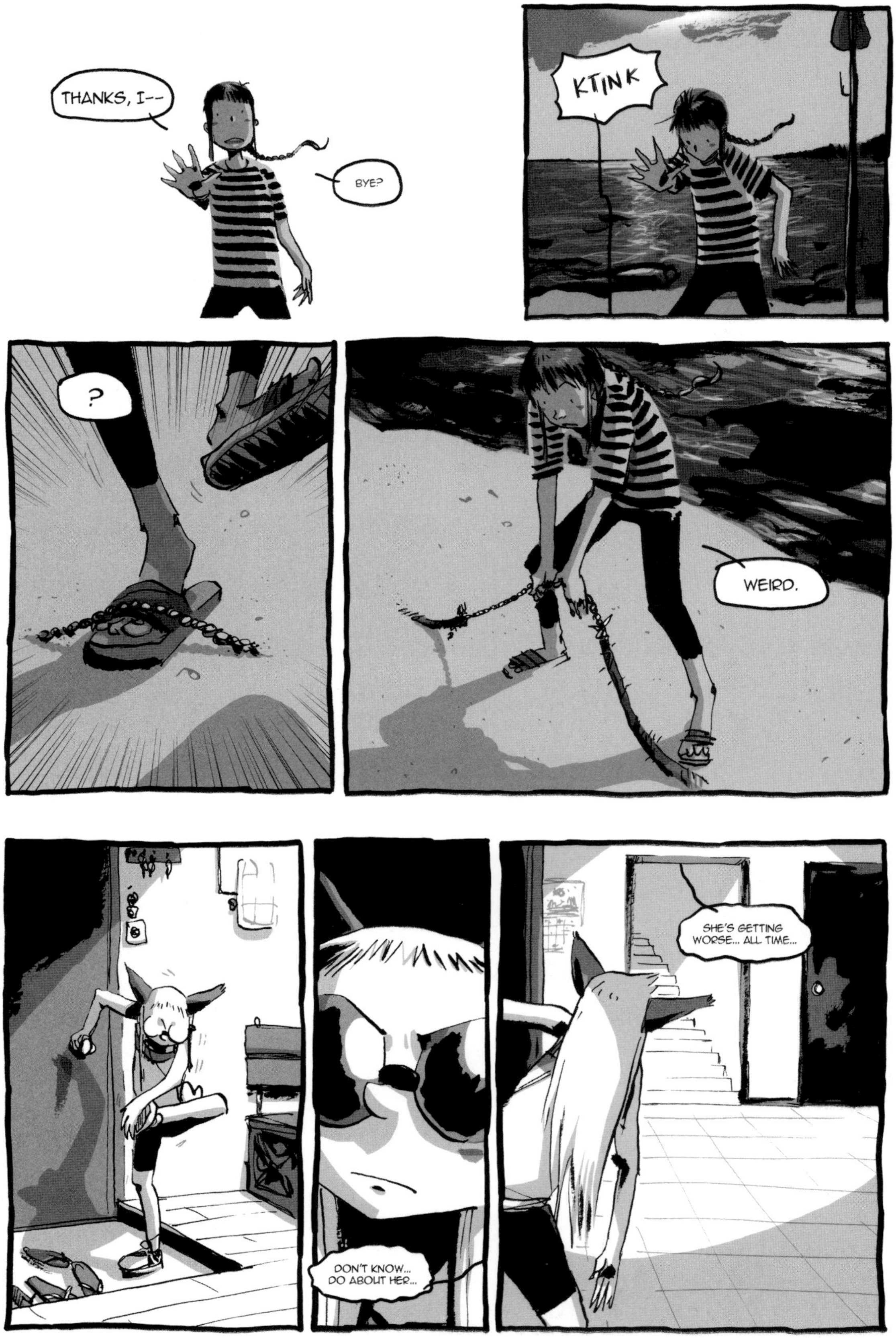
THANKS, I--
BYE?
KTINK
?
WEIRD.
DON'T KNOW...
DO ABOUT HER...
SHE'S GETTING
WORSE... ALL TIME...

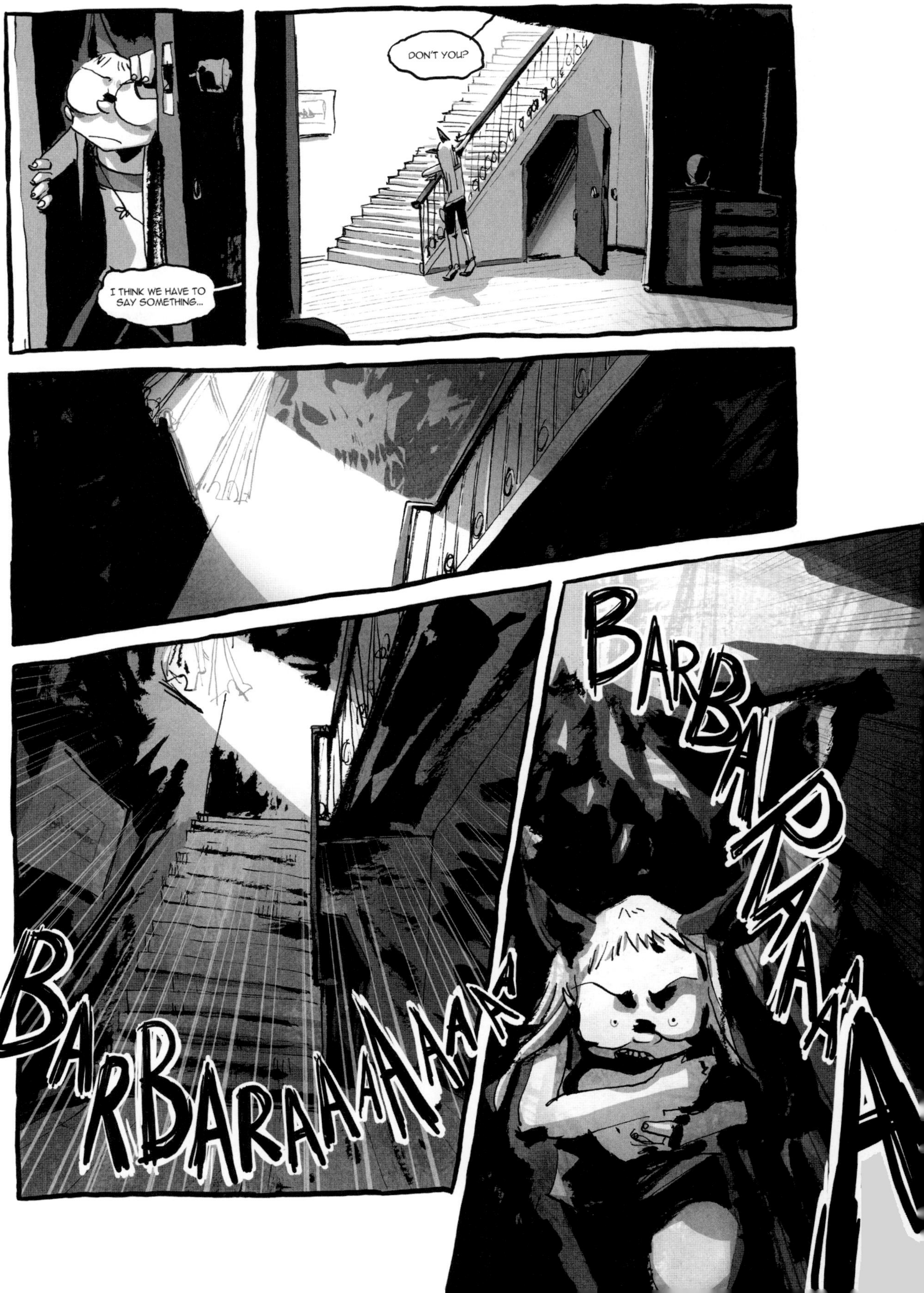
I THINK WE HAVE TO SAY SOMETHING...
DON'T YOU?
BARBARAAAAAAA
BARBARAAAAA

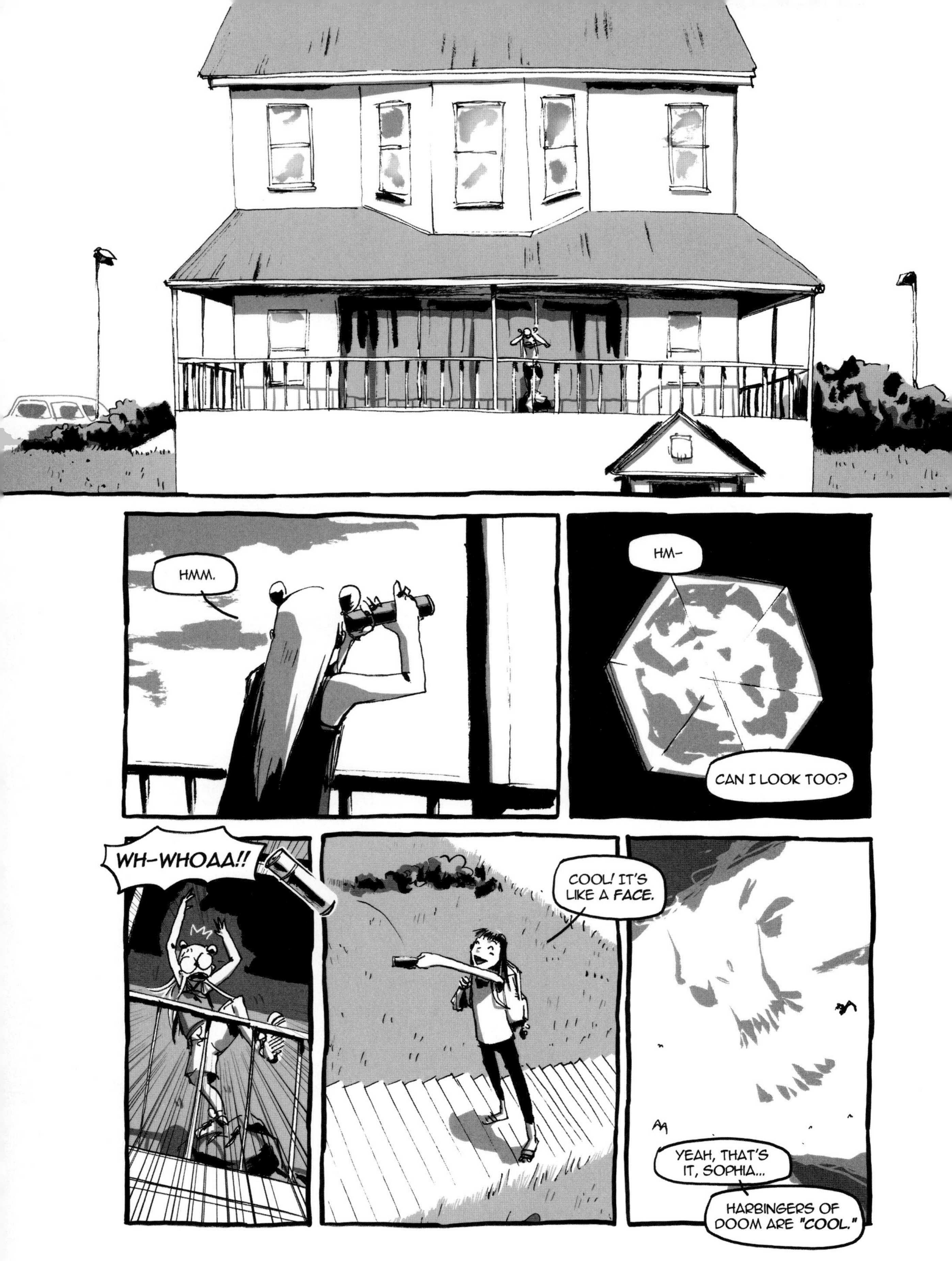
HMM.
HM-
CAN I LOOK TOO?
WH-WHOAA!!
COOL! IT'S LIKE A FACE.
YEAH, THAT'S IT, SOPHIA...
HARBINGERS OF DOOM ARE "COOL."

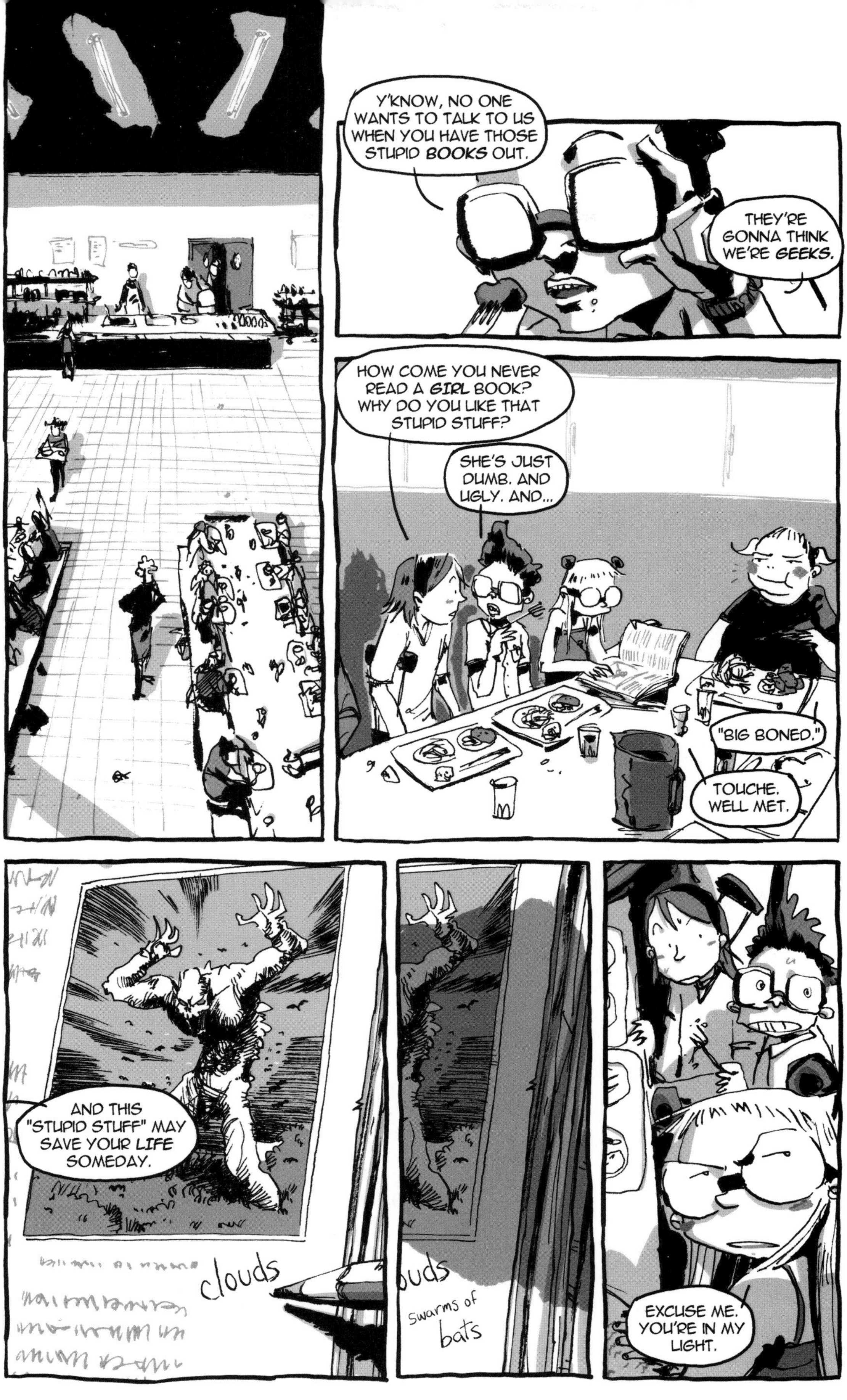
Y'KNOW, NO ONE WANTS TO TALK TO US WHEN YOU HAVE THOSE STUPID BOOKS OUT.
THEY'RE GONNA THINK WE'RE GEEKS.
HOW COME YOU NEVER READ A GIRL BOOK? WHY DO YOU LIKE THAT STUPID STUFF?
SHE'S JUST DUMB. AND UGLY. AND...
"BIG BONED."
TOUCHE. WELL MET.
AND THIS "STUPID STUFF" MAY SAVE YOUR LIFE SOMEDAY.
clouds
ouds
Swarms of bats
EXCUSE ME. YOU'RE IN MY LIGHT.

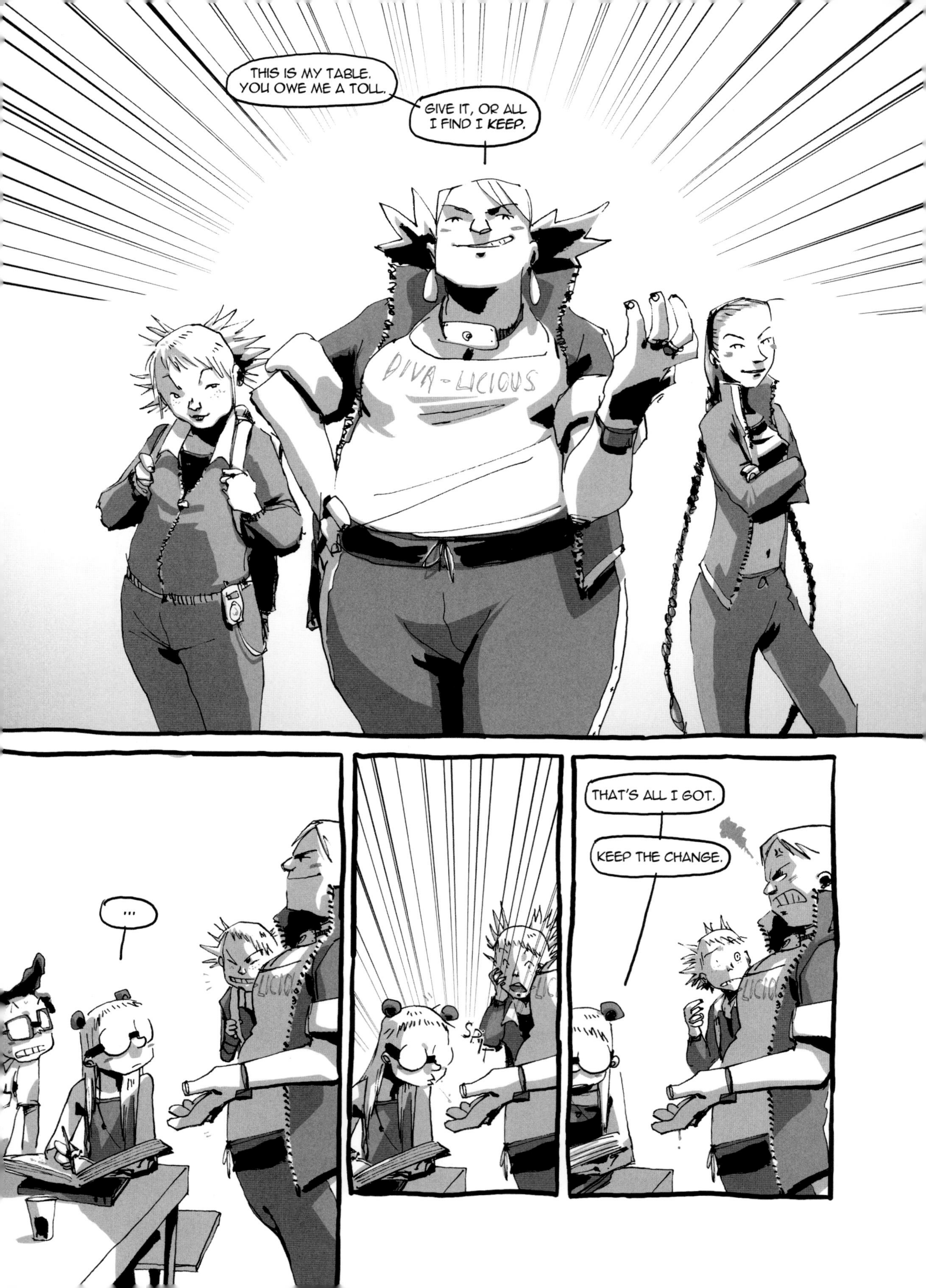
THIS IS MY TABLE. YOU OWE ME A TOLL.
GIVE IT, OR ALL I FIND I KEEP.
DIVA-LICIOUS
...
SPIT
THAT'S ALL I GOT.
KEEP THE CHANGE.

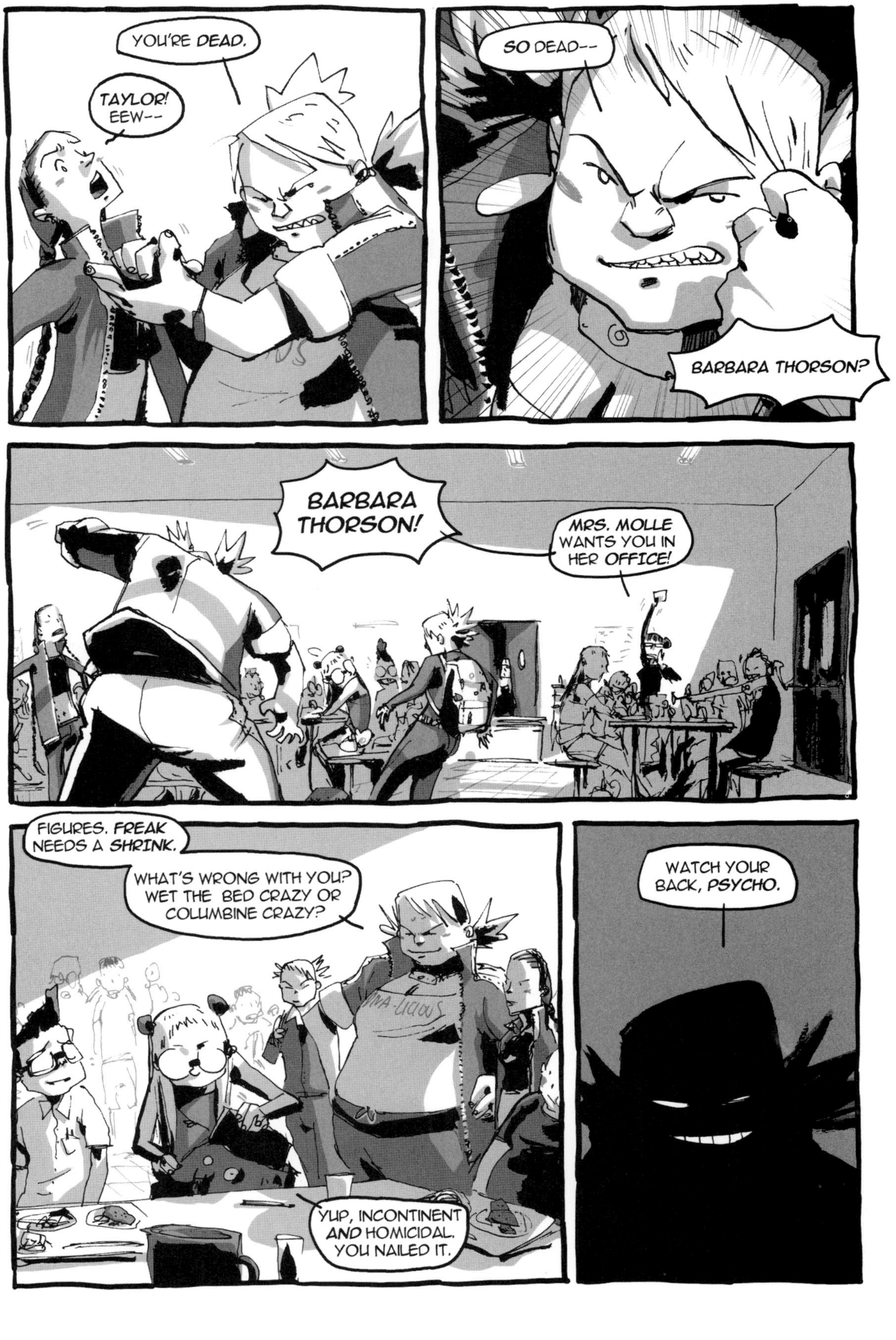
TAYLOR! EEW--
YOU'RE DEAD.
SO DEAD--
BARBARA THORSON?
BARBARA THORSON!
MRS. MOLLE WANTS YOU IN HER OFFICE!
FIGURES. FREAK NEEDS A SHRINK.
WHAT'S WRONG WITH YOU? WET THE BED CRAZY OR COLUMBINE CRAZY?
YUP, INCONTINENT AND HOMICIDAL. YOU NAILED IT.
WATCH YOUR BACK, PSYCHO.

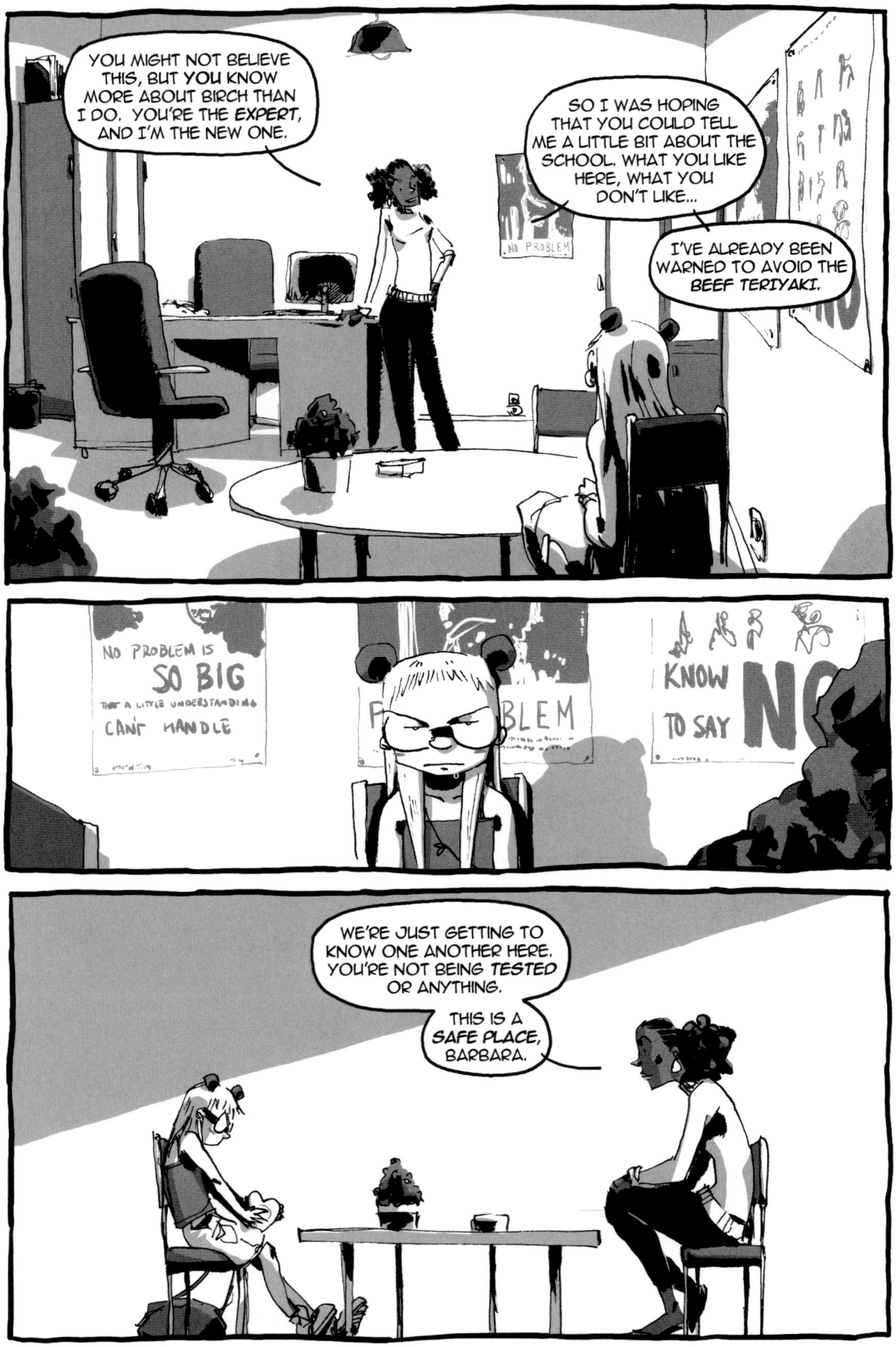
YOU MIGHT NOT BELIEVE THIS, BUT YOU KNOW MORE ABOUT BIRCH THAN I DO. YOU'RE THE EXPERT, AND I'M THE NEW ONE.
SO I WAS HOPING THAT YOU COULD TELL ME A LITTLE BIT ABOUT THE SCHOOL. WHAT YOU LIKE HERE, WHAT YOU DON'T LIKE...
I'VE ALREADY BEEN WARNED TO AVOID THE BEEF TERIYAKI.
NO PROBLEM
NO PROBLEM IS SO BIG THAT A LITTLE UNDERSTANDING CAN'T HANDLE
KNOW TO SAY NO
WE'RE JUST GETTING TO KNOW ONE ANOTHER HERE. YOU'RE NOT BEING TESTED OR ANYTHING.
THIS IS A SAFE PLACE, BARBARA.

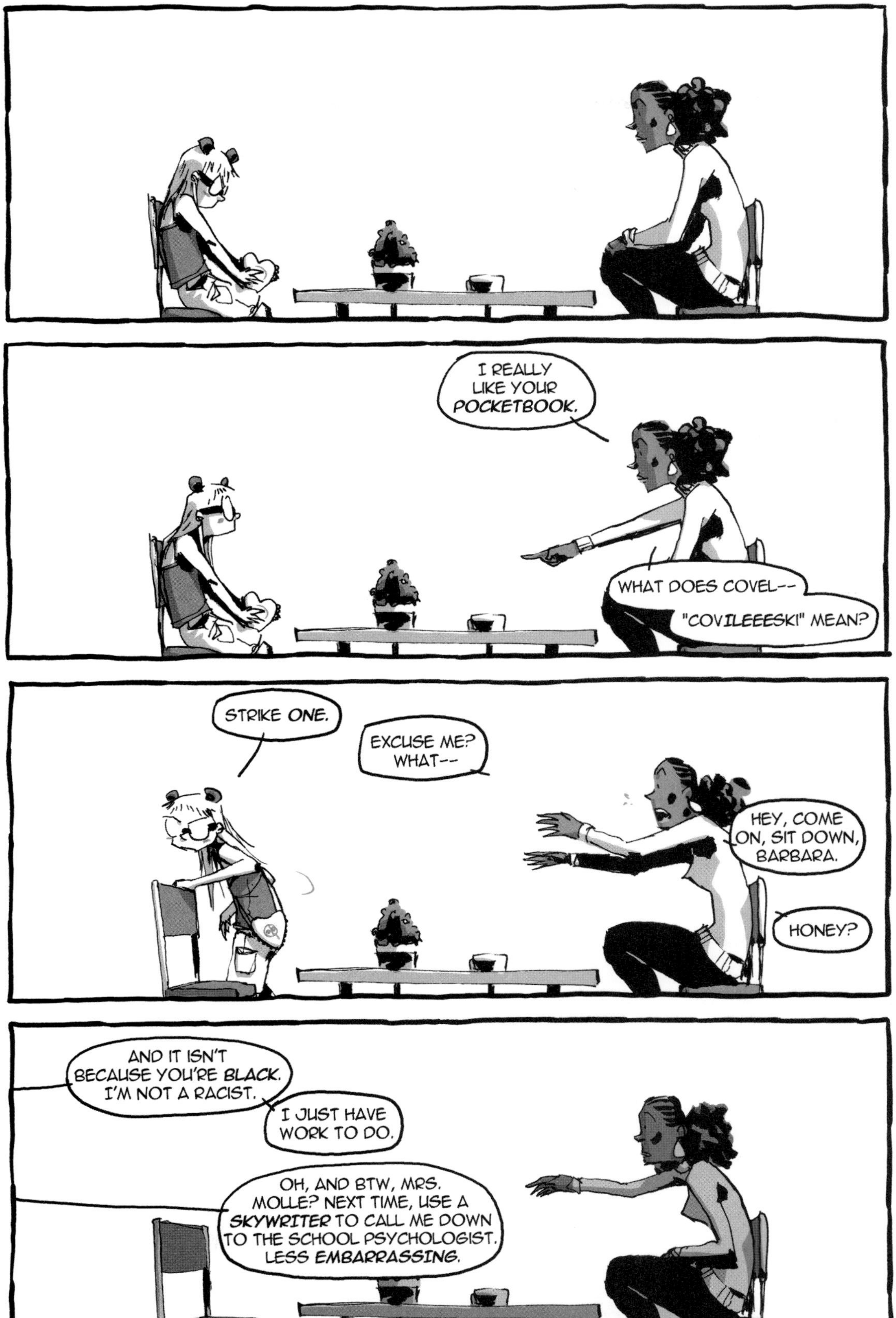

I REALLY LIKE YOUR POCKETBOOK.
WHAT DOES COVEL--
"COVILEEESKI" MEAN?
STRIKE ONE.
EXCUSE ME? WHAT--
HEY, COME ON, SIT DOWN, BARBARA.
HONEY?
AND IT ISN'T BECAUSE YOU'RE BLACK. I'M NOT A RACIST.
I JUST HAVE WORK TO DO.
OH, AND BTW, MRS. MOLLE? NEXT TIME, USE A SKYWRITER TO CALL ME DOWN TO THE SCHOOL PSYCHOLOGIST. LESS EMBARRASSING.

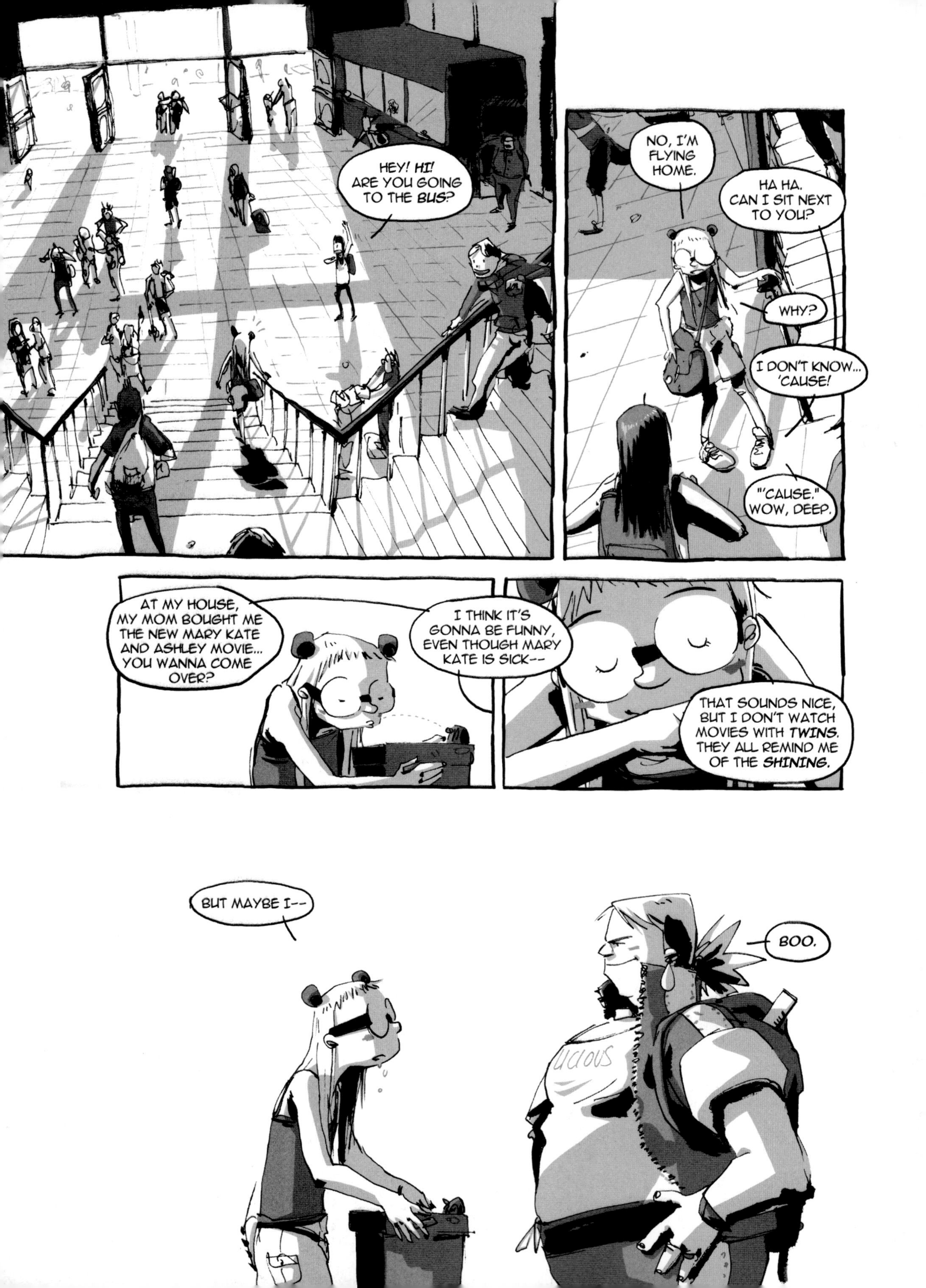
HEY! HI! ARE YOU GOING TO THE BUS?
NO, I'M FLYING HOME.
HA HA. CAN I SIT NEXT TO YOU?
WHY?
I DON'T KNOW... 'CAUSE!
"'CAUSE." WOW, DEEP.
AT MY HOUSE, MY MOM BOUGHT ME THE NEW MARY KATE AND ASHLEY MOVIE... YOU WANNA COME OVER?
I THINK IT'S GONNA BE FUNNY, EVEN THOUGH MARY KATE IS SICK--
THAT SOUNDS NICE, BUT I DON'T WATCH MOVIES WITH TWINS. THEY ALL REMIND ME OF THE SHINING.
BUT MAYBE I--
BOO.
LICIOUS

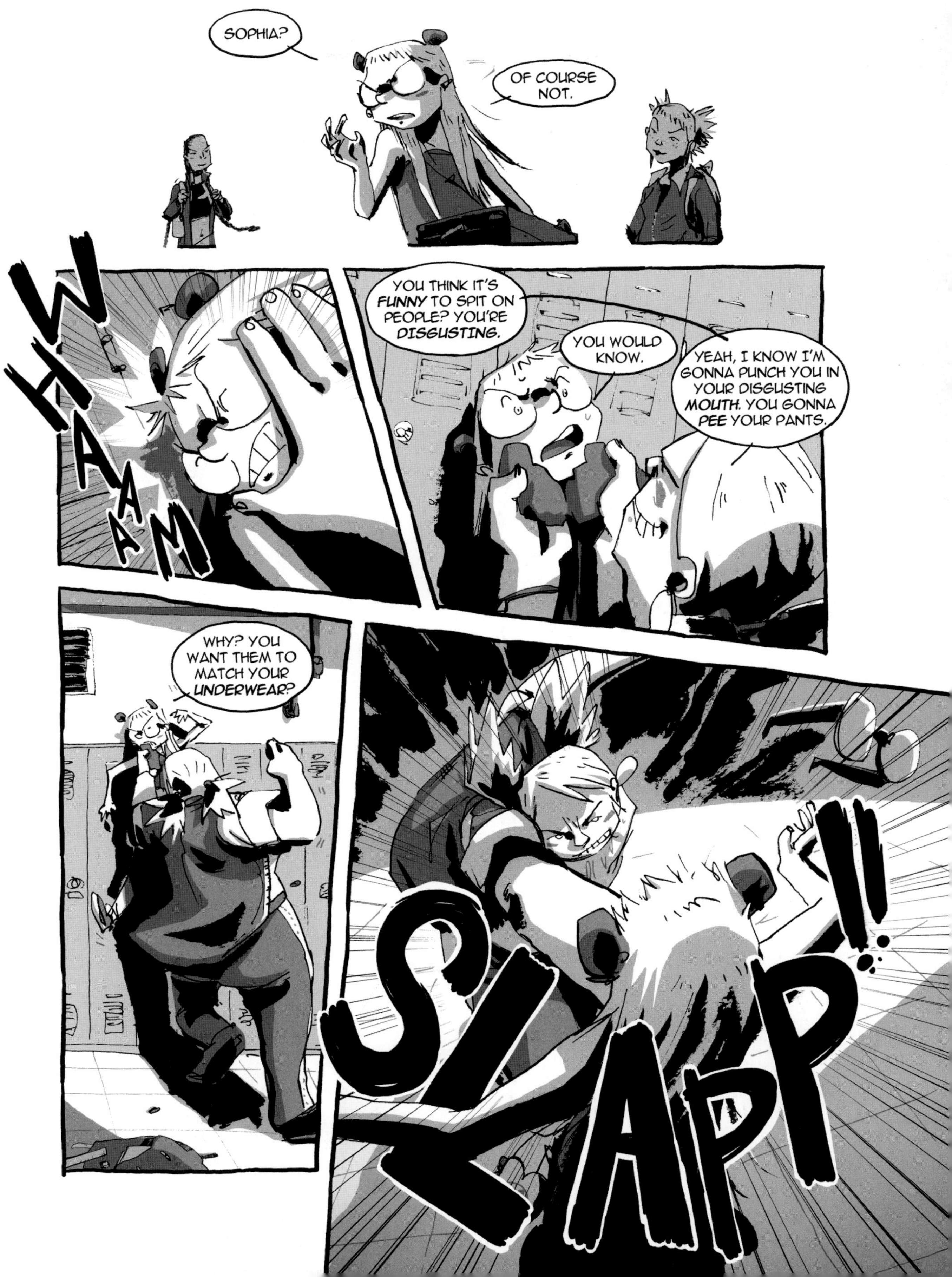
SOPHIA?
OF COURSE NOT.
WHAAAAM
YOU THINK IT'S FUNNY TO SPIT ON PEOPLE? YOU'RE DISGUSTING.
YOU WOULD KNOW.
YEAH, I KNOW I'M GONNA PUNCH YOU IN YOUR DISGUSTING MOUTH. YOU GONNA PEE YOUR PANTS.
WHY? YOU WANT THEM TO MATCH YOUR UNDERWEAR?
SLAPP!!

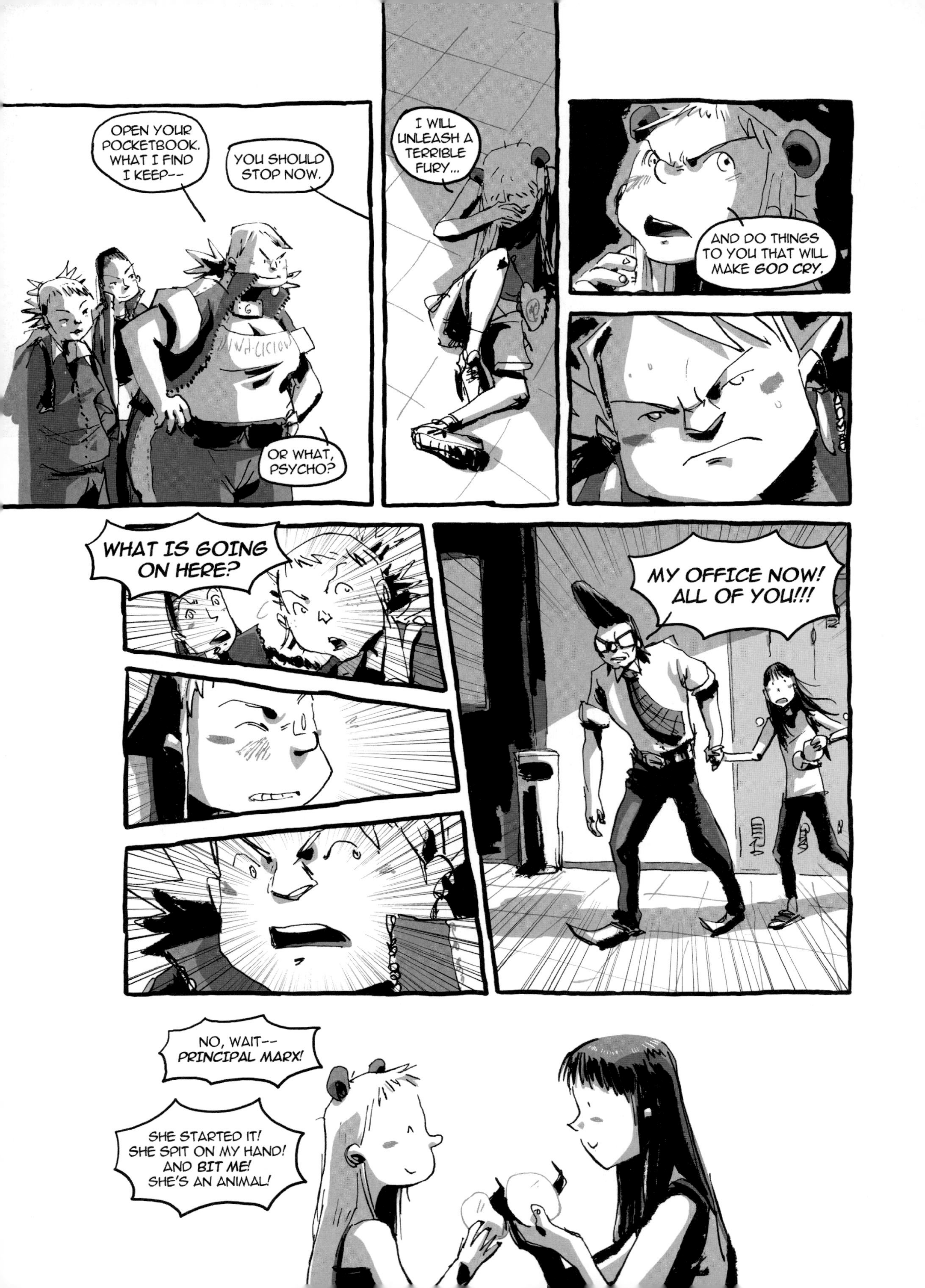
OPEN YOUR POCKETBOOK. WHAT I FIND I KEEP--
YOU SHOULD STOP NOW.
OR WHAT, PSYCHO?
I WILL UNLEASH A TERRIBLE FURY...
AND DO THINGS TO YOU THAT WILL MAKE GOD CRY.
WHAT IS GOING ON HERE?
MY OFFICE NOW! ALL OF YOU!!!
NO, WAIT-- PRINCIPAL MARX!
SHE STARTED IT! SHE SPIT ON MY HAND! AND BIT ME! SHE'S AN ANIMAL!

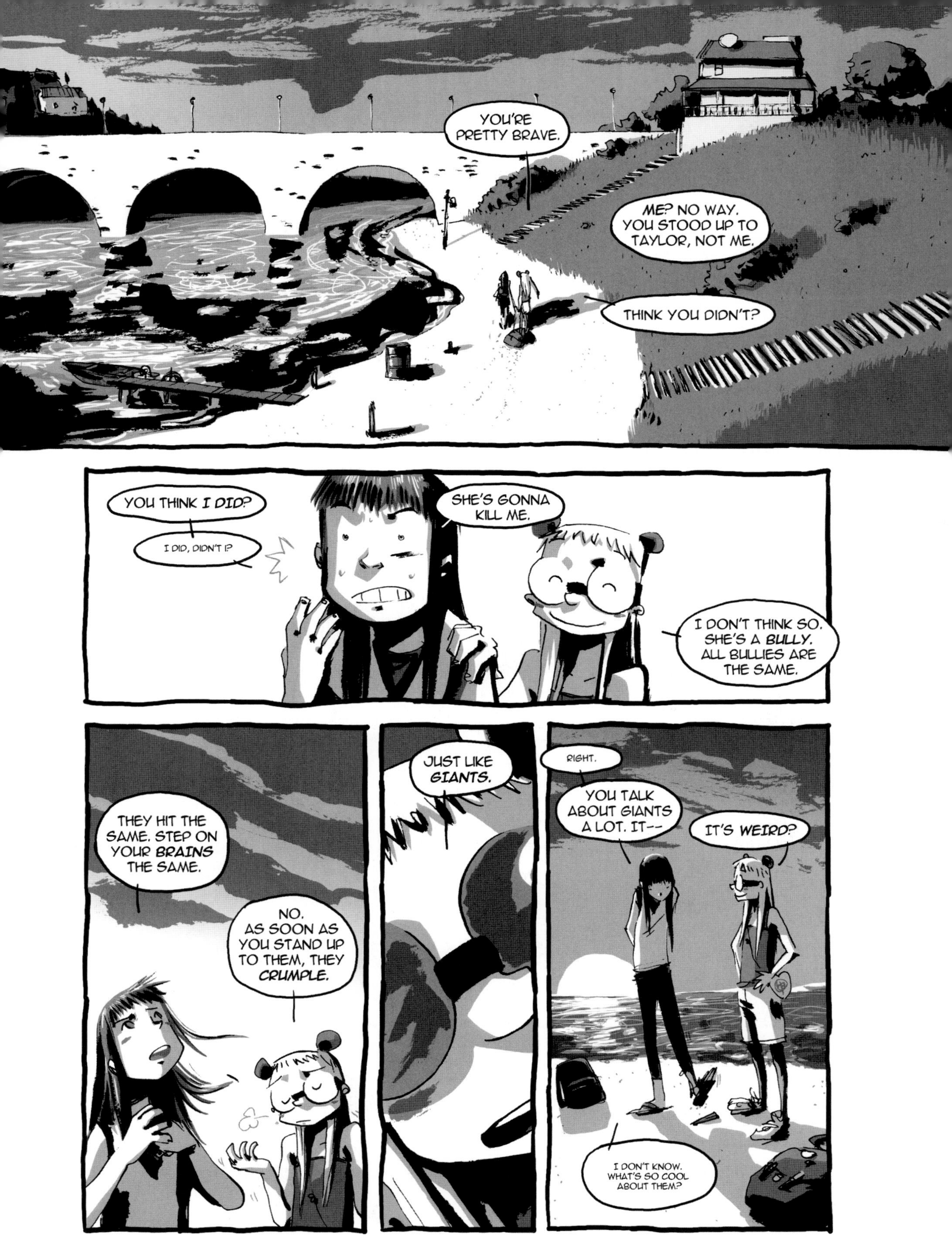
YOU'RE PRETTY BRAVE.
ME? NO WAY. YOU STOOD UP TO TAYLOR, NOT ME.
THINK YOU DIDN'T?
YOU THINK I DID?
I DID, DIDN'T I?
SHE'S GONNA KILL ME.
I DON'T THINK SO. SHE'S A BULLY. ALL BULLIES ARE THE SAME.
THEY HIT THE SAME. STEP ON YOUR BRAINS THE SAME.
NO. AS SOON AS YOU STAND UP TO THEM, THEY CRUMPLE.
JUST LIKE GIANTS.
RIGHT.
YOU TALK ABOUT GIANTS A LOT. IT--
IT'S WEIRD?
I DON'T KNOW. WHAT'S SO COOL ABOUT THEM?

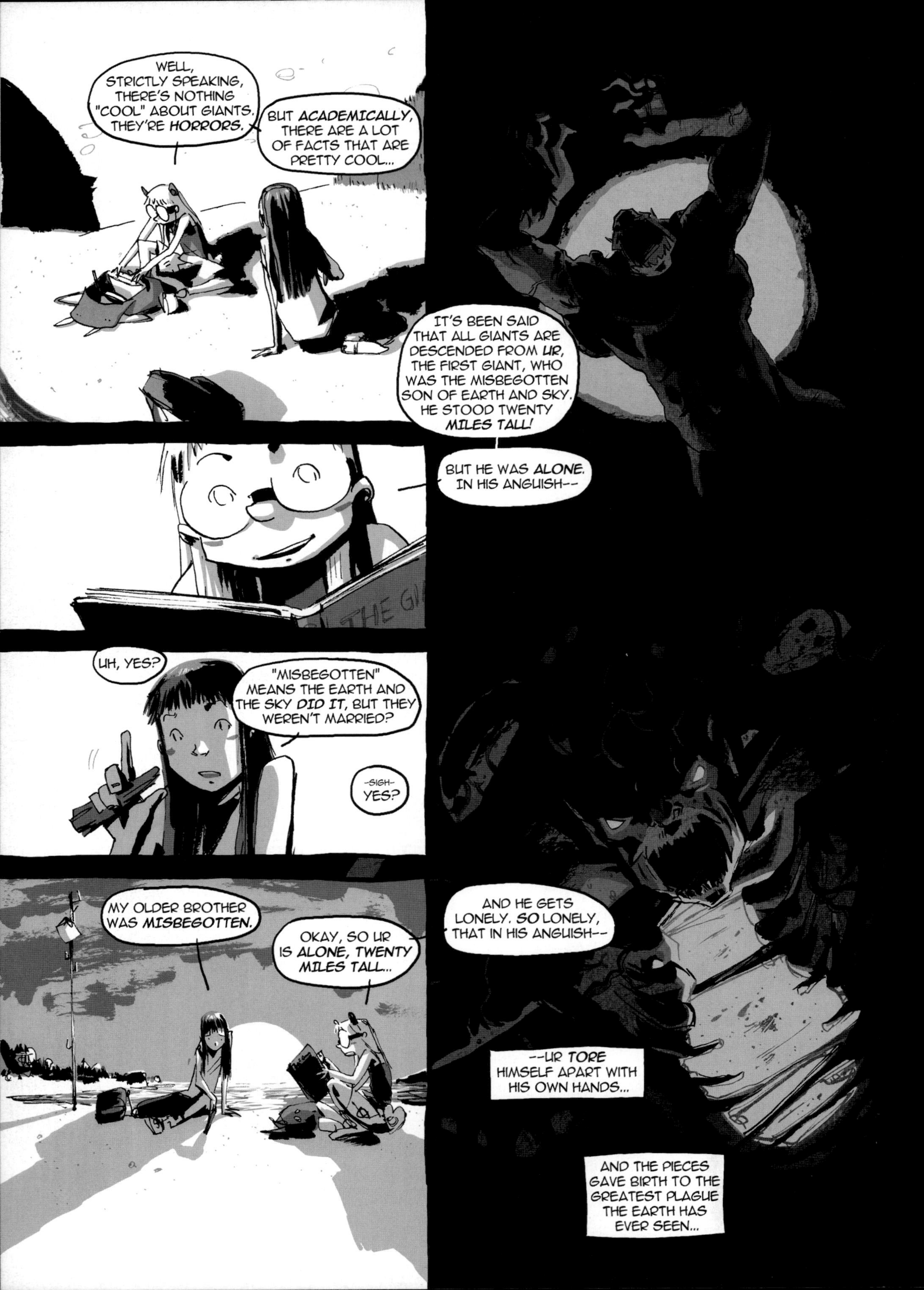
WELL, STRICTLY SPEAKING, THERE'S NOTHING "COOL" ABOUT GIANTS. THEY'RE HORRORS.
BUT ACADEMICALLY, THERE ARE A LOT OF FACTS THAT ARE PRETTY COOL...
IT'S BEEN SAID THAT ALL GIANTS ARE DESCENDED FROM UR, THE FIRST GIANT, WHO WAS THE MISBEGOTTEN SON OF EARTH AND SKY. HE STOOD TWENTY MILES TALL!
BUT HE WAS ALONE. IN HIS ANGUISH--
THE GI
UH, YES?
"MISBEGOTTEN" MEANS THE EARTH AND THE SKY DID IT, BUT THEY WEREN'T MARRIED?
-SIGH- YES?
MY OLDER BROTHER WAS MISBEGOTTEN.
OKAY, SO UR IS ALONE, TWENTY MILES TALL...
AND HE GETS LONELY. SO LONELY, THAT IN HIS ANGUISH--
--UR TORE HIMSELF APART WITH HIS OWN HANDS...
AND THE PIECES GAVE BIRTH TO THE GREATEST PLAGUE THE EARTH HAS EVER SEEN...

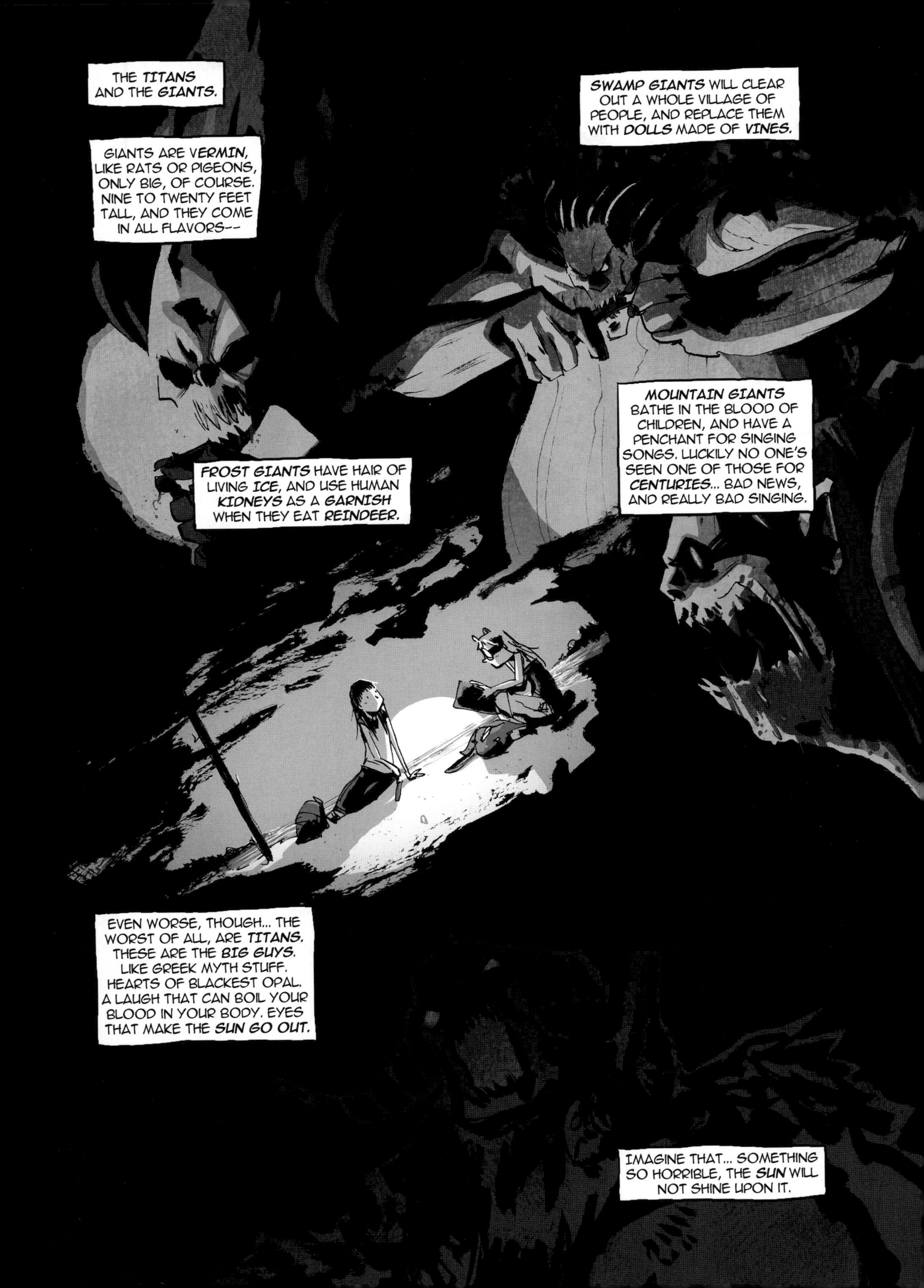
THE TITANS AND THE GIANTS.
GIANTS ARE VERMIN, LIKE RATS OR PIGEONS, ONLY BIG, OF COURSE. NINE TO TWENTY FEET TALL, AND THEY COME IN ALL FLAVORS--
SWAMP GIANTS WILL CLEAR OUT A WHOLE VILLAGE OF PEOPLE, AND REPLACE THEM WITH DOLLS MADE OF VINES.
FROST GIANTS HAVE HAIR OF LIVING ICE, AND USE HUMAN KIDNEYS AS A GARNISH WHEN THEY EAT REINDEER.
MOUNTAIN GIANTS BATHE IN THE BLOOD OF CHILDREN, AND HAVE A PENCHANT FOR SINGING SONGS. LUCKILY NO ONE'S SEEN ONE OF THOSE FOR CENTURIES... BAD NEWS, AND REALLY BAD SINGING.
EVEN WORSE, THOUGH... THE WORST OF ALL, ARE TITANS. THESE ARE THE BIG GUYS. LIKE GREEK MYTH STUFF. HEARTS OF BLACKEST OPAL. A LAUGH THAT CAN BOIL YOUR BLOOD IN YOUR BODY. EYES THAT MAKE THE SUN GO OUT.
IMAGINE THAT... SOMETHING SO HORRIBLE, THE SUN WILL NOT SHINE UPON IT.

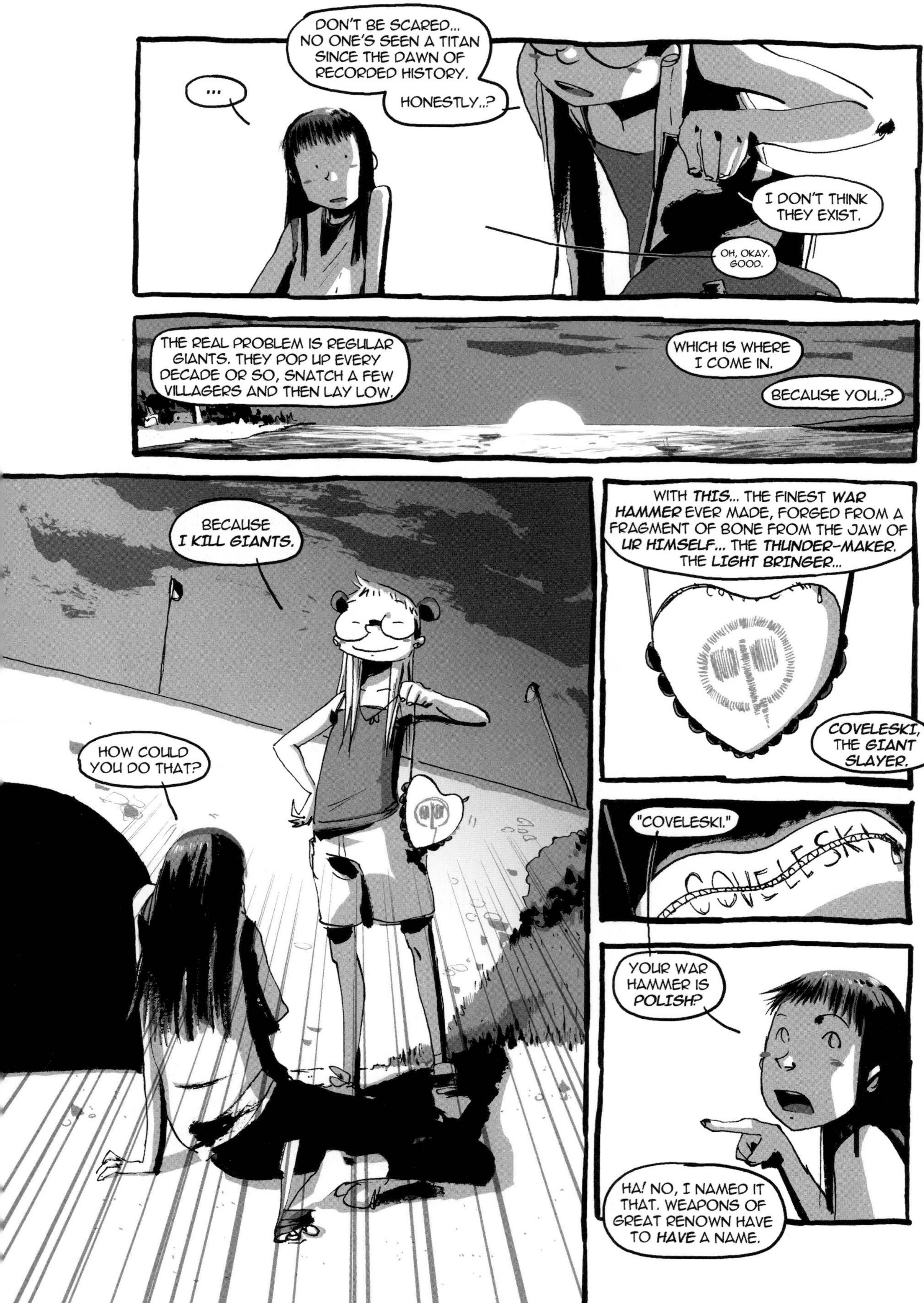
DON'T BE SCARED... NO ONE'S SEEN A TITAN SINCE THE DAWN OF RECORDED HISTORY.
...
HONESTLY..?
I DON'T THINK THEY EXIST.
OH, OKAY. GOOD.
THE REAL PROBLEM IS REGULAR GIANTS. THEY POP UP EVERY DECADE OR SO, SNATCH A FEW VILLAGERS AND THEN LAY LOW.
WHICH IS WHERE I COME IN.
BECAUSE YOU..?
BECAUSE I KILL GIANTS.
HOW COULD YOU DO THAT?
WITH THIS... THE FINEST WAR HAMMER EVER MADE, FORGED FROM A FRAGMENT OF BONE FROM THE JAW OF UR HIMSELF... THE THUNDER-MAKER. THE LIGHT BRINGER...
COVELESKI, THE GIANT SLAYER.
"COVELESKI."
COVELESKI
YOUR WAR HAMMER IS POLISH?
HA! NO, I NAMED IT THAT. WEAPONS OF GREAT RENOWN HAVE TO HAVE A NAME.

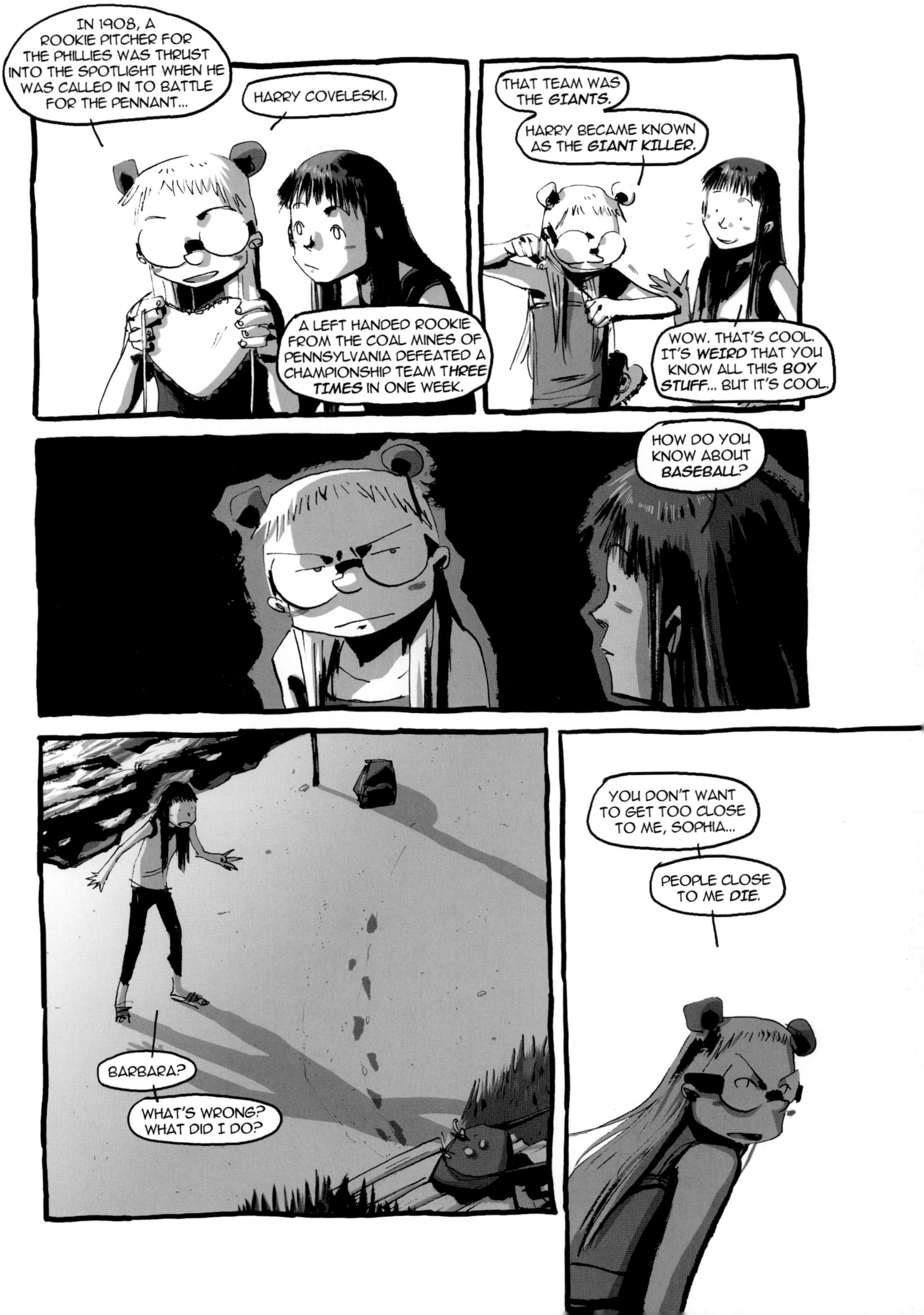
IN 1908, A ROOKIE PITCHER FOR THE PHILLIES WAS THRUST INTO THE SPOTLIGHT WHEN HE WAS CALLED IN TO BATTLE FOR THE PENNANT...
HARRY COVELESKI.
A LEFT HANDED ROOKIE FROM THE COAL MINES OF PENNSYLVANIA DEFEATED A CHAMPIONSHIP TEAM THREE TIMES IN ONE WEEK.
THAT TEAM WAS THE GIANTS.
HARRY BECAME KNOWN AS THE GIANT KILLER.
WOW. THAT'S COOL. IT'S WEIRD THAT YOU KNOW ALL THIS BOY STUFF... BUT IT'S COOL.
HOW DO YOU KNOW ABOUT BASEBALL?
BARBARA?
WHAT'S WRONG? WHAT DID I DO?
YOU DON'T WANT TO GET TOO CLOSE TO ME, SOPHIA...
PEOPLE CLOSE TO ME DIE.

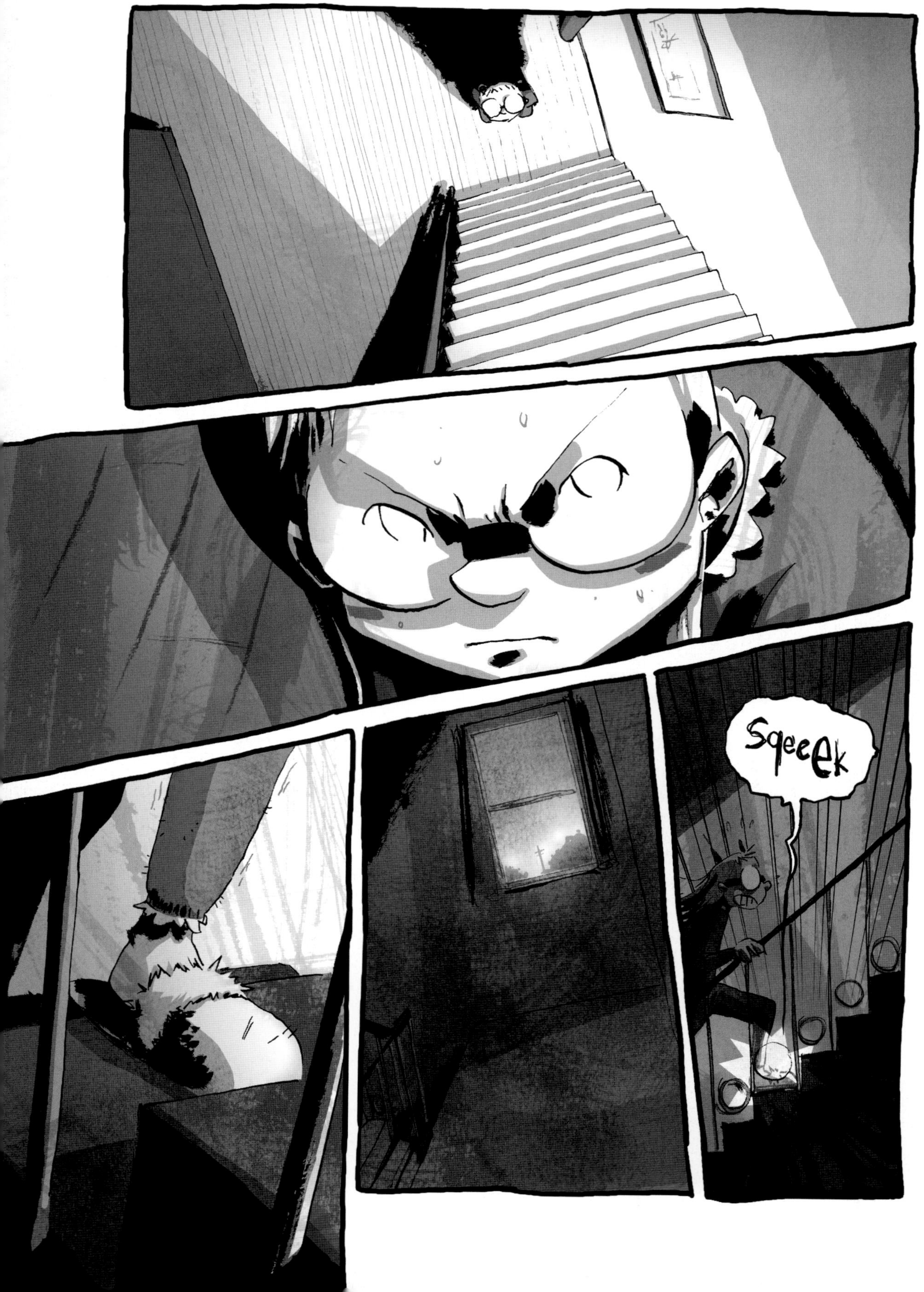
Sqeeek

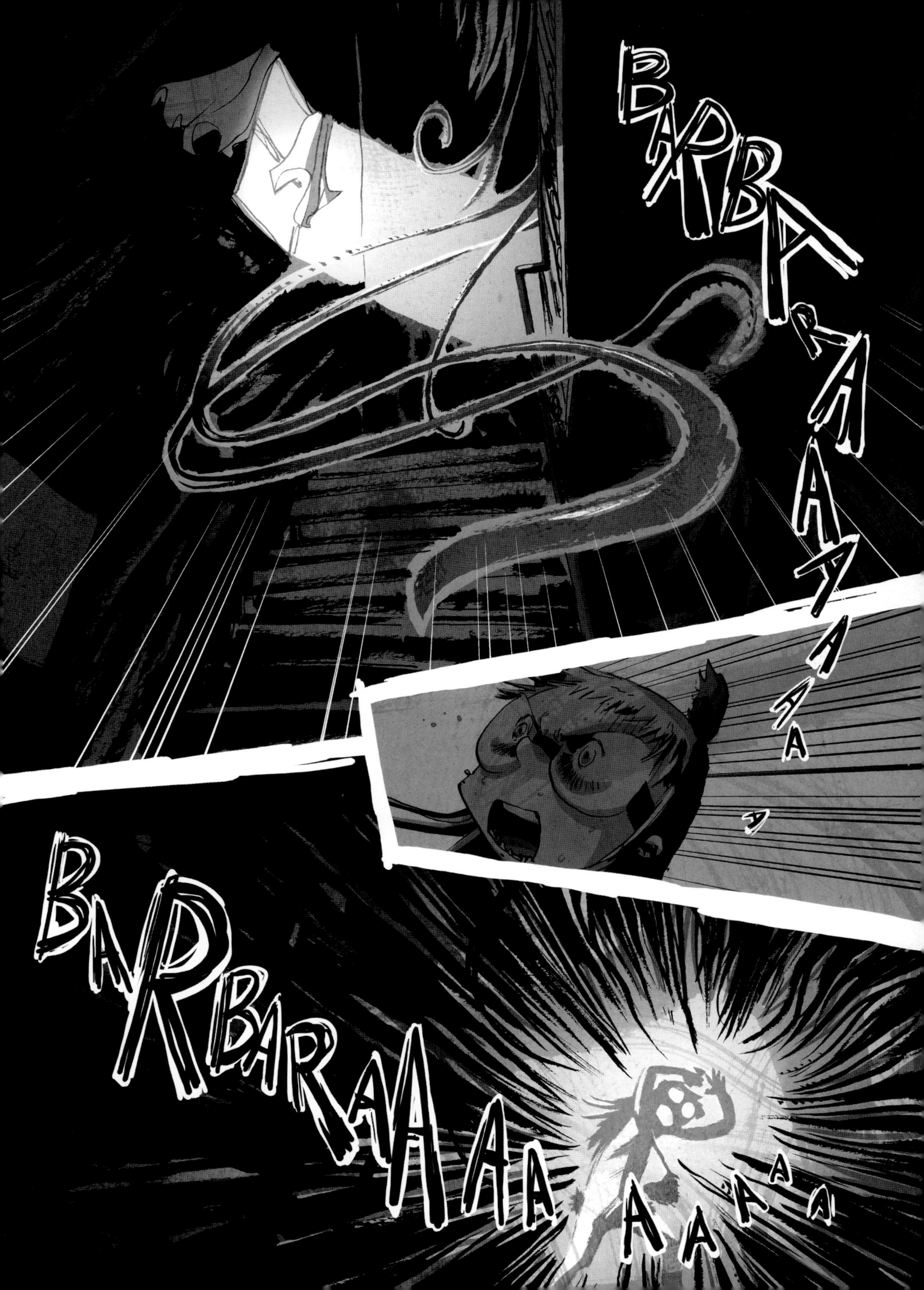
BARBARAAAAAAA
BARBARAAAAAAAAA

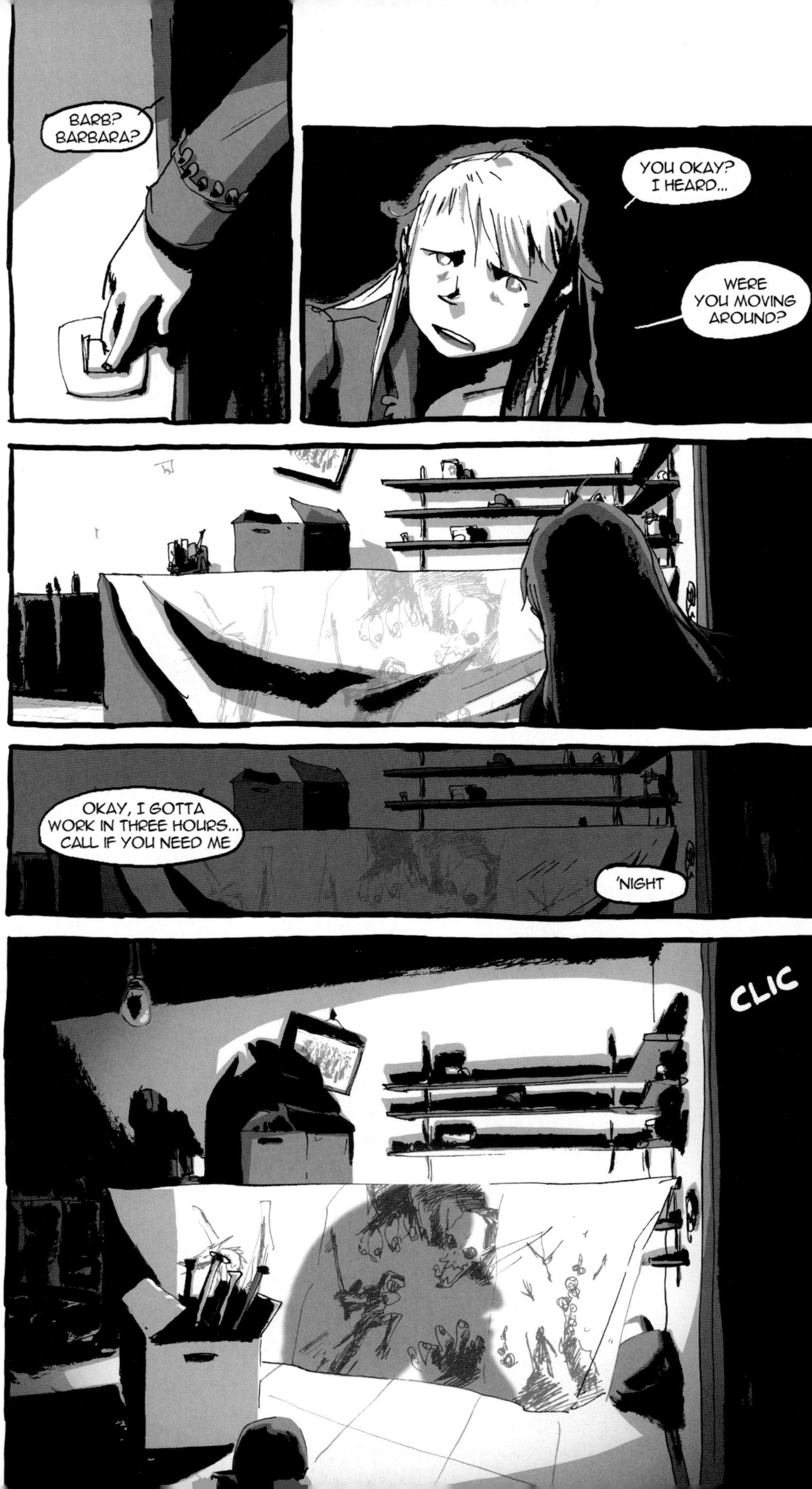
BARB? BARBARA?
YOU OKAY? I HEARD...
WERE YOU MOVING AROUND?
OKAY, I GOTTA WORK IN THREE HOURS... CALL IF YOU NEED ME
'NIGHT
CLIC

CHAPTER3: THE ARMOR

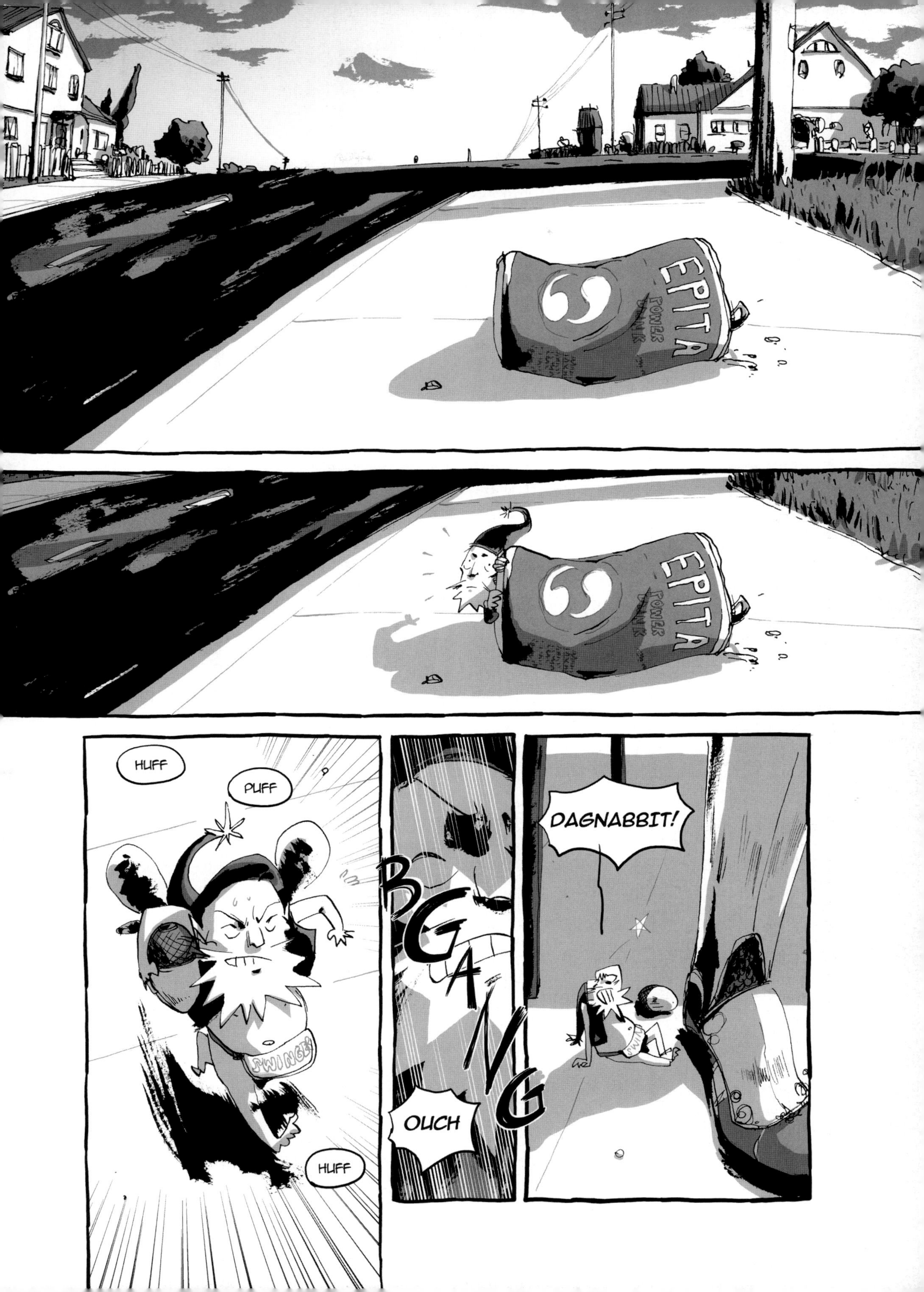

EPITA
POWER DRINK
EPITA
POWER DRINK
HUFF
PUFF
HUFF
BGANG
OUCH
DAGNABBIT!

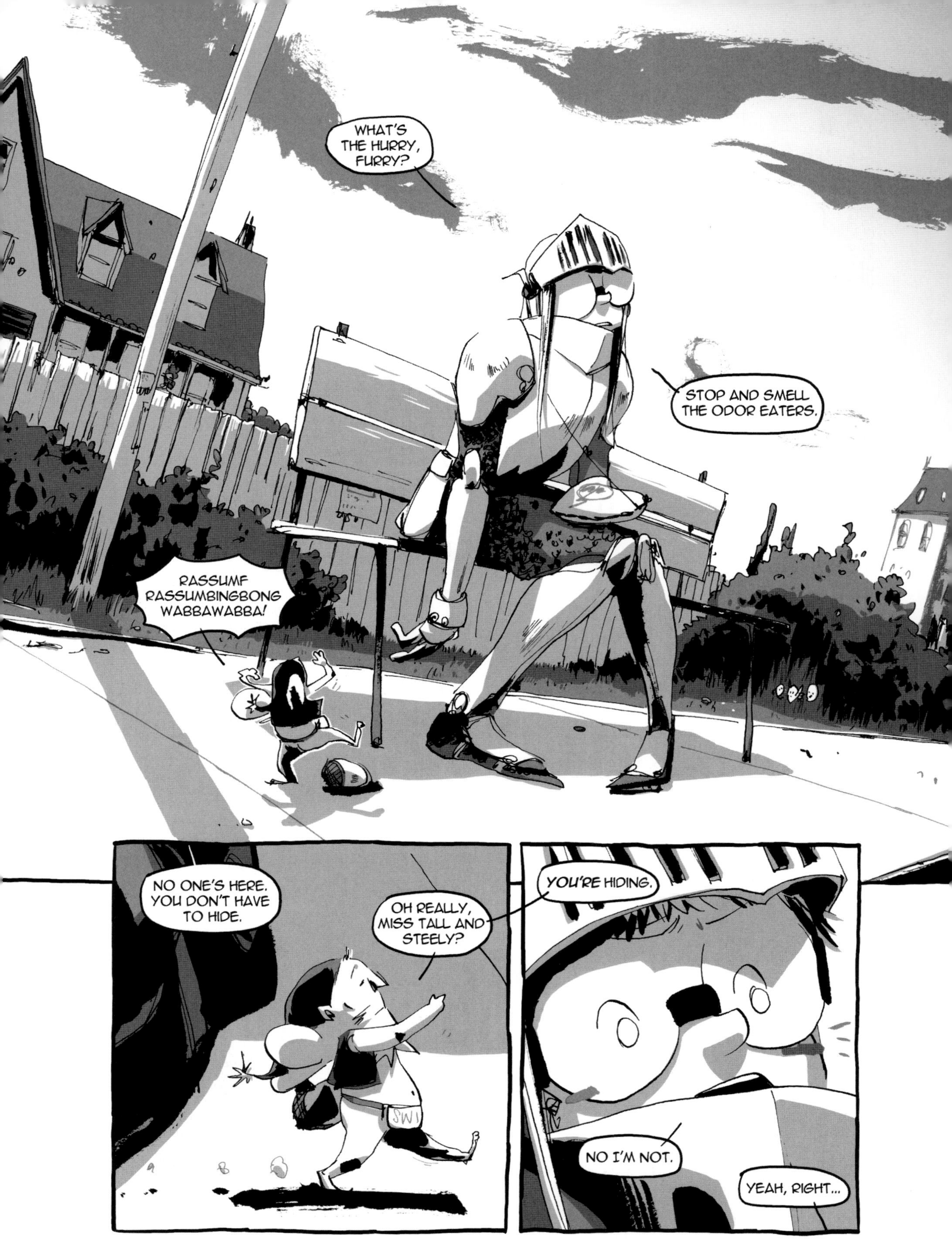
WHAT'S THE HURRY, FURRY?
STOP AND SMELL THE ODOR EATERS.
RASSUMF RASSUMBINGBONG WABBAWABBA!
NO ONE'S HERE. YOU DON'T HAVE TO HIDE.
OH REALLY, MISS TALL AND STEELY?
YOU'RE HIDING.
NO I'M NOT.
YEAH, RIGHT...

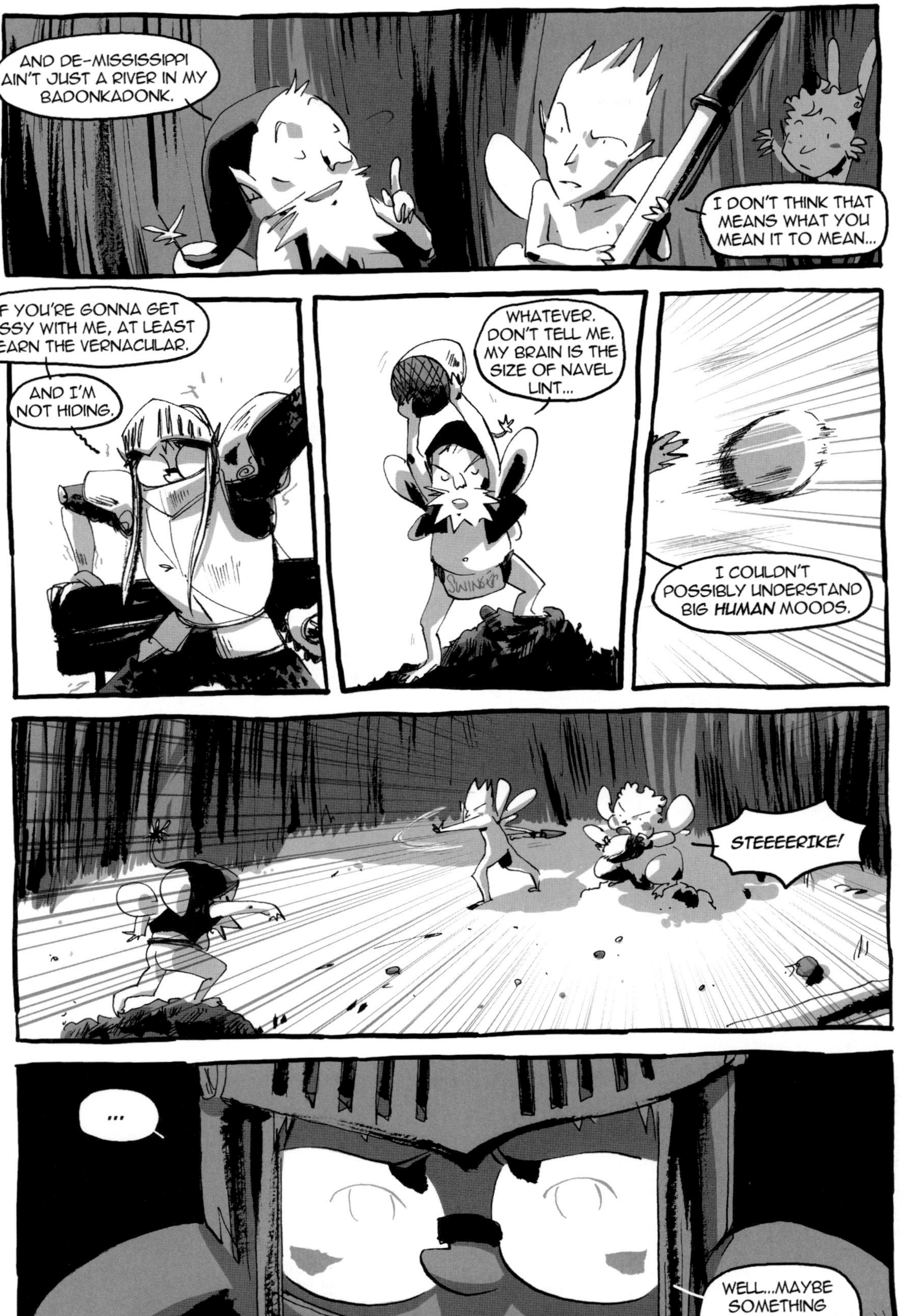
AND DE-MISSISSIPPI AIN'T JUST A RIVER IN MY BADONKADONK.
I DON'T THINK THAT MEANS WHAT YOU MEAN IT TO MEAN...
IF YOU'RE GONNA GET SASSY WITH ME, AT LEAST LEARN THE VERNACULAR.
AND I'M NOT HIDING.
WHATEVER. DON'T TELL ME. MY BRAIN IS THE SIZE OF NAVEL LINT...
I COULDN'T POSSIBLY UNDERSTAND BIG HUMAN MOODS.
STEEEERIKE!
...
WELL...MAYBE SOMETHING HAPPENED TODAY.

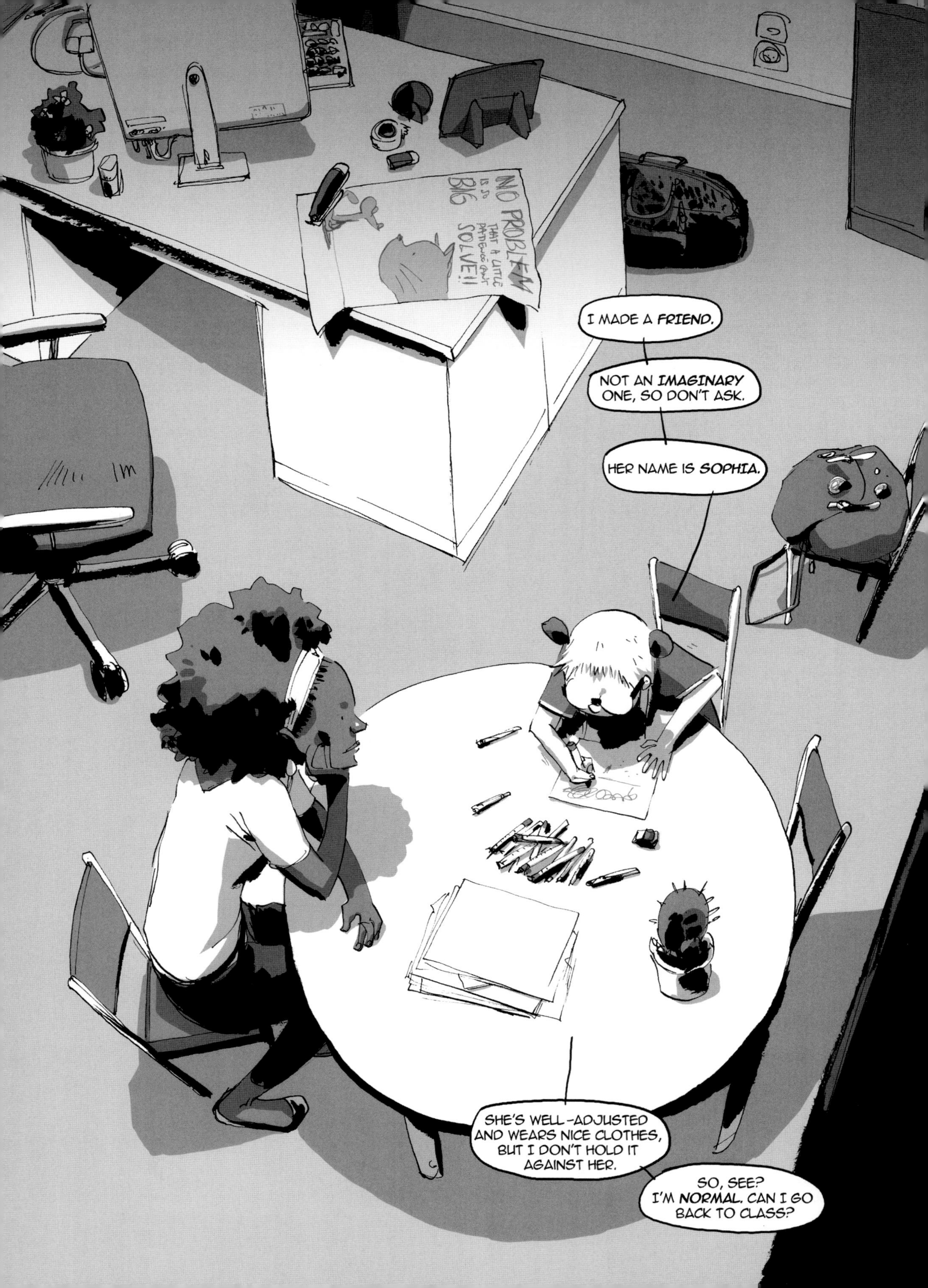

I MADE A FRIEND.
NOT AN IMAGINARY ONE, SO DON'T ASK.
HER NAME IS SOPHIA.
SHE'S WELL-ADJUSTED AND WEARS NICE CLOTHES, BUT I DON'T HOLD IT AGAINST HER.
SO, SEE? I'M NORMAL. CAN I GO BACK TO CLASS?

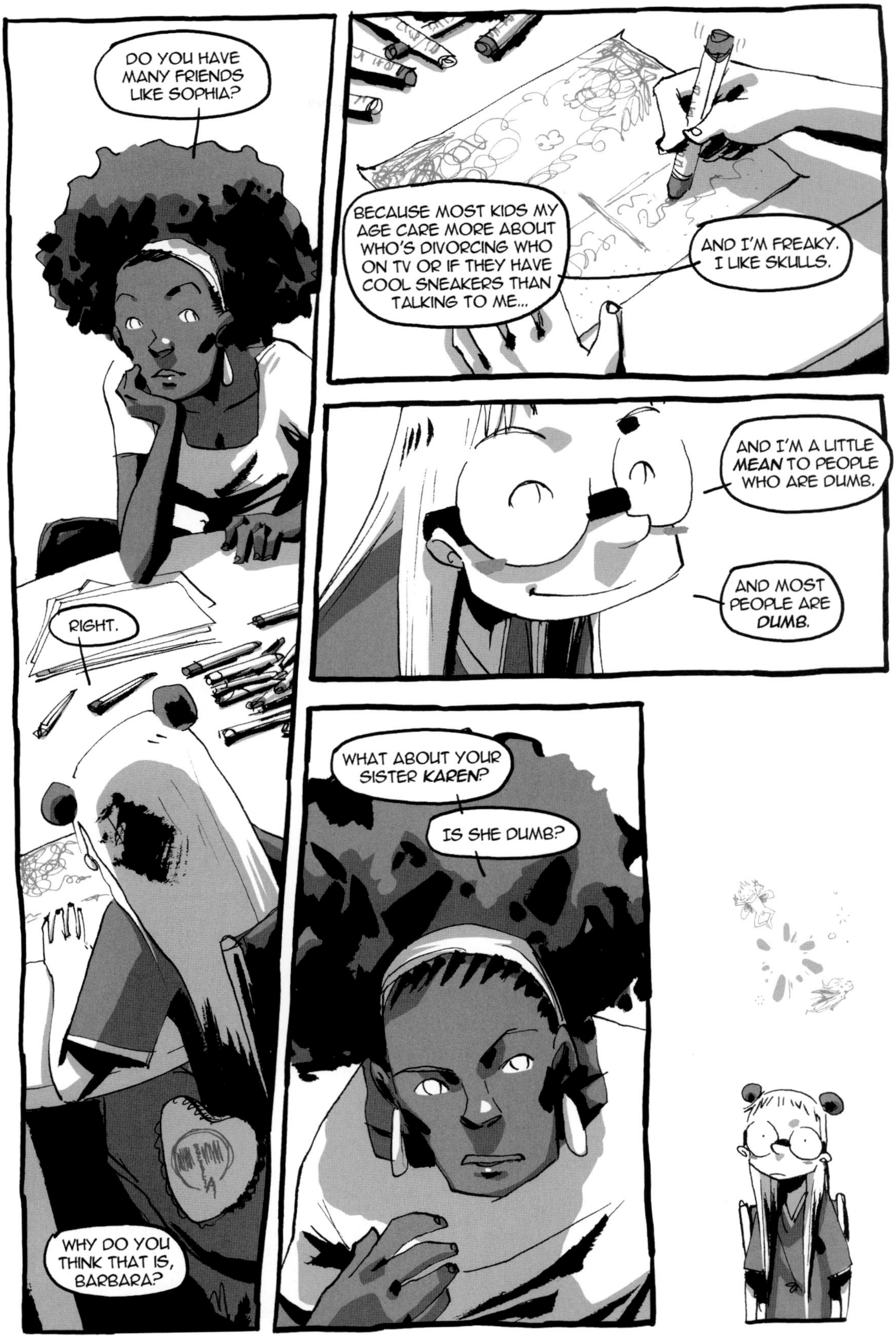
DO YOU HAVE MANY FRIENDS LIKE SOPHIA?
RIGHT.
WHY DO YOU THINK THAT IS, BARBARA?
BECAUSE MOST KIDS MY AGE CARE MORE ABOUT WHO'S DIVORCING WHO ON TV OR IF THEY HAVE COOL SNEAKERS THAN TALKING TO ME...
AND I'M FREAKY. I LIKE SKULLS.
AND I'M A LITTLE MEAN TO PEOPLE WHO ARE DUMB.
AND MOST PEOPLE ARE DUMB.
WHAT ABOUT YOUR SISTER KAREN?
IS SHE DUMB?

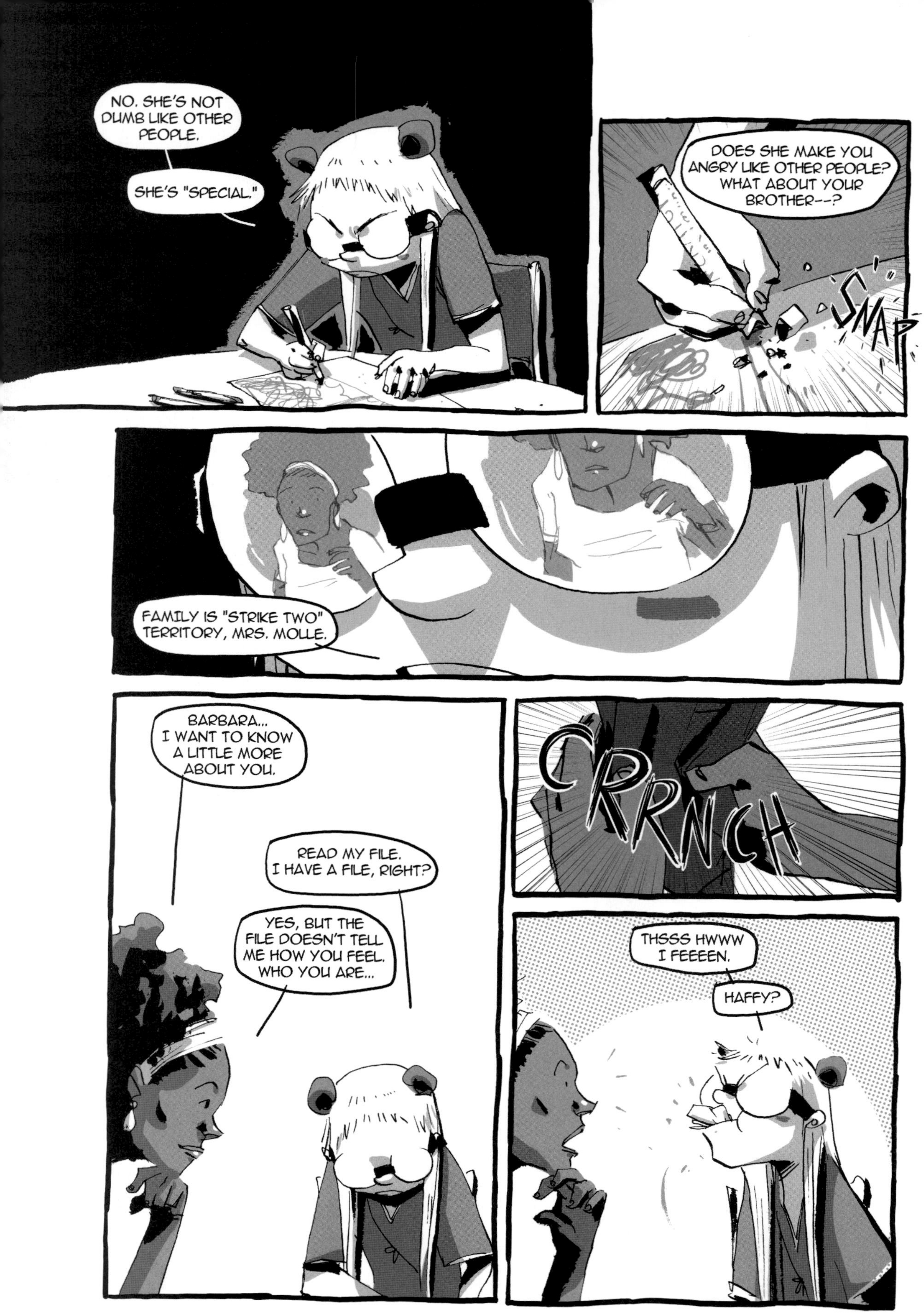
NO. SHE'S NOT DUMB LIKE OTHER PEOPLE.
SHE'S "SPECIAL."
DOES SHE MAKE YOU ANGRY LIKE OTHER PEOPLE? WHAT ABOUT YOUR BROTHER--?
SNAP
FAMILY IS "STRIKE TWO" TERRITORY, MRS. MOLLE.
BARBARA... I WANT TO KNOW A LITTLE MORE ABOUT YOU.
READ MY FILE. I HAVE A FILE, RIGHT?
YES, BUT THE FILE DOESN'T TELL ME HOW YOU FEEL. WHO YOU ARE...
CRRNCH
THSSS HWWW I FEEEEN.
HAFFY?

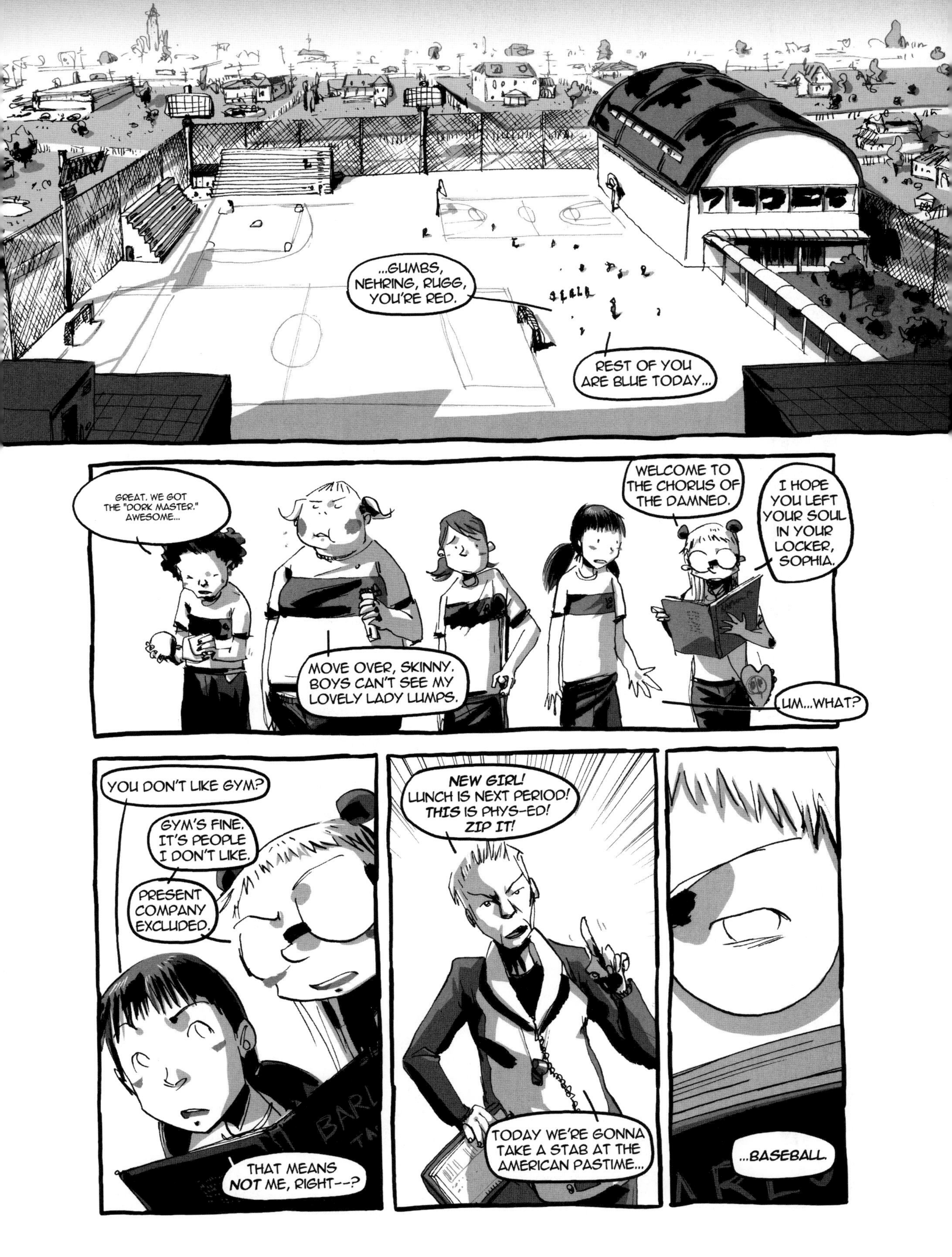

...GUMBS, NEHRING, RUGG, YOU'RE RED.
REST OF YOU ARE BLUE TODAY...
GREAT. WE GOT THE "DORK MASTER." AWESOME...
MOVE OVER, SKINNY. BOYS CAN'T SEE MY LOVELY LADY LUMPS.
WELCOME TO THE CHORUS OF THE DAMNED.
I HOPE YOU LEFT YOUR SOUL IN YOUR LOCKER, SOPHIA.
UM...WHAT?
YOU DON'T LIKE GYM?
GYM'S FINE. IT'S PEOPLE I DON'T LIKE.
PRESENT COMPANY EXCLUDED.
THAT MEANS NOT ME, RIGHT--?
NEW GIRL! LUNCH IS NEXT PERIOD! THIS IS PHYS-ED! ZIP IT!
TODAY WE'RE GONNA TAKE A STAB AT THE AMERICAN PASTIME...
...BASEBALL.

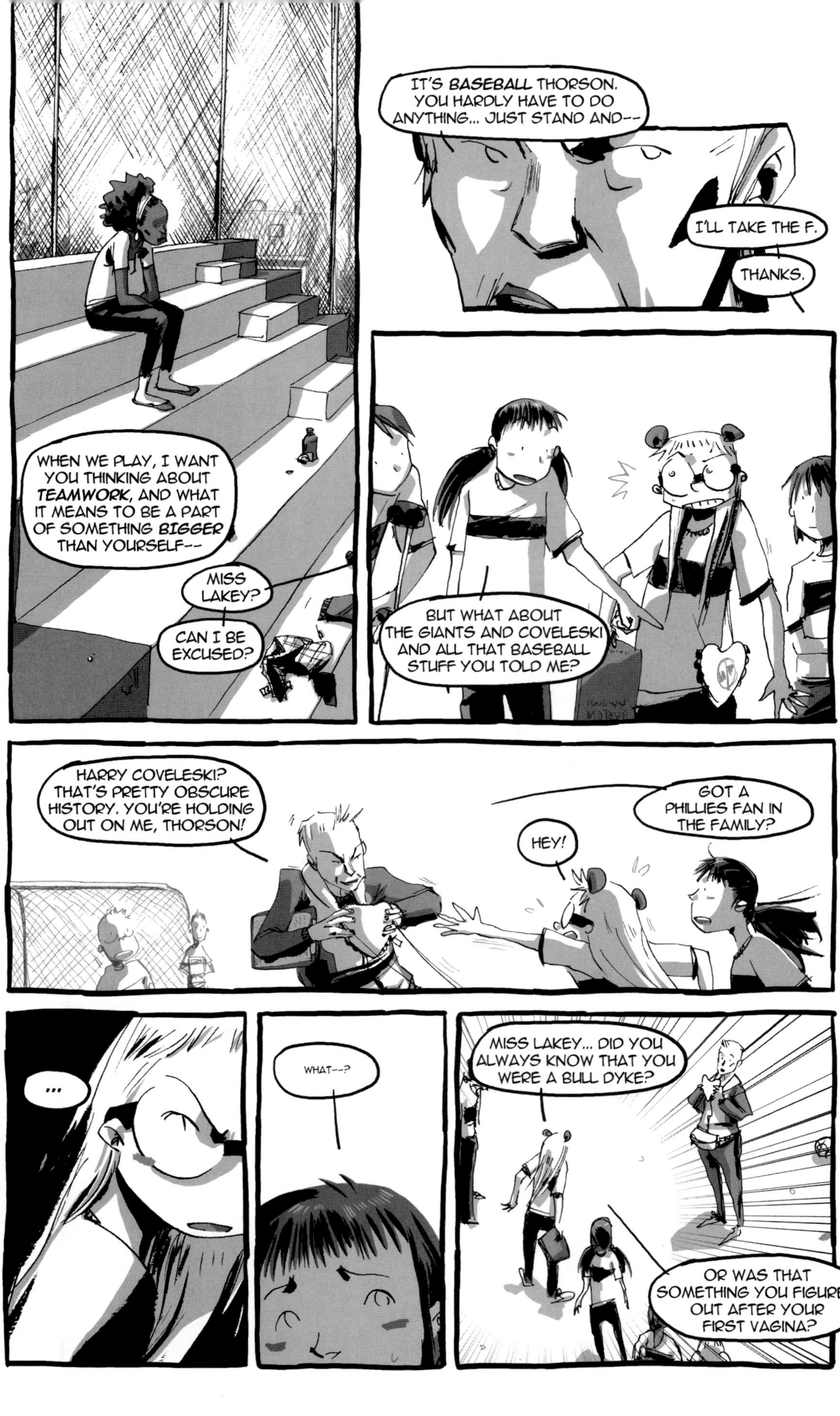

IT'S BASEBALL THORSON. YOU HARDLY HAVE TO DO ANYTHING... JUST STAND AND--
I'LL TAKE THE F.
THANKS.
WHEN WE PLAY, I WANT YOU THINKING ABOUT TEAMWORK, AND WHAT IT MEANS TO BE A PART OF SOMETHING BIGGER THAN YOURSELF--
MISS LAKEY?
CAN I BE EXCUSED?
BUT WHAT ABOUT THE GIANTS AND COVELESKI AND ALL THAT BASEBALL STUFF YOU TOLD ME?
HARRY COVELESKI? THAT'S PRETTY OBSCURE HISTORY. YOU'RE HOLDING OUT ON ME, THORSON!
GOT A PHILLIES FAN IN THE FAMILY?
HEY!
...
WHAT--?
MISS LAKEY... DID YOU ALWAYS KNOW THAT YOU WERE A BULL DYKE?
OR WAS THAT SOMETHING YOU FIGURED OUT AFTER YOUR FIRST VAGINA?

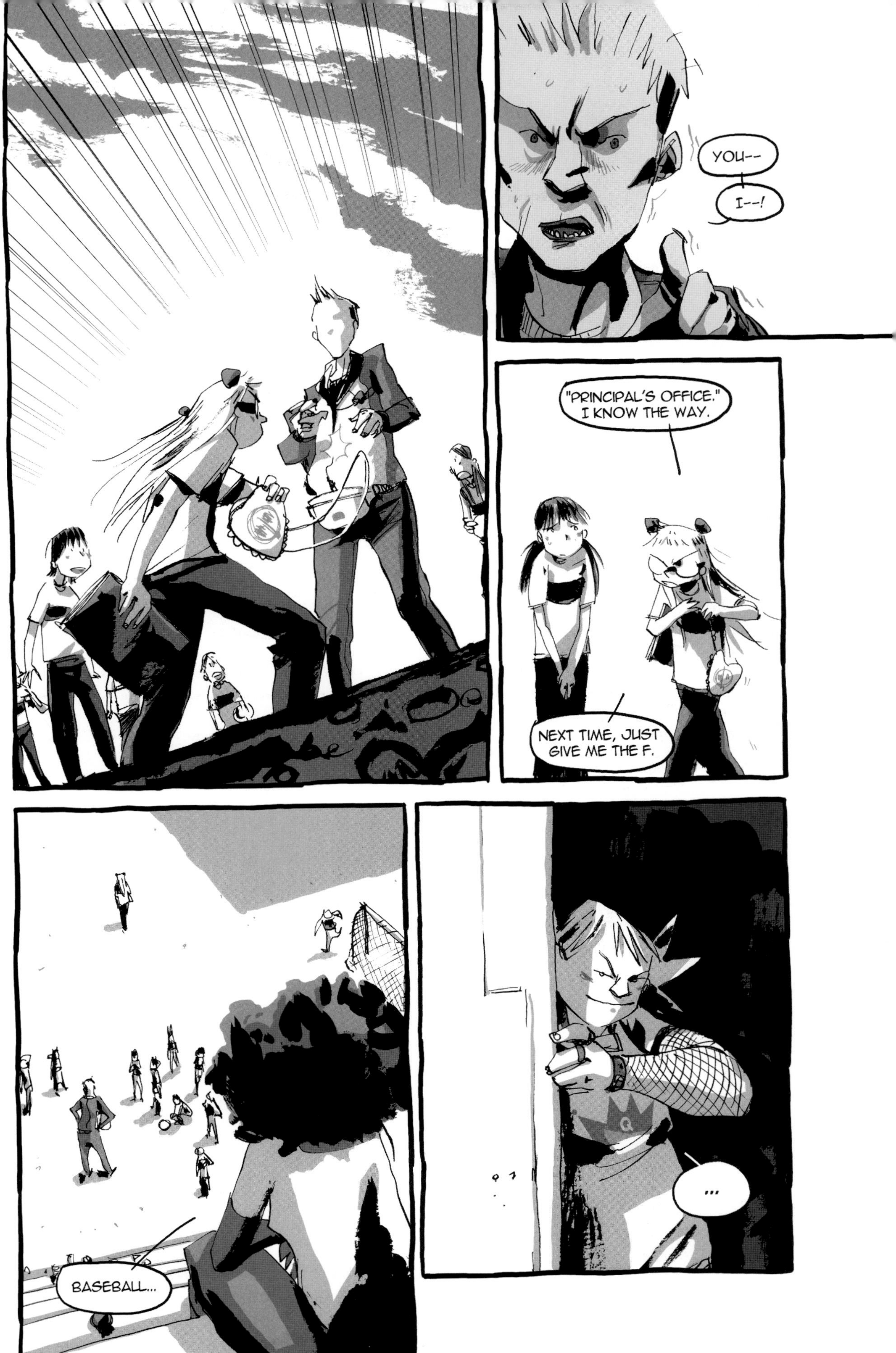
YOU--
I--!
"PRINCIPAL'S OFFICE."
I KNOW THE WAY.
NEXT TIME, JUST
GIVE ME THE F.
BASEBALL...
...

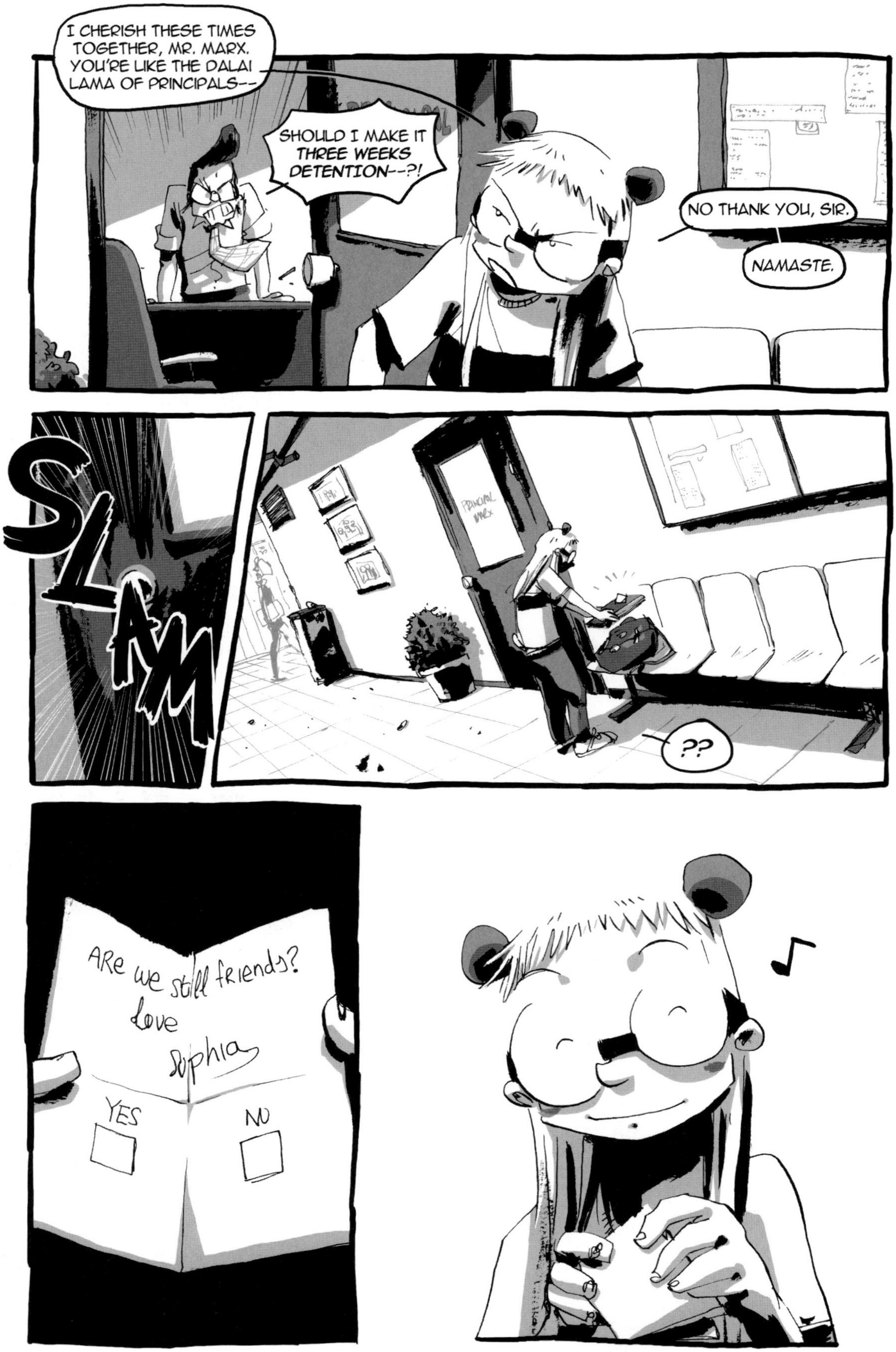
I CHERISH THESE TIMES TOGETHER, MR. MARX. YOU'RE LIKE THE DALAI LAMA OF PRINCIPALS--
SHOULD I MAKE IT THREE WEEKS DETENTION--?!
NO THANK YOU, SIR.
NAMASTE.
SLAM
??
Are we still friends?
love
Sophia
YES
NO

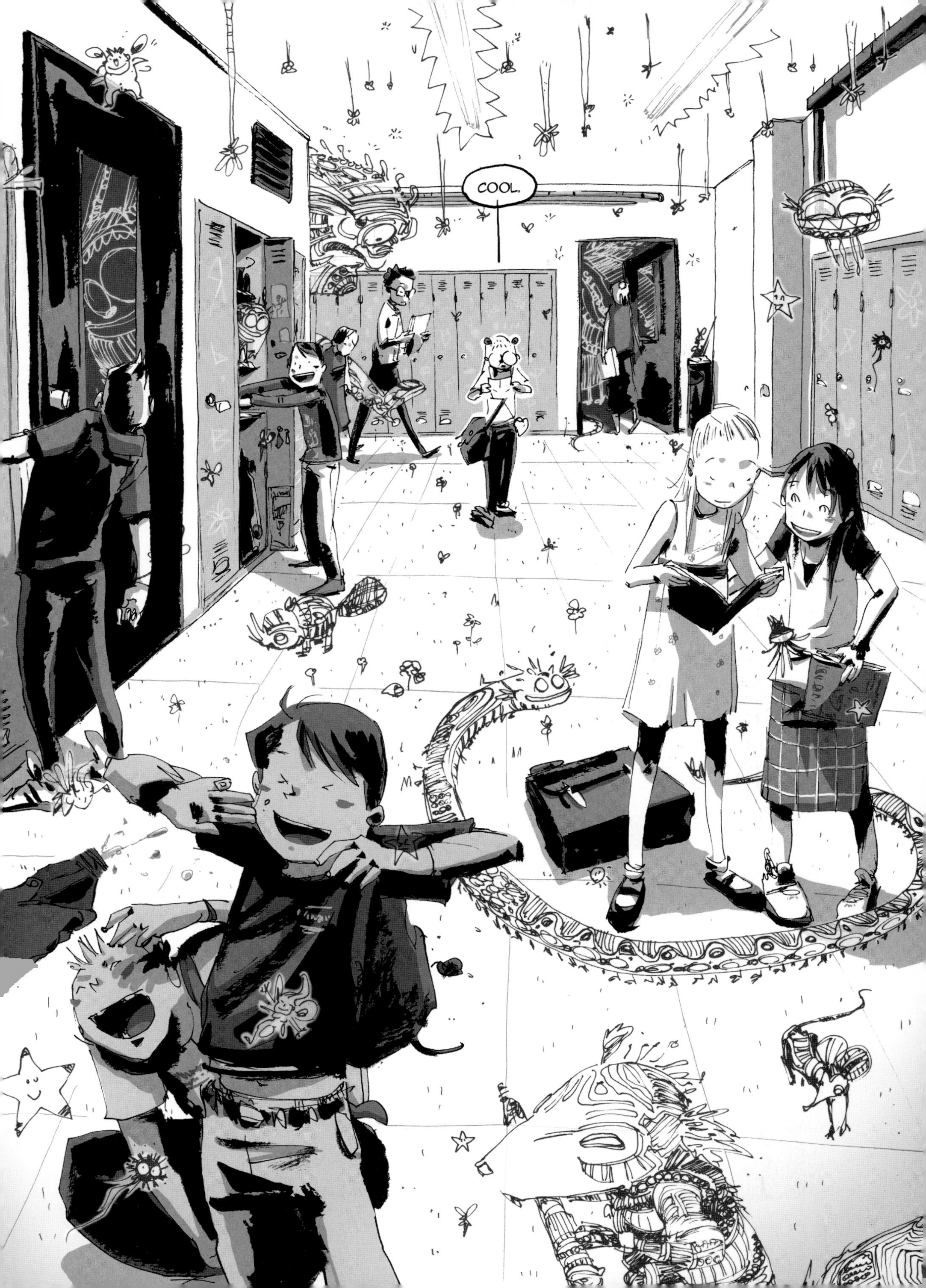
COOL.

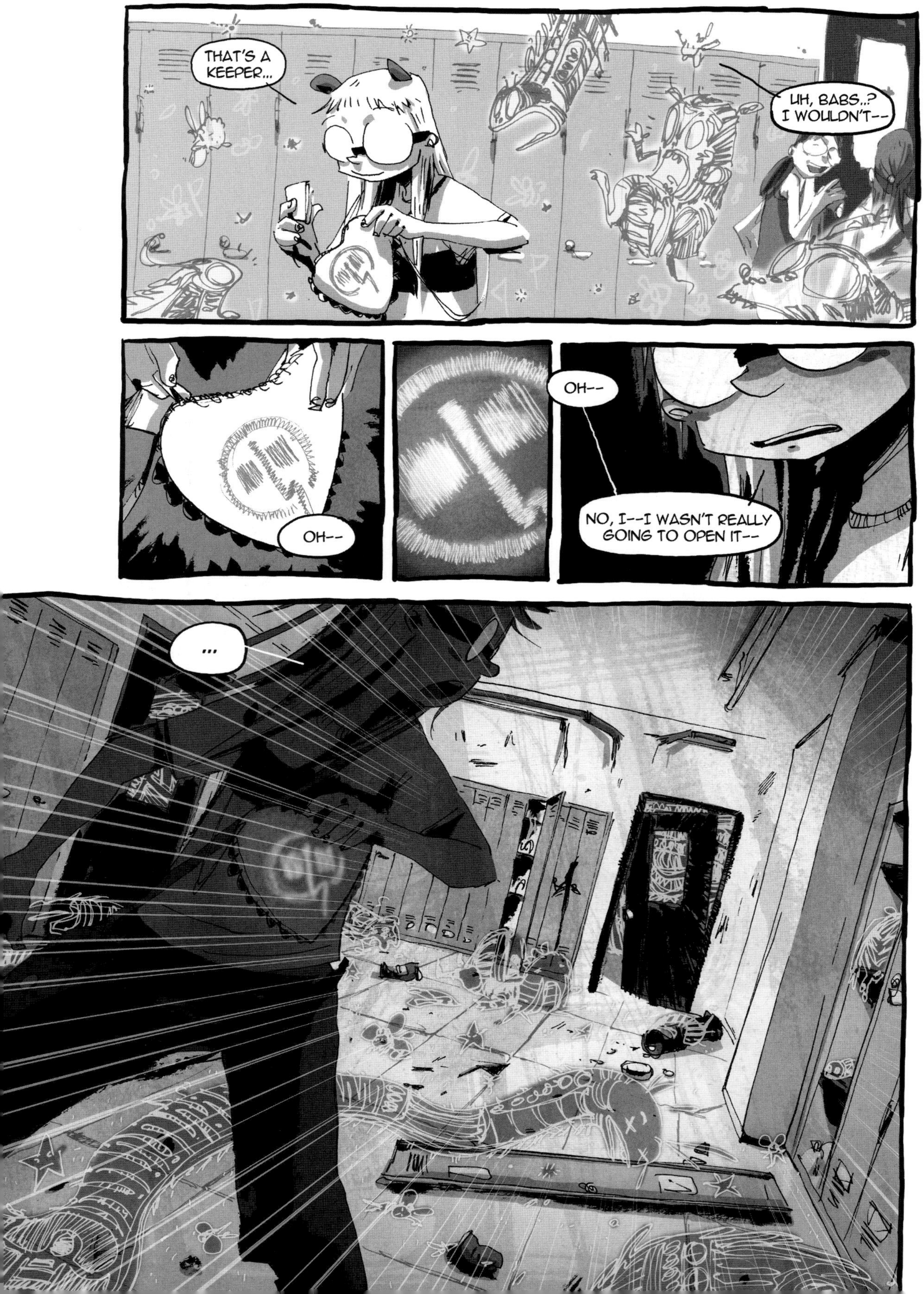
THAT'S A KEEPER...
UH, BABS..? I WOULDN'T--
OH--
OH--
NO, I--I WASN'T REALLY GOING TO OPEN IT--
...

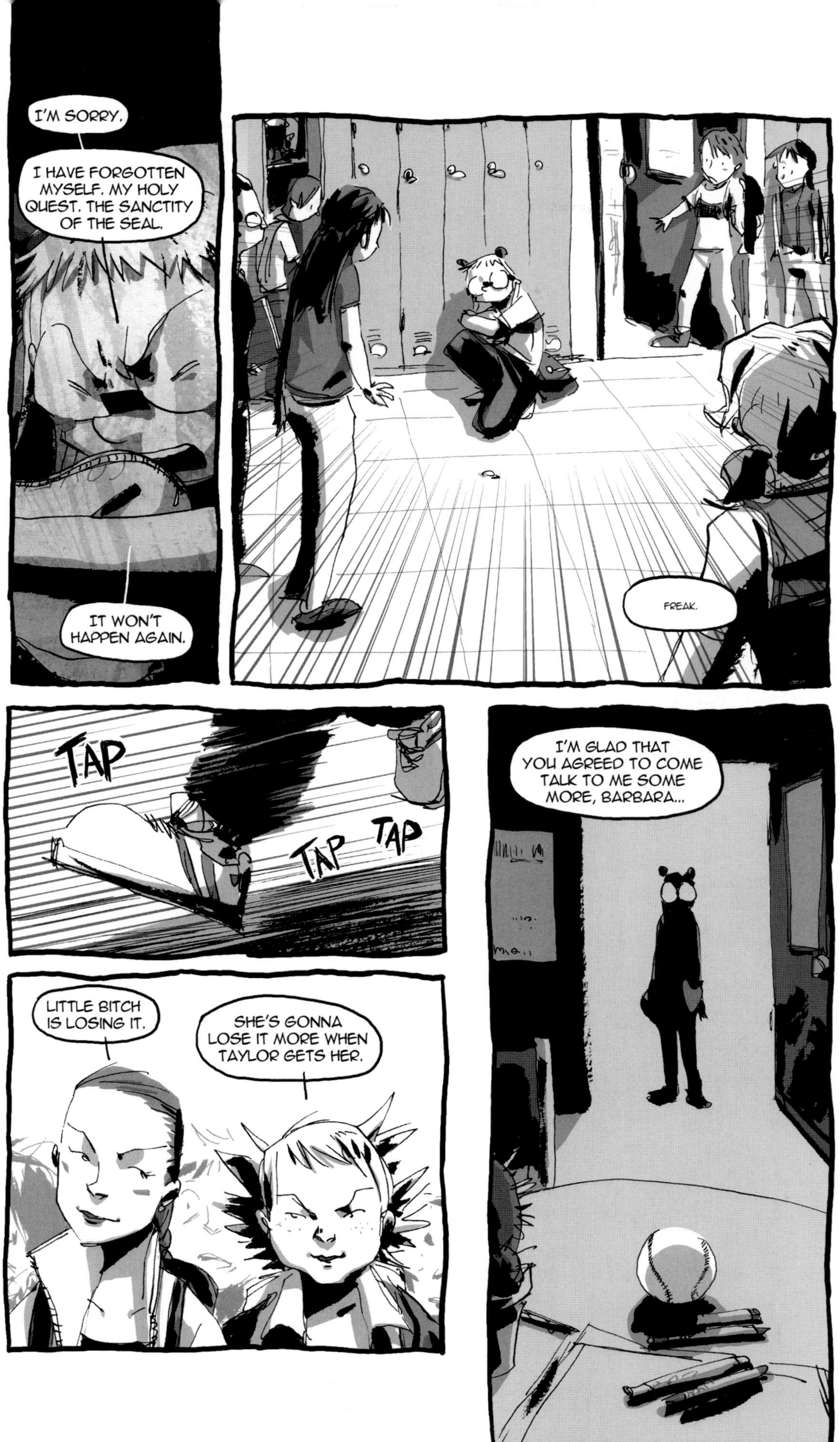
I'M SORRY.
I HAVE FORGOTTEN MYSELF. MY HOLY QUEST. THE SANCTITY OF THE SEAL.
IT WON'T HAPPEN AGAIN.
FREAK.
TAP
TAP TAP
LITTLE BITCH IS LOSING IT.
SHE'S GONNA LOSE IT MORE WHEN TAYLOR GETS HER.
I'M GLAD THAT YOU AGREED TO COME TALK TO ME SOME MORE, BARBARA...

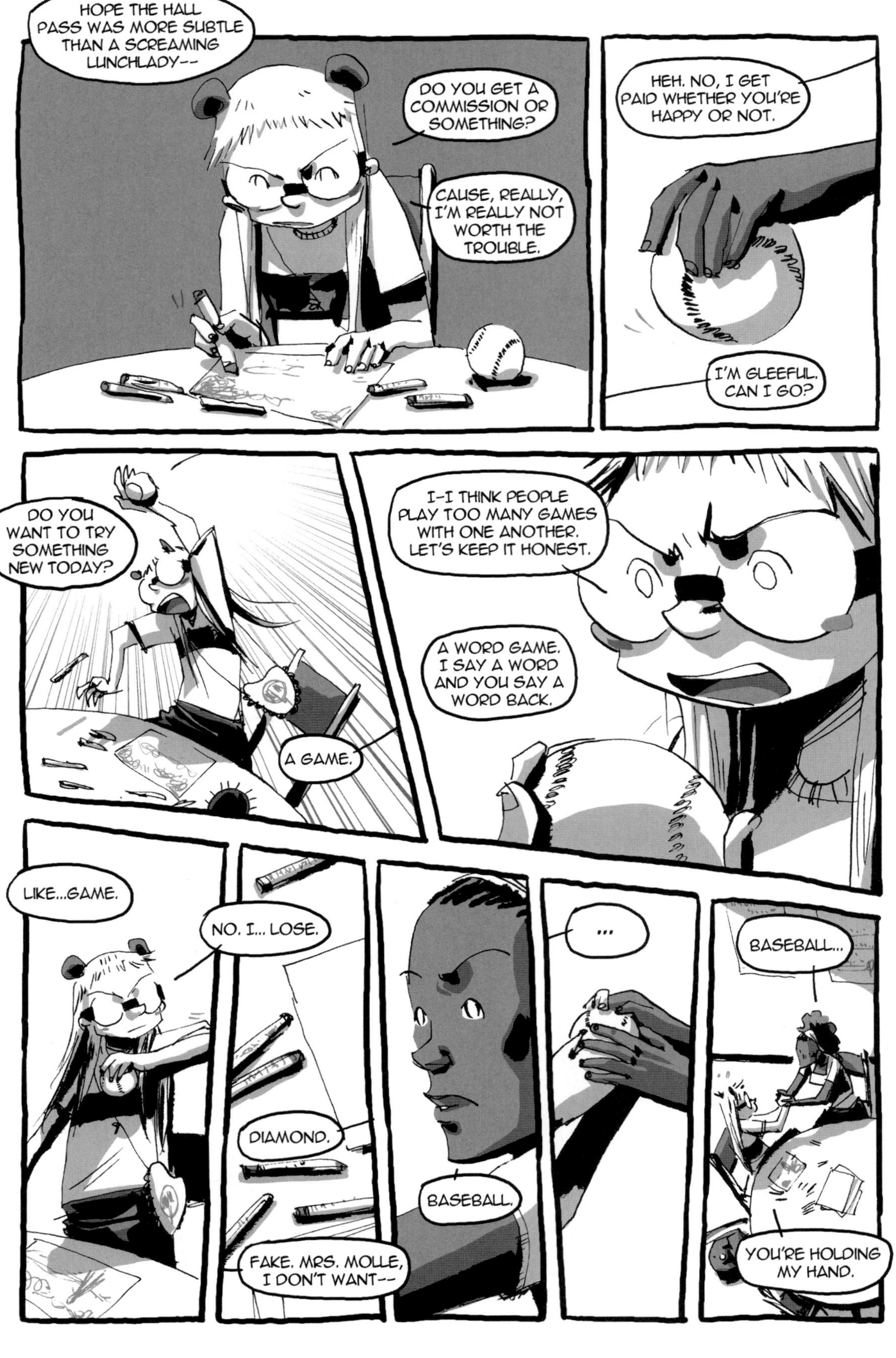
HOPE THE HALL PASS WAS MORE SUBTLE THAN A SCREAMING LUNCHLADY--
DO YOU GET A COMMISSION OR SOMETHING?
CAUSE, REALLY, I'M REALLY NOT WORTH THE TROUBLE.
HEH. NO, I GET PAID WHETHER YOU'RE HAPPY OR NOT.
I'M GLEEFUL. CAN I GO?
DO YOU WANT TO TRY SOMETHING NEW TODAY?
A GAME.
I-I THINK PEOPLE PLAY TOO MANY GAMES WITH ONE ANOTHER. LET'S KEEP IT HONEST.
A WORD GAME. I SAY A WORD AND YOU SAY A WORD BACK.
LIKE...GAME.
NO. I... LOSE.
DIAMOND.
FAKE. MRS. MOLLE, I DON'T WANT--
BASEBALL.
...
BASEBALL...
YOU'RE HOLDING MY HAND.

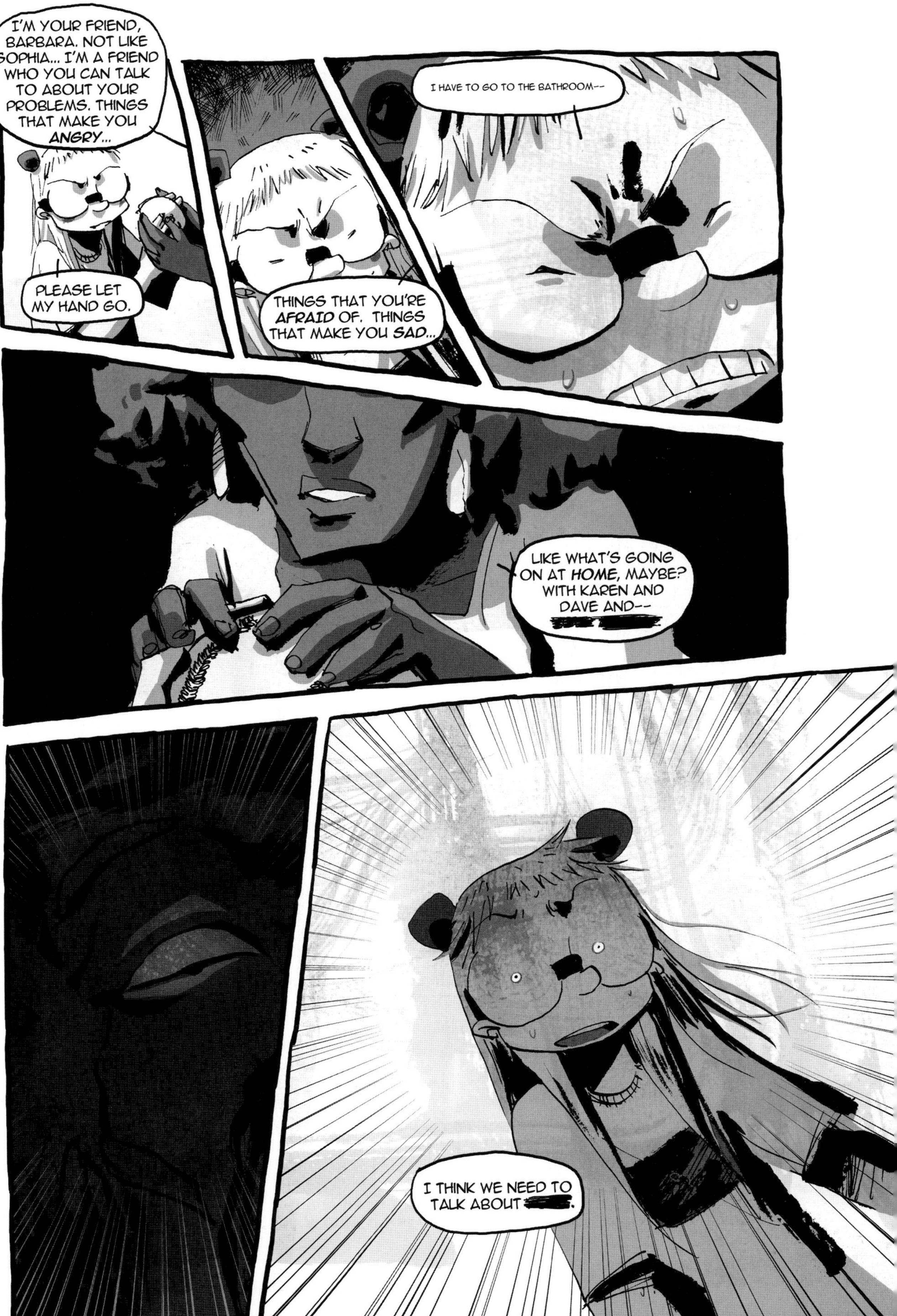
I'M YOUR FRIEND, BARBARA. NOT LIKE SOPHIA... I'M A FRIEND WHO YOU CAN TALK TO ABOUT YOUR PROBLEMS. THINGS THAT MAKE YOU ANGRY...
PLEASE LET MY HAND GO.
THINGS THAT YOU'RE AFRAID OF. THINGS THAT MAKE YOU SAD...
I HAVE TO GO TO THE BATHROOM--
LIKE WHAT'S GOING ON AT HOME, MAYBE? WITH KAREN AND DAVE AND-- [redacted]
I THINK WE NEED TO TALK ABOUT [redacted].

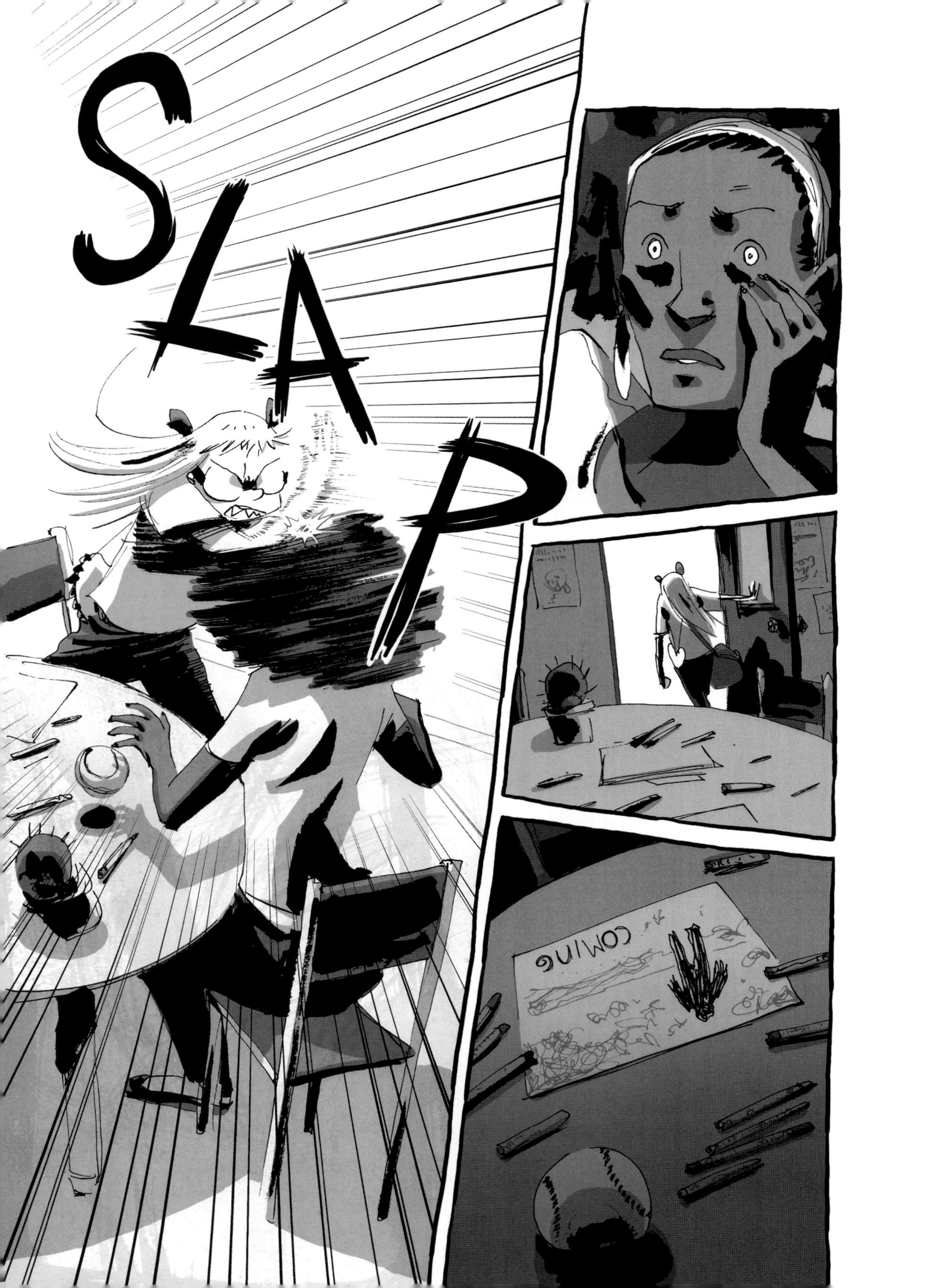
SLAP
COMING

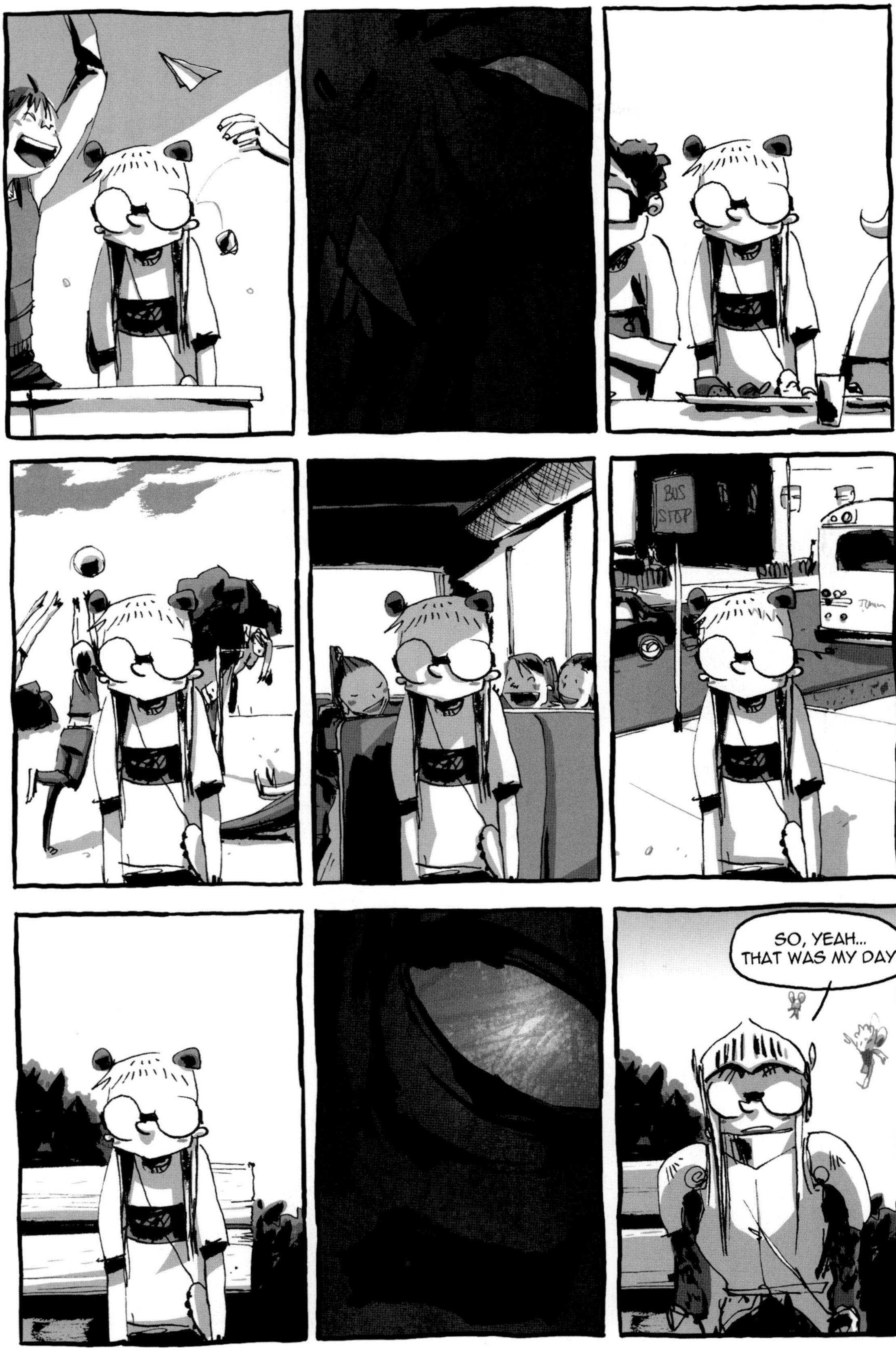
BUS STOP
SO, YEAH... THAT WAS MY DAY.

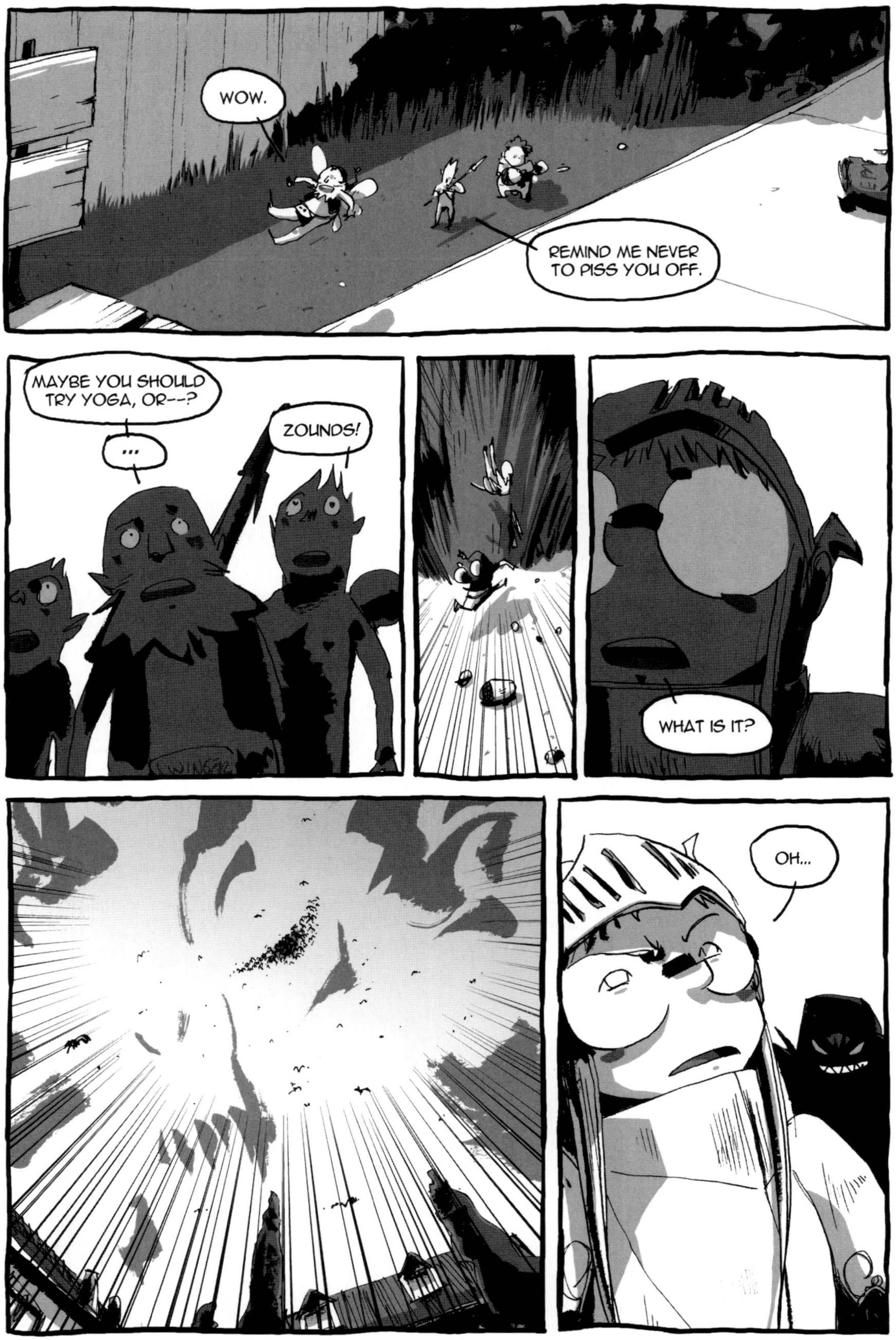
WOW.
REMIND ME NEVER TO PISS YOU OFF.
MAYBE YOU SHOULD TRY YOGA, OR--?
...
ZOUNDS!
WHAT IS IT?
OH...

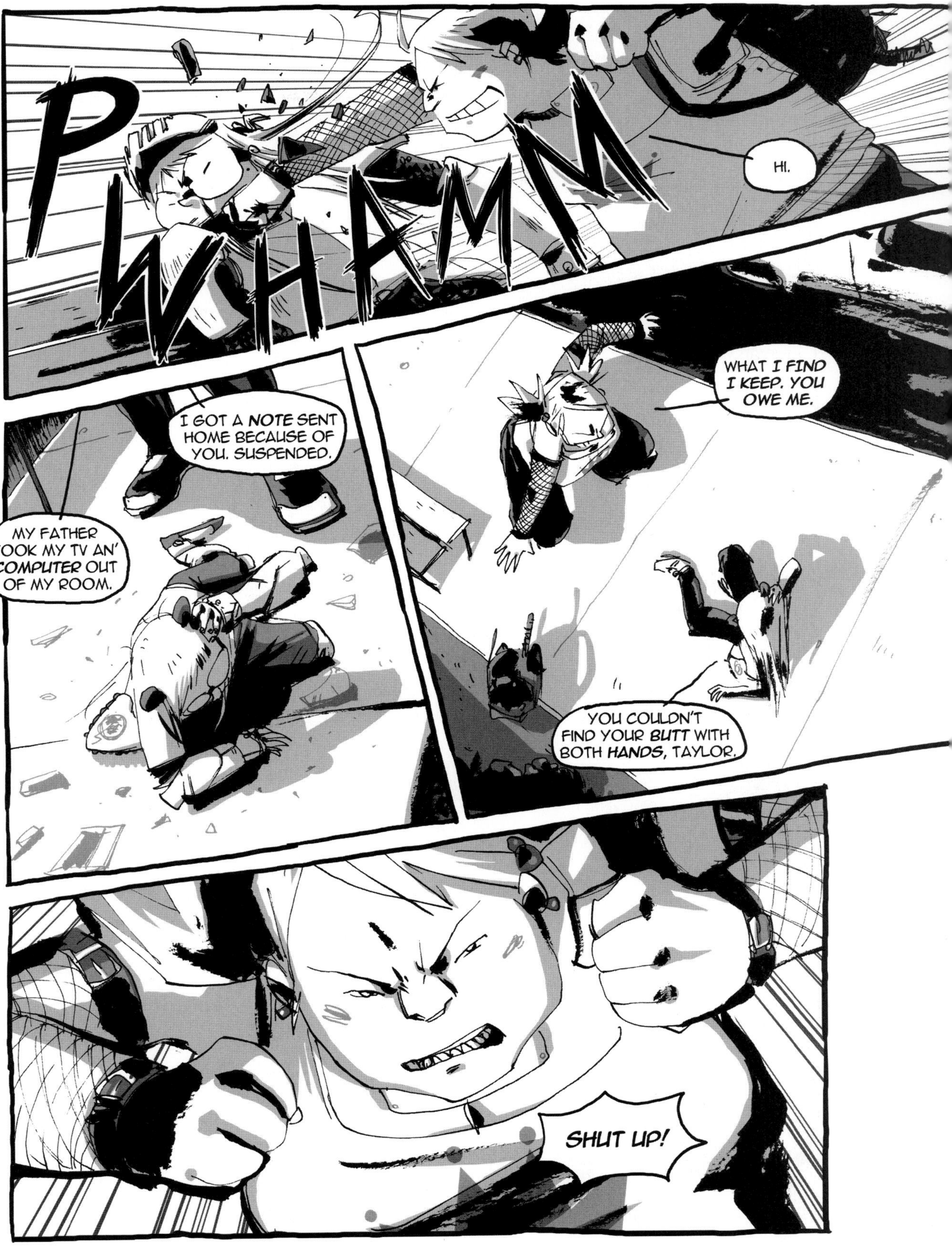
PWHAMM
HI.
I GOT A NOTE SENT HOME BECAUSE OF YOU. SUSPENDED.
MY FATHER TOOK MY TV AN' COMPUTER OUT OF MY ROOM.
WHAT I FIND I KEEP. YOU OWE ME.
YOU COULDN'T FIND YOUR BUTT WITH BOTH HANDS, TAYLOR.
SHUT UP!

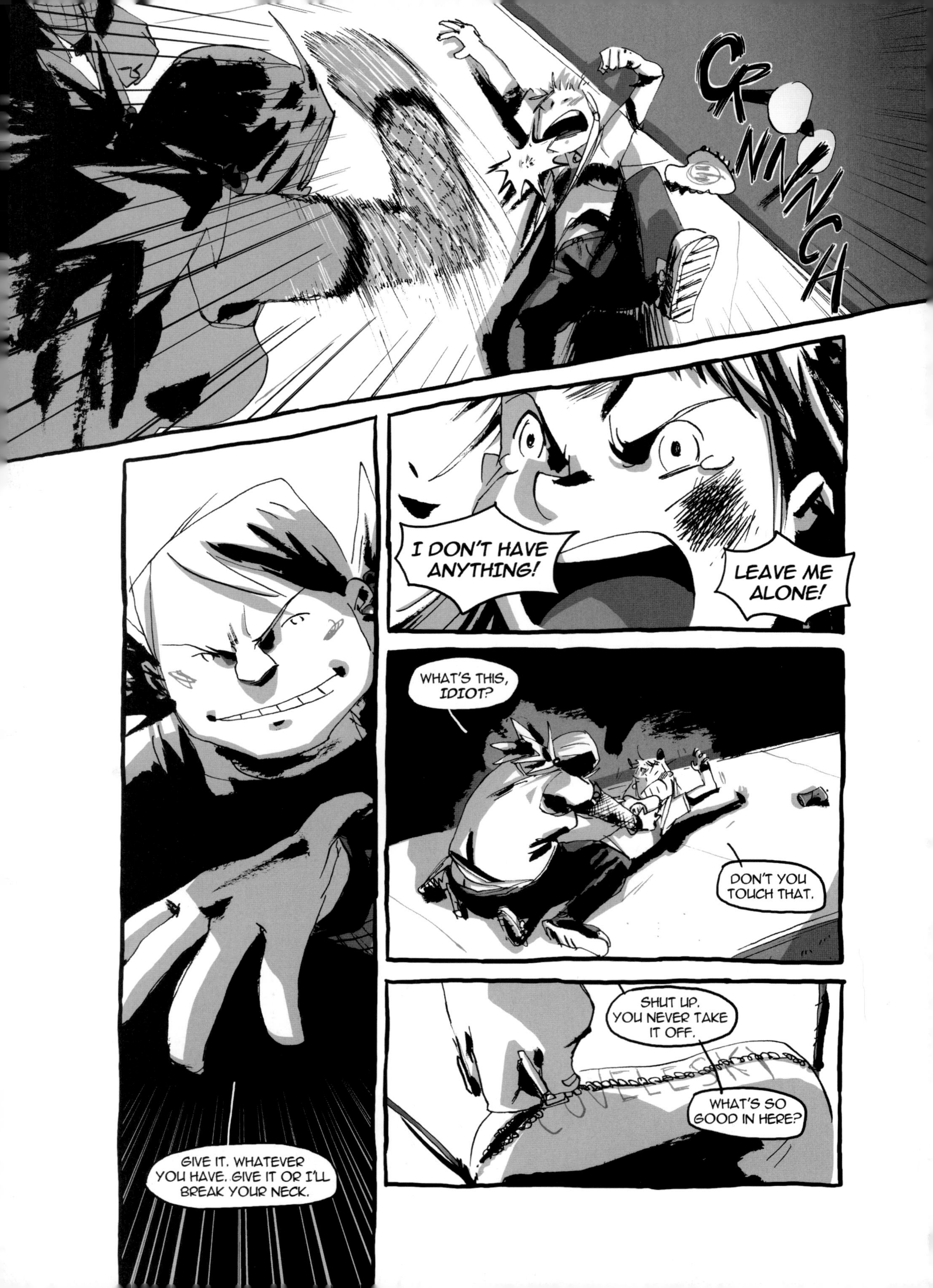

CRNNNCHA
I DON'T HAVE ANYTHING!
LEAVE ME ALONE!
GIVE IT. WHATEVER YOU HAVE. GIVE IT OR I'LL BREAK YOUR NECK.
WHAT'S THIS, IDIOT?
DON'T YOU TOUCH THAT.
SHUT UP. YOU NEVER TAKE IT OFF.
COVELESKY
WHAT'S SO GOOD IN HERE?

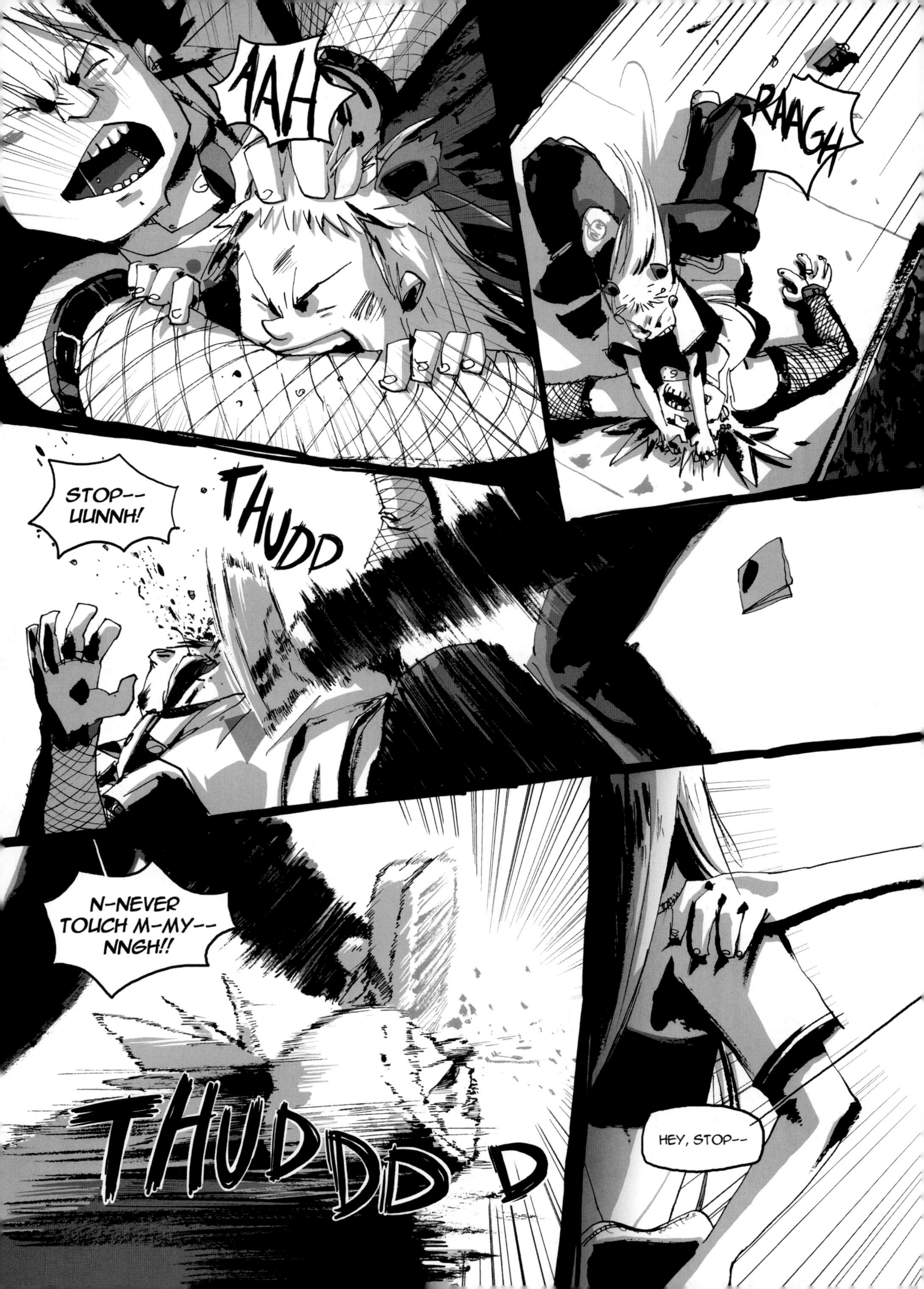
AAH
RAAGH
STOP--
UUNNH!
THUDD
N-NEVER
TOUCH M-MY--
NNGH!!
THUDDD D
HEY, STOP--

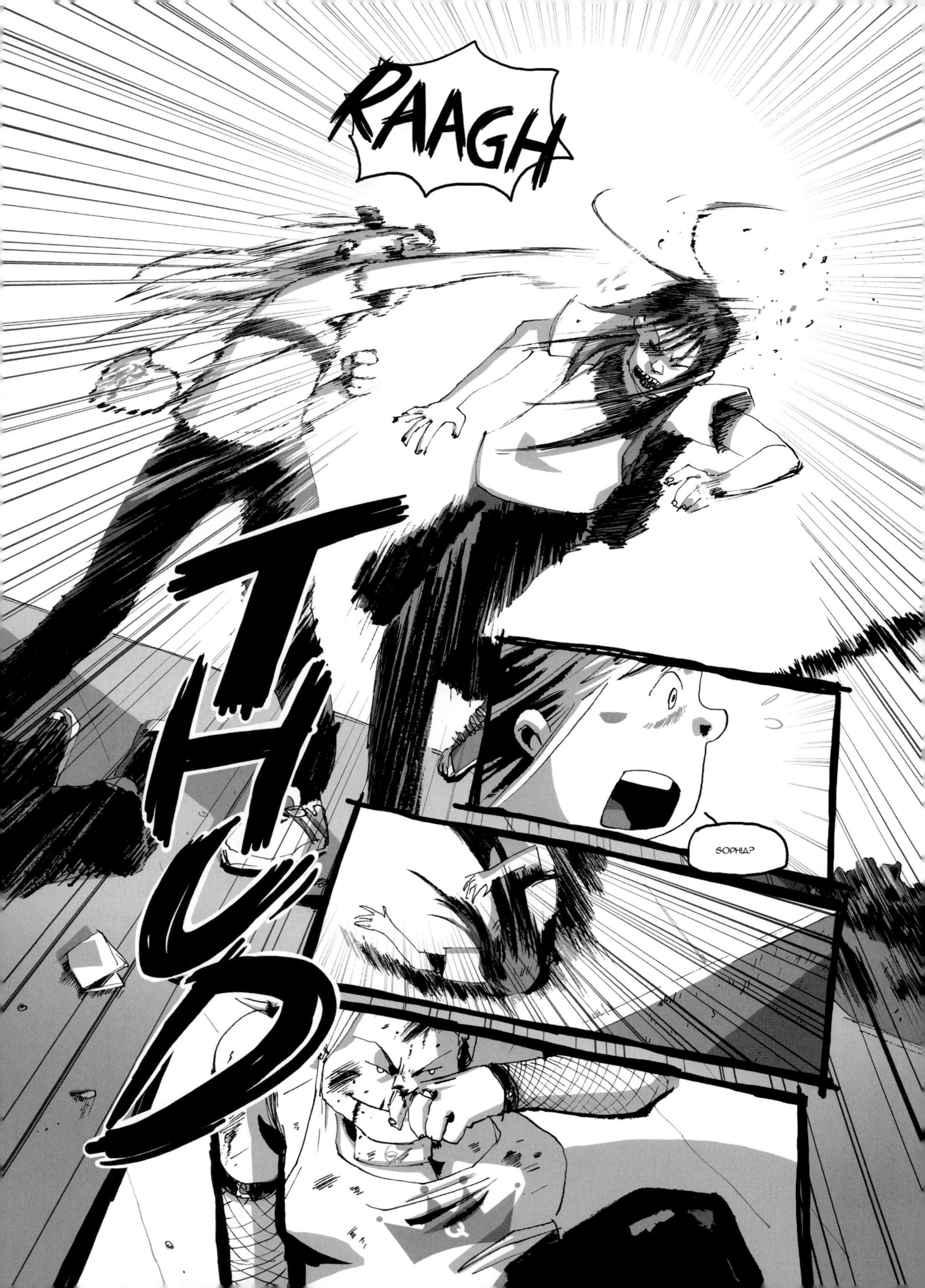
RAAGH
THUD
SOPHIA?

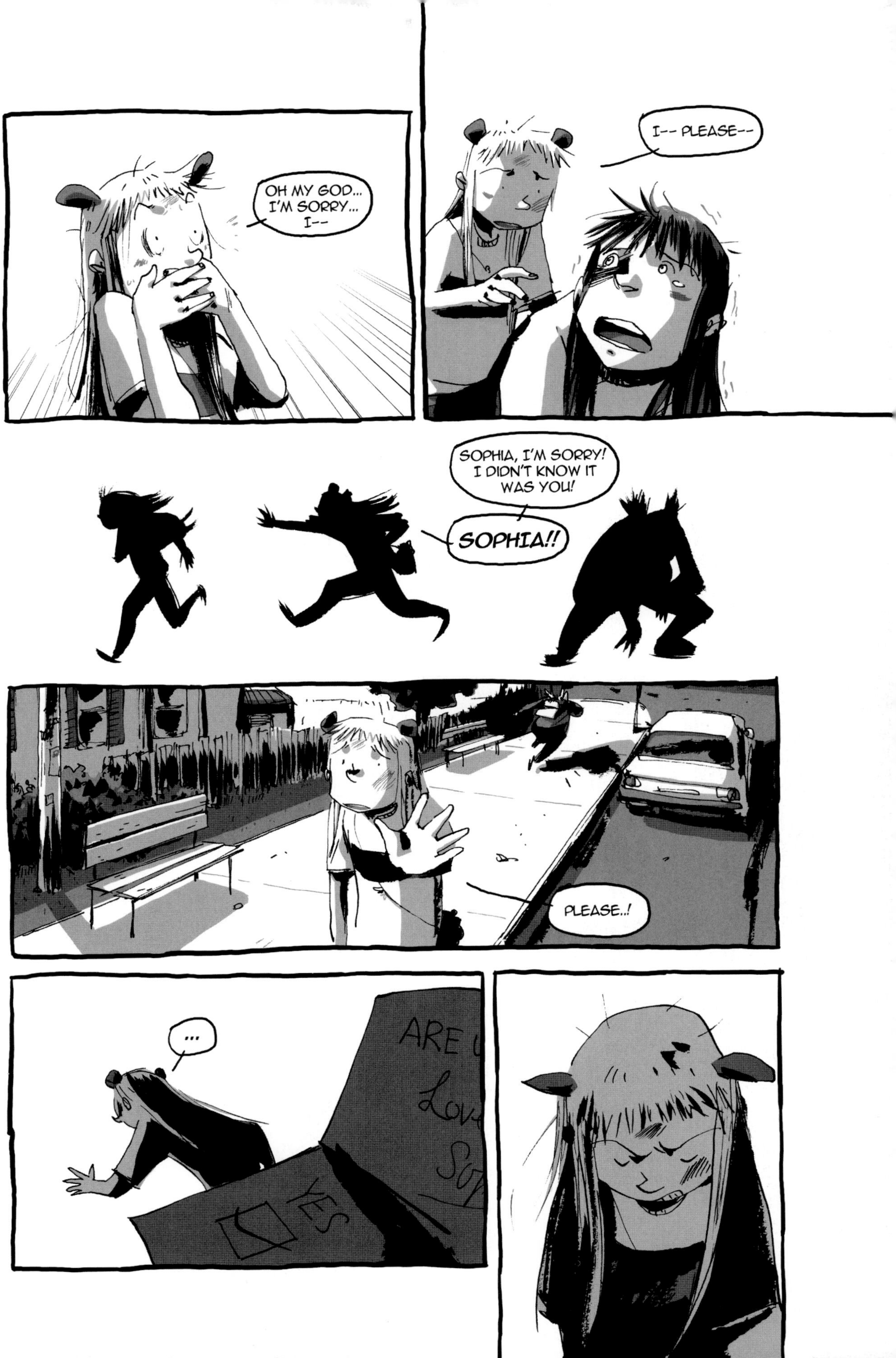

OH MY GOD... I'M SORRY... I--
I-- PLEASE--
SOPHIA, I'M SORRY! I DIDN'T KNOW IT WAS YOU!
SOPHIA!!
PLEASE..!
...

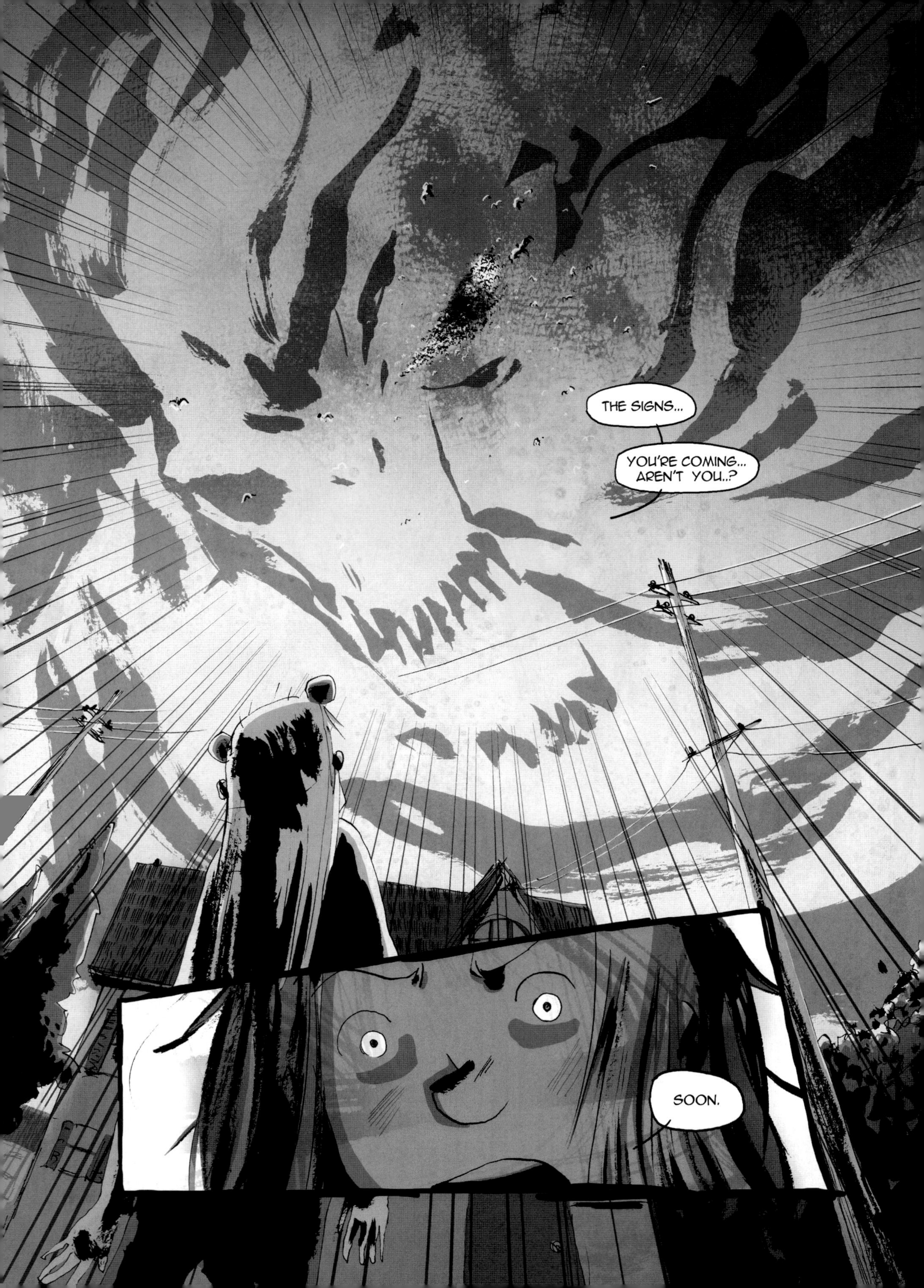
THE SIGNS...
YOU'RE COMING... AREN'T YOU..?
SOON.

CHAPTER**4**: THE GHOUL

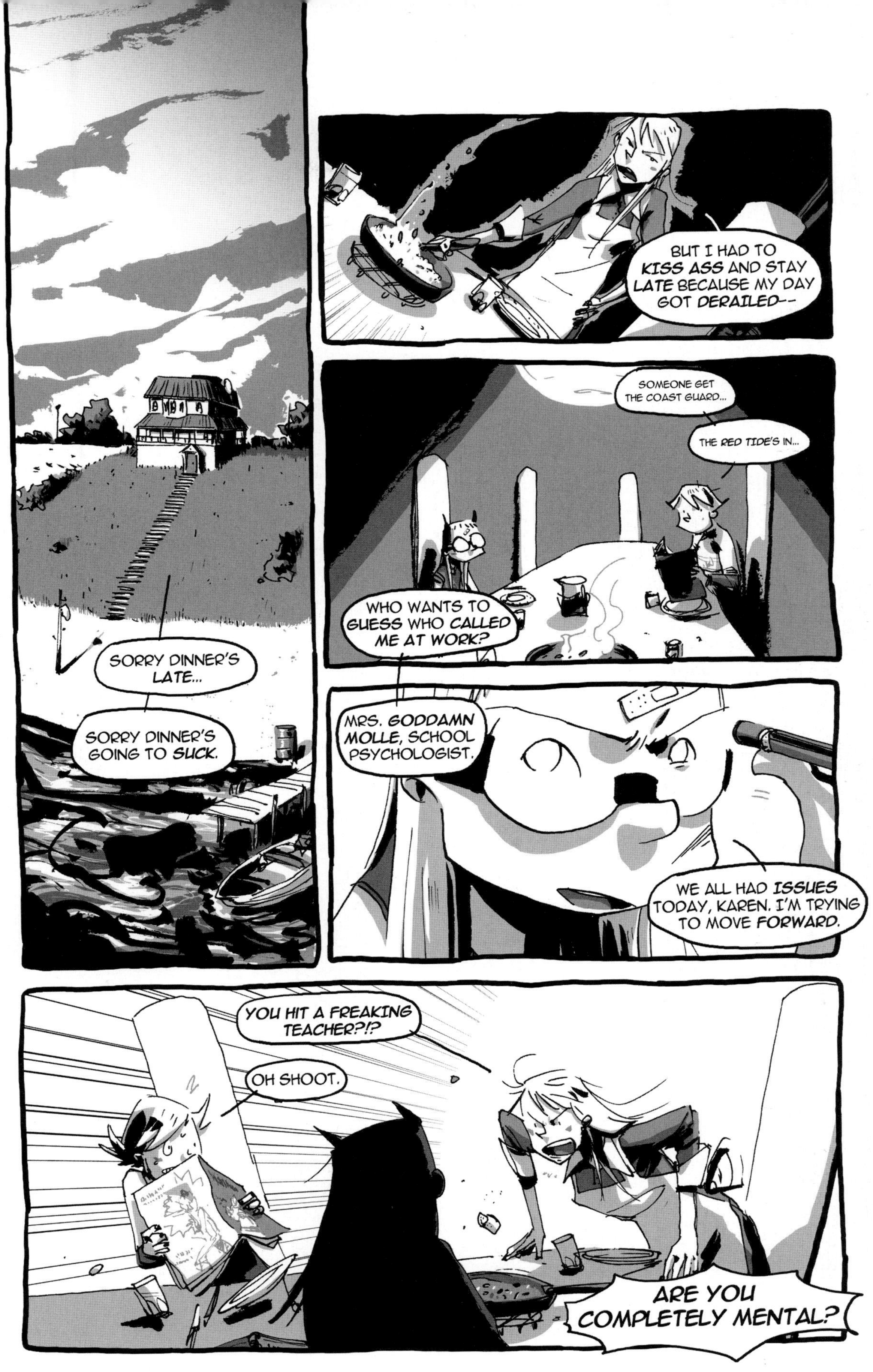
SORRY DINNER'S LATE...
SORRY DINNER'S GOING TO SUCK.
BUT I HAD TO KISS ASS AND STAY LATE BECAUSE MY DAY GOT DERAILED--
SOMEONE GET THE COAST GUARD...
THE RED TIDE'S IN...
WHO WANTS TO GUESS WHO CALLED ME AT WORK?
MRS. GODDAMN MOLLE, SCHOOL PSYCHOLOGIST.
WE ALL HAD ISSUES TODAY, KAREN. I'M TRYING TO MOVE FORWARD.
YOU HIT A FREAKING TEACHER?!?
OH SHOOT.
ARE YOU COMPLETELY MENTAL?

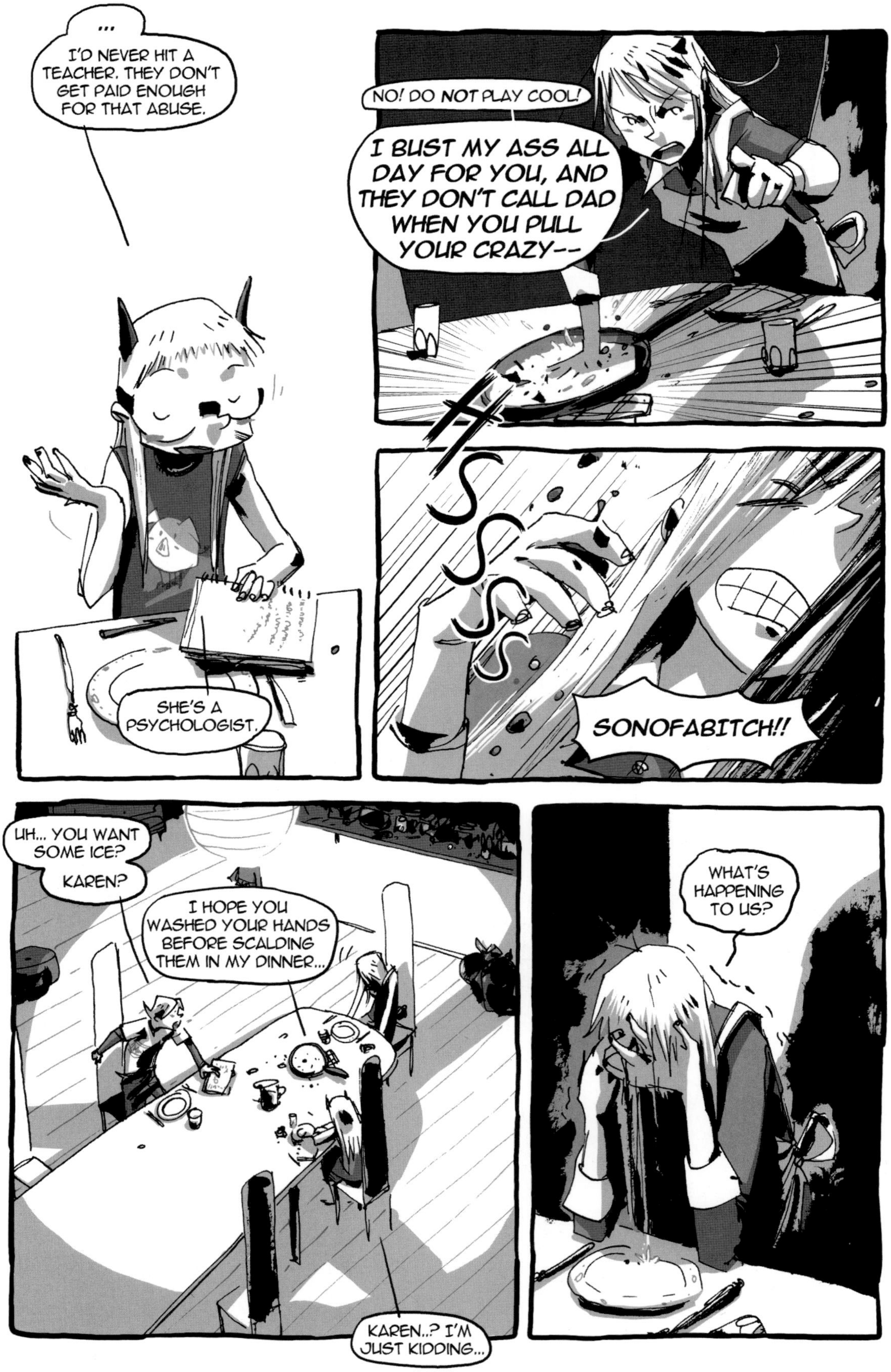
...
I'D NEVER HIT A TEACHER. THEY DON'T GET PAID ENOUGH FOR THAT ABUSE.
SHE'S A PSYCHOLOGIST.
NO! DO NOT PLAY COOL!
I BUST MY ASS ALL DAY FOR YOU, AND THEY DON'T CALL DAD WHEN YOU PULL YOUR CRAZY--
HISSSS
SONOFABITCH!!
UH... YOU WANT SOME ICE?
KAREN?
I HOPE YOU WASHED YOUR HANDS BEFORE SCALDING THEM IN MY DINNER...
KAREN..? I'M JUST KIDDING...
WHAT'S HAPPENING TO US?

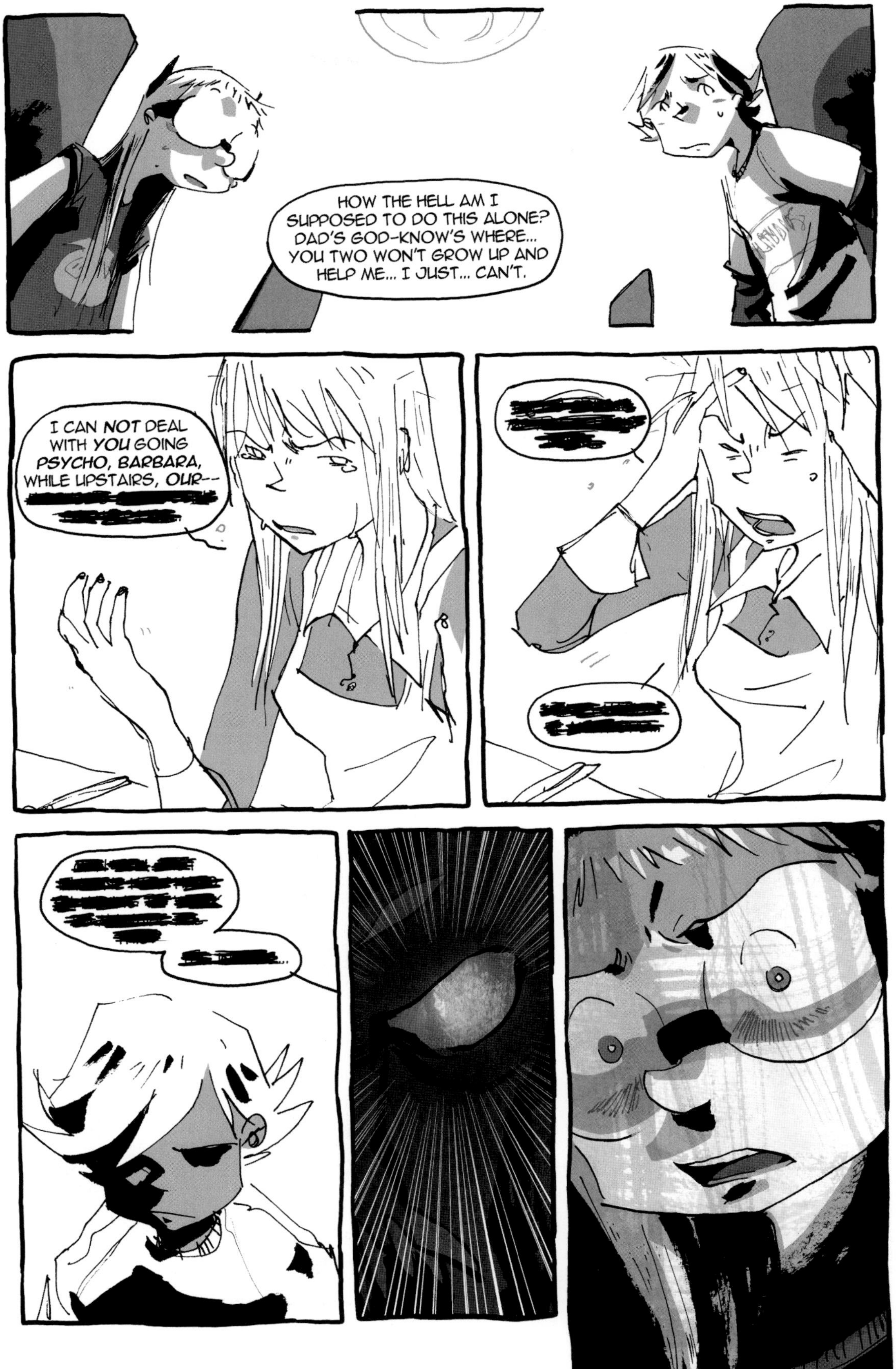
HOW THE HELL AM I SUPPOSED TO DO THIS ALONE? DAD'S GOD-KNOW'S WHERE... YOU TWO WON'T GROW UP AND HELP ME... I JUST... CAN'T.
I CAN **NOT** DEAL WITH **YOU** GOING **PSYCHO**, BARBARA, WHILE UPSTAIRS, **OUR**-- [redacted]
[redacted]
[redacted]
[redacted]
[redacted]...

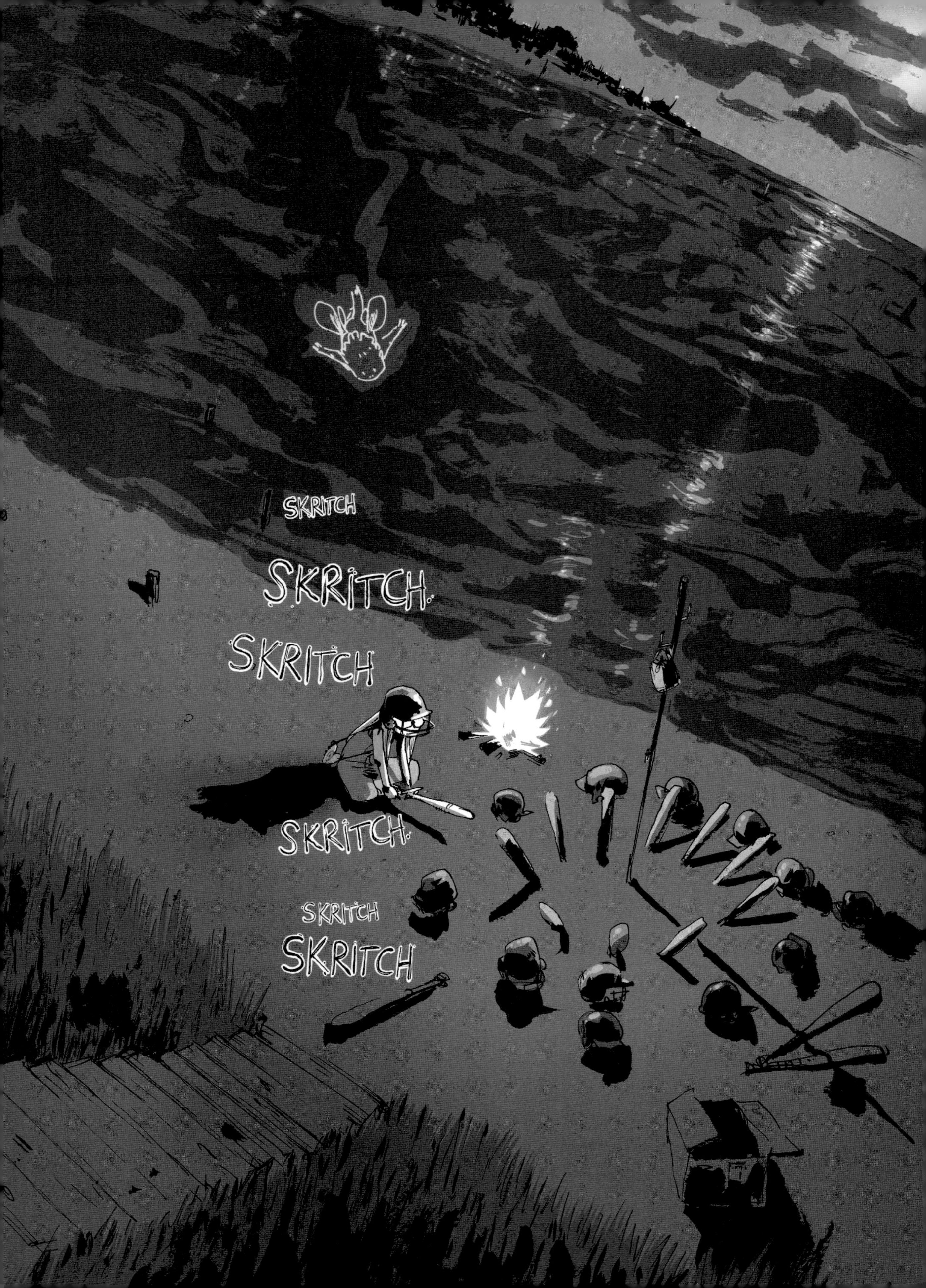
SKRITCH
SKRITCH
SKRITCH
SKRITCH
SKRITCH
SKRITCH

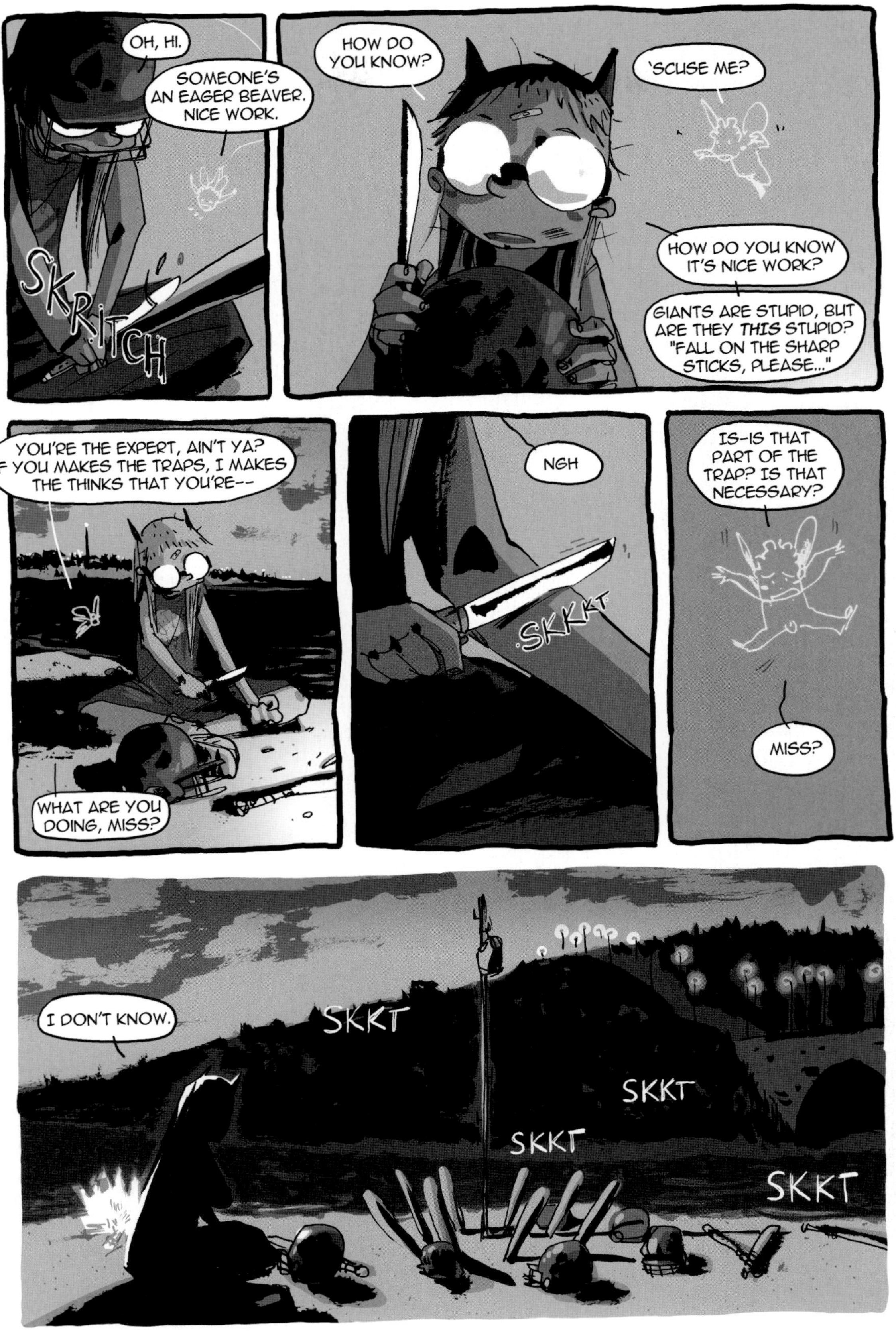
OH, HI.
SOMEONE'S AN EAGER BEAVER. NICE WORK.
SKRITCH
HOW DO YOU KNOW?
'SCUSE ME?
HOW DO YOU KNOW IT'S NICE WORK?
GIANTS ARE STUPID, BUT ARE THEY THIS STUPID? "FALL ON THE SHARP STICKS, PLEASE..."
YOU'RE THE EXPERT, AIN'T YA? 'F YOU MAKES THE TRAPS, I MAKES THE THINKS THAT YOU'RE--
WHAT ARE YOU DOING, MISS?
NGH
SKKKT
IS-IS THAT PART OF THE TRAP? IS THAT NECESSARY?
MISS?
I DON'T KNOW.
SKKT
SKKT
SKKT
SKKT

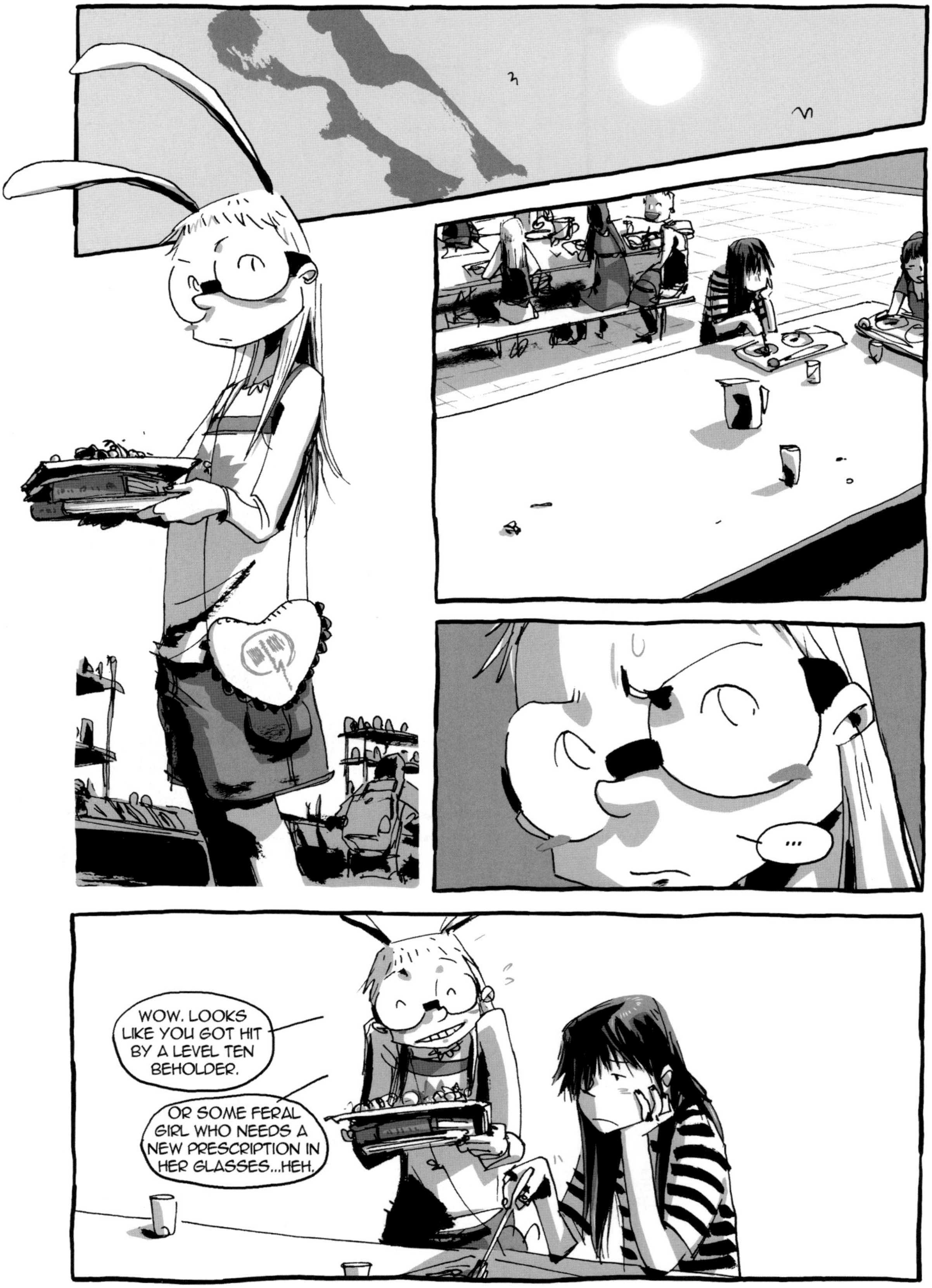
...
WOW. LOOKS LIKE YOU GOT HIT BY A LEVEL TEN BEHOLDER.
OR SOME FERAL GIRL WHO NEEDS A NEW PRESCRIPTION IN HER GLASSES...HEH.

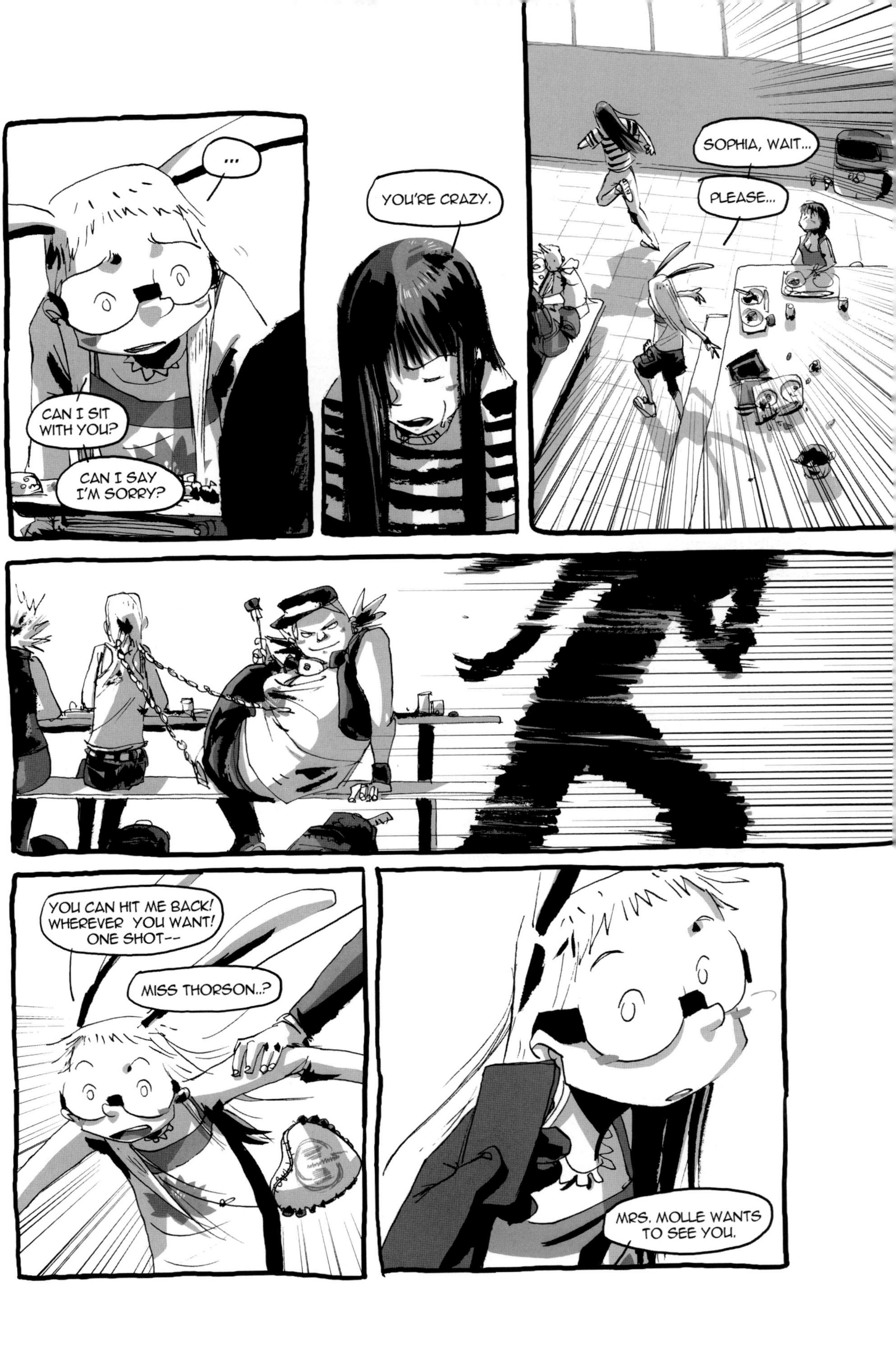
...
YOU'RE CRAZY.
CAN I SIT WITH YOU?
CAN I SAY I'M SORRY?
SOPHIA, WAIT...
PLEASE...
YOU CAN HIT ME BACK! WHEREVER YOU WANT! ONE SHOT--
MISS THORSON..?
MRS. MOLLE WANTS TO SEE YOU.

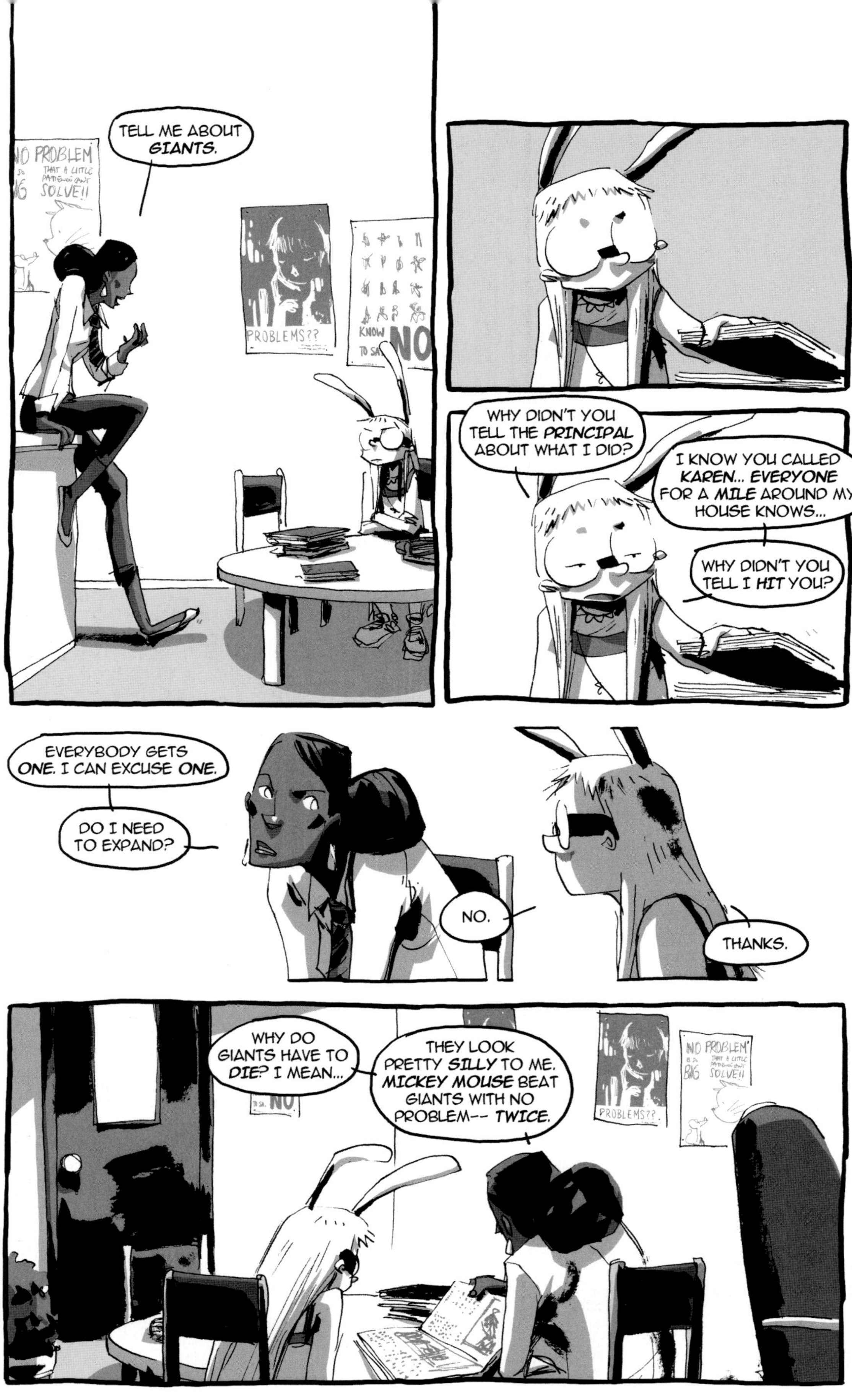
NO PROBLEM IS SO BIG THAT A LITTLE PATIENCE CAN'T SOLVE!!
TELL ME ABOUT GIANTS.
PROBLEMS??
KNOW TO SAY NO
WHY DIDN'T YOU TELL THE PRINCIPAL ABOUT WHAT I DID?
I KNOW YOU CALLED KAREN... EVERYONE FOR A MILE AROUND MY HOUSE KNOWS...
WHY DIDN'T YOU TELL I HIT YOU?
EVERYBODY GETS ONE. I CAN EXCUSE ONE.
DO I NEED TO EXPAND?
NO.
THANKS.
WHY DO GIANTS HAVE TO DIE? I MEAN...
THEY LOOK PRETTY SILLY TO ME. MICKEY MOUSE BEAT GIANTS WITH NO PROBLEM-- TWICE.

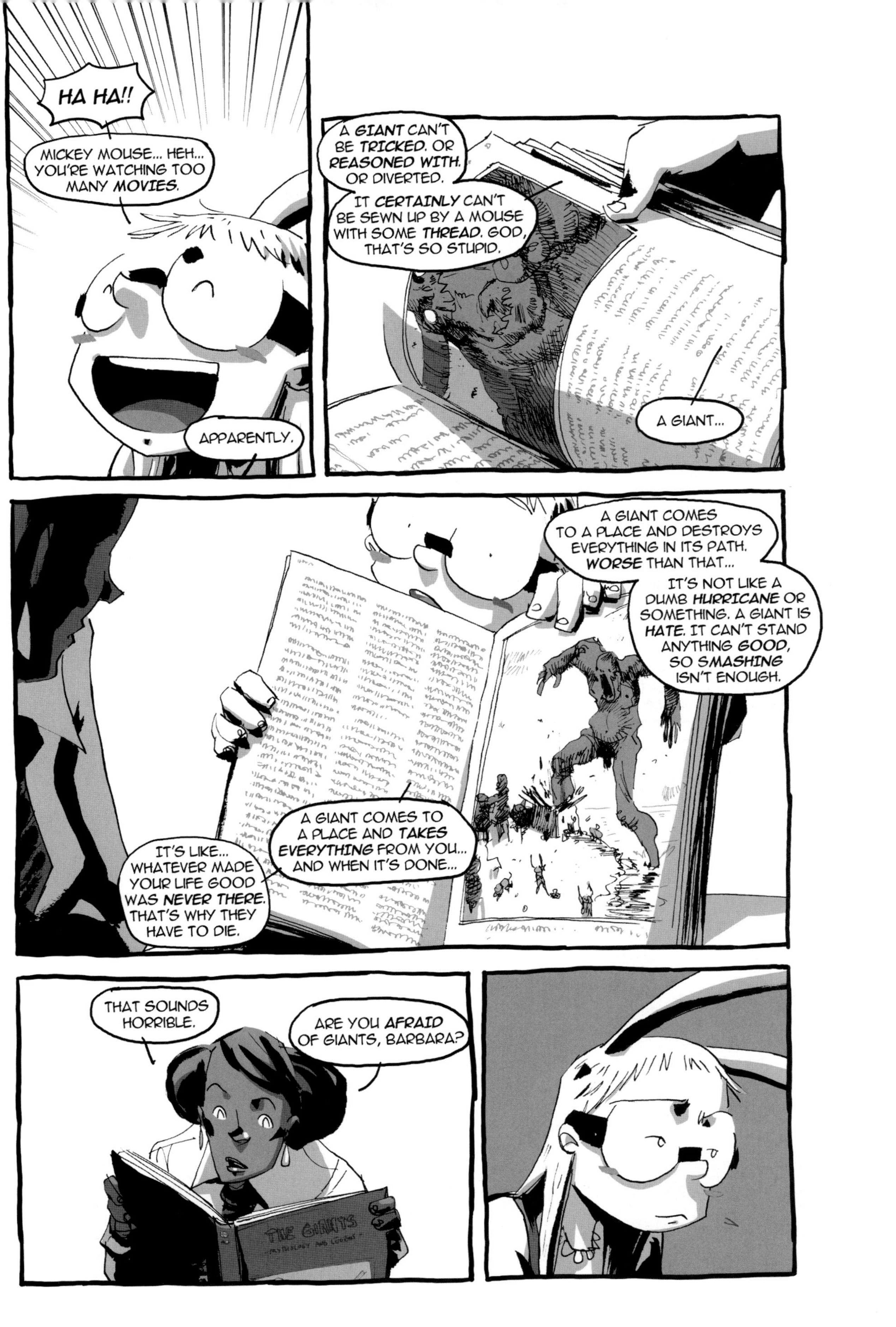
HA HA!!
MICKEY MOUSE... HEH... YOU'RE WATCHING TOO MANY MOVIES.
APPARENTLY.
A GIANT CAN'T BE TRICKED. OR REASONED WITH. OR DIVERTED.
IT CERTAINLY CAN'T BE SEWN UP BY A MOUSE WITH SOME THREAD. GOD, THAT'S SO STUPID.
A GIANT...
A GIANT COMES TO A PLACE AND DESTROYS EVERYTHING IN ITS PATH. WORSE THAN THAT...
IT'S NOT LIKE A DUMB HURRICANE OR SOMETHING. A GIANT IS HATE. IT CAN'T STAND ANYTHING GOOD, SO SMASHING ISN'T ENOUGH.
A GIANT COMES TO A PLACE AND TAKES EVERYTHING FROM YOU... AND WHEN IT'S DONE...
IT'S LIKE... WHATEVER MADE YOUR LIFE GOOD WAS NEVER THERE. THAT'S WHY THEY HAVE TO DIE.
THAT SOUNDS HORRIBLE.
ARE YOU AFRAID OF GIANTS, BARBARA?
THE GIANTS

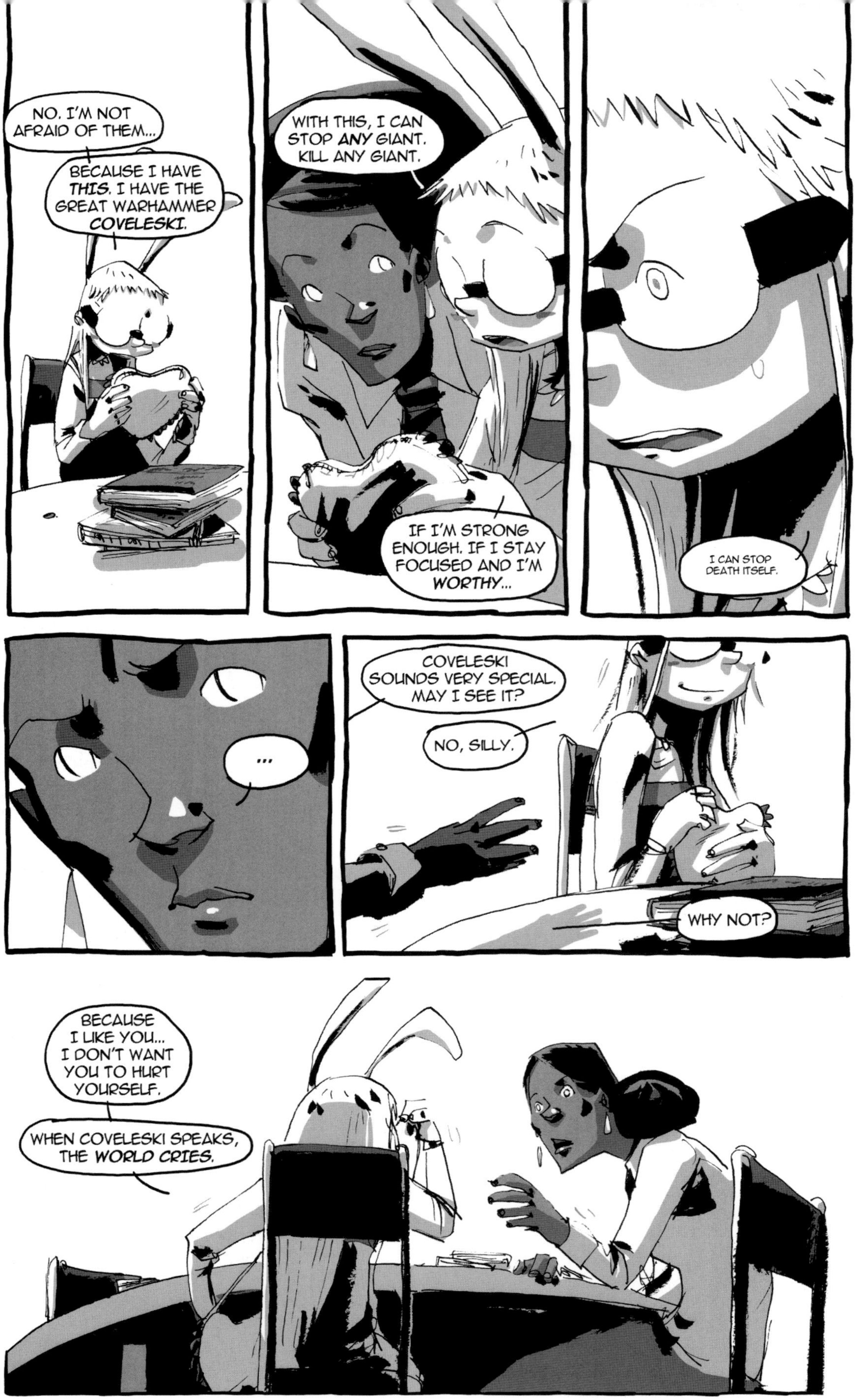
NO. I'M NOT AFRAID OF THEM...
BECAUSE I HAVE **THIS**. I HAVE THE GREAT WARHAMMER **COVELESKI**.
WITH THIS, I CAN STOP **ANY** GIANT. KILL ANY GIANT.
IF I'M STRONG ENOUGH. IF I STAY FOCUSED AND I'M **WORTHY**...
I CAN STOP DEATH ITSELF.
...
COVELESKI SOUNDS VERY SPECIAL. MAY I SEE IT?
NO, SILLY.
WHY NOT?
BECAUSE I LIKE YOU... I DON'T WANT YOU TO HURT YOURSELF.
WHEN COVELESKI SPEAKS, THE **WORLD CRIES**.

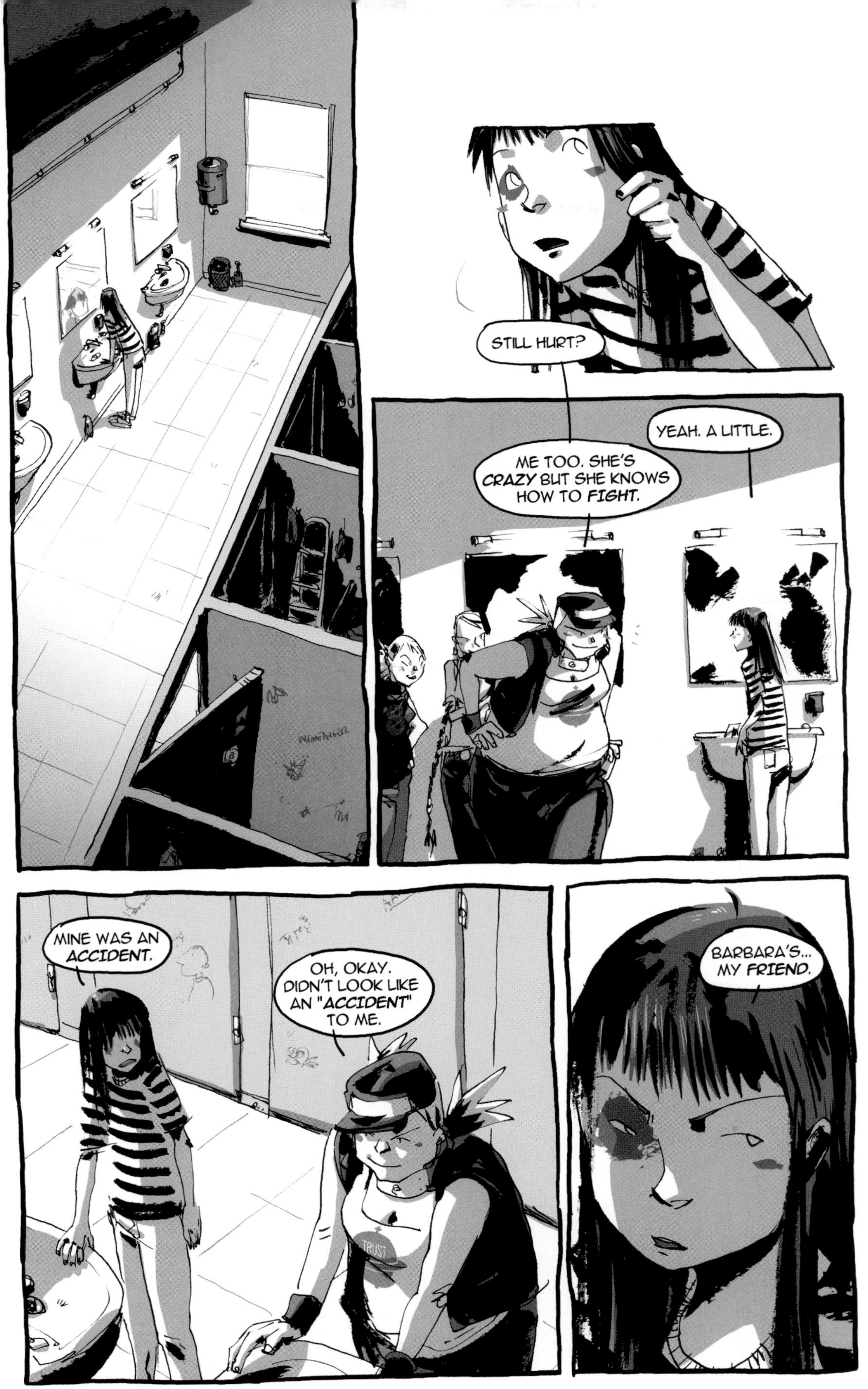
STILL HURT?
YEAH. A LITTLE.
ME TOO. SHE'S CRAZY BUT SHE KNOWS HOW TO FIGHT.
MINE WAS AN ACCIDENT.
OH, OKAY. DIDN'T LOOK LIKE AN "ACCIDENT" TO ME.
BARBARA'S... MY FRIEND.

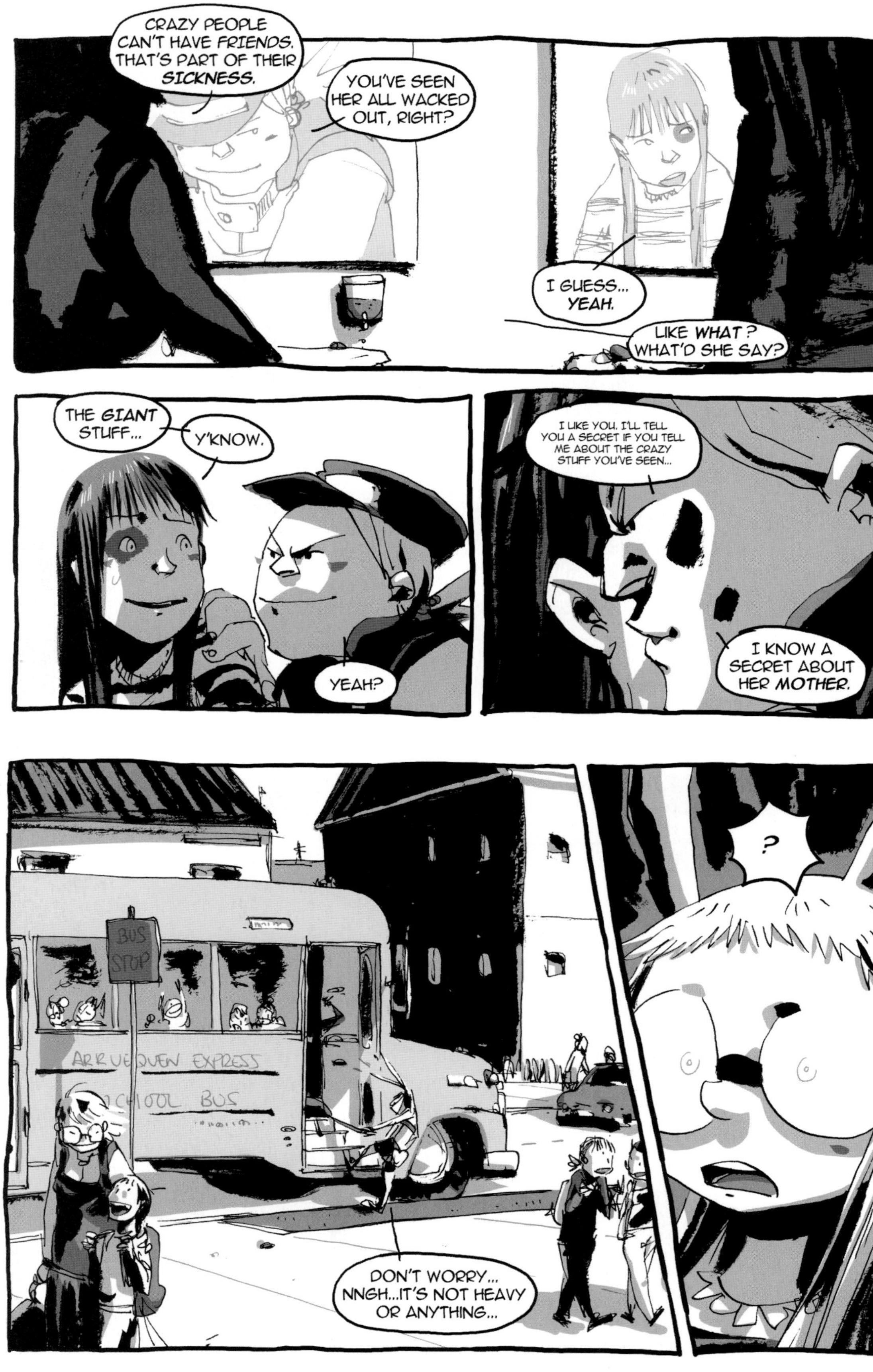
CRAZY PEOPLE CAN'T HAVE FRIENDS. THAT'S PART OF THEIR SICKNESS.
YOU'VE SEEN HER ALL WACKED OUT, RIGHT?
I GUESS... YEAH.
LIKE WHAT? WHAT'D SHE SAY?
THE GIANT STUFF...
Y'KNOW.
YEAH?
I LIKE YOU. I'LL TELL YOU A SECRET IF YOU TELL ME ABOUT THE CRAZY STUFF YOU'VE SEEN...
I KNOW A SECRET ABOUT HER MOTHER.
BUS STOP
DON'T WORRY... NNGH...IT'S NOT HEAVY OR ANYTHING...
?

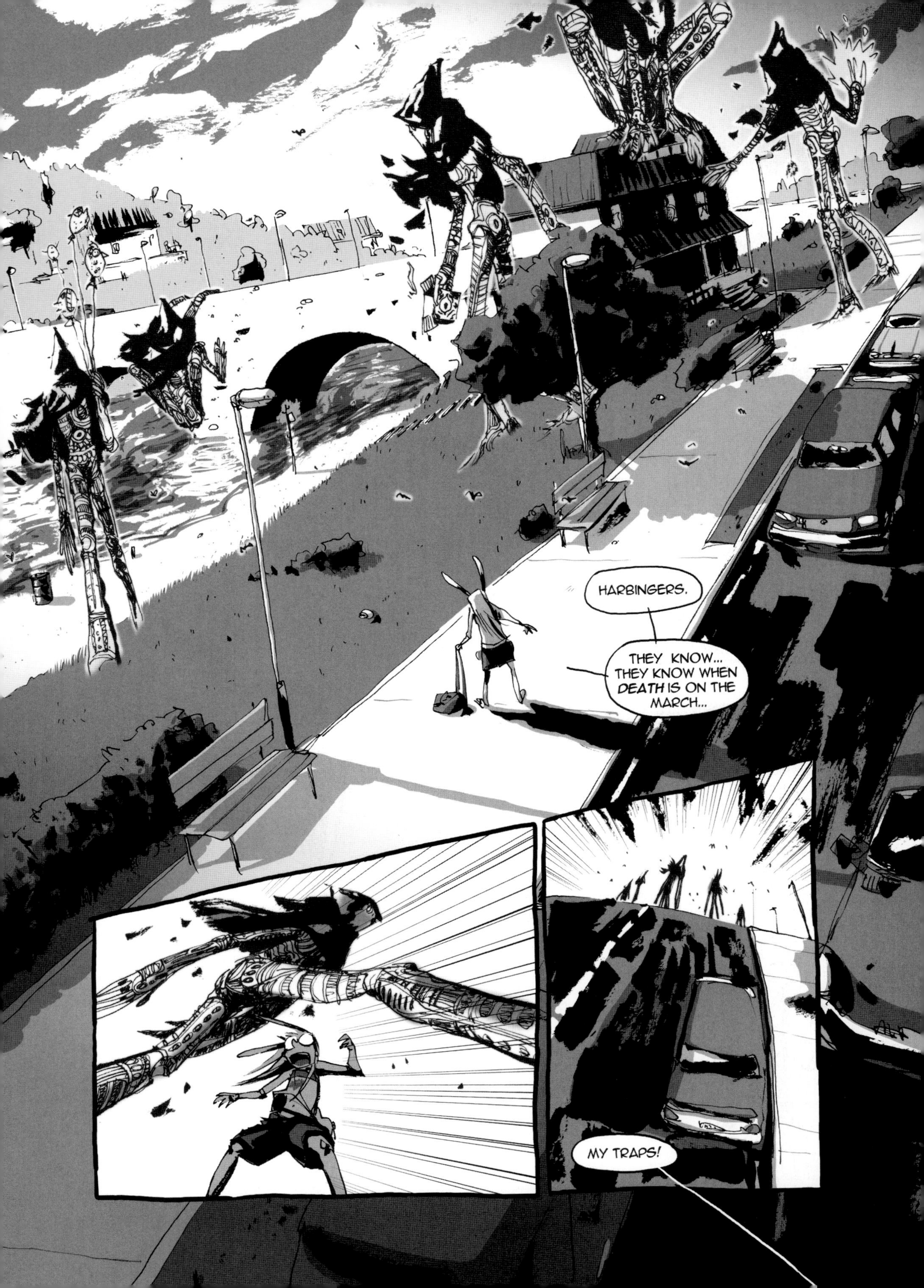
HARBINGERS.
THEY KNOW... THEY KNOW WHEN DEATH IS ON THE MARCH...
MY TRAPS!

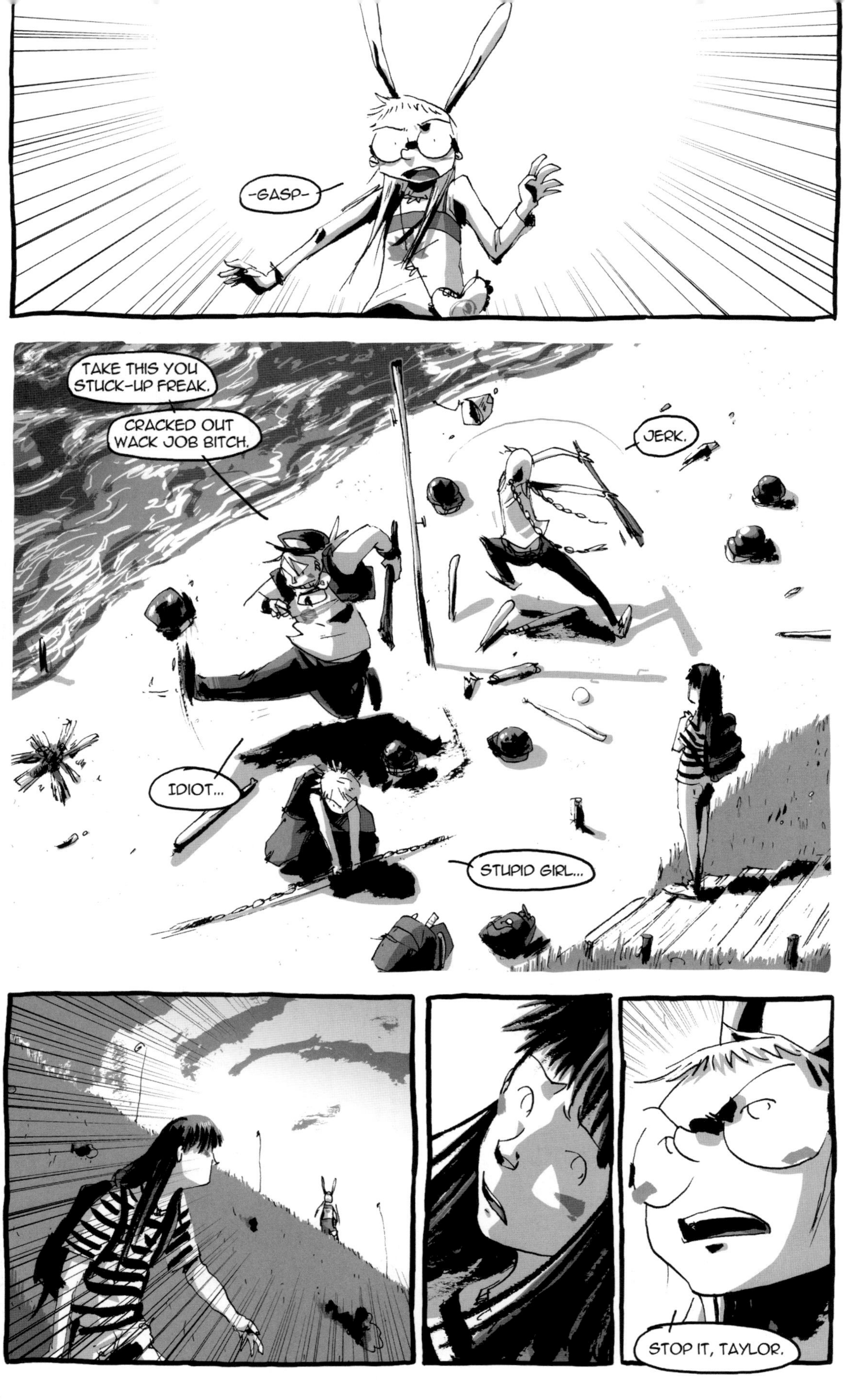
-GASP-
TAKE THIS YOU STUCK-UP FREAK.
CRACKED OUT WACK JOB BITCH.
JERK.
IDIOT...
STUPID GIRL...
STOP IT, TAYLOR.

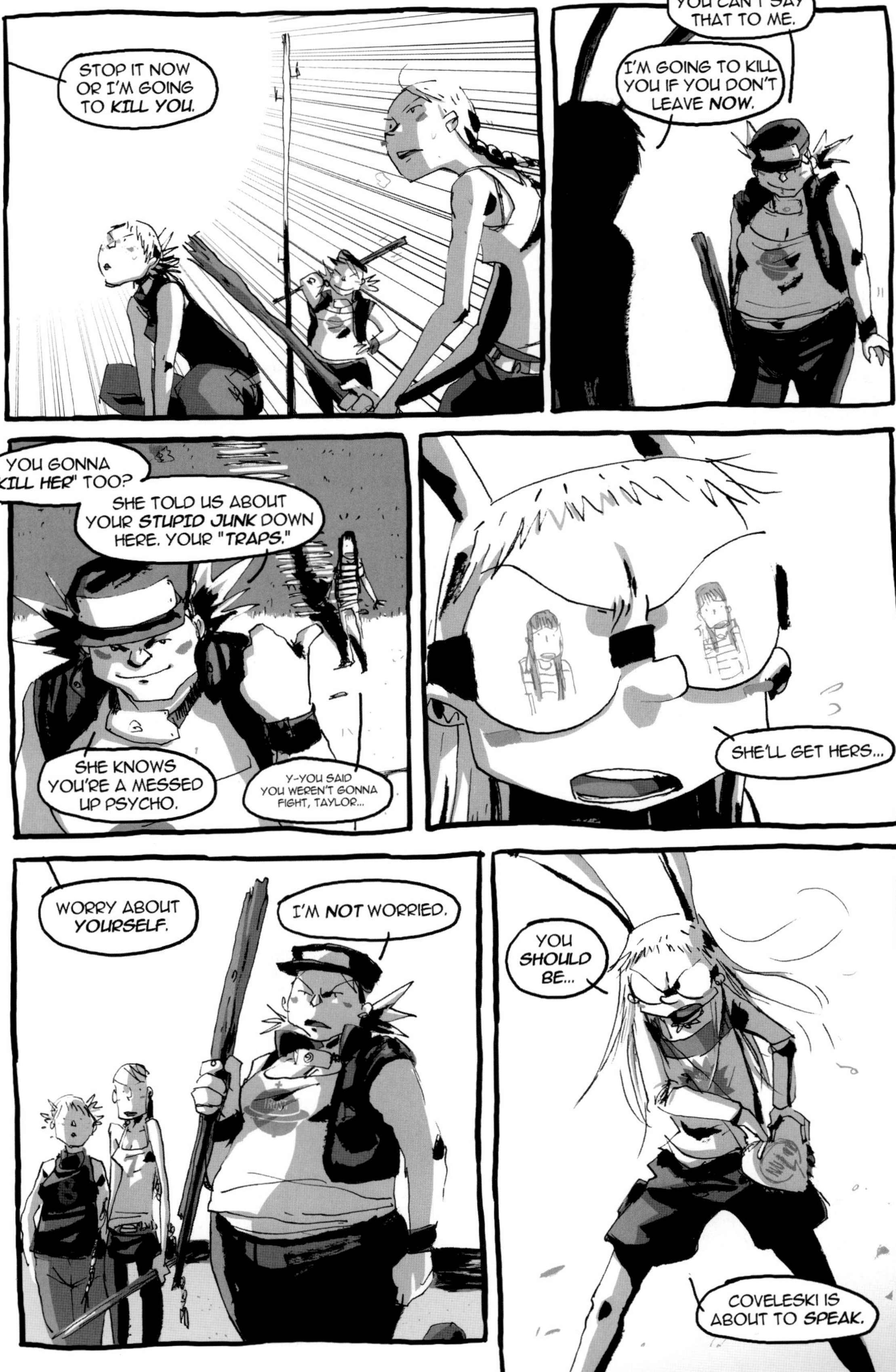
STOP IT NOW OR I'M GOING TO KILL YOU.
YOU CAN'T SAY THAT TO ME.
I'M GOING TO KILL YOU IF YOU DON'T LEAVE NOW.
YOU GONNA "KILL HER" TOO?
SHE TOLD US ABOUT YOUR STUPID JUNK DOWN HERE. YOUR "TRAPS."
SHE KNOWS YOU'RE A MESSED UP PSYCHO.
Y-YOU SAID YOU WEREN'T GONNA FIGHT, TAYLOR...
SHE'LL GET HERS...
WORRY ABOUT YOURSELF.
I'M NOT WORRIED.
YOU SHOULD BE...
COVELESKI IS ABOUT TO SPEAK.

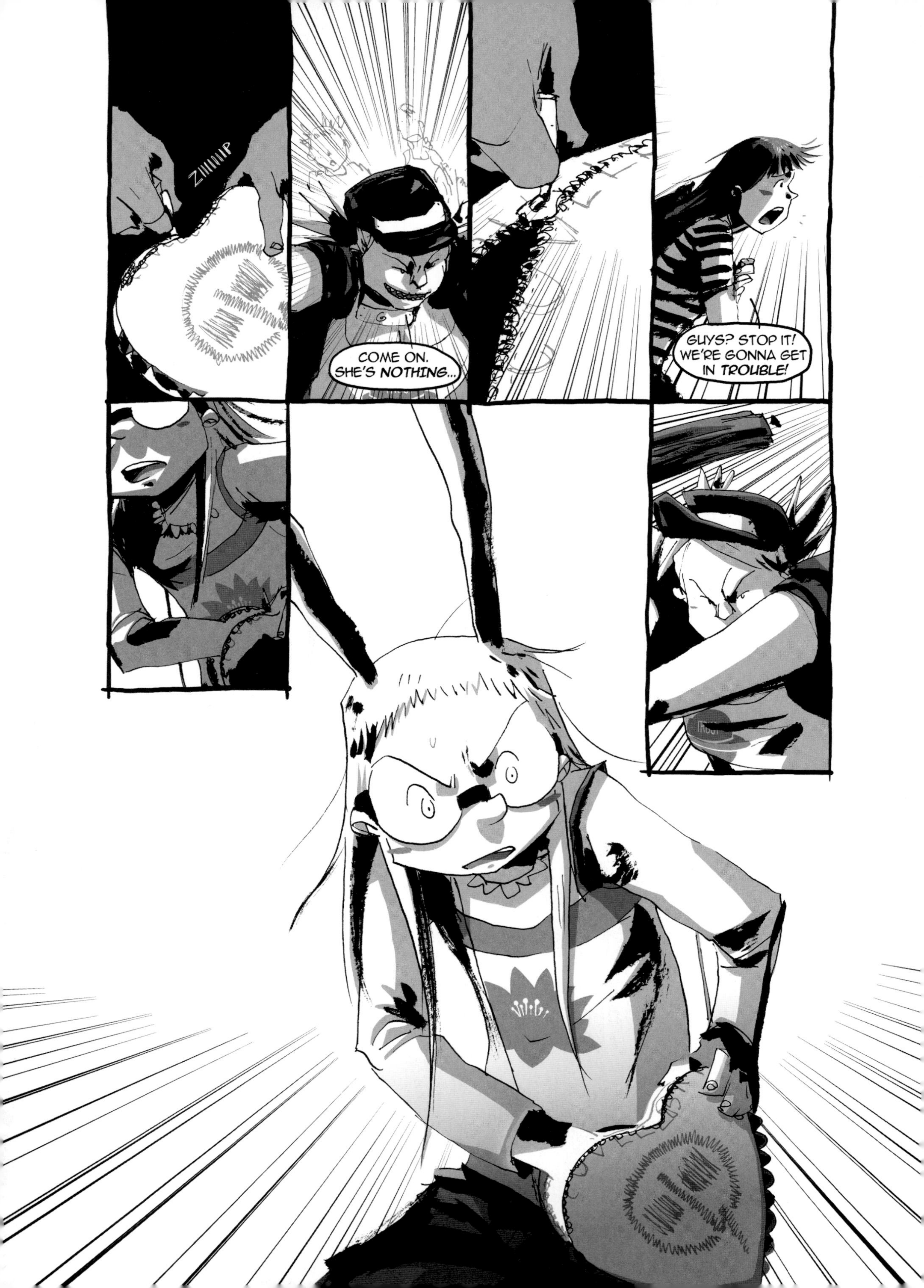
ZIIIIIP
COME ON.
SHE'S NOTHING...
GUYS? STOP IT!
WE'RE GONNA GET
IN TROUBLE!

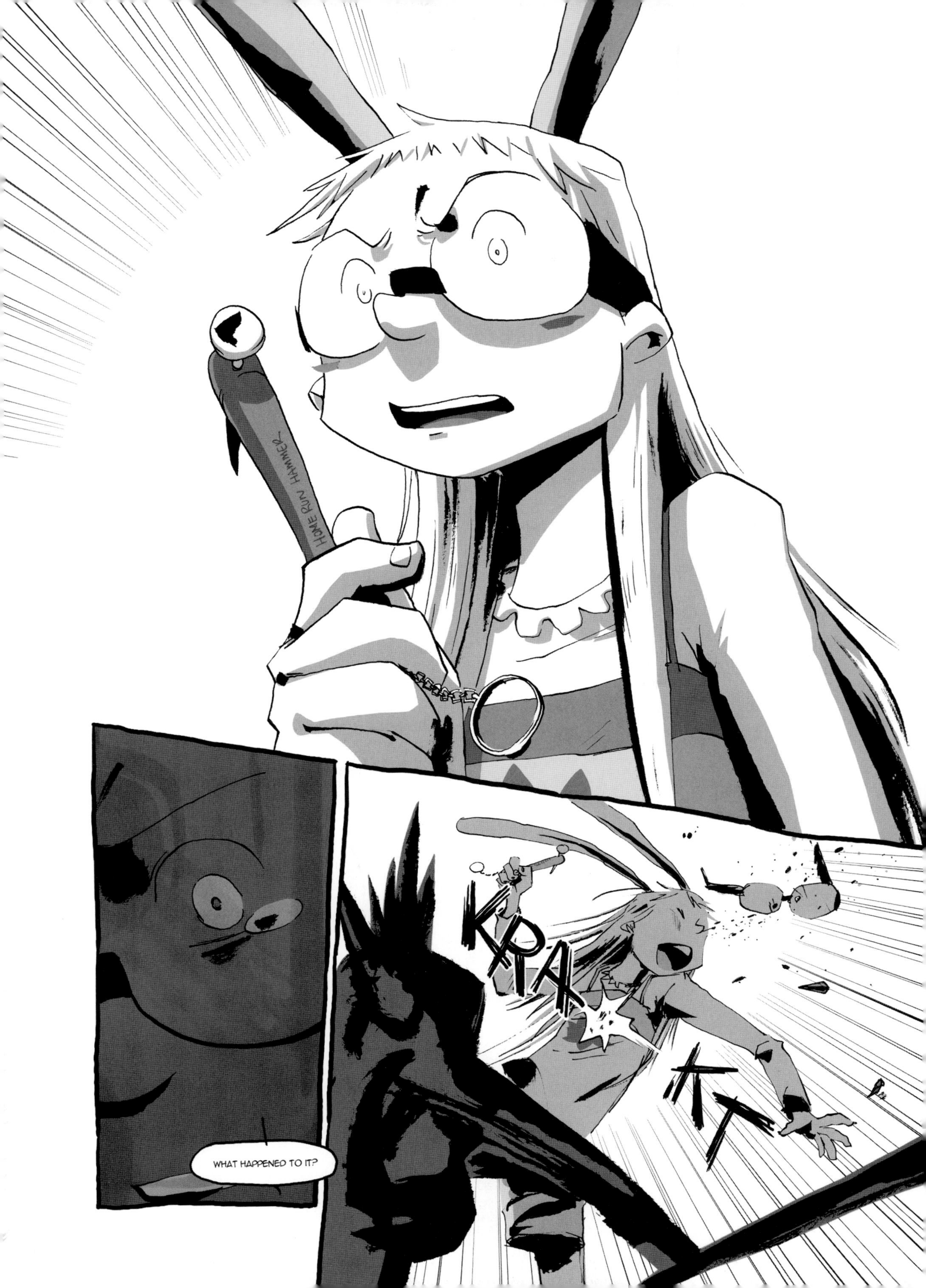
HOME RUN HAMMER
WHAT HAPPENED TO IT?
KRA
KT

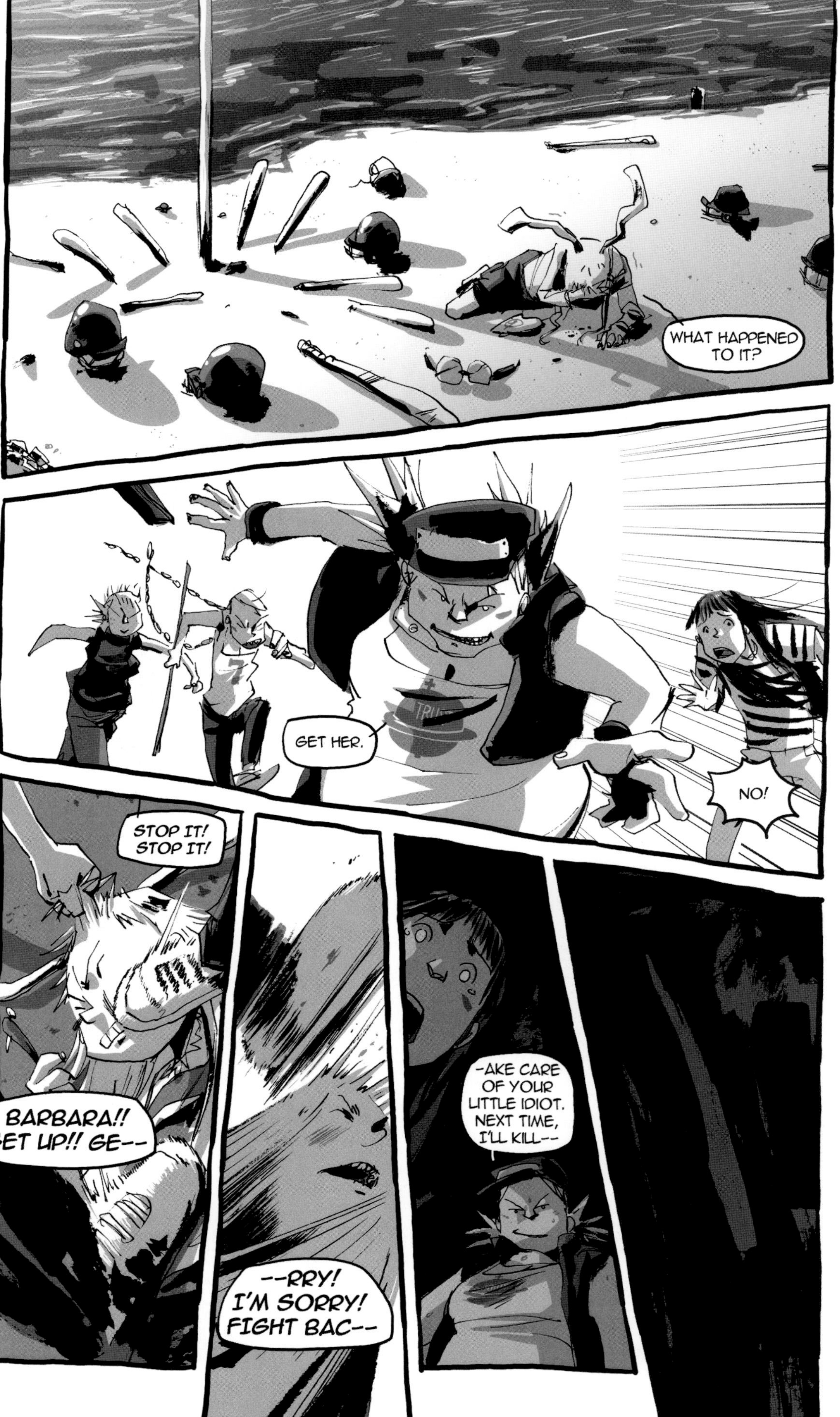
WHAT HAPPENED TO IT?
GET HER.
NO!
STOP IT! STOP IT!
BARBARA!! GET UP!! GE--
--RRY! I'M SORRY! FIGHT BAC--
-AKE CARE OF YOUR LITTLE IDIOT. NEXT TIME, I'LL KILL--

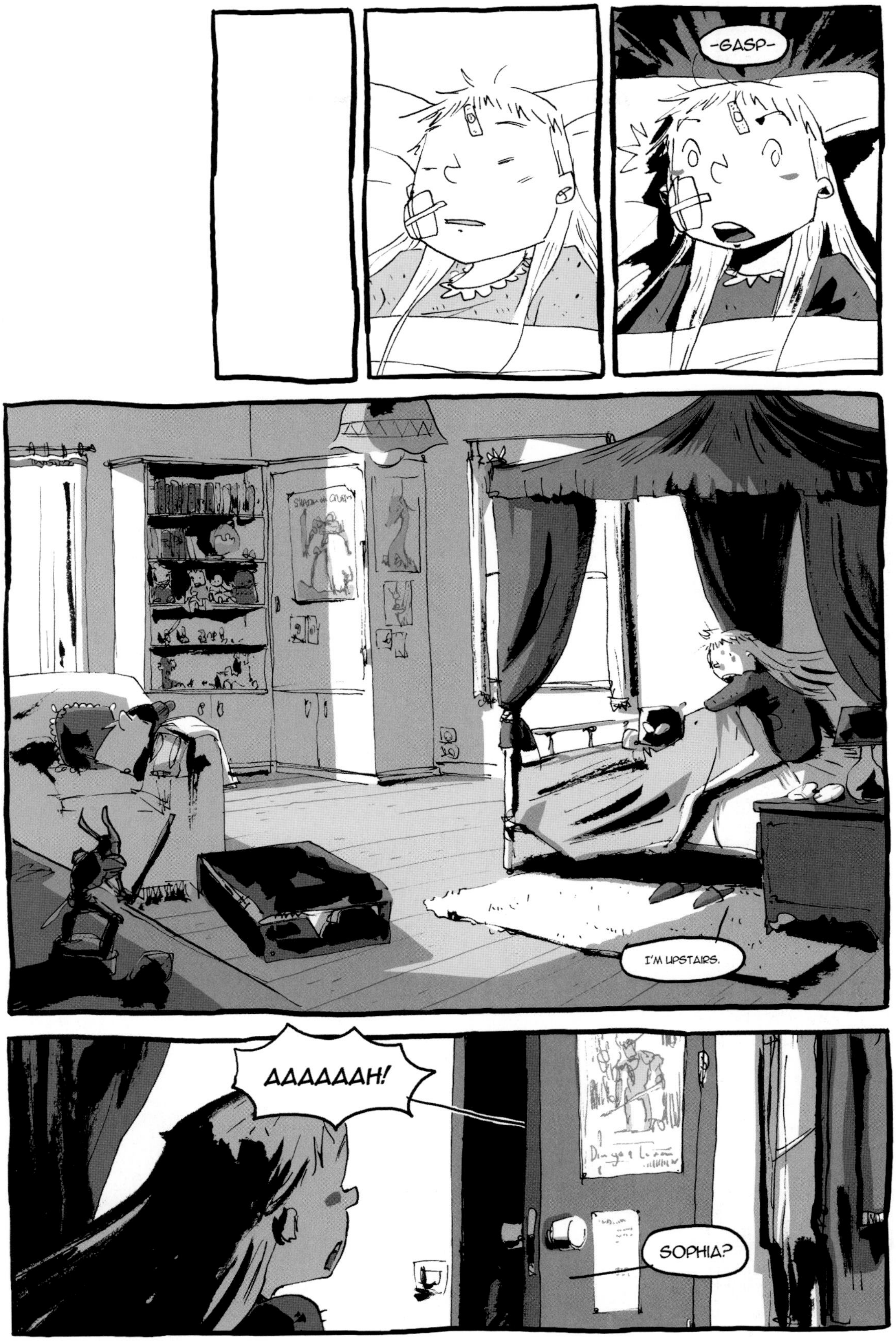
-GASP-
I'M UPSTAIRS.
AAAAAAH!
SOPHIA?

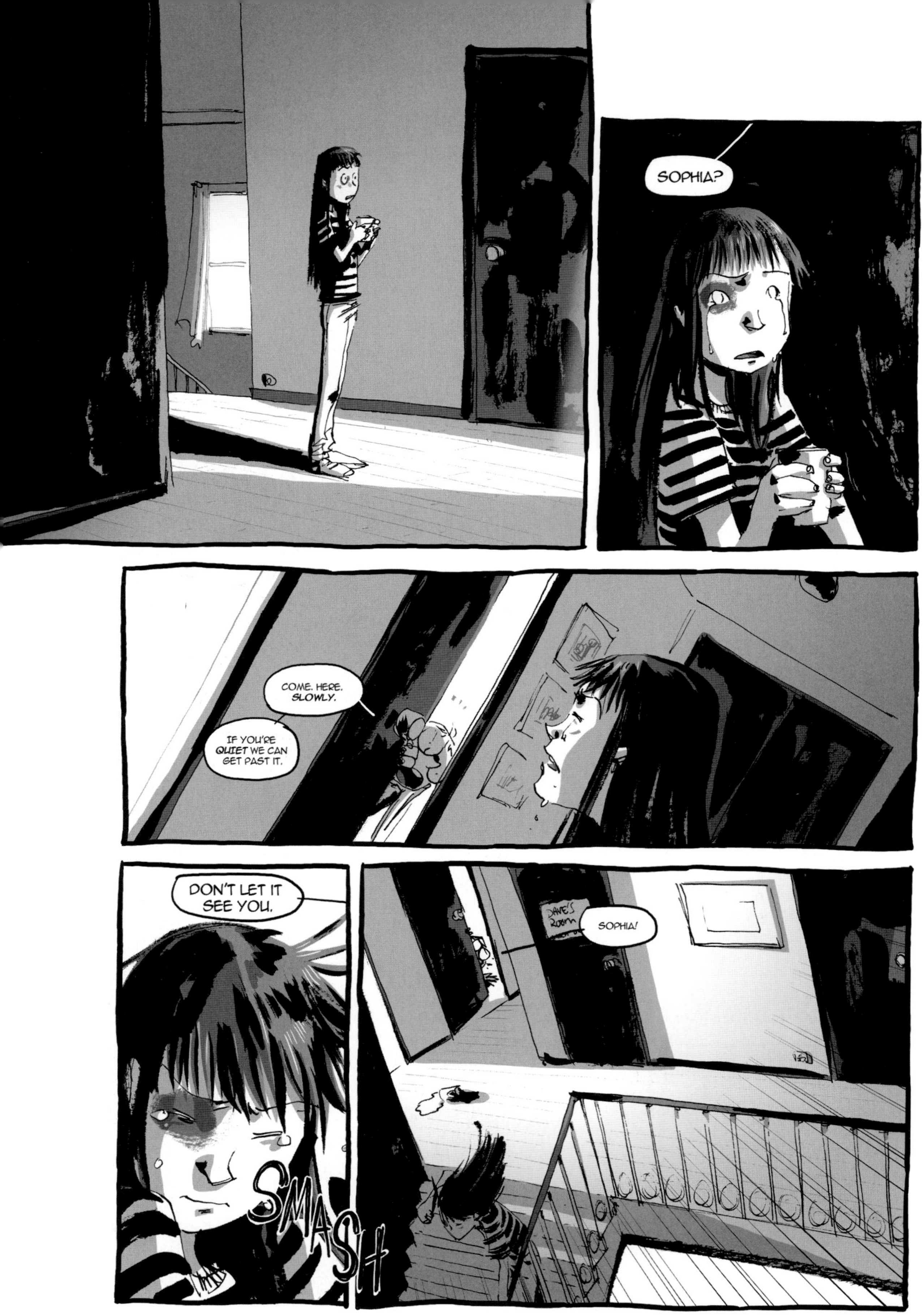
SOPHIA?
COME. HERE. SLOWLY.
IF YOU'RE QUIET WE CAN GET PAST IT.
DON'T LET IT SEE YOU.
SMASH
DAVE'S ROOM
SOPHIA!

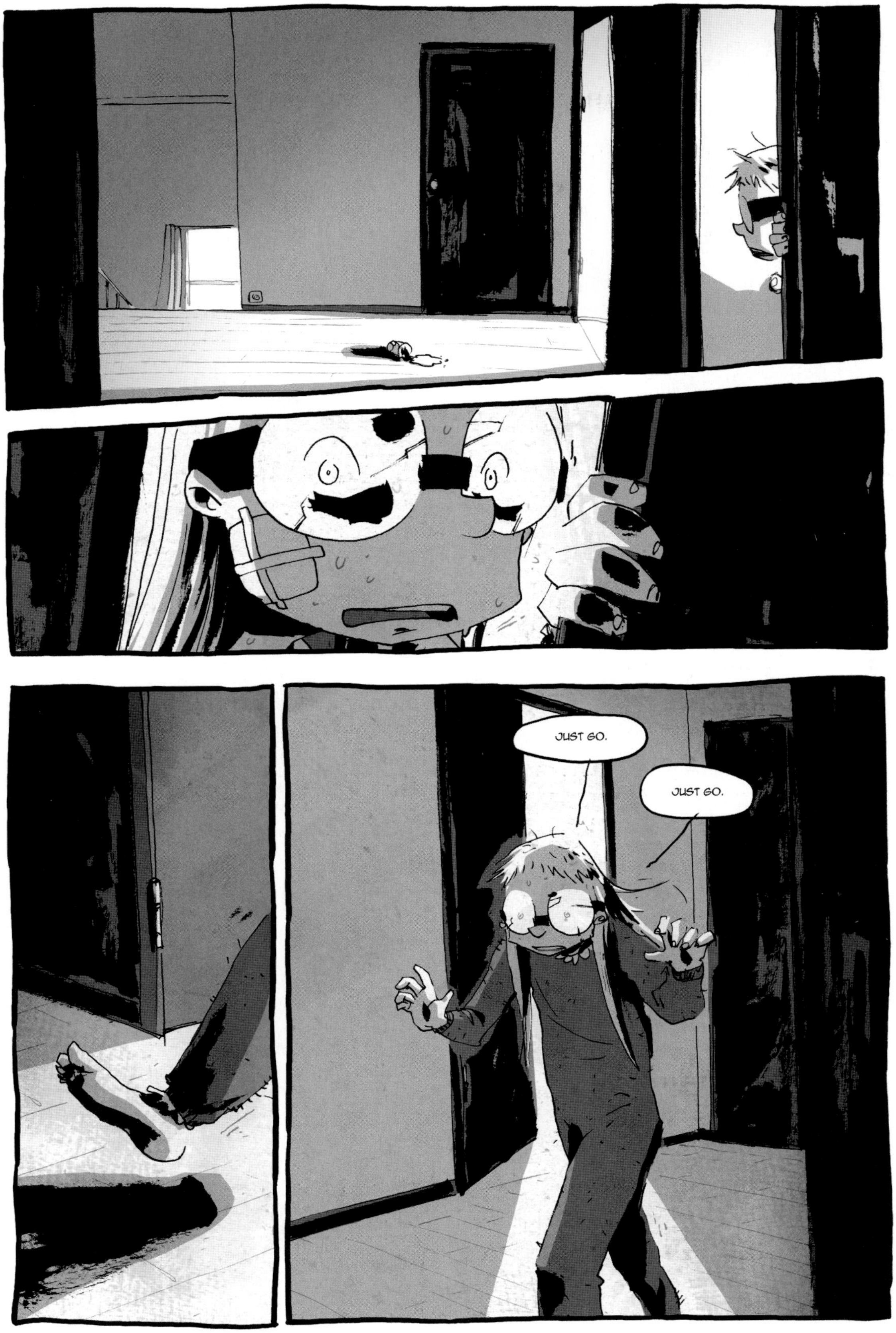
JUST GO.
JUST GO.

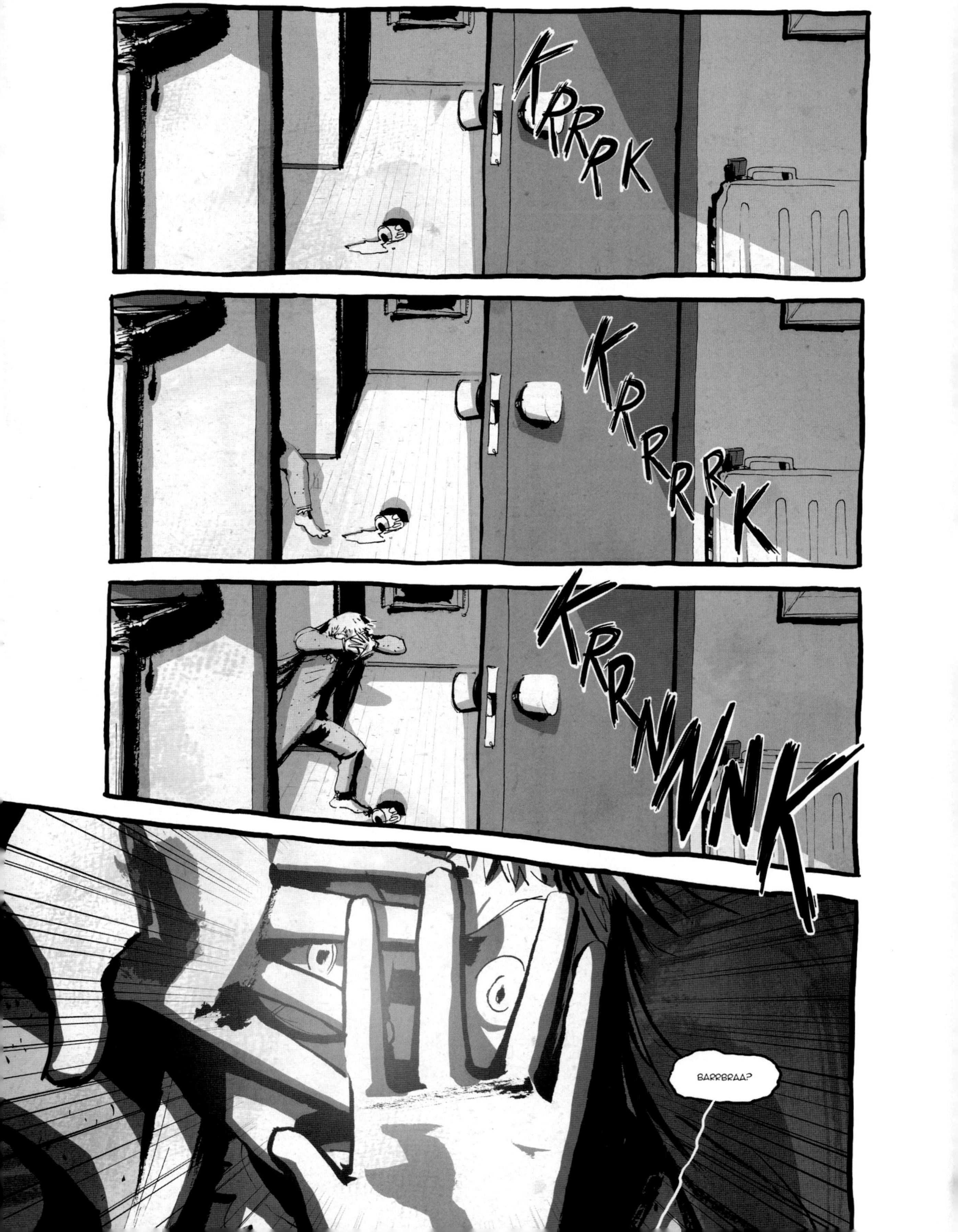
KRRRRK
KRRRRRRK
KRRRNNNK
BARRBRAA?

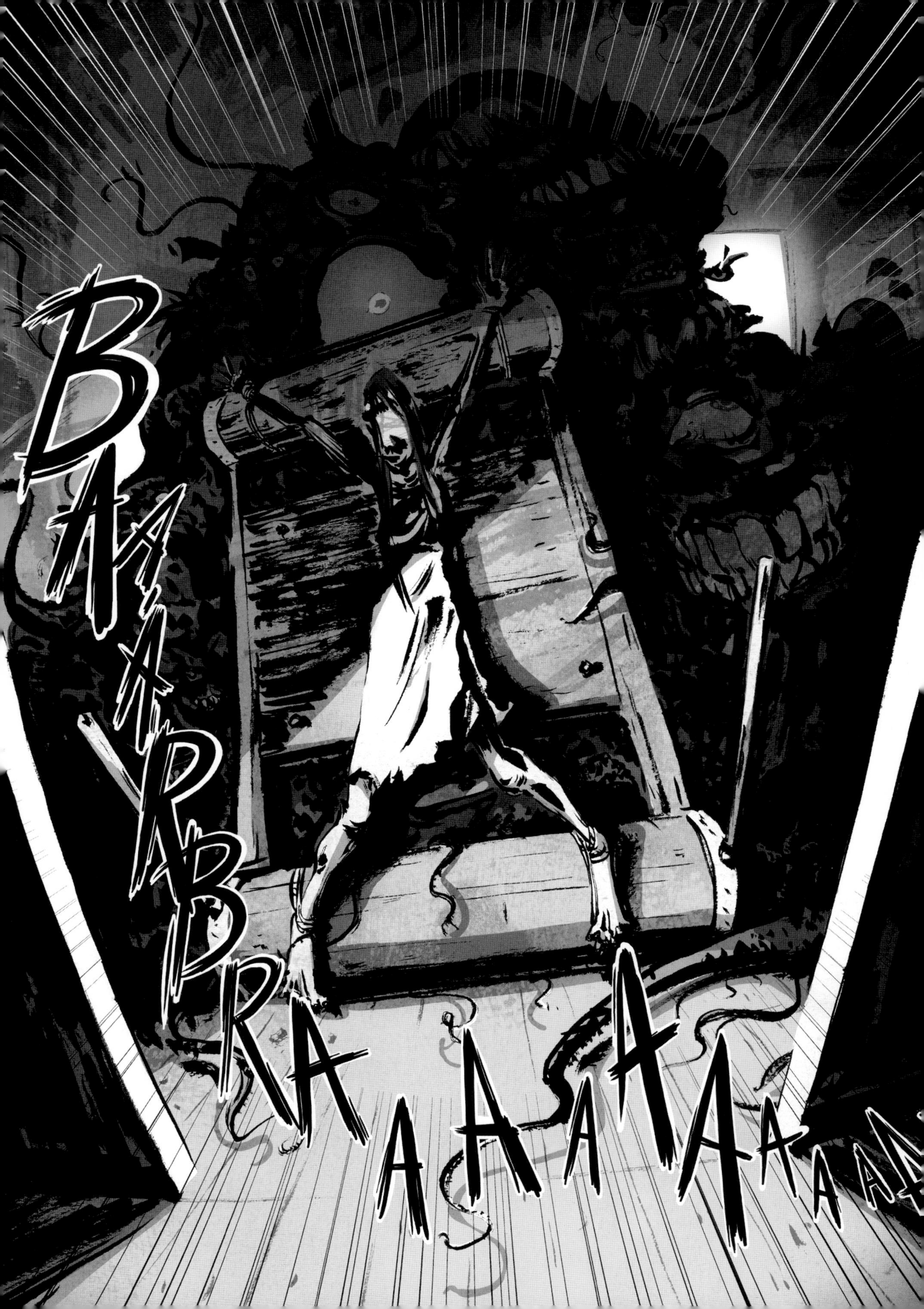
BAAARABRAAAAAAAAAA

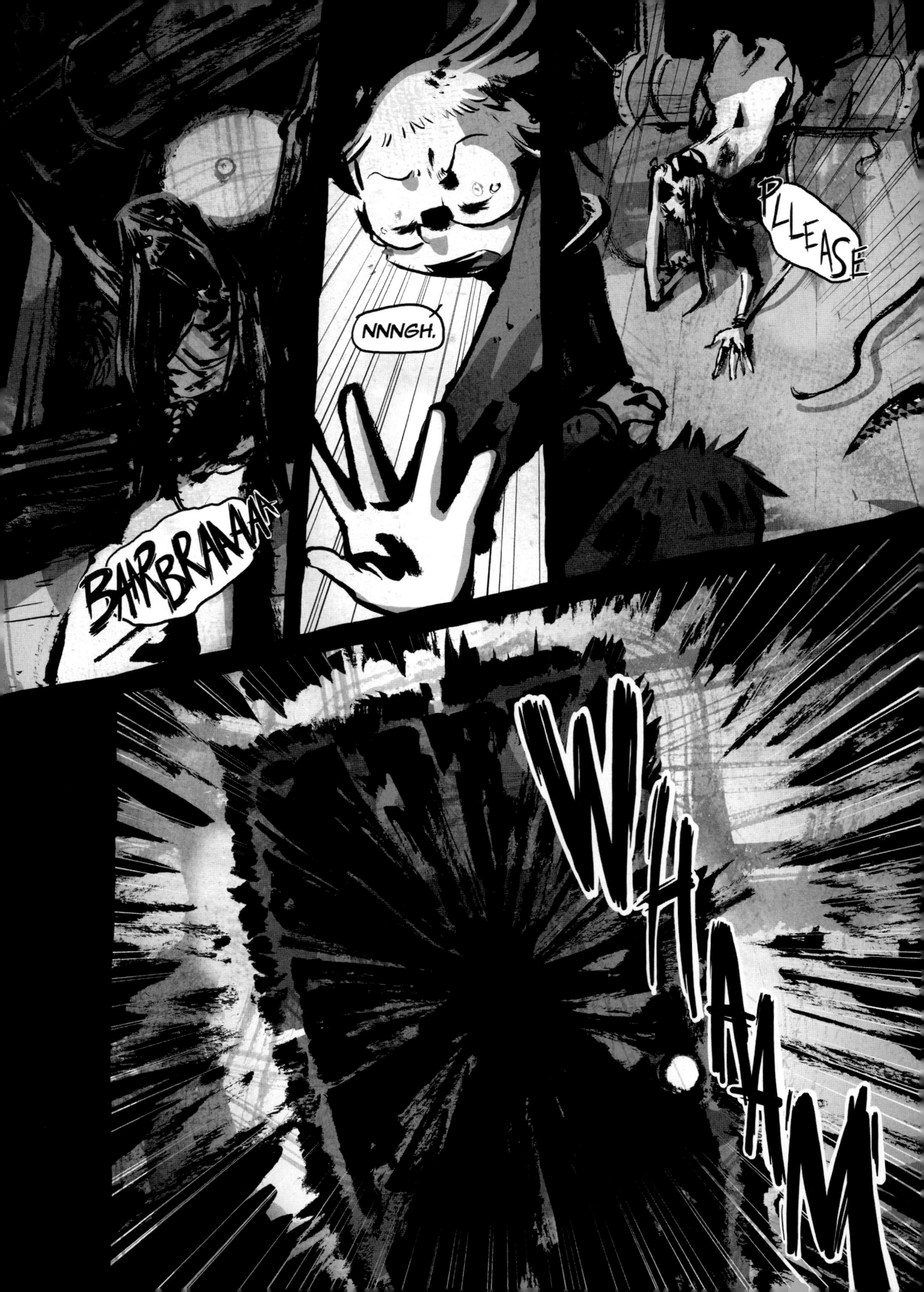
PLLEASE
NNNGH.
BAARBRAAAAA
WHAAM

CHAPTER**5**: THE SACRIFICE

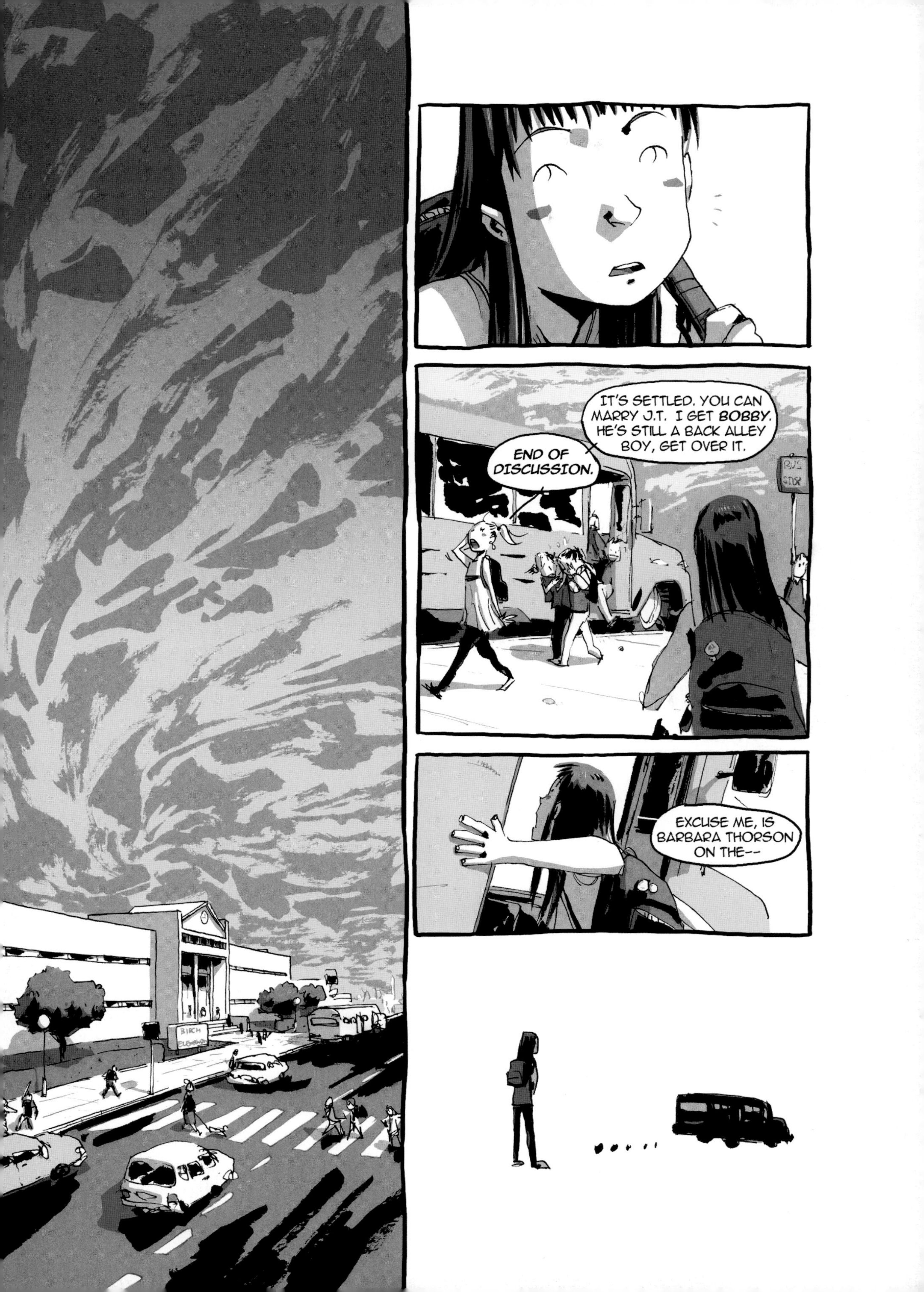
IT'S SETTLED. YOU CAN MARRY J.T. I GET BOBBY. HE'S STILL A BACK ALLEY BOY, GET OVER IT.
END OF DISCUSSION.
EXCUSE ME, IS BARBARA THORSON ON THE--

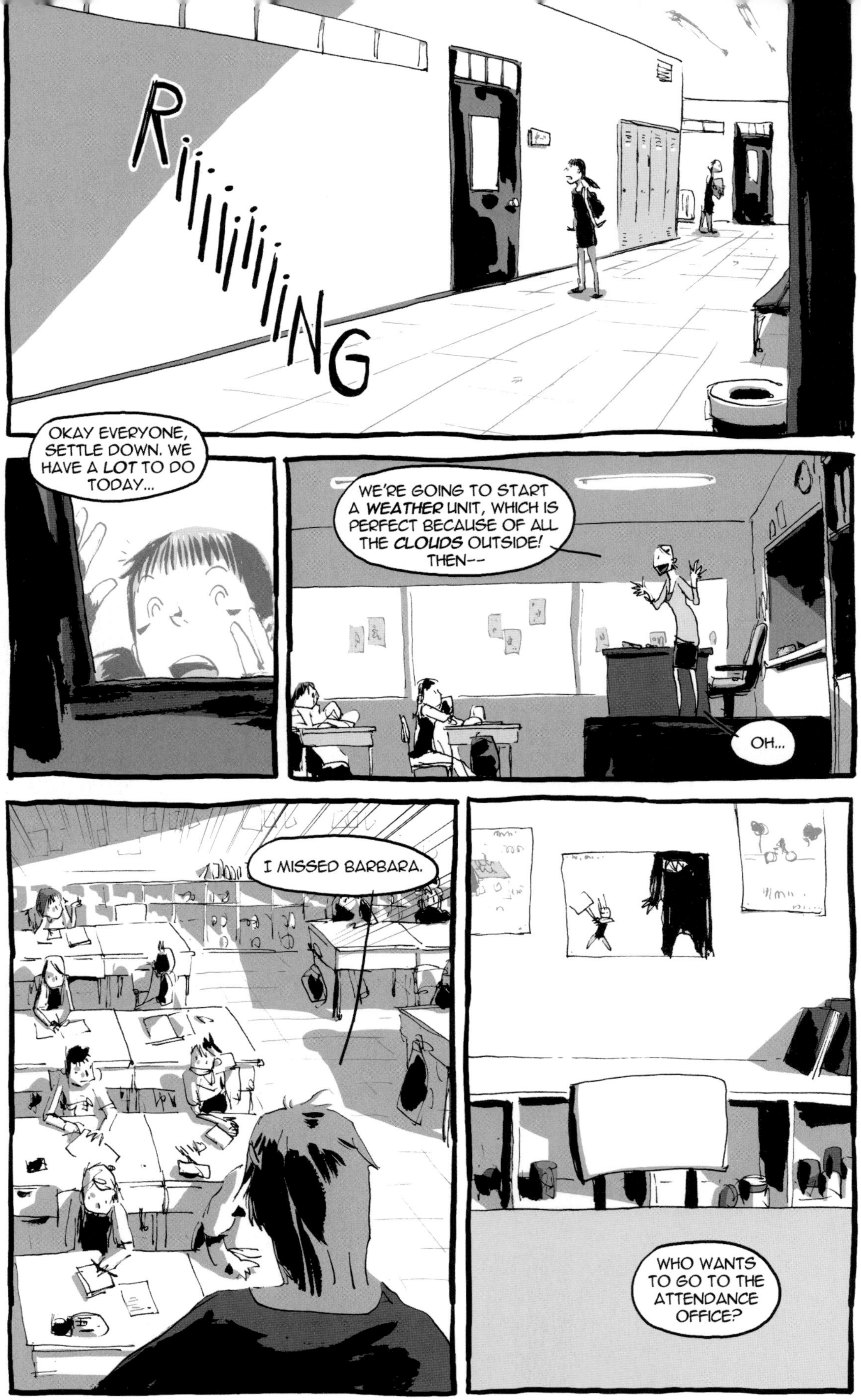
RIIIIIIIIING
OKAY EVERYONE, SETTLE DOWN. WE HAVE A LOT TO DO TODAY...
WE'RE GOING TO START A WEATHER UNIT, WHICH IS PERFECT BECAUSE OF ALL THE CLOUDS OUTSIDE! THEN--
OH...
I MISSED BARBARA.
WHO WANTS TO GO TO THE ATTENDANCE OFFICE?

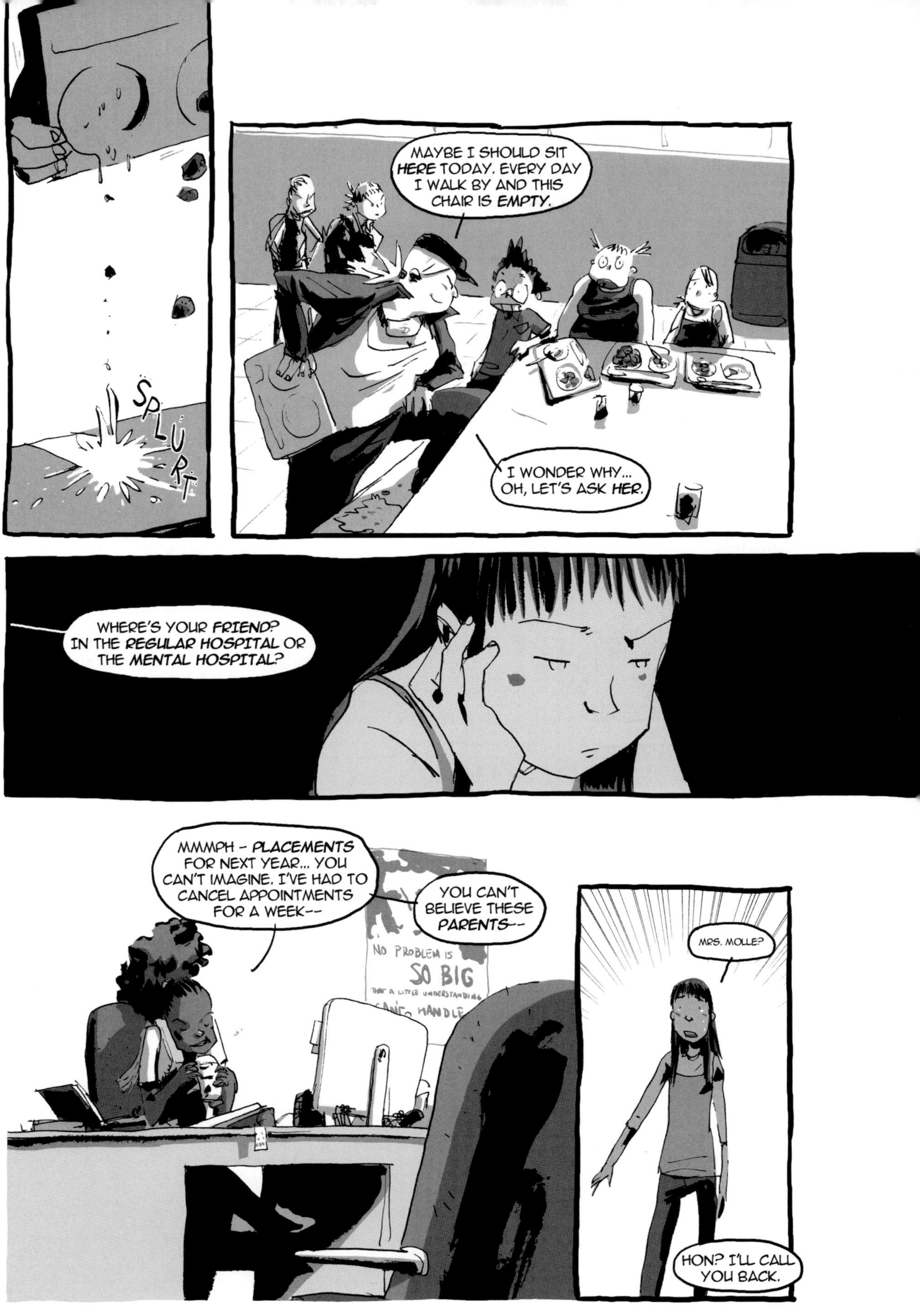
SPLURT
MAYBE I SHOULD SIT HERE TODAY. EVERY DAY I WALK BY AND THIS CHAIR IS EMPTY.
I WONDER WHY... OH, LET'S ASK HER.
WHERE'S YOUR FRIEND? IN THE REGULAR HOSPITAL OR THE MENTAL HOSPITAL?
MMMPH - PLACEMENTS FOR NEXT YEAR... YOU CAN'T IMAGINE. I'VE HAD TO CANCEL APPOINTMENTS FOR A WEEK--
YOU CAN'T BELIEVE THESE PARENTS--
NO PROBLEM IS SO BIG
MRS. MOLLE?
HON? I'LL CALL YOU BACK.

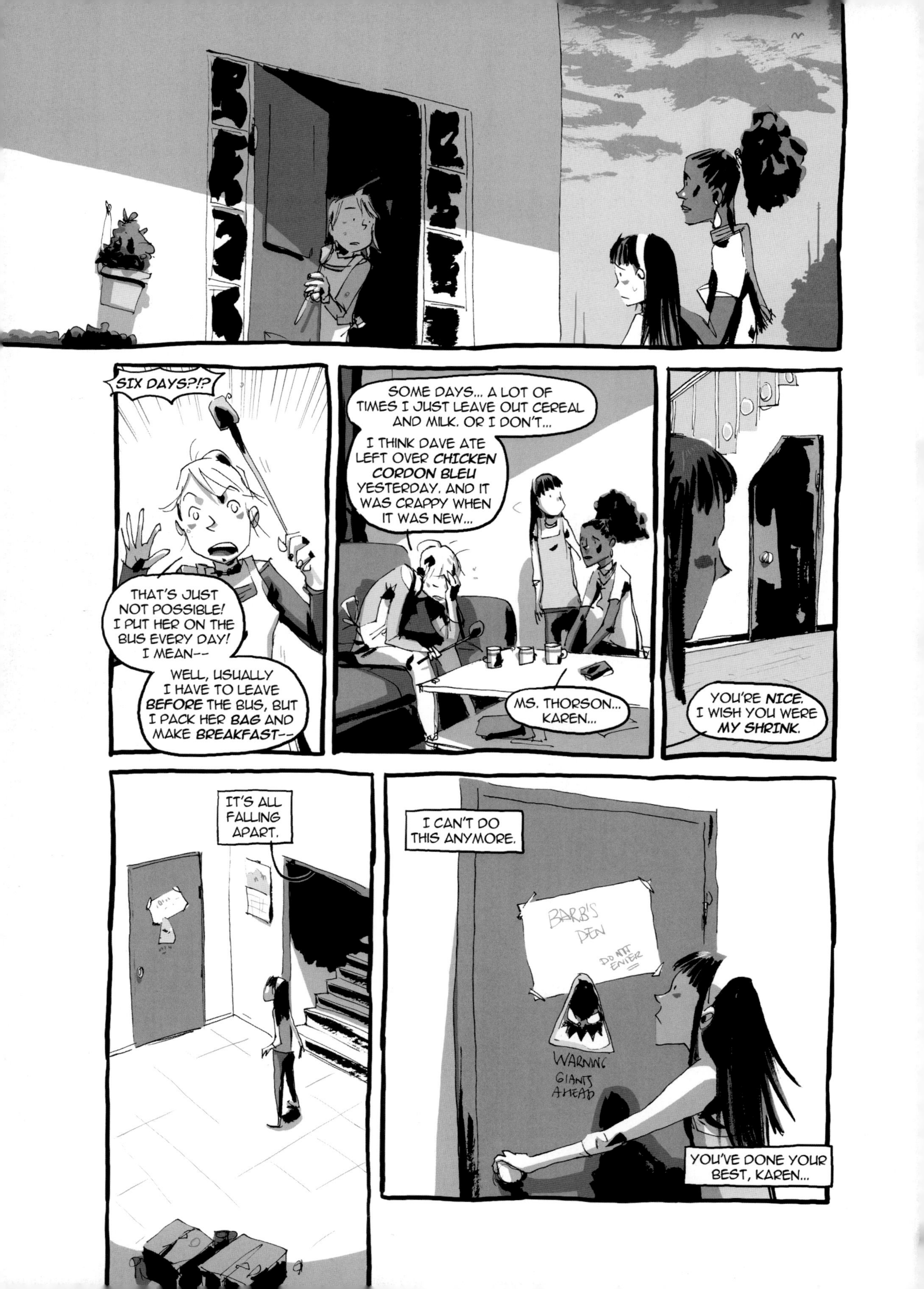
SIX DAYS?!?
THAT'S JUST NOT POSSIBLE! I PUT HER ON THE BUS EVERY DAY! I MEAN--
WELL, USUALLY I HAVE TO LEAVE BEFORE THE BUS, BUT I PACK HER BAG AND MAKE BREAKFAST--
SOME DAYS... A LOT OF TIMES I JUST LEAVE OUT CEREAL AND MILK. OR I DON'T...
I THINK DAVE ATE LEFT OVER CHICKEN CORDON BLEU YESTERDAY. AND IT WAS CRAPPY WHEN IT WAS NEW...
MS. THORSON... KAREN...
YOU'RE NICE. I WISH YOU WERE MY SHRINK.
IT'S ALL FALLING APART.
I CAN'T DO THIS ANYMORE.
BARB'S DEN
DO NOT ENTER
WARNING GIANTS AHEAD
YOU'VE DONE YOUR BEST, KAREN...

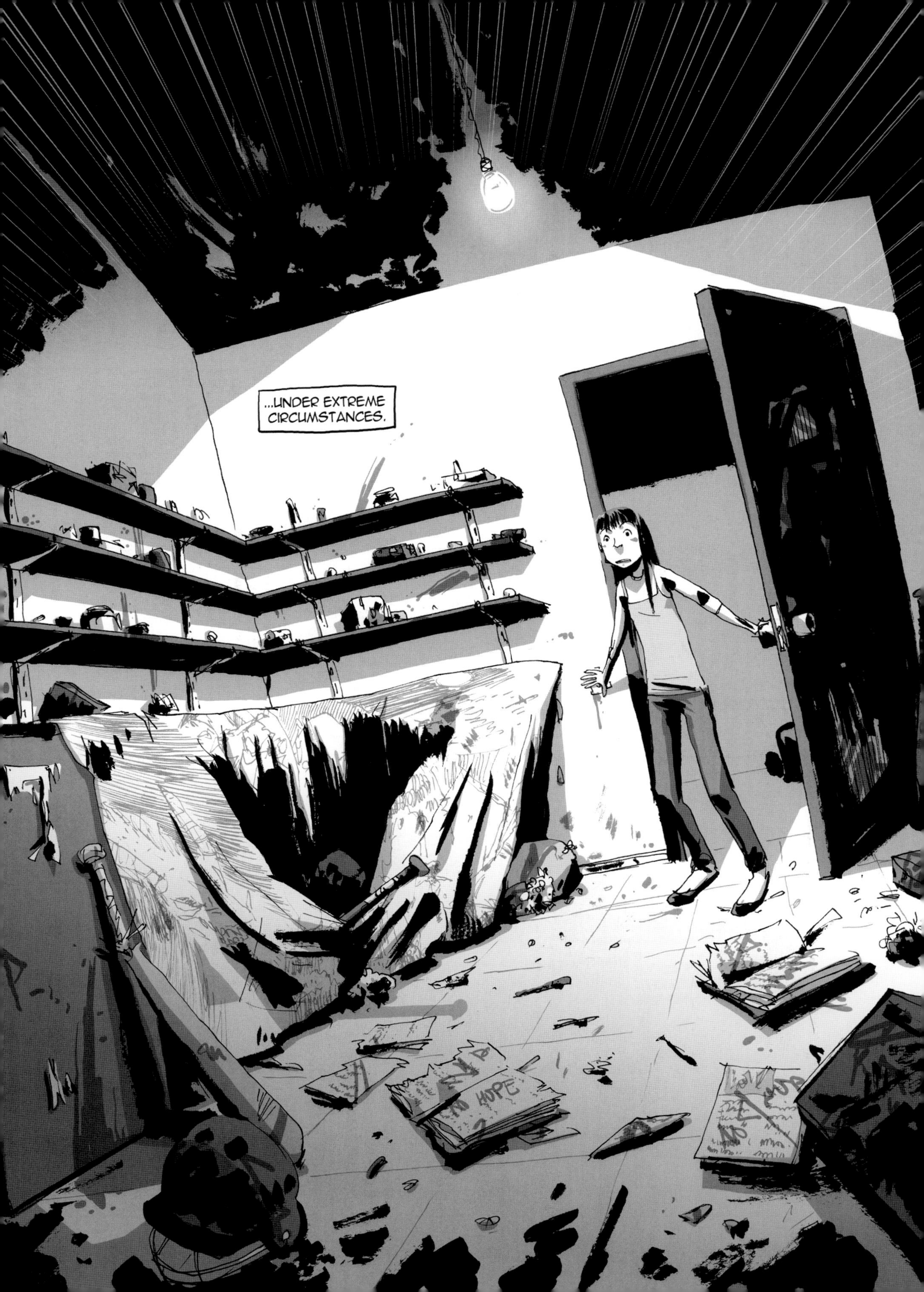
...UNDER EXTREME CIRCUMSTANCES.
NO HOPE

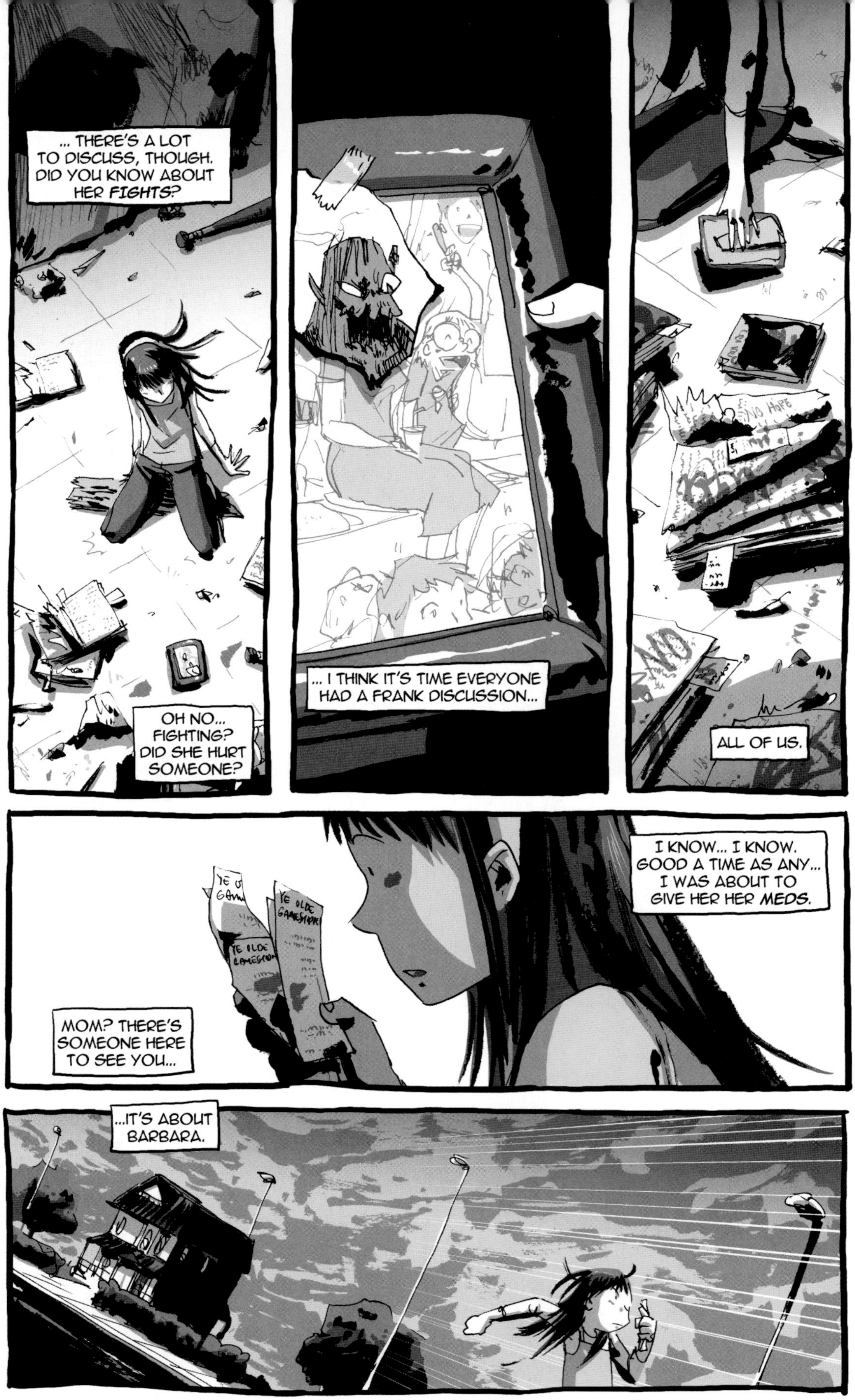
... THERE'S A LOT TO DISCUSS, THOUGH. DID YOU KNOW ABOUT HER FIGHTS?
OH NO... FIGHTING? DID SHE HURT SOMEONE?
... I THINK IT'S TIME EVERYONE HAD A FRANK DISCUSSION...
NO HOPE
NO
ALL OF US.
I KNOW... I KNOW. GOOD A TIME AS ANY... I WAS ABOUT TO GIVE HER HER MEDS.
YE OLDE GAMESTORE
YE OLDE GAMESTORE
MOM? THERE'S SOMEONE HERE TO SEE YOU...
...IT'S ABOUT BARBARA.

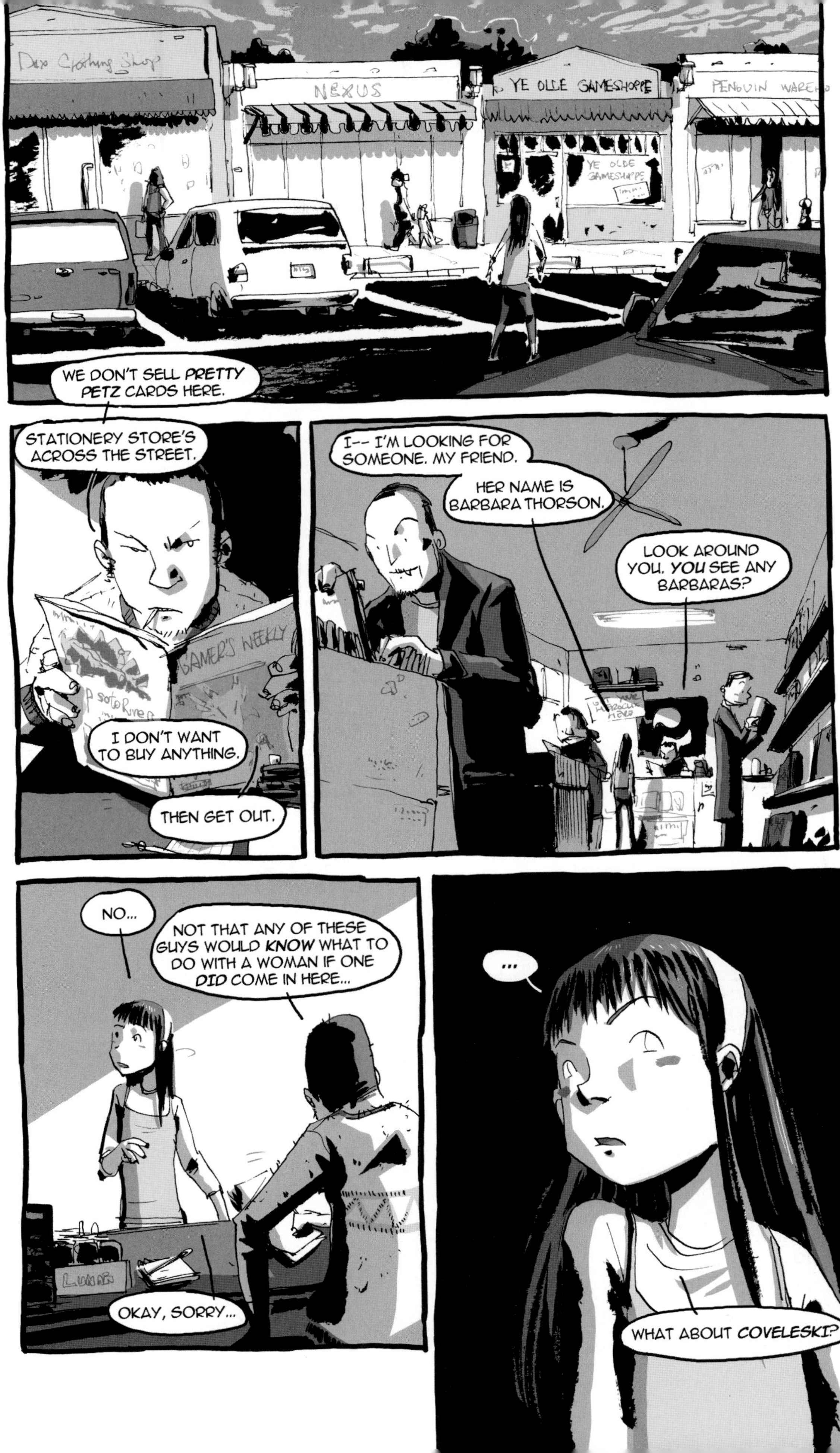
Dax Clothing Shop
NEXUS
YE OLDE GAMESHOPPE
PENGUIN WAREH
YE OLDE GAMESHOPPE
WE DON'T SELL PRETTY PETZ CARDS HERE.
STATIONERY STORE'S ACROSS THE STREET.
GAMER'S WEEKLY
I DON'T WANT TO BUY ANYTHING.
THEN GET OUT.
I-- I'M LOOKING FOR SOMEONE. MY FRIEND.
HER NAME IS BARBARA THORSON.
LOOK AROUND YOU. YOU SEE ANY BARBARAS?
NO...
NOT THAT ANY OF THESE GUYS WOULD KNOW WHAT TO DO WITH A WOMAN IF ONE DID COME IN HERE...
OKAY, SORRY...
...
WHAT ABOUT COVELESKI?

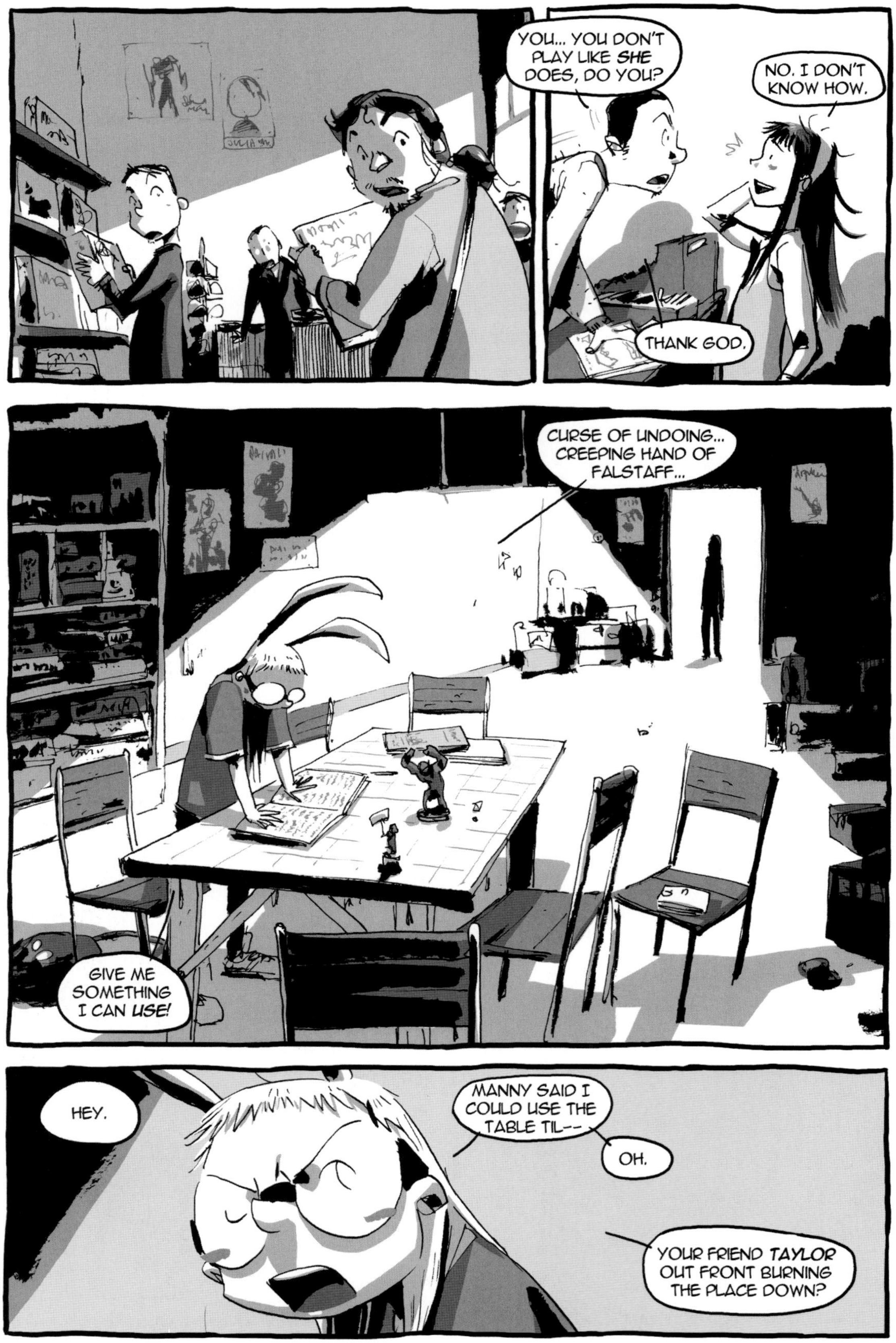
YOU... YOU DON'T PLAY LIKE SHE DOES, DO YOU?
NO. I DON'T KNOW HOW.
THANK GOD.
CURSE OF UNDOING... CREEPING HAND OF FALSTAFF...
GIVE ME SOMETHING I CAN USE!
HEY.
MANNY SAID I COULD USE THE TABLE TIL--
OH.
YOUR FRIEND TAYLOR OUT FRONT BURNING THE PLACE DOWN?

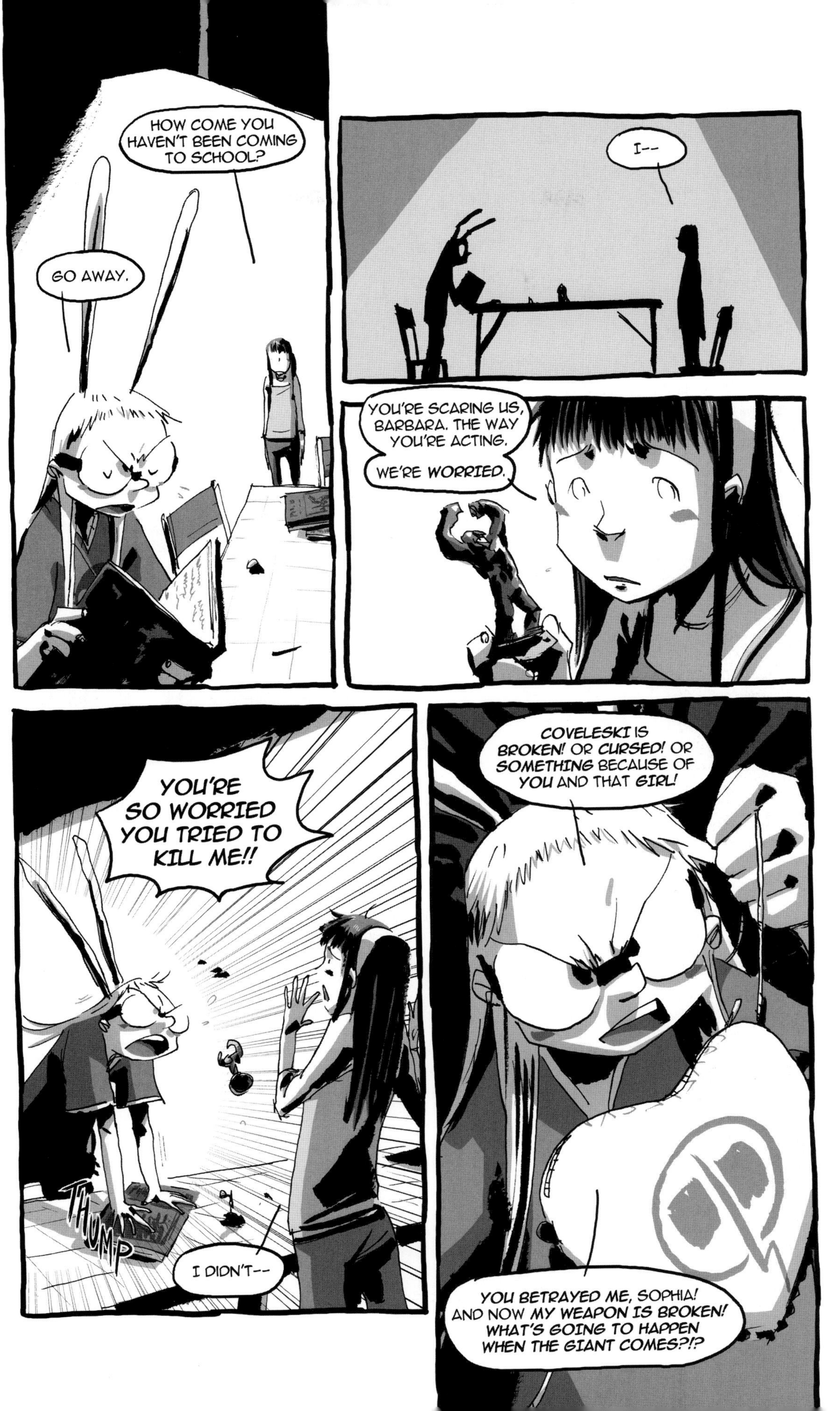
HOW COME YOU HAVEN'T BEEN COMING TO SCHOOL?
GO AWAY.
I--
YOU'RE SCARING US, BARBARA. THE WAY YOU'RE ACTING.
WE'RE WORRIED.
YOU'RE SO WORRIED YOU TRIED TO KILL ME!!
THUMP
I DIDN'T--
COVELESKI IS BROKEN! OR CURSED! OR SOMETHING BECAUSE OF YOU AND THAT GIRL!
YOU BETRAYED ME, SOPHIA! AND NOW MY WEAPON IS BROKEN! WHAT'S GOING TO HAPPEN WHEN THE GIANT COMES?!?

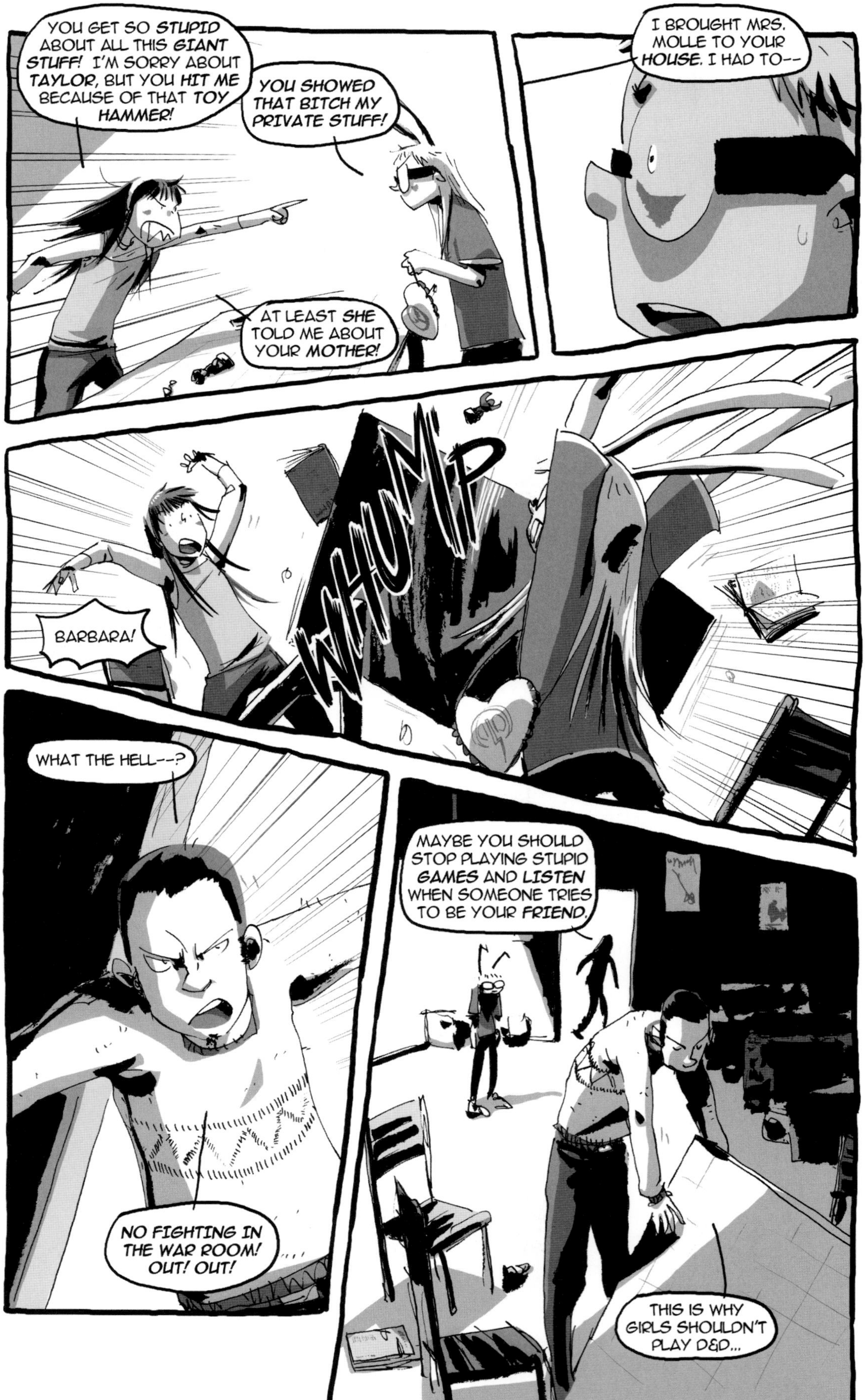
YOU GET SO STUPID ABOUT ALL THIS GIANT STUFF! I'M SORRY ABOUT TAYLOR, BUT YOU HIT ME BECAUSE OF THAT TOY HAMMER!
YOU SHOWED THAT BITCH MY PRIVATE STUFF!
AT LEAST SHE TOLD ME ABOUT YOUR MOTHER!
I BROUGHT MRS. MOLLE TO YOUR HOUSE. I HAD TO--
WHUMP
BARBARA!
WHAT THE HELL--?
NO FIGHTING IN THE WAR ROOM! OUT! OUT!
MAYBE YOU SHOULD STOP PLAYING STUPID GAMES AND LISTEN WHEN SOMEONE TRIES TO BE YOUR FRIEND.
THIS IS WHY GIRLS SHOULDN'T PLAY D&D...

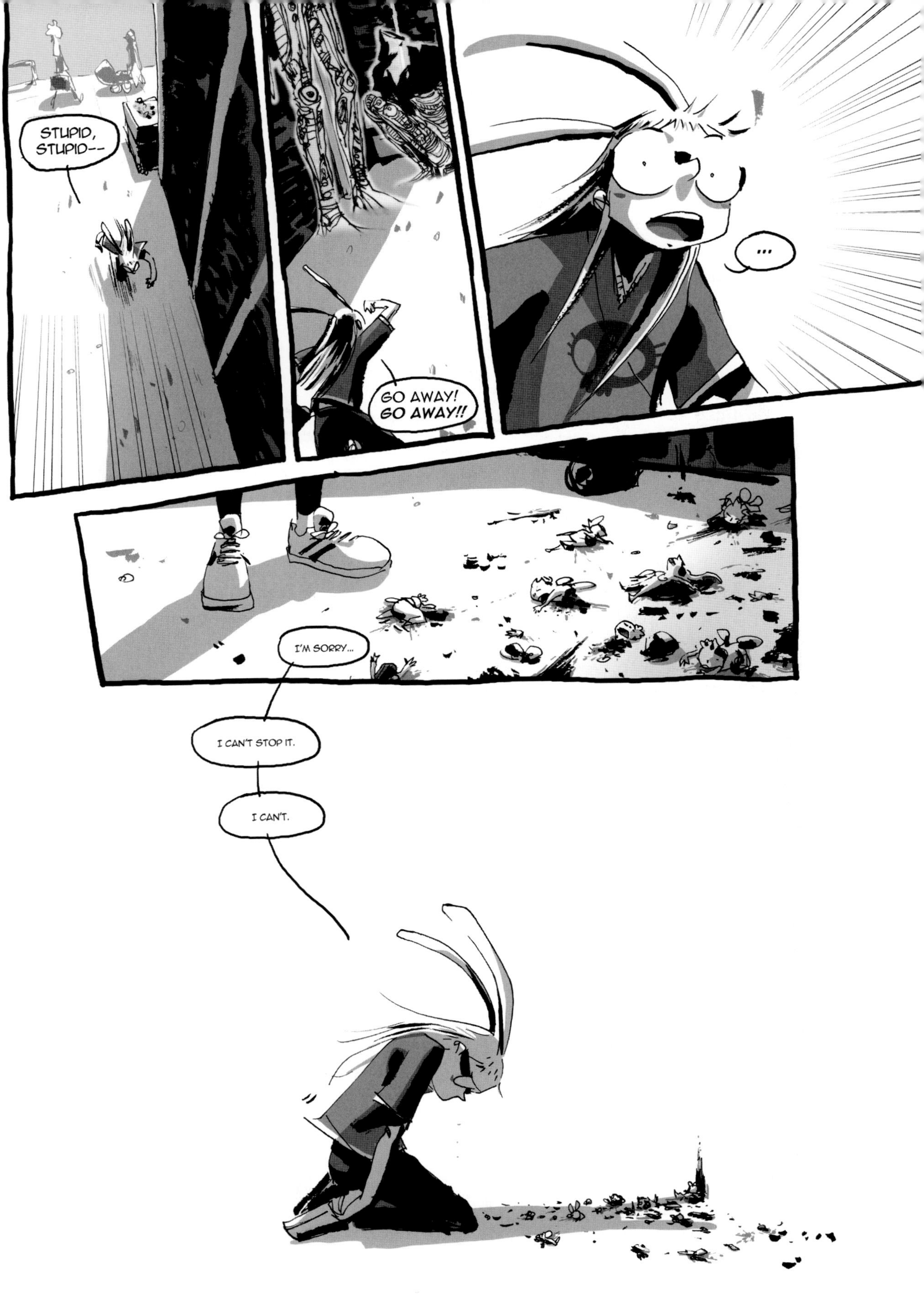
STUPID, STUPID--
GO AWAY! GO AWAY!!
...
I'M SORRY...
I CAN'T STOP IT.
I CAN'T.

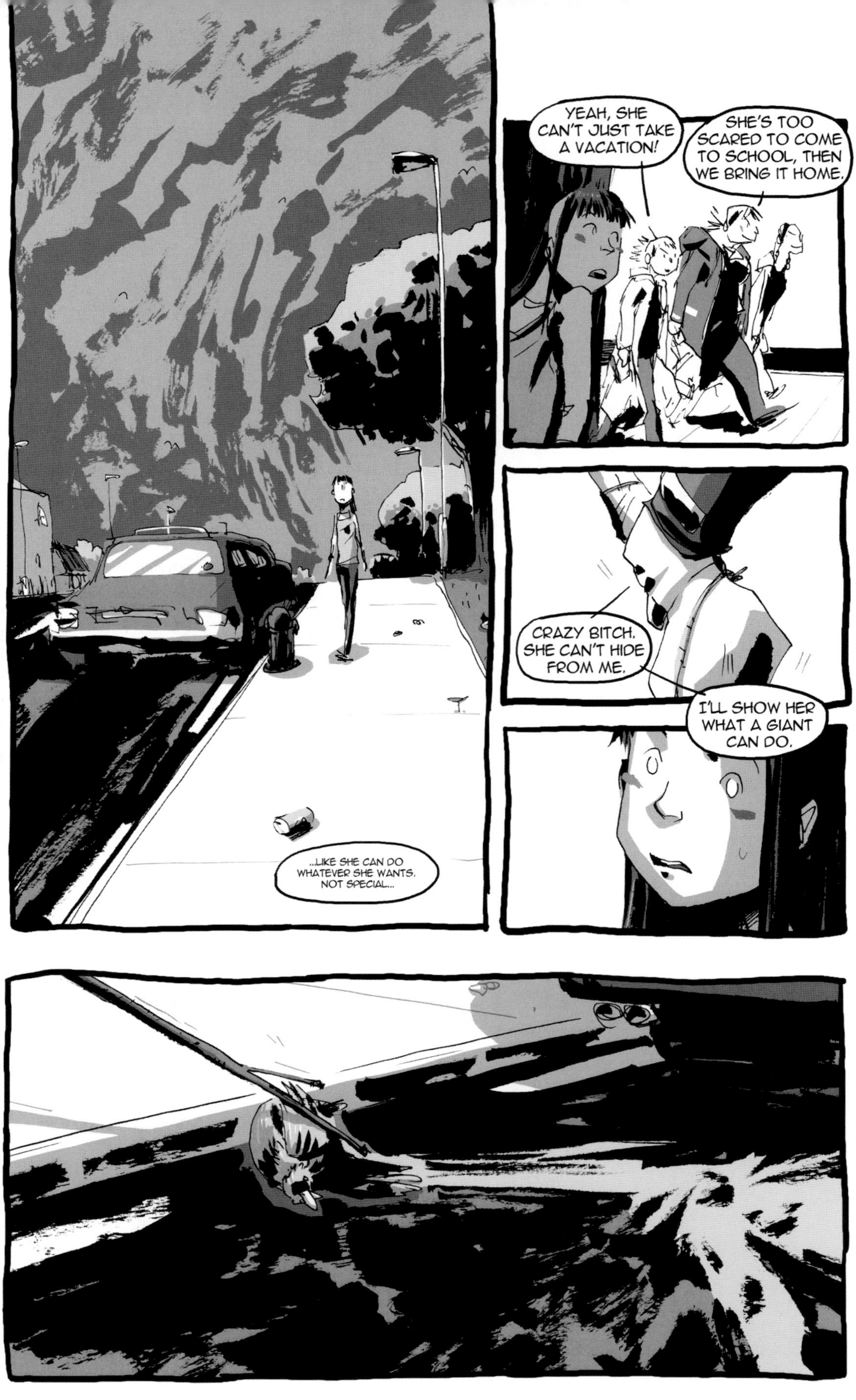
...LIKE SHE CAN DO WHATEVER SHE WANTS. NOT SPECIAL...
YEAH, SHE CAN'T JUST TAKE A VACATION!
SHE'S TOO SCARED TO COME TO SCHOOL, THEN WE BRING IT HOME.
CRAZY BITCH. SHE CAN'T HIDE FROM ME.
I'LL SHOW HER WHAT A GIANT CAN DO.

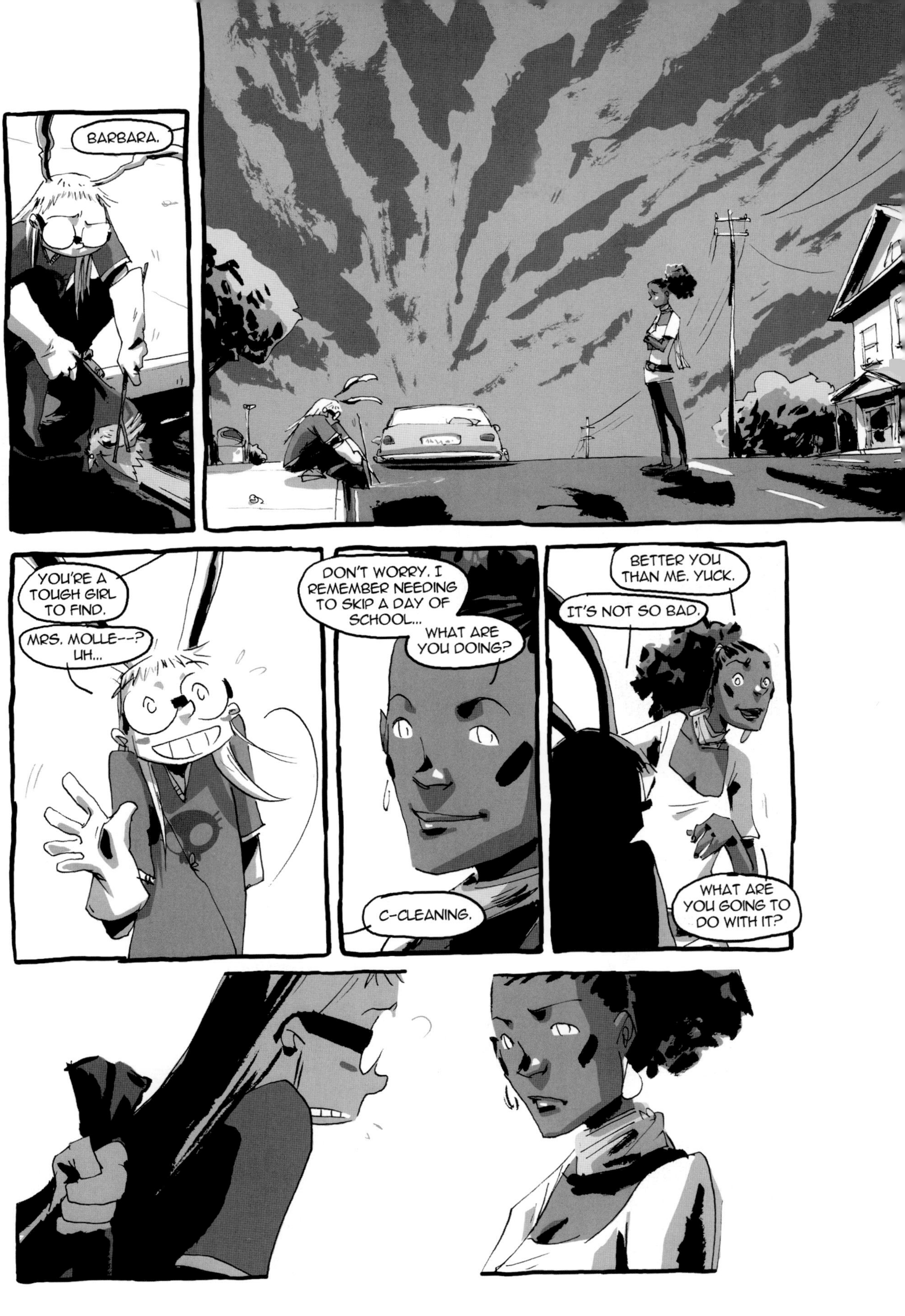
BARBARA.
YOU'RE A TOUGH GIRL TO FIND.
MRS. MOLLE--? UH...
DON'T WORRY. I REMEMBER NEEDING TO SKIP A DAY OF SCHOOL...
WHAT ARE YOU DOING?
C-CLEANING.
BETTER YOU THAN ME. YUCK.
IT'S NOT SO BAD.
WHAT ARE YOU GOING TO DO WITH IT?

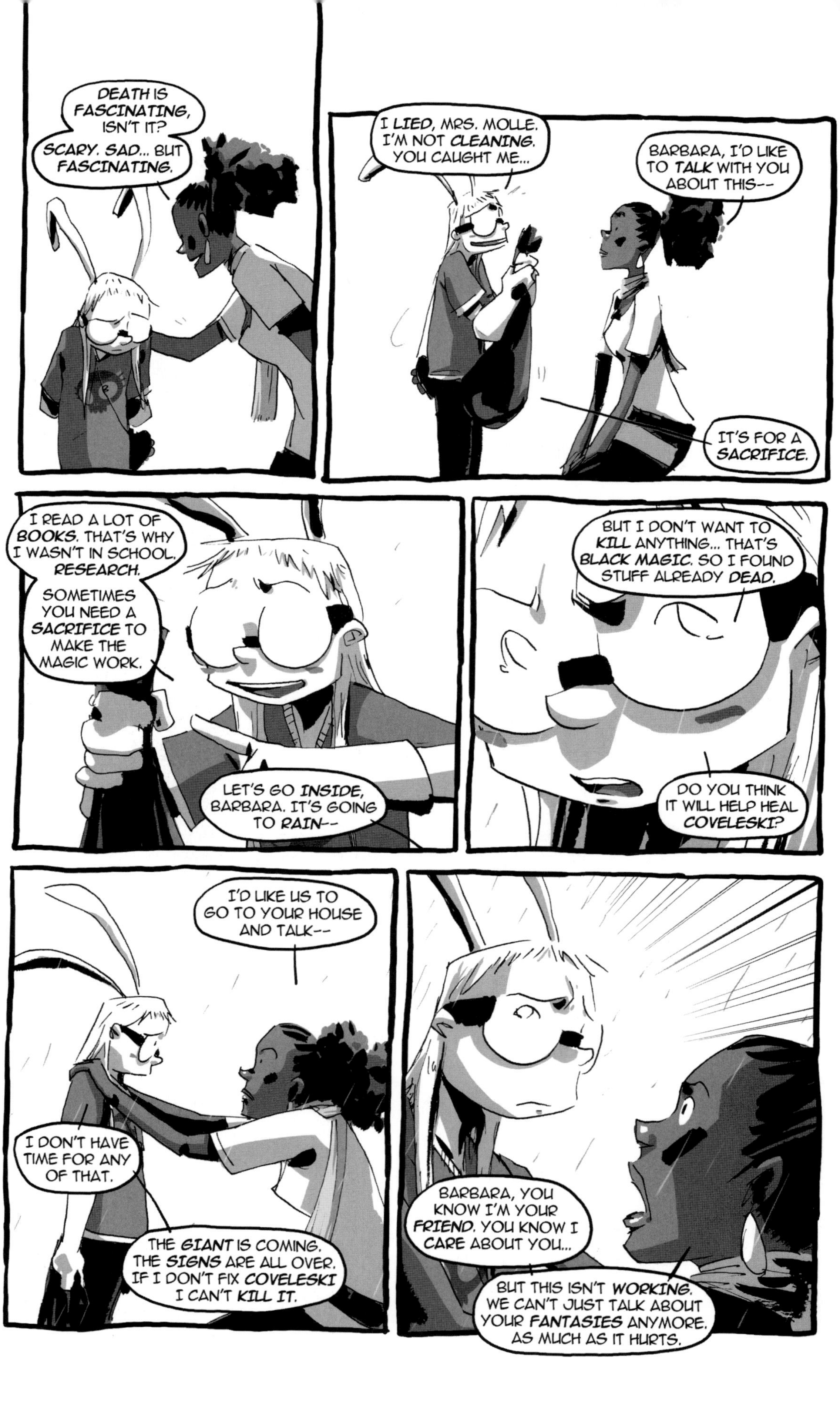
DEATH IS FASCINATING, ISN'T IT?
SCARY. SAD... BUT FASCINATING.
I LIED, MRS. MOLLE. I'M NOT CLEANING. YOU CAUGHT ME...
BARBARA, I'D LIKE TO TALK WITH YOU ABOUT THIS--
IT'S FOR A SACRIFICE.
I READ A LOT OF BOOKS. THAT'S WHY I WASN'T IN SCHOOL. RESEARCH.
SOMETIMES YOU NEED A SACRIFICE TO MAKE THE MAGIC WORK.
LET'S GO INSIDE, BARBARA. IT'S GOING TO RAIN--
BUT I DON'T WANT TO KILL ANYTHING... THAT'S BLACK MAGIC. SO I FOUND STUFF ALREADY DEAD.
DO YOU THINK IT WILL HELP HEAL COVELESKI?
I'D LIKE US TO GO TO YOUR HOUSE AND TALK--
I DON'T HAVE TIME FOR ANY OF THAT.
THE GIANT IS COMING. THE SIGNS ARE ALL OVER. IF I DON'T FIX COVELESKI I CAN'T KILL IT.
BARBARA, YOU KNOW I'M YOUR FRIEND. YOU KNOW I CARE ABOUT YOU...
BUT THIS ISN'T WORKING. WE CAN'T JUST TALK ABOUT YOUR FANTASIES ANYMORE. AS MUCH AS IT HURTS.

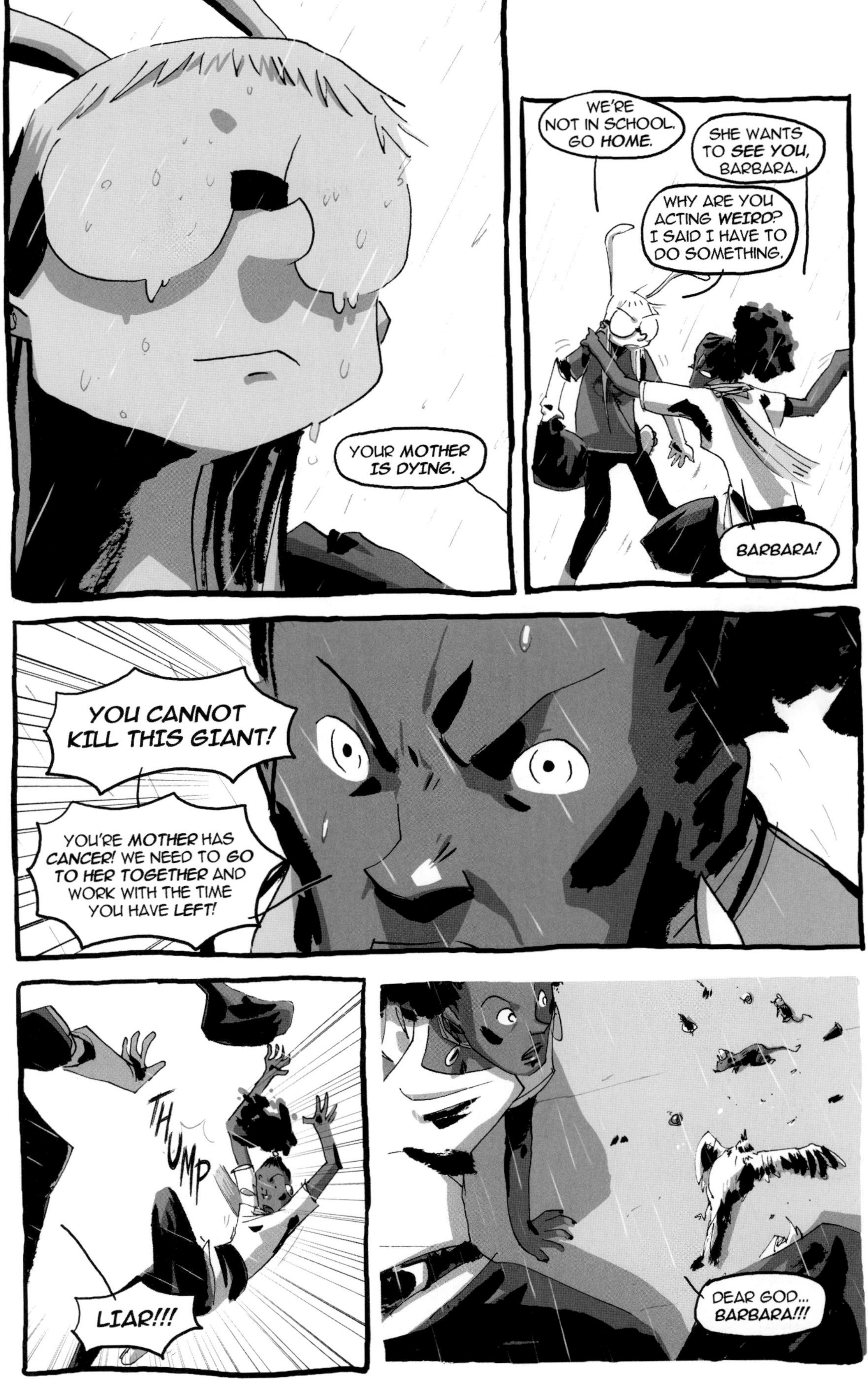
YOUR MOTHER IS DYING.
WE'RE NOT IN SCHOOL. GO HOME.
SHE WANTS TO SEE YOU, BARBARA.
WHY ARE YOU ACTING WEIRD? I SAID I HAVE TO DO SOMETHING.
BARBARA!
YOU CANNOT KILL THIS GIANT!
YOU'RE MOTHER HAS CANCER! WE NEED TO GO TO HER TOGETHER AND WORK WITH THE TIME YOU HAVE LEFT!
THUMP
LIAR!!!
DEAR GOD... BARBARA!!!

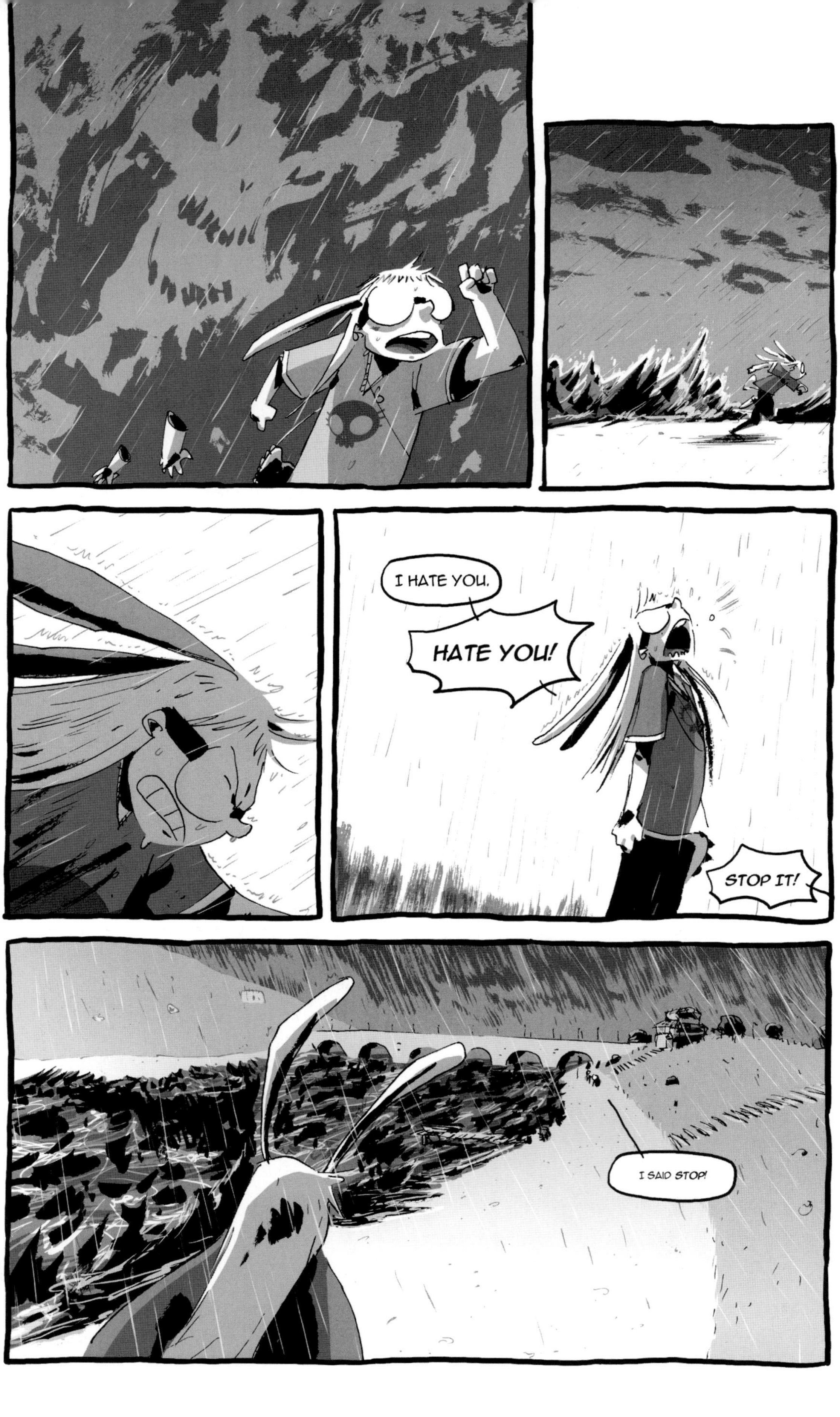
I HATE YOU.
HATE YOU!
STOP IT!
I SAID STOP!

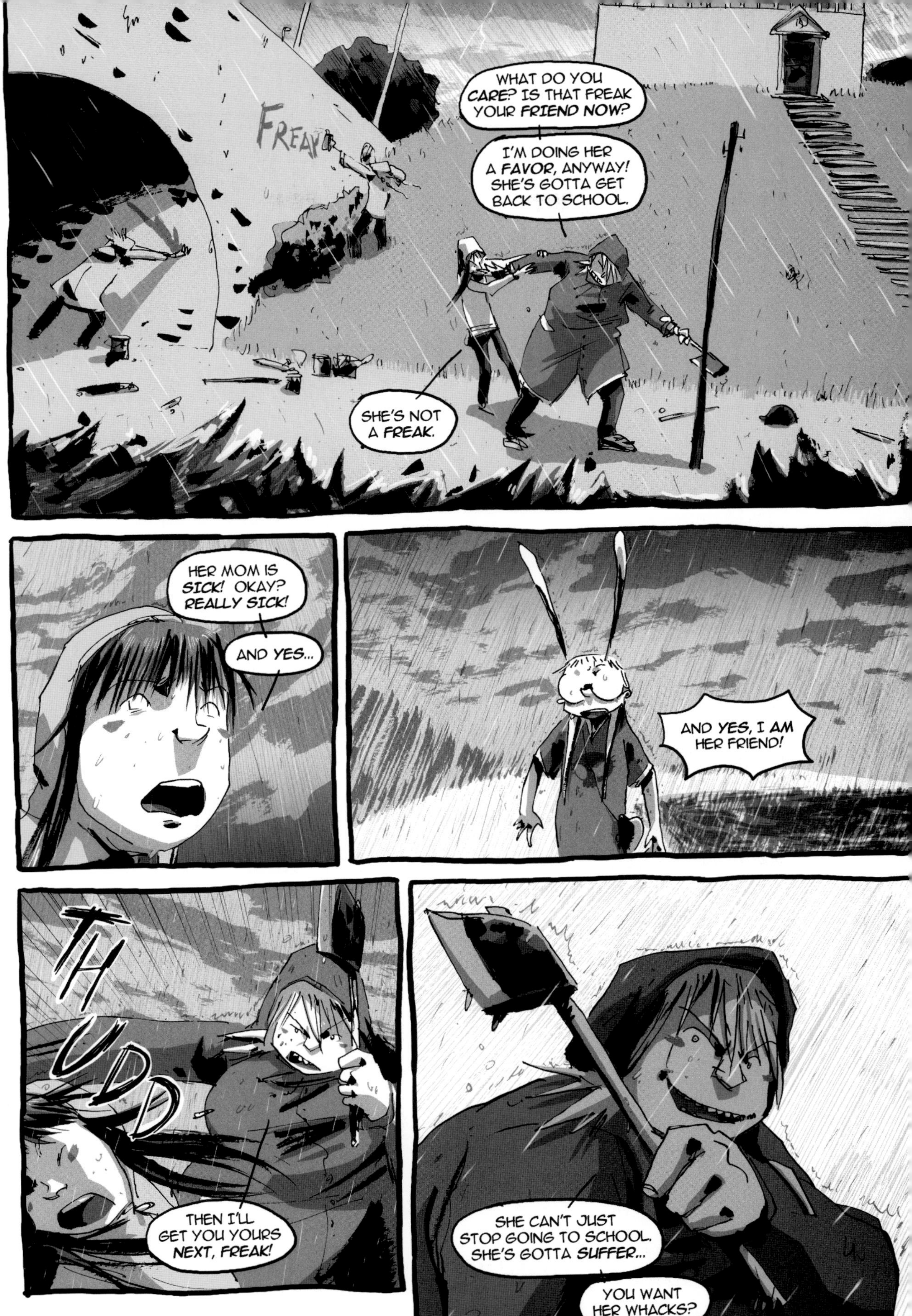
FREAK
WHAT DO YOU CARE? IS THAT FREAK YOUR FRIEND NOW?
I'M DOING HER A FAVOR, ANYWAY! SHE'S GOTTA GET BACK TO SCHOOL.
SHE'S NOT A FREAK.
HER MOM IS SICK! OKAY? REALLY SICK!
AND YES...
AND YES, I AM HER FRIEND!
THUDD
THEN I'LL GET YOU YOURS NEXT, FREAK!
SHE CAN'T JUST STOP GOING TO SCHOOL. SHE'S GOTTA SUFFER...
YOU WANT HER WHACKS?

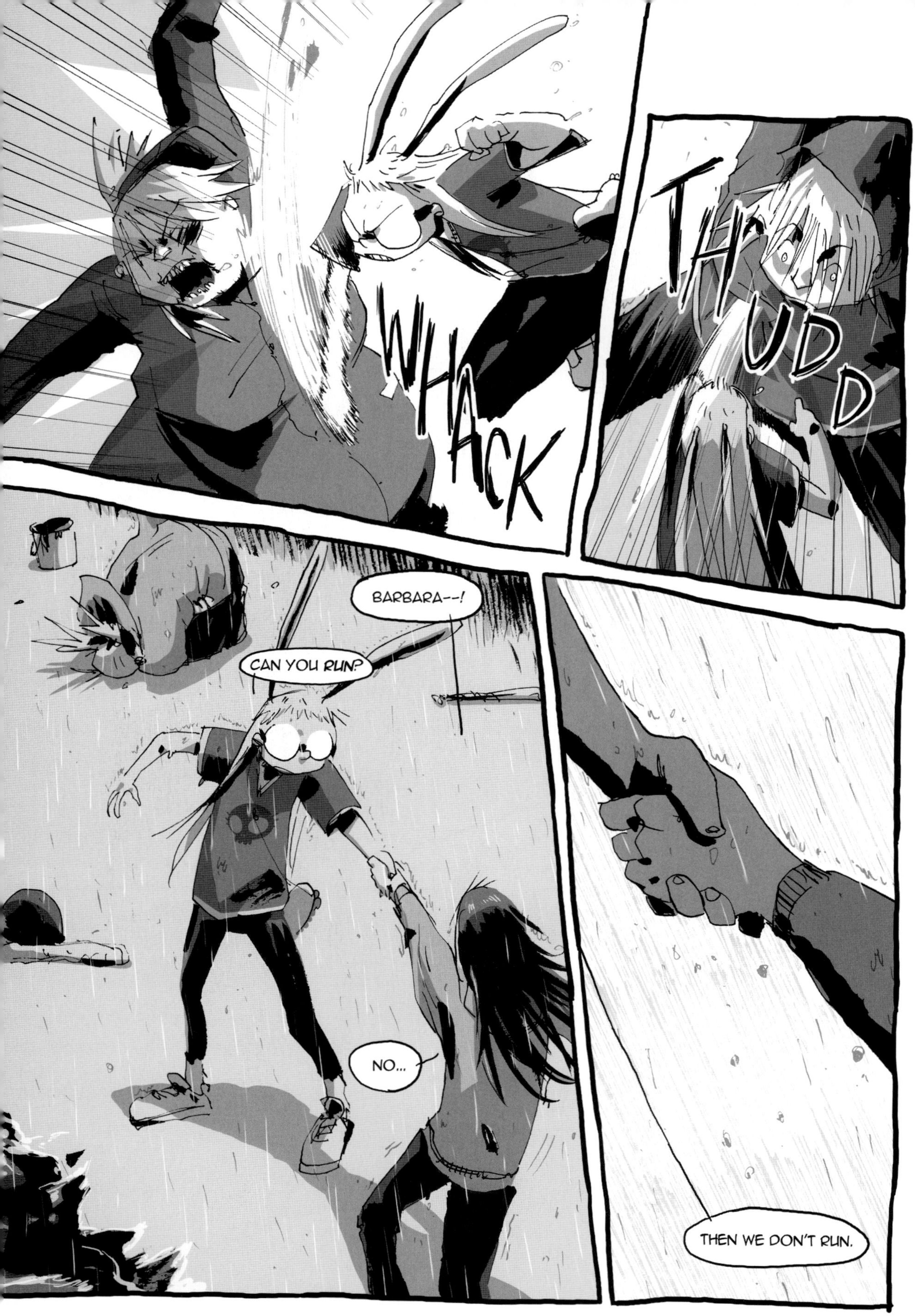
WHACK
THUDD
BARBARA--!
CAN YOU RUN?
NO...
THEN WE DON'T RUN.

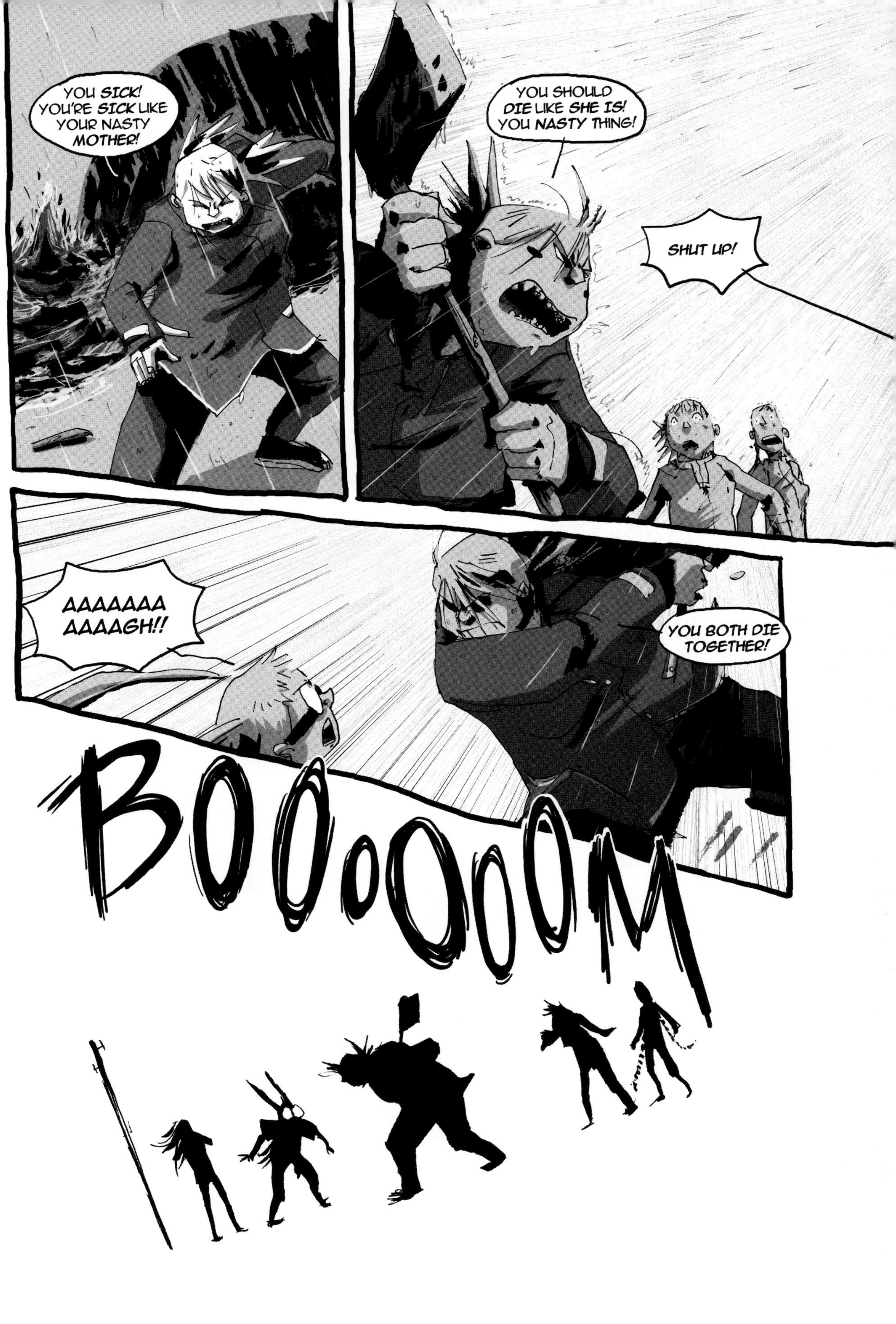
YOU SICK! YOU'RE SICK LIKE YOUR NASTY MOTHER!
YOU SHOULD DIE LIKE SHE IS! YOU NASTY THING!
SHUT UP!
AAAAAAA AAAAGH!!
YOU BOTH DIE TOGETHER!
BOOoOOOM

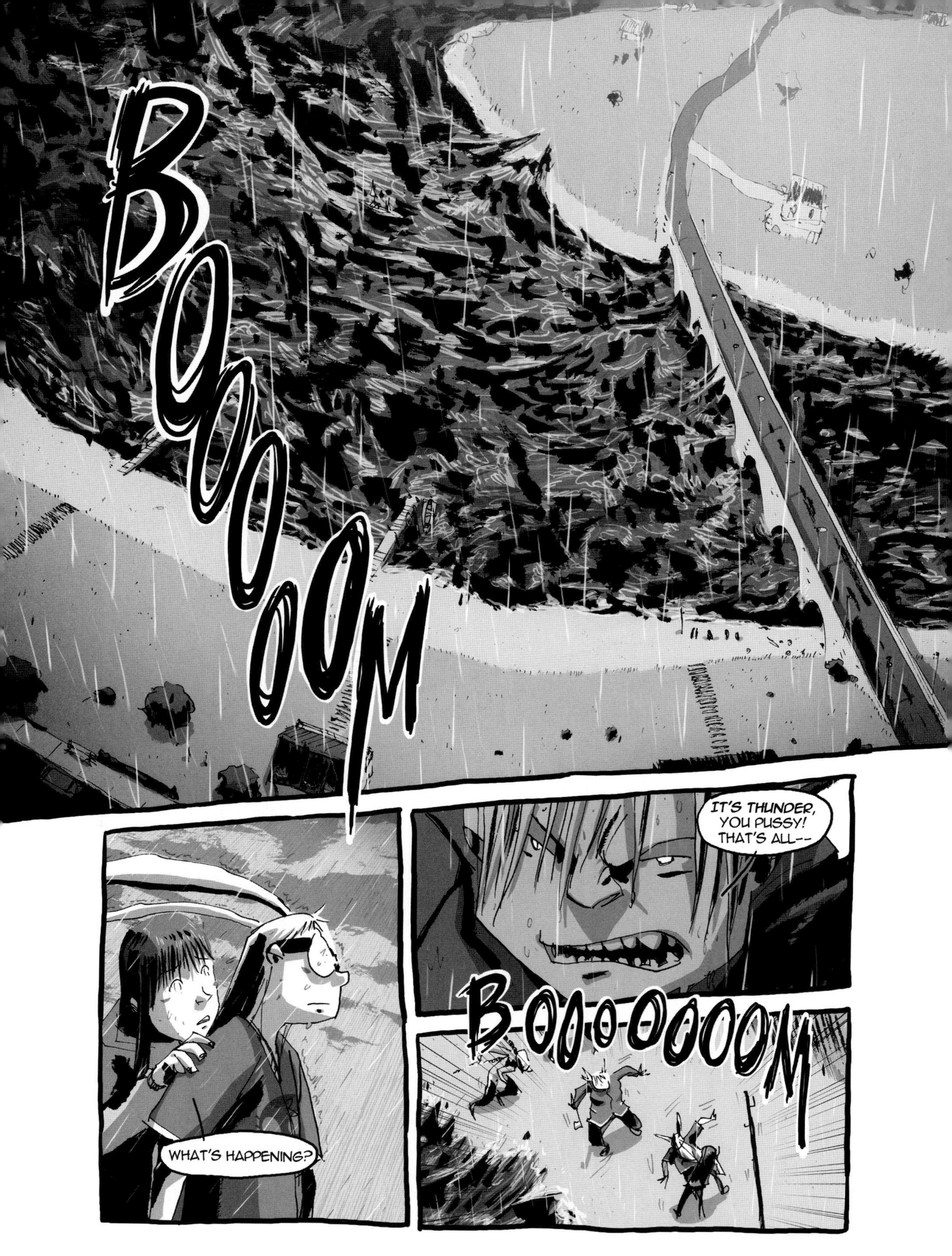
BOOOOOOOM
IT'S THUNDER, YOU PUSSY! THAT'S ALL--
WHAT'S HAPPENING?
BOOOOOOOM

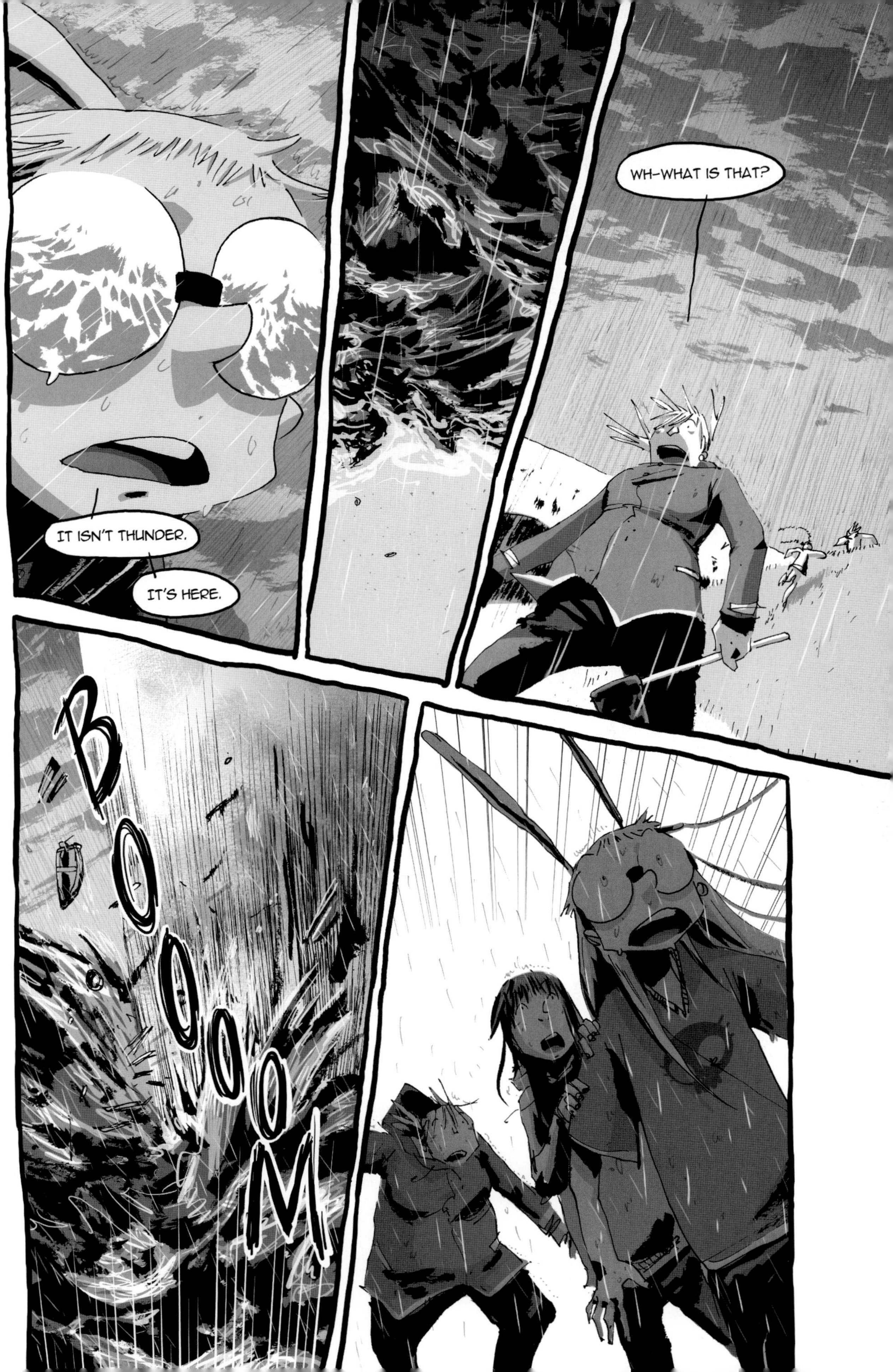
IT ISN'T THUNDER.
IT'S HERE.
WH-WHAT IS THAT?
BOOOOOM

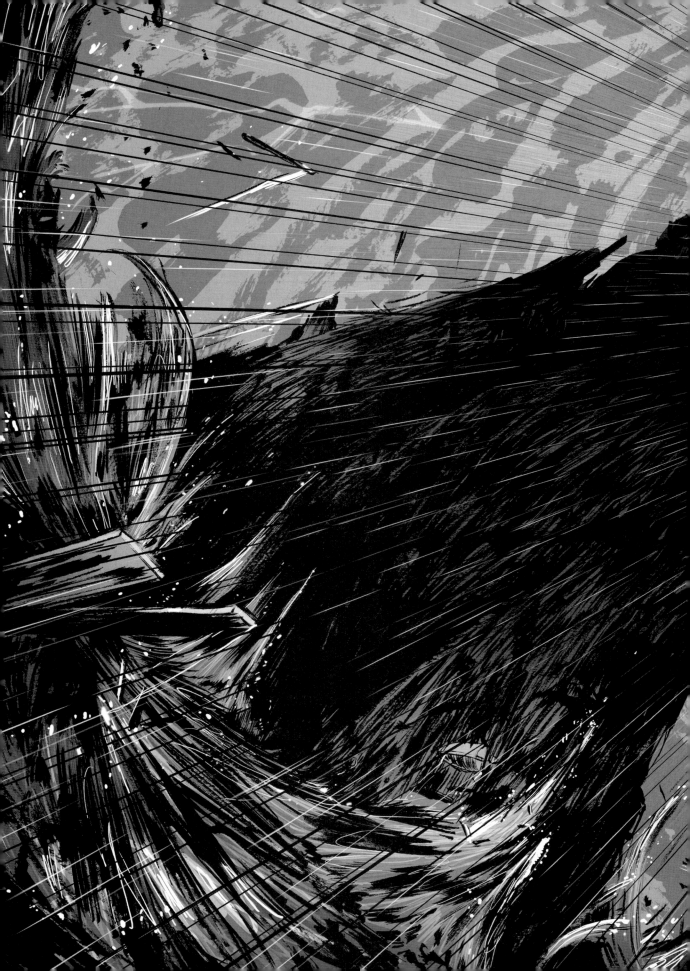

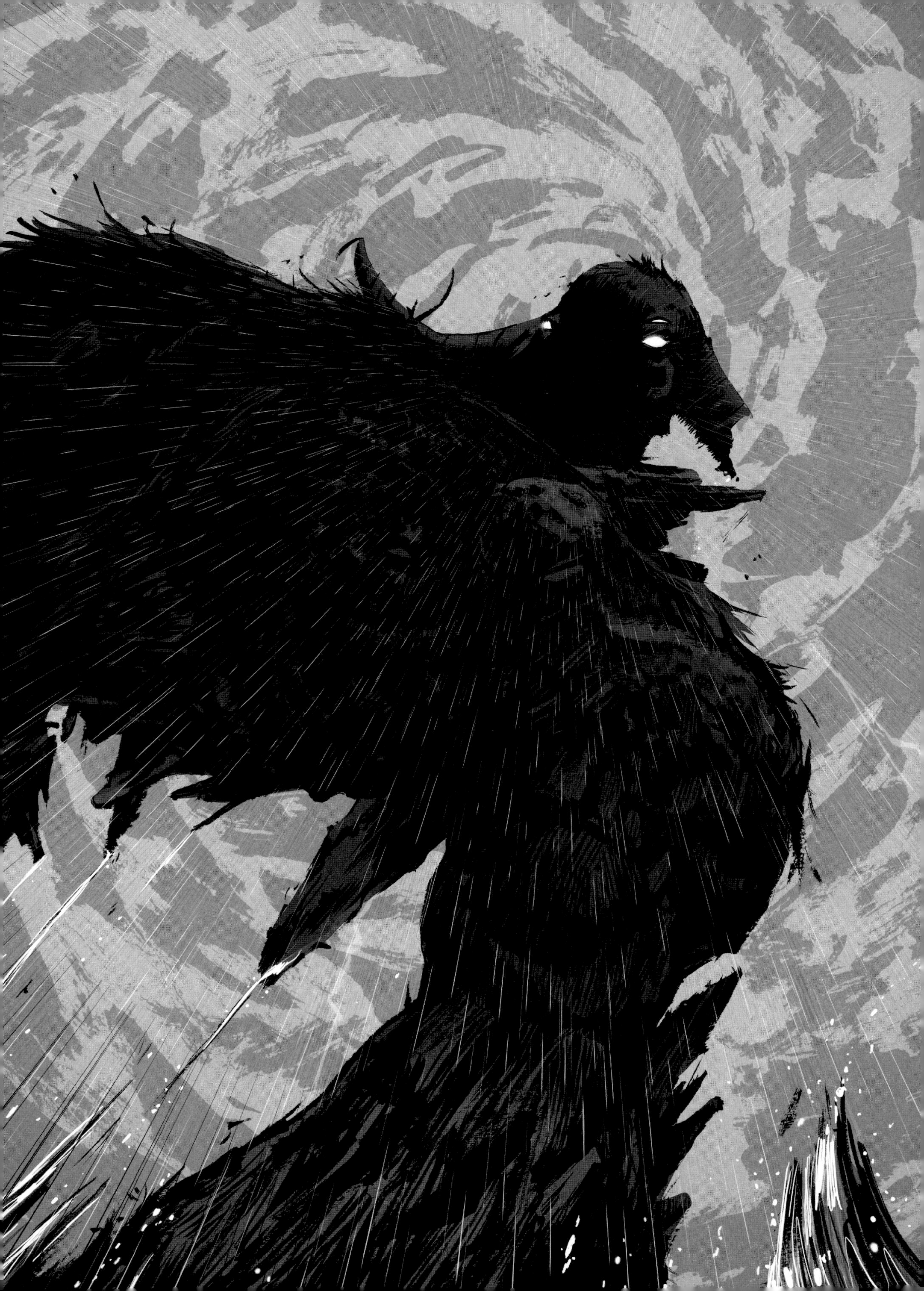

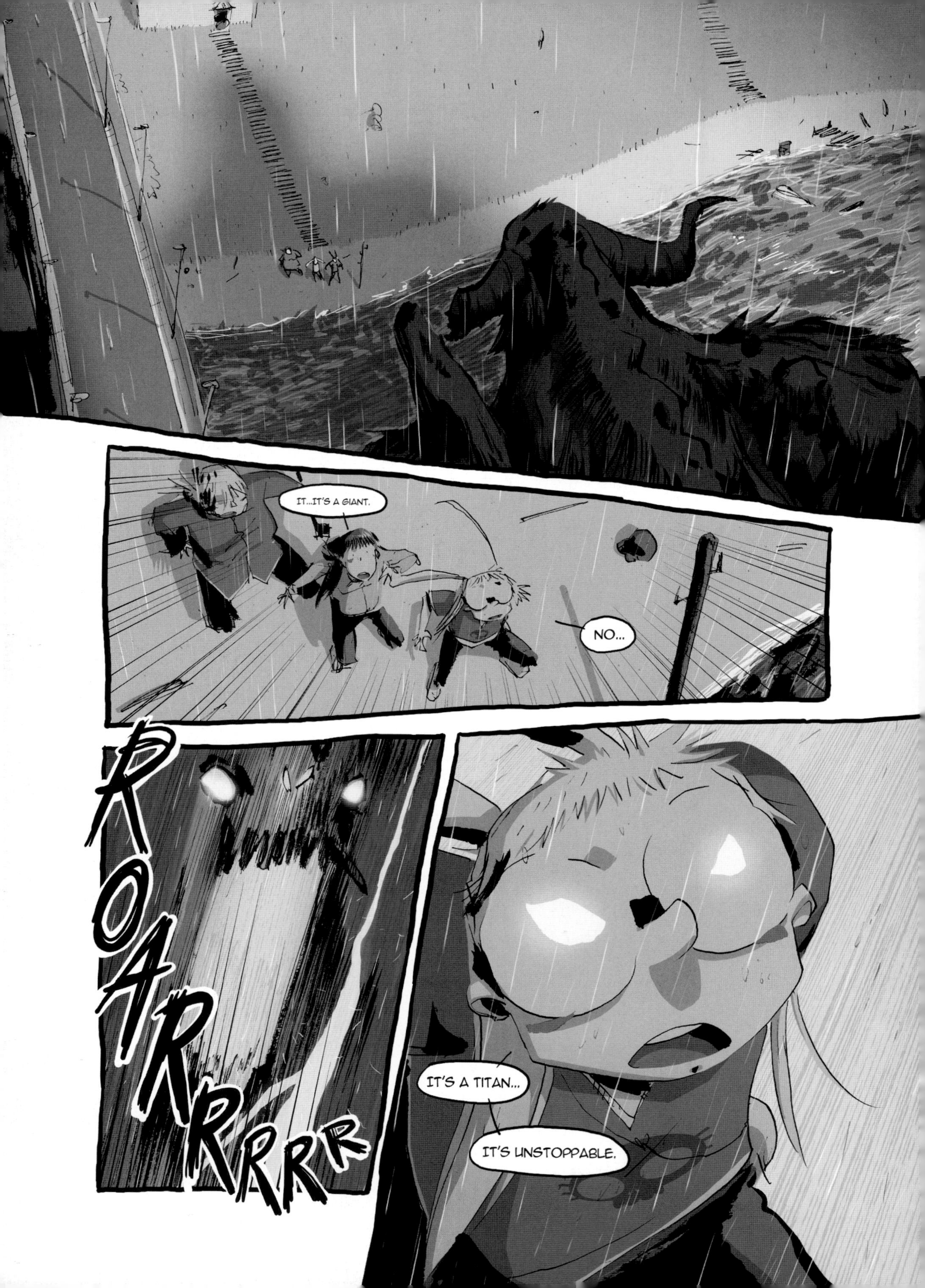
IT...IT'S A GIANT.
NO...
ROARRRRR
IT'S A TITAN...
IT'S UNSTOPPABLE.

CHAPTER6: THE TITAN

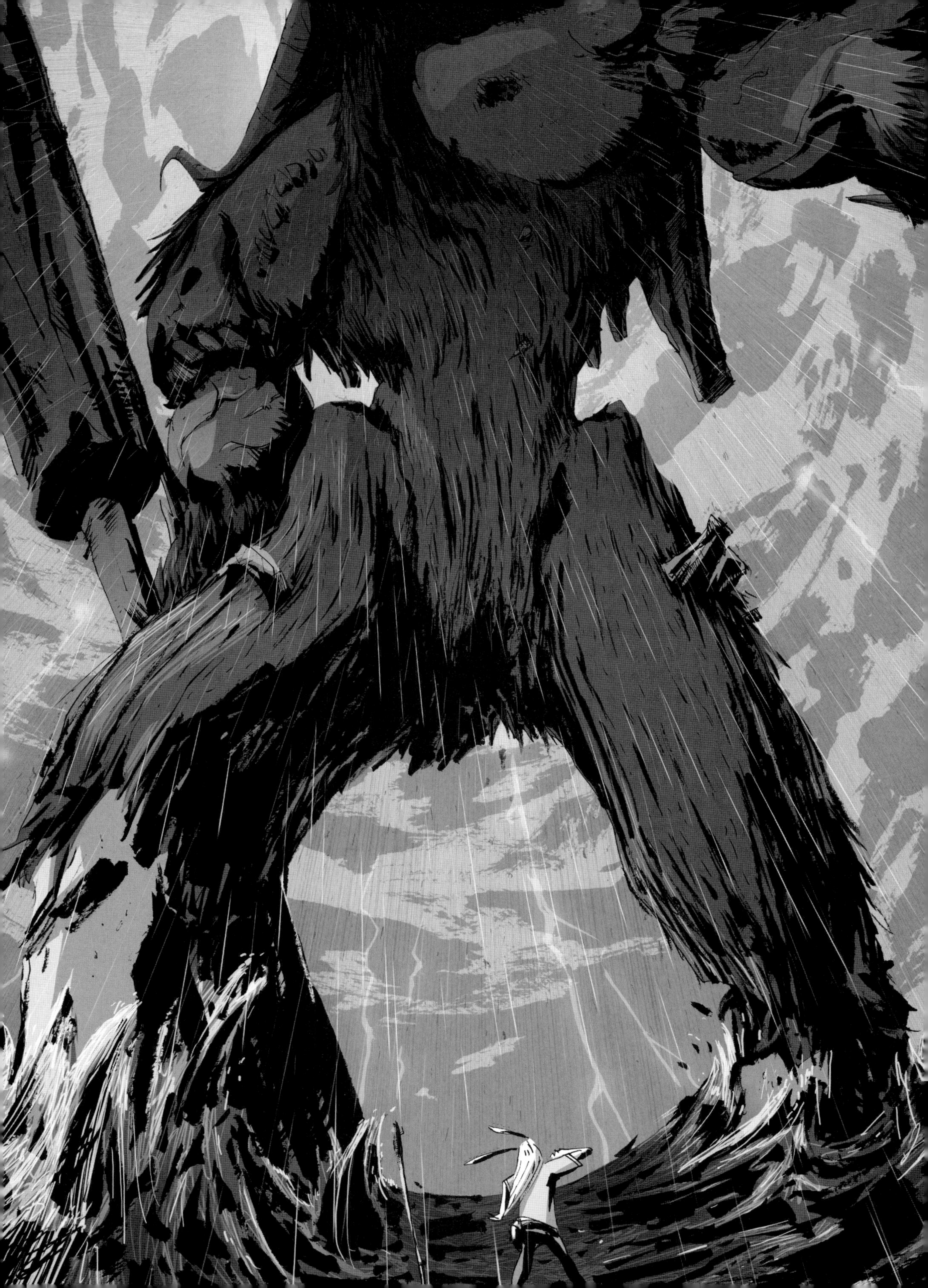

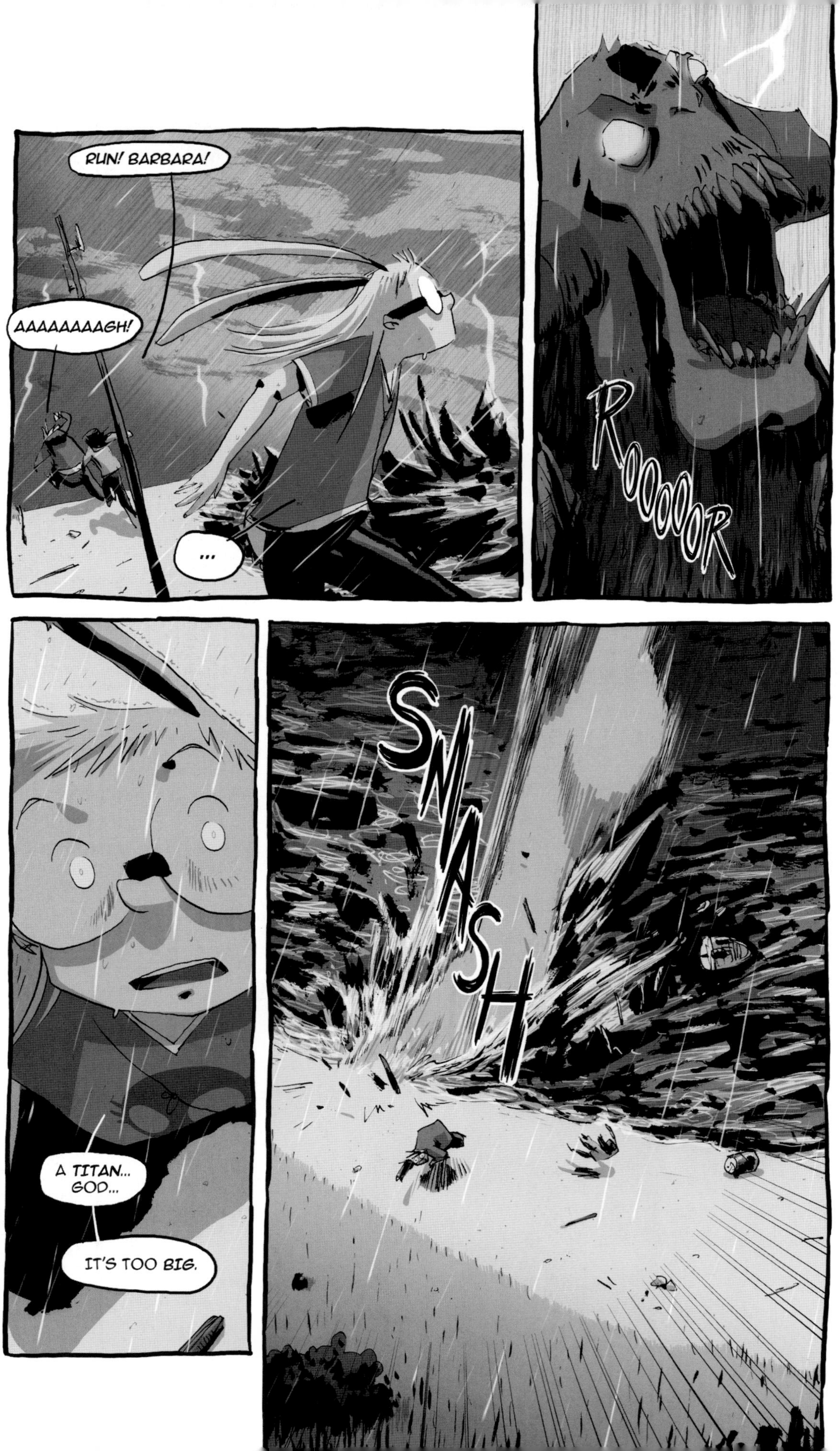
RUN! BARBARA!
AAAAAAAAGH!
...
ROOOOOR
A TITAN... GOD...
IT'S TOO BIG.
SMASH

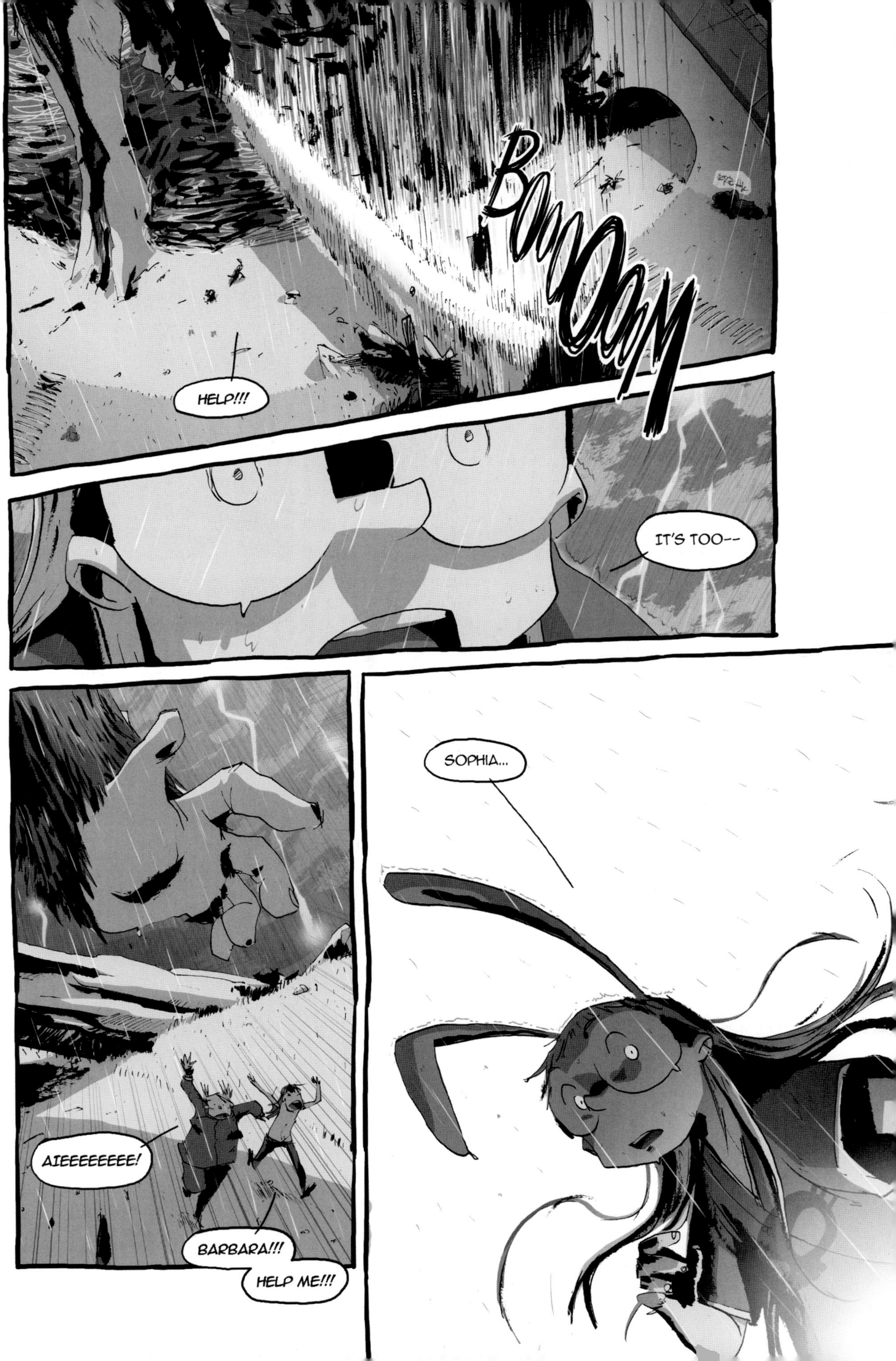

BOOOOM
HELP!!!
IT'S TOO--
AIEEEEEEEE!
BARBARA!!!
HELP ME!!!
SOPHIA...

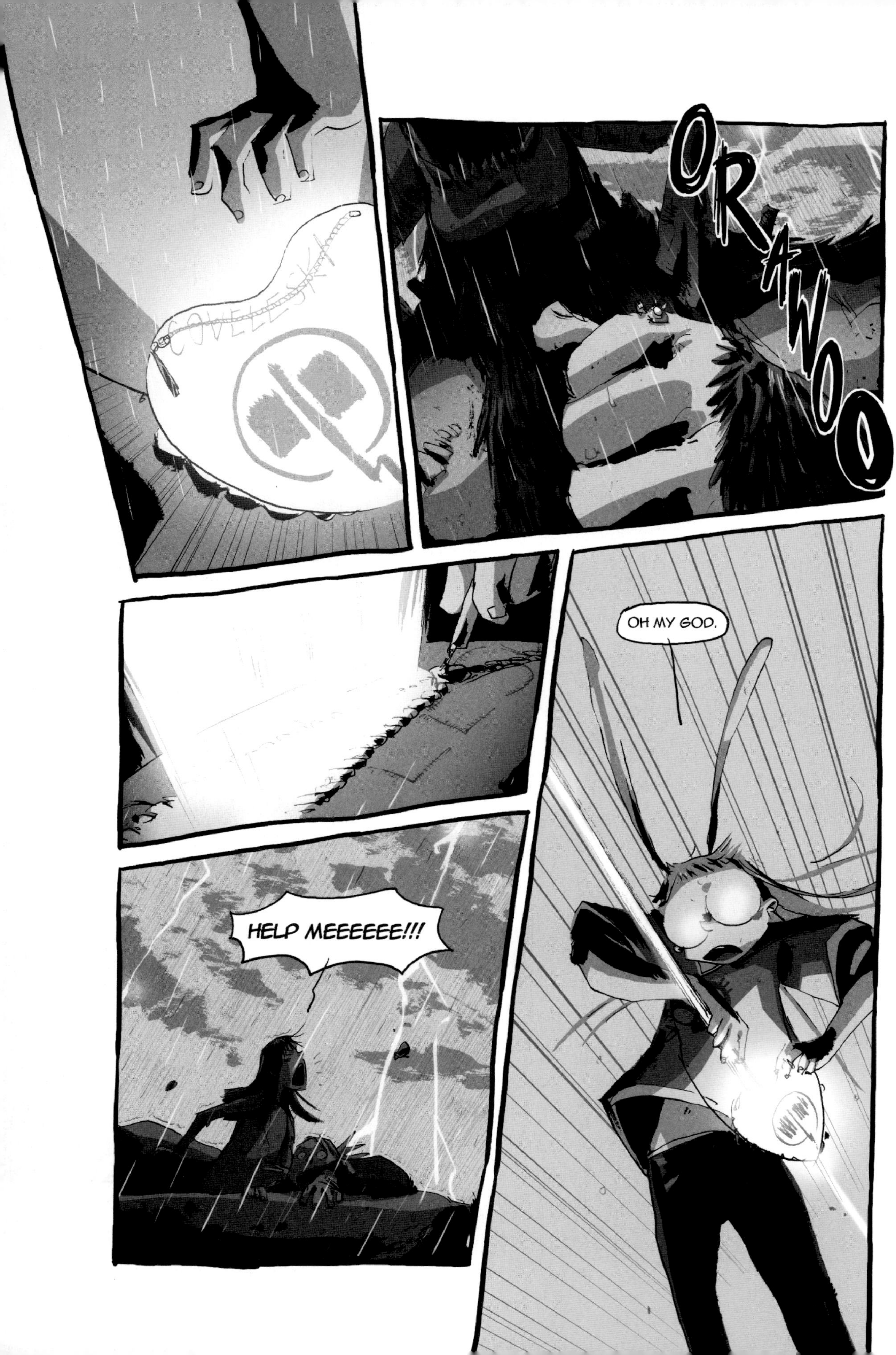
COVELESKI
ORAWOO
OH MY GOD.
HELP MEEEEEE!!!

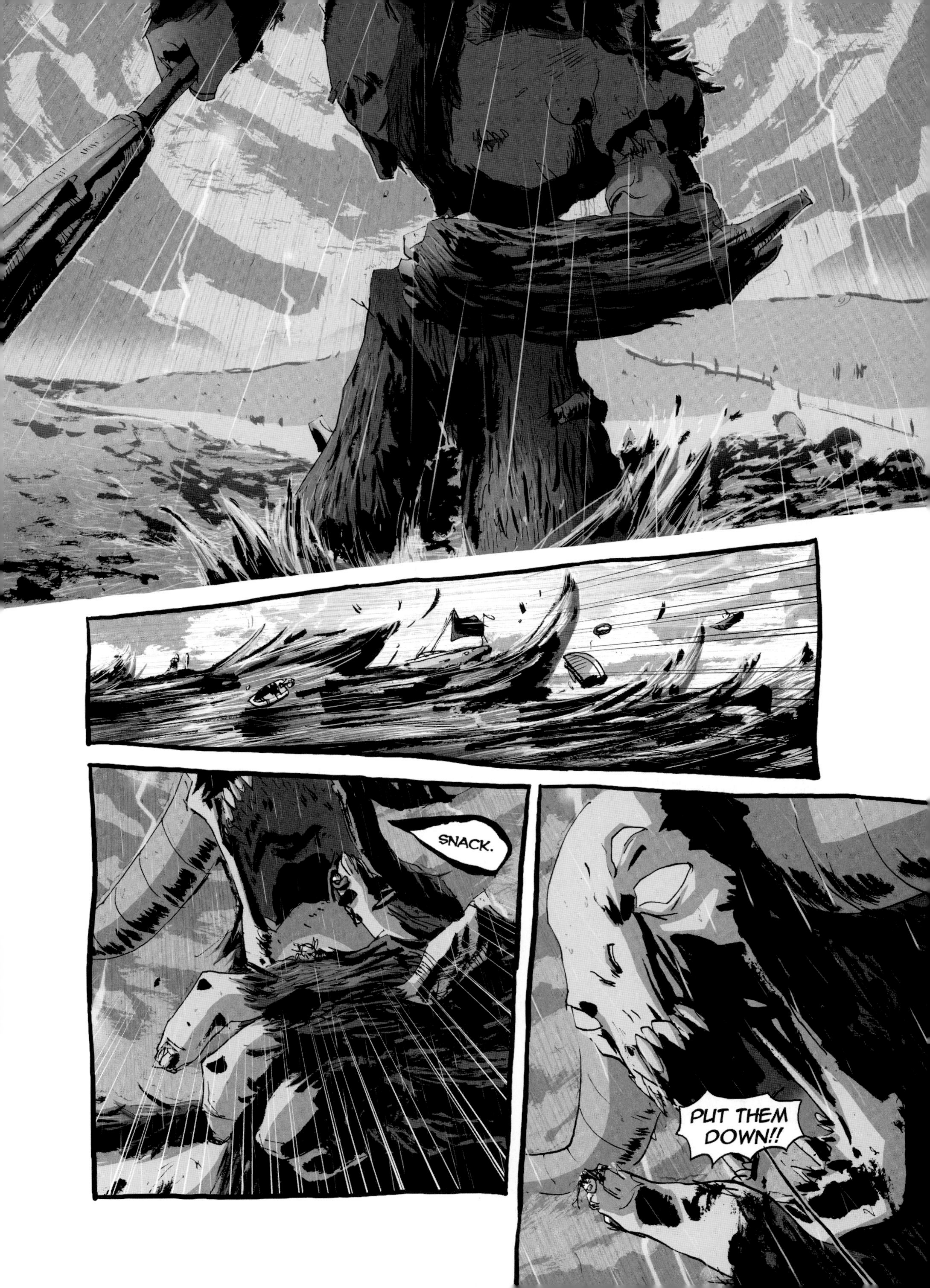
SNACK.
PUT THEM DOWN!!

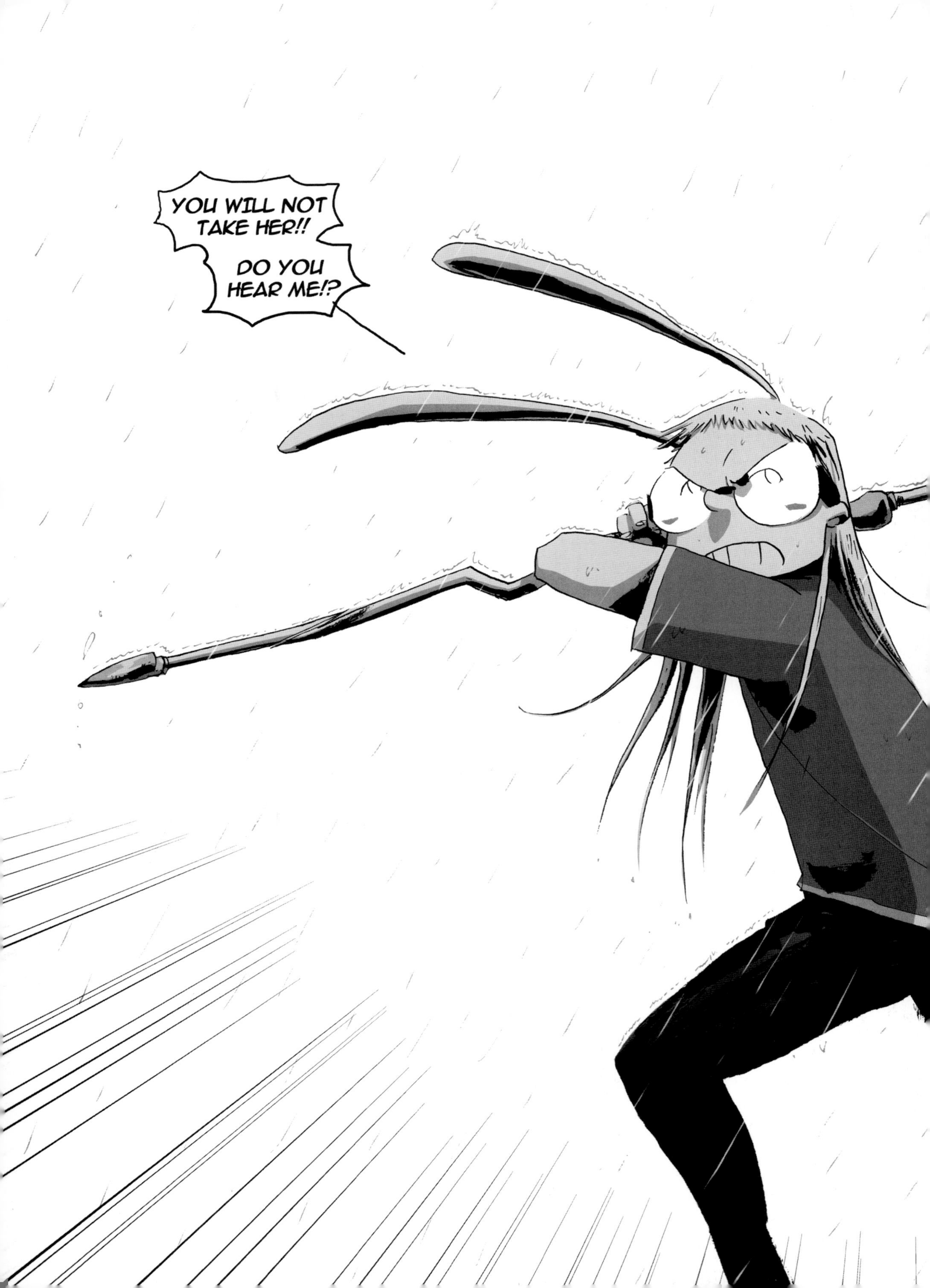
YOU WILL NOT TAKE HER!!
DO YOU HEAR ME!?

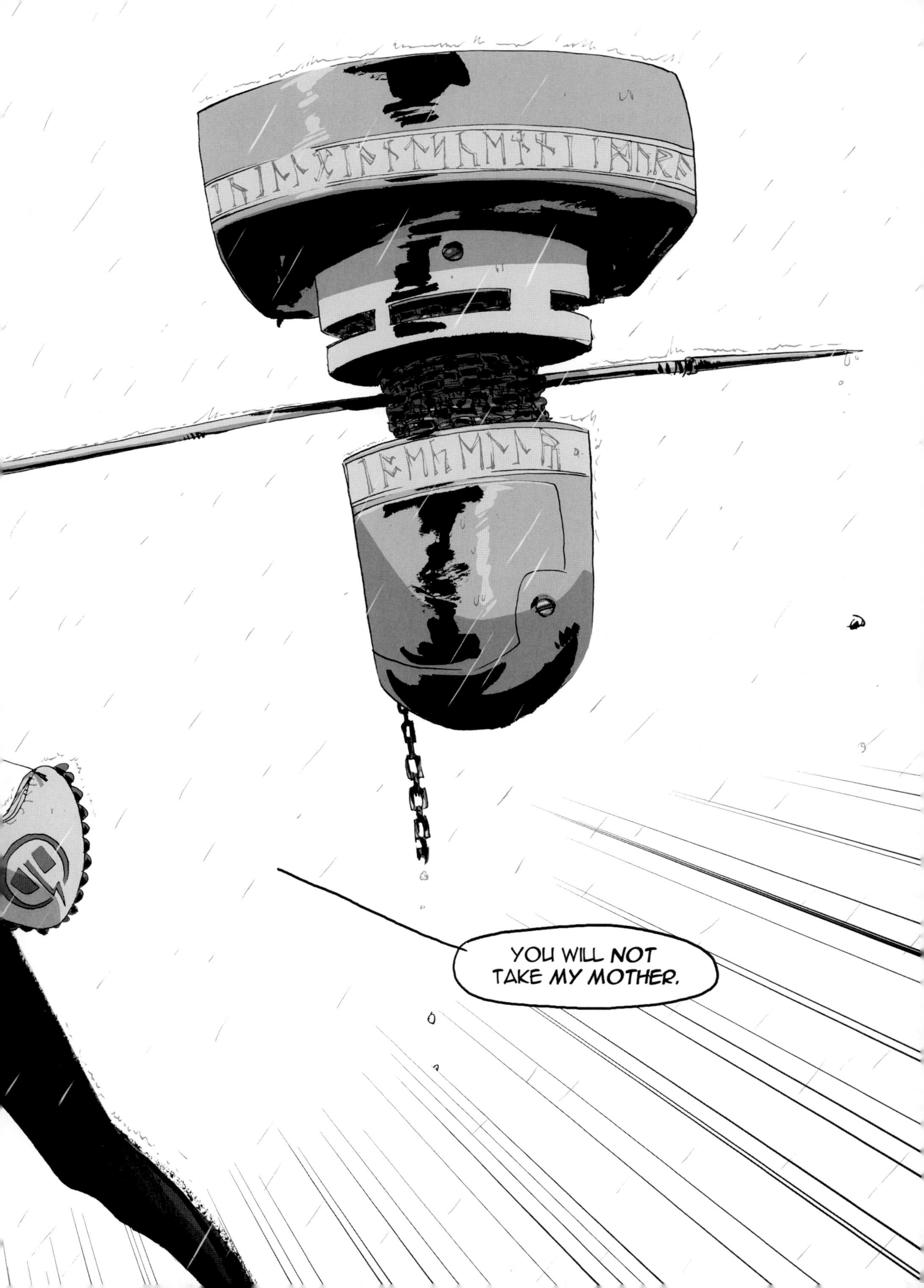
YOU WILL NOT TAKE MY MOTHER.

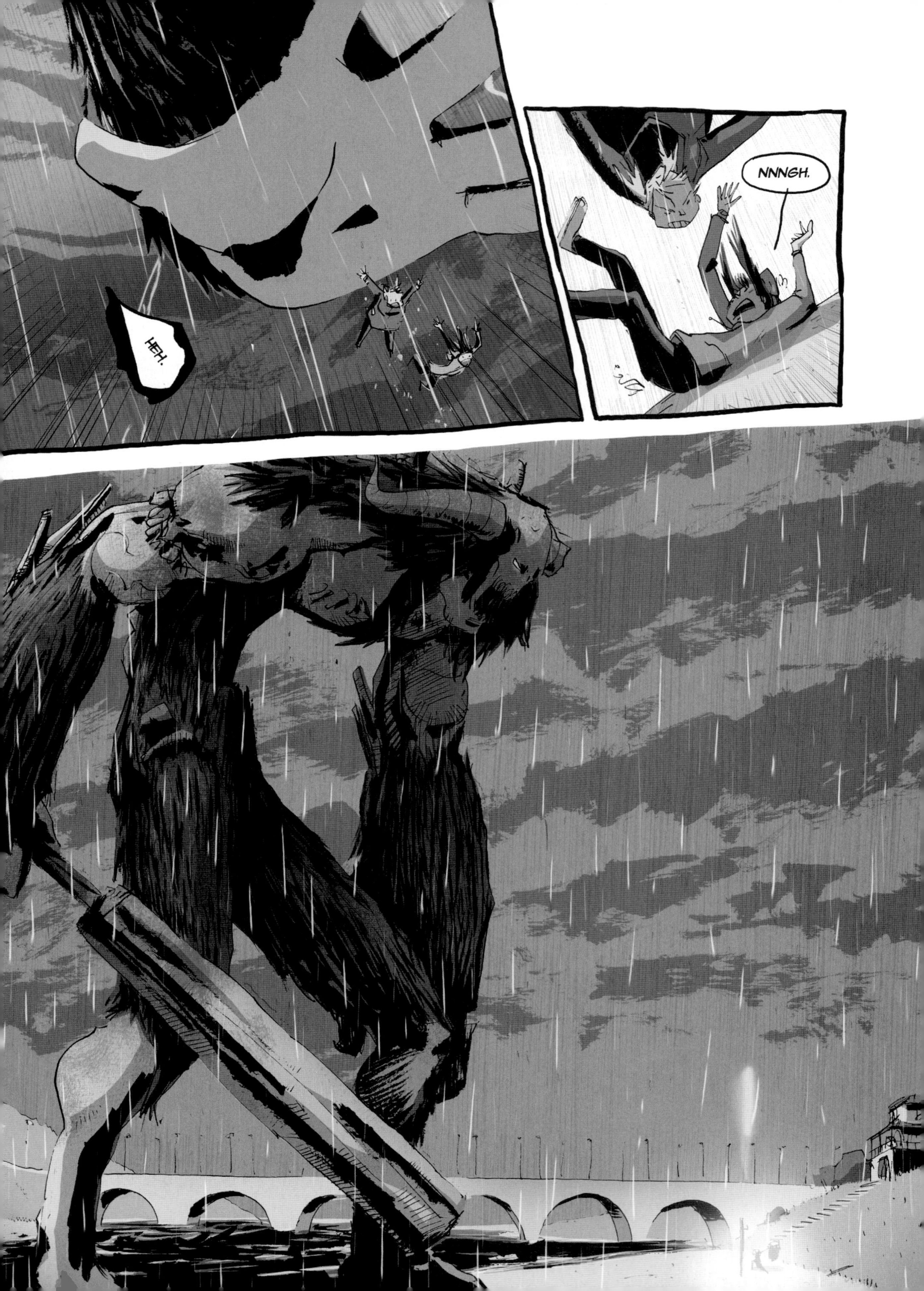
HEH.
NNNGH.

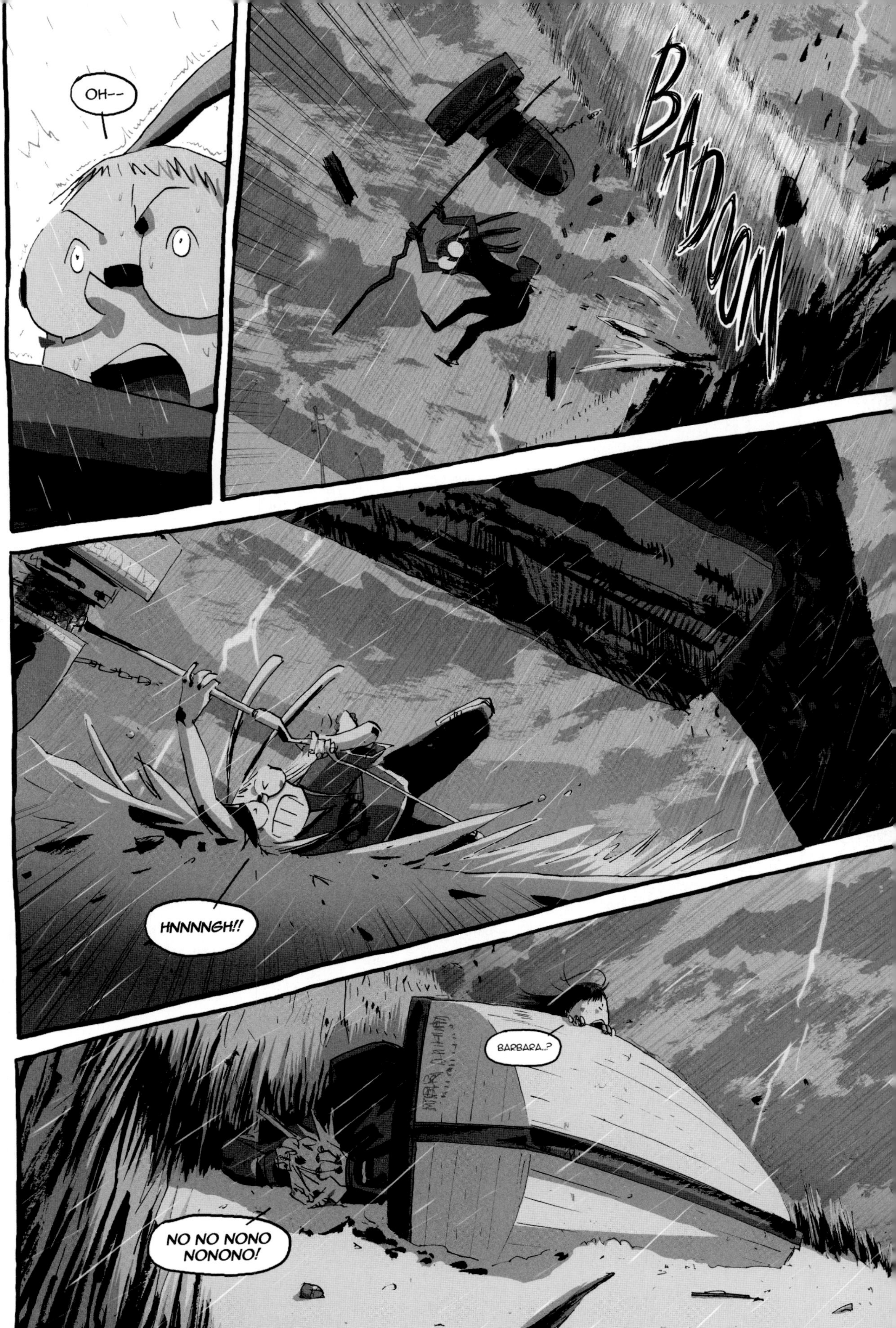
OH--
BADOOM
HNNNNGH!!
BARBARA..?
NO NO NONO NONONO!

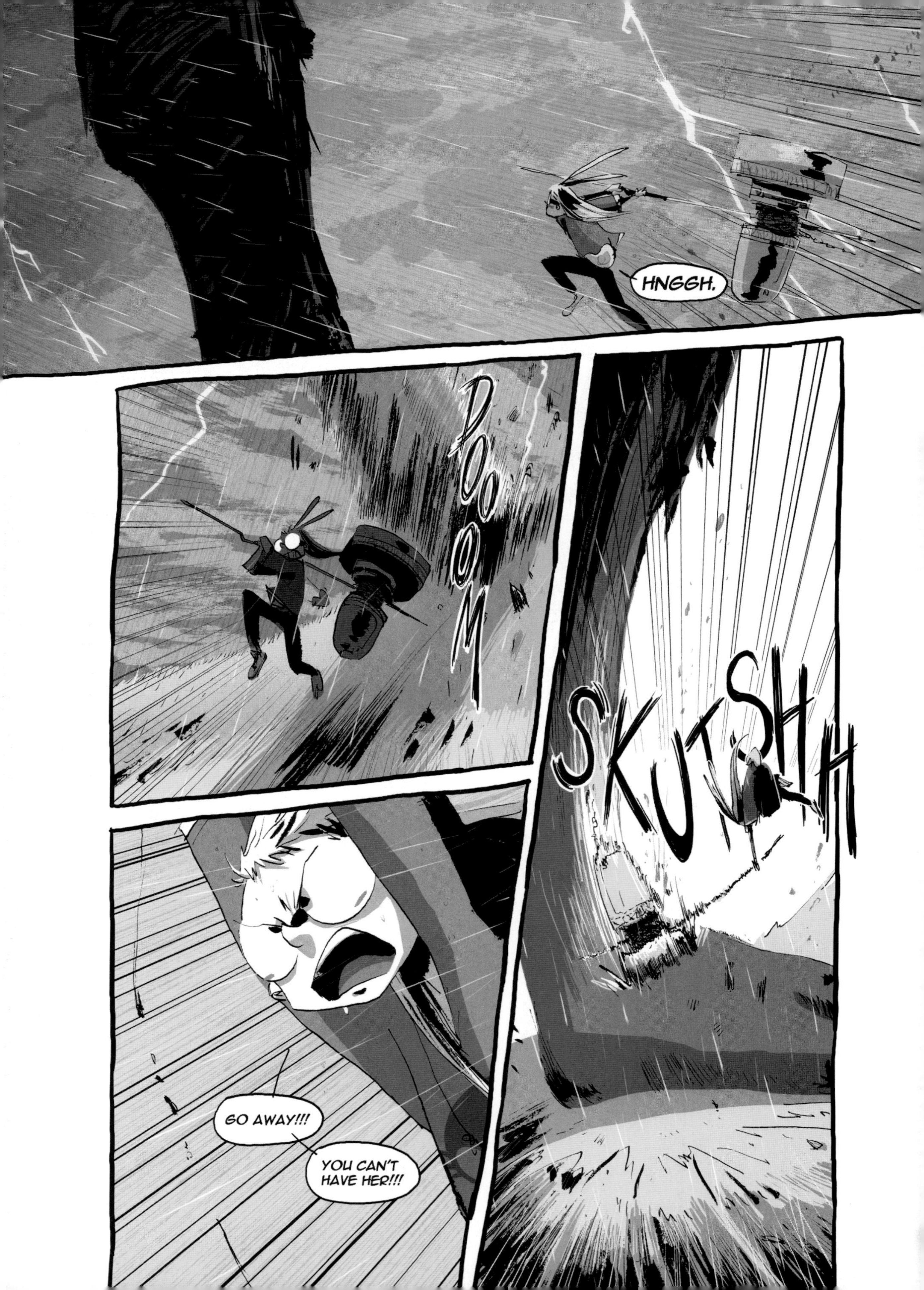
HNGGH.
DOOOOM
SKUTSHH
GO AWAY!!!
YOU CAN'T HAVE HER!!!

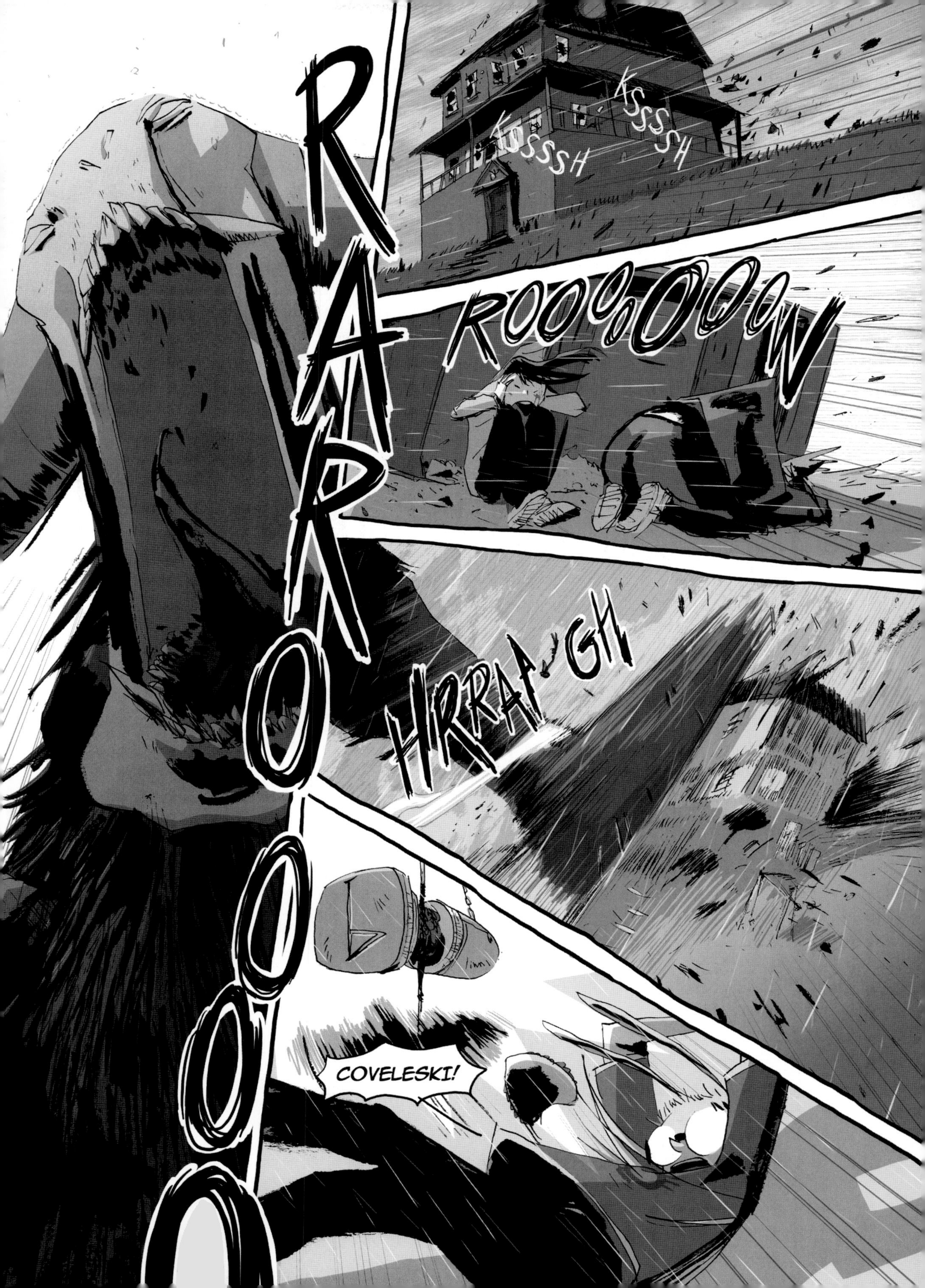

RAAROOOOOO
KSSSSH
KSSSSH
ROOOOOOOW
HRRAAGH
COVELESKI!

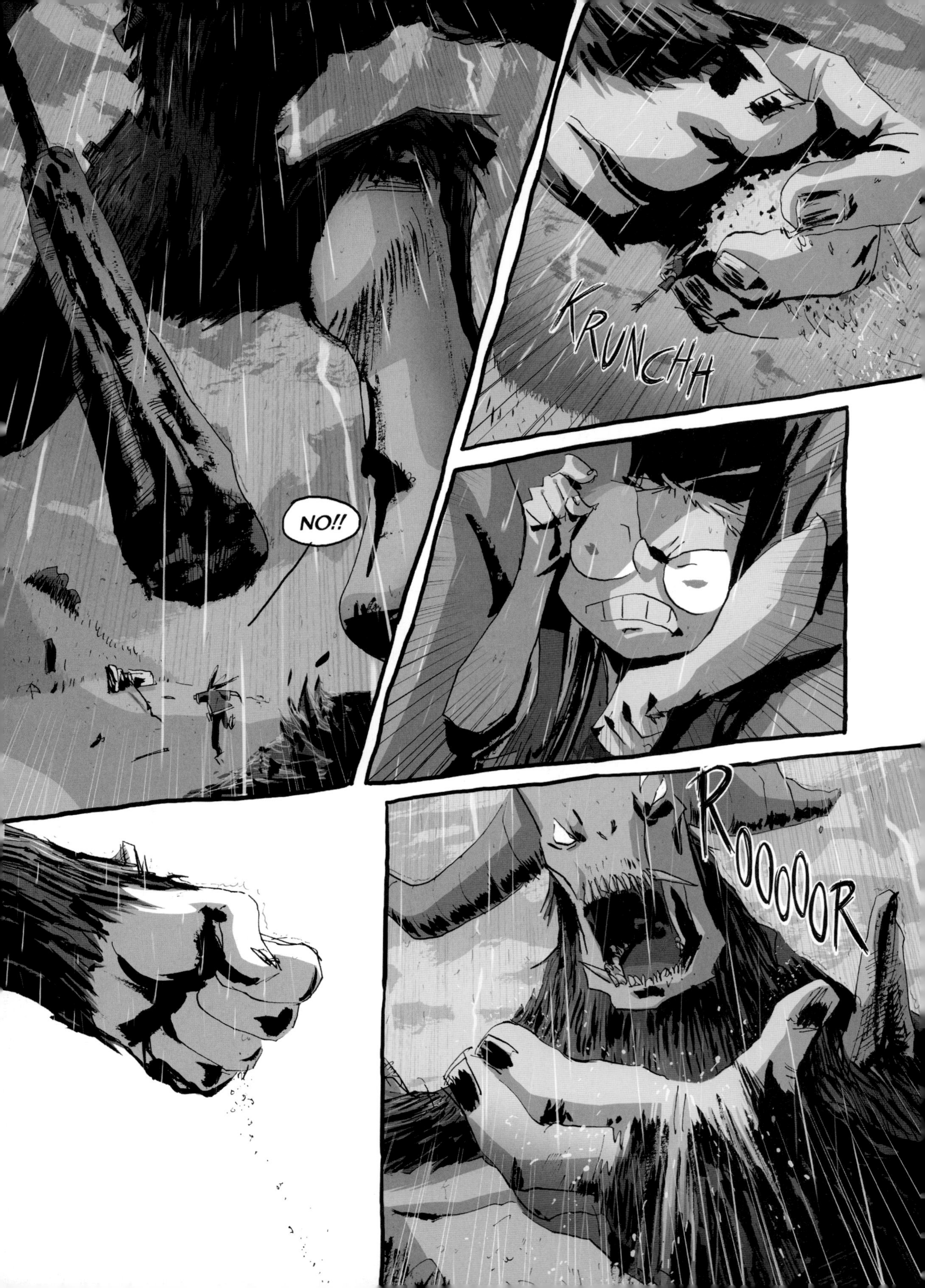
NO!!
KRUNCHH
ROOOOOOR

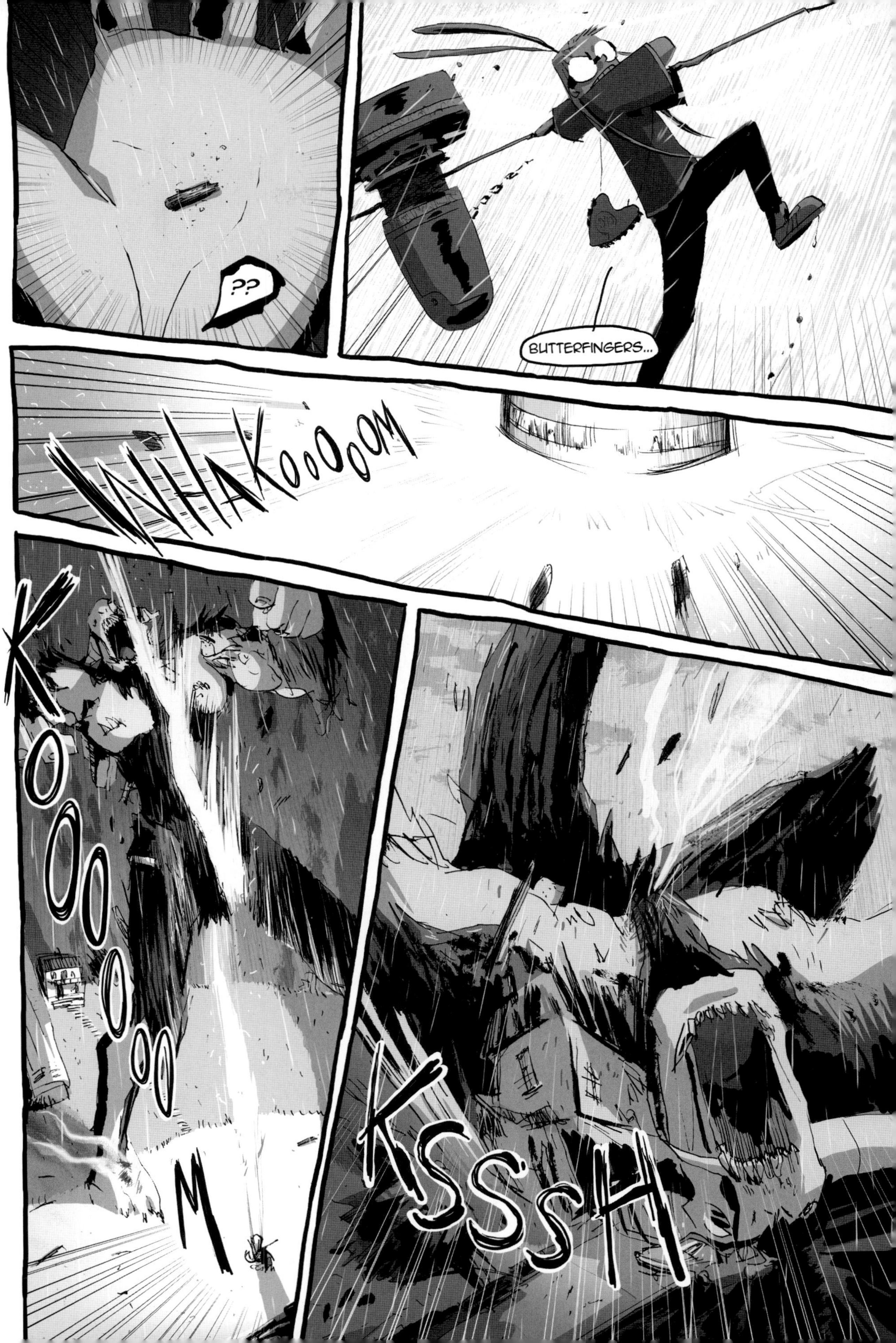
??
BUTTERFINGERS...
WHAKOOOOOM
KOOOOOOOOM
KSSSH

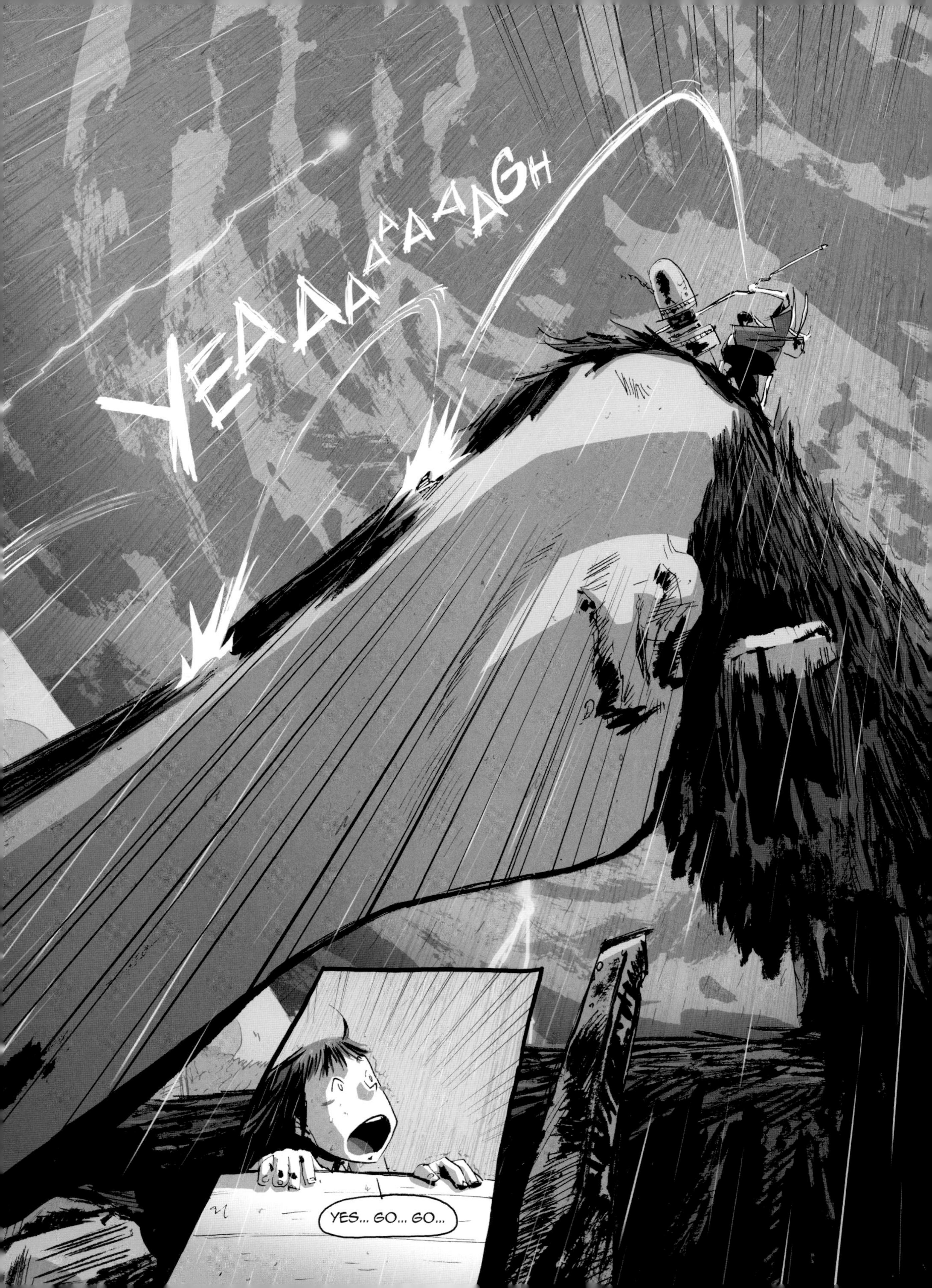
YEAAAAAAAGH
YES... GO... GO...

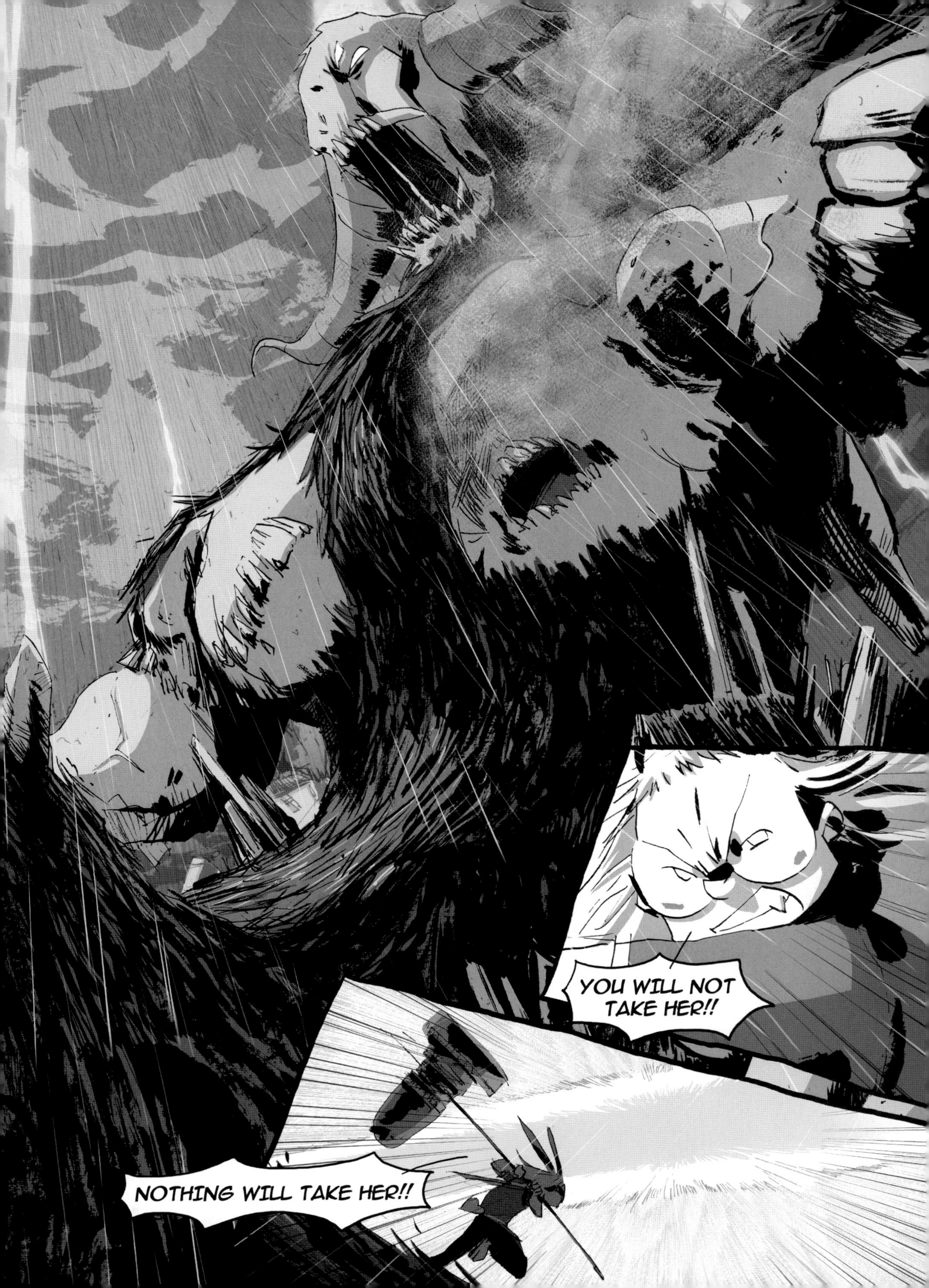
YOU WILL NOT TAKE HER!!
NOTHING WILL TAKE HER!!

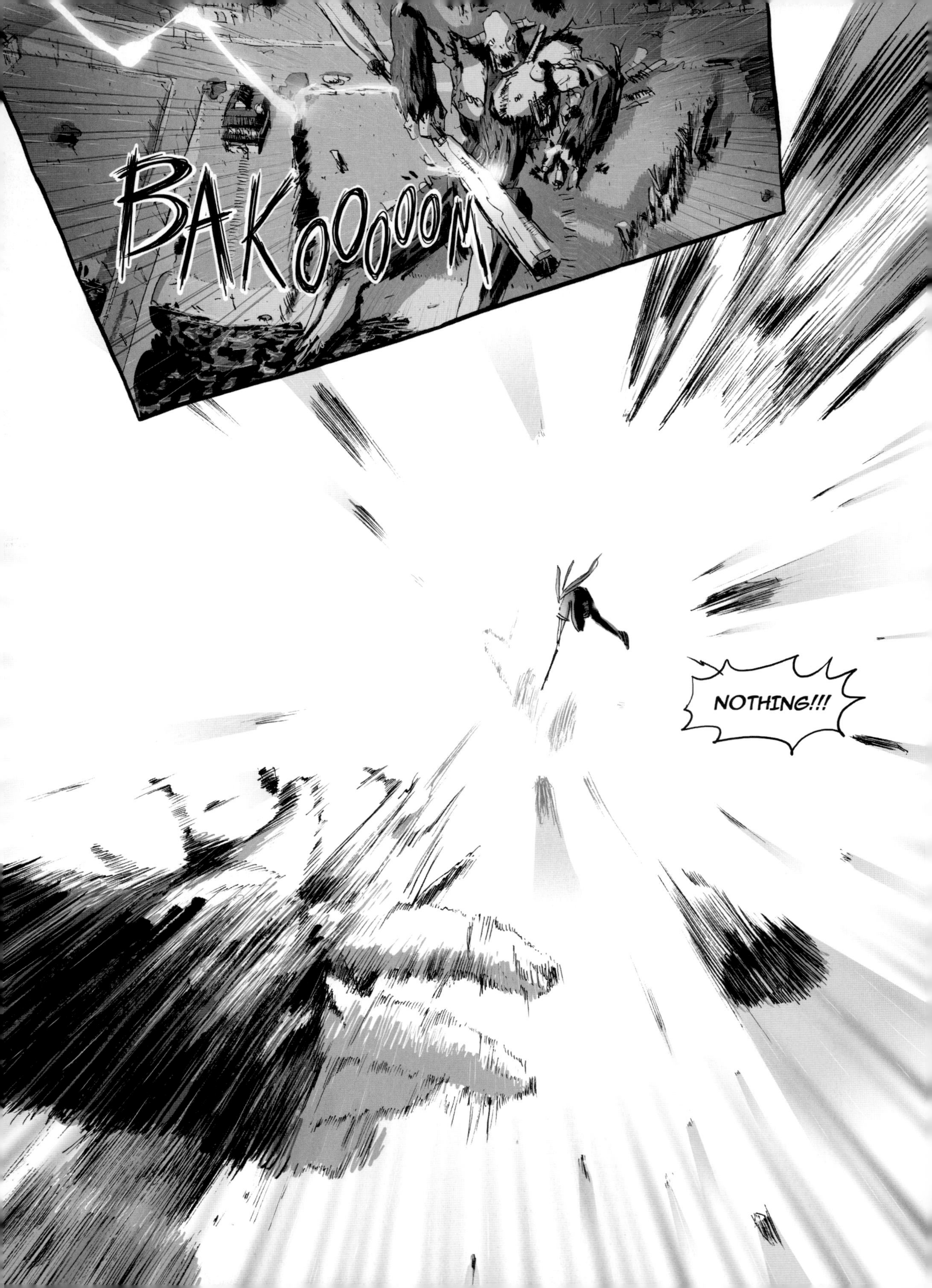
BAKOOOOOOM
NOTHING!!!

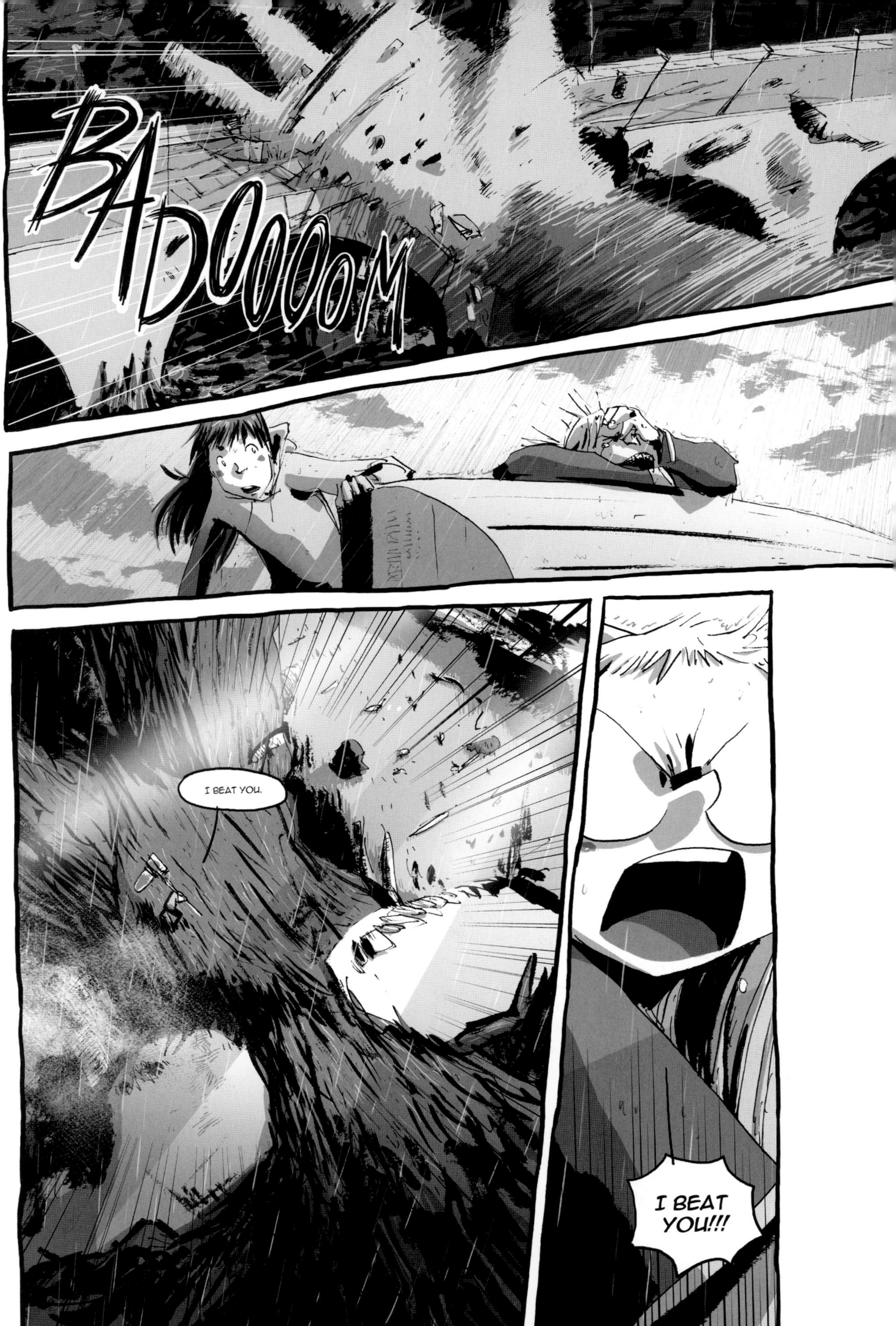
BADOOOOM
I BEAT YOU.
I BEAT YOU!!!

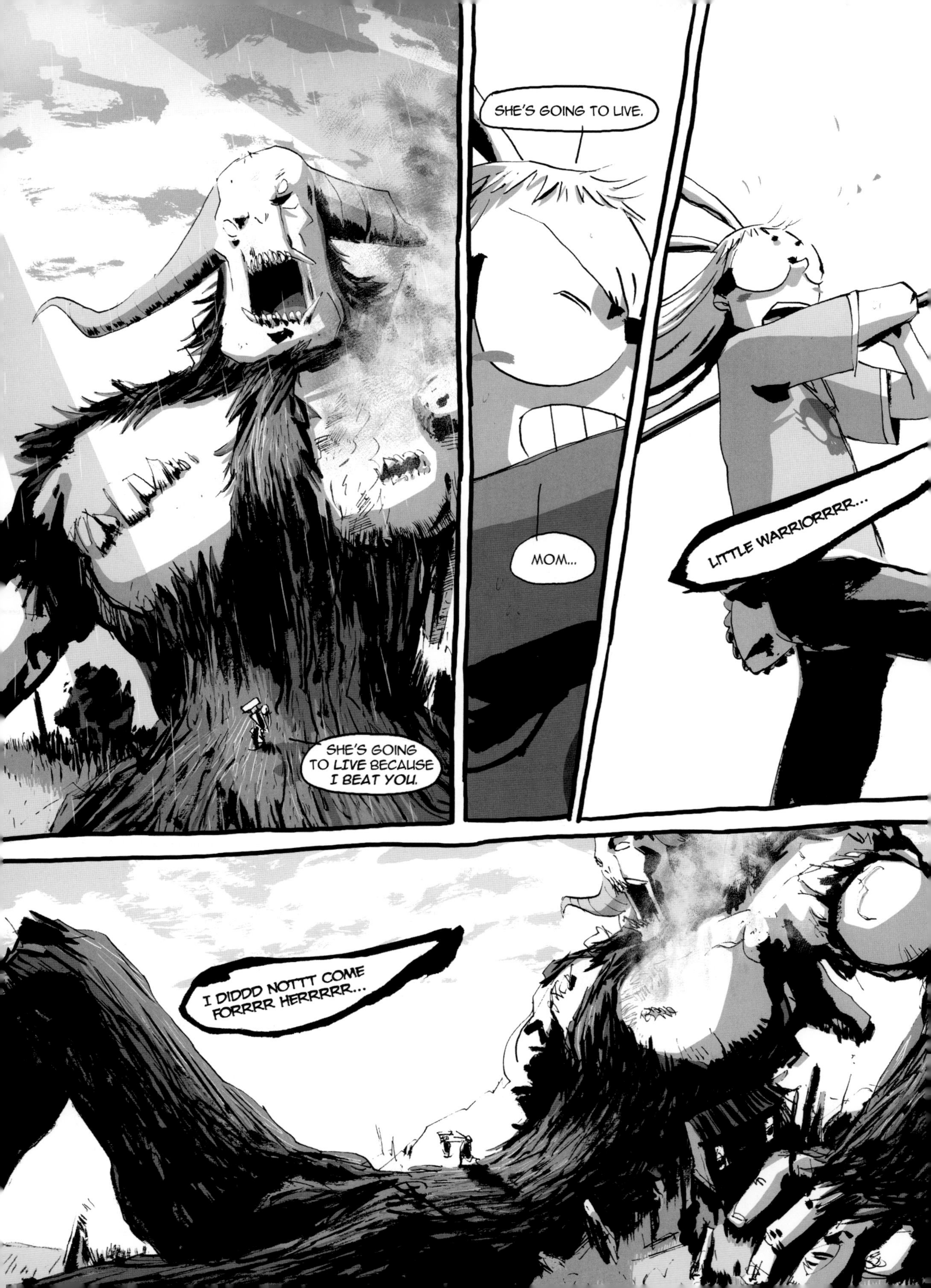
SHE'S GOING TO LIVE.
MOM...
LITTLE WARRIORRRR...
SHE'S GOING TO LIVE BECAUSE I BEAT YOU.
I DIDDD NOTTT COME FORRRR HERRRRR...

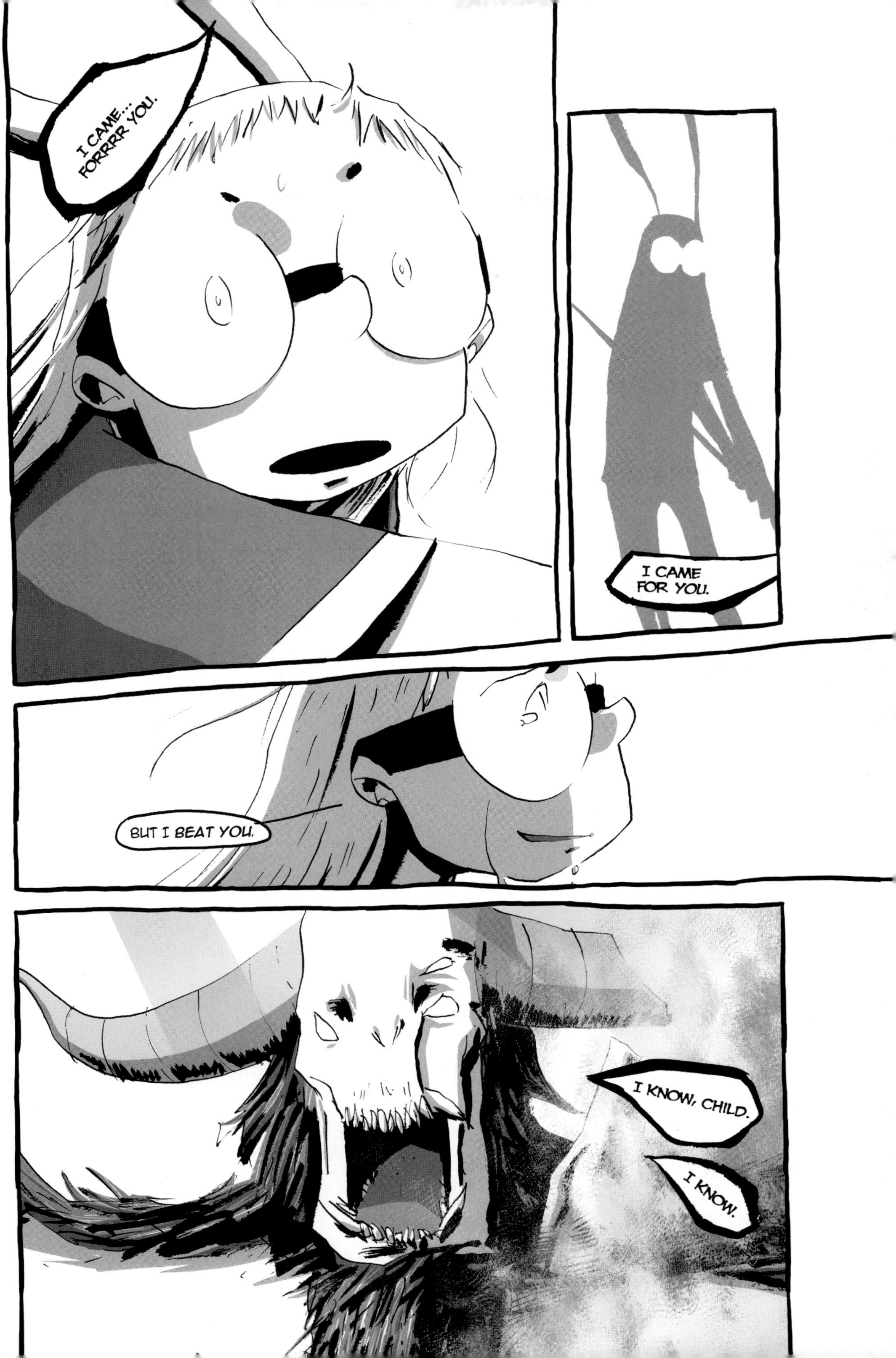
I CAME... FORRRR YOU.
I CAME FOR YOU.
BUT I BEAT YOU.
I KNOW, CHILD.
I KNOW.

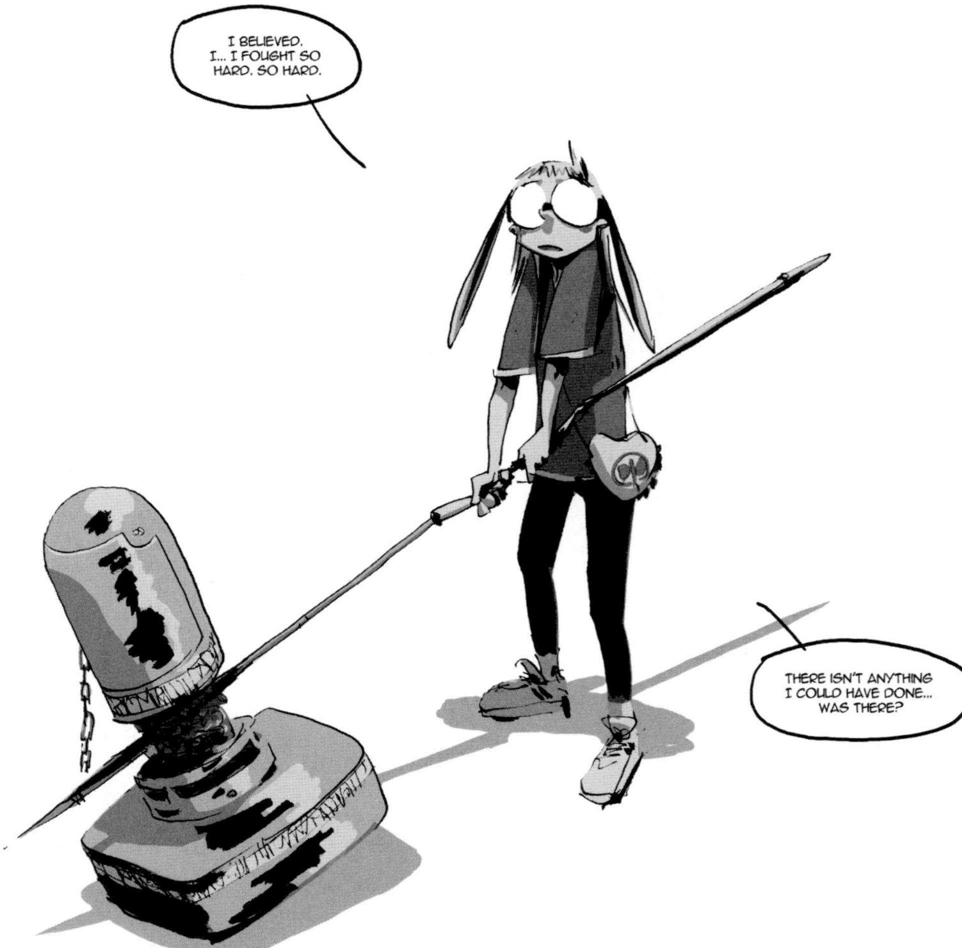
I BELIEVED.
I... I FOUGHT SO HARD. SO HARD.
THERE ISN'T ANYTHING I COULD HAVE DONE... WAS THERE?

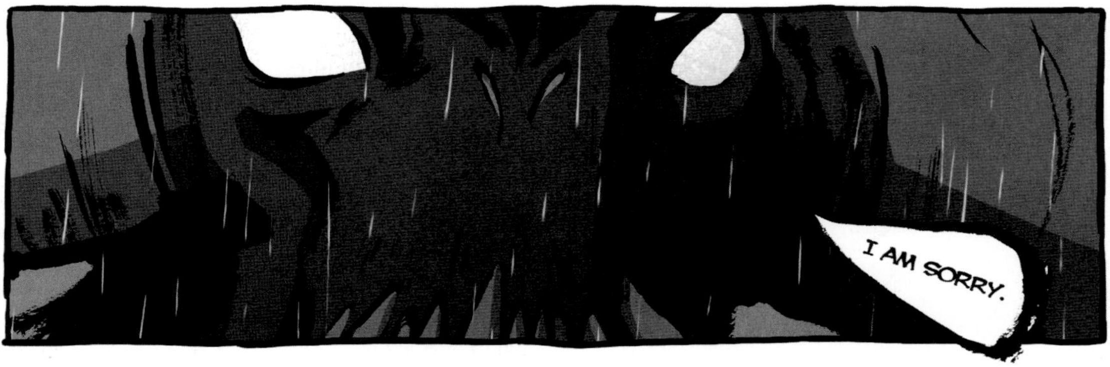
I AM SORRY.

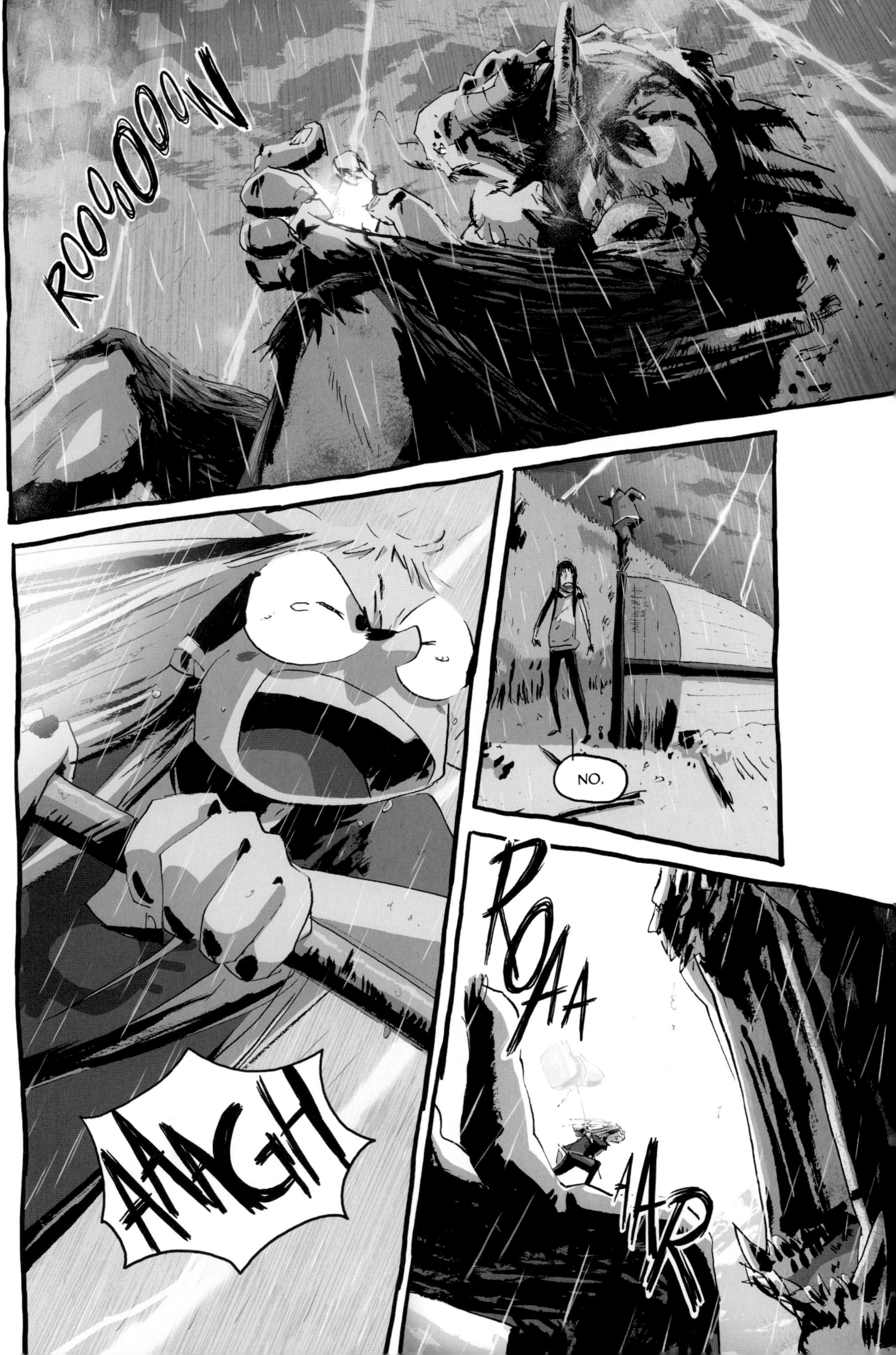
ROOOOOOW
NO.
AAAGH
ROAAAAR

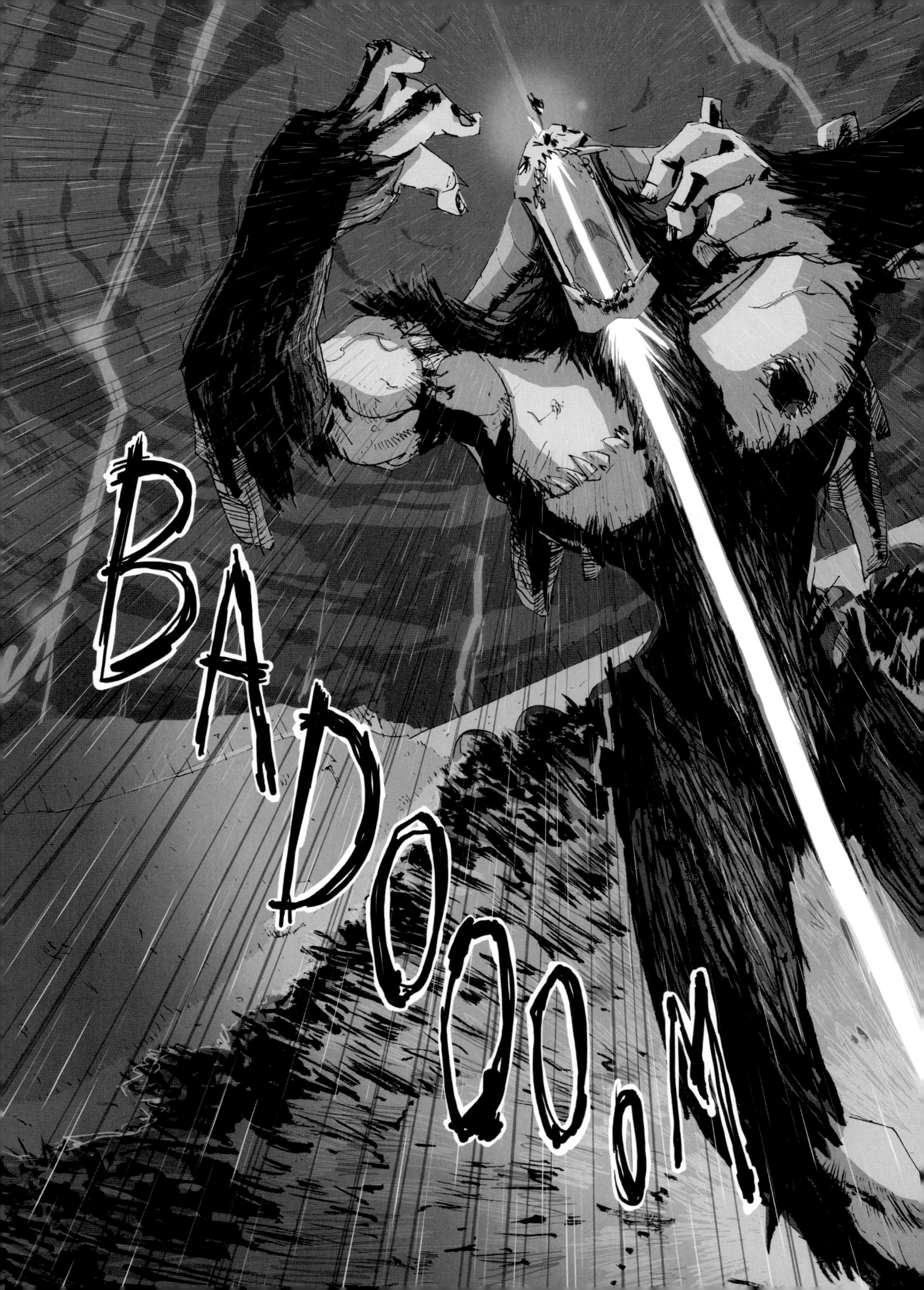
BADOOOoM

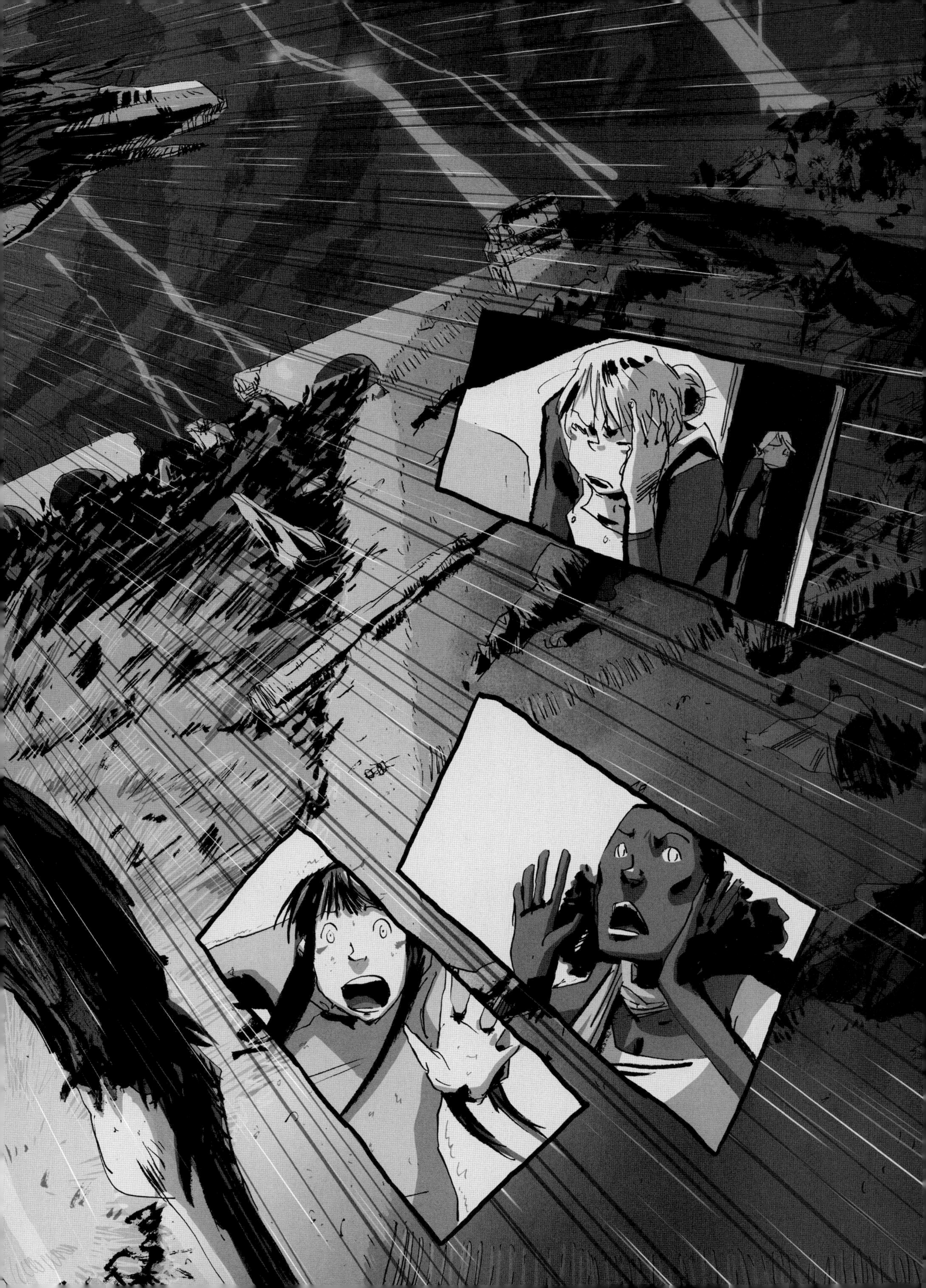

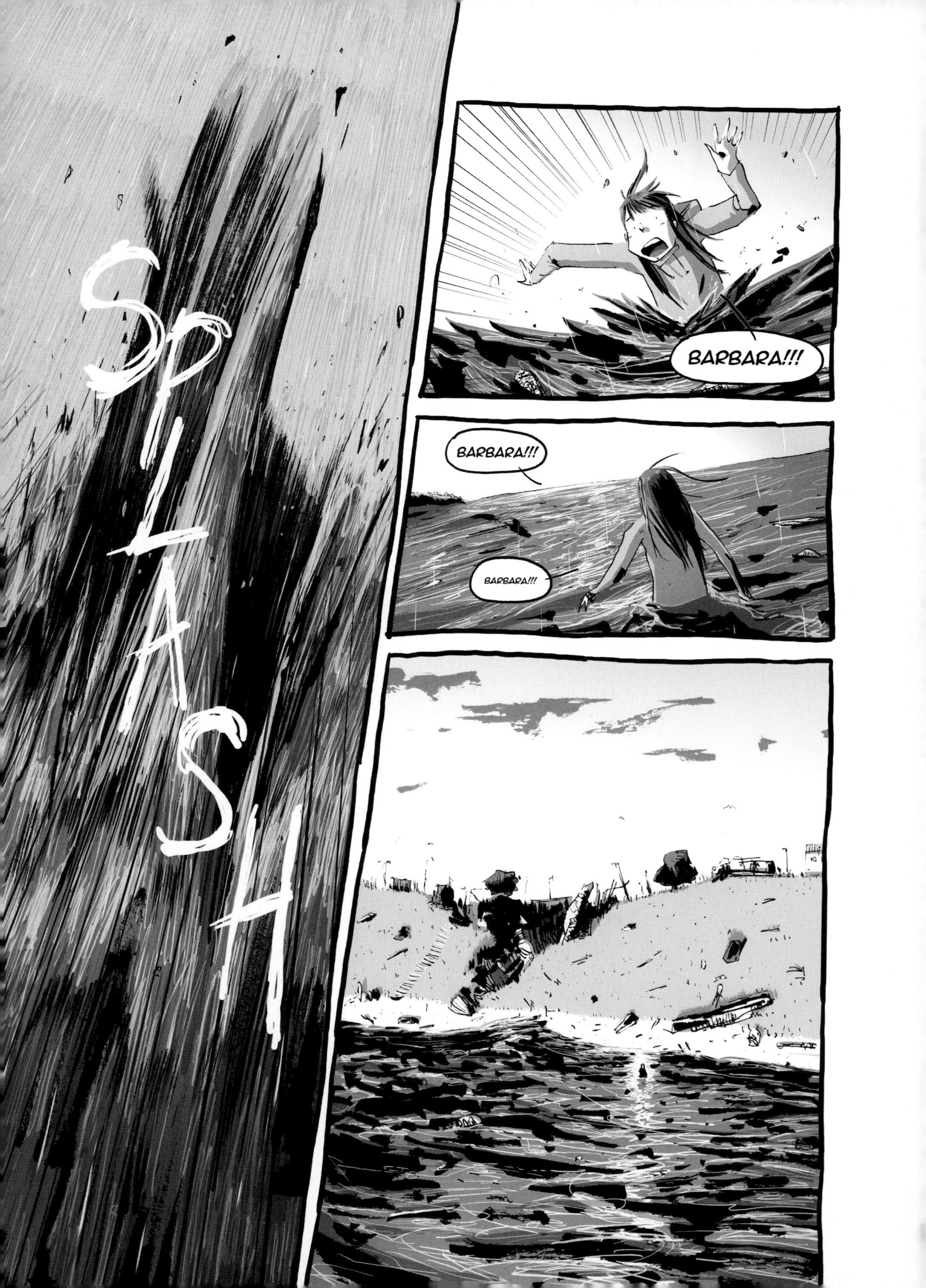
SPLASH
BARBARA!!!
BARBARA!!!
BARBARA!!!

CHAPTER**7:** THE END

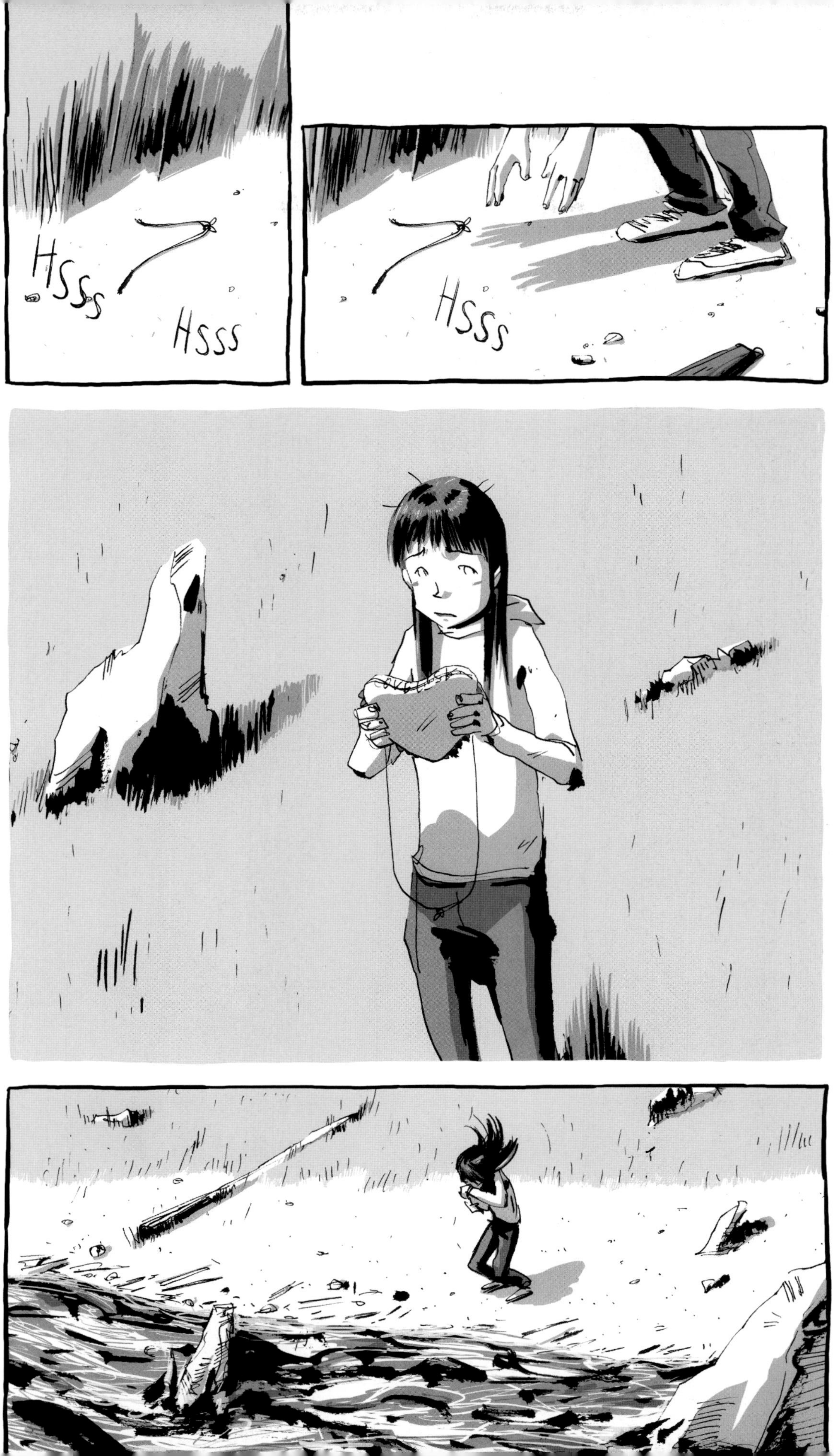
Hssss
Hsss
Hssss

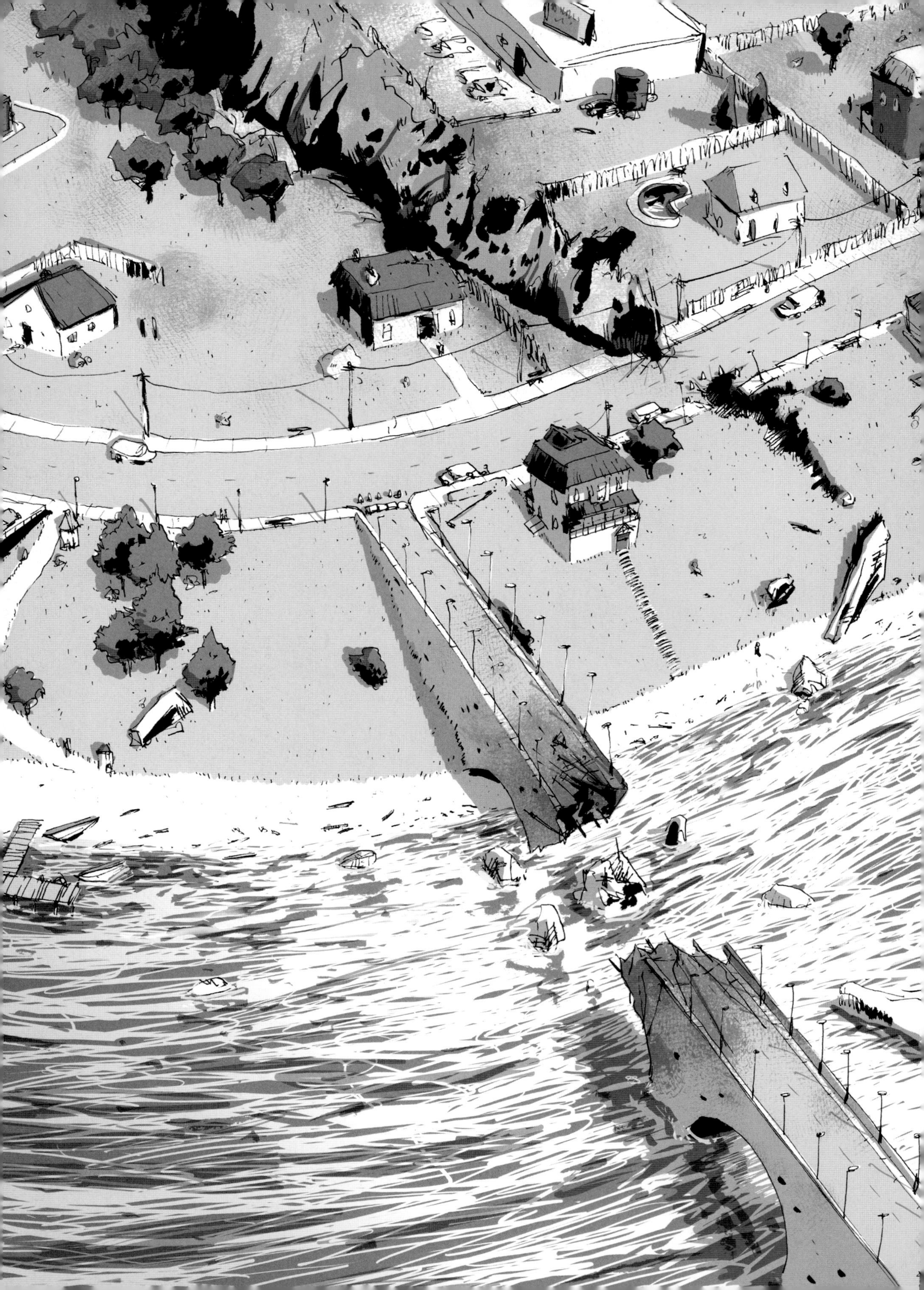

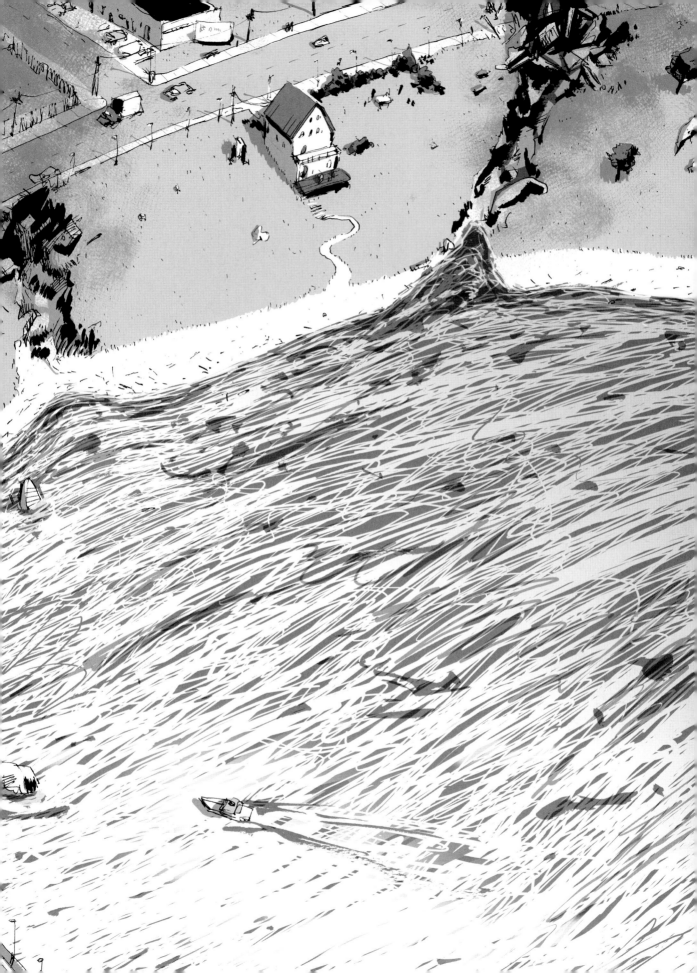

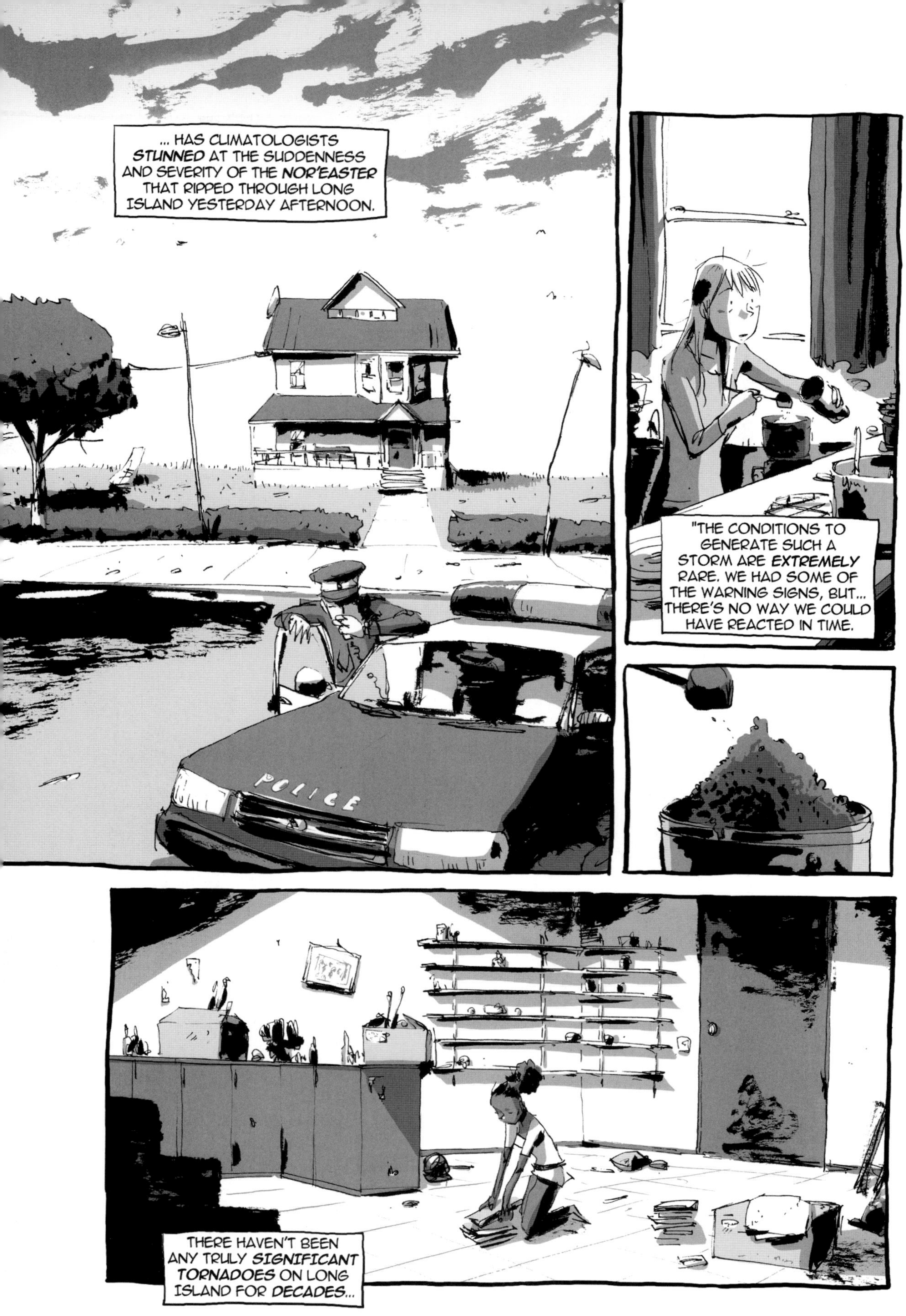
... HAS CLIMATOLOGISTS STUNNED AT THE SUDDENNESS AND SEVERITY OF THE NOR'EASTER THAT RIPPED THROUGH LONG ISLAND YESTERDAY AFTERNOON.
POLICE
"THE CONDITIONS TO GENERATE SUCH A STORM ARE EXTREMELY RARE. WE HAD SOME OF THE WARNING SIGNS, BUT... THERE'S NO WAY WE COULD HAVE REACTED IN TIME.
THERE HAVEN'T BEEN ANY TRULY SIGNIFICANT TORNADOES ON LONG ISLAND FOR DECADES...

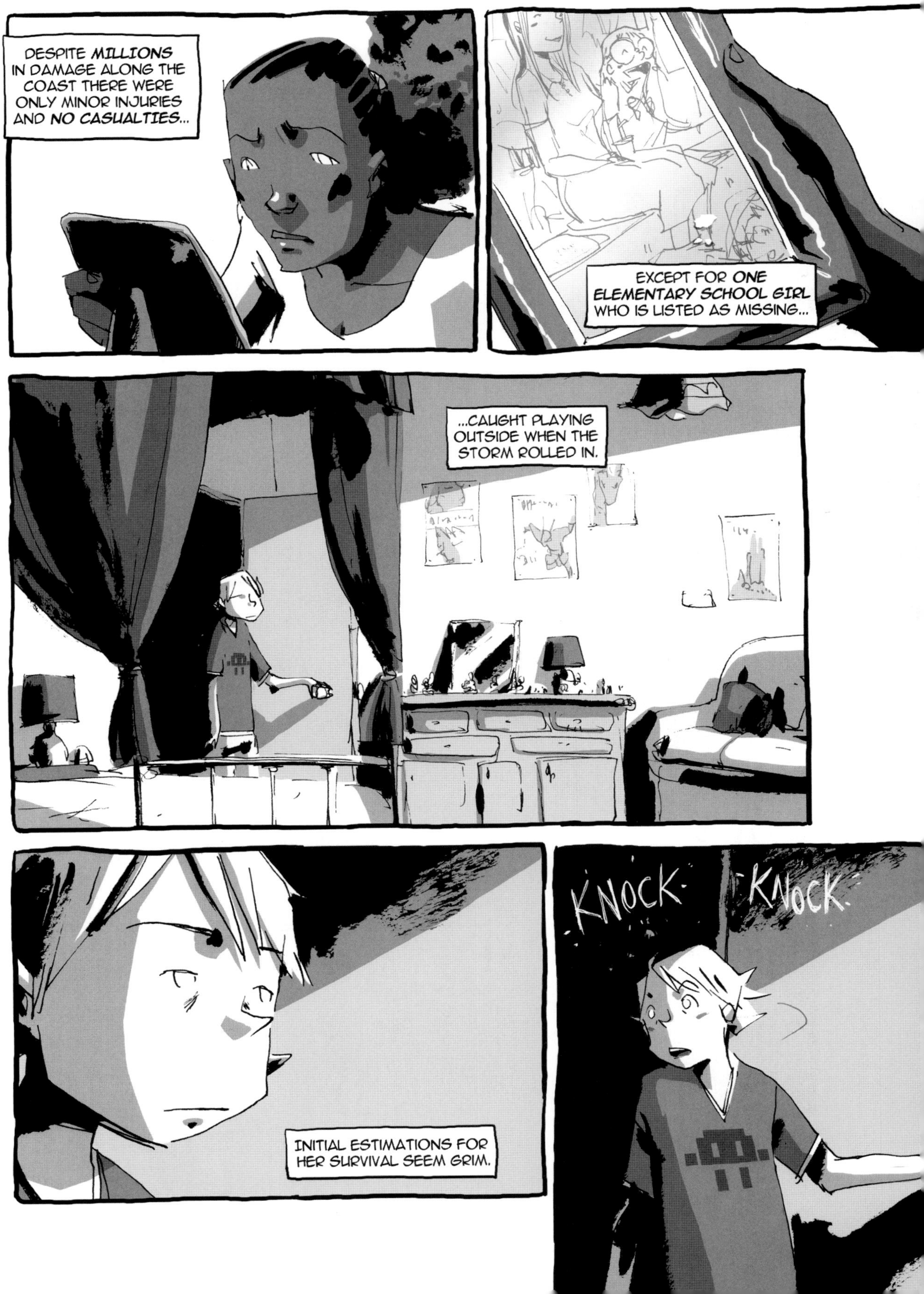
DESPITE MILLIONS IN DAMAGE ALONG THE COAST THERE WERE ONLY MINOR INJURIES AND NO CASUALTIES...
EXCEPT FOR ONE ELEMENTARY SCHOOL GIRL WHO IS LISTED AS MISSING...
...CAUGHT PLAYING OUTSIDE WHEN THE STORM ROLLED IN.
INITIAL ESTIMATIONS FOR HER SURVIVAL SEEM GRIM.
KNOCK
KNOCK

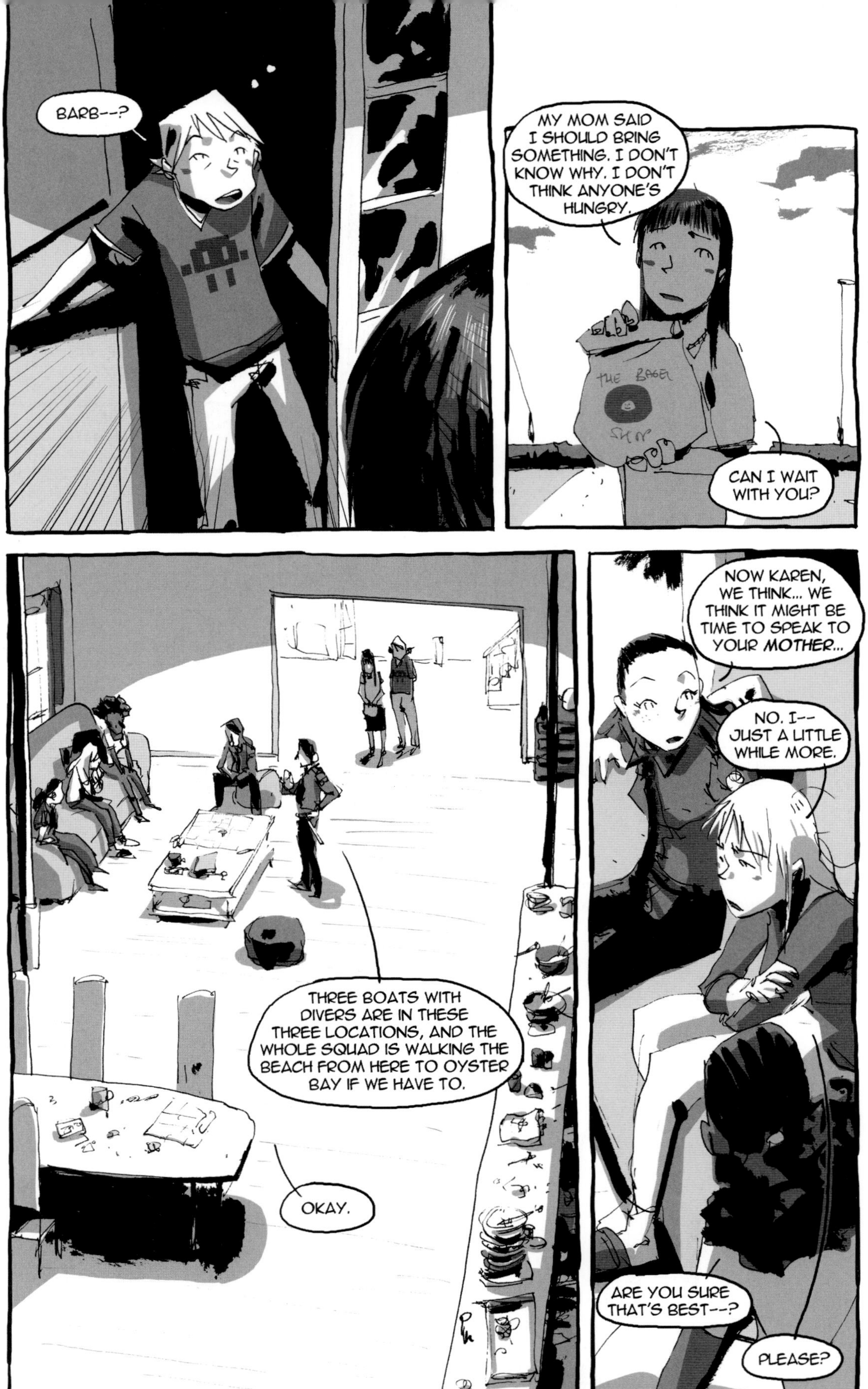
BARB--?
MY MOM SAID I SHOULD BRING SOMETHING. I DON'T KNOW WHY. I DON'T THINK ANYONE'S HUNGRY.
THE BAGEL SHOP
CAN I WAIT WITH YOU?
THREE BOATS WITH DIVERS ARE IN THESE THREE LOCATIONS, AND THE WHOLE SQUAD IS WALKING THE BEACH FROM HERE TO OYSTER BAY IF WE HAVE TO.
OKAY.
NOW KAREN, WE THINK... WE THINK IT MIGHT BE TIME TO SPEAK TO YOUR **MOTHER**...
NO. I-- JUST A LITTLE WHILE MORE.
ARE YOU SURE THAT'S BEST--?
PLEASE?

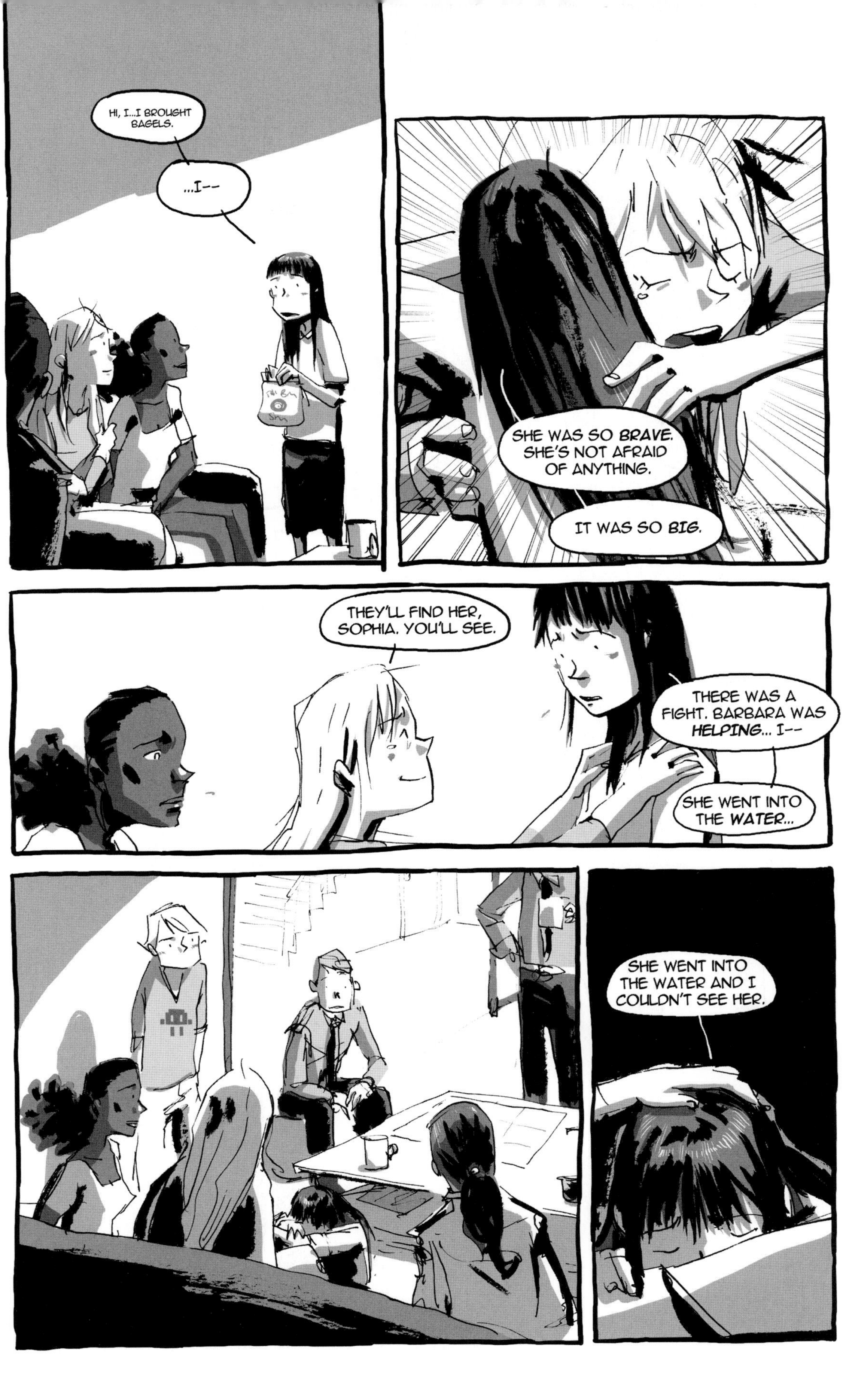
HI, I...I BROUGHT BAGELS.
...I--
SHE WAS SO BRAVE. SHE'S NOT AFRAID OF ANYTHING.
IT WAS SO BIG.
THEY'LL FIND HER, SOPHIA. YOU'LL SEE.
THERE WAS A FIGHT. BARBARA WAS HELPING... I--
SHE WENT INTO THE WATER...
SHE WENT INTO THE WATER AND I COULDN'T SEE HER.

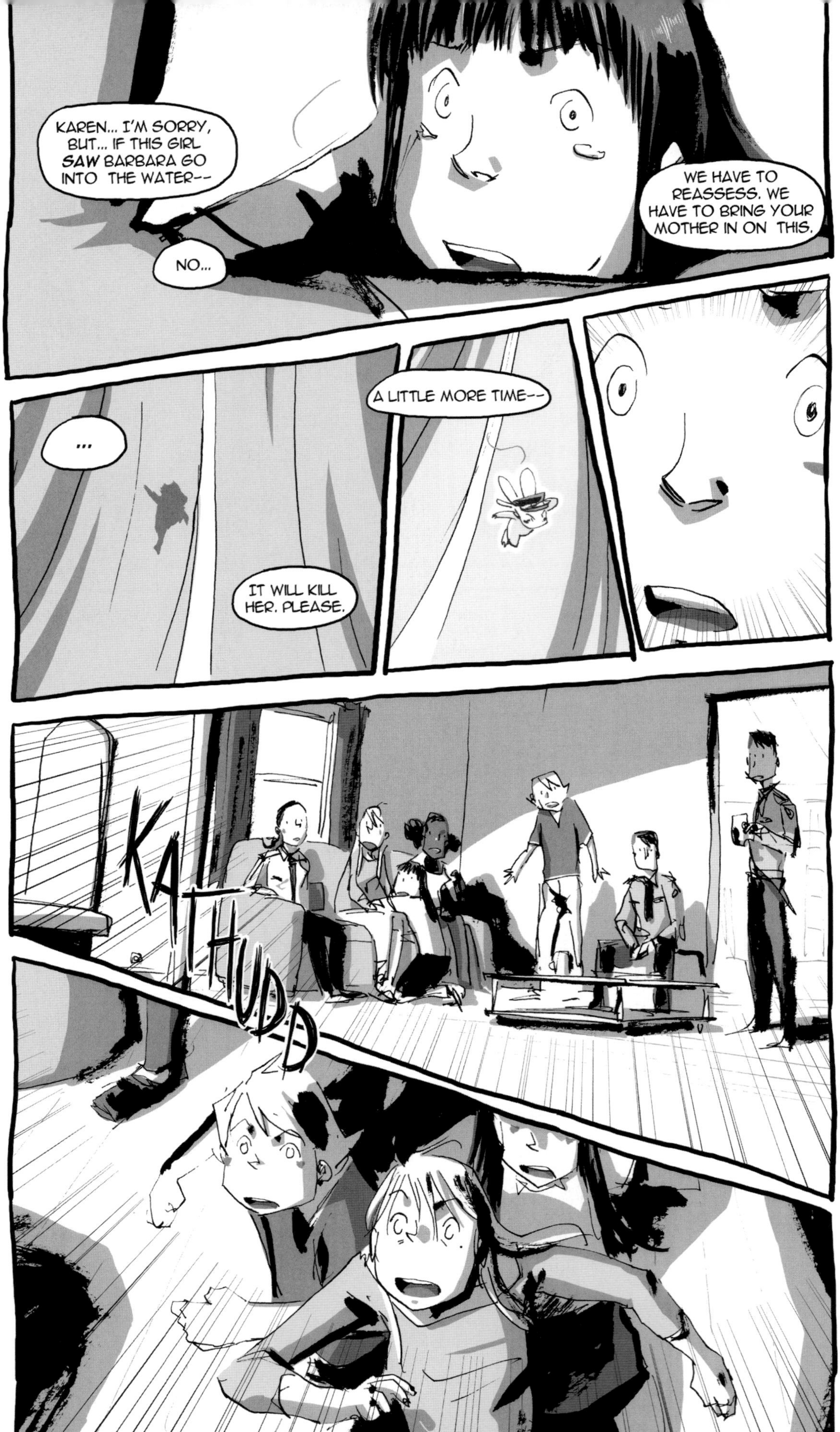
KAREN... I'M SORRY, BUT... IF THIS GIRL SAW BARBARA GO INTO THE WATER--
NO...
WE HAVE TO REASSESS. WE HAVE TO BRING YOUR MOTHER IN ON THIS.
...
IT WILL KILL HER. PLEASE.
A LITTLE MORE TIME--
KATHUDD

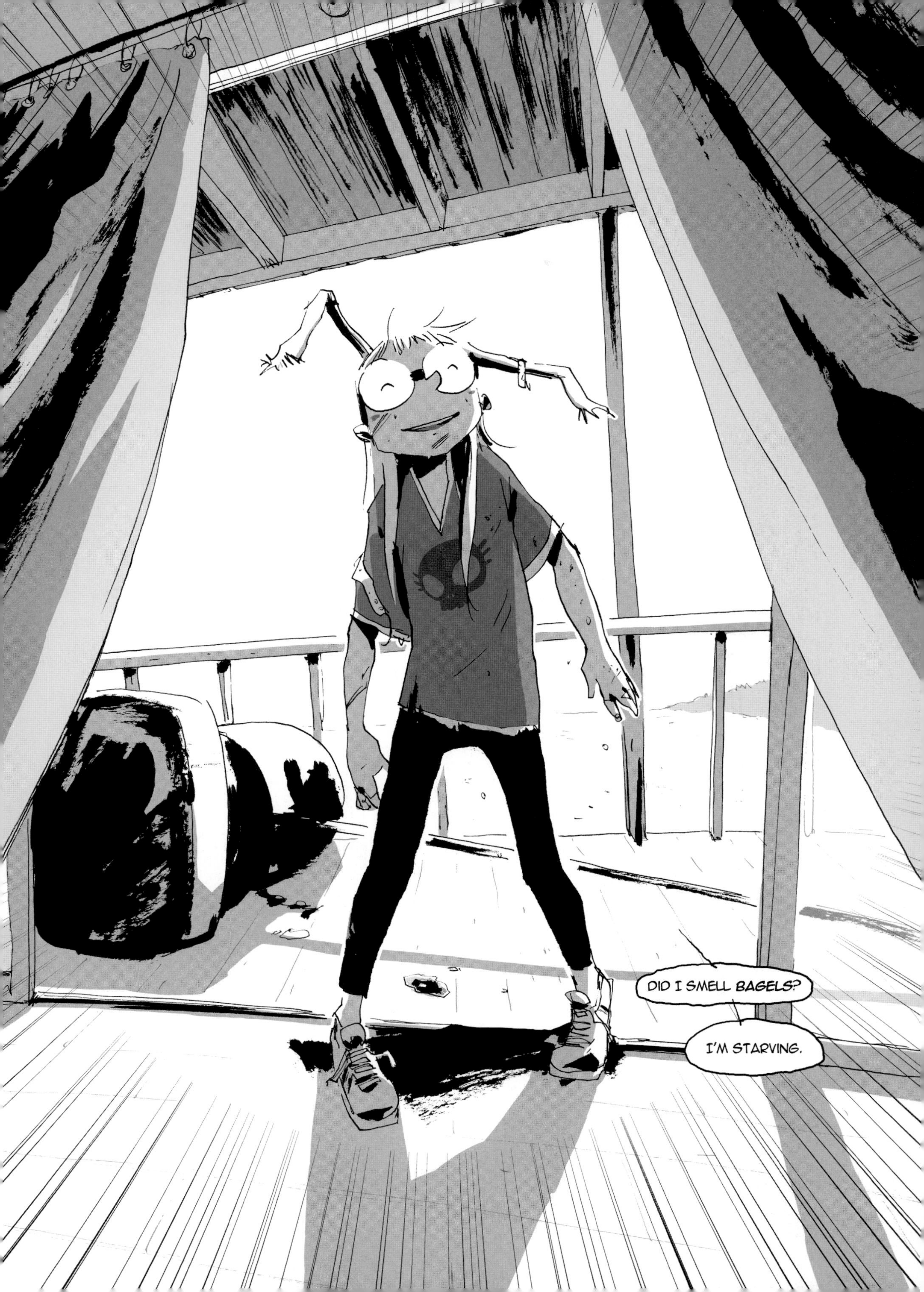
DID I SMELL BAGELS?
I'M STARVING.

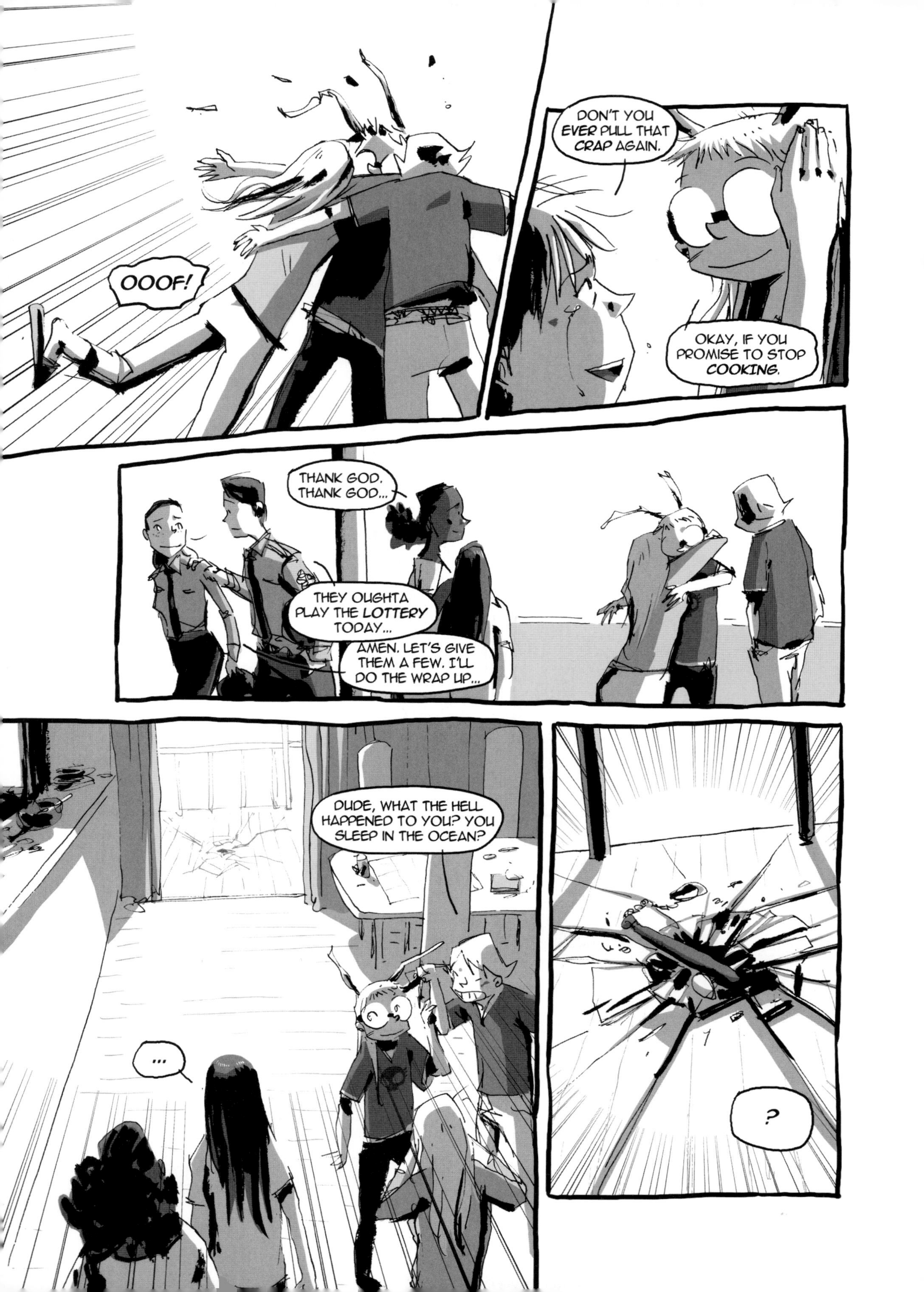

OOOF!
DON'T YOU EVER PULL THAT CRAP AGAIN.
OKAY, IF YOU PROMISE TO STOP COOKING.
THANK GOD. THANK GOD...
THEY OUGHTA PLAY THE LOTTERY TODAY...
AMEN. LET'S GIVE THEM A FEW. I'LL DO THE WRAP UP...
DUDE, WHAT THE HELL HAPPENED TO YOU? YOU SLEEP IN THE OCEAN?
...
?

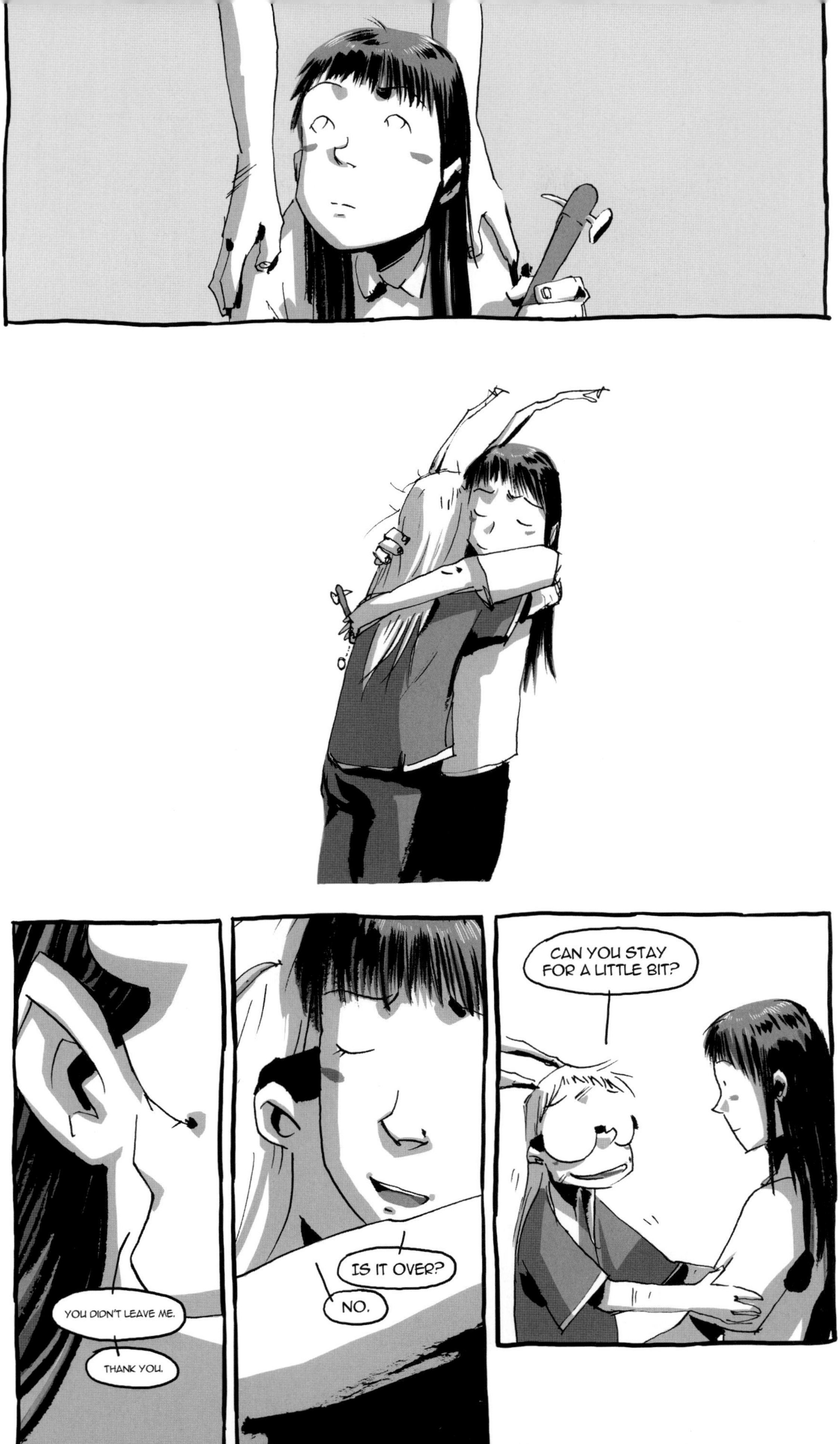
YOU DIDN'T LEAVE ME.
THANK YOU.
IS IT OVER?
NO.
CAN YOU STAY FOR A LITTLE BIT?

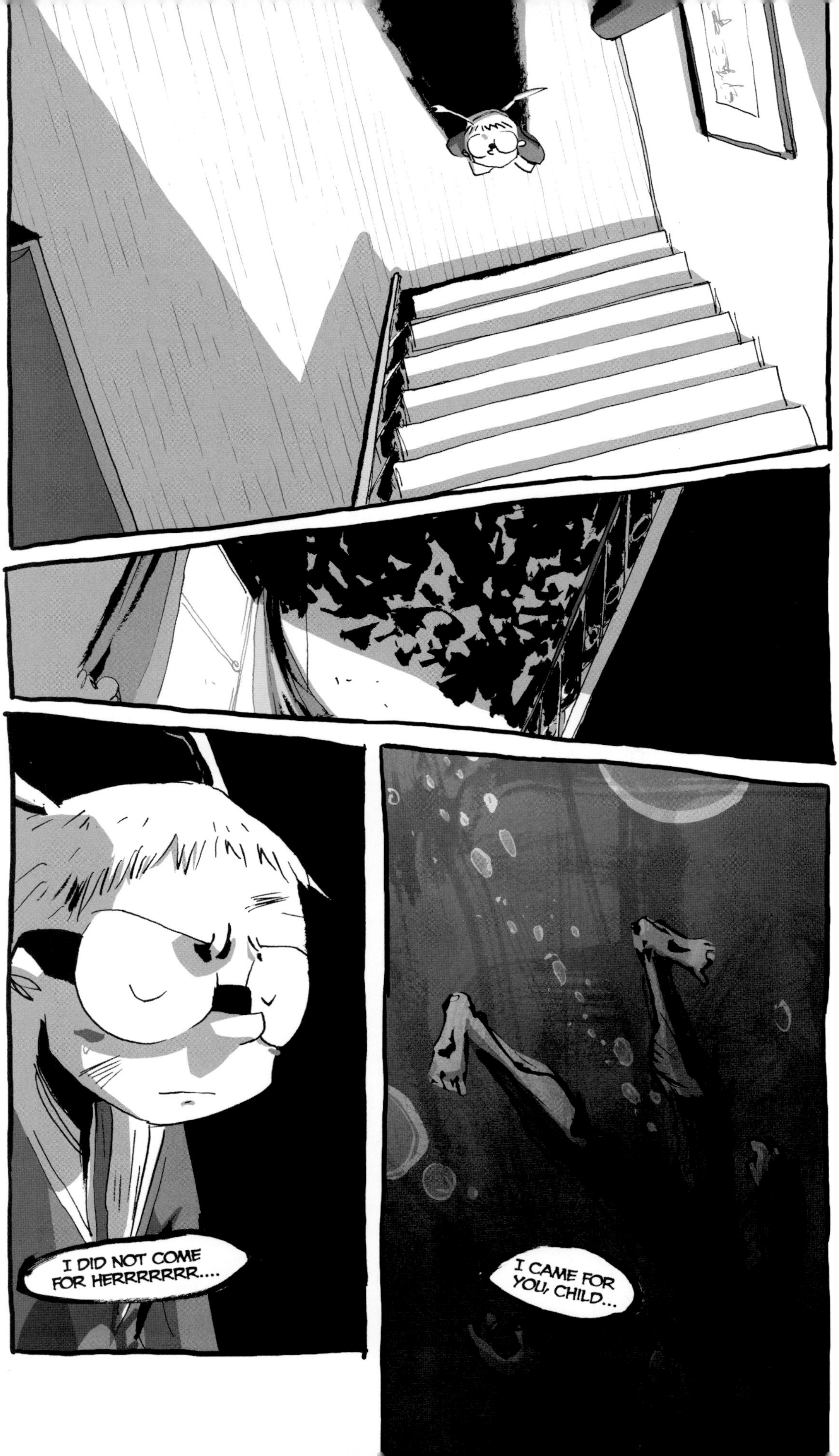
I DID NOT COME FOR HERRRRRRR....
I CAME FOR YOU, CHILD...

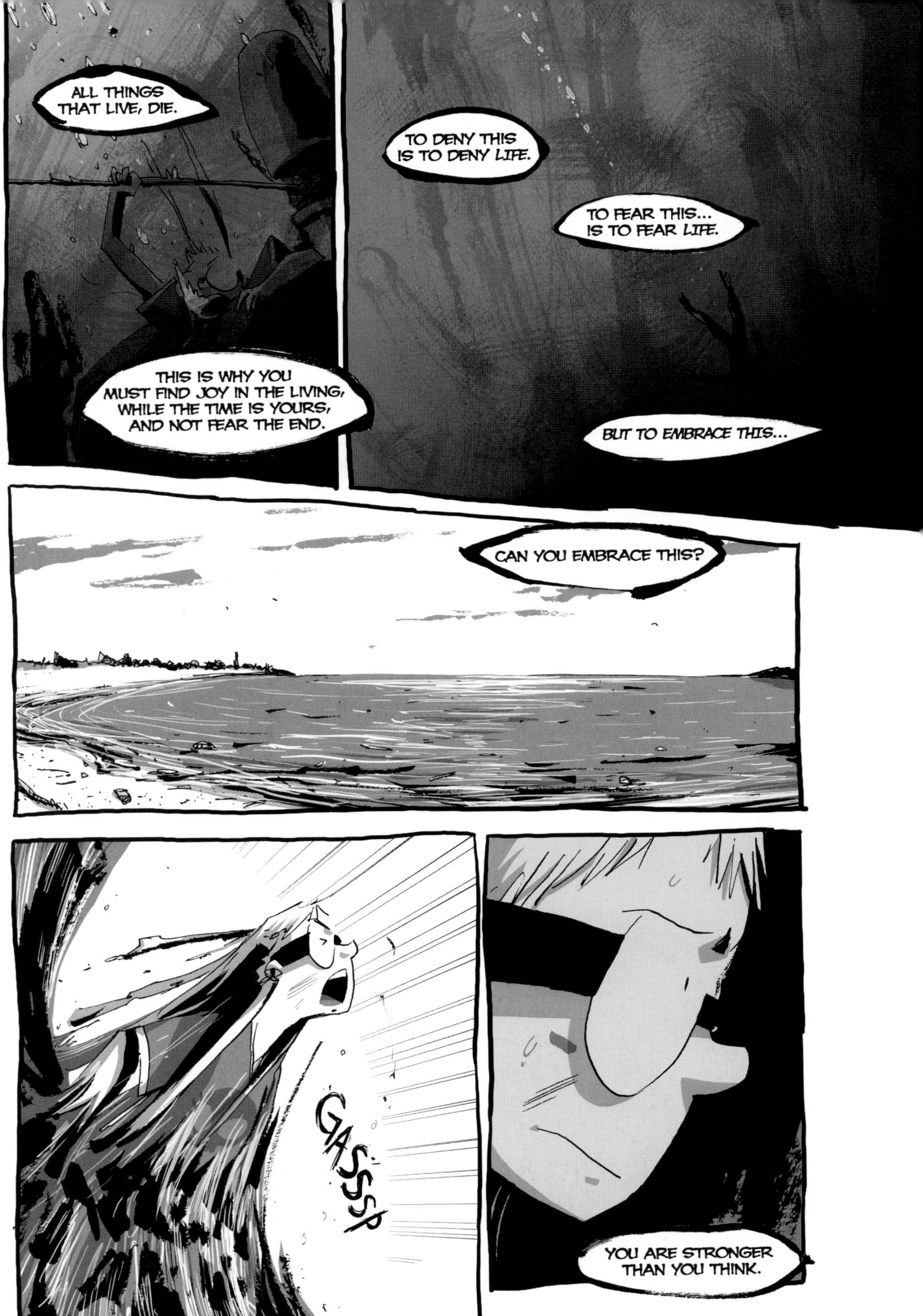
ALL THINGS THAT LIVE, DIE.
TO DENY THIS IS TO DENY LIFE.
TO FEAR THIS... IS TO FEAR LIFE.
THIS IS WHY YOU MUST FIND JOY IN THE LIVING, WHILE THE TIME IS YOURS, AND NOT FEAR THE END.
BUT TO EMBRACE THIS...
CAN YOU EMBRACE THIS?
GASSSP
YOU ARE STRONGER THAN YOU THINK.

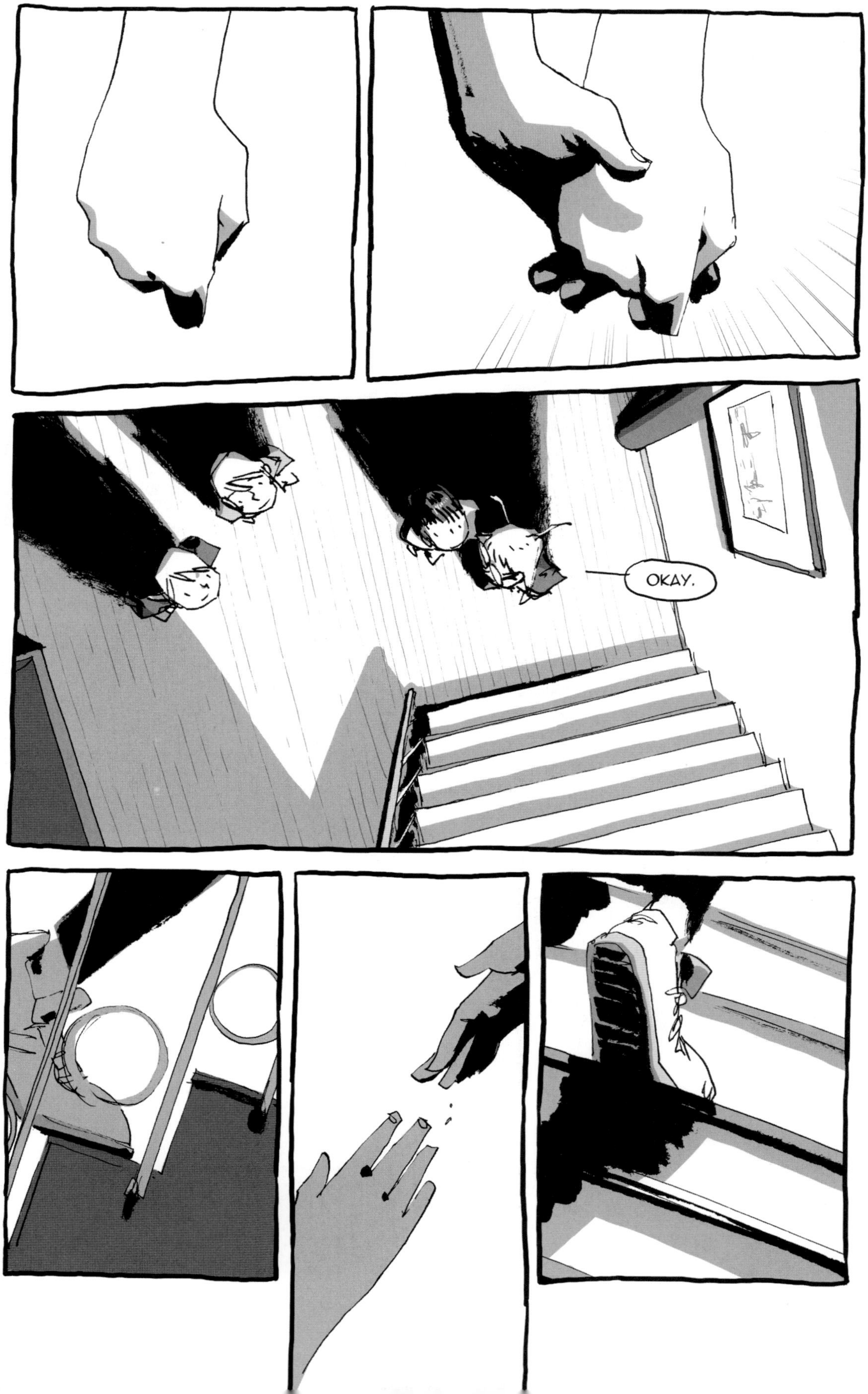
OKAY.

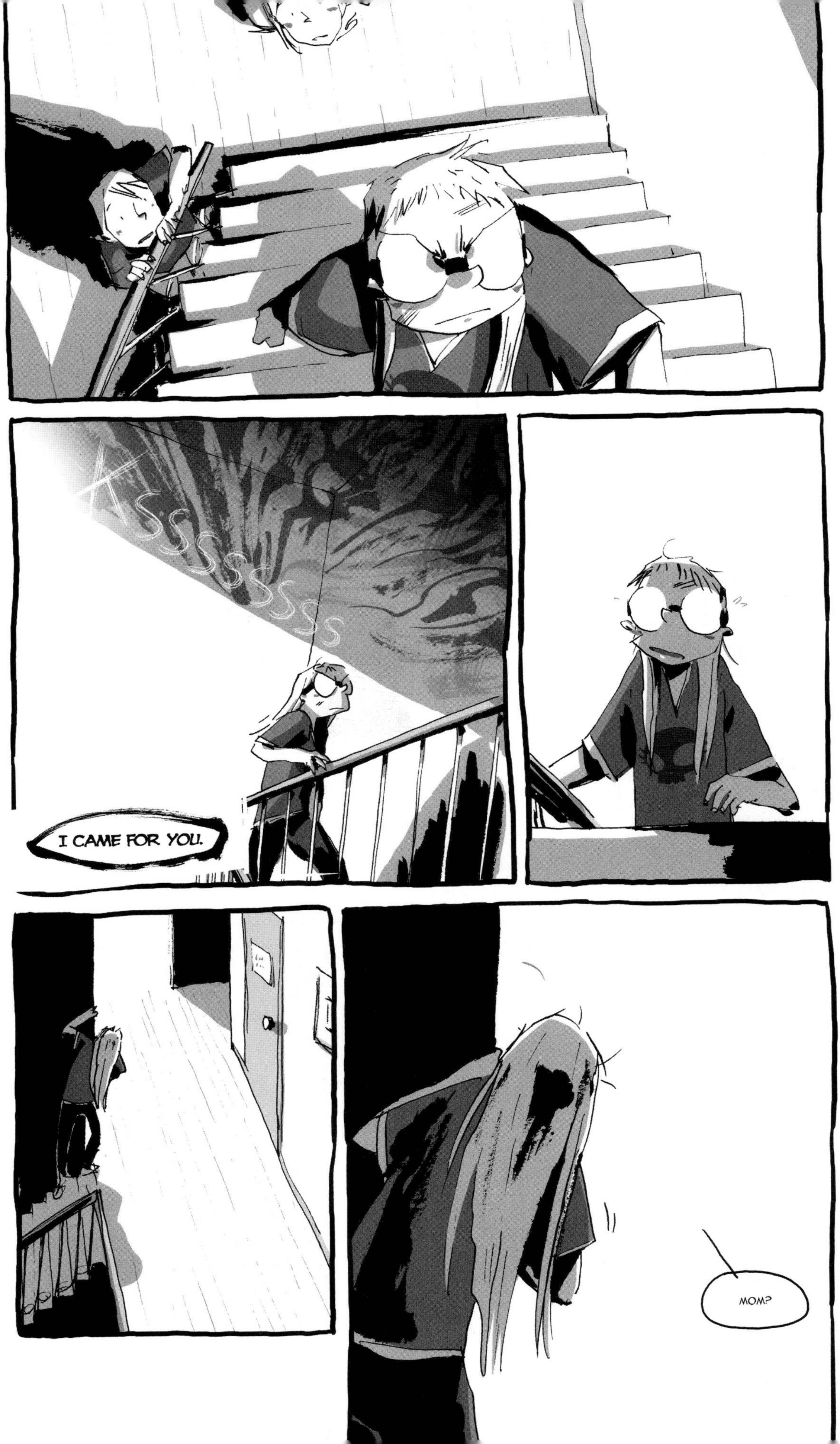
SSSSSSSSSS
I CAME FOR YOU.
MOM?

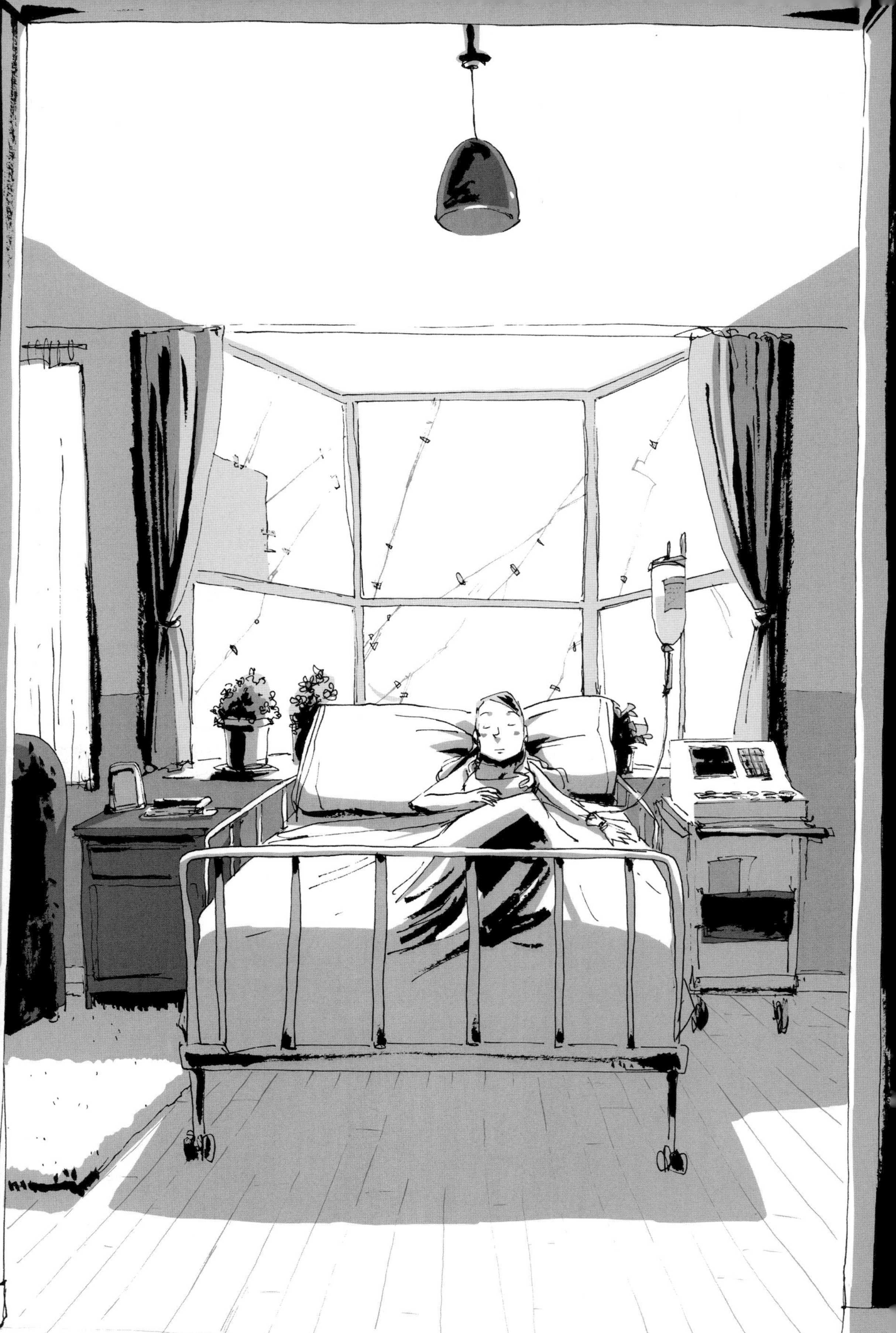

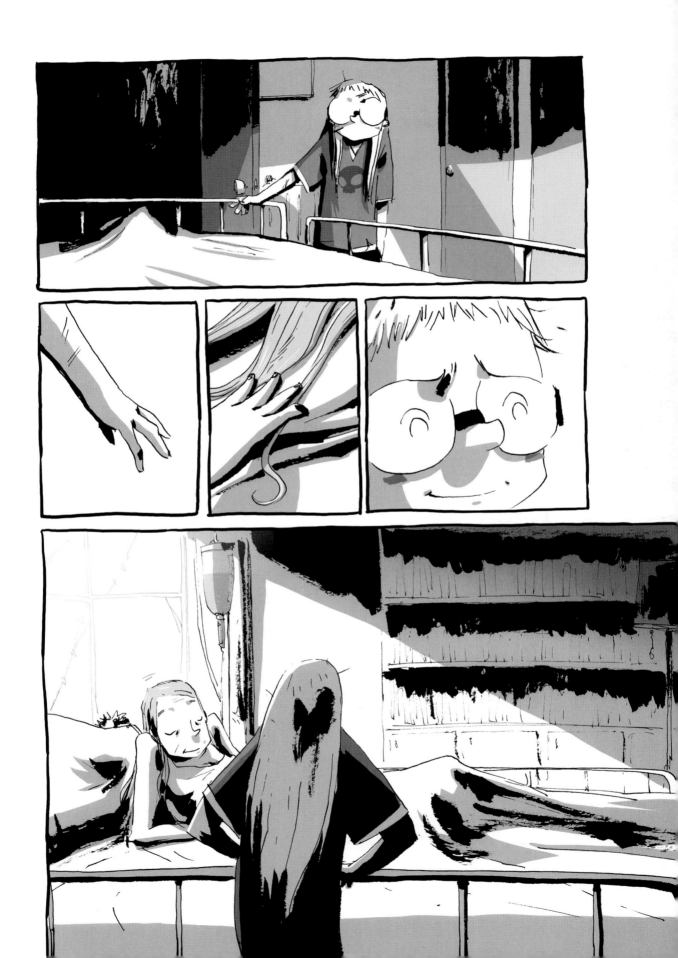

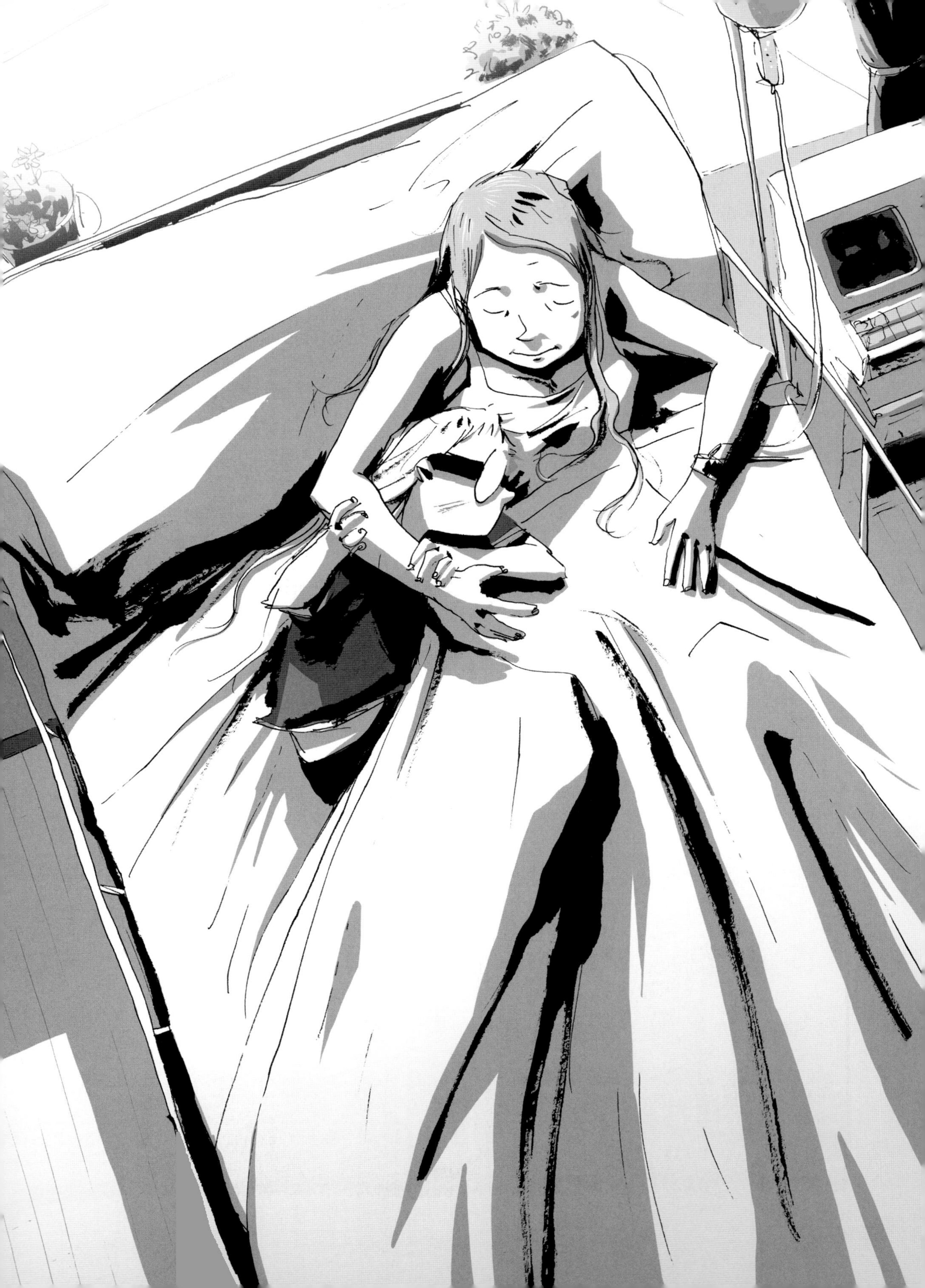

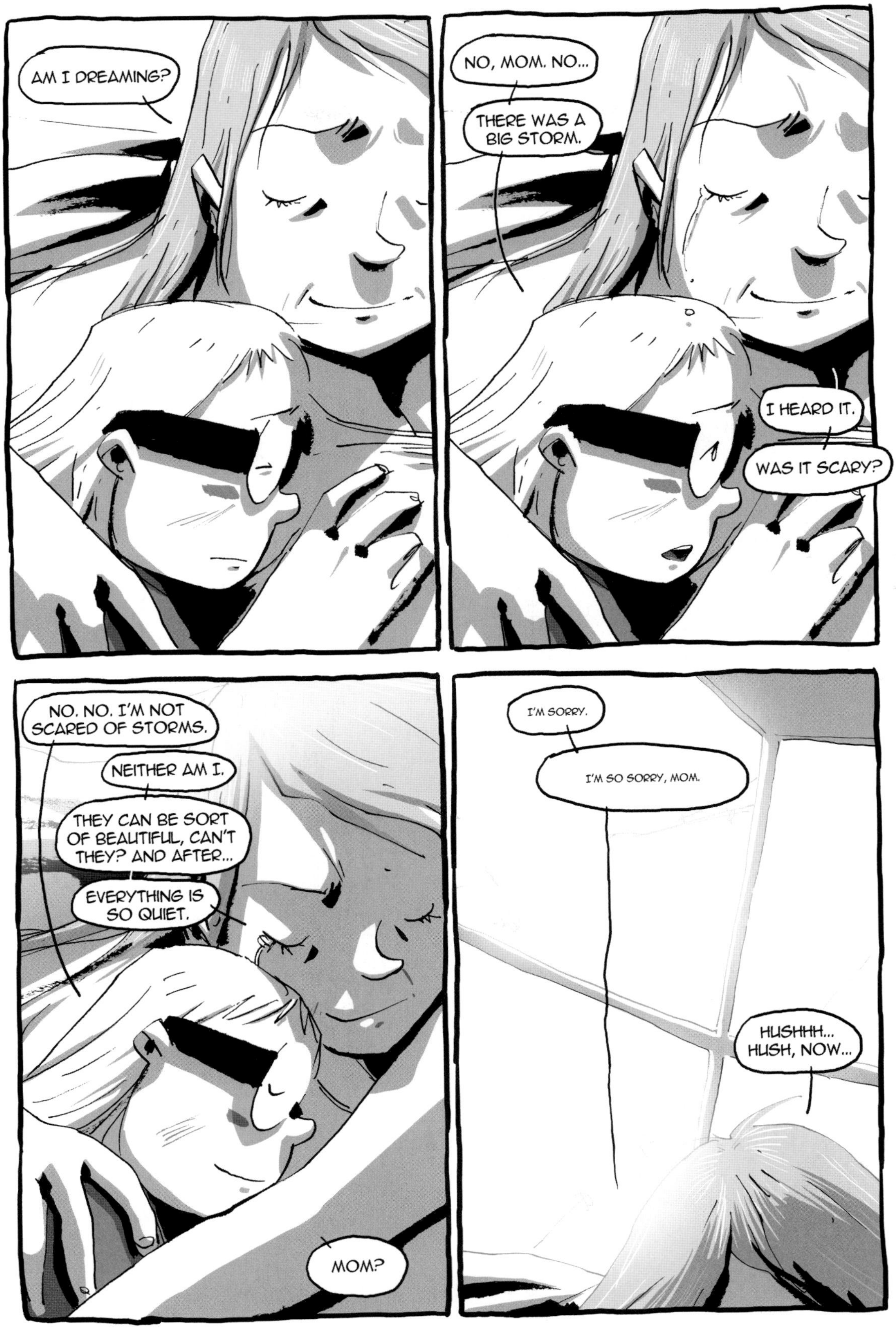
AM I DREAMING?
NO, MOM. NO...
THERE WAS A BIG STORM.
I HEARD IT.
WAS IT SCARY?
NO. NO. I'M NOT SCARED OF STORMS.
NEITHER AM I.
THEY CAN BE SORT OF BEAUTIFUL, CAN'T THEY? AND AFTER...
EVERYTHING IS SO QUIET.
MOM?
I'M SORRY.
I'M SO SORRY, MOM.
HUSHHH... HUSH, NOW...

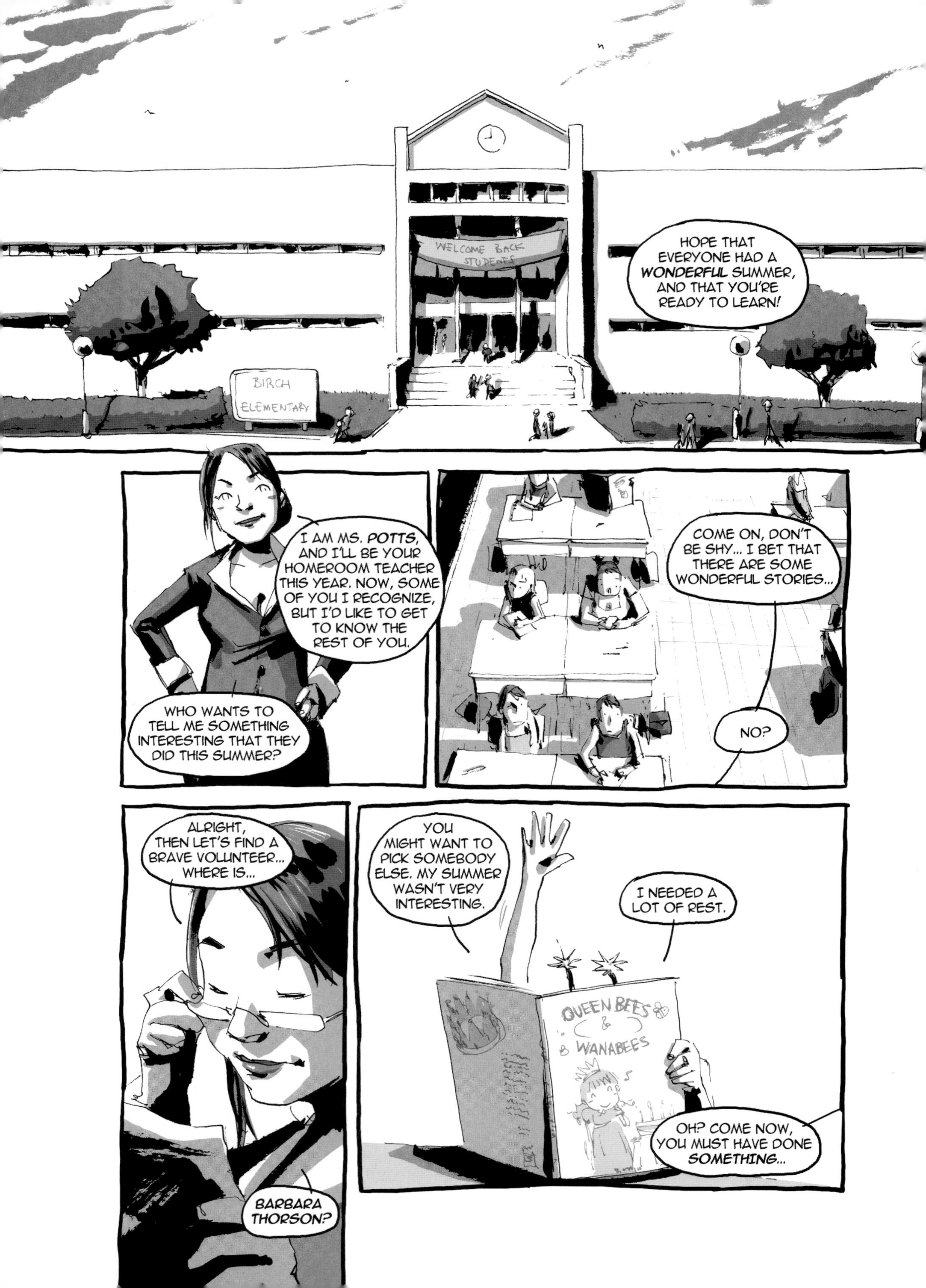
WELCOME BACK STUDENTS
BIRCH ELEMENTARY
HOPE THAT EVERYONE HAD A **WONDERFUL** SUMMER, AND THAT YOU'RE READY TO LEARN!
I AM MS. **POTTS**, AND I'LL BE YOUR HOMEROOM TEACHER THIS YEAR. NOW, SOME OF YOU I RECOGNIZE, BUT I'D LIKE TO GET TO KNOW THE REST OF YOU.
WHO WANTS TO TELL ME SOMETHING INTERESTING THAT THEY DID THIS SUMMER?
COME ON, DON'T BE SHY... I BET THAT THERE ARE SOME WONDERFUL STORIES...
NO?
ALRIGHT, THEN LET'S FIND A BRAVE VOLUNTEER... WHERE IS...
BARBARA THORSON?
YOU MIGHT WANT TO PICK SOMEBODY ELSE. MY SUMMER WASN'T VERY INTERESTING.
I NEEDED A LOT OF REST.
QUEEN BEES & WANABEES
OH? COME NOW, YOU MUST HAVE DONE **SOMETHING**...

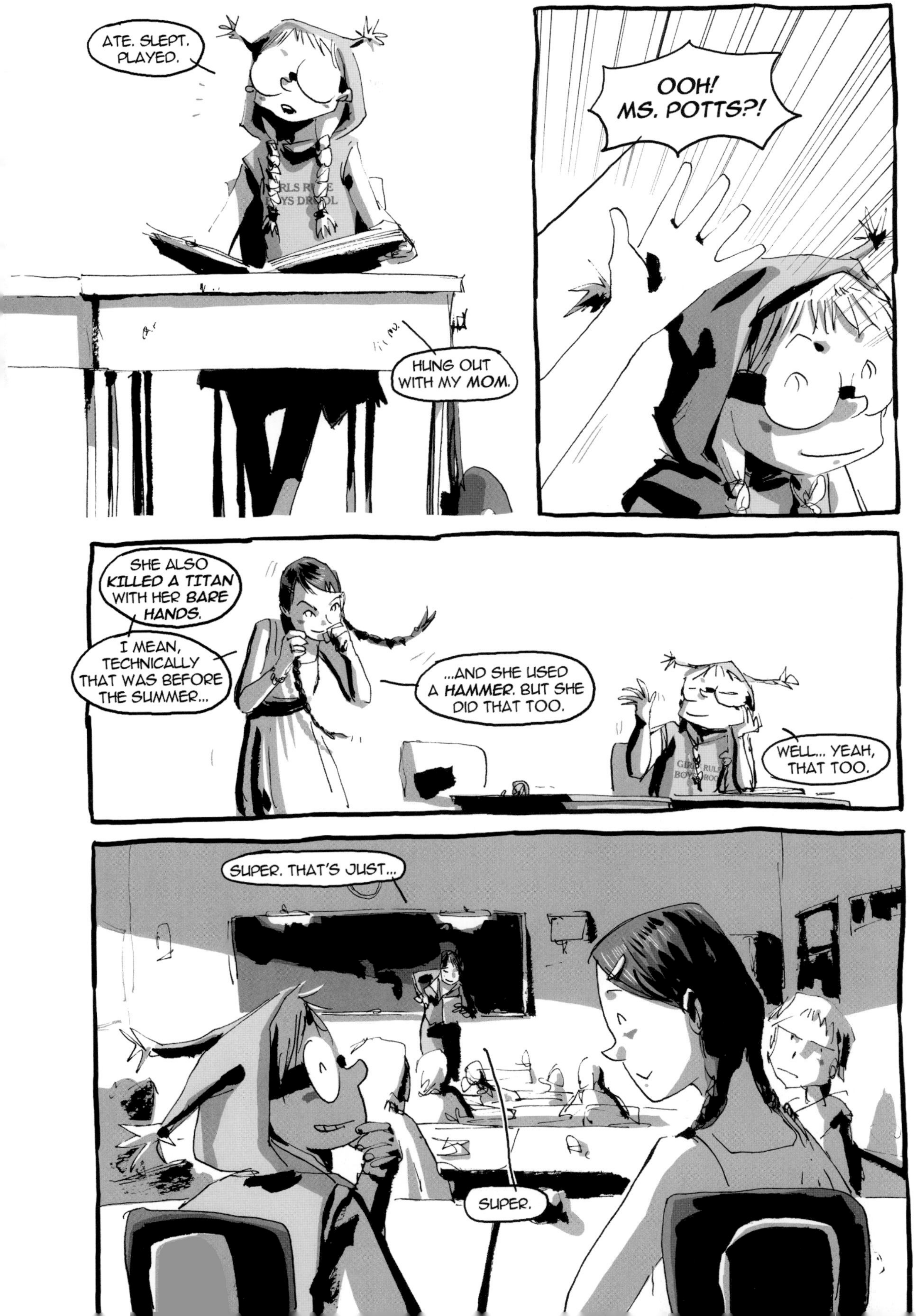
ATE. SLEPT. PLAYED.
HUNG OUT WITH MY MOM.
OOH! MS. POTTS?!
SHE ALSO KILLED A TITAN WITH HER BARE HANDS.
I MEAN, TECHNICALLY THAT WAS BEFORE THE SUMMER...
...AND SHE USED A HAMMER. BUT SHE DID THAT TOO.
WELL... YEAH, THAT TOO.
SUPER. THAT'S JUST...
SUPER.

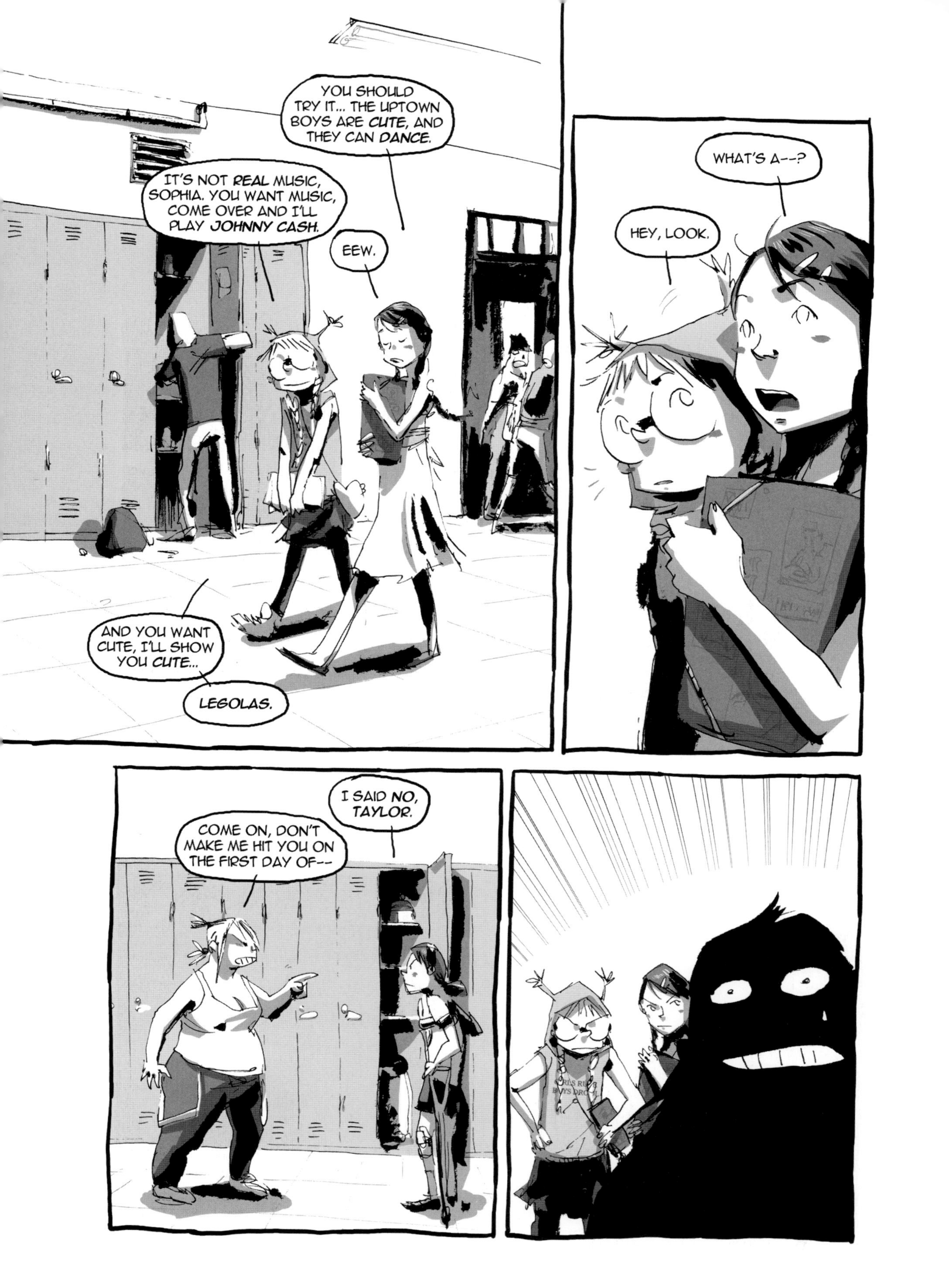
YOU SHOULD TRY IT... THE UPTOWN BOYS ARE CUTE, AND THEY CAN DANCE.
IT'S NOT REAL MUSIC, SOPHIA. YOU WANT MUSIC, COME OVER AND I'LL PLAY JOHNNY CASH.
EEW.
AND YOU WANT CUTE, I'LL SHOW YOU CUTE...
LEGOLAS.
WHAT'S A--?
HEY, LOOK.
I SAID NO, TAYLOR.
COME ON, DON'T MAKE ME HIT YOU ON THE FIRST DAY OF--

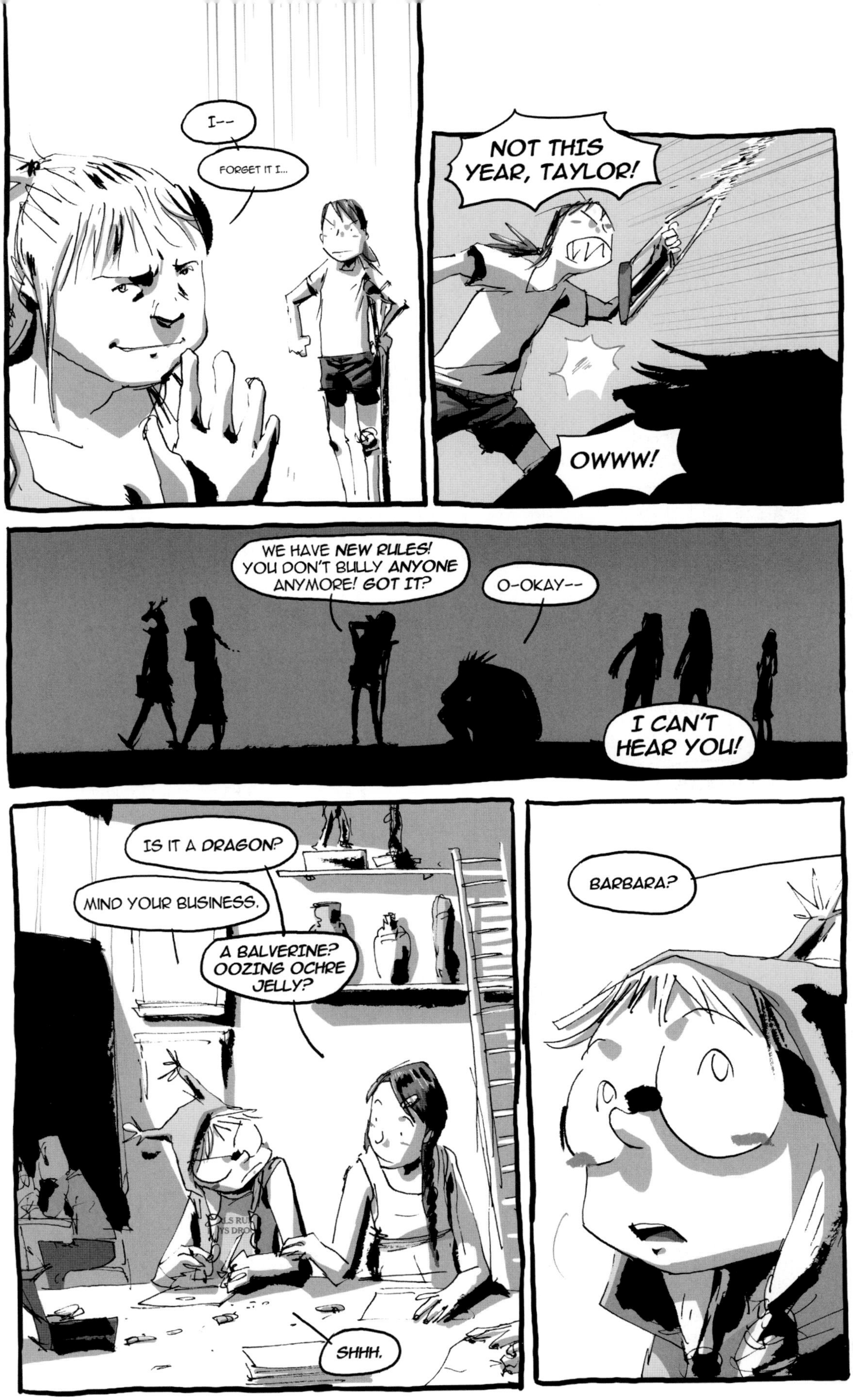
I--
FORGET IT I...
NOT THIS YEAR, TAYLOR!
OWWW!
WE HAVE NEW RULES! YOU DON'T BULLY ANYONE ANYMORE! GOT IT?
O-OKAY--
I CAN'T HEAR YOU!
IS IT A DRAGON?
MIND YOUR BUSINESS.
A BALVERINE? OOZING OCHRE JELLY?
SHHH.
BARBARA?

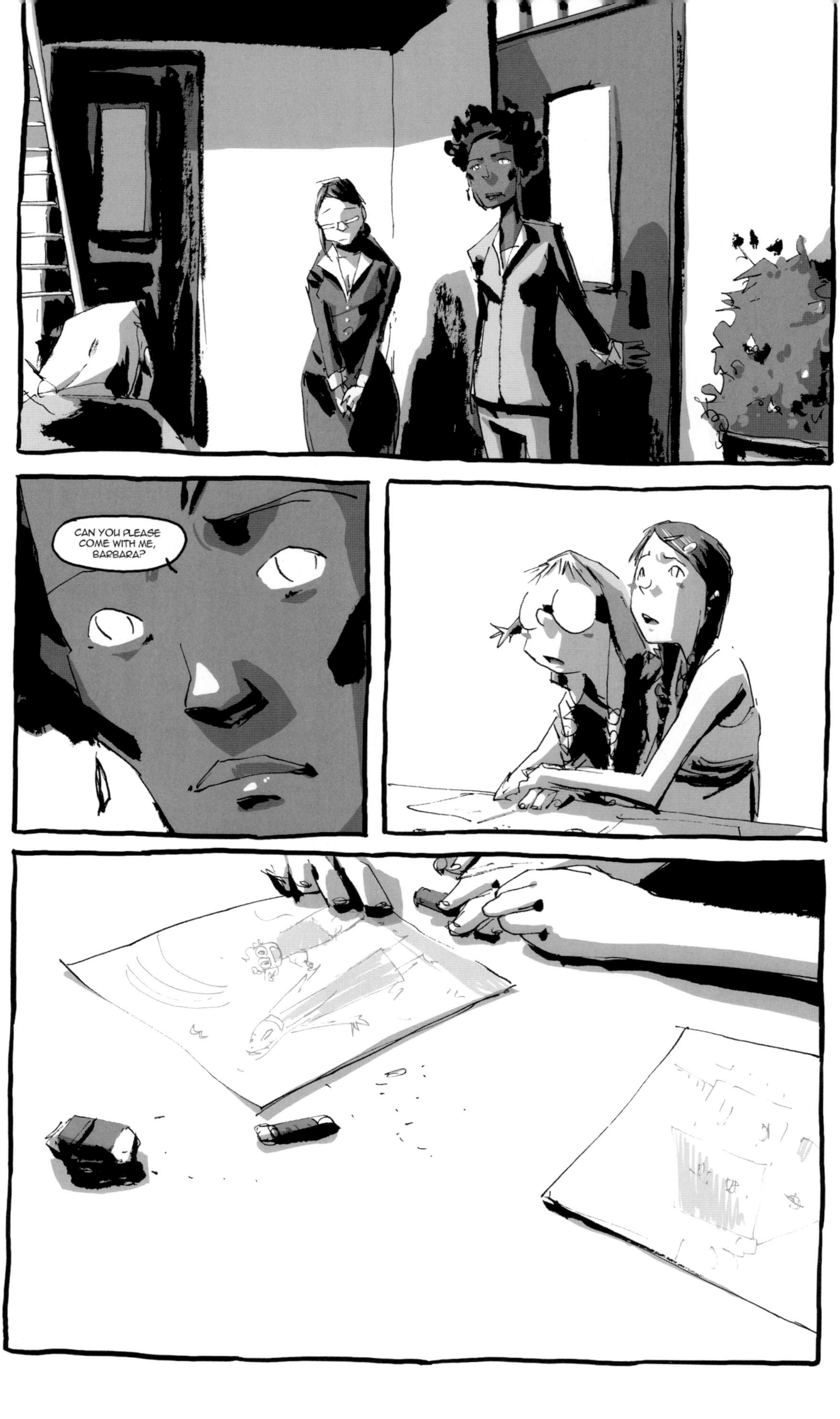
CAN YOU PLEASE COME WITH ME, BARBARA?

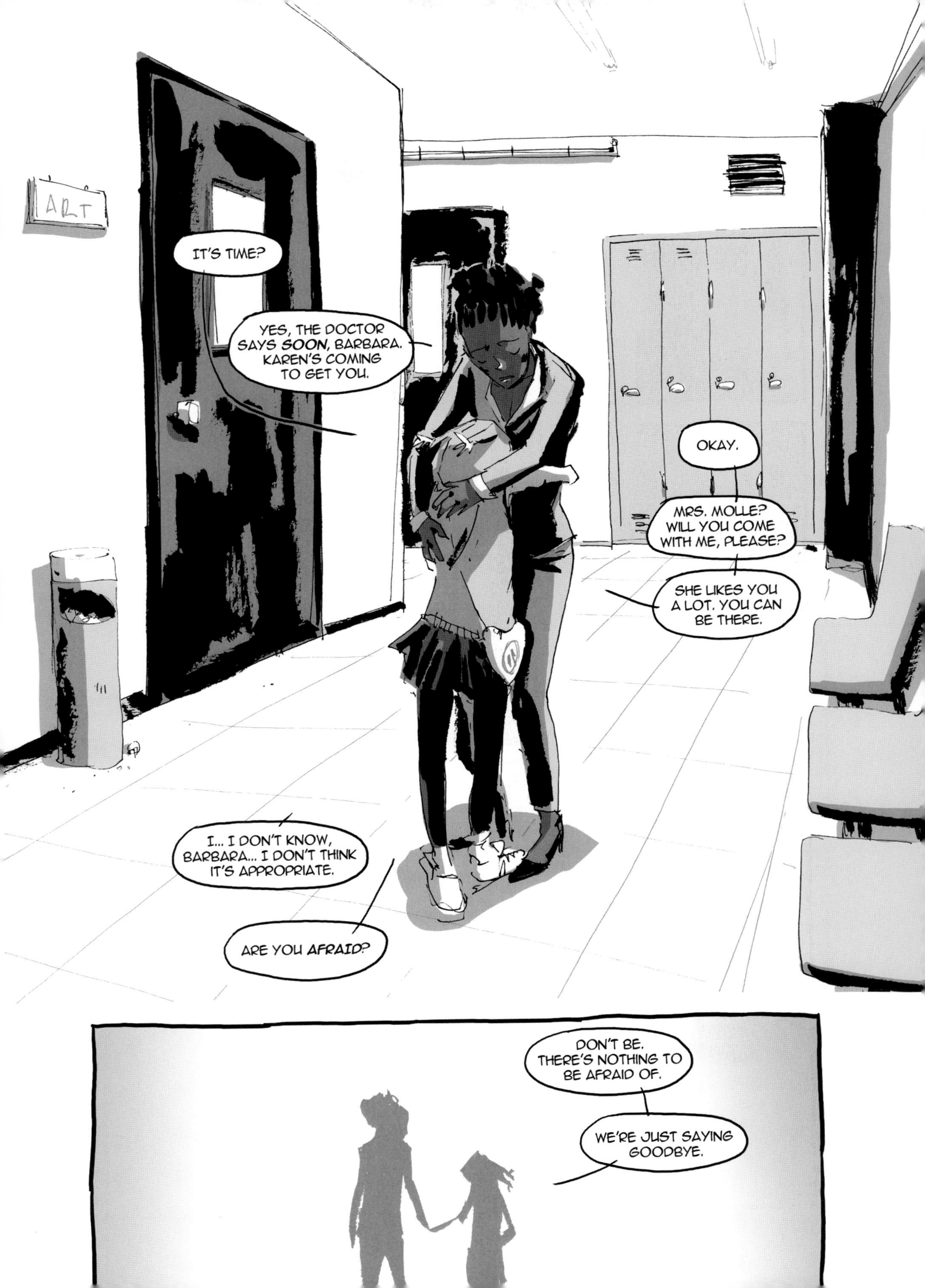
ART
IT'S TIME?
YES, THE DOCTOR SAYS SOON, BARBARA. KAREN'S COMING TO GET YOU.
OKAY.
MRS. MOLLE? WILL YOU COME WITH ME, PLEASE?
SHE LIKES YOU A LOT. YOU CAN BE THERE.
I... I DON'T KNOW, BARBARA... I DON'T THINK IT'S APPROPRIATE.
ARE YOU AFRAID?
DON'T BE. THERE'S NOTHING TO BE AFRAID OF.
WE'RE JUST SAYING GOODBYE.

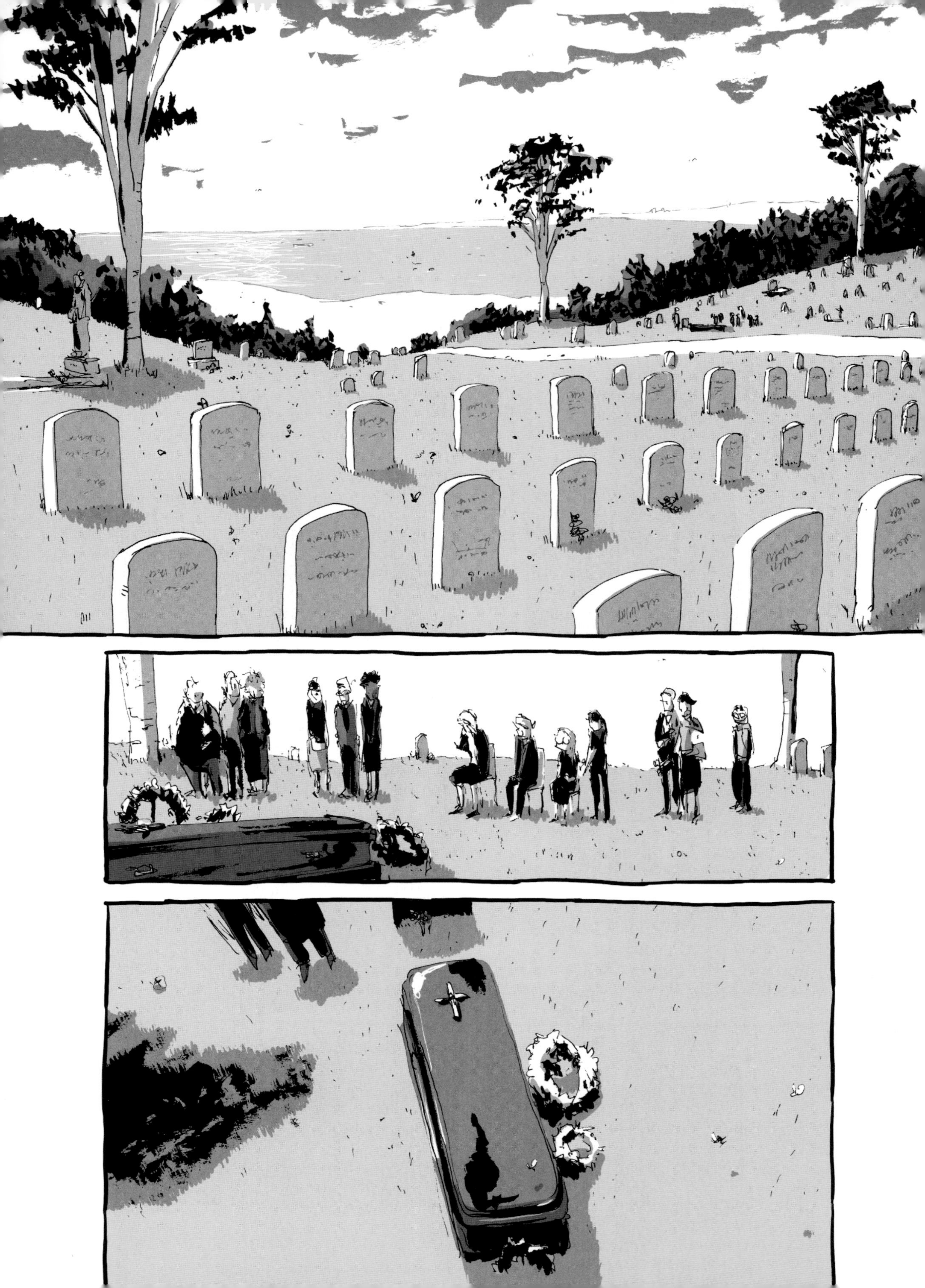

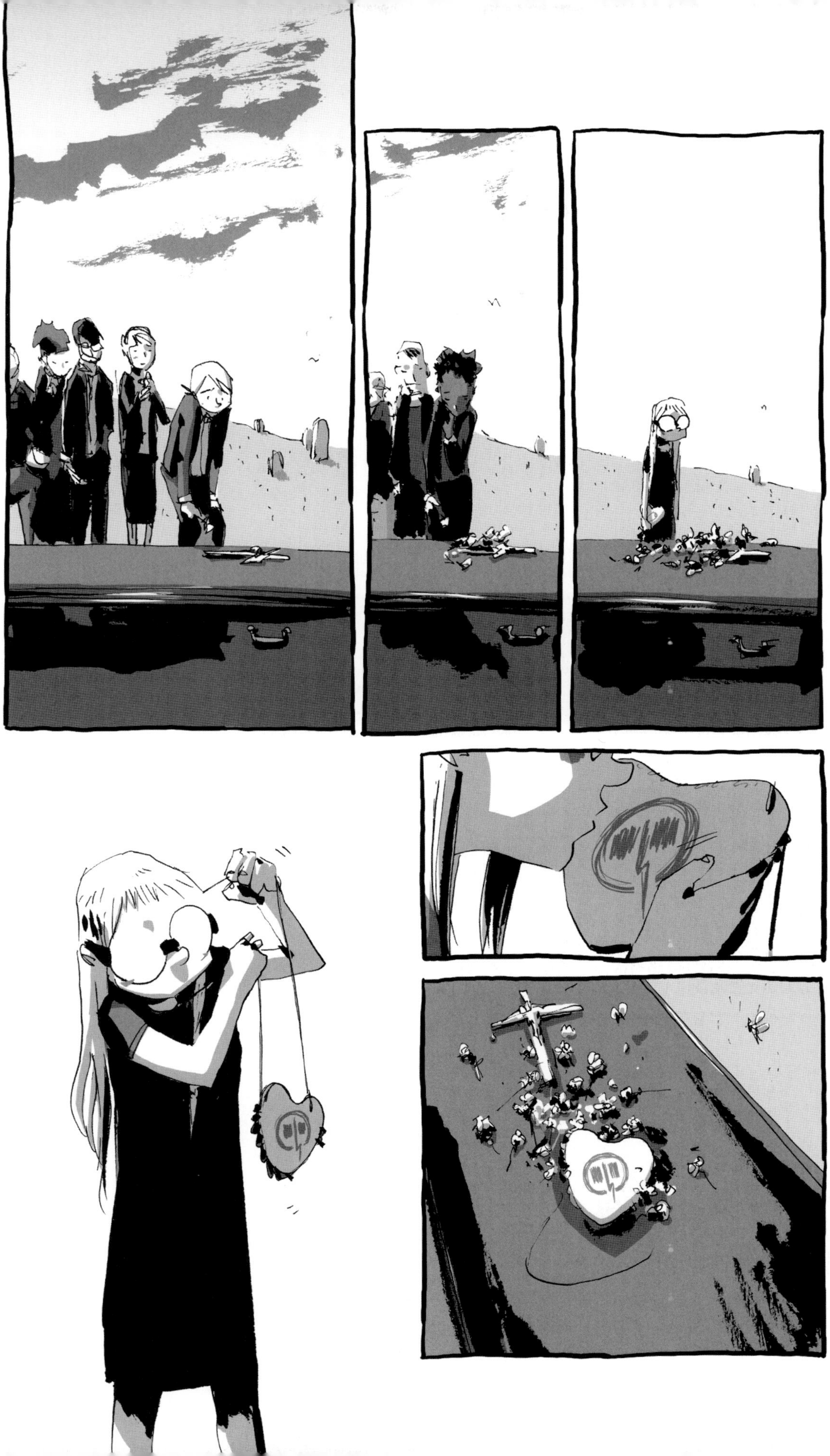

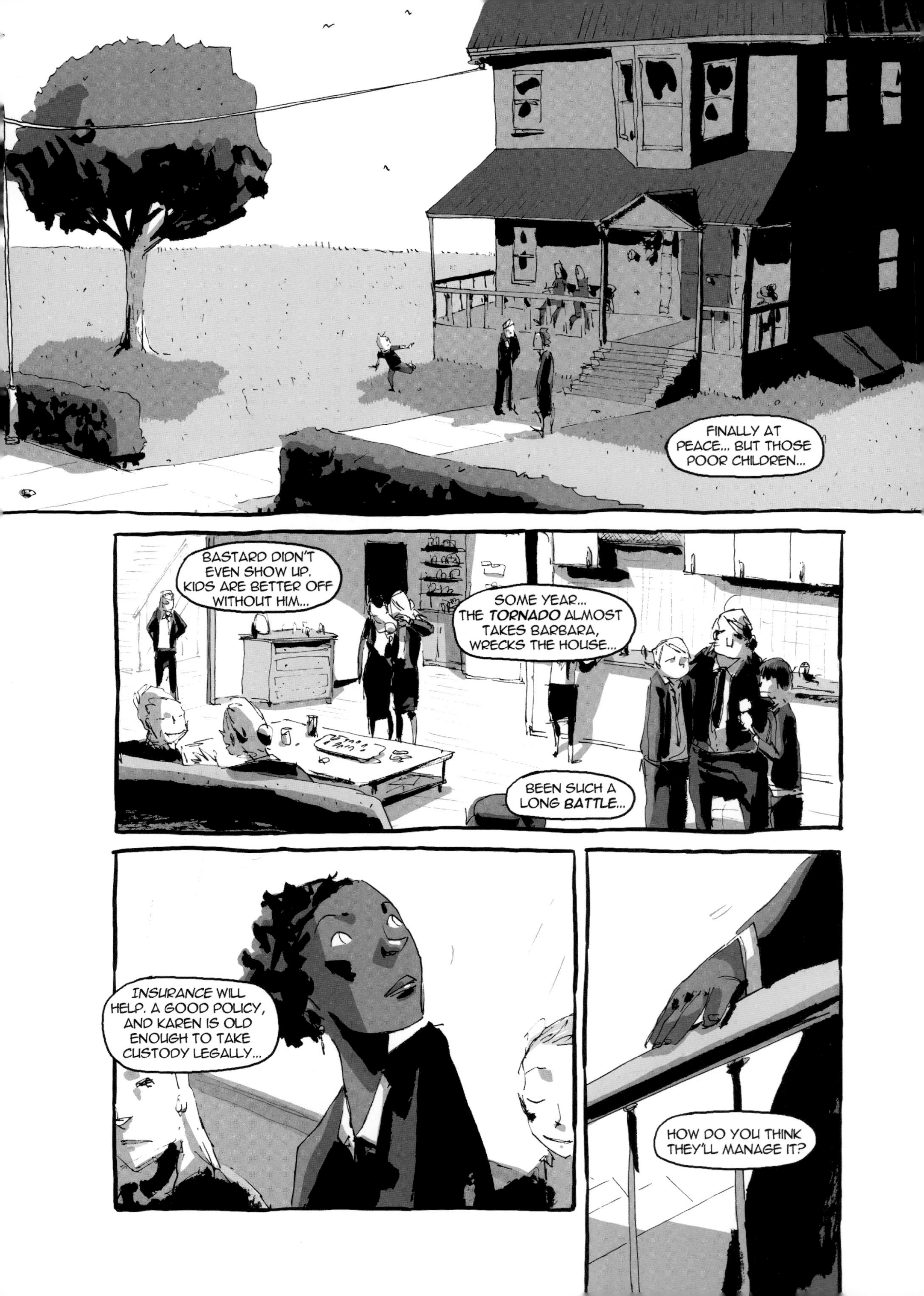
FINALLY AT PEACE... BUT THOSE POOR CHILDREN...
BASTARD DIDN'T EVEN SHOW UP. KIDS ARE BETTER OFF WITHOUT HIM...
SOME YEAR... THE TORNADO ALMOST TAKES BARBARA, WRECKS THE HOUSE...
BEEN SUCH A LONG BATTLE...
INSURANCE WILL HELP. A GOOD POLICY, AND KAREN IS OLD ENOUGH TO TAKE CUSTODY LEGALLY...
HOW DO YOU THINK THEY'LL MANAGE IT?

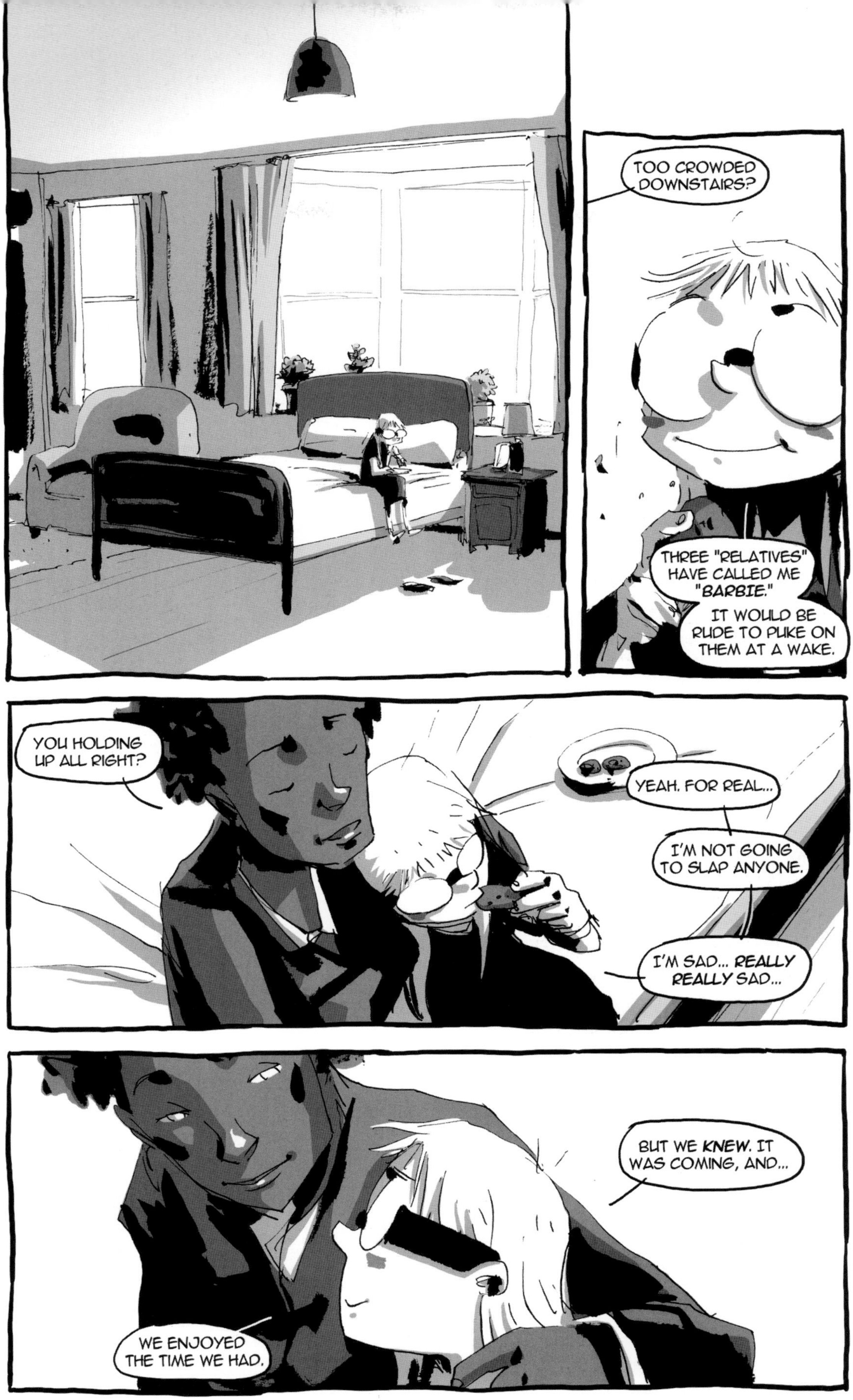
TOO CROWDED DOWNSTAIRS?
THREE "RELATIVES" HAVE CALLED ME "BARBIE."
IT WOULD BE RUDE TO PUKE ON THEM AT A WAKE.
YOU HOLDING UP ALL RIGHT?
YEAH. FOR REAL...
I'M NOT GOING TO SLAP ANYONE.
I'M SAD... REALLY REALLY SAD...
BUT WE KNEW. IT WAS COMING, AND...
WE ENJOYED THE TIME WE HAD.

YOU DID A LOT FOR ME. THANK YOU.

MOM THANKS YOU TOO.

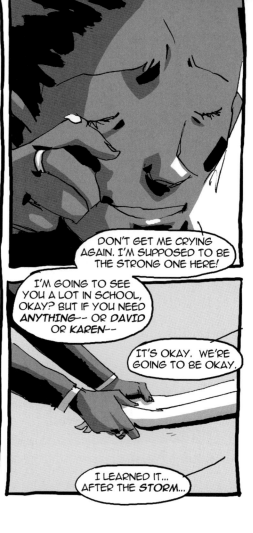

DON'T GET ME CRYING AGAIN. I'M SUPPOSED TO BE THE STRONG ONE HERE!

I'M GOING TO SEE YOU A LOT IN SCHOOL, OKAY? BUT IF YOU NEED *ANYTHING*-- OR DAVID OR *KAREN*--

IT'S OKAY. WE'RE GOING TO BE OKAY.

I LEARNED IT... AFTER THE *STORM*...

WE'RE A LOT STRONGER THAN WE THINK WE ARE.

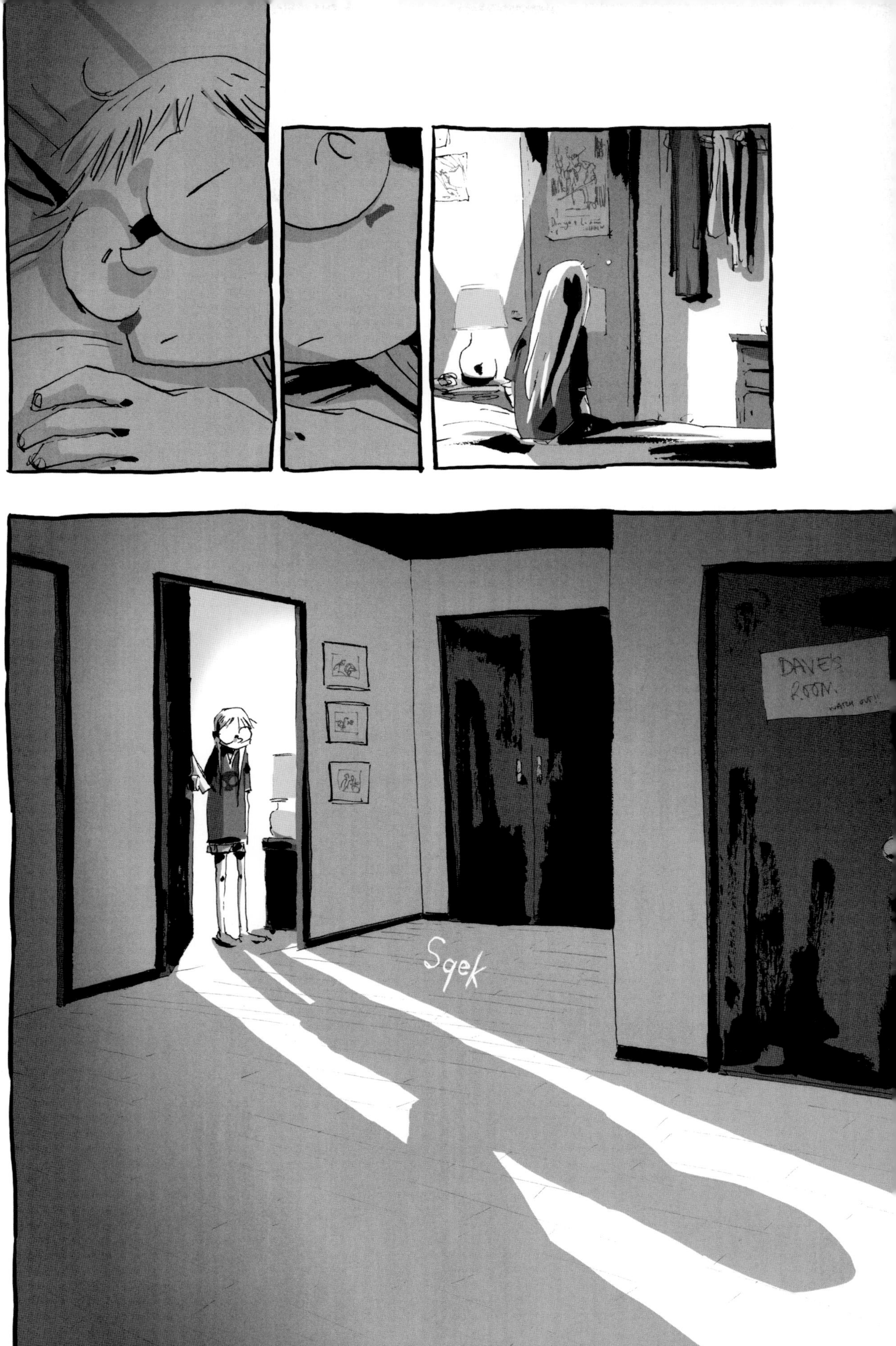
DAVE'S ROOM.
WATCH OUT!!
Sqek

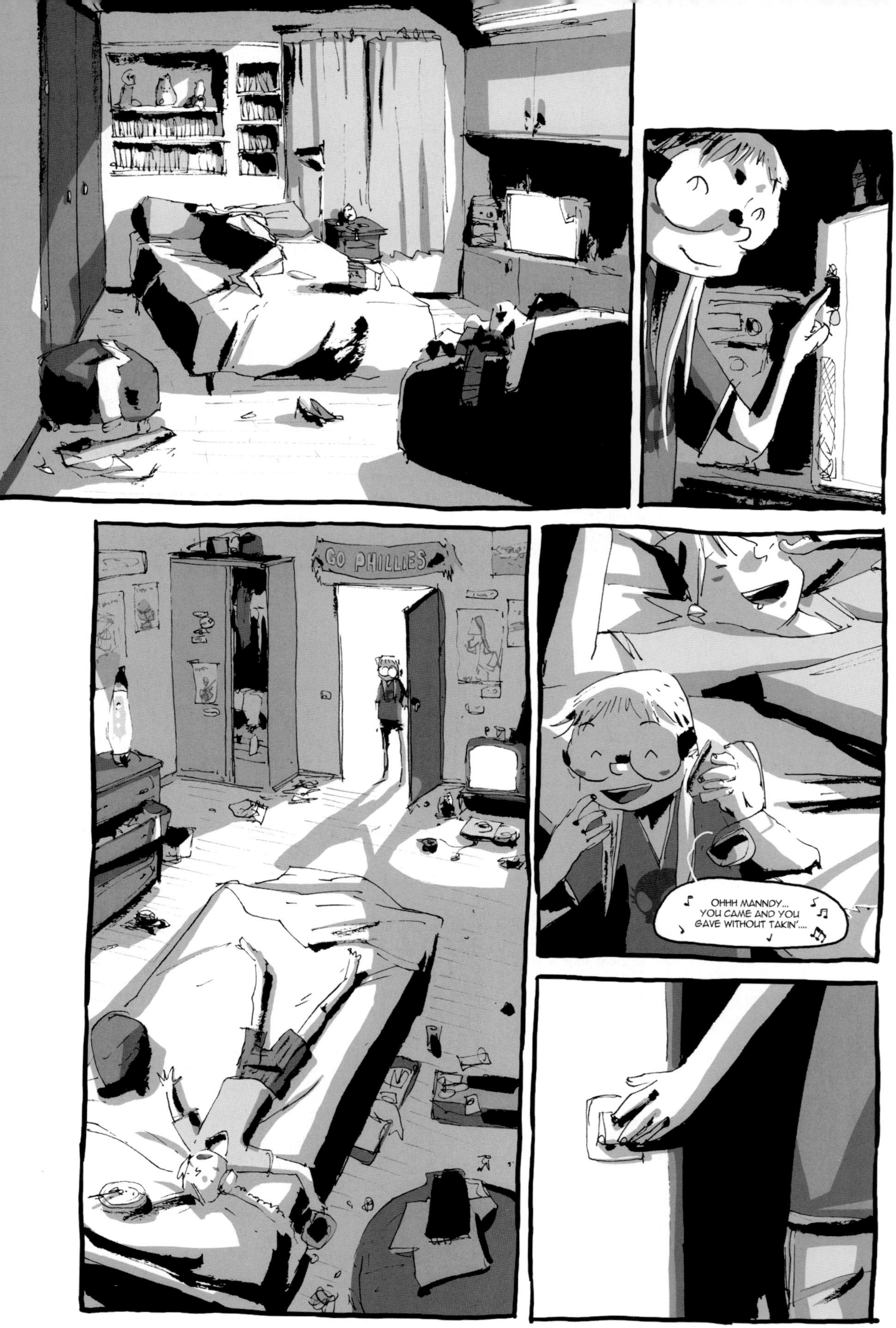
GO PHILLIES
OHHH MANNDY... YOU CAME AND YOU GAVE WITHOUT TAKIN'....

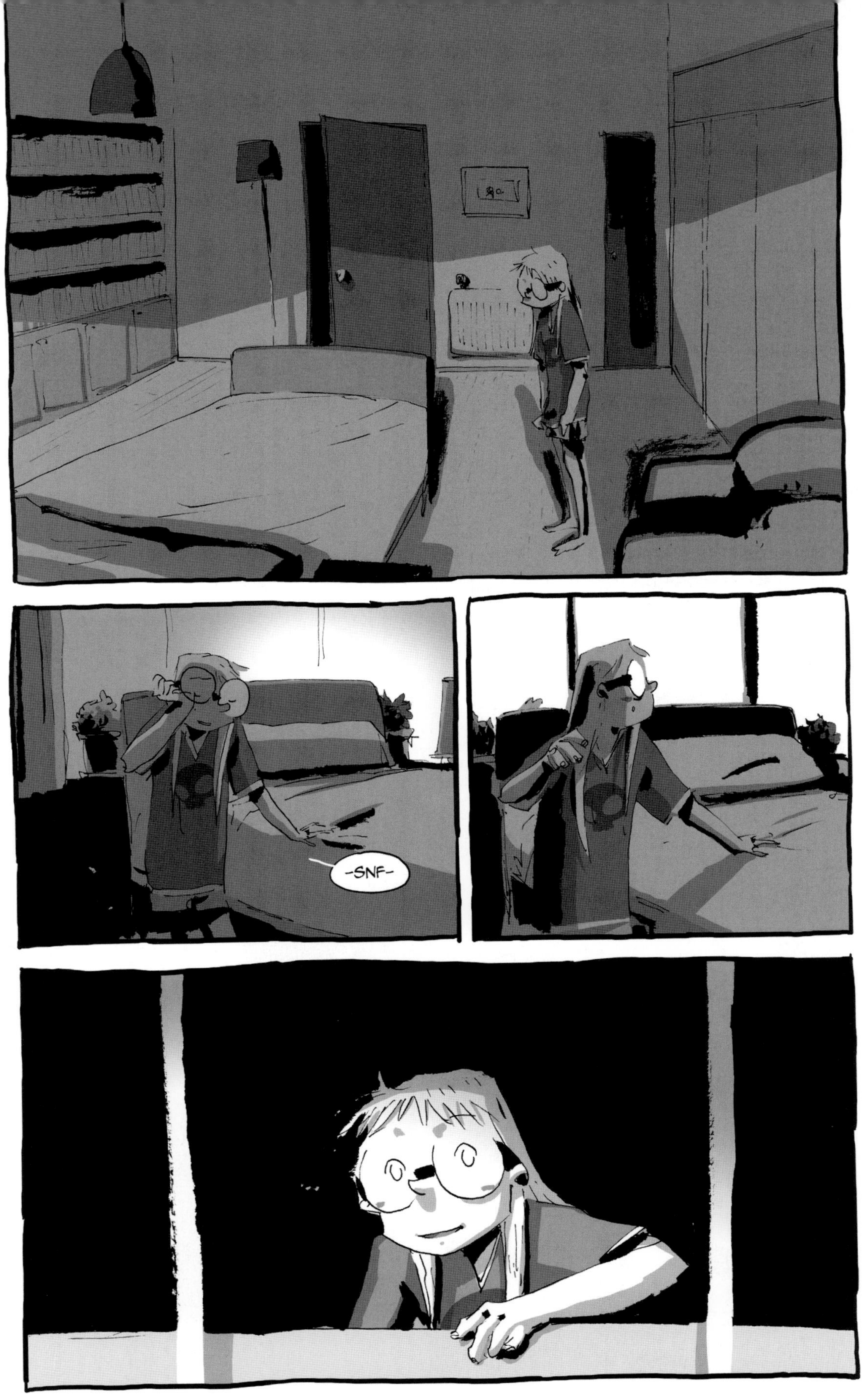
-SNF-

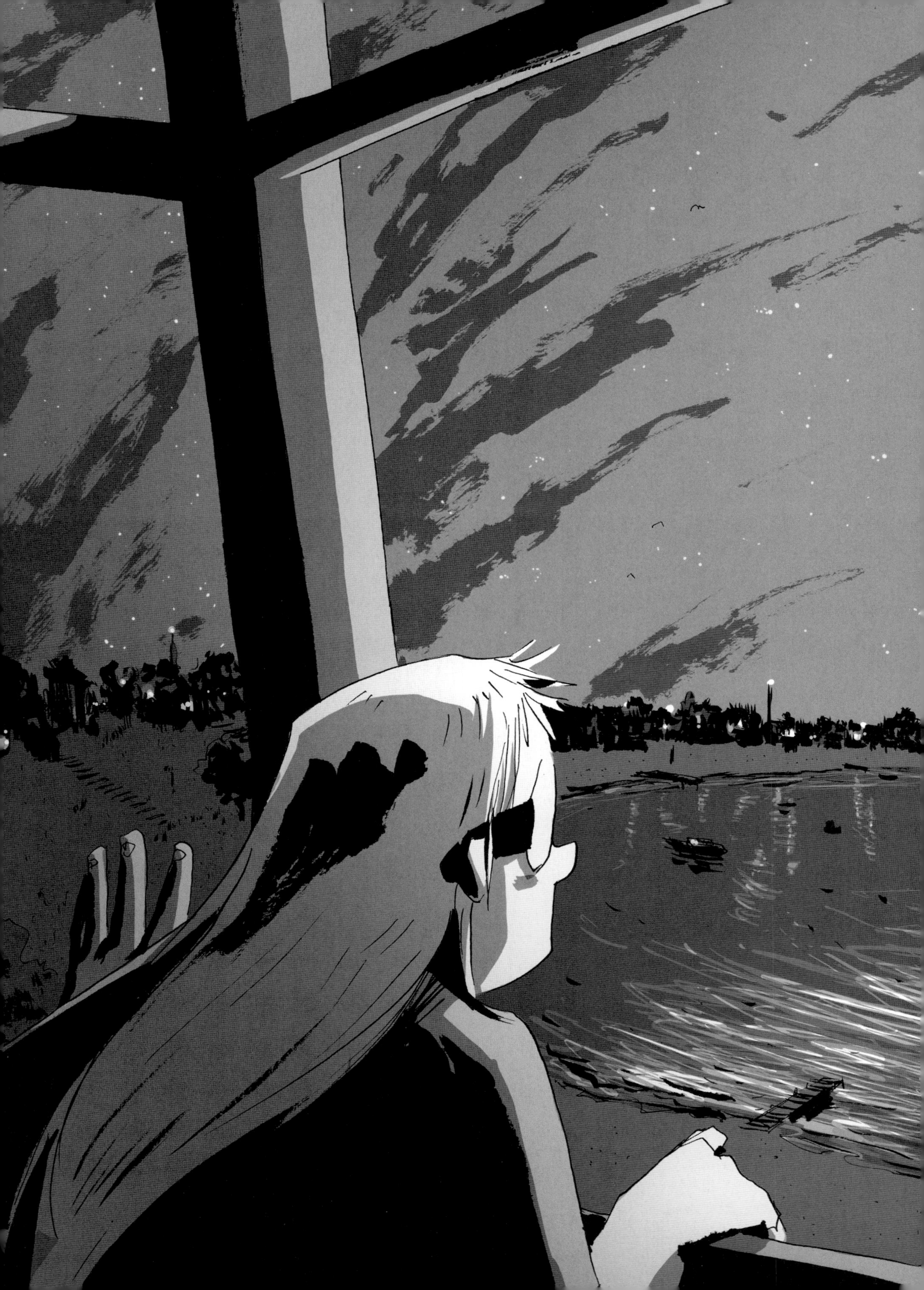

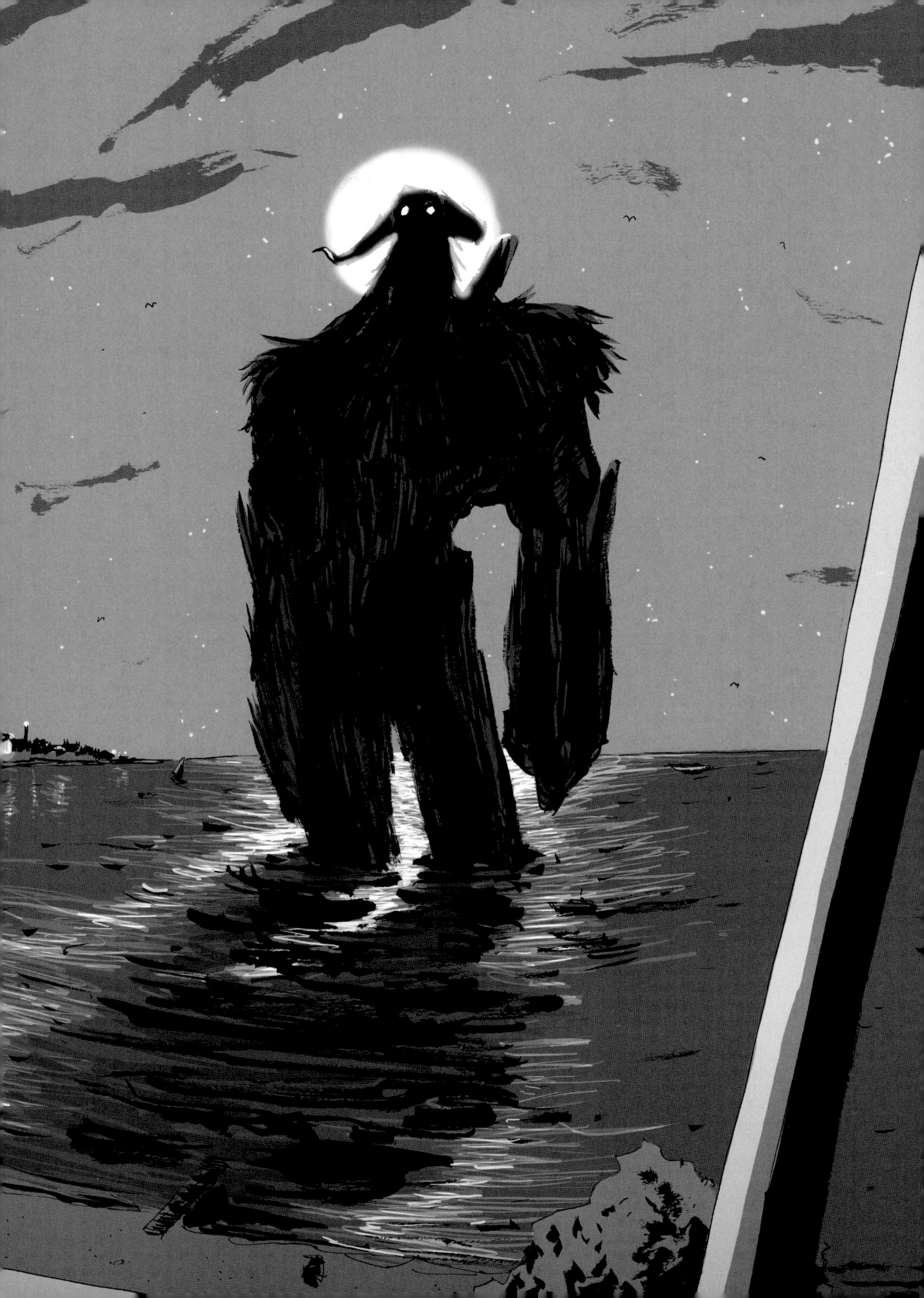

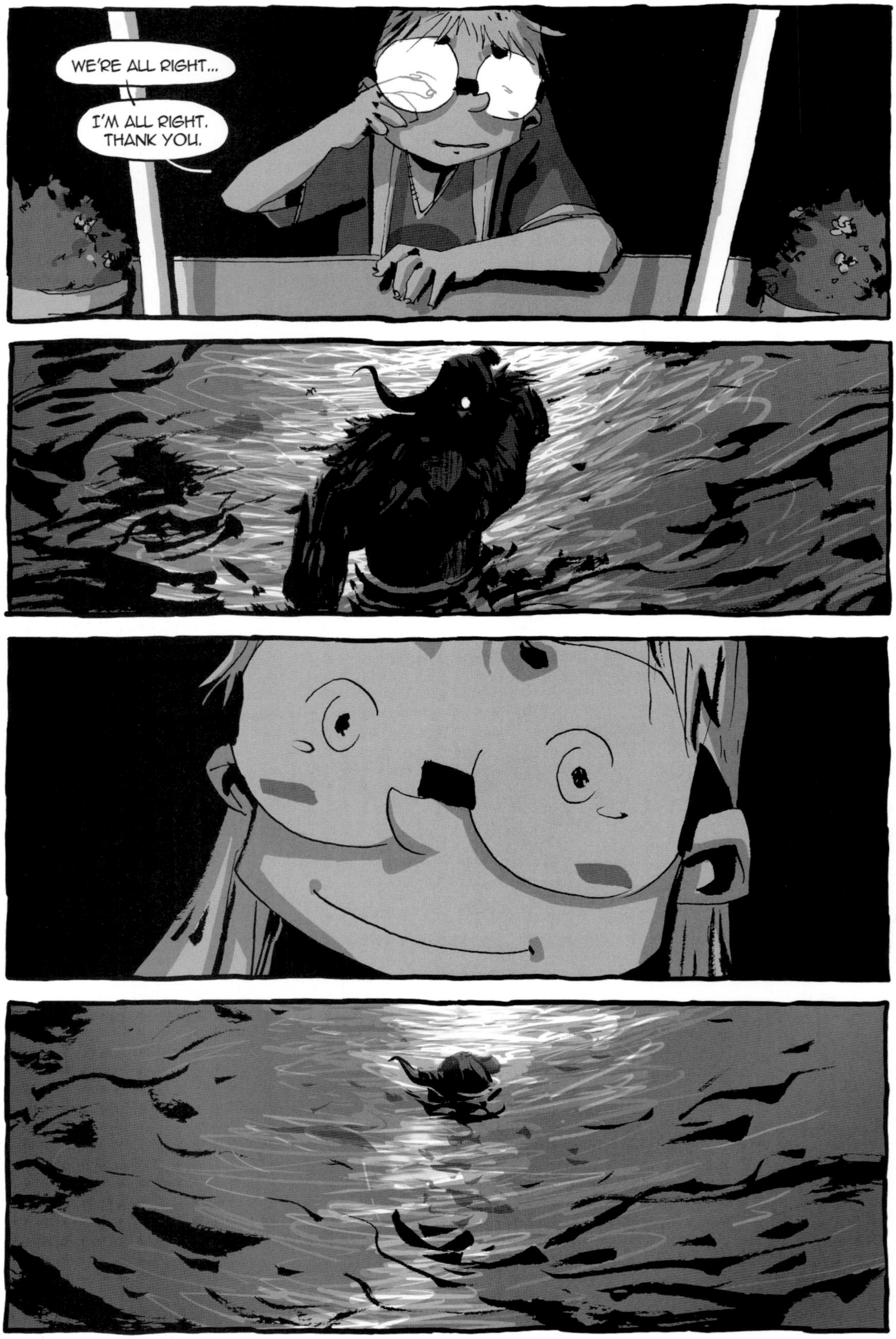
WE'RE ALL RIGHT...
I'M ALL RIGHT. THANK YOU.

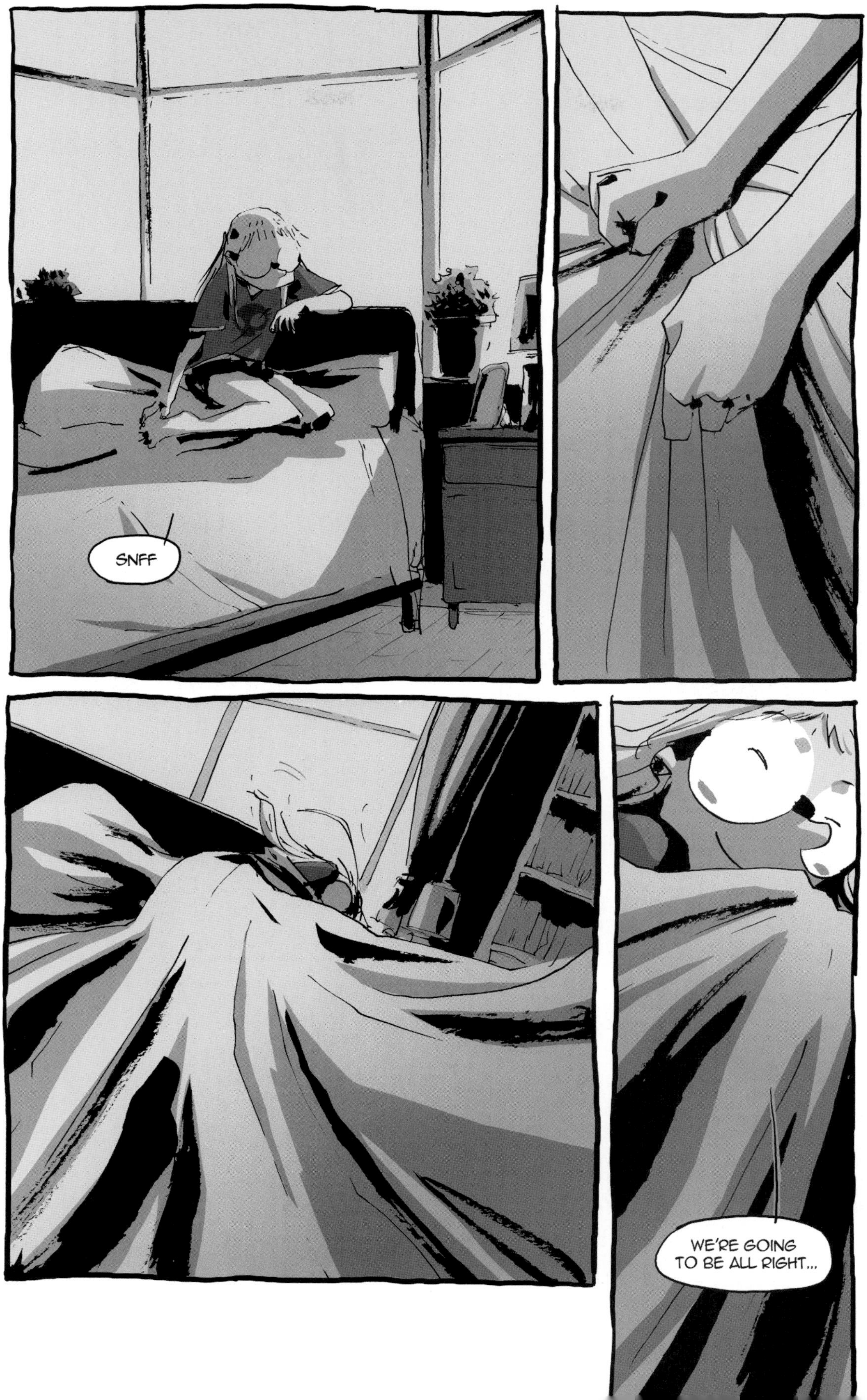
SNFF
WE'RE GOING TO BE ALL RIGHT...

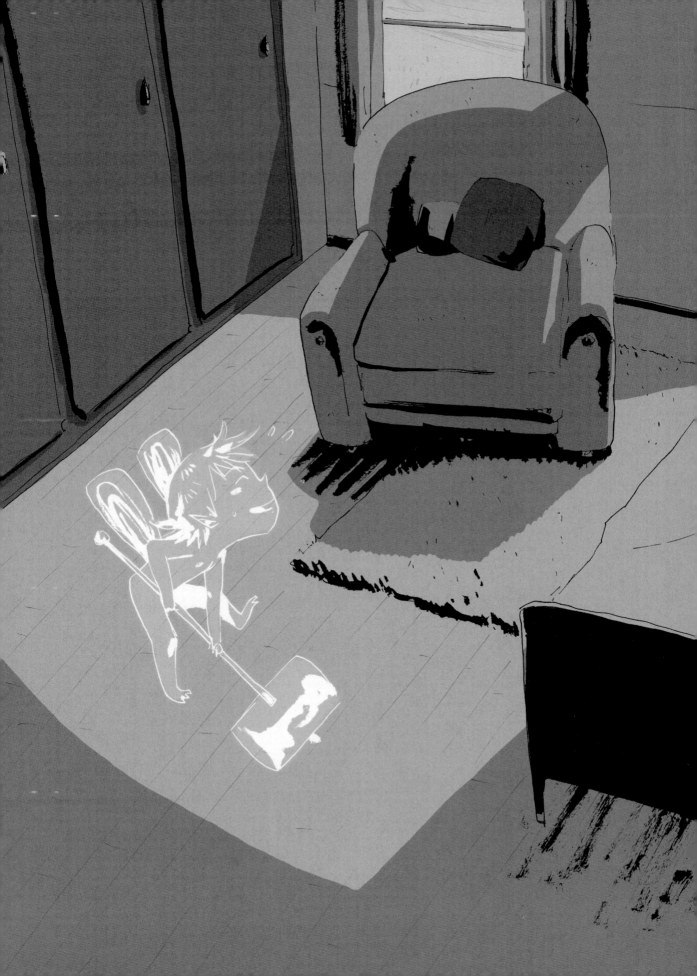

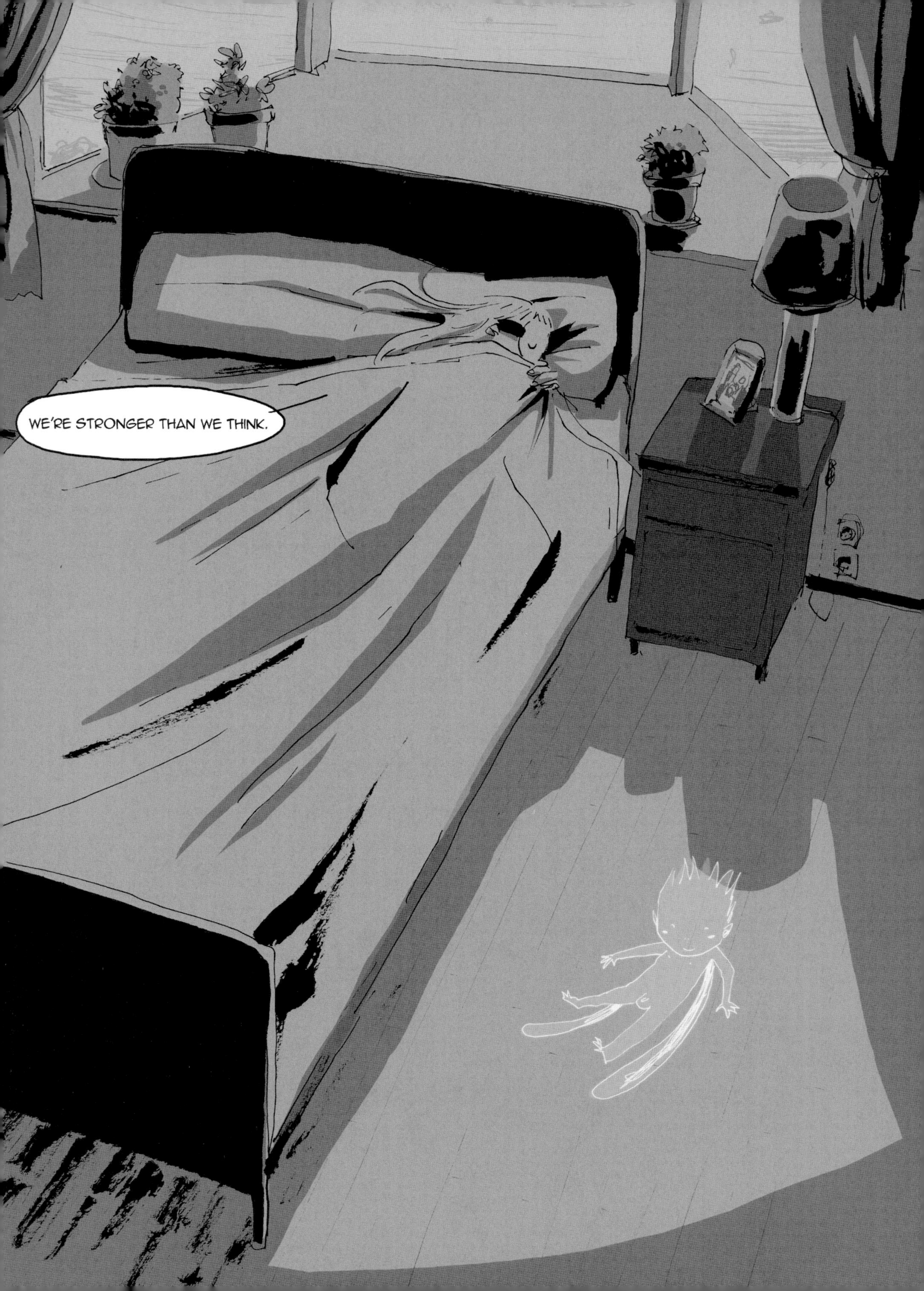
WE'RE STRONGER THAN WE THINK.

THE END

IKGIMAGESGALLERY

WARNING:
PIXIES
CROSSING

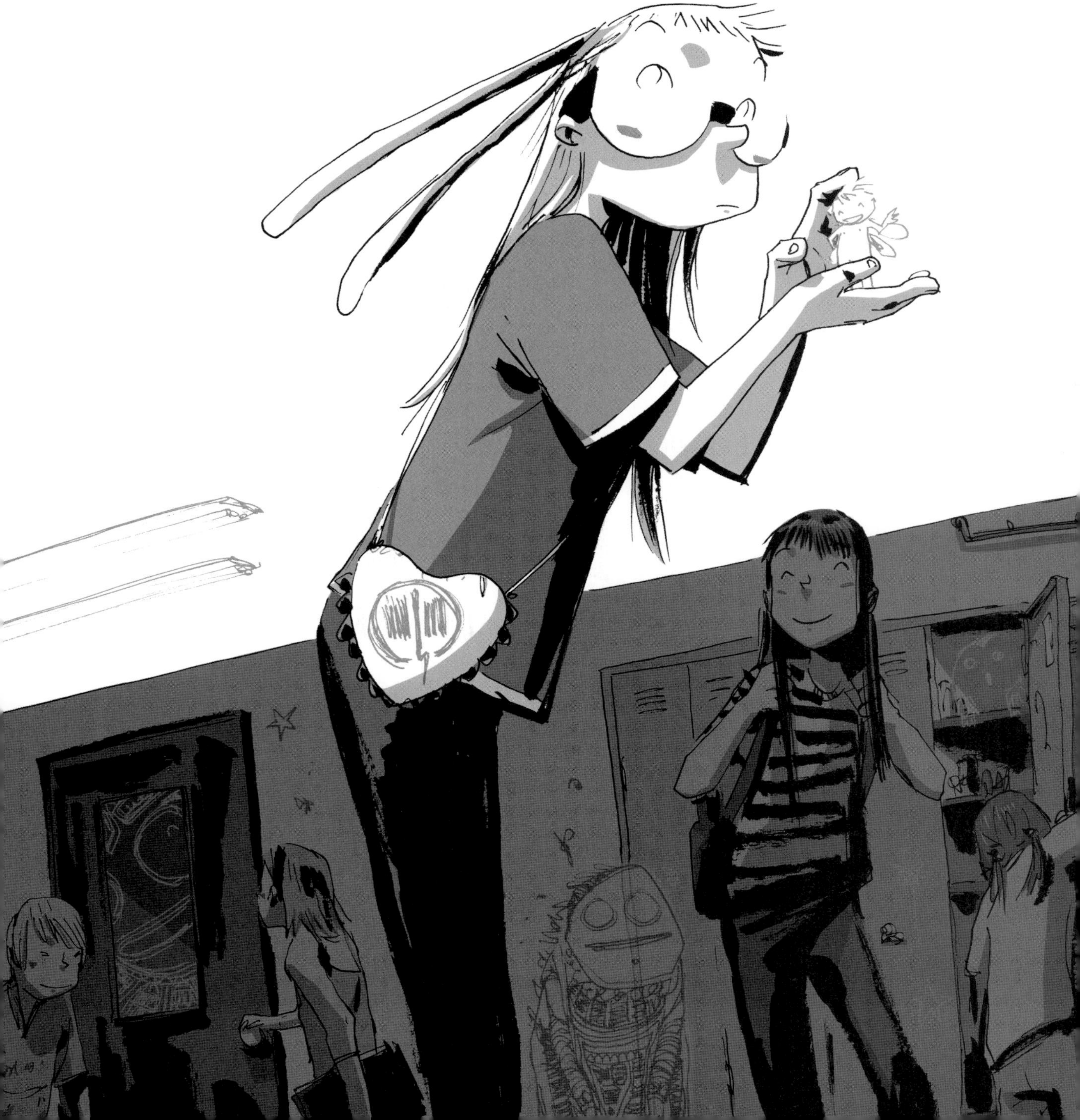

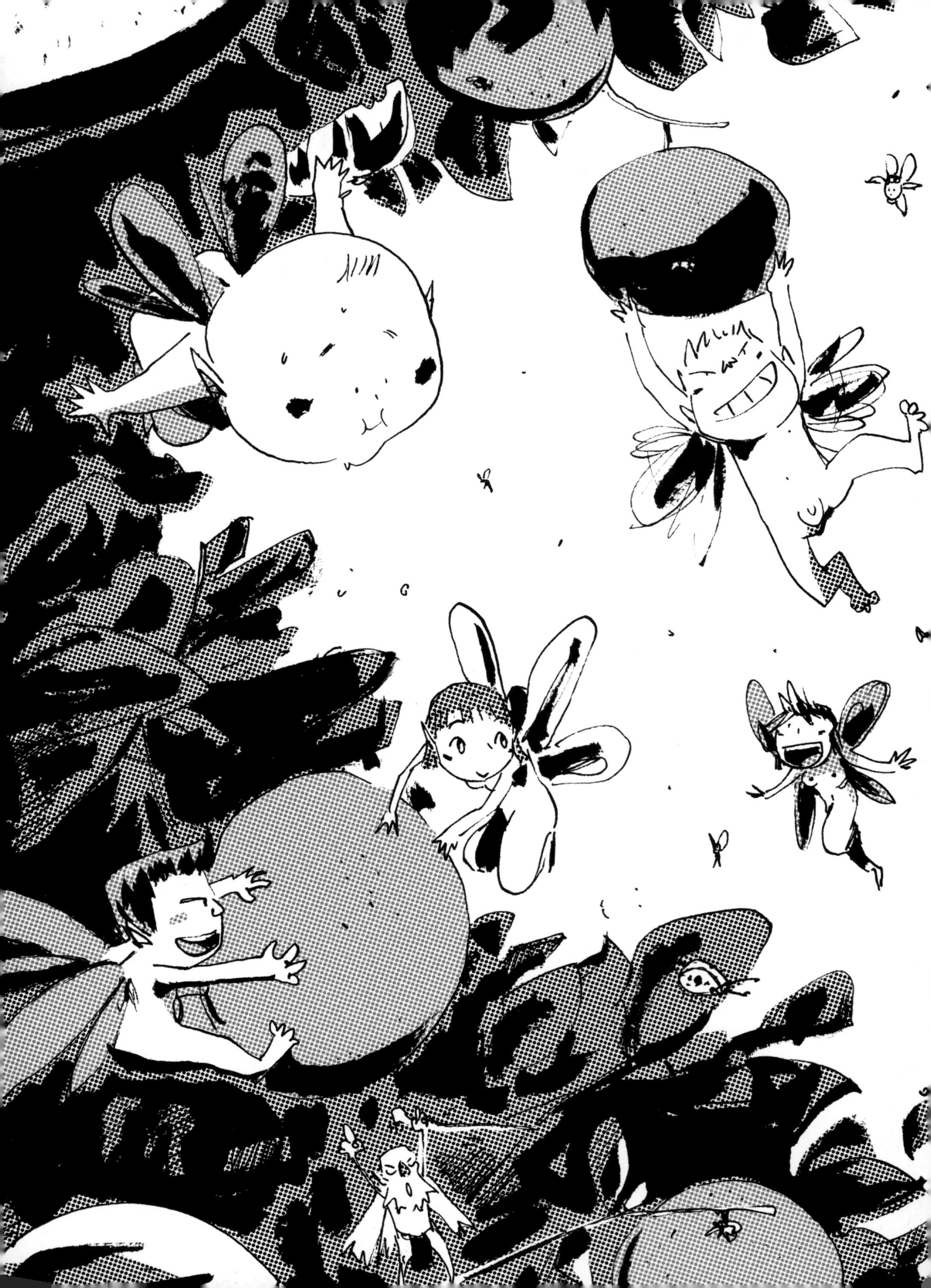

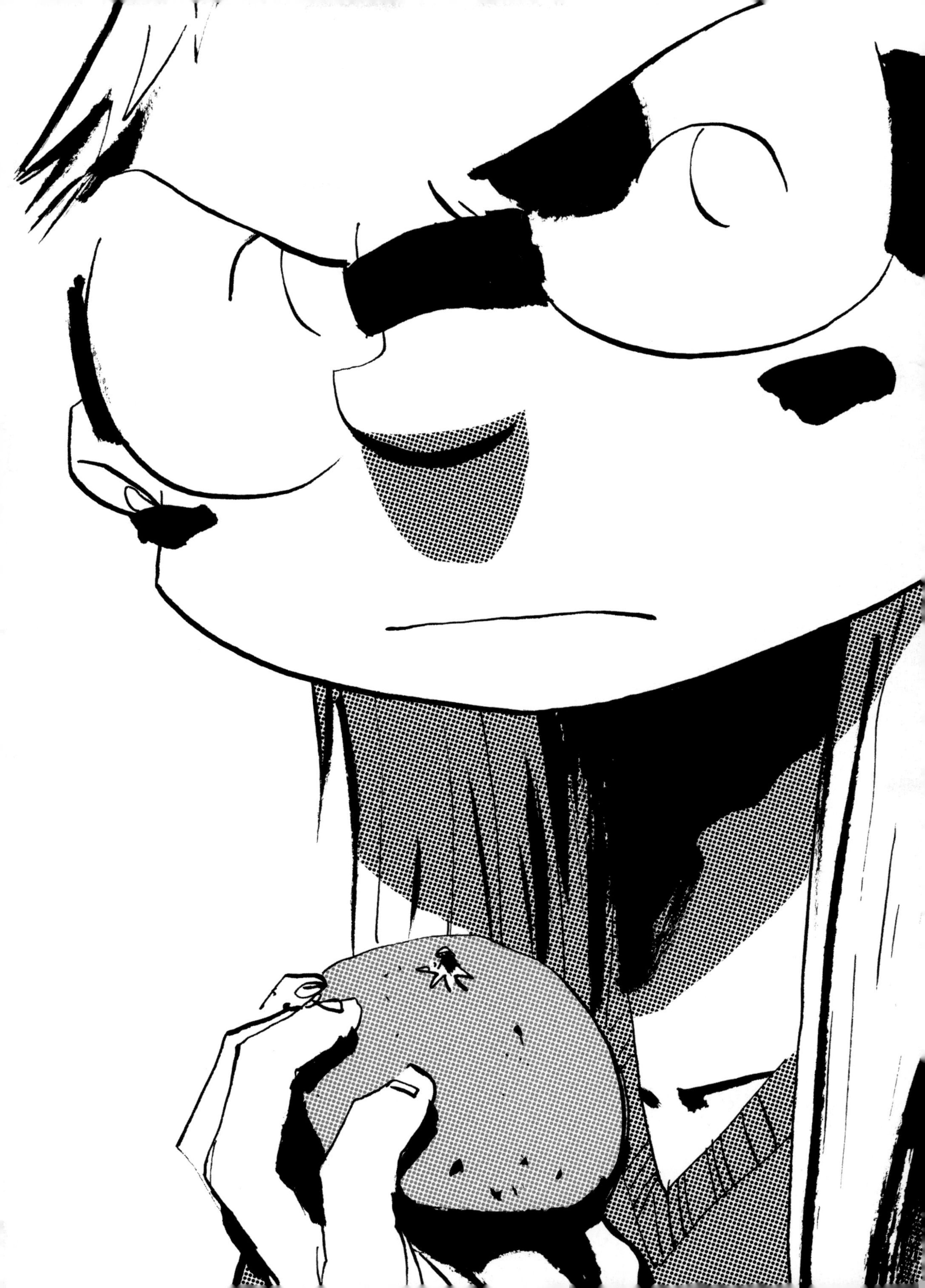

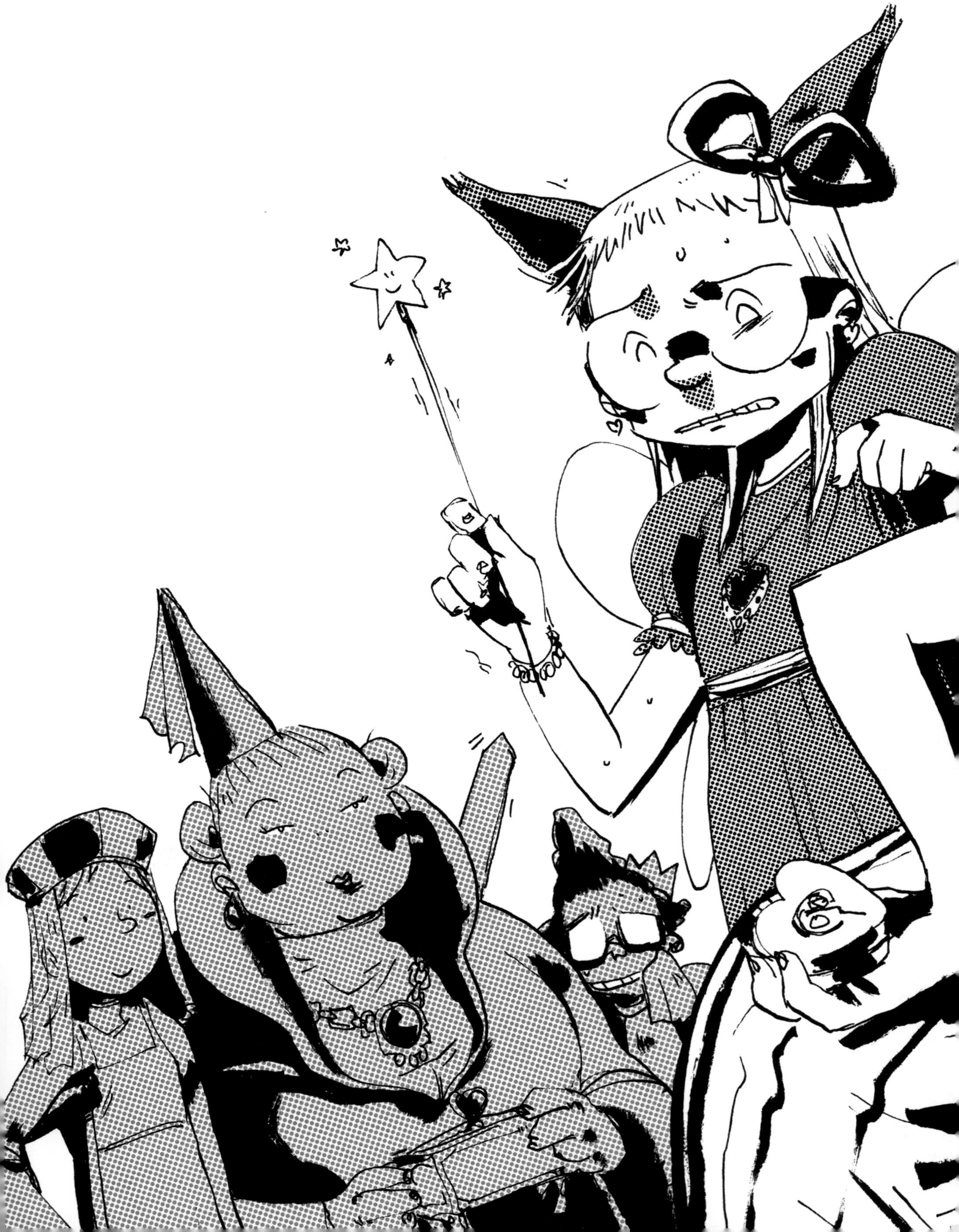

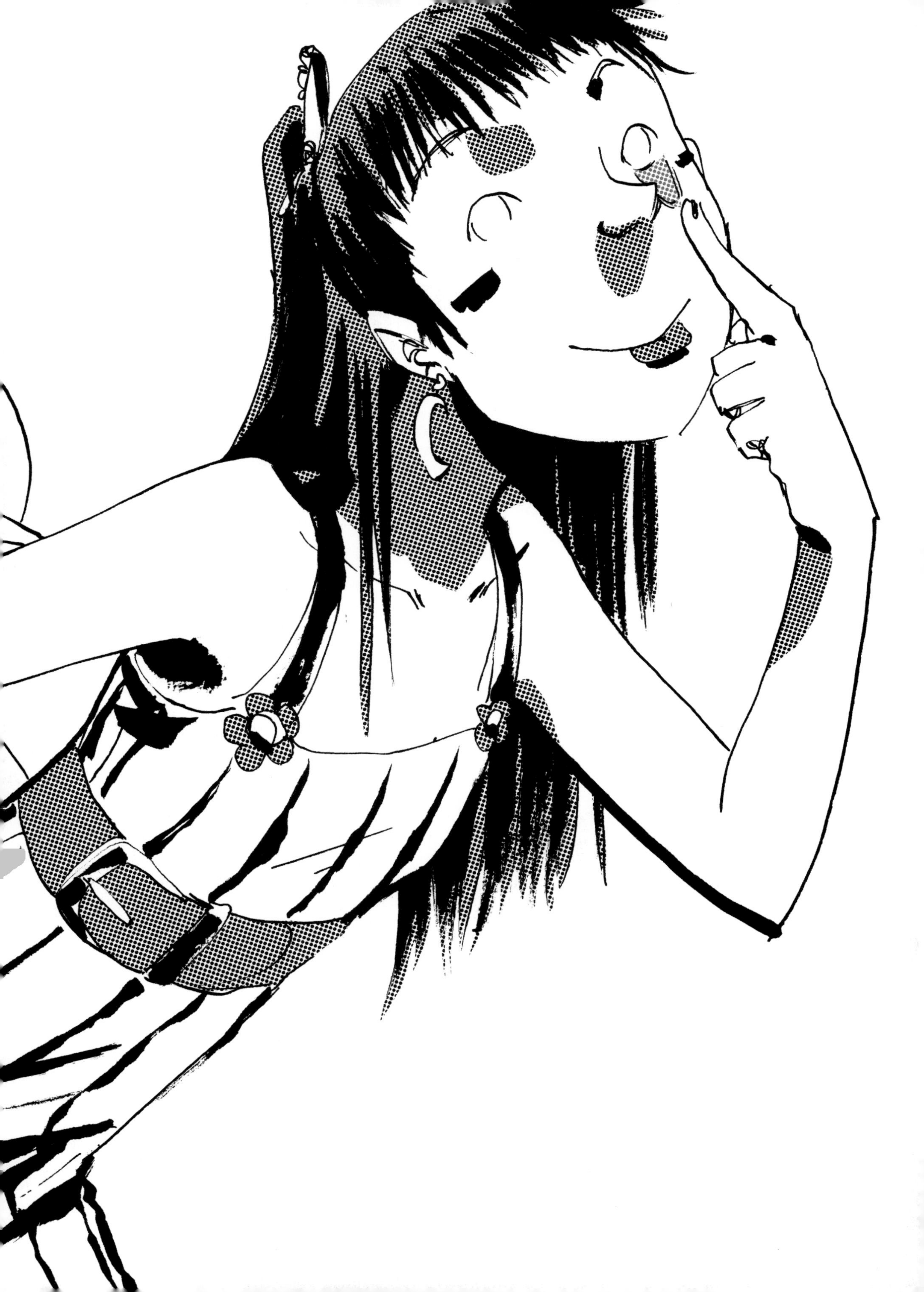

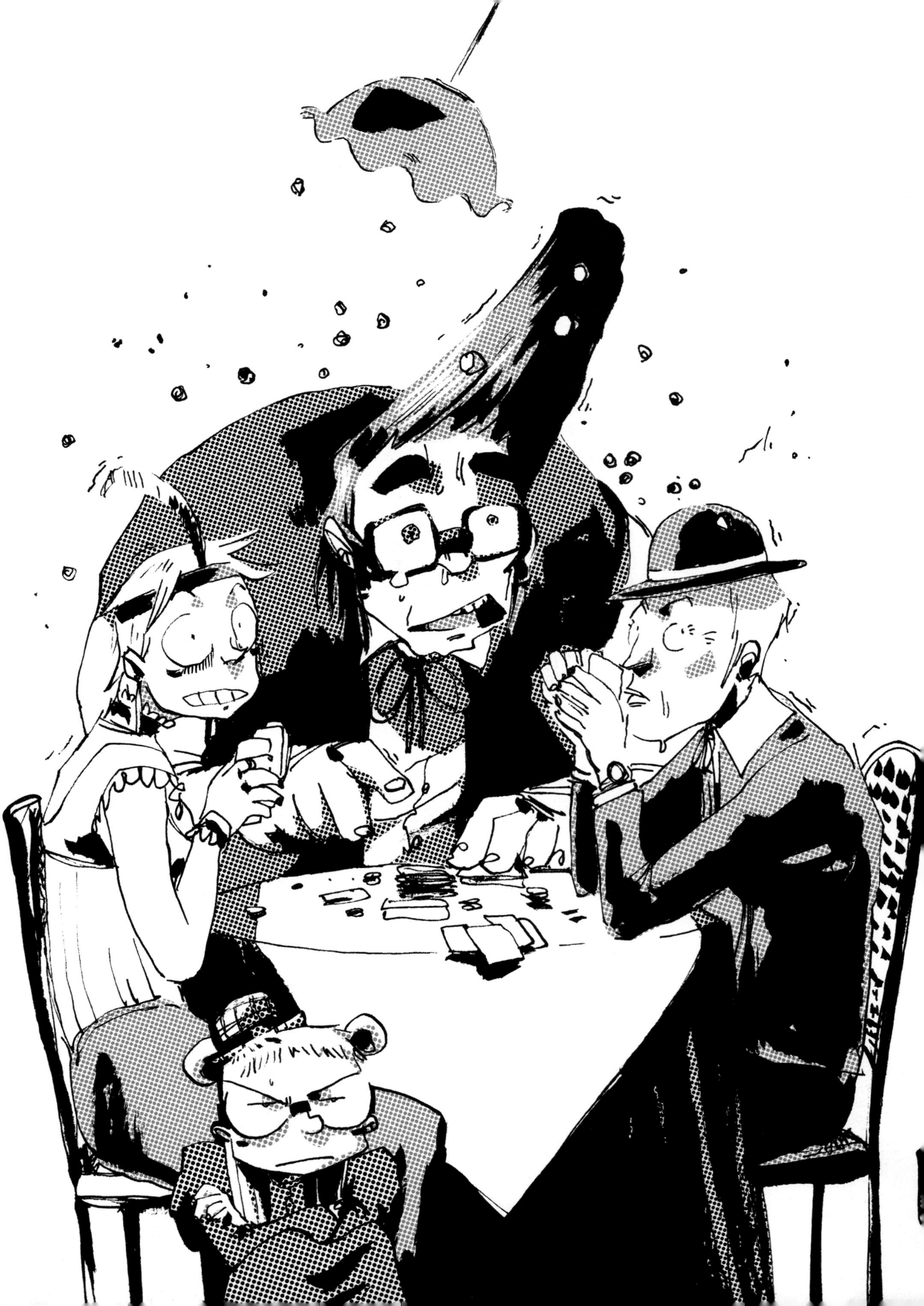

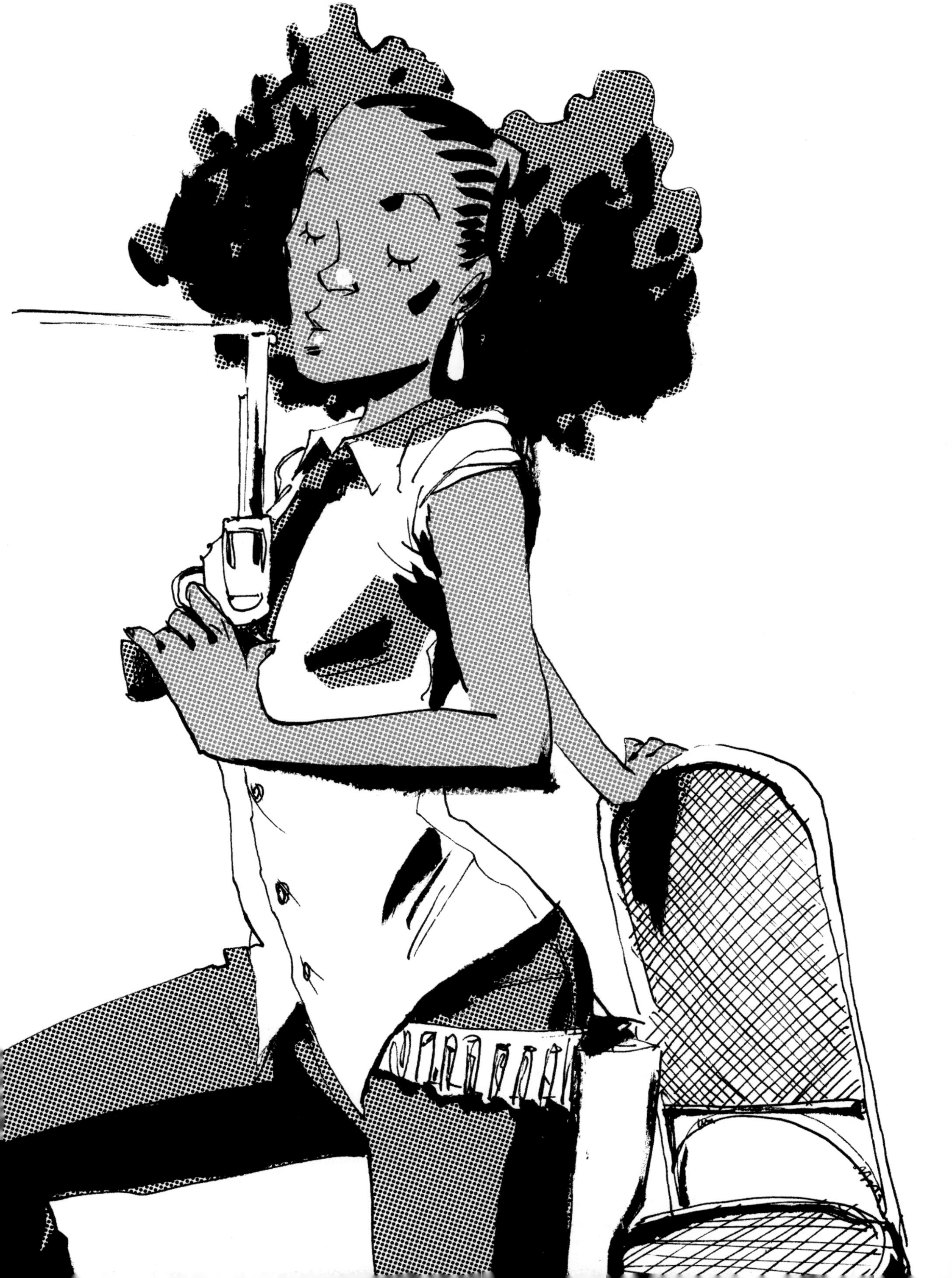

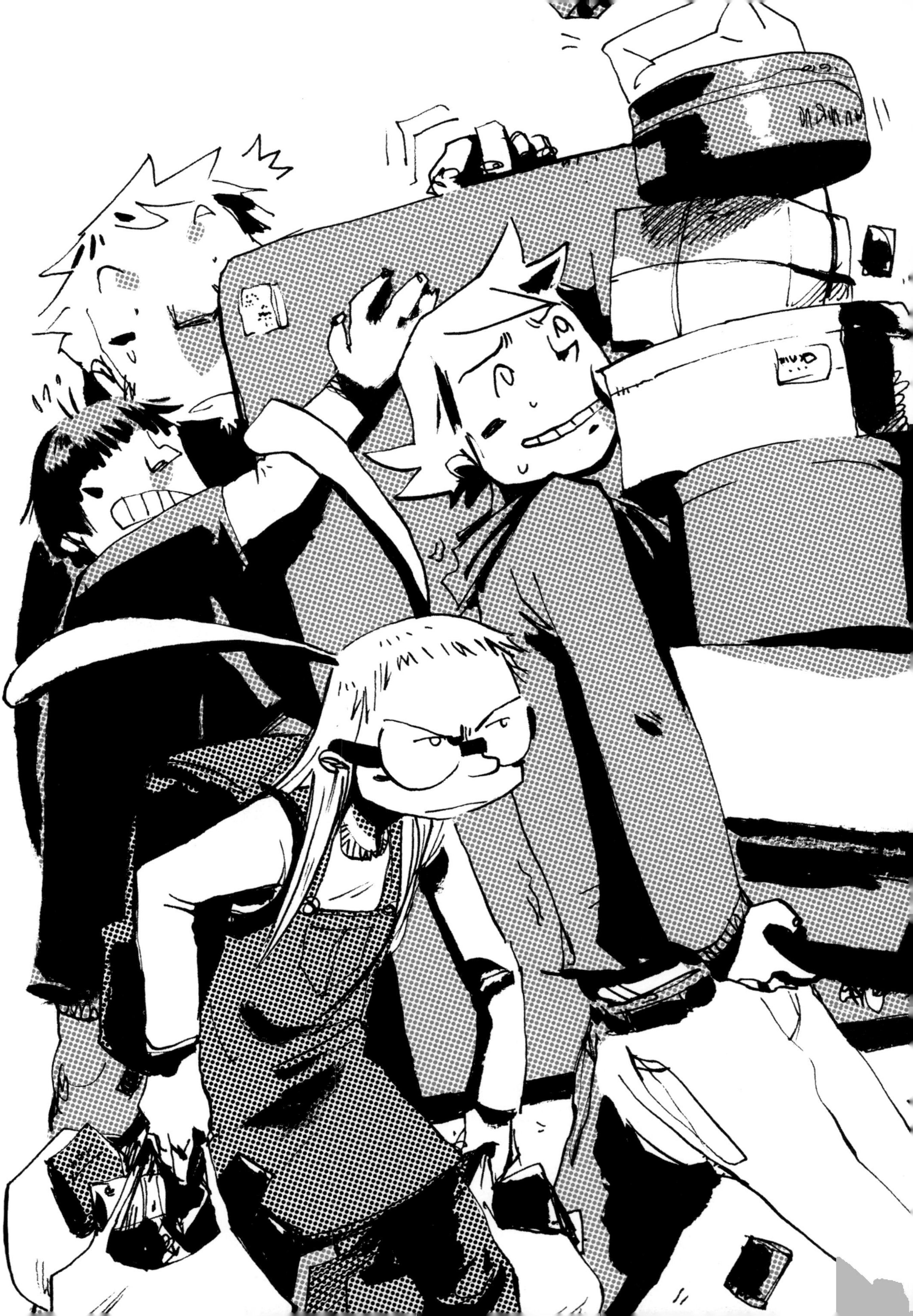

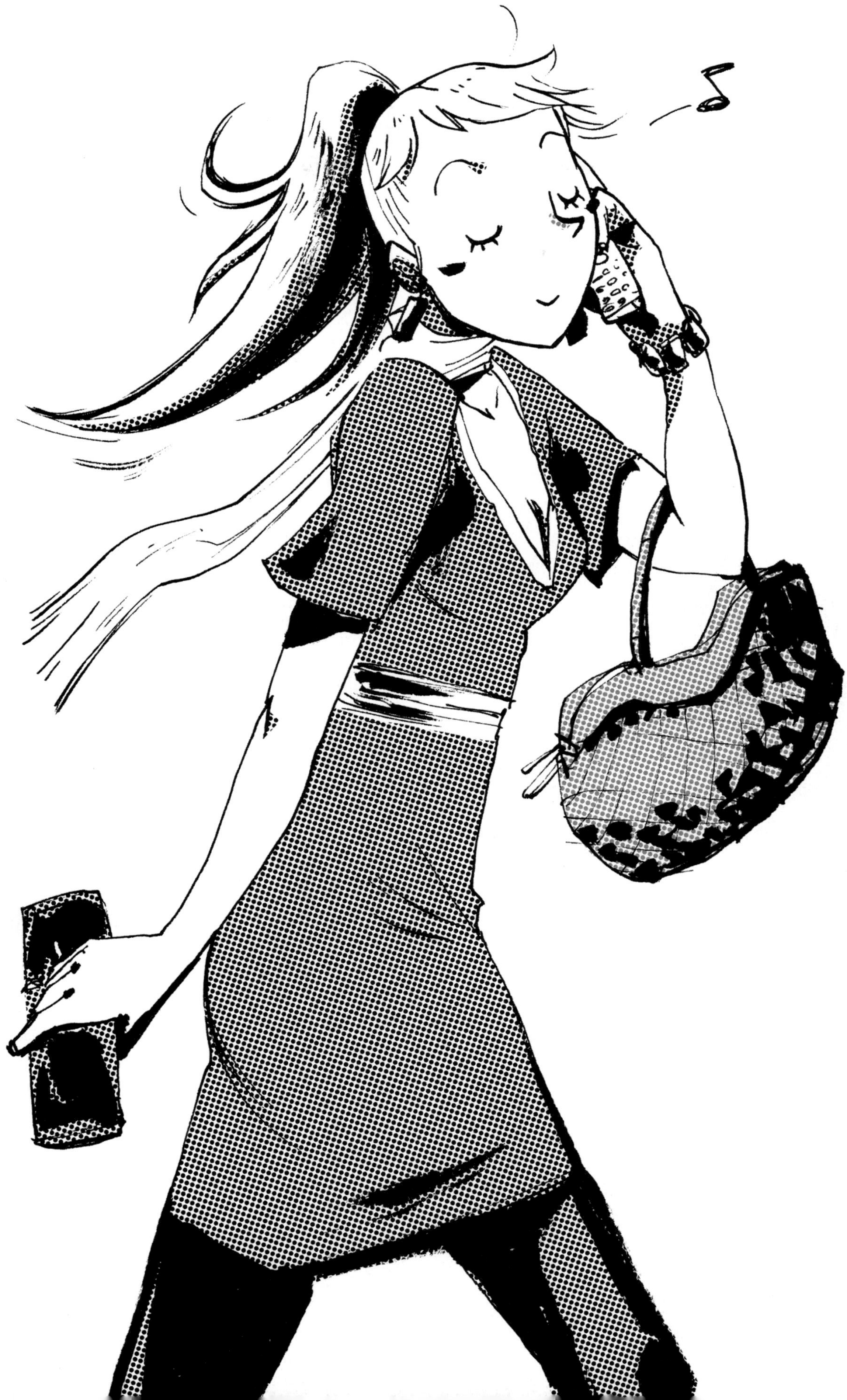

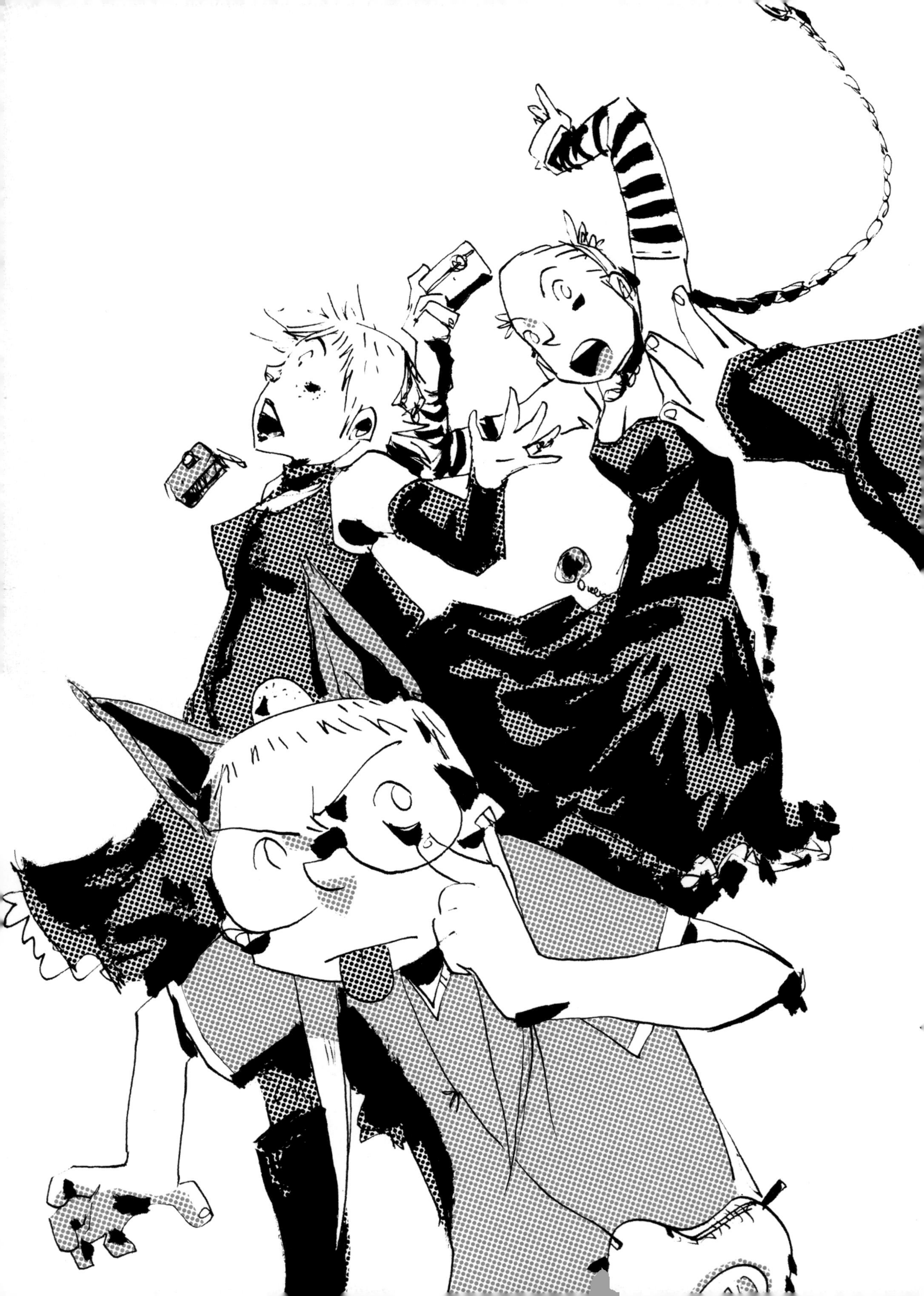

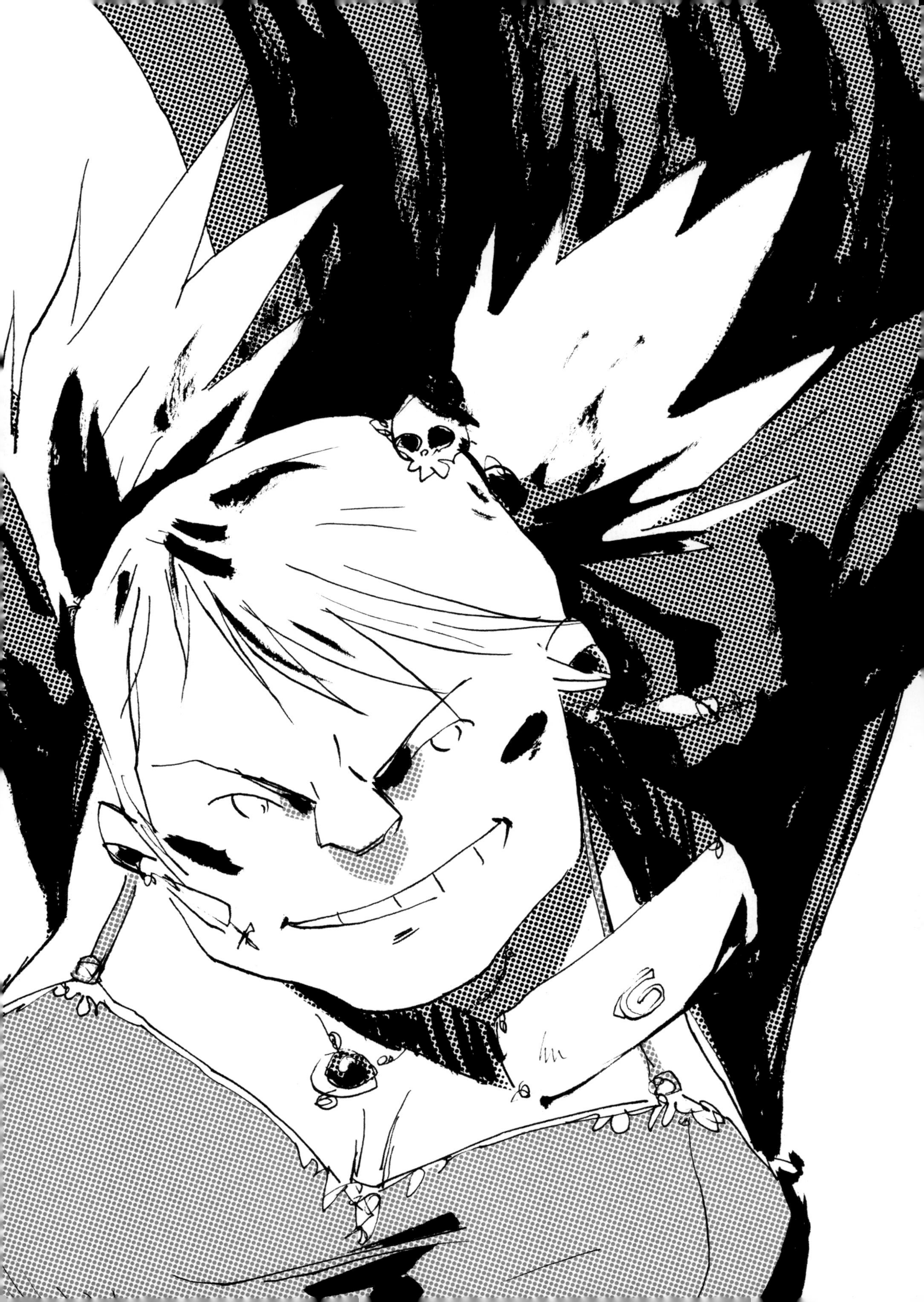

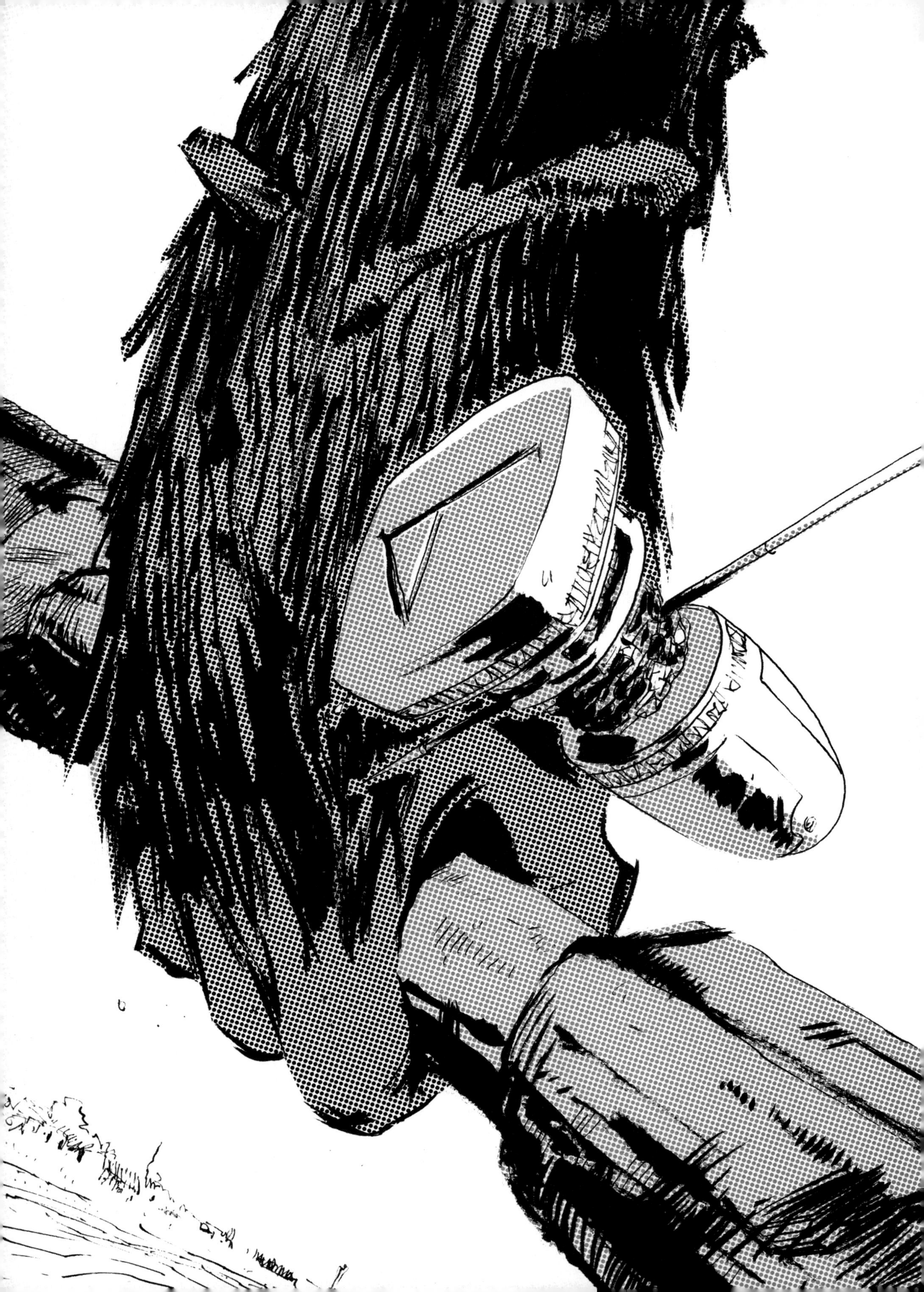

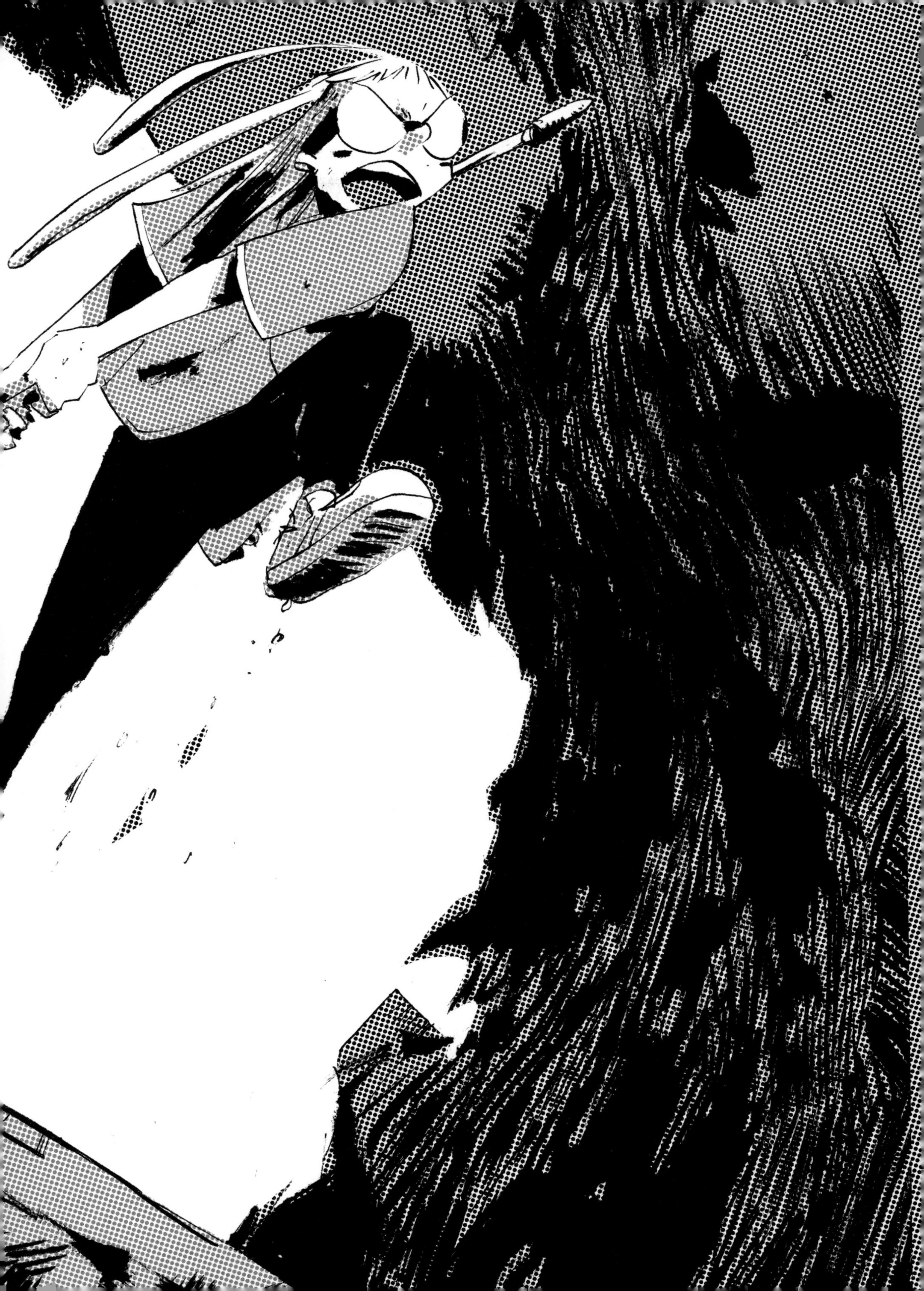

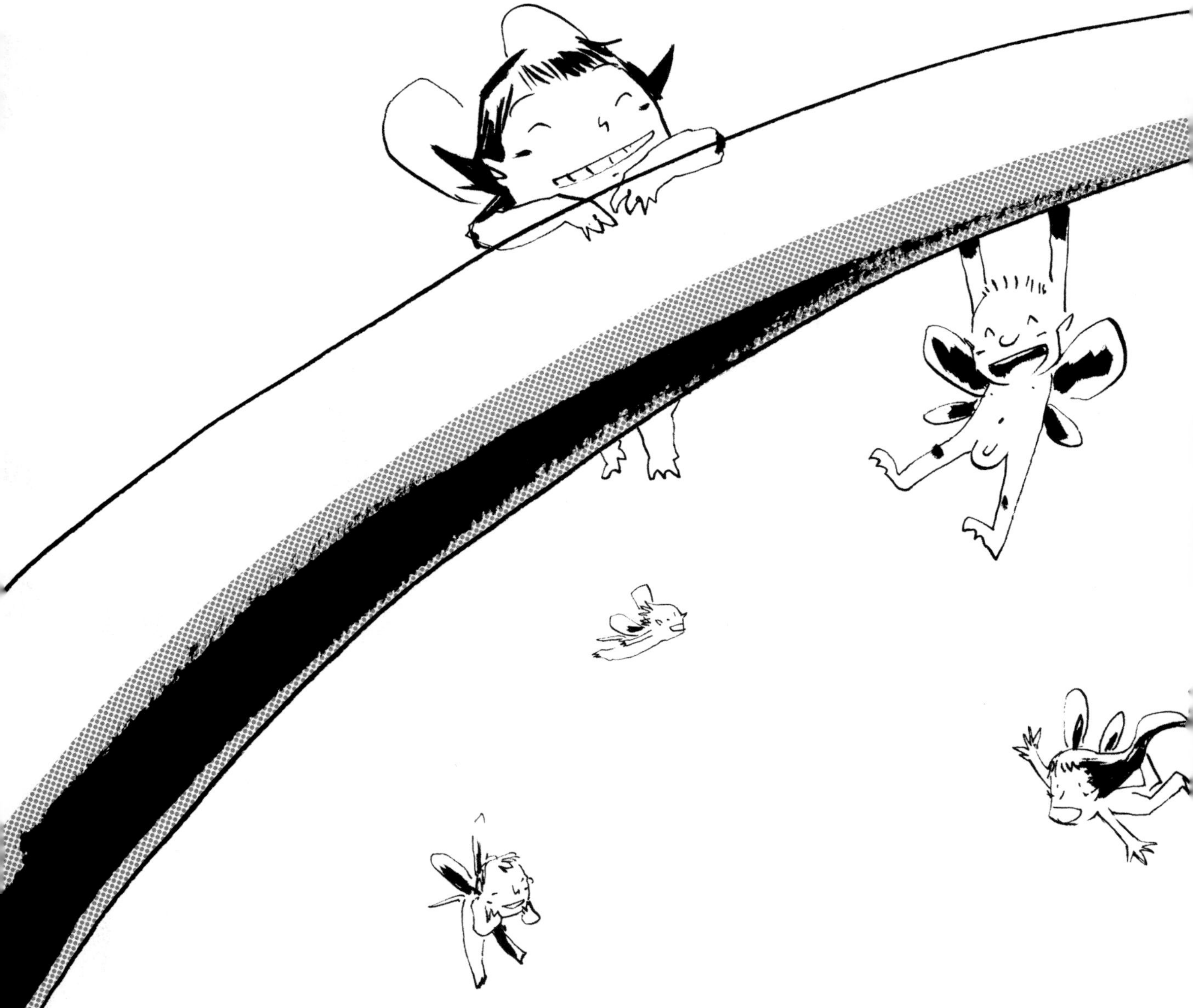

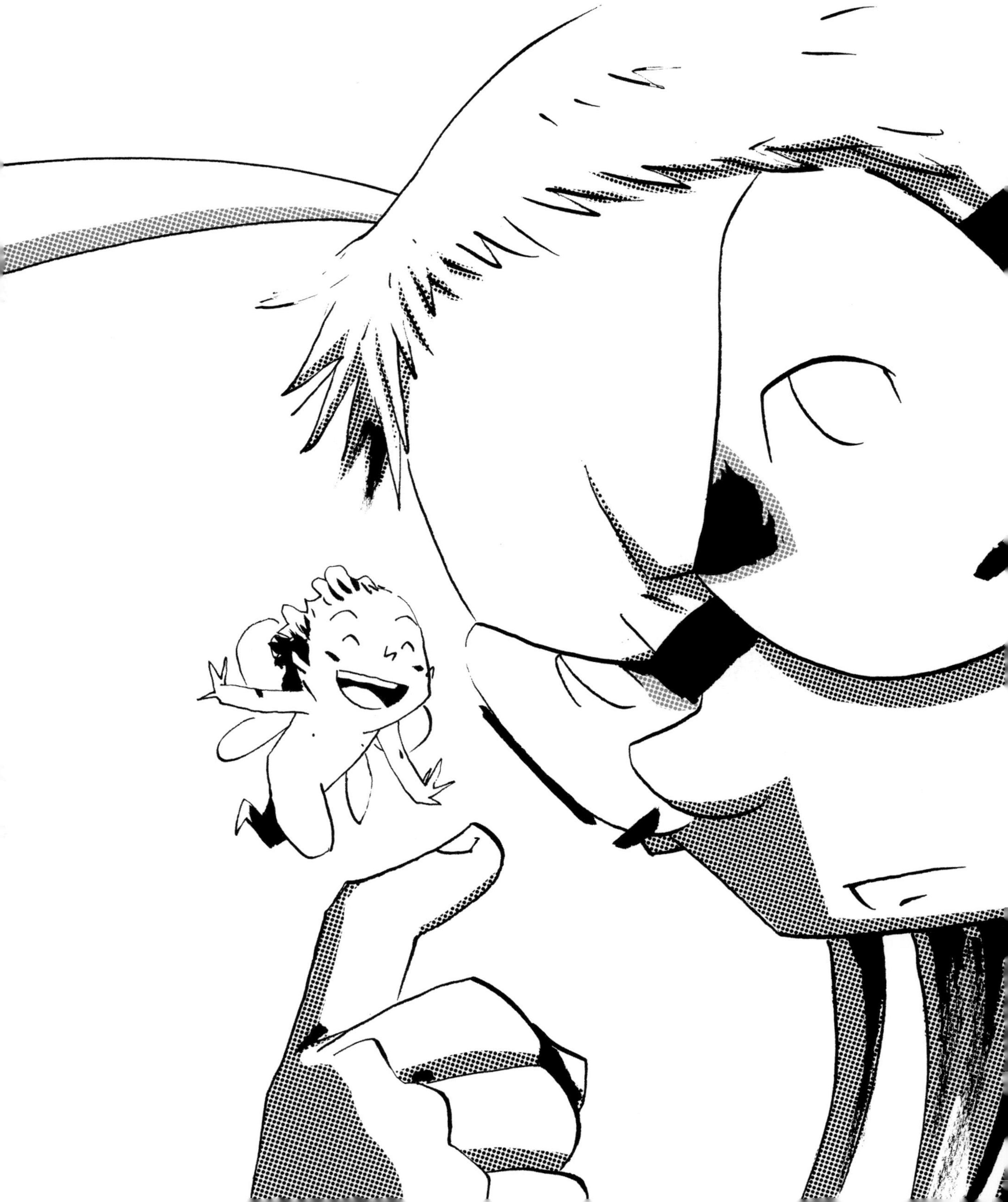

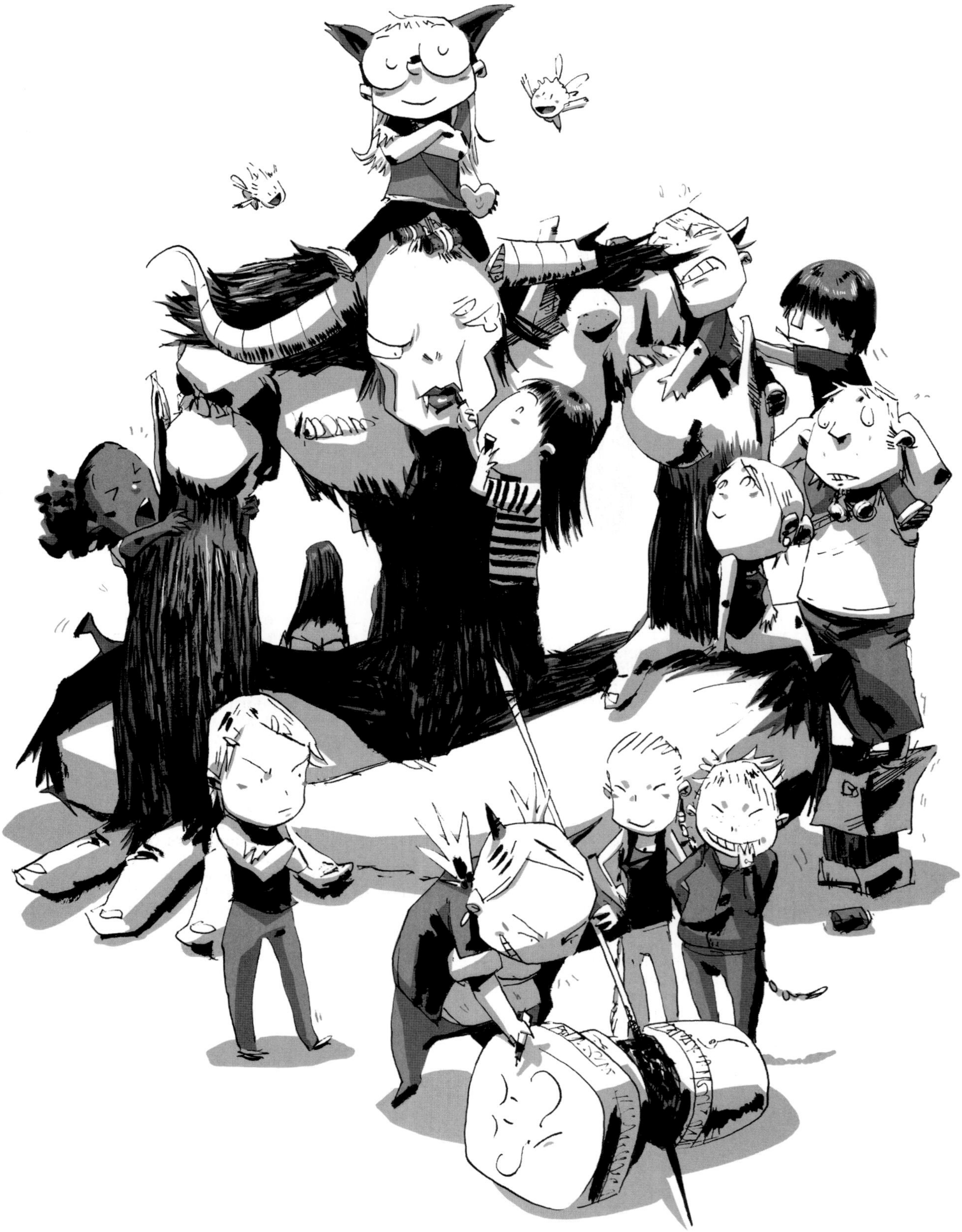

BEHIND THE SCENES

Writing is different for every person who's ever put pen to paper. For some it's a brutish, painful, bloody act of labor. For others, a methodical archeological expedition where bits of the whole are dusted off day by day until a civilization is revealed. After over a dozen years doing this professionally, I still don't know what my "method" is, unless you count guilty procrastination and overwriting as "method." However, I can always tell when a story is alive for me - because it literally claws its way through my guts and brains, consuming all other thoughts until I let it out in one furious burst. Invariably, when I get that feeling, I know I've uncovered a story I can tell the hell out of.

"I Kill Giants" was exactly that sort of story.

I scribbled Barbara's entire journey on a yellow legal pad in less than an hour while waiting for my dad to finish a physical therapy session. The idea for a story about a kid dealing with the death of a parent had been kicking about in my brain for a while, mostly because my Dad had spent a few months in the hospital for diabetes, which led to the loss of one leg - hence the PT session. Ironically, the year Giants finally saw print, 2008, was the year he succumbed to that same disease. (The last issue of "I Kill Giants" will hit the shelves almost exactly one year after his death.) Even though it took a few years for "I Kill Giants" to see print, the story never really diverged from those first dozen or so handwritten pages. Barbara aged up from her initial eight years. Scenes were moved. Thanks to generous and insightful notes from my friend Megan Casey, more of the "magic stuff" was worked through the story line and some of the "overtly sappy" bits were cut. But the spine was always there. More importantly, so was the heart.

As a general rule, I don't read my work once it sees print. I've lived with it for so long already - seen the layers of sinew, muscle, and skin added by my artists at every stage - that flipping through the printed final product doesn't hold much allure for me. Not so with Giants. Giants is a book I WANT to read, especially thanks to Ken's masterful drawing. I am not exaggerating when I tell you that Ken's breakdowns of the last few issues literally brought tears to my eyes, and each subsequent pass has only gotten stronger and stronger. I am fiercely proud of this book, and honored that Ken brought it to life with such care and affection. Barbara's story has become as much Ken's as it ever was mine, and, I hope, yours as well.

As always, thanks for reading.

JOE KELLY
New York, 2008

This has been my first long professional work in comics. Its mix of reality and fantasy has been the canvas on which Joe has kindly allowed me to work. I hope it was an enjoyable book to read.

JM KEN NIIMURA
Paris, 2008

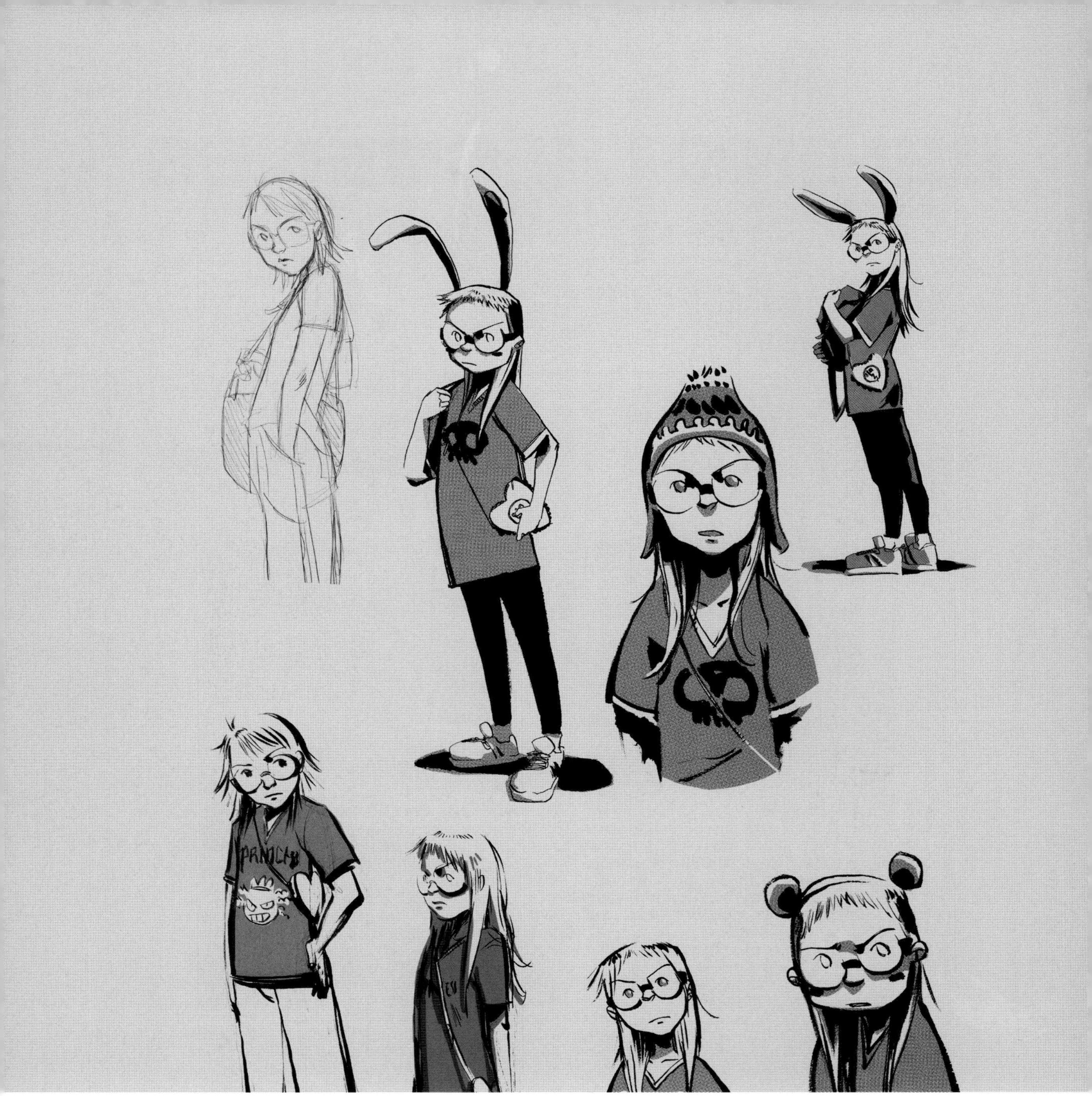

JK Barbara went through a lot of changes during the development of the book. She was loosely based on a 5th grade version of my daughter, who was in Kindergarten at the time I wrote the book. My daughter had a head of crazy curls, and I'd originally pictured Barbara with a barely managed head of flaming red locks. But when Ken started playing with her design, it just didn't sing to him. Especially in black and white, we both felt that the look lost something, and would just look like spaghetti. Being an insightful super-genius, Ken asked me what the hair was all about. I explained that I was gunning for an expression of Barbara's character, wild, unpredictable, a little weird. Since he was toying with the manga style anyway, Ken suggested "funny hats, animal ears really" to achieve the same goal. The second i saw those bunny ears in place, I was hooked.

KN I absolutely wanted Barbara to have a unique look, to have a something that with a single glance could tell us Barbara is a complete alien compared to the other characters. The animal ears were perfect for this: they allowed us to individualize her as well as making her much more expressive. Since the original script didn't say anything about this and Joe wisely didn't add any latter comment, all the characters seem to find it completely normal. That's precisely what I like the most, having this bizarre and somehow superficial element in a dramatic story.

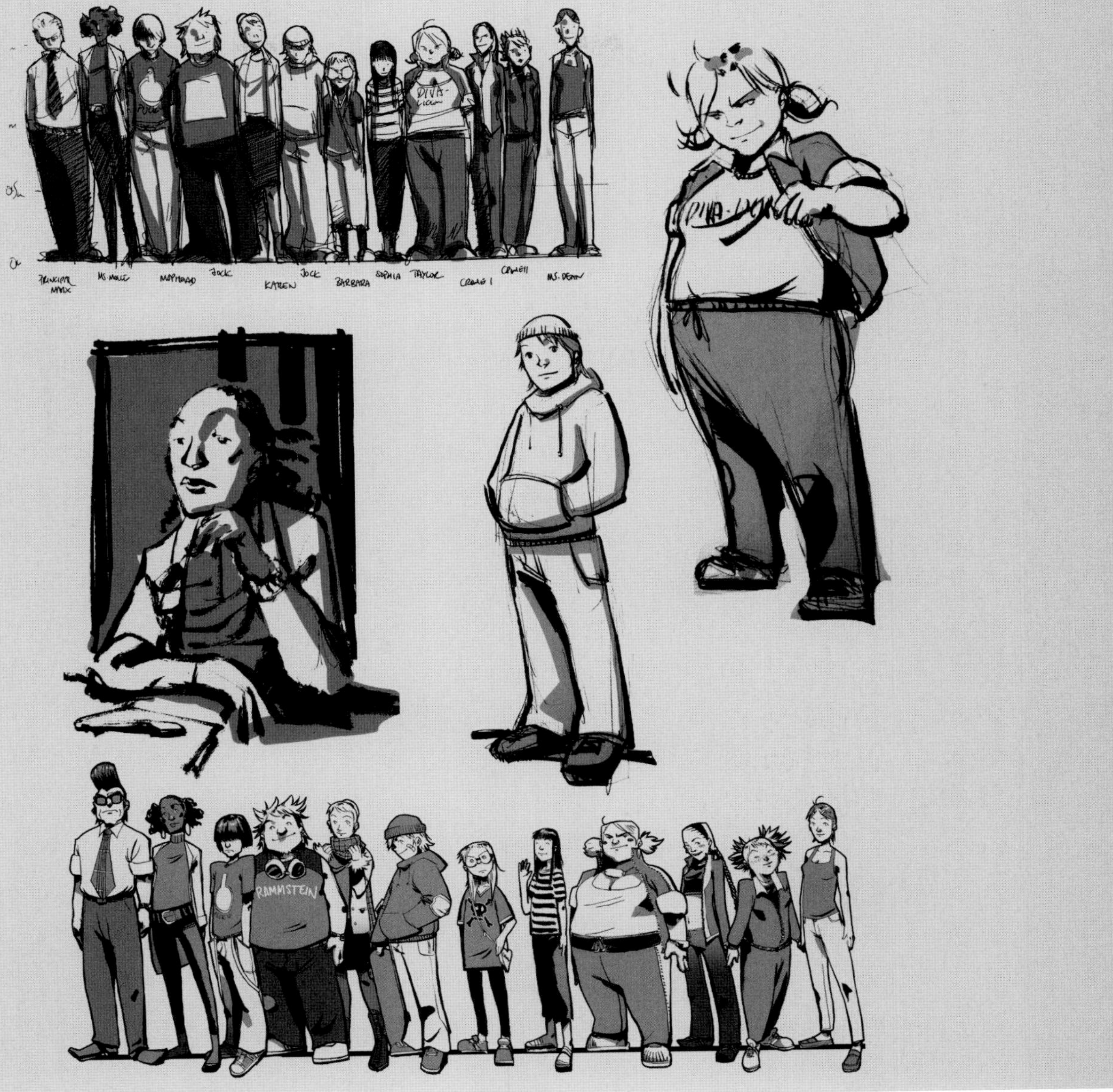
PRINCIPAL MARX
MS. MOLLE
MOPHEAD
JOCK
KAREN
JOCK
BARBARA
SOPHIA
TAYLOR
CRAIG I
MS. DEAN
RAMMSTEIN

JK I love the way Ken develops characters. He gives each one of them a ton of thought, experiments with styles, and ultimately collaborates with me to try and find the best expression of what I threw down on the page. In general, we spent a lot of time working out the ages of everyone in the cast, and he was extremely patient with all of my "help" in the designs.

KN This is my first attempt on a long story, and Joe's depiction of the characters was so accurate (both on a physical and psychological level) that it became a much easier task than I had thought. For months I made sketches of all the cast that we worked later individually. I came up with a first line-up that I found satisfying... but after a while, thanks to some of my friend's comments, I decided to make a second version of them all. It was also at this stage that I also brushed up the graphic style, becoming mostly what was seen on the comic. Sophia's character took very little to create, as well as Ms. Molle's, while Taylor took quite longer. I especially appreciate Mr. Marx, which is my personal homage to Finnish filmmaker Aki Kaurismäki: all the principals should rock as this one! There are of course friends that have been cast to appear on the comic, since it was much easier to imagine the character's body language if I had a real person as a reference. I hope they remain my friends despite their role!

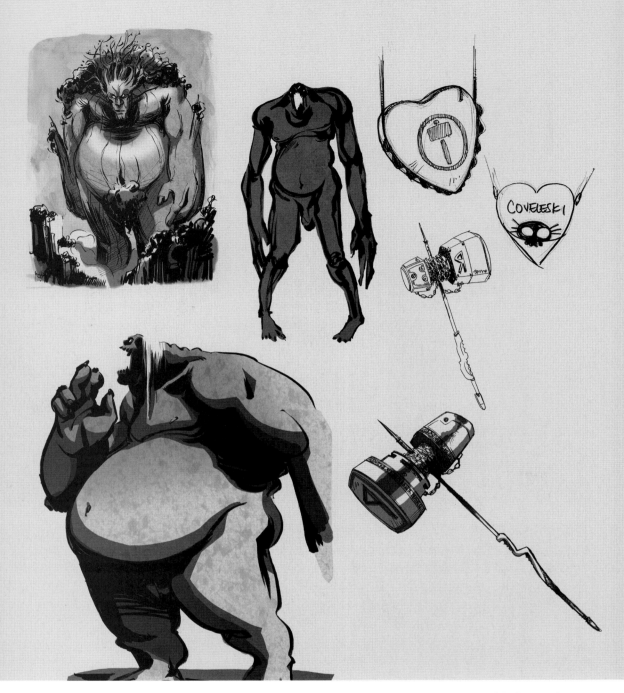

JK Ken threw down about a dozen Giant designs, even though they're really only used for one spread! But it was important to set the tone with them and show the depth of Barbara's imagination. A funny note, as you may notice, the giants are sporting... um... "little giants" of their own in the underpants area. I talked to Ken a bit about the difference in taste between the European and American markets - how here the wee wee tends to be a no no over here, silly as that is. Ken's response was something to the effect of, "Well, you wanted them to be scary, and I figured a monster chasing someone with a giant wang was pretty scary!" Scary indeed. We also put lots of attention on the designs for the pocketbook and Coveleski, both of which are critical props in Barbara's story. He was extremely patient as I'd hem and haw, "Well, that's too girly... that's too rough... try leather... try denim... what if it was a wrench instead of a hammer... or a broom!?! No... a hammer..." The design he ultimately came up with was a great amalgam of both our ideas - with subtle additions from Ken like the handle (a lightning bolt if you look at it!), the rune on the head, etc. I could not have asked for a greater weapon of choice for Barbara.

KN Even though I knew they weren't going to be shown during the story, I drew lots of different giants. I'm absolutely unable to imagine a giant sewing clothes, not to mention underwear. Let them be naked, I say.

JK The Titan had to be the scariest giant we could come up with, and I think I asked Ken for about 50 versions. It was important to me that he be asymmetrical if possible, hideous and malformed. What's so cool to me about the ultimate design Ken came up with is that he's not only pee-your-pants scary, but on a second glance, especially in the context of the story, he's sort of cute in his monstrosity. That face can "act" and emote, which is critical for it to work.

KN This was quite a challenge to me. The key to a succesful story was in well portraying the Titan's character. Something too childish or too explicit would have killed its charm. I found it difficult since we're hiding its identity for almost all the story, so we couldn't allow his appearance to be deceiving. This was the same for all of Barbara's nightmares and visions, where rather than making them very specific, I thought a more abstract look would allow us to find common points with the readers on what is thought to be scary or dangerous. The Titan had also to be grotesque, deformed, but fought and moved a lot, so it had to be a figure that worked in different positions. I am aware that there could have been better possibilities for the Titan, but unfortunately found myself reaching my present limitations. Maybe in some years I'll be able to draw it as I imagine it. Meanwhile, I hope you all find it scary enough...

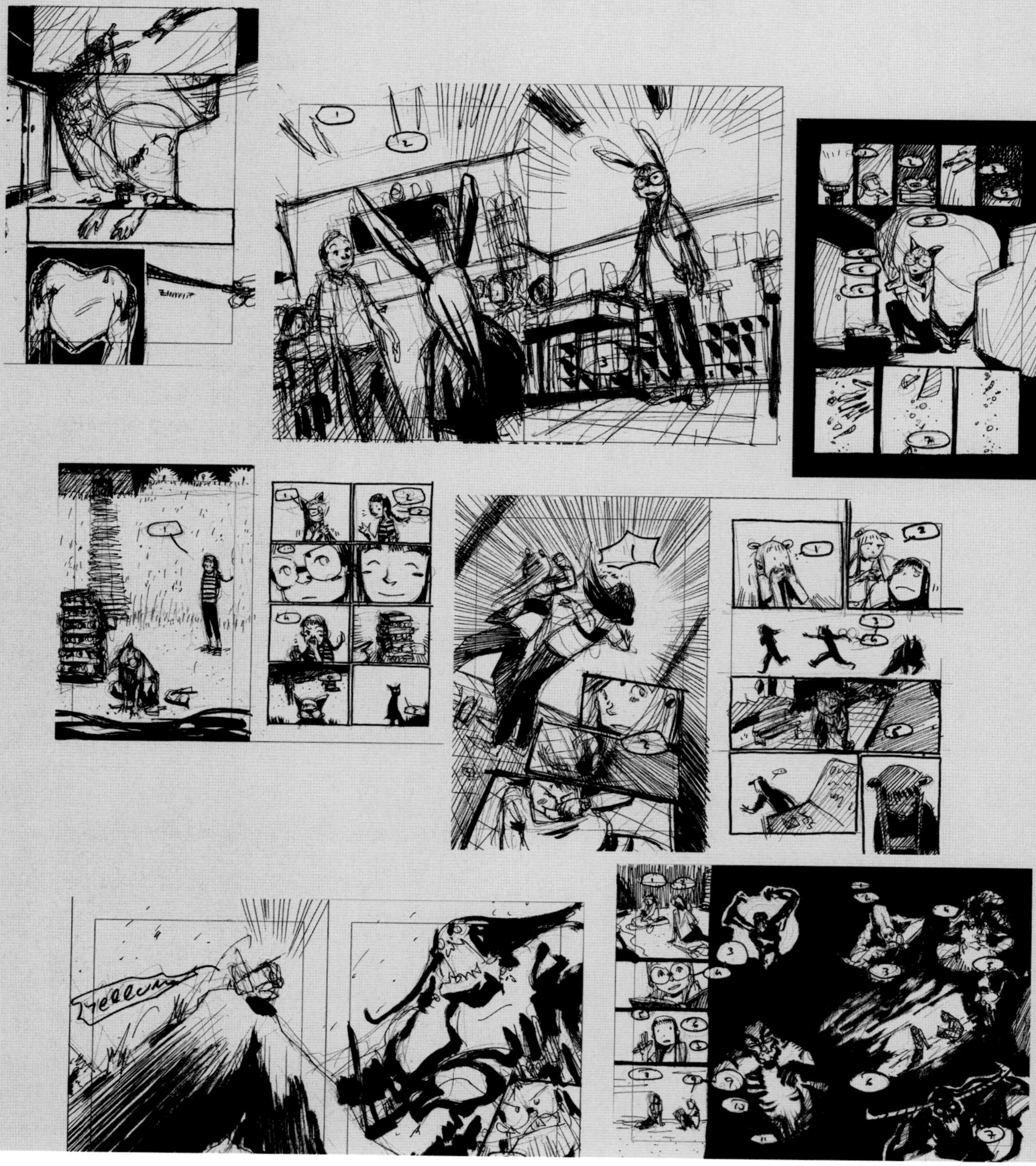

JK I'll let Ken talk about these, but one thing that continually amazed me was how accurate his breakdowns were compared to the final pages. Ken "sees" it all from the second he puts pencil to paper, it's just a matter of slow methodical construction to get everything just right. Even though his style looks "loose," it's a complete illusion. Ken is a perfectioinist of thie highest order, and it shows!

KN The way I make breakdowns is a good reflection of what I understand by comics. I very much appreciate those artists that not only take care on what they tell, but also HOW. As far as I am concerned, it doesn't mean drawing perfect figures or cool pin-ups, but rather being able to create a good reading rhythm, being able to suggest different moods and especially allowing the reader to flow from one panel to the other. Drawings only underline and help to complete the ideas thrown by the script and the breakdowns. I did thousands of versions of each page's composition before sending a final version to Joe. Being the first encounter between words and images, it was a great challenge to mingle them up to a point in which they become one. I also put lot of attention in making them very accurate. Funnily enough, the solution to most of the problems not only came from other artist's works, but also from the music I listen to (I need to have music all the time). It's all about rhythm!

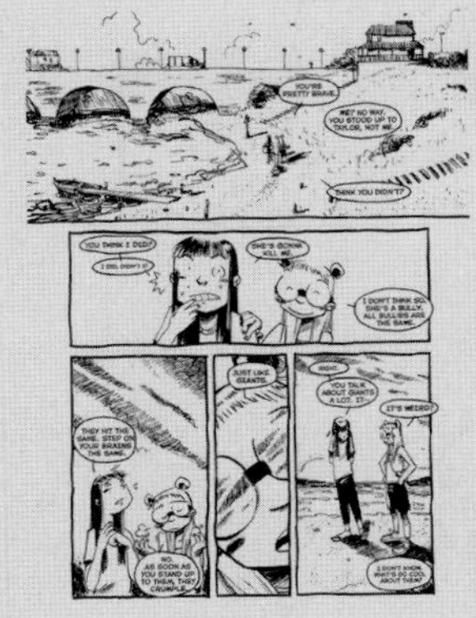

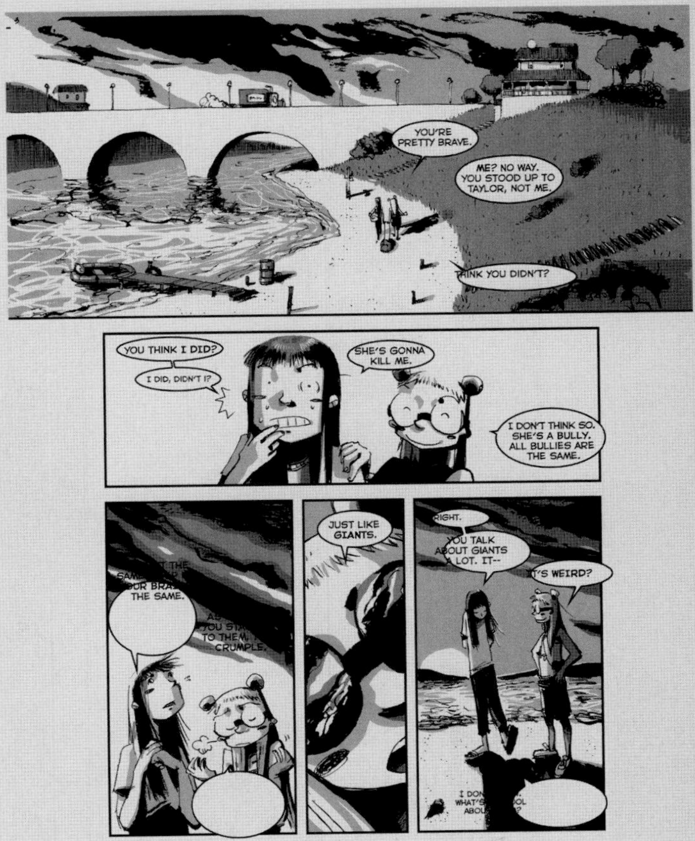
YOU'RE PRETTY BRAVE.
ME? NO WAY. YOU STOOD UP TO TAYLOR, NOT ME.
YOU THINK I DID?
I DID, DIDN'T I?
SHE'S GONNA KILL ME.
I DON'T THINK SO. SHE'S A BULLY. ALL BULLIES ARE THE SAME.
JUST LIKE GIANTS.
RIGHT.

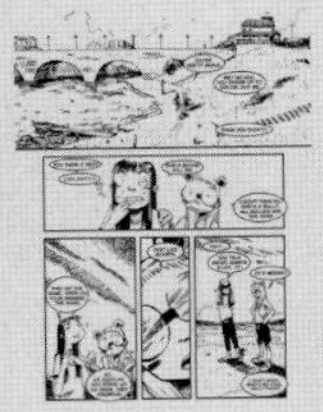

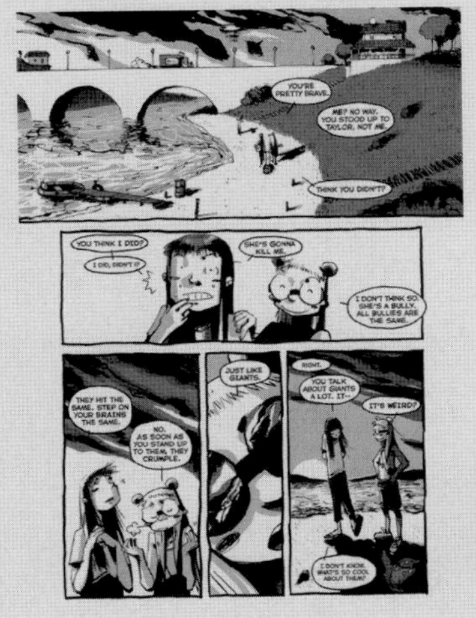
YOU'RE PRETTY BRAVE.
ME? NO WAY. YOU STOOD UP TO TAYLOR, NOT ME.
THINK YOU DIDN'T?
YOU THINK I DID?
I DID, DIDN'T I?
SHE'S GONNA KILL ME.
I DON'T THINK SO. SHE'S A BULLY. ALL BULLIES ARE THE SAME.
JUST LIKE GIANTS.
RIGHT.
YOU TALK ABOUT GIANTS A LOT. IT--
IT'S WEIRD?

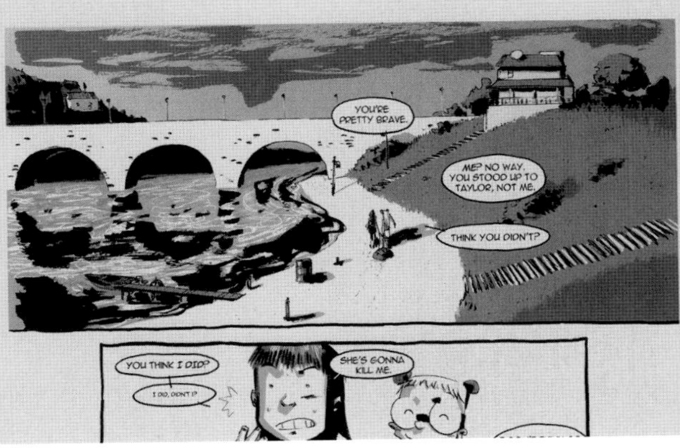
YOU'RE PRETTY BRAVE.
ME? NO WAY. YOU STOOD UP TO TAYLOR, NOT ME.
THINK YOU DIDN'T?
YOU THINK I DID?
I DID, DIDN'T I?
SHE'S GONNA KILL ME.

JK Again, this is Ken's area of expertise, so he should discuss the process, but it's incredible to me how many layers of work he put into a B/W book! The subtleties are incredible and sublime as you move from one stage to the next.

KN My main challenge when I accepted to work on IKG was to create a black and white comic. So far I've been spoiled by being able to use color in my stories, so this time my personal goal was to achieve a good black and white drawing with which I could feel at ease. Some of my favourite authors in this field include Osamu Tezuka, José Muñoz, Nicolas de Crécy, Taiyou Matsumoto, Will Eisner, Hugo Pratt, Iou Kuroda or Katsuhiro Otomo, not to mention classics such as Goya or Hokusai. Unlike them, so far I haven't succeded in drawing with only black lines as I firstly intended: suggesting textures, an atmosphere and movement by only adding black traces remains as a future challenge. At a given moment, I decided to add grey layers to help me complete the images. For the last year, I've been watching plenty of old movies, and it was there by chance that I found many solutions that I used on the panels. Special credit goes to Robert Wise's "The Haunting" for its striking compositions and incredible tension. I kept all of these ideas for my working method while adapting them so as not to make as flashy as to eclipse the storytelling.

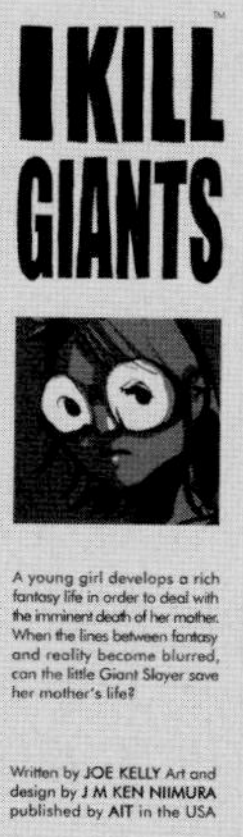
I KILL GIANTS
A young girl develops a rich fantasy life in order to deal with the imminent death of her mother. When the lines between fantasy and reality become blurred, can the little Giant Slayer save her mother's life?
Written by JOE KELLY Art and design by J M KEN NIIMURA published by AIT in the USA

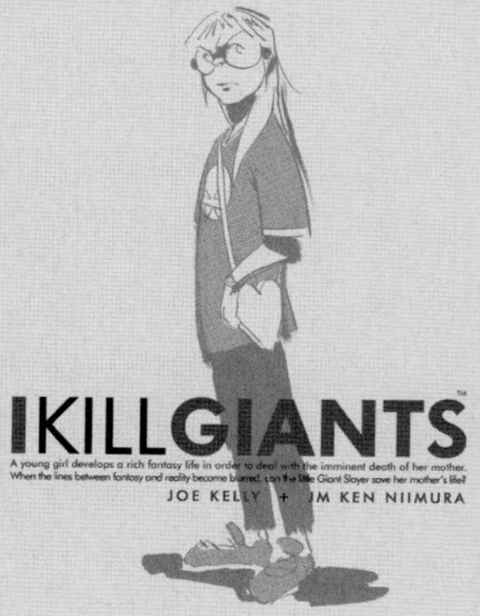
IKILLGIANTS
A young girl develops a rich fantasy life in order to deal with the imminent death of her mother. When the lines between fantasy and reality become blurred, can the little Giant Slayer save her mother's life?
JOE KELLY + JM KEN NIIMURA

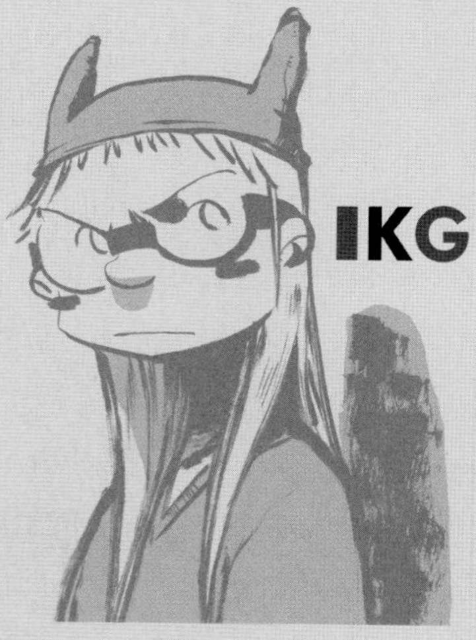
IKG

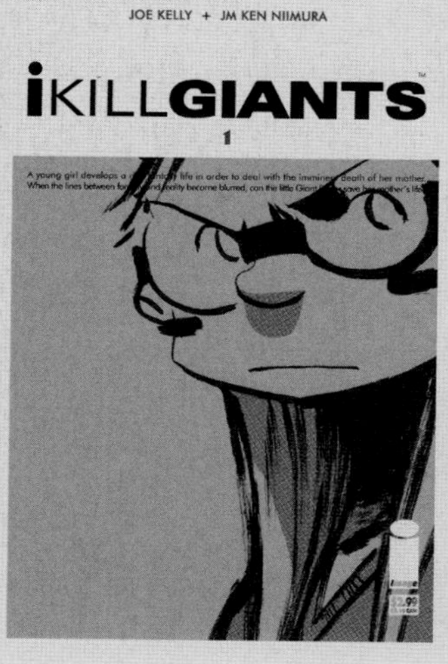
JOE KELLY + JM KEN NIIMURA
IKILLGIANTS
1

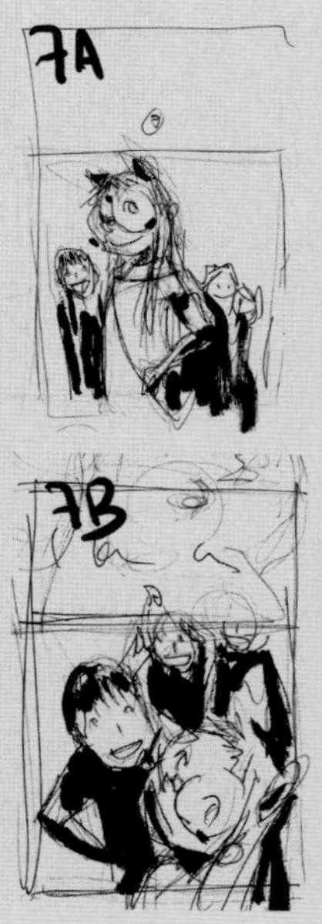
7A
7B

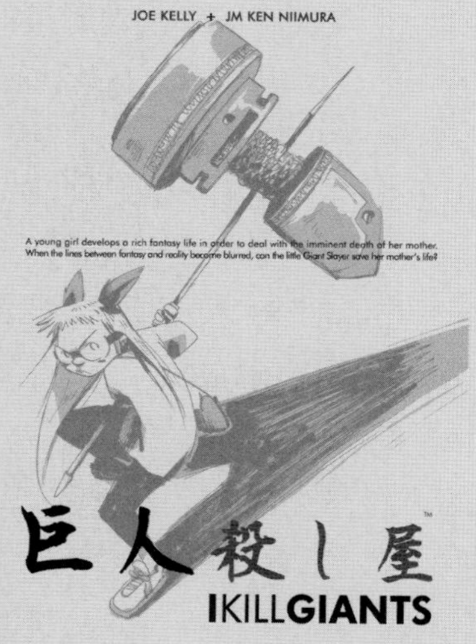
JOE KELLY + JM KEN NIIMURA
A young girl develops a rich fantasy life in order to deal with the imminent death of her mother. When the lines between fantasy and reality become blurred, can the little Giant Slayer save her mother's life?
巨人殺し屋
IKILLGIANTS

JK Ken's sense of design is amazing. I love watching him work through a visual problem as if it's a complicated mathematical equation - only to come up with a solution that at the same time feels organic and effortless. The graphic elements of this book make me smile every time - from the symbols on Barbara's shirts and pocketbook to the little glyphs on the IFC of each issue.

KN I come from a fanzine background where we had to do from the drawings to the graphic design and printing (and eventually selling and distribution). For some reason, I haven't been able to separate these elements from the comics I've done so far. A reader's experience with a comic starts from the very moment he looks at the cover and picks the book. Everything from the paper to the logotype, colors and composition are part of the storytelling. I'm aware I'm not the best graphic designer ever, but I intend creating effective objects through the books I do. Working on a comic doesn't only mean doing the pencilling or inking, but developing a series of symbols, a graphic identity that's particular to this story. Some of my idols in this field include artists such as Chris Ware or Dave McKean, whose books not only are amazingly well done, but have a unique look to them that makes them especially appealling to me. I'm of course way far from them, but hope to modestly follow their steps from now on...

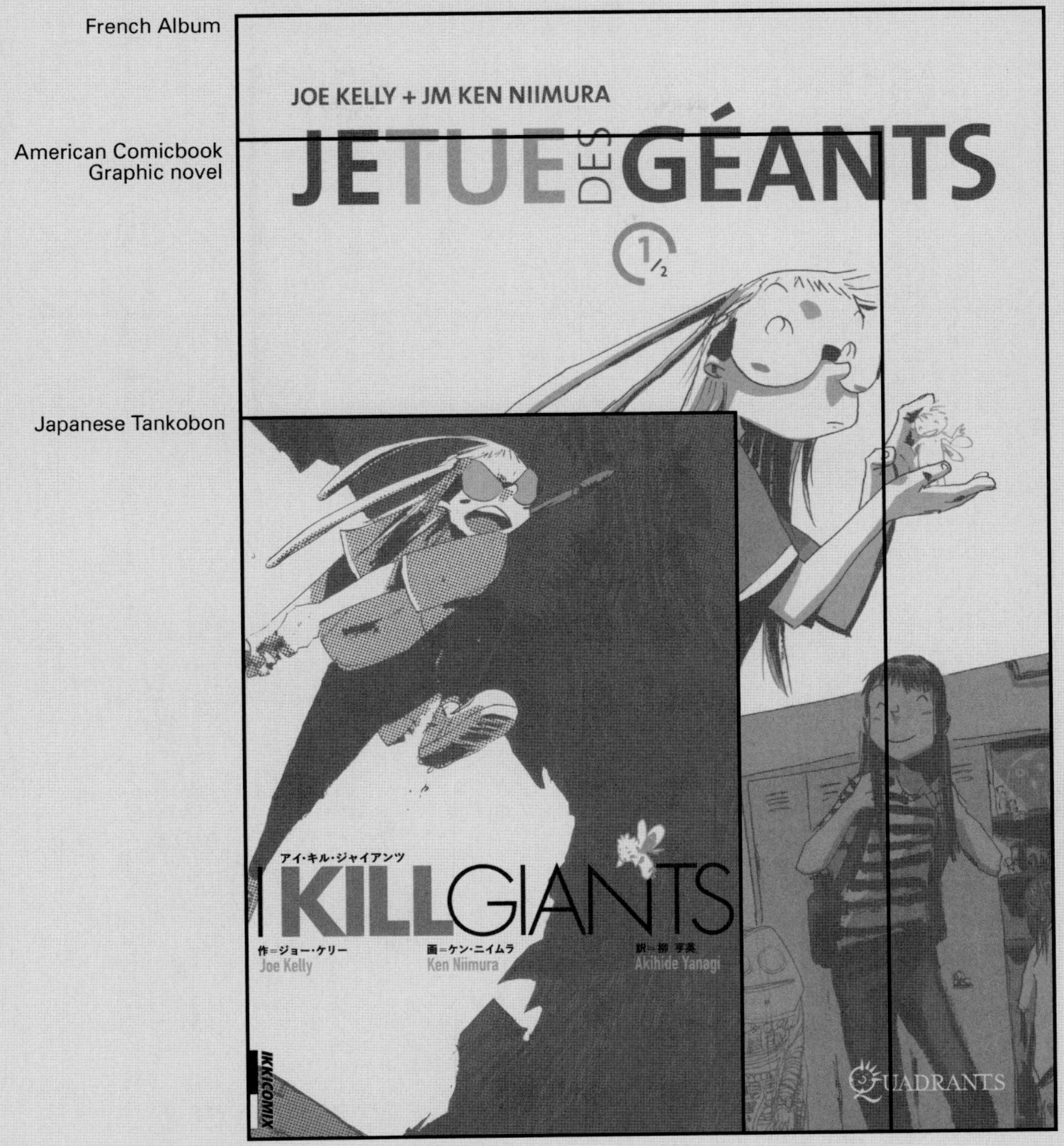
French Album
American Comicbook Graphic novel
Japanese Tankobon
JOE KELLY + JM KEN NIIMURA
JE TUE DES GÉANTS
1/2
アイ・キル・ジャイアンツ
I KILL GIANTS
作=ジョー・ケリー
Joe Kelly
画=ケン・ニイムラ
Ken Niimura
Akihide Yanagi
IKKI COMIX
QUADRANTS

KN Since IKG's first publication in the US, there have been many foreign editions (France, Spain, Italy, Holland, Japan, Brazil and counting), something that's been a source of joy for both Joe and me.

Whenever I read a foreign book, I often find it has a different "feel" to it depending on whether it's a European album, an American comicbook or a Japanese manga.

Being something of a comic storyte-lling geek, my theory is that comics are a very peculiar medium where, for historical and tech-nical reasons, each market has had its own for-mat, rarely found in the rest of markets.

To me, these the differences in format influence the storytelling and pacing, as well as the amount of details and complexity found in the panels, making overall for a whole different reading experience.

It was interesting to see through IKG's foreign editions that it's possible to have a comic published in each of the major marke-t's format (French album, American comicbo-ok, Japanese tankobon) without altering in any way its contents. I wonder what the rea-ding experience might be depending on what kind of comics each person is used to rea-ding.

In the end, this means that the book's message may have reached people from dif-ferent cultures in a more straightforward way, which in the end is what really counts.

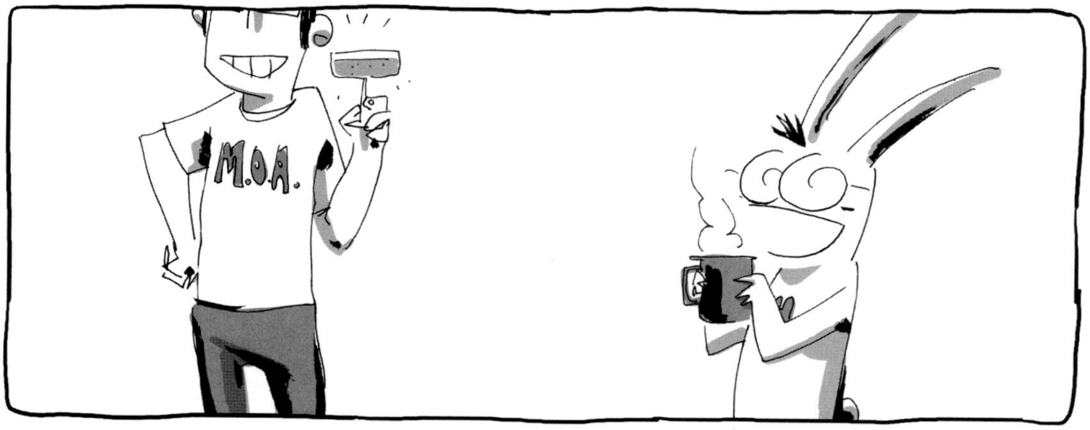
M.O.A.

Since the release of the book, it's been amazing and humbling to me to meet readers of IKG. More often than not, these conversations wind up with one or both of us getting misty eyed - often with just a few words exchanged. I feel very privileged to have been a part of something that people find in times of crisis in their lives.

The first time I met a young woman who was cosplaying as Barbara I almost lost it. When I met a guy who had tattooed the cover of the Titan Edition on his arm I really did lose it. I've always loved this book, but it's taken on a special resonance thanks to the feedback from the fans. They say that the reader is the "final collaborator." I am very lucky to have met so many of these collaborators, and I look forward to meeting more as word of the book spreads.

IKG has really become a part of me. As a general rule I don't look back at stuff I've written - I find it uncomfortable and strange, but never with Giants. You have to remember too that my connection to this project runs very deep. I cooked up the story taking my Dad to rehab after he'd lost a leg to diabetes. Years later after meeting Ken, I was finishing the single issues when he fell ill again and ultimately passed away. So any time I revisit the book, a whole slew of emotions come with it - which is why I relate so deeply to the folks who are kind enough to come to a con or drop me a letter and let me know what the book means to them.

We're in the same boat, really.

JOE KELLY
New York, 2014

Looking back at IKG, I often find many things I didn't see at the time of its creation.

For instance, every time I play "Shadow of the Colossus", it strikes me how much it influenced the way I drew and showed the giants. I wasn't too conscious at the time, but it's certainly thanks to Fumito Ueda's masterpiece that IKG looks the way it looks.

Man of Action's Steve Seagle gave us some wise advice concerning IKG's covers. It's been a matter of him suggesting to just add one color to the design, but he managed to give a totally different amosphere to be whole and I'm really thankful for that.

After its initial release in the US, there have been several foreign editions of IKG. Every time I attend a signing session, I'm always surprised to see that regardless of the country, this book appeals to a very wide audience.

Having the readers telling us what the book means to them and sharing their story with us is a constant reminder that we're not the only ones dealing with similar situations. and it also means thers's a reason for the book to exist.

I sincerely feel I owe all I am as an artist to IKG - never in my life had I had someone trusting me as much as Joe did, and helping me go step by step though all the process although I didn't have that much experience. Working with Joe helped me raise the bar on self-demanding.

It's been every creator's dream project - a school, both on the artistic side as well as the human side.

KEN NIIMURA
Tokyo, 2014

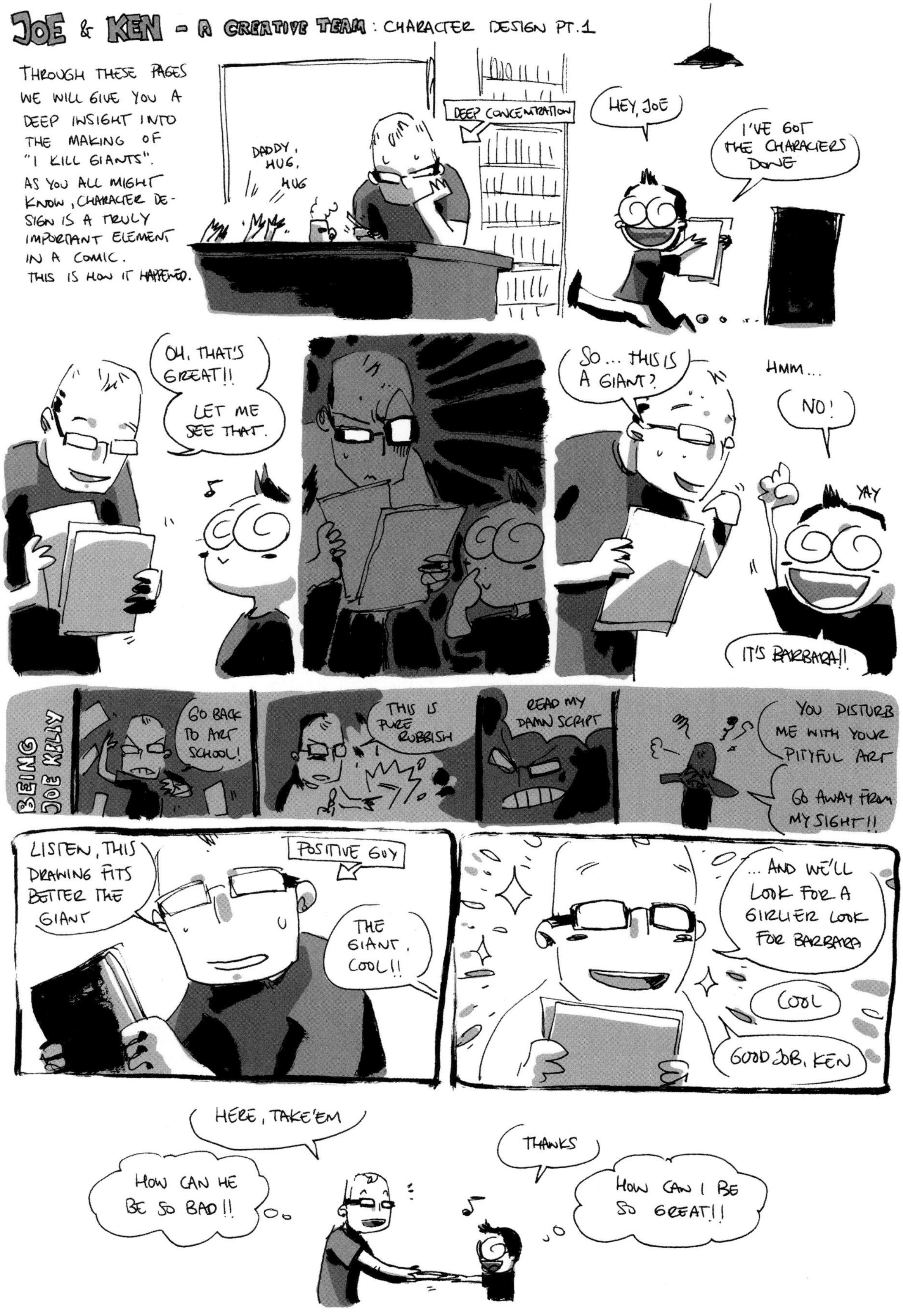
JOE & KEN - A CREATIVE TEAM : CHARACTER DESIGN PT. 1
THROUGH THESE PAGES WE WILL GIVE YOU A DEEP INSIGHT INTO THE MAKING OF "I KILL GIANTS". AS YOU ALL MIGHT KNOW, CHARACTER DESIGN IS A TRULY IMPORTANT ELEMENT IN A COMIC. THIS IS HOW IT HAPPENED.
DEEP CONCENTRATION
DADDY, HUG, HUG
HEY, JOE
I'VE GOT THE CHARACTERS DONE
OH, THAT'S GREAT!!
LET ME SEE THAT.
SO... THIS IS A GIANT?
HMM...
NO!
YAY
IT'S BARBARA!!
BEING JOE KELLY
GO BACK TO ART SCHOOL!
THIS IS PURE RUBBISH
READ MY DAMN SCRIPT
YOU DISTURB ME WITH YOUR PITYFUL ART
GO AWAY FROM MY SIGHT!!
LISTEN, THIS DRAWING FITS BETTER THE GIANT
POSITIVE GUY
THE GIANT. COOL!!
... AND WE'LL LOOK FOR A GIRLIER LOOK FOR BARBARA
COOL
GOOD JOB, KEN
HERE, TAKE'EM
THANKS
HOW CAN HE BE SO BAD!!
HOW CAN I BE SO GREAT!!

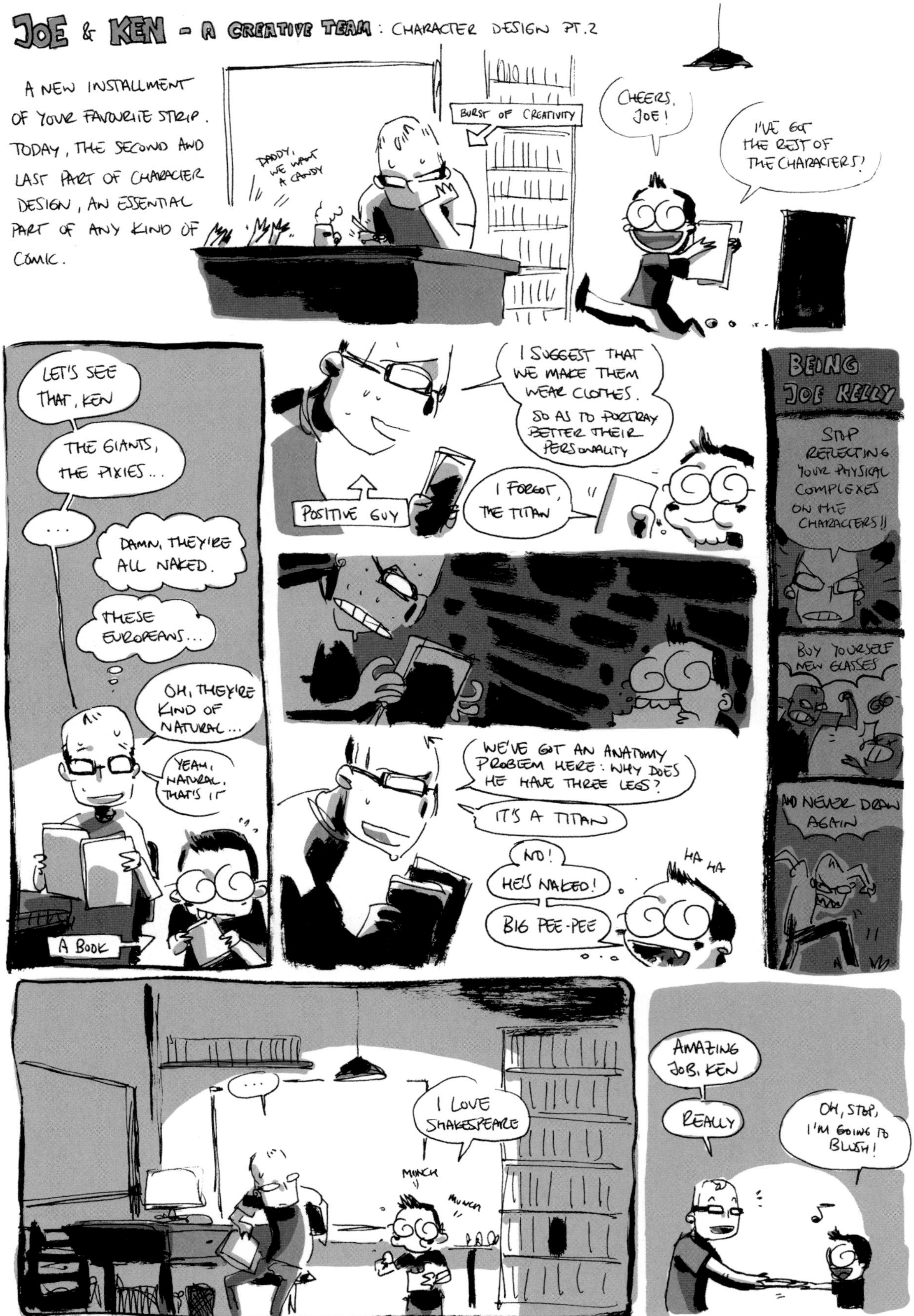
JOE & KEN - A CREATIVE TEAM: CHARACTER DESIGN PT.2
A NEW INSTALLMENT OF YOUR FAVOURITE STRIP. TODAY, THE SECOND AND LAST PART OF CHARACTER DESIGN, AN ESSENTIAL PART OF ANY KIND OF COMIC.
BURST OF CREATIVITY
DADDY, WE WANT A CANDY
CHEERS, JOE!
I'VE GOT THE REST OF THE CHARACTERS!
LET'S SEE THAT, KEN
THE GIANTS, THE PIXIES...
...
DAMN, THEY'RE ALL NAKED.
THESE EUROPEANS...
OH, THEY'RE KIND OF NATURAL...
YEAH, NATURAL, THAT'S IT
A BOOK
I SUGGEST THAT WE MAKE THEM WEAR CLOTHES.
SO AS TO PORTRAY BETTER THEIR PERSONALITY
POSITIVE GUY
I FORGOT THE TITAN
WE'VE GOT AN ANATOMY PROBLEM HERE: WHY DOES HE HAVE THREE LEGS?
IT'S A TITAN
NO!
HE'S NAKED!
BIG PEE-PEE
HA HA
BEING JOE KELLY
STOP REFLECTING YOUR PHYSICAL COMPLEXES ON THE CHARACTERS!!
BUY YOURSELF NEW GLASSES
AND NEVER DRAW AGAIN
...
I LOVE SHAKESPEARE
MUNCH
MUNCH
AMAZING JOB, KEN
REALLY
OH, STOP, I'M GOING TO BLUSH!

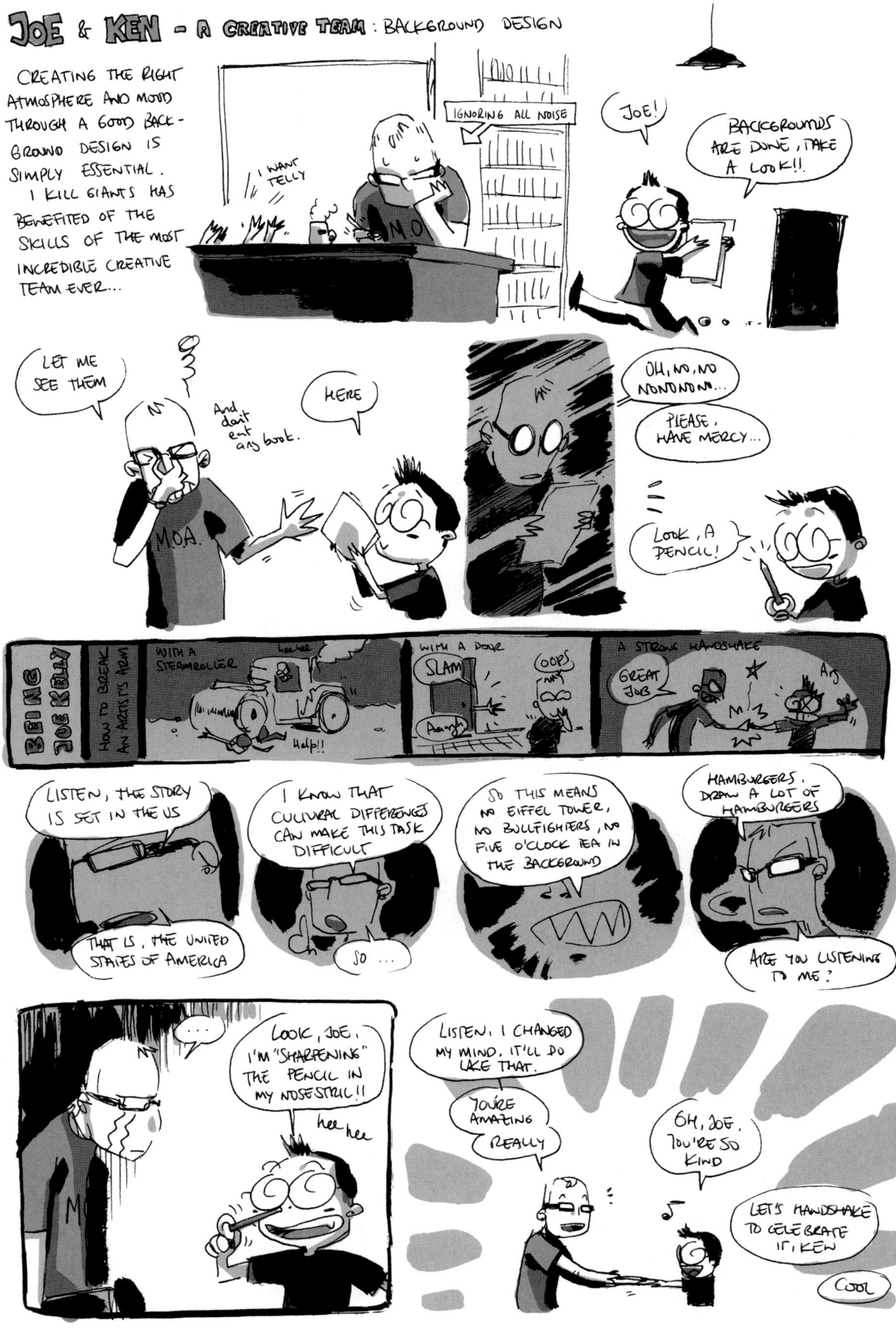
JOE & KEN - A CREATIVE TEAM: BACKGROUND DESIGN
CREATING THE RIGHT ATMOSPHERE AND MOOD THROUGH A GOOD BACKGROUND DESIGN IS SIMPLY ESSENTIAL. I KILL GIANTS HAS BENEFITED OF THE SKILLS OF THE MOST INCREDIBLE CREATIVE TEAM EVER...
I WANT TELLY
M.O
IGNORING ALL NOISE
JOE!
BACKGROUNDS ARE DONE, TAKE A LOOK!!
LET ME SEE THEM
And don't eat any book.
M.O.A.
HERE
OH, NO, NO NONONONO...
PLEASE, HAVE MERCY...
LOOK, A PENCIL!
BEING JOE KELLY
HOW TO BREAK AN ARTIST'S ARM
WITH A STEAMROLLER
hee hee
Help!!
WITH A DOOR
SLAM
OOPS
Aaargh
A STRONG HANDSHAKE
GREAT JOB
Arg
LISTEN, THE STORY IS SET IN THE US
THAT IS, THE UNITED STATES OF AMERICA
I KNOW THAT CULTURAL DIFFERENCES CAN MAKE THIS TASK DIFFICULT
SO ...
SO THIS MEANS NO EIFFEL TOWER, NO BULLFIGHTERS, NO FIVE O'CLOCK TEA IN THE BACKGROUND
HAMBURGERS. DRAW A LOT OF HAMBURGERS
ARE YOU LISTENING TO ME?
...
LOOK, JOE, I'M "SHARPENING" THE PENCIL IN MY NOSESTRIL!!
hee hee
M
LISTEN, I CHANGED MY MIND, IT'LL DO LIKE THAT.
YOU'RE AMAZING
REALLY
OH, JOE, YOU'RE SO KIND
LET'S HANDSHAKE TO CELEBRATE IT, KEN
COOL

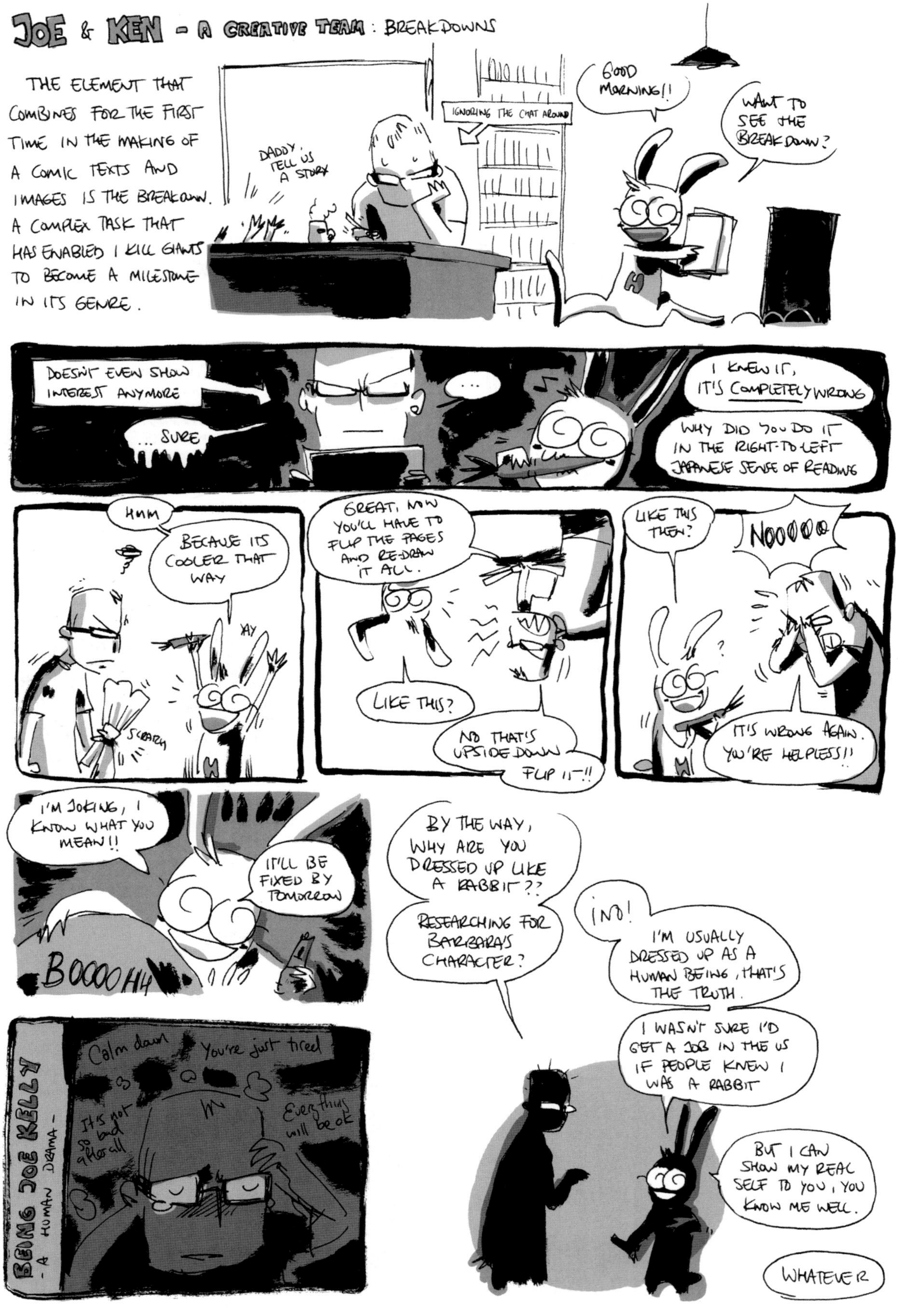
JOE & KEN - A CREATIVE TEAM : BREAKDOWNS
THE ELEMENT THAT COMBINES FOR THE FIRST TIME IN THE MAKING OF A COMIC TEXTS AND IMAGES IS THE BREAKDOWN. A COMPLEX TASK THAT HAS ENABLED I KILL GIANTS TO BECOME A MILESTONE IN ITS GENRE.
DADDY, TELL US A STORY
IGNORING THE CHAT AROUND
GOOD MORNING!!
WANT TO SEE THE BREAKDOWN?
DOESN'T EVEN SHOW INTEREST ANYMORE
...
... SURE
I KNEW IT, IT'S COMPLETELY WRONG
WHY DID YOU DO IT IN THE RIGHT-TO-LEFT JAPANESE SENSE OF READING
HMM
BECAUSE ITS COOLER THAT WAY
YAY
SCRATCH
GREAT, NOW YOU'LL HAVE TO FLIP THE PAGES AND RE-DRAW IT ALL.
LIKE THIS?
NO THAT'S UPSIDE DOWN FLIP IT!!
LIKE THIS THEN?
NOOOOO
IT'S WRONG AGAIN. YOU'RE HELPLESS!!
I'M JOKING, I KNOW WHAT YOU MEAN!!
IT'LL BE FIXED BY TOMORROW
BOOOOHH
BY THE WAY, WHY ARE YOU DRESSED UP LIKE A RABBIT??
RESEARCHING FOR BARBARA'S CHARACTER?
NO!
I'M USUALLY DRESSED UP AS A HUMAN BEING, THAT'S THE TRUTH.
I WASN'T SURE I'D GET A JOB IN THE US IF PEOPLE KNEW I WAS A RABBIT
BUT I CAN SHOW MY REAL SELF TO YOU, YOU KNOW ME WELL.
WHATEVER
BEING JOE KELLY - A HUMAN DRAMA -
Calm down
You're just tired
It's not so bad after all
Everything will be ok

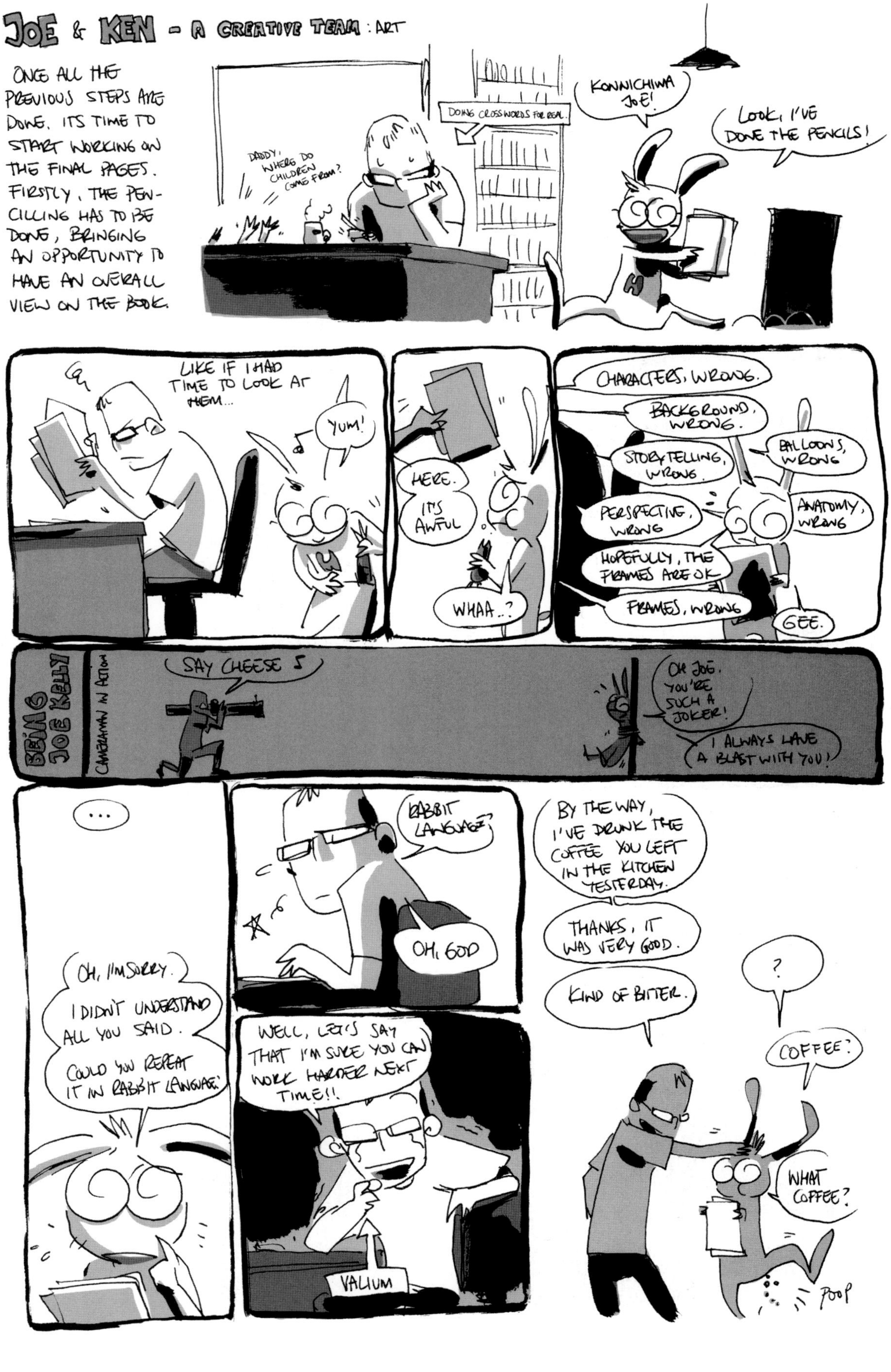
JOE & KEN - A CREATIVE TEAM : ART
ONCE ALL THE PREVIOUS STEPS ARE DONE, ITS TIME TO START WORKING ON THE FINAL PAGES. FIRSTLY, THE PENCILLING HAS TO BE DONE, BRINGING AN OPPORTUNITY TO HAVE AN OVERALL VIEW ON THE BOOK.
DOING CROSSWORDS FOR REAL.
DADDY, WHERE DO CHILDREN COME FROM?
KONNICHIWA JOE!
LOOK, I'VE DONE THE PENCILS!
LIKE IF I HAD TIME TO LOOK AT THEM...
YUM!
HERE.
IT'S AWFUL
WHAA..?
CHARACTERS, WRONG.
BACKGROUND, WRONG.
STORYTELLING, WRONG.
BALLOONS, WRONG
PERSPECTIVE, WRONG
ANATOMY, WRONG
HOPEFULLY, THE FRAMES ARE OK
FRAMES, WRONG
GEE.
BEING JOE KELLY
CAMERAMAN IN ACTION
SAY CHEESE
OH JOE, YOU'RE SUCH A JOKER!
I ALWAYS HAVE A BLAST WITH YOU!
...
OH, I'M SORRY.
I DIDN'T UNDERSTAND ALL YOU SAID.
COULD YOU REPEAT IT IN RABBIT LANGUAGE?
RABBIT LANGUAGE?
OH, GOD
WELL, LET'S SAY THAT I'M SURE YOU CAN WORK HARDER NEXT TIME!!
VALIUM
BY THE WAY, I'VE DRUNK THE COFFEE YOU LEFT IN THE KITCHEN YESTERDAY.
THANKS, IT WAS VERY GOOD.
KIND OF BITTER.
?
COFFEE?
WHAT COFFEE?
POOP

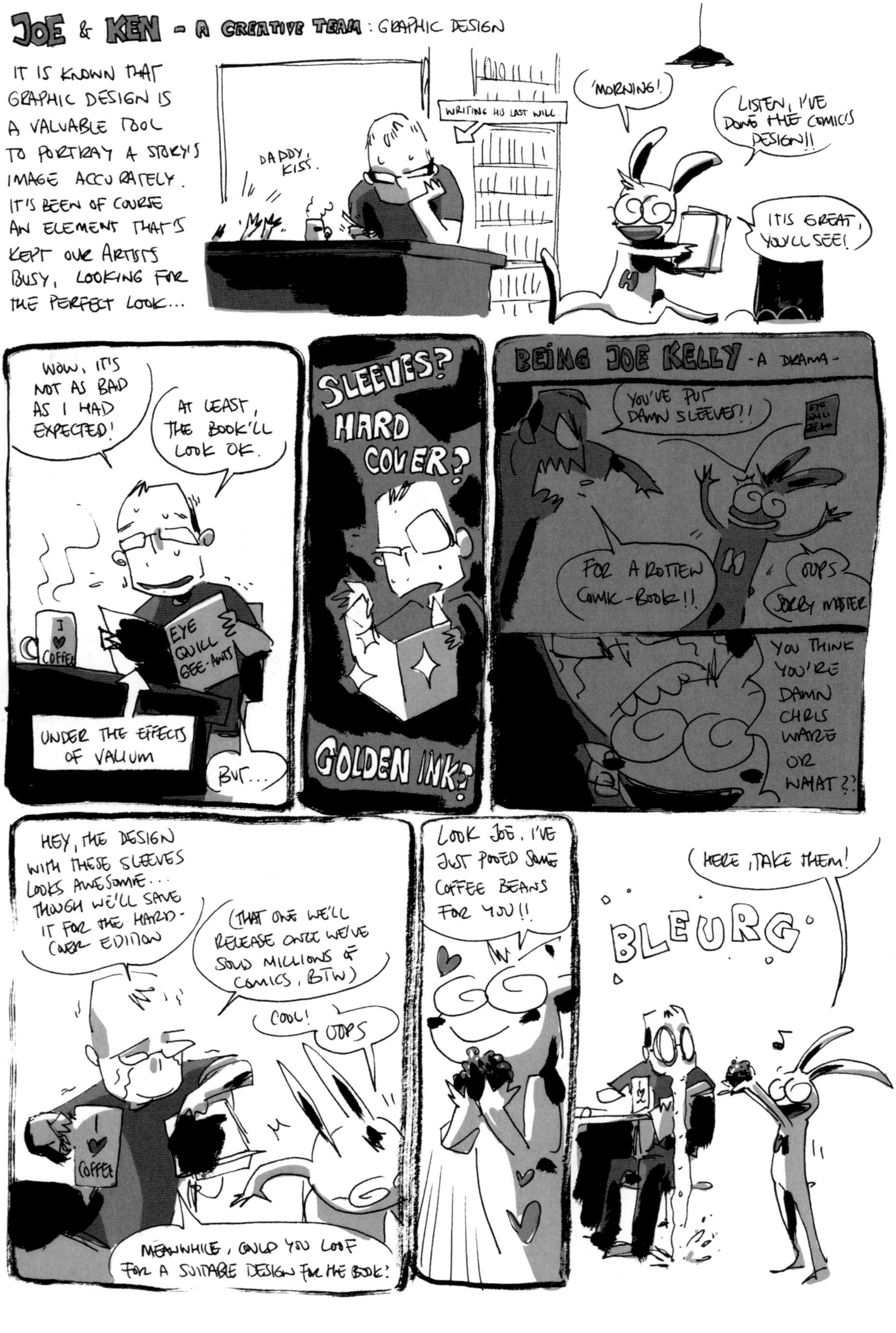
JOE & KEN - A CREATIVE TEAM : GRAPHIC DESIGN
IT IS KNOWN THAT GRAPHIC DESIGN IS A VALUABLE TOOL TO PORTRAY A STORY'S IMAGE ACCURATELY. IT'S BEEN OF COURSE AN ELEMENT THAT'S KEPT OUR ARTISTS BUSY, LOOKING FOR THE PERFECT LOOK...
DADDY, KISS.
WRITING HIS LAST WILL
'MORNING!
LISTEN, I'VE DONE THE COMICS DESIGN!!
IT'S GREAT, YOU'LL SEE!
WOW, IT'S NOT AS BAD AS I HAD EXPECTED!
AT LEAST, THE BOOK'LL LOOK OK.
EYE QUILL GEE-ANTS
I ♥ COFFEE
UNDER THE EFFECTS OF VALIUM
BUT...
SLEEVES?
HARD COVER?
GOLDEN INK?
BEING JOE KELLY - A DRAMA -
YOU'VE PUT DAMN SLEEVES!!
FOR A ROTTEN COMIC-BOOK!!
OOPS
SORRY MASTER
YOU THINK YOU'RE DAMN CHRIS WARE OR WHAT?!
HEY, THE DESIGN WITH THESE SLEEVES LOOKS AWESOME... THOUGH WE'LL SAVE IT FOR THE HARD-COVER EDITION
(THAT ONE WE'LL RELEASE ONCE WE'VE SOLD MILLIONS OF COMICS, BTW)
COOL!
OOPS
I ♥ COFFEE
MEANWHILE, COULD YOU LOOK FOR A SUITABLE DESIGN FOR THE BOOK?
LOOK JOE, I'VE JUST POOED SOME COFFEE BEANS FOR YOU!!
HERE, TAKE THEM!
BLEURG

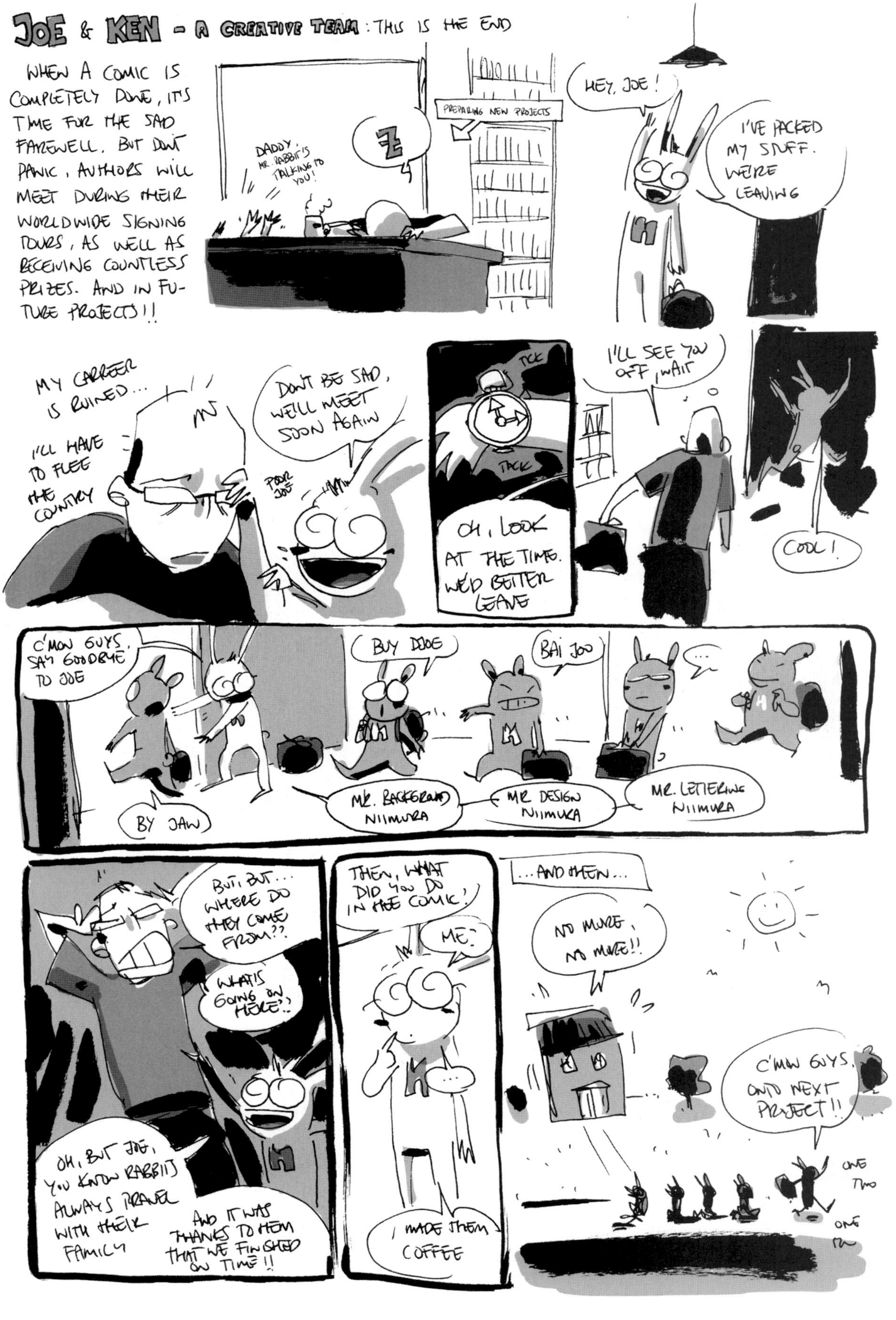
JOE & KEN - A CREATIVE TEAM: THIS IS THE END
WHEN A COMIC IS COMPLETELY DONE, IT'S TIME FOR THE SAD FAREWELL. BUT DON'T PANIC, AUTHORS WILL MEET DURING THEIR WORLDWIDE SIGNING TOURS, AS WELL AS RECEIVING COUNTLESS PRIZES. AND IN FUTURE PROJECTS!!
DADDY, MR RABBIT'S TALKING TO YOU!
Z
PREPARING NEW PROJECTS
HEY, JOE!
I'VE PACKED MY STUFF. WE'RE LEAVING
MY CAREER IS RUINED...
I'LL HAVE TO FLEE THE COUNTRY
DON'T BE SAD, WE'LL MEET SOON AGAIN
POOR JOE
TICK
TACK
OH, LOOK AT THE TIME. WE'D BETTER LEAVE
I'LL SEE YOU OFF, WAIT
COOL!
C'MON GUYS, SAY GOODBYE TO JOE
BY JAW
BUY DJOE
MR. BACKGROUND NIIMURA
BAI JOO
MR DESIGN NIIMURA
...
MR. LETTERING NIIMURA
BUT, BUT... WHERE DO THEY COME FROM??
WHAT'S GOING ON HERE?!
OH, BUT JOE, YOU KNOW RABBITS ALWAYS TRAVEL WITH THEIR FAMILY
AND IT WAS THANKS TO THEM THAT WE FINISHED ON TIME!!
THEN, WHAT DID YOU DO IN THE COMIC?
ME?
...
I MADE THEM COFFEE
...AND THEN...
NO MORE, NO MORE!!
C'MON GUYS, ONTO NEXT PROJECT!!
ONE
TWO
ONE
TWO

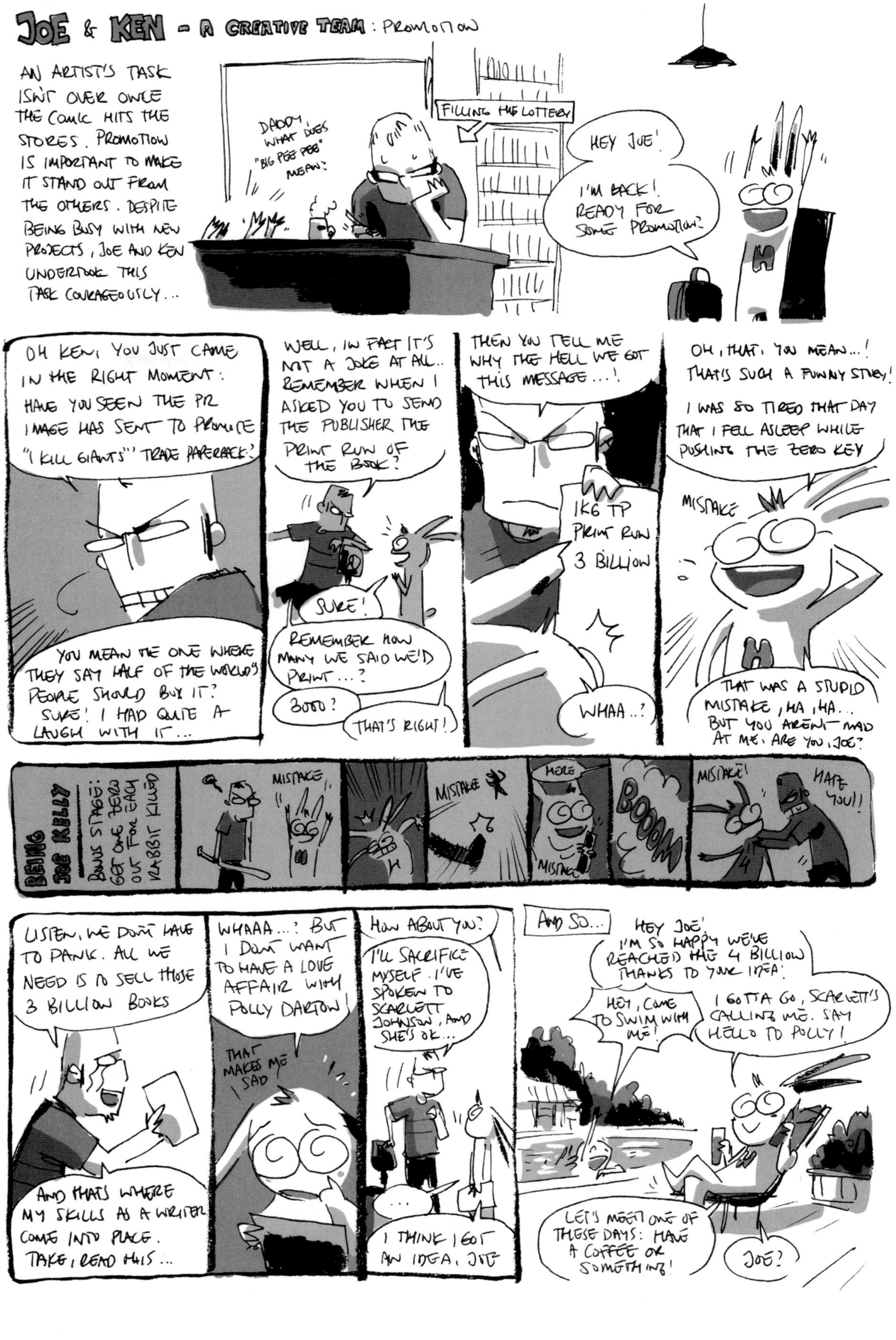
JOE & KEN - A CREATIVE TEAM : PROMOTION
AN ARTIST'S TASK ISN'T OVER ONCE THE COMIC HITS THE STORES. PROMOTION IS IMPORTANT TO MAKE IT STAND OUT FROM THE OTHERS. DESPITE BEING BUSY WITH NEW PROJECTS, JOE AND KEN UNDERTOOK THIS TASK COURAGEOUSLY...
DADDY, WHAT DOES "BIG PEE PEE" MEAN?
FILLING THE LOTTERY
HEY JOE!
I'M BACK! READY FOR SOME PROMOTION?
OH KEN, YOU JUST CAME IN THE RIGHT MOMENT: HAVE YOU SEEN THE PR IMAGE HAS SENT TO PROMOTE "I KILL GIANTS" TRADE PAPERBACK?
YOU MEAN THE ONE WHERE THEY SAY HALF OF THE WORLD'S PEOPLE SHOULD BUY IT? SURE! I HAD QUITE A LAUGH WITH IT...
WELL, IN FACT IT'S NOT A JOKE AT ALL.. REMEMBER WHEN I ASKED YOU TO SEND THE PUBLISHER THE PRINT RUN OF THE BOOK?
SURE!
REMEMBER HOW MANY WE SAID WE'D PRINT...?
3000?
THAT'S RIGHT!
THEN YOU TELL ME WHY THE HELL WE GOT THIS MESSAGE...!
IKG TP PRINT RUN 3 BILLION
WHAA...?
OH, THAT YOU MEAN...! THAT'S SUCH A FUNNY STORY!
I WAS SO TIRED THAT DAY THAT I FELL ASLEEP WHILE PUSHING THE ZERO KEY
MISTAKE
THAT WAS A STUPID MISTAKE, HA, HA... BUT YOU AREN'T MAD AT ME, ARE YOU, JOE?
BEING JOE KELLY
BONUS STAGE: GET ONE ZERO OUT FOR EACH RABBIT KILLED
MISTAKE
MISTAKE
HERE
BOOOM
MISTAKE
MISTAKE!
HATE YOU!!
LISTEN, WE DON'T HAVE TO PANIC. ALL WE NEED IS TO SELL THOSE 3 BILLION BOOKS
AND THAT'S WHERE MY SKILLS AS A WRITER COME INTO PLACE. TAKE, READ THIS...
WHAAA...? BUT I DON'T WANT TO HAVE A LOVE AFFAIR WITH POLLY DARTON!
THAT MAKES ME SAD
HOW ABOUT YOU?
I'LL SACRIFICE MYSELF. I'VE SPOKEN TO SCARLETT JOHNSON, AND SHE'S OK...
...
I THINK I GOT AN IDEA, JOE
AND SO...
HEY JOE! I'M SO HAPPY WE'VE REACHED THE 4 BILLION THANKS TO YOUR IDEA!
HEY, COME TO SWIM WITH ME!
I GOTTA GO, SCARLETT'S CALLING ME. SAY HELLO TO POLLY!
LET'S MEET ONE OF THESE DAYS: HAVE A COFFEE OR SOMETHING!
JOE?